A SCARLET PIMPERNEL COLLECTION

The Scarlet Pimpernel, I Will Repay, The Elusive Pimpernel, The League of the Scarlet Pimpernel

BARONESS ORCZY

This work is a product of its time and place and may include values, images, events, and language that are offensive to modern sensibilities. Reader discretion is advised.

The Scarlet Pimpernel: Originally published in 1905, this work is in the public domain in the United States.

I Will Repay: Originally published in 1906, this work is in the public domain in the United States.

The Elusive Pimpernel: Originally published in 1908, this work is in the public domain in the United States.

The League of the Scarlet Pimpernel: Originally published in 1920, this work is in the public domain in the United States.

No copyright claim is made with respect to public domain works.

This work reflects minor editorial revisions to the original texts.

Cover design created using Canva.com and reproduced pursuant to its free media license agreement. Cover art is "The Billiard Room," by Nicolas Taunay (1755-830), after 1810, courtesy of the Metropolitan Museum of Art, Open Access/Public Domain.

CONTENTS

THE SCARLET PIMPERNEL	1
I WILL REPAY	151
THE ELUSIVE PIMPERNEL	269
THE LEAGUE OF THE SCARLET PIMPERNEL	417

THE SCARLET PIMPERNEL

THE SCARLET PIMPERNEL

I. PARIS: SEPTEMBER, 1792

A SURGING, seething, murmuring crowd of beings that are human only in name, for to the eye and ear they seem naught but savage creatures, animated by vile passions and by the lust of vengeance and of hate. The hour, some little time before sunset, and the place, the West Barricade, at the very spot where, a decade later, a proud tyrant raised an undying monument to the nation's glory and his own vanity.

During the greater part of the day the guillotine had been kept busy at its ghastly work: all that France had boasted of in the past centuries, of ancient names, and blue blood, had paid toll to her desire for liberty and for fraternity. The carnage had only ceased at this late hour of the day because there were other more interesting sights for the people to witness, a little while before the final closing of the barricades for the night.

And so the crowd rushed away from the Place de la Grève and made for the various barricades in order to watch this interesting and amusing sight.

It was to be seen every day, for those aristos were such fools! They were traitors to the people of course, all of them, men, women, and children, who happened to be descendants of the great men who since the Crusades had made the glory of France: her old *noblesse*. Their ancestors had oppressed the people, had crushed them under the scarlet heels of their dainty buckled shoes, and now the people had become the rulers of France and crushed their former masters—not beneath their heel, for they went shoeless mostly in these days—but beneath a more effectual weight, the knife of the guillotine.

And daily, hourly, the hideous instrument of torture claimed its many victims—old men, young women, tiny children, even until the day when it would finally demand the head of a King and of a beautiful young Queen.

But this was as it should be: were not the people now the rulers of France? Every aristocrat was a traitor, as his ancestors had been before him: for two hundred years now the people had sweated, and toiled, and starved, to keep a lustful court in lavish extravagance; now the descendants of those who had helped to make those courts brilliant had to hide for their lives—to fly, if they wished to avoid the tardy vengeance of the people.

And they did try to hide, and tried to fly: that was just the fun of the whole thing. Every afternoon before the gates closed and the market carts went out in procession by the various barricades, some fool of an aristo endeavoured to evade the clutches of the Committee of Public Safety. In various disguises, under various pretexts, they tried to slip through the barriers which were so well guarded by citizen soldiers of the Republic. Men in women's clothes, women in male attire, children disguised in beggars' rags: there were some of all sorts: *ci-devant* counts, marquises, even dukes, who wanted to fly from France, reach England or some other equally accursed country, and there try to rouse foreign feeling against the glorious Revolution, or to raise an army in order to liberate the wretched prisoners in the Temple, who had once called themselves sovereigns of France.

But they were nearly always caught at the barricades. Sergeant Bibot especially at the West Gate had a wonderful nose for scenting an aristo in the most perfect disguise. Then, of course, the fun began. Bibot would look at his prey as a cat looks upon the mouse, play with him, sometimes for quite a quarter of an hour, pretend to be hoodwinked by the disguise, by the wigs and other bits of theatrical make-up which hid the identity of a *ci-devant* noble marquise or count.

Oh! Bibot had a keen sense of humour, and it was well worth hanging round that West Barricade, in order to see him catch an aristo in the very act of trying to flee from the vengeance of the people.

Sometimes Bibot would let his prey actually out by the gates, allowing him to think for the space of two minutes at least that he really had escaped out of Paris, and might even manage to reach the coast of England in safety, but Bibot would let the unfortunate wretch walk about ten mètres towards the open country, then he would send two men after him and bring him back, stripped of his disguise.

Oh! that was extremely funny, for as often as not the fugitive would prove to be a woman, some proud marchioness, who looked terribly comical when she found herself in Bibot's clutches after all, and knew that a summary trial would await her the next day and after that, the fond embrace of Madame la Guillotine.

No wonder that on this fine afternoon in September the crowd round Bibot's gate was eager and excited. The lust of blood grows with its satisfaction, there is no satiety: the crowd had seen a hundred noble heads fall beneath the guillotine to-day, it wanted to make sure that it would see another hundred fall on the morrow.

Bibot was sitting on an overturned and empty cask close by the gate of the barricade; a small detachment of citoyen soldiers was under his command. The work had been very hot lately. Those cursed aristos were becoming terrified and tried their hardest to slip out of Paris: men, women and children, whose ancestors, even in remote ages, had served those traitorous Bourbons, were all traitors themselves and right food for the guillotine. Every day Bibot had had the satisfaction of unmasking some fugitive royalists and sending them back to be tried by the Committee of Public Safety, presided over by that good patriot, Citoyen Foucquier-Tinville.

Robespierre and Danton both had commended Bibot for his zeal, and Bibot was proud of the fact that he on his own initiative had sent at least fifty aristos to the guillotine.

But to-day all the sergeants in command at the various barricades had had special orders. Recently a very great number of aristos had succeeded in escaping out of France and in reaching England safely. There were curious rumours about these escapes; they had become very frequent and singularly daring; the people's minds were becoming strangely excited about it all. Sergeant Grospierre had been sent to the guillotine for allowing a whole family of aristos to slip out of the North Gate under his very nose.

It was asserted that these escapes were organised by a band of Englishmen, whose daring seemed to be unparalleled, and who, from sheer desire to meddle in what did not concern them, spent their spare time in snatching away lawful victims destined for Madame la Guillotine. These rumours soon grew in extravagance; there was no doubt that this band of meddlesome Englishmen did exist; moreover, they seemed to be under the leadership of a man whose pluck and audacity were almost fabulous. Strange stories were afloat of how he and those aristos whom he rescued became suddenly invisible as they reached the barricades and escaped out of the gates by sheer supernatural agency.

No one had seen these mysterious Englishmen; as for their leader, he was never spoken of, save with a superstitious shudder. Citoyen Foucquier-Tinville would in the course of the day receive a scrap of paper from some mysterious source; sometimes he would find it in the pocket of his coat, at others it would be handed to him by someone in the crowd, whilst he was on his way to the sitting of the Committee of Public Safety. The paper always contained a brief notice that the band of meddlesome Englishmen were at work, and it was always signed with a device drawn in red—a little star-shaped flower, which we in England call the Scarlet Pimpernel. Within a few hours of the receipt of this impudent notice, the citoyens of the Committee of Public Safety would hear that so many royalists and aristocrats had succeeded in reaching the coast, and were on their way to England and safety.

The guards at the gates had been doubled, the sergeants in command had been threatened with death, whilst liberal rewards were offered for the capture of these daring and impudent Englishmen. There was a sum of five thousand francs promised to the man who laid hands on the mysterious and elusive Scarlet Pimpernel.

Everyone felt that Bibot would be that man, and Bibot allowed that belief to take firm root in everybody's mind; and so, day after day, people came to watch him at the West Gate, so as to be present when he laid hands on any fugitive aristo who perhaps might be accompanied by that mysterious Englishman.

"Bah!" he said to his trusted corporal, "Citoyen Grospierre was a fool! Had it been me now, at that North Gate last week . . ."

Citoyen Bibot spat on the ground to express his contempt for his comrade's stupidity.

"How did it happen, citoyen?" asked the corporal.

"Grospierre was at the gate, keeping good watch," began Bibot, pompously, as the crowd closed in round him, listening eagerly to his narrative. "We've all heard of this meddlesome Englishman, this accursed Scarlet Pimpernel. He won't get through *my* gate, *morbleu!* unless he be the devil himself. But Grospierre was a fool. The market carts were going through the gates; there was one laden with casks, and driven by an old man, with a boy beside him. Grospierre was a bit drunk, but he thought himself very clever; he looked into the casks—most of them, at least—and saw they were empty, and let the cart go through."

A murmur of wrath and contempt went round the group of ill-clad wretches, who crowded round Citoyen Bibot.

"Half an hour later," continued the sergeant, "up comes a captain of the guard with a squad of some dozen soldiers with him. 'Has a cart gone through?' he asks of Grospierre, breathlessly. 'Yes,' says Grospierre, 'not half an hour ago.' 'And you have let them escape,' shouts the captain furiously. 'You'll go to the guillotine for this, citoyen sergeant! that cart held concealed the *ci-devant* Duc de Chalis and all his family!' 'What!' thunders Grospierre, aghast. 'Aye! and the driver was none other than that cursed Englishman, the Scarlet Pimpernel.'"

A howl of execration greeted this tale. Citoyen Grospierre had paid for his blunder on the guillotine, but what a fool! oh! what a fool!

Bibot was laughing so much at his own tale that it was some time before he could continue.

"'After them, my men,' shouts the captain," he said, after a while, "'remember the reward; after them, they cannot have gone far!' And with that he rushes through the gate, followed by his dozen soldiers."

"But it was too late!" shouted the crowd, excitedly.

"They never got them!"

"Curse that Grospierre for his folly!"

"He deserved his fate!"

"Fancy not examining those casks properly!"

But these sallies seemed to amuse Citoyen Bibot exceedingly; he laughed until his sides ached, and the tears streamed down his cheeks.

"Nay, nay!" he said at last, "those aristos weren't in the cart; the driver was not the Scarlet Pimpernel!"

"What?"

"No! The captain of the guard was that damned Englishman in disguise, and every one of his soldiers aristos!"

The crowd this time said nothing: the story certainly savoured of the supernatural, and though the Republic had abolished God, it had not quite succeeded in killing the fear of the supernatural in the hearts of the people. Truly that Englishman must be the devil himself.

The sun was sinking low down in the west. Bibot prepared himself to close the gates.

"*En avant* the carts," he said.

Some dozen covered carts were drawn up in a row, ready to leave town, in order to fetch the produce from the country close by, for market the next morning. They were mostly well known to Bibot, as they went through his gate twice every day on their way to and from the town. He spoke to one or two of their drivers—mostly women—and was at great pains to examine the inside of the carts.

"You never know," he would say, "and I'm not going to be caught like that fool Grospierre."

The women who drove the carts usually spent their day on the Place de la Grève, beneath the platform of the guillotine, knitting and gossiping, whilst they watched the rows of tumbrils arriving with the victims the Reign of Terror claimed every day. It was great fun to see the aristos arriving for the reception of Madame la Guillotine, and the places close by the platform were very much sought after. Bibot, during the day, had been on duty on the Place. He recognized most of the old hags, "tricotteuses," as they were called, who sat there and knitted, whilst head after head fell beneath the knife, and they themselves got quite bespattered with the blood of those cursed aristos.

"Hé! la mère!" said Bibot to one of these horrible hags, "what have you got there?"

He had seen her earlier in the day, with her knitting and the whip of her cart close beside her. Now she had fastened a row of curly locks to the whip handle, all colours, from gold to silver, fair to dark, and she stroked them with her huge, bony fingers as she laughed at Bibot.

"I made friends with Madame Guillotine's lover," she said with a coarse laugh, "he cut these off for me from the heads as they rolled down. He has promised me some more to-morrow, but I don't know if I shall be at my usual place."

"Ah! how is that, la mère?" asked Bibot, who, hardened soldier though he was, could not help shuddering at the awful loathsomeness of this semblance of a woman, with her ghastly trophy on the handle of her whip.

"My grandson has got the small-pox," she said with a jerk of her thumb towards the inside of her cart, "some say it's the plague! If it is, I sha'n't be allowed to come into Paris to-morrow."

At the first mention of the word small-pox, Bibot had stepped hastily backwards, and when the old hag spoke of the plague, he retreated from her as fast as he could.

"Curse you!" he muttered, whilst the whole crowd hastily avoided the cart, leaving it standing all alone in the midst of the place.

The old hag laughed.

"Curse you, citoyen, for being a coward," she said. "Bah! what a man to be afraid of sickness."

"*Morbleu!* the plague!"

Everyone was awe-struck and silent, filled with horror for the loathsome malady, the one thing which still had the power to arouse terror and disgust in these savage, brutalised creatures.

"Get out with you and with your plague-stricken brood!" shouted Bibot, hoarsely.

And with another rough laugh and coarse jest, the old hag whipped up her lean nag and drove her cart out of the gate.

This incident had spoilt the afternoon. The people were terrified of these two horrible curses, the two maladies which nothing could cure, and which were the precursors of an awful and lonely death. They hung about the barricades, silent and sullen for a while, eyeing one another suspiciously, avoiding each other as if by instinct, lest the plague lurked already in their midst. Presently, as in the case of Grospierre, a captain of the guard appeared suddenly. But he was known to Bibot, and there was no fear of his turning out to be a sly Englishman in disguise.

"A cart, . . ." he shouted breathlessly, even before he had reached the gates.

"What cart?" asked Bibot, roughly.

"Driven by an old hag. . . . A covered cart . . ."

"There were a dozen . . ."

"An old hag who said her son had the plague?"

"Yes . . ."

"You have not let them go?"

"*Morbleu!*" said Bibot, whose purple cheeks had suddenly become white with fear.

"The cart contained the *ci-devant* Comtesse de Tournay and her two children, all of them traitors and condemned to death."

"And their driver?" muttered Bibot, as a superstitious shudder ran down his spine.

"*Sacré tonnerre*," said the captain, "but it is feared that it was that accursed Englishman himself—the Scarlet Pimpernel."

II. "THE FISHERMAN'S REST"

In the kitchen Sally was extremely busy—saucepans and frying-pans were standing in rows on the gigantic hearth, the huge stock-pot stood in a corner, and the jack turned with slow deliberation, and presented alternately to the glow every side of a noble sirloin of beef. The two little kitchen-maids bustled around, eager to help, hot and panting, with cotton sleeves well tucked up above the dimpled elbows, and giggling over some private jokes of their own, whenever Miss Sally's back was turned for a moment. And old Jemima, stolid in temper and solid in bulk, kept up a long and subdued grumble, while she stirred the stock-pot methodically over the fire.

"What ho! Sally!" came in cheerful if none too melodious accents from the coffee-room close by.

"Lud bless my soul!" exclaimed Sally, with a good-humoured laugh, "what be they all wanting now, I wonder!"

"Beer, of course," grumbled Jemima, "you don't 'xpect Jimmy Pitkin to 'ave done with one tankard, do ye?"

"Mr. 'Arry, 'e looked uncommon thirsty too," simpered Martha, one of the little kitchen-maids; and her beady black eyes twinkled as they met those of her companion, whereupon both started on a round of short and suppressed giggles.

Sally looked cross for a moment, and thoughtfully rubbed her hands against her shapely hips; her palms were itching, evidently, to come in contact with Martha's rosy cheeks—but inherent good-humour prevailed, and with a pout and a shrug of the shoulders, she turned her attention to the fried potatoes.

"What ho, Sally! hey, Sally!"

And a chorus of pewter mugs, tapped with impatient hands against the oak tables of the coffee-room, accompanied the shouts for mine host's buxom daughter.

"Sally!" shouted a more persistent voice, "are ye goin' to be all night with that there beer?"

"I do think father might get the beer for them," muttered Sally, as Jemima, stolidly and without further comment, took a couple of foam-crowned jugs from the shelf, and began filling a number of pewter tankards with some of that home-brewed ale for which "The Fisherman's Rest" had been famous since the days of King Charles. "'E knows 'ow busy we are in 'ere."

"Your father is too busy discussing politics with Mr. 'Empseed to worry 'isself about you and the kitchen," grumbled Jemima under her breath.

Sally had gone to the small mirror which hung in a corner of the kitchen, and was hastily smoothing her hair and setting her frilled cap at its most becoming angle over her dark curls; then she took up the tankards by their handles, three in each strong, brown hand, and laughing, grumbling, blushing, carried them through into the coffee-room.

There, there was certainly no sign of that bustle and activity which kept four women busy and hot in the glowing kitchen beyond.

The coffee-room of "The Fisherman's Rest" is a show place now at the beginning of the twentieth century. At the end of the eighteenth, in the year of grace 1792, it had not yet gained that notoriety and importance which a hundred additional years and the craze of the age have since bestowed upon it. Yet it was an old place, even then, for the oak rafters and beams were already black with age—as were the panelled seats, with their tall backs, and the long polished tables between, on which innumerable pewter tankards had left fantastic patterns of many-sized rings. In the leaded window, high up, a row of pots of scarlet geraniums and blue larkspur gave the bright note of colour against the dull background of the oak.

That Mr. Jellyband, landlord of "The Fisherman's Rest" at Dover, was a prosperous man, was of course clear to the most casual observer. The pewter on the fine old dressers, the brass above the gigantic hearth, shone like silver and gold—the red-tiled floor was as brilliant as the scarlet geranium on the window sill—this meant that his servants were good and plentiful, that the custom was constant, and of that order which necessitated the keeping up of the coffee-room to a high standard of elegance and order.

As Sally came in, laughing through her frowns, and displaying a row of dazzling white teeth, she was greeted with shouts and chorus of applause.

"Why, here's Sally! What ho, Sally! Hurrah for pretty Sally!"

"I thought you'd grown deaf in that kitchen of yours," muttered Jimmy Pitkin, as he passed the back of his hand across his very dry lips.

"All ri'! all ri'!" laughed Sally, as she deposited the freshly-filled tankards upon the tables, "why, what a 'urry, to be sure! And is your gran'mother a-dyin' an' you wantin' to see the pore soul afore she'm gone! I never see'd such a mighty rushin'!"

A chorus of good-humoured laughter greeted this witticism, which gave the company there present food for many jokes, for some considerable time. Sally now seemed in less of a hurry to get back to her pots and pans. A young man with fair curly hair, and eager, bright blue eyes, was engaging most of her attention and the whole of her time, whilst broad witticisms anent Jimmy Pitkin's fictitious grandmother flew from mouth to mouth, mixed with heavy puffs of pungent tobacco smoke.

Facing the hearth, his legs wide apart, a long clay pipe in his mouth, stood mine host himself, worthy Mr. Jellyband, landlord of "The Fisherman's Rest," as his father had been before him, aye, and his grandfather and great-grandfather too, for that matter. Portly in build, jovial in countenance and somewhat bald of pate, Mr. Jellyband was indeed a typical rural John Bull of those days—the days when our prejudiced insularity was at its height, when to an Englishman, be he lord, yeoman, or peasant, the whole of the continent of Europe was a den of immorality, and the rest of the world an unexploited land of savages and cannibals.

There he stood, mine worthy host, firm and well set up on his limbs, smoking his long churchwarden and caring nothing for nobody at home, and despising everybody abroad. He wore the typical scarlet waistcoat, with shiny brass buttons, the corduroy breeches, the grey worsted stockings and smart buckled shoes, that characterised every self-respecting innkeeper in Great Britain in these days—and while pretty, motherless

Sally had need of four pairs of brown hands to do all the work that fell on her shapely shoulders, worthy Jellyband discussed the affairs of nations with his most privileged guests.

The coffee-room indeed, lighted by two well-polished lamps, which hung from the raftered ceiling, looked cheerful and cosy in the extreme. Through the dense clouds of tobacco smoke that hung about in every corner, the faces of Mr. Jellyband's customers appeared red and pleasant to look at, and on good terms with themselves, their host and all the world; from every side of the room loud guffaws accompanied pleasant, if not highly intellectual, conversation—while Sally's repeated giggles testified to the good use Mr. Harry Waite was making of the short time she seemed inclined to spare him.

They were mostly fisher-folk who patronised Mr. Jellyband's coffee-room, but fishermen are known to be very thirsty people; the salt which they breathe in, when they are on the sea, accounts for their parched throats when on shore. But "The Fisherman's Rest" was something more than a rendezvous for these humble folk. The London and Dover coach started from the hostel daily, and passengers who had come across the Channel, and those who started for the "grand tour," all became acquainted with Mr. Jellyband, his French wines and his home-brewed ales.

It was towards the close of September, 1792, and the weather which had been brilliant and hot throughout the month had suddenly broken up; for two days torrents of rain had deluged the south of England, doing its level best to ruin what chances the apples and pears and late plums had of becoming really fine, self-respecting fruit. Even now it was beating against the leaded windows, and tumbling down the chimney, making the cheerful wood fire sizzle in the hearth.

"Lud! did you ever see such a wet September, Mr. Jellyband?" asked Mr. Hempseed.

He sat in one of the seats inside the hearth, did Mr. Hempseed, for he was an authority and an important personage not only at "The Fisherman's Rest," where Mr. Jellyband always made a special selection of him as a foil for political arguments, but throughout the neighbourhood, where his learning and notably his knowledge of the Scriptures was held in the most profound awe and respect. With one hand buried in the capacious pockets of his corduroys underneath his elaborately-worked, well-worn smock, the other holding his long clay pipe, Mr. Hempseed sat there looking dejectedly across the room at the rivulets of moisture which trickled down the window panes.

"No," replied Mr. Jellyband, sententiously, "I dunno, Mr. 'Empseed, as I ever did. An' I've been in these parts nigh on sixty years."

"Aye! you wouldn't rec'llect the first three years of them sixty, Mr. Jellyband," quietly interposed Mr. Hempseed. "I dunno as I ever see'd an infant take much note of the weather, leastways not in these parts, an' I've lived 'ere nigh on seventy-five years, Mr. Jellyband."

The superiority of this wisdom was so incontestable that for the moment Mr. Jellyband was not ready with his usual flow of argument.

"It do seem more like April than September, don't it?" continued Mr. Hempseed, dolefully, as a shower of raindrops fell with a sizzle upon the fire.

"Aye! that it do," assented the worthy host, "but then what can you 'xpect, Mr. 'Empseed, I says, with sich a government as we've got?"

Mr. Hempseed shook his head with an infinity of wisdom, tempered by deeply-rooted mistrust of the British climate and the British Government.

"I don't 'xpect nothing, Mr. Jellyband," he said. "Pore folks like us is of no account up there in Lunnon, I knows that, and it's not often as I do complain. But when it comes to sich wet weather in September, and all me fruit a-rottin' and a-dyin' like the 'Guptian mother's first-born, and doin' no more good than they did, pore dears, save to a lot of Jews, pedlars and sich, with their oranges and sich like foreign ungodly fruit, which nobody'd buy if English apples and pears was nicely swelled. As the Scriptures say—"

"That's quite right, Mr. 'Empseed," retorted Jellyband, "and as I says, what can you 'xpect? There's all them Frenchy devils over the Channel yonder a-murderin' their king and nobility, and Mr. Pitt and Mr. Fox and Mr. Burke a-fightin' and a-wranglin' between them, if we Englishmen should 'low them to go on in their ungodly way. 'Let 'em murder!' says Mr. Pitt. 'Stop 'em!' says Mr. Burke."

"And let 'em murder, says I, and be demmed to 'em," said Mr. Hempseed, emphatically, for he had but little liking for his friend Jellyband's political arguments, wherein he always got out of his depth, and had but little chance for displaying those pearls of wisdom which had earned for him so high a reputation in the neighbourhood and so many free tankards of ale at "The Fisherman's Rest."

"Let 'em murder," he repeated again, "but don't let's 'ave sich rain in September, for that is agin the law and the Scriptures which says—"

"Lud! Mr. 'Arry, 'ow you made me jump!"

It was unfortunate for Sally and her flirtation that this remark of hers should have occurred at the precise moment when Mr. Hempseed was collecting his breath, in order to deliver himself of one of those Scriptural utterances which had made him famous, for it brought down upon her pretty head the full flood of her father's wrath.

"Now then, Sally, me girl, now then!" he said, trying to force a frown upon his good-humoured face, "stop that fooling with them young jackanapes and get on with the work."

"The work's gettin' on all ri', father."

But Mr. Jellyband was peremptory. He had other views for his buxom daughter, his only child, who would in God's good time become the owner of "The Fisherman's Rest," than to see her married to one of these young fellows who earned but a precarious livelihood with their net.

"Did ye hear me speak, me girl?" he said in that quiet tone, which no one inside the inn dared to disobey. "Get on with my Lord Tony's supper, for, if it ain't the best we can do, and 'e not satisfied, see what you'll get, that's all."

Reluctantly Sally obeyed.

"Is you 'xpecting special guests then to-night, Mr. Jellyband?" asked Jimmy Pitkin, in a loyal attempt to divert his host's attention from the circumstances connected with Sally's exit from the room.

"Aye! that I be," replied Jellyband, "friends of my Lord Tony hisself. Dukes and duchesses from over the water yonder, whom the young lord and his friend, Sir Andrew Ffoulkes, and other young noblemen have helped out of the clutches of them murderin' devils."

But this was too much for Mr. Hempseed's querulous philosophy.

"Lud!" he said, "what they do that for, I wonder? I don't 'old not with interferin' in other folks' ways. As the Scriptures say—"

"Maybe, Mr. 'Empseed," interrupted Jellyband, with biting sarcasm, "as you're a personal friend of Mr. Pitt, and as you says along with Mr. Fox: 'Let 'em murder!' says you."

"Pardon me, Mr. Jellyband," feebly protested Mr. Hempseed, "I dunno as I ever did."

But Mr. Jellyband had at last succeeded in getting upon his favourite hobby-horse, and had no intention of dismounting in any hurry.

"Or maybe you've made friends with some of them French chaps 'oo they do say have come over here o' purpose to make us Englishmen agree with their murderin' ways."

"I dunno what you mean, Mr. Jellyband," suggested Mr. Hempseed, "all I know is—"

"All *I* know is," loudly asserted mine host, "that there was my friend Peppercorn, 'oo owns the 'Blue-Faced Boar,' an' as true and loyal an Englishman as you'd see in the land. And now look at 'im!—'E made friends with some o' them frog-eaters, 'obnobbed with them just as if they was Englishmen, and not just a lot of immoral, God-forsaking furrin' spies. Well! and what happened? Peppercorn 'e now ups and talks of revolutions, and liberty, and down with the aristocrats, just like Mr. 'Empseed over 'ere!"

"Pardon me, Mr. Jellyband," again interposed Mr. Hempseed, feebly, "I dunno as I ever did—"

Mr. Jellyband had appealed to the company in general, who were listening awe-struck and open-mouthed at the recital of Mr. Peppercorn's defalcations. At one table two customers—gentlemen apparently by their clothes—had pushed aside their half-finished game of dominoes, and had been listening for some time, and evidently with much amusement at Mr. Jellyband's international opinions. One of them now, with a quiet, sarcastic smile still lurking round the corners of his mobile mouth, turned towards the centre of the room where Mr. Jellyband was standing.

"You seem to think, mine honest friend," he said quietly, "that these Frenchmen—spies I think you called them—are mighty clever fellows to have made mincemeat so to speak of your friend Mr. Peppercorn's opinions. How did they accomplish that now, think you?"

"Lud! sir, I suppose they talked 'im over. Those Frenchies, I've 'eard it said, 'ave got the gift of gab—and Mr. 'Empseed 'ere will tell you 'ow it is that they just twist some people round their little finger like."

"Indeed, and is that so, Mr. Hempseed?" inquired the stranger politely.

"Nay, sir!" replied Mr. Hempseed, much irritated, "I dunno as I can give you the information you require."

"Faith, then," said the stranger, "let us hope, my worthy host, that these clever spies will not succeed in upsetting your extremely loyal opinions."

But this was too much for Mr. Jellyband's pleasant equanimity. He burst into an uproarious fit of laughter, which was soon echoed by those who happened to be in his debt.

"Hahaha! hohoho! hehehe!" He laughed in every key, did my worthy host, and laughed until his sides ached, and his eyes streamed. "At me! hark at that! Did ye 'ear 'im say that they'd be upsettin' my opinions?—Eh?—Lud love you, sir, but you do say some queer things."

"Well, Mr. Jellyband," said Mr. Hempseed, sententiously, "you know what the Scriptures say: 'Let 'im 'oo stands take 'eed lest 'e fall.'"

"But then hark'ee, Mr. 'Empseed," retorted Jellyband, still holding his sides with laughter, "the Scriptures didn't know me. Why, I wouldn't so much as drink a glass of ale with one o' them murderin' Frenchmen, and nothin' 'd make me change my opinions. Why! I've 'eard it said that them frog-eaters can't even speak the King's English, so, of course, if any of 'em tried to speak their God-forsaken lingo to me, why, I should spot them directly, see!—and forewarned is forearmed, as the saying goes."

"Aye! my honest friend," assented the stranger cheerfully, "I see that you are much too sharp, and a match for any twenty Frenchmen, and here's to your very good health, my worthy host, if you'll do me the honour to finish this bottle of mine with me."

"I am sure you're very polite, sir," said Mr. Jellyband, wiping his eyes which were still streaming with the abundance of his laughter, "and I don't mind if I do."

The stranger poured out a couple of tankards full of wine, and having offered one to mine host, he took the other himself.

"Loyal Englishmen as we all are," he said, whilst the same humorous smile played round the corners of his thin lips—"loyal as we are, we must admit that this at least is one good thing which comes to us from France."

"Aye! we'll none of us deny that, sir," assented mine host.

"And here's to the best landlord in England, our worthy host, Mr. Jellyband," said the stranger in a loud tone of voice.

"Hip, hip, hurrah!" retorted the whole company present. Then there was loud clapping of hands, and mugs and tankards made a rattling music upon the tables to the accompaniment of loud laughter at nothing in particular, and of Mr. Jellyband's muttered exclamations:

"Just fancy *me* bein' talked over by any God-forsaken furriner!—What?—Lud love you, sir, but you do say some queer things."

To which obvious fact the stranger heartily assented. It was certainly a preposterous suggestion that anyone could ever upset Mr. Jellyband's firmly-rooted opinions anent the utter worthlessness of the inhabitants of the whole continent of Europe.

III. THE REFUGEES

Feeling in every part of England certainly ran very high at this time against the French and their doings. Smugglers and legitimate traders between the French and English coasts brought snatches of news from over the water, which made every honest Englishman's blood boil, and made him long to have "a good go" at those murderers, who had imprisoned their king and all his family, subjected the queen and the royal children to every species of indignity, and were even now loudly demanding the blood of the whole Bourbon family and of every one of its adherents.

The execution of the Princesse de Lamballe, Marie Antoinette's young and charming friend, had filled everyone in England with unspeakable horror, the daily execution of scores of royalists of good family, whose only sin was their aristocratic name, seemed to cry for vengeance to the whole of civilised Europe.

Yet, with all that, no one dared to interfere. Burke had exhausted all his eloquence in trying to induce the British Government to fight the revolutionary government of France, but Mr. Pitt, with characteristic prudence, did not feel that this country was fit yet to embark on another arduous and costly war. It was for Austria to take the initiative; Austria, whose fairest daughter was even now a dethroned queen, imprisoned and insulted by a howling mob; and surely 'twas not—so argued Mr. Fox—for the whole of England to take up arms, because one set of Frenchmen chose to murder another.

As for Mr. Jellyband and his fellow John Bulls, though they looked upon all foreigners with withering contempt, they were royalist and anti-revolutionists to a man, and at this present moment were furious with Pitt for his caution and moderation, although they naturally understood nothing of the diplomatic reasons which guided that great man's policy.

But now Sally came running back, very excited and very eager. The joyous company in the coffee-room had heard nothing of the noise outside, but she had spied a dripping horse and rider who had stopped at the door of "The Fisherman's Rest," and while the stable boy ran forward to take charge of the horse, pretty Miss Sally went to the front door to greet the welcome visitor.

"I think I see'd my Lord Antony's horse out in the yard, father," she said, as she ran across the coffee-room.

But already the door had been thrown open from outside, and the next moment an arm, covered in drab cloth and dripping with the heavy rain, was round pretty Sally's waist, while a hearty voice echoed along the polished rafters of the coffee-room.

"Aye, and bless your brown eyes for being so sharp, my pretty Sally," said the man who had just entered, whilst worthy Mr. Jellyband came bustling forward, eager, alert and fussy, as became the advent of one of the most favoured guests of his hostel.

"Lud, I protest, Sally," added Lord Antony, as he deposited a kiss on Miss Sally's blooming cheeks, "but you are growing prettier and prettier every time I see you—and my honest friend, Jellyband here, must have hard work to keep the fellows off that slim waist of yours. What say you, Mr. Waite?"

Mr. Waite—torn between his respect for my lord and his dislike of that particular type of joke—only replied with a doubtful grunt.

Lord Antony Dewhurst, one of the sons of the Duke of Exeter, was in those days a very perfect type of a young English gentleman—tall, well set-up, broad of shoulders and merry of face, his laughter rang loudly wherever he went. A good sportsman, a lively companion, a courteous, well-bred man of the world, with not too much brains to spoil his temper, he was a universal favourite in London drawing-rooms or in the coffee-rooms of village inns. At "The Fisherman's Rest" everyone knew him—for he was fond of a trip across to France, and always spent a night under worthy Mr. Jellyband's roof on his way there or back.

He nodded to Waite, Pitkin and the others as he at last released Sally's waist, and crossed over to the hearth to warm and dry himself: as he did so, he cast a quick, somewhat suspicious glance at the two strangers, who had quietly resumed their game of dominoes, and for a moment a look of deep earnestness, even of anxiety, clouded his jovial young face.

But only for a moment; the next he had turned to Mr. Hempseed, who was respectfully touching his forelock.

"Well, Mr. Hempseed, and how is the fruit?"

"Badly, my lord, badly," replied Mr. Hempseed, dolefully, "but what can you 'xpect with this 'ere government favourin' them rascals over in France, who would murder their king and all their nobility."

"Odd's life!" retorted Lord Antony; "so they would, honest Hempseed,—at least those they can get hold of, worse luck! But we have got some friends coming here to-night, who at any rate have evaded their clutches."

It almost seemed, when the young man said these words, as if he threw a defiant look towards the quiet strangers in the corner.

"Thanks to you, my lord, and to your friends, so I've heard it said," said Mr. Jellyband.

But in a moment Lord Antony's hand fell warningly on mine host's arm.

"Hush!" he said peremptorily, and instinctively once again looked towards the strangers.

"Oh! Lud love you, they are all right, my lord," retorted Jellyband; "don't you be afraid. I wouldn't have spoken, only I knew we were among friends. That gentleman over there is as true and loyal a subject of King George as you are yourself, my lord, saving your presence. He is but lately arrived in Dover, and is settling down in business in these parts."

"In business? Faith, then, it must be as an undertaker, for I vow I never beheld a more rueful countenance."

"Nay, my lord, I believe that the gentleman is a widower, which no doubt would account for the melancholy of his bearing—but he is a friend, nevertheless, I'll vouch for that—and you will own, my lord, that who should judge of a face better than the landlord of a popular inn—"

"Oh, that's all right, then, if we are among friends," said Lord Antony, who evidently did not care to discuss the subject with his host. "But, tell me, you have no one else staying here, have you?"

"No one, my lord, and no one coming, either, leastways—"

"Leastways?"

"No one your lordship would object to, I know."

"Who is it?"

"Well, my lord, Sir Percy Blakeney and his lady will be here presently, but they ain't a-goin' to stay—"

"Lady Blakeney?" queried Lord Antony, in some astonishment.

"Aye, my lord. Sir Percy's skipper was here just now. He says that my lady's brother is crossing over to France to-day in the *Day Dream,* which is Sir Percy's yacht, and Sir Percy and my lady will come with him as far as here to see the last of him. It don't put you out, do it, my lord?"

"No, no, it doesn't put me out, friend; nothing will put me out, unless that supper is not the very best which Miss Sally can cook, and which has ever been served in 'The Fisherman's Rest.'"

"You need have no fear of that, my lord," said Sally, who all this while had been busy setting the table for supper. And very gay and inviting it looked, with a large bunch of brilliantly coloured dahlias in the centre, and the bright pewter goblets and blue china about.

"How many shall I lay for, my lord?"

"Five places, pretty Sally, but let the supper be enough for ten at least—our friends will be tired, and, I hope, hungry. As for me, I vow I could demolish a baron of beef to-night."

"Here they are, I do believe," said Sally, excitedly, as a distant clatter of horses and wheels could now be distinctly heard, drawing rapidly nearer.

There was general commotion in the coffee-room. Everyone was curious to see my Lord Antony's swell friends from over the water. Miss Sally cast one or two quick glances at the little bit of mirror which hung on the wall, and worthy Mr. Jellyband bustled out in order to give the first welcome himself to his distinguished guests. Only the two strangers in the corner did not participate in the general excitement. They were calmly finishing their game of dominoes, and did not even look once towards the door.

"Straight ahead, Comtesse, the door on your right," said a pleasant voice outside.

"Aye! there they are, all right enough," said Lord Antony, joyfully; "off with you, my pretty Sally, and see how quickly you can dish up the soup."

The door was thrown wide open, and, preceded by Mr. Jellyband, who was profuse in his bows and welcomes, a party of four—two ladies and two gentlemen—entered the coffee-room.

"Welcome! Welcome to old England!" said Lord Antony, effusively, as he came eagerly forward with both hands outstretched towards the newcomers.

"Ah, you are Lord Antony Dewhurst, I think," said one of the ladies, speaking with a strong foreign accent.

"At your service, Madame," he replied, as he ceremoniously kissed the hands of both the ladies, then turned to the men and shook them both warmly by the hand.

Sally was already helping the ladies to take off their travelling cloaks, and both turned, with a shiver, towards the brightly-blazing hearth.

There was a general movement among the company in the coffee-room. Sally had bustled off to her kitchen, whilst Jellyband, still profuse with his respectful salutations, arranged one or two chairs around the fire. Mr. Hempseed, touching his forelock, was quietly vacating the seat in the hearth. Everyone was staring curiously, yet deferentially, at the foreigners.

"Ah, Messieurs! what can I say?" said the elder of the two ladies, as she stretched a pair of fine, aristocratic hands to the warmth of the blaze, and looked with unspeakable gratitude first at Lord Antony, then at one of the young men who had accompanied her party, and who was busy divesting himself of his heavy, caped coat.

"Only that you are glad to be in England, Comtesse," replied Lord Antony, "and that you have not suffered too much from your trying voyage."

"Indeed, indeed, we are glad to be in England," she said, while her eyes filled with tears, "and we have already forgotten all that we have suffered."

Her voice was musical and low, and there was a great deal of calm dignity and of many sufferings nobly endured marked in the handsome, aristocratic face, with its wealth of snow-white hair dressed high above the forehead, after the fashion of the times.

"I hope my friend, Sir Andrew Ffoulkes, proved an entertaining travelling companion, Madame?"

"Ah, indeed, Sir Andrew was kindness itself. How could my children and I ever show enough gratitude to you all, Messieurs?"

Her companion, a dainty, girlish figure, childlike and pathetic in its look of fatigue and of sorrow, had said nothing as yet, but her eyes, large, brown, and full of tears, looked up from the fire and sought those of Sir Andrew Ffoulkes, who had drawn near to the hearth and to her; then, as they met his, which were fixed with unconcealed admiration upon the sweet face before him, a thought of warmer colour rushed up to her pale cheeks.

"So this is England," she said, as she looked round with childlike curiosity at the great open hearth, the oak rafters, and the yokels with their elaborate smocks and jovial, rubicund, British countenances.

"A bit of it, Mademoiselle," replied Sir Andrew, smiling, "but all of it, at your service."

The young girl blushed again, but this time a bright smile, fleet and sweet, illumined her dainty face. She said nothing, and Sir Andrew too was silent, yet those two young people understood one another, as young people have a way of doing all the world over, and have done since the world began.

"But, I say, supper!" here broke in Lord Antony's jovial voice, "supper, honest Jellyband. Where is that pretty wench of yours and the dish of soup? Zooks, man, while you stand there gaping at the ladies, they will faint with hunger."

"One moment! one moment, my lord," said Jellyband, as he threw open the door that led to the kitchen and shouted lustily: "Sally! Hey, Sally there, are ye ready, my girl?"

Sally was ready, and the next moment she appeared in the doorway carrying a gigantic tureen, from which rose a cloud of steam and an abundance of savoury odour.

"Odd's my life, supper at last!" ejaculated Lord Antony, merrily, as he gallantly offered his arm to the Comtesse.

"May I have the honour?" he added ceremoniously, as he led her towards the supper table.

There was general bustle in the coffee-room: Mr. Hempseed and most of the yokels and fisher-folk had gone to make way for "the quality," and to finish smoking their pipes elsewhere. Only the two strangers stayed on, quietly and unconcernedly playing their game of dominoes and sipping their wine; whilst at another table Harry Waite, who was fast losing his temper, watched pretty Sally bustling round the table.

She looked a very dainty picture of English rural life, and no wonder that the susceptible young Frenchman could scarce take his eyes off her pretty face. The Vicomte de Tournay was scarce nineteen, a beardless boy, on whom the terrible tragedies which were being enacted in his own country had made but little impression. He was elegantly and even foppishly dressed, and once safely landed in England he was evidently ready to forget the horrors of the Revolution in the delights of English life.

"Pardi, if zis is England," he said as he continued to ogle Sally with marked satisfaction, "I am of it satisfied."

It would be impossible at this point to record the exact exclamation which escaped through Mr. Harry Waite's clenched teeth. Only respect for "the quality," and notably for my Lord Antony, kept his marked disapproval of the young foreigner in check.

"Nay, but this *is* England, you abandoned young reprobate," interposed Lord Antony with a laugh, "and do not, I pray, bring your loose foreign ways into this most moral country."

Lord Antony had already sat down at the head of the table with the Comtesse on his right. Jellyband was bustling round, filling glasses and putting chairs straight. Sally waited, ready to hand round the soup. Mr. Harry Waite's friends had at last succeeded in taking him out of the room, for his temper was growing more and more violent under the Vicomte's obvious admiration for Sally.

"Suzanne," came in stern, commanding accents from the rigid Comtesse.

Suzanne blushed again; she had lost count of time and of place whilst she had stood beside the fire, allowing the handsome young Englishman's eyes to dwell upon her sweet face, and his hand, as if unconsciously, to rest upon hers. Her mother's voice brought her back to reality once more, and with a submissive "Yes, Mama," she too took her place at the supper table.

IV. THE LEAGUE OF THE SCARLET PIMPERNEL

They all looked a merry, even a happy party, as they sat round the table; Sir Andrew Ffoulkes and Lord Antony Dewhurst, two typical good-looking, well-born and well-bred Englishmen of that year of grace 1792, and the aristocratic French comtesse with her two children, who had just escaped from such dire perils, and found a safe retreat at last on the shores of protecting England.

In the corner the two strangers had apparently finished their game; one of them arose, and standing with his back to the merry company at the table, he adjusted with much deliberation his large triple caped coat. As he did so, he gave one quick glance all around him. Everyone was busy laughing and chatting, and he murmured the words "All safe!": his companion then, with the alertness borne of long practice, slipped on to his knees in a moment, and the next had crept noiselessly under the oak bench. The stranger then, with a loud "Good-night," quietly walked out of the coffee-room.

Not one of those at the supper table had noticed this curious and silent manœuvre, but when the stranger finally closed the door of the coffee-room behind him, they all instinctively sighed a sigh of relief.

"Alone, at last!" said Lord Antony, jovially.

Then the young Vicomte de Tournay rose, glass in hand, and with the graceful affectation peculiar to the times, he raised it aloft, and said in broken English,—

"To His Majesty George Three of England. God bless him for his hospitality to us all, poor exiles from France."

"His Majesty the King!" echoed Lord Antony and Sir Andrew as they drank loyally to the toast.

"To His Majesty King Louis of France," added Sir Andrew, with solemnity. "May God protect him, and give him victory over his enemies."

Everyone rose and drank this toast in silence. The fate of the unfortunate King of France, then a prisoner of his own people, seemed to cast a gloom even over Mr. Jellyband's pleasant countenance.

"And to M. le Comte de Tournay de Basserive," said Lord Antony, merrily. "May we welcome him in England before many days are over."

"Ah, Monsieur," said the Comtesse, as with a slightly trembling hand she conveyed her glass to her lips, "I scarcely dare to hope."

But already Lord Antony had served out the soup, and for the next few moments all conversation ceased, while Jellyband and Sally handed round the plates and everyone began to eat.

"Faith, Madame!" said Lord Antony, after a while, "mine was no idle toast; seeing yourself, Mademoiselle Suzanne and my friend the Vicomte safely in England now, surely you must feel reassured as to the fate of Monsieur le Comte."

"Ah, Monsieur," replied the Comtesse, with a heavy sigh, "I trust in God—I can but pray—and hope . . ."

"Aye, Madame!" here interposed Sir Andrew Ffoulkes, "trust in God by all means, but believe also a little in your English friends, who have sworn to bring the Count safely across the Channel, even as they have brought you to-day."

"Indeed, indeed, Monsieur," she replied, "I have the fullest confidence in you and in your friends. Your fame, I assure you, has spread throughout the whole of France. The way some of my own friends have escaped from the clutches of that awful revolutionary tribunal was nothing short of a miracle—and all done by you and your friends—"

"We were but the hands, Madame la Comtesse . . ."

"But my husband, Monsieur," said the Comtesse, whilst unshed tears seemed to veil her voice, "he is in such deadly peril—I would never have left him, only . . . there were my children . . . I was torn between my duty to him, and to them. They refused to go without me . . . and you and your friends assured me so solemnly that my husband would be safe. But, oh! now that I am here—amongst you all—in this beautiful, free England—I think of him, flying for his life, hunted like a poor beast . . . in such peril. . . . Ah! I should not have left him . . . I should not have left him! . . ."

The poor woman had completely broken down; fatigue, sorrow and emotion had overmastered her rigid, aristocratic bearing. She was crying gently to herself, whilst Suzanne ran up to her and tried to kiss away her tears.

Lord Antony and Sir Andrew had said nothing to interrupt the Comtesse whilst she was speaking. There was no doubt that they felt deeply for her; their very silence testified to that—but in every century, and ever since England has been what it is, an Englishman has always felt somewhat ashamed of his own emotion and of his own sympathy. And so the two young men said nothing, and busied themselves in trying to hide their feelings, only succeeding in looking immeasurably sheepish.

"As for me, Monsieur," said Suzanne, suddenly, as she looked through a wealth of brown curls across at Sir Andrew, "I trust you absolutely, and I *know* that you will bring my dear father safely to England, just as you brought us to-day."

This was said with so much confidence, such unuttered hope and belief, that it seemed as if by magic to dry the mother's eyes, and to bring a smile upon everybody's lips.

"Nay! you shame me, Mademoiselle," replied Sir Andrew; "though my life is at your service, I have been but a humble tool in the hands of our great leader, who organised and effected your escape."

He had spoken with so much warmth and vehemence that Suzanne's eyes fastened upon him in undisguised wonder.

"Your leader, Monsieur?" said the Comtesse, eagerly. "Ah! of course, you must have a leader. And I did not think of that before! But tell me where is he? I must go to him at once, and I and my children must throw ourselves at his feet, and thank him for all that he has done for us."

"Alas, Madame!" said Lord Antony, "that is impossible."

"Impossible?—Why?"

"Because the Scarlet Pimpernel works in the dark, and his identity is only known under a solemn oath of secrecy to his immediate followers."

"The Scarlet Pimpernel?" said Suzanne, with a merry laugh. "Why! what a droll name! What is the Scarlet Pimpernel, Monsieur?"

She looked at Sir Andrew with eager curiosity. The young man's face had become almost transfigured. His eyes shone with enthusiasm; hero-worship, love, admiration for his leader seemed literally to glow upon his face.

"The Scarlet Pimpernel, Mademoiselle," he said at last, "is the name of a humble English wayside flower; but it is also the name chosen to hide the identity of the best and bravest man in all the world, so that he may better succeed in accomplishing the noble task he has set himself to do."

"Ah, yes," here interposed the young Vicomte, "I have heard speak of this Scarlet Pimpernel. A little flower—red?—yes! They say in Paris that every time a royalist escapes to England that devil, Foucquier-Tinville, the Public Prosecutor, receives a paper with that little flower dessinated in red upon it.... Yes?"

"Yes, that is so," assented Lord Antony.

"Then he will have received one such paper to-day?"

"Undoubtedly."

"Oh! I wonder what he will say!" said Suzanne, merrily. "I have heard that the picture of that little red flower is the only thing that frightens him."

"Faith, then," said Sir Andrew, "he will have many more opportunities of studying the shape of that small scarlet flower."

"Ah! Monsieur," sighed the Comtesse, "it all sounds like a romance, and I cannot understand it all."

"Why should you try, Madame?"

"But, tell me, why should your leader—why should you all—spend your money and risk your lives—for it is your lives you risk, Messieurs, when you set foot in France—and all for us French men and women, who are nothing to you?"

"Sport, Madame la Comtesse, sport," asserted Lord Antony, with his jovial, loud and pleasant voice; "we are a nation of sportsmen, you know, and just now it is the fashion to pull the hare from between the teeth of the hound."

"Ah, no, no, not sport only, Monsieur ... you have a more noble motive, I am sure, for the good work you do."

"Faith, Madame, I would like you to find it then ... as for me, I vow, I love the game, for this is the finest sport I have yet encountered.—Hair-breadth escapes ... the devil's own risks!—Tally ho!—and away we go!"

But the Comtesse shook her head, still incredulously. To her it seemed preposterous that these young men and their great leader, all of them rich, probably well-born, and young, should for no other motive than sport, run the terrible risks, which she knew they were constantly doing. Their nationality, once they had set foot in France, would be no safeguard to them. Anyone found harbouring or assisting suspected royalists would be ruthlessly condemned and summarily executed, whatever his nationality might be. And this band of young Englishmen had, to her own knowledge, bearded the implacable and bloodthirsty tribunal of the Revolution, within the very walls of Paris itself, and had snatched away condemned victims, almost from the very foot of the guillotine. With a shudder, she recalled the events of the last few days, her escape from Paris with her two children, all three of them hidden beneath the hood of a rickety cart, and lying amidst a heap of turnips and cabbages, not daring to breathe, whilst the mob howled "À la lanterne les aristos!" at that awful West Barricade.

It had all occurred in such a miraculous way; she and her husband had understood that they had been placed on the list of "suspected persons," which meant that their trial and death were but a matter of days—of hours, perhaps.

Then came the hope of salvation; the mysterious epistle, signed with the enigmatical scarlet device; the clear, peremptory directions; the parting from the Comte de Tournay, which had torn the poor wife's heart in two; the hope of reunion; the flight with her two children; the covered cart; that awful hag driving it, who looked like some horrible evil demon, with the ghastly trophy on her whip handle!

The Comtesse looked round at the quaint, old-fashioned English inn, the peace of this land of civil and religious liberty, and she closed her eyes to shut out the haunting vision of that West Barricade, and of the mob retreating panic-stricken when the old hag spoke of the plague.

Every moment under that cart she expected recognition, arrest, herself and her children tried and condemned, and these young Englishmen, under the guidance of their brave and mysterious leader, had risked their lives to save them all, as they had already saved scores of other innocent people.

And all only for sport? Impossible! Suzanne's eyes as she sought those of Sir Andrew plainly told him that she thought that *he* at any rate rescued his fellow-men from terrible and unmerited death, through a higher and nobler motive than his friend would have her believe.

"How many are there in your brave league, Monsieur?" she asked timidly.

"Twenty all told, Mademoiselle," he replied, "one to command, and nineteen to obey. All of us Englishmen, and all pledged to the same cause—to obey our leader and to rescue the innocent."

"May God protect you all, Messieurs," said the Comtesse, fervently.

"He has done that so far, Madame."

"It is wonderful to me, wonderful!—That you should all be so brave, so devoted to your fellow-men—yet you are English!—and in France treachery is rife—all in the name of liberty and fraternity."

"The women even, in France, have been more bitter against us aristocrats than the men," said the Vicomte, with a sigh.

"Ah, yes," added the Comtesse, whilst a look of haughty disdain and intense bitterness shot through her melancholy eyes. "There was that woman, Marguerite St. Just, for instance. She denounced the Marquis de St. Cyr and all his family to the awful tribunal of the Terror."

"Marguerite St. Just?" said Lord Antony, as he shot a quick and apprehensive glance across at Sir Andrew. "Marguerite St. Just?—Surely..."

"Yes!" replied the Comtesse, "surely you know her. She was a leading actress of the Comédie Française, and she married an Englishman lately. You must know her—"

"Know her?" said Lord Antony. "Know Lady Blakeney—the most fashionable woman in London—the wife of the richest man in England? Of course, we all know Lady Blakeney."

"She was a school-fellow of mine at the convent in Paris," interposed Suzanne, "and we came over to England together to learn your language. I was very fond of Marguerite, and I cannot believe that she ever did anything so wicked."

"It certainly seems incredible," said Sir Andrew. "You say that she actually denounced the Marquis de St. Cyr? Why should she have done such a thing? Surely there must be some mistake—"

"No mistake is possible, Monsieur," rejoined the Comtesse, coldly. "Marguerite St. Just's brother is a noted republican. There was some talk of a family feud between him and my cousin, the Marquis de St. Cyr. The St. Justs' are quite plebeian, and the republican government employs many spies. I assure you there is no mistake. . . . You had not heard this story?"

"Faith, Madame, I did hear some vague rumours of it, but in England no one would credit it. . . . Sir Percy Blakeney, her husband, is a very wealthy man, of high social position, the intimate friend of the Prince of Wales . . . and Lady Blakeney leads both fashion and society in London."

"That may be, Monsieur, and we shall, of course, lead a very quiet life in England, but I pray God that while I remain in this beautiful country, I may never meet Marguerite St. Just."

The proverbial wet-blanket seemed to have fallen over the merry little company gathered round the table. Suzanne looked sad and silent; Sir Andrew fidgeted uneasily with his fork, whilst the Comtesse, encased in the plate-armour of her aristocratic prejudices, sat, rigid and unbending, in her straight-backed chair. As for Lord Antony, he looked extremely uncomfortable, and glanced once or twice apprehensively towards Jellyband, who looked just as uncomfortable as himself.

"At what time do you expect Sir Percy and Lady Blakeney?" he contrived to whisper unobserved, to mine host.

"Any moment, my lord," whispered Jellyband in reply.

Even as he spoke, a distant clatter was heard of an approaching coach; louder and louder it grew, one or two shouts became distinguishable, then the rattle of horses' hoofs on the uneven cobble stones, and the next moment a stable boy had thrown open the coffee-room door and rushed in excitedly.

"Sir Percy Blakeney and my lady," he shouted at the top of his voice, "they're just arriving."

And with more shouting, jingling of harness, and iron hoofs upon the stones, a magnificent coach, drawn by four superb bays, had halted outside the porch of "The Fisherman's Rest."

V. MARGUERITE

In a moment the pleasant oak-raftered coffee-room of the inn became the scene of hopeless confusion and discomfort. At the first announcement made by the stable boy, Lord Antony, with a fashionable oath, had jumped up from his seat and was now giving many and confused directions to poor bewildered Jellyband, who seemed at his wits' end what to do.

"For goodness' sake, man," admonished his lordship, "try to keep Lady Blakeney talking outside for a moment, while the ladies withdraw. Zounds!" he added, with another more emphatic oath, "this is most unfortunate."

"Quick, Sally! the candles!" shouted Jellyband, as hopping about from one leg to another, he ran hither and thither, adding to the general discomfort of everybody.

The Comtesse, too, had risen to her feet: rigid and erect, trying to hide her excitement beneath more becoming *sang-froid,* she repeated mechanically,—

"I will not see her!—I will not see her!"

Outside, the excitement attendant upon the arrival of very important guests grew apace.

"Good-day, Sir Percy!—Good-day to your ladyship! Your servant, Sir Percy!"—was heard in one long, continued chorus, with alternate more feeble tones of—"Remember the poor blind man! of your charity, lady and gentleman!"

Then suddenly a singularly sweet voice was heard through all the din.

"Let the poor man be—and give him some supper at my expense."

The voice was low and musical, with a slight sing-song in it, and a faint *soupçon* of foreign intonation in the pronunciation of the consonants.

Everyone in the coffee-room heard it and paused, instinctively listening to it for a moment. Sally was holding the candles by the opposite door, which led to the bedrooms upstairs, and the Comtesse was in the act of beating a hasty retreat before that enemy who owned such a sweet musical voice; Suzanne reluctantly was preparing to follow her mother, whilst casting regretful glances towards the door, where she hoped still to see her dearly-beloved, erstwhile school-fellow.

Then Jellyband threw open the door, still stupidly and blindly hoping to avert the catastrophe which he felt was in the air, and the same low, musical voice said, with a merry laugh and mock consternation,—

"B-r-r-r-r! I am as wet as a herring! *Dieu!* has anyone ever seen such a contemptible climate?"

"Suzanne, come with me at once—I wish it," said the Comtesse, peremptorily.

"Oh! Mama!" pleaded Suzanne.

"My lady . . . er . . . h'm! . . . my lady! . . ." came in feeble accents from Jellyband, who stood clumsily trying to bar the way.

"*Pardieu*, my good man," said Lady Blakeney, with some impatience, "what are you standing in my way for, dancing about like a turkey with a sore foot? Let me get to the fire, I am perished with the cold."

And the next moment Lady Blakeney, gently pushing mine host on one side, had swept into the coffee-room.

There are many portraits and miniatures extant of Marguerite St. Just—Lady Blakeney as she was then—but it is doubtful if any of these really do her singular beauty justice. Tall, above the average, with magnificent presence and regal figure, it is small wonder that even the Comtesse paused for a moment in involuntary admiration before turning her back on so fascinating an apparition.

Marguerite Blakeney was then scarcely five-and-twenty, and her beauty was at its most dazzling stage. The large hat, with its undulating and waving plumes, threw a soft shadow across the classic brow with the aureole of auburn hair—free at the moment from any powder; the sweet, almost childlike mouth, the straight chiselled nose, round chin, and delicate throat, all seemed set off by the picturesque costume of the period. The rich blue velvet robe moulded in its every line the graceful contour of the figure, whilst one tiny hand held, with a dignity all its own, the tall stick adorned with a large bunch of ribbons which fashionable ladies of the period had taken to carrying recently.

With a quick glance all around the room, Marguerite Blakeney had taken stock of everyone there. She nodded pleasantly to Sir Andrew Ffoulkes, whilst extending a hand to Lord Antony.

"Hello! my Lord Tony, why—what are *you* doing here in Dover?" she said merrily.

Then, without waiting for a reply, she turned and faced the Comtesse and Suzanne. Her whole face lighted up with additional brightness, as she stretched out both arms towards the young girl.

"Why! if that isn't my little Suzanne over there. *Pardieu*, little citizeness, how came you to be in England? And Madame too!"

She went up effusively to them both, with not a single touch of embarrassment in her manner or in her smile. Lord Tony and Sir Andrew watched the little scene with eager apprehension. English though they were, they had often been in France, and had mixed sufficiently with the French to realise the unbending hauteur, the bitter hatred with which the old *noblesse* of France viewed all those who had helped to contribute to their downfall. Armand St. Just, the brother of beautiful Lady Blakeney—though known to hold moderate and conciliatory views—was an ardent republican; his feud with the ancient family of St. Cyr—the rights and wrongs of which no outsider ever knew—had culminated in the downfall, the almost total extinction, of the latter. In France, St. Just and his party had triumphed, and here in England, face to face with these three refugees driven from their country, flying for their lives, bereft of all which centuries of luxury had given them, there stood a fair scion of those same republican families which had hurled down a throne, and uprooted an aristocracy whose origin was lost in the dim and distant vista of bygone centuries.

She stood there before them, in all the unconscious insolence of beauty, and stretched out her dainty hand to them, as if she would, by that one act, bridge over the conflict and bloodshed of the past decade.

"Suzanne, I forbid you to speak to that woman," said the Comtesse, sternly, as she placed a restraining hand upon her daughter's arm.

She had spoken in English, so that all might hear and understand; the two young English gentlemen as well as the common innkeeper and his daughter. The latter literally gasped with horror at this foreign insolence, this impudence before her ladyship—who was English, now that she was Sir Percy's wife, and a friend of the Princess of Wales to boot.

As for Lord Antony and Sir Andrew Ffoulkes, their very hearts seemed to stand still with horror at this gratuitous insult. One of them uttered an exclamation of appeal, the other one of warning, and instinctively both glanced hurriedly towards the door, whence a slow, drawly, not unpleasant voice had already been heard.

Alone among those present Marguerite Blakeney and the Comtesse de Tournay had remained seemingly unmoved. The latter, rigid, erect and defiant, with one hand still upon her daughter's arm, seemed the very personification of unbending pride. For the moment Marguerite's sweet face had become as white as the soft fichu which swathed her throat, and a very keen observer might have noted that the hand which held the tall, beribboned stick was clenched, and trembled somewhat.

But this was only momentary; the next instant the delicate eyebrows were raised slightly, the lips curved sarcastically upwards, the clear blue eyes looked straight at the rigid Comtesse, and with a slight shrug of the shoulders—

"Hoity-toity, citizeness," she said gaily, "what fly stings you, pray?"

"We are in England now, Madame," rejoined the Comtesse, coldly, "and I am at liberty to forbid my daughter to touch your hand in friendship. Come, Suzanne."

She beckoned to her daughter, and without another look at Marguerite Blakeney, but with a deep, old-fashioned curtsey to the two young men, she sailed majestically out of the room.

There was silence in the old inn parlour for a moment, as the rustle of the Comtesse's skirts died away down the passage. Marguerite, rigid as a statue, followed with hard, set eyes the upright figure, as it disappeared through the doorway—but as little Suzanne, humble and obedient, was about to follow her mother, the hard, set expression suddenly vanished, and a wistful, almost pathetic and childlike look stole into Lady Blakeney's eyes.

Little Suzanne caught that look; the child's sweet nature went out to the beautiful woman, scarce older than herself; filial obedience vanished before girlish sympathy; at the door she turned, ran back to Marguerite, and putting her arms round her, kissed her effusively; then only did she follow her mother, Sally bringing up the rear, with a pleasant smile on her dimpled face, and with a final curtsey to my lady.

Suzanne's sweet and dainty impulse had relieved the unpleasant tension. Sir Andrew's eyes followed the pretty little figure, until it had quite disappeared, then they met Lady Blakeney's with unassumed merriment.

Marguerite, with dainty affectation, had kissed her hand to the ladies, as they disappeared through the door, then a humorous smile began hovering round the corners of her mouth.

"So that's it, is it?" she said gaily. "La! Sir Andrew, did you ever see such an unpleasant person? I hope when I grow old I sha'n't look like that."

She gathered up her skirts, and assuming a majestic gait, stalked towards the fireplace.

"Suzanne," she said, mimicking the Comtesse's voice, "I forbid you to speak to that woman!"

The laugh which accompanied this sally sounded perhaps a trifle forced and hard, but neither Sir Andrew nor Lord Tony were very keen observers. The mimicry was so perfect, the tone of the voice so accurately reproduced, that both the young men joined in a hearty cheerful "Bravo!"

"Ah! Lady Blakeney!" added Lord Tony, "how they must miss you at the Comédie Française, and how the Parisians must hate Sir Percy for having taken you away."

"Lud, man," rejoined Marguerite, with a shrug of her graceful shoulders, "'tis impossible to hate Sir Percy for anything; his witty sallies would disarm even Madame la Comtesse herself."

The young Vicomte, who had not elected to follow his mother in her dignified exit, now made a step forward, ready to champion the Comtesse should Lady Blakeney aim any further shafts at her. But before he could utter a preliminary word of protest, a pleasant, though distinctly inane laugh, was heard from outside, and the next moment an unusually tall and very richly dressed figure appeared in the doorway.

VI. AN EXQUISITE OF '92

Sir Percy Blakeney, as the chronicles of the time inform us, was in this year of grace 1792, still a year or two on the right side of thirty. Tall, above the average, even for an Englishman, broad-shouldered and massively built, he would have been called unusually good-looking, but for a certain lazy expression in his deep-set blue eyes, and that perpetual inane laugh which seemed to disfigure his strong, clearly-cut mouth.

It was nearly a year ago now that Sir Percy Blakeney, Bart., one of the richest men in England, leader of all the fashions, and intimate friend of the Prince of Wales, had astonished fashionable society in London and Bath by bringing home, from one of his journeys abroad, a beautiful, fascinating, clever, French wife. He, the sleepiest, dullest, most British Britisher that had ever set a pretty woman yawning, had secured a brilliant matrimonial prize for which, as all chroniclers aver, there had been many competitors.

Marguerite St. Just had first made her *début* in artistic Parisian circles, at the very moment when the greatest social upheaval the world has ever known was taking place within its very walls. Scarcely eighteen, lavishly gifted with beauty and talent, chaperoned only by a young and devoted brother, she had soon gathered round her, in her charming apartment in the Rue Richelieu, a coterie which was as brilliant as it was exclusive—exclusive, that is to say, only from one point of view: Marguerite St. Just was from principle and by conviction a republican—equality of birth was her motto—inequality of fortune was in her eyes a mere untoward accident, but the only inequality she admitted was that of talent. "Money and titles may be hereditary," she would say, "but brains are not," and thus her charming salon was reserved for originality and intellect, for brilliance and wit, for clever men and talented women, and the entrance into it was soon looked upon in the world of intellect—which even in those days and in those troublous times found its pivot in Paris—as the seal to an artistic career.

Clever men, distinguished men, and even men of exalted station formed a perpetual and brilliant court round the fascinating young actress of the Comédie Française, and she glided through republican, revolutionary, bloodthirsty Paris like a shining comet with a trail behind her of all that was most distinguished, most interesting, in intellectual Europe.

Then the climax came. Some smiled indulgently and called it an artistic eccentricity, others looked upon it as a wise provision, in view of the many events which were crowding thick and fast in Paris just then, but to all, the real motive of that climax remained a puzzle and a mystery. Anyway, Marguerite St. Just married Sir Percy Blakeney one fine day, just like that, without any warning to her friends, without a *soirée de contrat* or *dîner de fiançailles* or other appurtenances of a fashionable French wedding.

How that stupid, dull Englishman ever came to be admitted within the intellectual circle which revolved round "the cleverest woman in Europe," as her friends unanimously called her, no one ventured to guess—a golden key is said to open every door, asserted the more malignantly inclined.

Enough, she married him, and "the cleverest woman in Europe" had linked her fate to that "demmed idiot" Blakeney, and not even her most intimate friends could assign to this strange step any other motive than that of supreme eccentricity. Those friends who knew, laughed to scorn the idea that Marguerite St. Just had married a fool for the sake of the worldly advantages with which he might endow her. They knew, as a matter of fact, that Marguerite St. Just cared nothing about money, and still less about a title; moreover, there were at least half a dozen other men in the cosmopolitan world equally well-born, if not so wealthy as Blakeney, who would have been only too happy to give Marguerite St. Just any position she might choose to covet.

As for Sir Percy himself, he was universally voted to be totally unqualified for the onerous post he had taken upon himself. His chief qualifications for it seemed to consist in his blind adoration for her, his great wealth, and the high favour in which he stood at the English court; but London society thought that, taking into consideration his own intellectual limitations, it would have been wiser on his part had he bestowed those worldly advantages upon a less brilliant and witty wife.

Although lately he had been so prominent a figure in fashionable English society, he had spent most of his early life abroad. His father, the late Sir Algernon Blakeney, had had the terrible misfortune of seeing an idolized young wife become hopelessly insane after two years of happy married life. Percy had just been born when the late Lady Blakeney fell a prey to the terrible malady which in those days was looked upon as hopelessly incurable and nothing short of a curse of God upon the entire family. Sir Algernon took his afflicted young wife abroad, and there presumably Percy was educated, and grew up between an imbecile mother and a distracted father, until he attained his majority. The death of his parents following close upon one another left him a free man, and as Sir Algernon had led a forcibly simple and retired life, the large Blakeney fortune had increased tenfold.

Sir Percy Blakeney had travelled a great deal abroad, before he brought home his beautiful, young, French wife. The fashionable circles of the time were ready to receive them both with open arms. Sir Percy was rich, his wife was accomplished, the Prince of Wales took a very great liking to them both. Within six months they were the acknowledged leaders of fashion and of style. Sir Percy's coats were the talk of the town, his inanities were quoted, his foolish laugh copied by the gilded youth at Almack's or the Mall. Everyone knew that he was hopelessly stupid, but then that was scarcely to be wondered at, seeing that all the Blakeneys, for generations, had been notoriously dull, and that his mother had died an imbecile.

Thus society accepted him, petted him, made much of him, since his horses were the finest in the country, his *fêtes* and wines the most sought after. As for his marriage with "the cleverest woman in Europe," well! the inevitable came with sure and rapid footsteps. No one pitied him, since his fate was of his own making. There were plenty of young ladies in England, of high birth and good looks, who would have been quite willing to help him to spend the Blakeney fortune, whilst smiling indulgently at his inanities and his good-humoured foolishness. Moreover, Sir Percy got no pity, because he seemed to require none—he seemed very proud of his clever wife, and to care little that she took no pains to disguise that good-natured contempt which she evidently felt for him, and that she even amused herself by sharpening her ready wits at his expense.

But then Blakeney was really too stupid to notice the ridicule with which his clever wife covered him, and if his matrimonial relations with the fascinating Parisienne had not turned out all that his hopes and his dog-like devotion for her had pictured, society could never do more than vaguely guess at it.

In his beautiful house at Richmond he played second fiddle to his clever wife with imperturbable *bonhomie*; he lavished jewels and luxuries of all kinds upon her, which she took with inimitable grace, dispensing the hospitality of his superb mansion with the same graciousness with which she had welcomed the intellectual coterie of Paris.

Physically, Sir Percy Blakeney was undeniably handsome—always excepting the lazy, bored look which was habitual to him. He was always irreproachably dressed, and wore the exaggerated "Incroyable" fashions, which had just crept across from Paris to England, with the perfect good taste innate in an English gentleman. On this special afternoon in September, in spite of the long journey by coach, in spite of rain and mud, his coat set irreproachably across his fine shoulders, his hands looked almost femininely white, as they emerged through billowy frills of finest Mechlin lace: the extravagantly short-waisted satin coat, wide-lapelled waistcoat, and tight-fitting striped breeches, set off his massive figure to perfection, and in repose one might have admired so fine a specimen of English manhood, until the foppish ways, the affected movements, the perpetual inane laugh, brought one's admiration of Sir Percy Blakeney to an abrupt close.

He had lolled into the old-fashioned inn parlour, shaking the wet off his fine overcoat; then putting up a gold-rimmed eye-glass to his lazy blue eye, he surveyed the company, upon whom an embarrassed silence had suddenly fallen.

"How do, Tony? How do, Ffoulkes?" he said, recognising the two young men and shaking them by the hand. "Zounds, my dear fellow," he added, smothering a slight yawn, "did you ever see such a beastly day? Demmed climate this."

With a quaint little laugh, half of embarrassment and half of sarcasm, Marguerite had turned towards her husband, and was surveying him from head to foot, with an amused little twinkle in her merry blue eyes.

"La!" said Sir Percy, after a moment or two's silence, as no one offered any comment, "how sheepish you all look.... What's up?"

"Oh, nothing, Sir Percy," replied Marguerite, with a certain amount of gaiety, which, however, sounded somewhat forced, "nothing to disturb your equanimity—only an insult to your wife."

The laugh which accompanied this remark was evidently intended to reassure Sir Percy as to the gravity of the incident. It apparently succeeded in that, for, echoing the laugh, he rejoined placidly—

"La, m'dear! you don't say so. Begad! who was the bold man who dared to tackle you—eh?"

Lord Tony tried to interpose, but had no time to do so, for the young Vicomte had already quickly stepped forward.

"Monsieur," he said, prefixing his little speech with an elaborate bow, and speaking in broken English, "my mother, the Comtesse de Tournay de Basserive, has offenced Madame, who, I see, is your wife. I cannot ask your pardon for my mother; what she does is right in my eyes. But I am ready to offer you the usual reparation between men of honour."

The young man drew up his slim stature to its full height and looked very enthusiastic, very proud, and very hot as he gazed at six foot odd of gorgeousness, as represented by Sir Percy Blakeney, Bart.

"Lud, Sir Andrew," said Marguerite, with one of her merry infectious laughs, "look on that pretty picture—the English turkey and the French bantam."

The simile was quite perfect, and the English turkey looked down with complete bewilderment upon the dainty little French bantam, which hovered quite threateningly around him.

"La! sir," said Sir Percy at last, putting up his eye-glass and surveying the young Frenchman with undisguised wonderment, "where, in the cuckoo's name, did you learn to speak English?"

"Monsieur!" protested the Vicomte, somewhat abashed at the way his warlike attitude had been taken by the ponderous-looking Englishman.

"I protest 'tis marvellous!" continued Sir Percy, imperturbably, "demmed marvellous! Don't you think so, Tony—eh? I vow I can't speak the French lingo like that. What?"

"Nay, I'll vouch for that!" rejoined Marguerite. "Sir Percy has a British accent you could cut with a knife."

"Monsieur," interposed the Vicomte earnestly, and in still more broken English, "I fear you have not understand. I offer you the only posseeble reparation among gentlemen."

"What the devil is that?" asked Sir Percy, blandly.

"My sword, Monsieur," replied the Vicomte, who, though still bewildered, was beginning to lose his temper.

"You are a sportsman, Lord Tony," said Marguerite, merrily; "ten to one on the little bantam."

But Sir Percy was staring sleepily at the Vicomte for a moment or two, through his partly closed heavy lids, then he smothered another yawn, stretched his long limbs, and turned leisurely away.

"Lud love you, sir," he muttered good-humouredly. "Demmit, young man, what's the good of your sword to me?"

What the Vicomte thought and felt at that moment, when that long-limbed Englishman treated him with such marked insolence, might fill volumes of sound reflections. . . . What he said resolved itself into a single articulate word, for all the others were choked in his throat by his surging wrath—

"A duel, Monsieur," he stammered.

Once more Blakeney turned, and from his high altitude looked down on the choleric little man before him; but not even for a second did he seem to lose his own imperturbable good-humour. He laughed his own pleasant and inane laugh, and burying his slender, long hands into the capacious pockets of his overcoat, he said leisurely—

"A duel? La! is that what he meant? Odd's fish! you are a bloodthirsty young ruffian. Do you want to make a hole in a law-abiding man? . . . As for me, sir, I never fight duels," he added, as he placidly sat down and stretched his long, lazy legs out before him. "Demmed uncomfortable things, duels, ain't they, Tony?"

Now the Vicomte had no doubt vaguely heard that in England the fashion of duelling amongst gentlemen had been suppressed by the law with a very stern hand; still to him, a Frenchman, whose notions of bravery and honour were based upon a code that had centuries of tradition to back it, the spectacle of a gentleman actually refusing to fight a duel was little short of an enormity. In his mind he vaguely pondered whether he should strike that long-legged Englishman in the face and call him a coward, or whether such conduct in a lady's presence might be deemed ungentlemanly, when Marguerite happily interposed.

"I pray you, Lord Tony," she said in that gentle, sweet, musical voice of hers, "I pray you play the peacemaker. The child is bursting with rage, and," she added with a *soupçon* of dry sarcasm, "might do Sir Percy an injury." She laughed a mocking little laugh, which, however, did not in the least disturb her husband's placid equanimity. "The British turkey has had the day," she said. "Sir Percy would provoke all the saints in the calendar and keep his temper the while."

But already Blakeney, good-humoured as ever, had joined in the laugh against himself.

"Demmed smart that now, wasn't it?" he said, turning pleasantly to the Vicomte. "Clever woman my wife, sir. . . . You will find *that* out if you live long enough in England."

"Sir Percy is in the right, Vicomte," here interposed Lord Antony, laying a friendly hand on the young Frenchman's shoulder. "It would hardly be fitting that you should commence your career in England by provoking him to a duel."

For a moment longer the Vicomte hesitated, then with a slight shrug of the shoulders directed against the extraordinary code of honour prevailing in this fog-ridden island, he said with becoming dignity,—

"Ah, well! if Monsieur is satisfied, I have no griefs. You, mi'lor', are our protector. If I have done wrong, I withdraw myself."

"Aye, do!" rejoined Blakeney, with a long sigh of satisfaction, "withdraw yourself over there. Demmed excitable little puppy," he added under his breath. "Faith, Ffoulkes, if that's a specimen of the goods you and your friends bring over from France, my advice to you is, drop 'em 'mid Channel, my friend, or I shall have to see old Pitt about it, get him to clap on a prohibitive tariff, and put you in the stocks an you smuggle."

"La, Sir Percy, your chivalry misguides you," said Marguerite, coquettishly, "you forget that you yourself have imported one bundle of goods from France."

Blakeney slowly rose to his feet, and, making a deep and elaborate bow before his wife, he said with consummate gallantry,—

"I had the pick of the market, Madame, and my taste is unerring."

"More so than your chivalry, I fear," she retorted sarcastically.

"Odd's life, m'dear! be reasonable! Do you think I am going to allow my body to be made a pincushion of, by every little frog-eater who don't like the shape of your nose?"

"Lud, Sir Percy!" laughed Lady Blakeney as she bobbed him a quaint and pretty curtsey, "you need not be afraid! 'Tis not the *men* who dislike the shape of my nose."

"Afraid be demmed! Do you impugn my bravery, Madame? I don't patronise the ring for nothing, do I, Tony? I've put up the fists with Red Sam before now, and—and he didn't get it all his own way either—"

"S'faith, Sir Percy," said Marguerite, with a long and merry laugh, that went echoing along the old oak rafters of the parlour, "I would I had seen you then . . . ha! ha! ha! ha!— you must have looked a pretty picture . . . and . . . and to be afraid of a little French boy . . . ha! ha! . . . ha! ha!"

"Ha! ha! ha! he! he! he!" echoed Sir Percy, good-humouredly. "La, Madame, you honour me! Zooks! Ffoulkes, mark ye that! I have made my wife laugh!—The cleverest woman in Europe! . . . Odd's fish, we must have a bowl on that!" and he tapped vigorously on the table near him. "Hey! Jelly! Quick, man! Here, Jelly!"

Harmony was once more restored. Mr. Jellyband, with a mighty effort, recovered himself from the many emotions he had experienced within the last half hour.

"A bowl of punch, Jelly, hot and strong, eh?" said Sir Percy. "The wits that have just made a clever woman laugh must be whetted! Ha! ha! ha! Hasten, my good Jelly!"

"Nay, there is no time, Sir Percy," interposed Marguerite. "The skipper will be here directly and my brother must get on board, or the *Day Dream* will miss the tide."

"Time, m'dear? There is plenty of time for any gentleman to get drunk and get on board before the turn of the tide."

"I think, your ladyship," said Jellyband, respectfully, "that the young gentleman is coming along now with Sir Percy's skipper."

"That's right," said Blakeney, "then Armand can join us in the merry bowl. Think you, Tony," he added, turning towards the Vicomte, "that that jackanapes of yours will join us in a glass? Tell him that we drink in token of reconciliation."

"In fact you are all such merry company," said Marguerite, "that I trust you will forgive me if I bid my brother good-bye in another room."

It would have been bad form to protest. Both Lord Antony and Sir Andrew felt that Lady Blakeney could not altogether be in tune with them at that moment. Her love for her brother, Armand St. Just, was deep and touching in the extreme. He had just spent a few weeks with her in her English home, and was going back to serve his country, at a moment when death was the usual reward for the most enduring devotion.

Sir Percy also made no attempt to detain his wife. With that perfect, somewhat affected gallantry which characterised his every movement, he opened the coffee-room door for her, and made her the most approved and elaborate bow, which the fashion of the time dictated, as she sailed out of the room without bestowing on him more than a passing, slightly contemptuous glance. Only Sir Andrew Ffoulkes, whose every thought since he had met Suzanne de Tournay seemed keener, more gentle, more innately sympathetic, noted the curious look of intense longing, of deep and hopeless passion, with which the inane and flippant Sir Percy followed the retreating figure of his brilliant wife.

VII. THE SECRET ORCHARD

Once outside the noisy coffee-room, alone in the dimly-lighted passage, Marguerite Blakeney seemed to breathe more freely. She heaved a deep sigh, like one who had long been oppressed with the heavy weight of constant self-control, and she allowed a few tears to fall unheeded down her cheeks.

Outside the rain had ceased, and through the swiftly passing clouds, the pale rays of an after-storm sun shone upon the beautiful white coast of Kent and the quaint, irregular houses that clustered round the Admiralty Pier. Marguerite Blakeney stepped on to the porch and looked out to sea. Silhouetted against the ever-changing sky, a graceful schooner, with white sails set, was gently dancing in the breeze. The *Day Dream* it was, Sir Percy Blakeney's yacht, which was ready to take Armand St. Just back to France into the very midst of that seething, bloody Revolution which was overthrowing a monarchy, attacking a religion, destroying a society, in order to try and rebuild upon the ashes of tradition a new Utopia, of which a few men dreamed, but which none had the power to establish.

In the distance two figures were approaching "The Fisherman's Rest": one, an oldish man, with a curious fringe of grey hairs round a rotund and massive chin, and who walked with that peculiar rolling gait which invariably betrays the seafaring man: the other, a young, slight figure, neatly and becomingly dressed in a dark, many-caped overcoat; he was clean-shaved, and his dark hair was taken well back over a clear and noble forehead.

"Armand!" said Marguerite Blakeney, as soon as she saw him approaching from the distance, and a happy smile shone on her sweet face, even through the tears.

A minute or two later brother and sister were locked in each other's arms, while the old skipper stood respectfully on one side.

"How much time have we got, Briggs?" asked Lady Blakeney, "before M. St. Just need go on board?"

"We ought to weigh anchor before half an hour, your ladyship," replied the old man, pulling at his grey forelock.

Linking her arm in his, Marguerite led her brother towards the cliffs.

"Half an hour," she said, looking wistfully out to sea, "half an hour more and you'll be far from me, Armand! Oh! I can't believe that you are going, dear! These last few days—whilst Percy has been away, and I've had you all to myself, have slipped by like a dream."

"I am not going far, sweet one," said the young man gently, "a narrow channel to cross—a few miles of road—I can soon come back."

"Nay, 'tis not the distance, Armand—but that awful Paris . . . just now . . ."

They had reached the edge of the cliff. The gentle sea-breeze blew Marguerite's hair about her face, and sent the ends of her soft lace fichu waving round her, like a white and supple snake. She tried to pierce the distance far away, beyond which lay the shores of France: that relentless and stern France which was exacting her pound of flesh, the blood-tax from the noblest of her sons.

"Our own beautiful country, Marguerite," said Armand, who seemed to have divined her thoughts.

"They are going too far, Armand," she said vehemently. "You are a republican, so am I . . . we have the same thoughts, the same enthusiasm for liberty and equality . . . but even *you* must think that they are going too far . . ."

"Hush!—" said Armand, instinctively, as he threw a quick, apprehensive glance around him.

"Ah! you see: you don't think yourself that it is safe even to speak of these things—here in England!" She clung to him suddenly with strong, almost motherly, passion: "Don't go, Armand!" she begged; "don't go back! What should I do if . . . if . . . if . . ."

Her voice was choked in sobs, her eyes, tender, blue and loving, gazed appealingly at the young man, who in his turn looked steadfastly into hers.

"You would in any case be my own brave sister," he said gently, "who would remember that, when France is in peril, it is not for her sons to turn their backs on her."

Even as he spoke, that sweet, childlike smile crept back into her face, pathetic in the extreme, for it seemed drowned in tears.

"Oh! Armand!" she said quaintly, "I sometimes wish you had not so many lofty virtues. . . . I assure you little sins are far less dangerous and uncomfortable. But you *will* be prudent?" she added earnestly.

"As far as possible . . . I promise you."

"Remember, dear, I have only you . . . to . . . to care for me. . . ."

"Nay, sweet one, you have other interests now. Percy cares for you. . . ."

A look of strange wistfulness crept into her eyes as she murmured,—

"He did . . . once . . ."

"But surely . . ."

"There, there, dear, don't distress yourself on my account. Percy is very good . . ."

"Nay!" he interrupted energetically, "I will distress myself on your account, my Margot. Listen, dear, I have not spoken of these things to you before; something always seemed to stop me when I wished to question you. But, somehow, I feel as if I could not go away and leave you now without asking you one question. . . . You need not answer it if you do not wish," he added, as he noted a sudden hard look, almost of apprehension, darting through her eyes.

"What is it?" she asked simply.

"Does Sir Percy Blakeney know that . . . I mean, does he know the part you played in the arrest of the Marquis de St. Cyr?"

She laughed—a mirthless, bitter, contemptuous laugh, which was like a jarring chord in the music of her voice.

"That I denounced the Marquis de St. Cyr, you mean, to the tribunal that ultimately sent him and all his family to the guillotine? Yes, he does know. . . . I told him after I married him. . . ."

"You told him all the circumstances—which so completely exonerated you from any blame?"

"It was too late to talk of 'circumstances'; he heard the story from other sources; my confession came too tardily, it seems. I could no longer plead extenuating circumstances: I could not bemean myself by trying to explain—"

"And?"

"And now I have the satisfaction, Armand, of knowing that the biggest fool in England has the most complete contempt for his wife."

She spoke with vehement bitterness this time, and Armand St. Just, who loved her so dearly, felt that he had placed a somewhat clumsy finger upon an aching wound.

"But Sir Percy loved you, Margot," he repeated gently.

"Loved me?—Well, Armand, I thought at one time that he did, or I should not have married him. I daresay," she added, speaking very rapidly, as if she were glad at last to lay down a heavy burden, which had oppressed her for months, "I daresay that even you thought—as everybody else did—that I married Sir Percy because of his wealth—but I assure you, dear, that it was not so. He seemed to worship me with a curious intensity of concentrated passion, which went straight to my heart. I had never loved anyone before, as you know, and I was four-and-twenty then—so I naturally thought that it was not in my nature to love. But it has always seemed to me that it *must* be *heavenly* to be loved blindly, passionately, wholly . . . worshipped, in fact—and the very fact that Percy was slow and stupid was an attraction for me, as I thought he would love me all the more. A clever man would naturally have other interests, an ambitious man other hopes. . . . I thought that a fool would worship, and think of nothing else. And I was ready to respond, Armand; I would have allowed myself to be worshipped, and given infinite tenderness in return. . . ."

She sighed—and there was a world of disillusionment in that sigh. Armand St. Just had allowed her to speak on without interruption: he listened to her, whilst allowing his own thoughts to run riot. It was terrible to see a young and beautiful woman—a girl in all but name—still standing almost at the threshold of her life, yet bereft of hope, bereft of illusions, bereft of those golden and fantastic dreams, which should have made her youth one long, perpetual holiday.

Yet perhaps—though he loved his sister dearly—perhaps he understood: he had studied men in many countries, men of all ages, men of every grade of social and intellectual status, and inwardly he understood what Marguerite had left unsaid. Granted that Percy Blakeney was dull-witted, but in his slow-going mind, there would still be room for that ineradicable pride of a descendant of a long line of English gentlemen. A Blakeney had died on Bosworth Field, another had sacrificed life and fortune for the sake of a treacherous Stuart: and that same pride—foolish and prejudiced as the republican Armand would call it—must have been stung to the quick on hearing of the sin which lay at Lady Blakeney's door. She had been young, misguided, ill-advised perhaps. Armand knew that: and those who took advantage of Marguerite's youth, her impulses and imprudence, knew it still better; but Blakeney was slow-witted, he would not listen to "circumstances," he only clung to facts, and these had shown him Lady Blakeney denouncing a fellow-man to a tribunal that knew no pardon: and the contempt he would feel for the deed she had done, however unwittingly, would kill that same love in him, in which sympathy and intellectuality could never have had a part.

Yet even now, his own sister puzzled him. Life and love have such strange vagaries. Could it be that with the waning of her husband's love, Marguerite's heart had awakened with love for him? Strange extremes meet in love's pathway: this woman, who had had half intellectual Europe at her feet, might perhaps have set her affections on a fool. Marguerite was gazing out towards the sunset. Armand could not see her face, but presently it seemed to him that something which glittered for a moment in the golden evening light, fell from her eyes onto her dainty fichu of lace.

But he could not broach that subject with her. He knew her strange, passionate nature so well, and knew that reserve which lurked behind her frank, open ways.

They had always been together, these two, for their parents had died when Armand was still a youth, and Marguerite but a child. He, some eight years her senior, had watched over her until her marriage; had chaperoned her during those brilliant years spent in the flat of the Rue de Richelieu, and had seen her enter upon this new life of hers, here in England, with much sorrow and some foreboding.

This was his first visit to England since her marriage, and the few months of separation had already seemed to have built up a slight, thin partition between brother and sister; the same deep, intense love was still there, on both sides, but each now seemed to have a secret orchard, into which the other dared not penetrate.

There was much Armand St. Just could not tell his sister; the political aspect of the revolution in France was changing almost every day; she might not understand how his own views and sympathies might become modified, even as the excesses, committed by those who had been his friends, grew in horror and in intensity. And Marguerite could not speak to her brother about the secrets of her heart; she hardly understood them herself, she only knew that, in the midst of luxury, she felt lonely and unhappy.

And now Armand was going away; she feared for his safety, she longed for his presence. She would not spoil these last few sadly-sweet moments by speaking about herself. She led him gently along the cliffs, then down to the beach; their arms linked in one another's, they had still so much to say that lay just outside that secret orchard of theirs.

VIII. THE ACCREDITED AGENT

The afternoon was rapidly drawing to a close; and a long, chilly English summer's evening was throwing a misty pall over the green Kentish landscape.

The *Day Dream* had set sail, and Marguerite Blakeney stood alone on the edge of the cliff for over an hour, watching those white sails, which bore so swiftly away from her the only being who really cared for her, whom she dared to love, whom she knew she could trust.

Some little distance away to her left the lights from the coffee-room of "The Fisherman's Rest" glittered yellow in the gathering mist; from time to time it seemed to her aching nerves as if she could catch from thence the sound of merry-making and of jovial talk, or even that perpetual, senseless laugh of her husband's, which grated continually upon her sensitive ears.

Sir Percy had had the delicacy to leave her severely alone. She supposed that, in his own stupid, good-natured way, he may have understood that she would wish to remain alone, while those white sails disappeared into the vague horizon, so many miles away. He, whose notions of propriety and decorum were supersensitive, had not suggested even that an attendant should remain within call. Marguerite was grateful to her husband for all this; she always tried to be grateful to him for his thoughtfulness, which was constant, and for his generosity, which really was boundless. She tried even at times to curb the sarcastic, bitter thoughts of him, which made her—in spite of herself—say cruel, insulting things, which she vaguely hoped would wound him.

Yes! she often wished to wound him, to make him feel that she too held him in contempt, that she too had forgotten that once she had almost loved him. Loved that inane fop! whose thoughts seemed unable to soar beyond the tying of a cravat or the new cut of a coat. Bah! And yet! . . . vague memories, that were sweet and ardent and attuned to this calm summer's evening, came wafted back to her memory, on the invisible wings of the light sea-breeze: the time when first he worshipped her; he seemed so devoted—a very slave—and there was a certain latent intensity in that love which had fascinated her.

Then suddenly that love, that devotion, which throughout his courtship she had looked upon as the slavish fidelity of a dog, seemed to vanish completely. Twenty-four hours after the simple little ceremony at old St. Roch, she had told him the story of how, inadvertently, she had spoken of certain matters connected with the Marquis de St. Cyr before some men—her friends—who had used this information against the unfortunate Marquis, and sent him and his family to the guillotine.

She hated the Marquis. Years ago, Armand, her dear brother, had loved Angèle de St. Cyr, but St. Just was a plebeian, and the Marquis full of the pride and arrogant prejudices of his caste. One day Armand, the respectful, timid lover, ventured on sending a small poem—enthusiastic, ardent, passionate—to the idol of his dreams. The next night he was waylaid just outside Paris by the valets of the Marquis de St. Cyr, and ignominiously thrashed—thrashed like a dog within an inch of his life—because he had dared to raise his eyes to the daughter of the aristocrat. The incident was one which, in those days, some two years before the great Revolution, was of almost daily occurrence in France; incidents of that type, in fact, led to the bloody reprisals, which a few years later sent most of those haughty heads to the guillotine.

Marguerite remembered it all: what her brother must have suffered in his manhood and his pride must have been appalling; what she suffered through him and with him she never attempted even to analyse.

Then the day of retribution came. St. Cyr and his kind had found their masters, in those same plebeians whom they had despised. Armand and Marguerite, both intellectual, thinking beings, adopted with the enthusiasm of their years the Utopian doctrines of the Revolution, while the Marquis de St. Cyr and his family fought inch by inch for the retention of those privileges which had placed them socially above their fellow-men. Marguerite, impulsive, thoughtless, not calculating the purport of her words, still smarting under the terrible insult her brother had suffered at the Marquis' hands, happened to hear—amongst her own coterie—that the St. Cyrs were in treasonable correspondence with Austria, hoping to obtain the Emperor's support to quell the growing revolution in their own country.

In those days one denunciation was sufficient: Marguerite's few thoughtless words anent the Marquis de St. Cyr bore fruit within twenty-four hours. He was arrested. His papers were searched: letters from the Austrian Emperor, promising to send troops against the Paris populace, were found in his desk. He was arraigned for treason against the nation, and sent to the guillotine, whilst his family, his wife and his sons, shared this awful fate.

Marguerite, horrified at the terrible consequences of her own thoughtlessness, was powerless to save the Marquis: her own coterie, the leaders of the revolutionary movement, all proclaimed her as a heroine: and when she married Sir Percy Blakeney, she did not perhaps altogether realise how severely he would look upon the sin, which she had so inadvertently committed, and which still lay heavily upon her soul. She made full confession of it to her husband, trusting to his blind love for her, her boundless power over him, to soon make him forget what might have sounded unpleasant to an English ear.

Certainly at the moment he seemed to take it very quietly; hardly, in fact, did he appear to understand the meaning of all she said; but what was more certain still, was that never after that could she detect the slightest sign of that love, which she once believed had been wholly hers. Now they had drifted quite apart, and Sir Percy seemed to have laid aside his love for her, as he would an ill-fitting glove. She tried to rouse him by sharpening her ready wit against his dull intellect; endeavoured to excite his jealousy, if she could not rouse his love; tried to goad him to self-assertion, but all in vain. He remained the same, always passive, drawling, sleepy, always courteous, invariably a gentleman: she had all that the world and a wealthy husband can give to a pretty woman, yet on this beautiful summer's evening, with the white sails of the *Day Dream* finally hidden by the evening shadows, she felt more lonely than that poor tramp who plodded his way wearily along the rugged cliffs.

With another heavy sigh, Marguerite Blakeney turned her back upon the sea and cliffs, and walked slowly back towards "The Fisherman's Rest." As she drew near, the sound of revelry, of gay, jovial laughter, grew louder and more distinct. She could distinguish Sir Andrew Ffoulkes' pleasant voice, Lord Tony's boisterous guffaws, her husband's occasional, drawly, sleepy comments; then realising the loneliness of the road and the fast gathering gloom round her, she quickened her steps ... the next moment she perceived a stranger coming rapidly towards her. Marguerite did not look up: she was not the least nervous, and "The Fisherman's Rest" was now well within call.

The stranger paused when he saw Marguerite coming quickly towards him, and just as she was about to slip past him, he said very quietly:

"Citoyenne St. Just."

Marguerite uttered a little cry of astonishment, at thus hearing her own familiar maiden name uttered so close to her. She looked up at the stranger, and this time, with a cry of unfeigned pleasure, she put out both her hands effusively towards him.

"Chauvelin!" she exclaimed.

"Himself, citoyenne, at your service," said the stranger, gallantly kissing the tips of her fingers.

Marguerite said nothing for a moment or two, as she surveyed with obvious delight the not very prepossessing little figure before her. Chauvelin was then nearer forty than thirty—a clever, shrewd-looking personality, with a curious fox-like expression in the deep, sunken eyes. He was the same stranger who an hour or two previously had joined Mr. Jellyband in a friendly glass of wine.

"Chauvelin ... my friend ..." said Marguerite, with a pretty little sigh of satisfaction. "I am mightily pleased to see you."

No doubt poor Marguerite St. Just, lonely in the midst of her grandeur, and of her starchy friends, was happy to see a face that brought back memories of that happy time in Paris, when she reigned—a queen—over the intellectual coterie of the Rue de Richelieu. She did not notice the sarcastic little smile, however, that hovered round the thin lips of Chauvelin.

"But tell me," she added merrily, "what in the world, or whom in the world, are you doing here in England?"

She had resumed her walk towards the inn, and Chauvelin turned and walked beside her.

"I might return the subtle compliment, fair lady," he said. "What of yourself?"

"Oh, I?" she said, with a shrug of the shoulders. "Je m'ennuie, mon ami, that is all."

They had reached the porch of "The Fisherman's Rest," but Marguerite seemed loth to go within. The evening air was lovely after the storm, and she had found a friend who exhaled the breath of Paris, who knew Armand well, who could talk of all the merry, brilliant friends whom she had left behind. So she lingered on under the pretty porch, while through the gaily-lighted dormer-window of the coffee-room came sounds of laughter, of calls for "Sally" and for beer, of tapping of mugs, and clinking of dice, mingled with Sir Percy Blakeney's inane and mirthless laugh. Chauvelin stood beside her, his shrewd, pale, yellow eyes fixed on the pretty face, which looked so sweet and childlike in this soft English summer twilight.

"You surprise me, citoyenne," he said quietly, as he took a pinch of snuff.

"Do I now?" she retorted gaily. "Faith, my little Chauvelin, I should have thought that, with your penetration, you would have guessed that an atmosphere composed of fogs and virtues would never suit Marguerite St. Just."

"Dear me! is it as bad as that?" he asked, in mock consternation.

"Quite," she retorted, "and worse."

"Strange! Now, I thought that a pretty woman would have found English country life peculiarly attractive."

"Yes! so did I," she said with a sigh. "Pretty women," she added meditatively, "ought to have a good time in England, since all the pleasant things are forbidden them—the very things they do every day."

"Quite so!"

"You'll hardly believe it, my little Chauvelin," she said earnestly, "but I often pass a whole day—a whole day—without encountering a single temptation."

"No wonder," retorted Chauvelin, gallantly, "that the cleverest woman in Europe is troubled with *ennui*."

She laughed one of her melodious, rippling, childlike laughs.

"It must be pretty bad, mustn't it?" she said archly, "or I should not have been so pleased to see you."

"And this within a year of a romantic love match! . . ."

"Yes! . . . a year of a romantic love match . . . that's just the difficulty . . ."

"Ah! . . . that idyllic folly," said Chauvelin, with quiet sarcasm, "did not then survive the lapse of . . . weeks?"

"Idyllic follies never last, my little Chauvelin. . . . They come upon us like the measles . . . and are as easily cured."

Chauvelin took another pinch of snuff: he seemed very much addicted to that pernicious habit, so prevalent in those days; perhaps, too, he found the taking of snuff a convenient veil for disguising the quick, shrewd glances with which he strove to read the very souls of those with whom he came in contact.

"No wonder," he repeated, with the same gallantry, "that the most active brain in Europe is troubled with *ennui*."

"I was in hopes that you had a prescription against the malady, my little Chauvelin."

"How can I hope to succeed in that which Sir Percy Blakeney has failed to accomplish?"

"Shall we leave Sir Percy out of the question for the present, my dear friend?" she said drily.

"Ah! my dear lady, pardon me, but that is just what we cannot very well do," said Chauvelin, whilst once again his eyes, keen as those of a fox on the alert, darted a quick glance at Marguerite. "I have a most perfect prescription against the worst form of *ennui*, which I would have been happy to submit to you, but—"

"But what?"

"There *is* Sir Percy."

"What has he to do with it?"

"Quite a good deal, I am afraid. The prescription I would offer, fair lady, is called by a very plebeian name: Work!"

"Work?"

Chauvelin looked at Marguerite long and scrutinisingly. It seemed as if those keen, pale eyes of his were reading every one of her thoughts. They were alone together; the evening air was quite still, and their soft whispers were drowned in the noise which came from the coffee-room. Still, Chauvelin took a step or two from under the porch, looked quickly and keenly all round him, then, seeing that indeed no one was within earshot, he once more came back close to Marguerite.

"Will you render France a small service, citoyenne?" he asked, with a sudden change of manner, which lent his thin, fox-like face singular earnestness.

"La, man!" she replied flippantly, "how serious you look all of a sudden. . . . Indeed I do not know if I *would* render France a small service—at any rate, it depends upon the kind of service she—or you—want."

"Have you ever heard of the Scarlet Pimpernel, Citoyenne St. Just?" asked Chauvelin, abruptly.

"Heard of the Scarlet Pimpernel?" she retorted with a long and merry laugh, "Faith, man! we talk of nothing else. . . . We have hats 'à la Scarlet Pimpernel'; our horses are called 'Scarlet Pimpernel'; at the Prince of Wales' supper party the other night we had a 'oufflé à la Scarlet Pimpernel.' . . . Lud!" she added gaily, "the other day I ordered at my milliner's a blue dress trimmed with green, and bless me, if she did not call that 'à la Scarlet Pimpernel.'"

Chauvelin had not moved while she prattled merrily along; he did not even attempt to stop her when her musical voice and her childlike laugh went echoing through the still evening air. But he remained serious and earnest whilst she laughed, and his voice, clear, incisive, and hard, was not raised above his breath as he said,—

"Then, as you have heard of that enigmatical personage, citoyenne, you must also have guessed, and known, that the man who hides his identity under that strange pseudonym, is the most bitter enemy of our republic, of France . . . of men like Armand St. Just."

"La! . . ." she said, with a quaint little sigh, "I dare swear he is. . . . France has many bitter enemies these days."

"But you, citoyenne, are a daughter of France, and should be ready to help her in a moment of deadly peril."

"My brother Armand devotes his life to France," she retorted proudly; "as for me, I can do nothing . . . here in England. . . ."

"Yes, you . . ." he urged still more earnestly, whilst his thin fox-like face seemed suddenly to have grown impressive and full of dignity, "here, in England, citoyenne . . . you alone can help us. . . . Listen!—I have been sent over here by the Republican Government as its representative: I present my credentials to Mr. Pitt in London tomorrow. One of my duties here is to find out all about this League of the Scarlet Pimpernel, which has become a standing menace to France, since it is pledged to help our cursed aristocrats—traitors to their country, and enemies of the people—to escape from the just punishment which they deserve. You know as well as I do, citoyenne, that once they are over here, those French *émigrés* try to rouse public feeling against the Republic. . . . They are ready to join issue with any enemy bold enough to attack France. . . . Now, within the last month, scores of these *émigrés*, some only suspected of treason, others actually condemned by the Tribunal of Public Safety, have succeeded in crossing the Channel. Their escape in each instance was planned, organised and effected by this society of young English jackanapes, headed by a man whose brain seems as resourceful as his identity is mysterious. All the most strenuous efforts on the part of my spies have failed to discover who he is; whilst the others are the hands, he is the head, who beneath this strange anonymity calmly works at the destruction of France. I mean to strike at that head, and for this I want your help—through him afterwards I can reach the rest of the gang: he is a young buck in English society, of that I feel sure. Find that man for me, citoyenne!" he urged, "find him for France!"

Marguerite had listened to Chauvelin's impassioned speech without uttering a word, scarce making a movement, hardly daring to breathe. She had told him before that this mysterious hero of romance was the talk of the smart set to which she belonged; already, before this, her heart and her imagination had been stirred by the thought of the brave man, who, unknown to fame, had rescued hundreds of lives from a terrible, often an unmerciful fate. She had but little real sympathy with those haughty French aristocrats, insolent in their pride of caste, of whom the Comtesse de Tournay de Basserive was so typical an example; but, republican and liberal-minded though she was from principle, she hated and loathed the methods which the young Republic had chosen for establishing itself. She had not been in Paris for some months; the horrors and bloodshed of the Reign of Terror, culminating in the September massacres, had only come across the Channel to her as a faint echo. Robespierre, Danton, Marat, she had not known in their new guise of bloody justiciaries, merciless wielders of the guillotine. Her very soul recoiled in horror from these excesses, to which she feared her brother Armand—moderate republican as he was—might become one day the holocaust.

Then, when first she heard of this band of young English enthusiasts, who, for sheer love of their fellow-men, dragged women and children, old and young men, from a horrible death, her heart had glowed with pride for them, and now, as Chauvelin spoke, her very soul went out to the gallant and mysterious leader of the reckless little band, who risked his life daily, who gave it freely and without ostentation, for the sake of humanity.

Her eyes were moist when Chauvelin had finished speaking, the lace at her bosom rose and fell with her quick, excited breathing; she no longer heard the noise of drinking from the inn, she did not heed her husband's voice or his inane laugh, her thoughts had gone wandering in search of the mysterious hero! Ah! there was a man she might have loved, had he come her way: everything in him appealed to her romantic imagination; his personality, his strength, his bravery, the loyalty of those who served under him in the same noble cause, and, above all, that anonymity which crowned him, as if with a halo of romantic glory.

"Find him for France, citoyenne!"

Chauvelin's voice close to her ear roused her from her dreams. The mysterious hero had vanished, and, not twenty yards away from her, a man was drinking and laughing, to whom she had sworn faith and loyalty.

"La! man," she said with a return of her assumed flippancy, "you are astonishing. Where in the world am I to look for him?"

"You go everywhere, citoyenne," whispered Chauvelin, insinuatingly, "Lady Blakeney is the pivot of social London, so I am told . . . you see everything, you *hear* everything."

"Easy, my friend," retorted Marguerite, drawing herself up to her full height and looking down, with a slight thought of contempt on the small, thin figure before her. "Easy! you seem to forget that there are six feet of Sir Percy Blakeney, and a long line of ancestors to stand between Lady Blakeney and such a thing as you propose."

"For the sake of France, citoyenne!" reiterated Chauvelin, earnestly.

"Tush, man, you talk nonsense anyway; for even if you did know who this Scarlet Pimpernel is, you could do nothing to him—an Englishman!"

"I'd take my chance of that," said Chauvelin, with a dry, rasping little laugh. "At any rate we could send him to the guillotine first to cool his ardour, then, when there is a diplomatic fuss about it, we can apologise—humbly—to the British Government, and, if necessary, pay compensation to the bereaved family."

"What you propose is horrible, Chauvelin," she said, drawing away from him as from some noisome insect. "Whoever the man may be, he is brave and noble, and never —do you hear me?—never would I lend a hand to such villainy."

"You prefer to be insulted by every French aristocrat who comes to this country?"

Chauvelin had taken sure aim when he shot this tiny shaft. Marguerite's fresh young cheeks became a thought more pale and she bit her under lip, for she would not let him see that the shaft had struck home.

"That is beside the question," she said at last with indifference. "I can defend myself, but I refuse to do any dirty work for you—or for France. You have other means at your disposal; you must use them, my friend."

And without another look at Chauvelin, Marguerite Blakeney turned her back on him and walked straight into the inn.

"That is not your last word, citoyenne," said Chauvelin, as a flood of light from the passage illumined her elegant, richly-clad figure, "we meet in London, I hope!"

"We meet in London," she said, speaking over her shoulder at him, "but that is my last word."

She threw open the coffee-room door and disappeared from his view, but he remained under the porch for a moment or two, taking a pinch of snuff. He had received a rebuke and a snub, but his shrewd, fox-like face looked neither abashed nor disappointed; on the contrary, a curious smile, half sarcastic and wholly satisfied, played around the corners of his thin lips.

IX. THE OUTRAGE

A beautiful starlit night had followed on the day of incessant rain: a cool, balmy, late summer's night, essentially English in its suggestion of moisture and scent of wet earth and dripping leaves.

The magnificent coach, drawn by four of the finest thoroughbreds in England, had driven off along the London road, with Sir Percy Blakeney on the box, holding the reins in his slender feminine hands, and beside him Lady Blakeney wrapped in costly furs. A fifty-mile drive on a starlit summer's night! Marguerite had hailed the notion of it with delight. . . . Sir Percy was an enthusiastic whip; his four thoroughbreds, which had been sent down to Dover a couple of days before, were just sufficiently fresh and restive to add zest to the expedition, and Marguerite revelled in anticipation of the few hours of solitude, with the soft night breeze fanning her cheeks, her thoughts wandering, whither away? She knew from old experience that Sir Percy would speak little, if at all: he had often driven her on his beautiful coach for hours at night, from point to point, without making more than one or two casual remarks upon the weather or the state of the roads. He was very fond of driving by night, and she had very quickly adopted his fancy: as she sat next to him hour after hour, admiring the dexterous, certain way in which he handled the reins, she often wondered what went on in that slow-going head of his. He never told her, and she had never cared to ask.

At "The Fisherman's Rest" Mr. Jellyband was going the round, putting out the lights. His bar customers had all gone, but upstairs in the snug little bedrooms, Mr. Jellyband had quite a few important guests: the Comtesse de Tournay, with Suzanne, and the Vicomte, and there were two more bedrooms ready for Sir Andrew Ffoulkes and Lord Antony Dewhurst, if the two young men should elect to honour the ancient hostelry and stay the night.

For the moment these two young gallants were comfortably installed in the coffee-room, before the huge log-fire, which, in spite of the mildness of the evening, had been allowed to burn merrily.

"I say, Jelly, has everyone gone?" asked Lord Tony, as the worthy landlord still busied himself clearing away glasses and mugs.

"Everyone, as you see, my lord."

"And all your servants gone to bed?"

"All except the boy on duty in the bar, and," added Mr. Jellyband with a laugh, "I expect he'll be asleep afore long, the rascal."

"Then we can talk here undisturbed for half an hour?"

"At your service, my lord. . . . I'll leave your candles on the dresser . . . and your rooms are quite ready . . . I sleep at the top of the house myself, but if your lordship'll only call loudly enough, I daresay I shall hear."

"All right, Jelly . . . and . . . I say, put the lamp out—the fire'll give us all the light we need—and we don't want to attract the passer-by."

"All ri', my lord."

Mr. Jellyband did as he was bid—he turned out the quaint old lamp that hung from the raftered ceiling and blew out all the candles.

"Let's have a bottle of wine, Jelly," suggested Sir Andrew.

"All ri', sir!"

Jellyband went off to fetch the wine. The room now was quite dark, save for the circle of ruddy and fitful light formed by the brightly blazing logs in the hearth.

"Is that all, gentlemen?" asked Jellyband, as he returned with a bottle of wine and a couple of glasses, which he placed on the table.

"That'll do nicely, thanks, Jelly!" said Lord Tony.

"Good-night, my lord! Good-night, sir!"

"Good-night, Jelly!"

The two young men listened, whilst the heavy tread of Mr. Jellyband was heard echoing along the passage and staircase. Presently even that sound died out, and the whole of "The Fisherman's Rest" seemed wrapt in sleep, save the two young men drinking in silence beside the hearth.

For a while no sound was heard, even in the coffee-room, save the ticking of the old grandfather's clock and the crackling of the burning wood.

"All right again this time, Ffoulkes?" asked Lord Antony at last.

Sir Andrew had been dreaming evidently, gazing into the fire, and seeing therein, no doubt, a pretty, piquant face, with large brown eyes and a wealth of dark curls round a childish forehead.

"Yes!" he said, still musing, "all right!"

"No hitch?"

"None."

Lord Antony laughed pleasantly as he poured himself out another glass of wine.

"I need not ask, I suppose, whether you found the journey pleasant this time?"

"No, friend, you need not ask," replied Sir Andrew, gaily. "It was all right."

"Then here's to her very good health," said jovial Lord Tony. "She's a bonnie lass, though she *is* a French one. And here's to your courtship—may it flourish and prosper exceedingly."

He drained his glass to the last drop, then joined his friend beside the hearth.

"Well! you'll be doing the journey next, Tony, I expect," said Sir Andrew, rousing himself from his meditations, "you and Hastings, certainly; and I hope you may have as pleasant a task as I had, and as charming a travelling companion. You have no idea, Tony...."

"No! I haven't," interrupted his friend pleasantly, "but I'll take your word for it. And now," he added, whilst a sudden earnestness crept over his jovial young face, "how about business?"

The two young men drew their chairs closer together, and instinctively, though they were alone, their voices sank to a whisper.

"I saw the Scarlet Pimpernel alone, for a few moments in Calais," said Sir Andrew, "a day or two ago. He crossed over to England two days before we did. He had escorted the party all the way from Paris, dressed—you'll never credit it!—as an old market woman, and driving—until they were safely out of the city—the covered cart, under which the Comtesse de Tournay, Mlle. Suzanne, and the Vicomte lay concealed among the turnips and cabbages. They, themselves, of course, never suspected who their driver was. He drove them right through a line of soldiery and a yelling mob, who were screaming, 'À bas les aristos!' But the market cart got through along with some others, and the Scarlet Pimpernel, in shawl, petticoat and hood, yelled 'À bas les aristos!' louder than anybody. Faith!" added the young man, as his eyes glowed with enthusiasm for the beloved leader, "that man's a marvel! His cheek is preposterous, I vow!—and that's what carries him through."

Lord Antony, whose vocabulary was more limited than that of his friend, could only find an oath or two with which to show his admiration for his leader.

"He wants you and Hastings to meet him at Calais," said Sir Andrew, more quietly, "on the 2nd of next month. Let me see! that will be next Wednesday."

"Yes."

"It is, of course, the case of the Comte de Tournay, this time; a dangerous task, for the Comte, whose escape from his château, after he had been declared a 'suspect' by the Committee of Public Safety, was a masterpiece of the Scarlet Pimpernel's ingenuity, is now under sentence of death. It will be rare sport to get *him* out of France, and you will have a narrow escape, if you get through at all. St. Just has actually gone to meet him—of course, no one suspects St. Just as yet; but after that . . . to get them both out of the country! I'faith, 'twill be a tough job, and tax even the ingenuity of our chief. I hope I may yet have orders to be of the party."

"Have you any special instructions for me?"

"Yes! rather more precise ones than usual. It appears that the Republican Government have sent an accredited agent over to England, a man named Chauvelin, who is said to be terribly bitter against our league, and determined to discover the identity of our leader, so that he may have him kidnapped, the next time he attempts to set foot in France. This Chauvelin has brought a whole army of spies with him, and until the chief has sampled the lot, he thinks we should meet as seldom as possible on the business of the league, and on no account should talk to each other in public places for a time. When he wants to speak to us, he will contrive to let us know."

The two young men were both bending over the fire, for the blaze had died down, and only a red glow from the dying embers cast a lurid light on a narrow semicircle in front of the hearth. The rest of the room lay buried in complete gloom; Sir Andrew had taken a pocket-book from his pocket, and drawn therefrom a paper, which he unfolded, and together they tried to read it by the dim red firelight. So intent were they upon this, so wrapt up in the cause, the business they had so much at heart, so precious was this document which came from the very hand of their adored leader, that they had eyes and ears only for that. They lost count of the sounds around them, of the dropping of crisp ash from the grate, of the monotonous ticking of the clock, of the soft, almost imperceptible rustle of something on the floor close beside them. A figure had emerged from under one of the benches; with snake-like, noiseless movements it crept closer and closer to the two young men, not breathing, only gliding along the floor, in the inky blackness of the room.

"You are to read these instructions and commit them to memory," said Sir Andrew, "then destroy them."

He was about to replace the letter-case into his pocket, when a tiny slip of paper fluttered from it and fell on to the floor. Lord Antony stooped and picked it up.

"What's that?" he asked.

"I don't know," replied Sir Andrew.

"It dropped out of your pocket just now. It certainly did not seem to be with the other paper."

"Strange!—I wonder when it got there? It is from the chief," he added, glancing at the paper.

Both stooped to try and decipher this last tiny scrap of paper on which a few words had been hastily scrawled, when suddenly a slight noise attracted their attention, which seemed to come from the passage beyond.

"What's that?" said both instinctively. Lord Antony crossed the room towards the door, which he threw open quickly and suddenly; at that very moment he received a stunning blow between the eyes, which threw him back violently into the room. Simultaneously the crouching, snake-like figure in the gloom had jumped up and hurled itself from behind upon the unsuspecting Sir Andrew, felling him to the ground.

All this occurred within the short space of two or three seconds, and before either Lord Antony or Sir Andrew had time or chance to utter a cry or to make the faintest struggle. They were each seized by two men, a muffler was quickly tied round the mouth of each, and they were pinioned to one another back to back, their arms, hands, and legs securely fastened.

One man had in the meanwhile quietly shut the door; he wore a mask and now stood motionless while the others completed their work.

"All safe, citoyen!" said one of the men, as he took a final survey of the bonds which secured the two young men.

"Good!" replied the man at the door; "now search their pockets and give me all the papers you find."

This was promptly and quietly done. The masked man having taken possession of all the papers, listened for a moment or two if there were any sound within "The Fisherman's Rest." Evidently satisfied that this dastardly outrage had remained unheard, he once more opened the door and pointed peremptorily down the passage. The four men lifted Sir Andrew and Lord Antony from the ground, and as quietly, as noiselessly as they had come, they bore the two pinioned young gallants out of the inn and along the Dover Road into the gloom beyond.

In the coffee-room the masked leader of this daring attempt was quickly glancing through the stolen papers.

"Not a bad day's work on the whole," he muttered, as he quietly took off his mask, and his pale, fox-like eyes glittered in the red glow of the fire. "Not a bad day's work."

He opened one or two more letters from Sir Andrew Ffoulkes' pocket-book, noted the tiny scrap of paper which the two young men had only just had time to read; but one letter specially, signed Armand St. Just, seemed to give him strange satisfaction.

"Armand St. Just a traitor after all," he murmured. "Now, fair Marguerite Blakeney," he added viciously between his clenched teeth, "I think that you will help me to find the Scarlet Pimpernel."

X. IN THE OPERA BOX

It was one of the gala nights at Covent Garden Theatre, the first of the autumn season in this memorable year of grace 1792.

The house was packed, both in the smart orchestra boxes and the pit, as well as in the more plebeian balconies and galleries above. Glück's *Orpheus* made a strong appeal to the more intellectual portions of the house, whilst the fashionable women, the gaily-dressed and brilliant throng, spoke to the eye of those who cared but little for this "latest importation from Germany."

Selina Storace had been duly applauded after her grand *aria* by her numerous admirers; Benjamin Incledon, the acknowledged favourite of the ladies, had received special gracious recognition from the royal box; and now the curtain came down after the glorious finale to the second act, and the audience, which had hung spell-bound on the magic strains of the great maestro, seemed collectively to breathe a long sigh of satisfaction, previous to letting loose its hundreds of waggish and frivolous tongues.

In the smart orchestra boxes many well-known faces were to be seen. Mr. Pitt, overweighted with cares of state, was finding brief relaxation in to-night's musical treat; the Prince of Wales, jovial, rotund, somewhat coarse and commonplace in appearance, moved about from box to box, spending brief quarters of an hour with those of his more intimate friends.

In Lord Grenville's box, too, a curious, interesting personality attracted everyone's attention; a thin, small figure with shrewd, sarcastic face and deep-set eyes, attentive to the music, keenly critical of the audience, dressed in immaculate black, with dark hair free from any powder. Lord Grenville—Foreign Secretary of State—paid him marked, though frigid deference.

Here and there, dotted about among distinctly English types of beauty, one or two foreign faces stood out in marked contrast: the haughty aristocratic cast of countenance of the many French royalist *émigrés* who, persecuted by the relentless, revolutionary faction of their country, had found a peaceful refuge in England. On these faces sorrow and care were deeply writ; the women especially paid but little heed, either to the music or to the brilliant audience; no doubt their thoughts were far away with husband, brother, son maybe, still in peril, or lately succumbed to a cruel fate.

Among these the Comtesse de Tournay de Basserive, but lately arrived from France, was a most conspicuous figure: dressed in deep, heavy black silk, with only a white lace kerchief to relieve the aspect of mourning about her person, she sat beside Lady Portarles, who was vainly trying by witty sallies and somewhat broad jokes, to bring a smile to the Comtesse's sad mouth. Behind her sat little Suzanne and the Vicomte, both silent and somewhat shy among so many strangers. Suzanne's eyes seemed wistful; when she first entered the crowded house, she had looked eagerly all around, scanned every face, scrutinised every box. Evidently the one face she wished to see was not there, for she settled herself down quietly behind her mother, listened apathetically to the music, and took no further interest in the audience itself.

"Ah, Lord Grenville," said Lady Portarles, as following a discreet knock, the clever, interesting head of the Secretary of State appeared in the doorway of the box, "you could not arrive more *à propos*. Here is Madame la Comtesse de Tournay positively dying to hear the latest news from France."

The distinguished diplomatist had come forward and was shaking hands with the ladies.

"Alas!" he said sadly, "it is of the very worst. The massacres continue; Paris literally reeks with blood; and the guillotine claims a hundred victims a day."

Pale and tearful, the Comtesse was leaning back in her chair, listening horror-struck to this brief and graphic account of what went on in her own misguided country.

"Ah, Monsieur!" she said in broken English, "it is dreadful to hear all that—and my poor husband still in that awful country. It is terrible for me to be sitting here, in a theatre, all safe and in peace, whilst he is in such peril."

"Lud, Madame!" said honest, bluff Lady Portarles, "your sitting in a convent won't make your husband safe, and you have your children to consider: they are too young to be dosed with anxiety and premature mourning."

The Comtesse smiled through her tears at the vehemence of her friend. Lady Portarles, whose voice and manner would not have misfitted a jockey, had a heart of gold, and hid the most genuine sympathy and most gentle kindliness, beneath the somewhat coarse manners affected by some ladies at that time.

"Besides which, Madame," added Lord Grenville, "did you not tell me yesterday that the League of the Scarlet Pimpernel had pledged their honour to bring M. le Comte safely across the Channel?"

"Ah, yes!" replied the Comtesse, "and that is my only hope. I saw Lord Hastings yesterday . . . he reassured me again."

"Then I am sure you need have no fear. What the league have sworn, that they surely will accomplish. Ah!" added the old diplomatist with a sigh, "if I were but a few years younger . . ."

"La, man!" interrupted honest Lady Portarles, "you are still young enough to turn your back on that French scarecrow that sits enthroned in your box to-night."

"I wish I could . . . but your ladyship must remember that in serving our country we must put prejudices aside. M. Chauvelin is the accredited agent of his Government . . ."

"Odd's fish, man!" she retorted, "you don't call those bloodthirsty ruffians over there a government, do you?"

"It has not been thought advisable as yet," said the Minister, guardedly, "for England to break off diplomatic relations with France, and we cannot therefore refuse to receive with courtesy the agent she wishes to send to us."

"Diplomatic relations be demmed, my lord! That sly little fox over there is nothing but a spy, I'll warrant, and you'll find—an I'm much mistaken, that he'll concern himself little with diplomacy, beyond trying to do mischief to royalist refugees—to our heroic Scarlet Pimpernel and to the members of that brave little league."

"I am sure," said the Comtesse, pursing up her thin lips, "that if this Chauvelin wishes to do us mischief, he will find a faithful ally in Lady Blakeney."

"Bless the woman!" ejaculated Lady Portarles, "did ever anyone see such perversity? My Lord Grenville, you have the gift of the gab, will you please explain to Madame la Comtesse that she is acting like a fool. In your position here in England, Madame," she added, turning a wrathful and resolute face towards the Comtesse, "you cannot afford to put on the hoity-toity airs you French aristocrats are so fond of. Lady Blakeney may or may not be in sympathy with those ruffians in France; she may or may not have had anything to do with the arrest and condemnation of St. Cyr, or whatever the man's name is, but she is the leader of fashion in this country; Sir Percy Blakeney has more money than any half-dozen other men put together, he is hand and glove with royalty, and your trying to snub Lady Blakeney will not harm her, but will make you look a fool. Isn't that so, my lord?"

But what Lord Grenville thought of this matter, or to what reflections this homely tirade of Lady Portarles led the Comtesse de Tournay, remained unspoken, for the curtain had just risen on the third act of *Orpheus*, and admonitions to silence came from every part of the house.

Lord Grenville took a hasty farewell of the ladies and slipped back into his box, where M. Chauvelin had sat all through this *entr'acte*, with his eternal snuff-box in his hand, and with his keen pale eyes intently fixed upon a box opposite to him, where, with much frou-frou of silken skirts, much laughter and general stir of curiosity amongst the audience, Marguerite Blakeney had just entered, accompanied by her husband, and looking divinely pretty beneath the wealth of her golden, reddish curls, slightly besprinkled with powder, and tied back at the nape of her graceful neck with a gigantic black bow. Always dressed in the very latest vagary of fashion, Marguerite alone among the ladies that night had discarded the cross-over fichu and broad-lapelled over-dress, which had been in fashion for the last two or three years. She wore the short-waisted classical-shaped gown, which so soon was to become the approved mode in every country in Europe. It suited her graceful, regal figure to perfection, composed as it was of shimmering stuff which seemed a mass of rich gold embroidery.

As she entered, she leant for a moment out of the box, taking stock of all those present whom she knew. Many bowed to her as she did so, and from the royal box there came also a quick and gracious salute.

Chauvelin watched her intently all through the commencement of the third act, as she sat enthralled with the music, her exquisite little hand toying with a small jeweled fan, her regal head, her throat, arms and neck covered with magnificent diamonds and rare gems, the gift of the adoring husband who sprawled leisurely by her side.

Marguerite was passionately fond of music. *Orpheus* charmed her to-night. The very joy of living was writ plainly upon the sweet young face, it sparkled out of the merry blue eyes and lit up the smile that lurked around the lips. She was after all but five-and-twenty, in the heyday of youth, the darling of a brilliant throng, adored, *fêted*, petted, cherished. Two days ago the *Day Dream* had returned from Calais, bringing her news that her idolized brother had safely landed, that he thought of her, and would be prudent for her sake.

What wonder for the moment, and listening to Glück's impassioned strains, that she forgot her disillusionments, forgot her vanished love-dreams, forgot even the lazy, good-humoured nonentity who had made up for his lack of spiritual attainments by lavishing worldly advantages upon her.

He had stayed beside her in the box just as long as convention demanded, making way for His Royal Highness, and for the host of admirers who in a continued procession came to pay homage to the queen of fashion. Sir Percy had strolled away, to talk to more congenial friends probably. Marguerite did not even wonder whither he had gone—she cared so little; she had had a little court round her, composed of the *jeunesse dorée* of London, and had just dismissed them all, wishing to be alone with Glück for a brief while.

A discreet knock at the door roused her from her enjoyment.

"Come in," she said with some impatience, without turning to look at the intruder.

Chauvelin, waiting for his opportunity, noted that she was alone, and now, without pausing for that impatient "Come in," he quietly slipped into the box, and the next moment was standing behind Marguerite's chair.

"A word with you, citoyenne," he said quietly.

Marguerite turned quickly, in alarm, which was not altogether feigned.

"Lud, man! you frightened me," she said with a forced little laugh, "your presence is entirely inopportune. I want to listen to Glück, and have no mind for talking."

"But this is my only opportunity," he said, as quietly, and without waiting for permission, he drew a chair close behind her—so close that he could whisper in her ear, without disturbing the audience, and without being seen, in the dark background of the box. "This is my only opportunity," he repeated, as she vouchsafed him no reply, "Lady Blakeney is always so surrounded, so *fêted* by her court, that a mere old friend has but very little chance."

"Faith, man!" she said impatiently, "you must seek for another opportunity then. I am going to Lord Grenville's ball to-night after the opera. So are you, probably. I'll give you five minutes then...."

"Three minutes in the privacy of this box are quite sufficient for me," he rejoined placidly, "and I think that you would be wise to listen to me, Citoyenne St. Just."

Marguerite instinctively shivered. Chauvelin had not raised his voice above a whisper; he was now quietly taking a pinch of snuff, yet there was something in his attitude, something in those pale, foxy eyes, which seemed to freeze the blood in her veins, as would the sight of some deadly hitherto unguessed peril.

"Is that a threat, citoyen?" she asked at last.

"Nay, fair lady," he said gallantly, "only an arrow shot into the air."

He paused a moment, like a cat which sees a mouse running heedlessly by, ready to spring, yet waiting with that feline sense of enjoyment of mischief about to be done. Then he said quietly—

"Your brother, St. Just, is in peril."

Not a muscle moved in the beautiful face before him. He could only see it in profile, for Marguerite seemed to be watching the stage intently, but Chauvelin was a keen observer; he noticed the sudden rigidity of the eyes, the hardening of the mouth, the sharp, almost paralysed tension of the beautiful, graceful figure.

"Lud, then," she said, with affected merriment, "since 'tis one of your imaginary plots, you'd best go back to your own seat and leave me to enjoy the music."

And with her hand she began to beat time nervously against the cushion of the box. Selina Storace was singing the "Che farò" to an audience that hung spellbound upon the prima donna's lips. Chauvelin did not move from his seat; he quietly watched that tiny nervous hand, the only indication that his shaft had indeed struck home.

"Well?" she said suddenly and irrelevantly, and with the same feigned unconcern.

"Well, citoyenne?" he rejoined placidly.

"About my brother?"

"I have news of him for you which, I think, will interest you, but first let me explain. . . . May I?"

The question was unnecessary. He felt, though Marguerite still held her head steadily averted from him, that her every nerve was strained to hear what he had to say.

"The other day, citoyenne," he said, "I asked for your help. . . . France needed it, and I thought I could rely on you, but you gave me your answer. . . . Since then the exigencies of my own affairs and your own social duties have kept us apart . . . although many things have happened. . . ."

"To the point, I pray you, citoyen," she said lightly; "the music is entrancing, and the audience will get impatient of your talk."

"One moment, citoyenne. The day on which I had the honour of meeting you at Dover, and less than an hour after I had your final answer, I obtained possession of some papers, which revealed another of those subtle schemes for the escape of a batch of French aristocrats—that traitor de Tournay amongst others—all organised by that arch-meddler, the Scarlet Pimpernel. Some of the threads, too, of this mysterious organisation have fallen into my hands, but not all, and I want you—nay! you *must* help me to gather them together."

Marguerite seemed to have listened to him with marked impatience; she now shrugged her shoulders and said gaily—

"Bah! man. Have I not already told you that I care nought about your schemes or about the Scarlet Pimpernel. And had you not spoken about my brother . . ."

"A little patience, I entreat, citoyenne," he continued imperturbably. "Two gentlemen, Lord Antony Dewhurst and Sir Andrew Ffoulkes were at 'The Fisherman's Rest' at Dover that same night."

"I know. I saw them there."

"They were already known to my spies as members of that accursed league. It was Sir Andrew Ffoulkes who escorted the Comtesse de Tournay and her children across the Channel. When the two young men were alone, my spies forced their way into the coffee-room of the inn, gagged and pinioned the two gallants, seized their papers, and brought them to me."

In a moment she had guessed the danger. Papers? . . . Had Armand been imprudent? . . . The very thought struck her with nameless terror. Still she would not let this man see that she feared; she laughed gaily and lightly.

"Faith! and your impudence passes belief," she said merrily. "Robbery and violence! —in England!—in a crowded inn! Your men might have been caught in the act!"

"What if they had? They are children of France, and have been trained by your humble servant. Had they been caught they would have gone to jail, or even to the gallows, without a word of protest or indiscretion; at any rate it was well worth the risk. A crowded inn is safer for these little operations than you think, and my men have experience."

"Well? And those papers?" she asked carelessly.

"Unfortunately, though they have given me cognisance of certain names . . . certain movements . . . enough, I think, to thwart their projected *coup* for the moment, it would only be for the moment, and still leaves me in ignorance of the identity of the Scarlet Pimpernel."

"La! my friend," she said, with the same assumed flippancy of manner, "then you are where you were before, aren't you? and you can let me enjoy the last strophe of the *aria*. Faith!" she added, ostentatiously smothering an imaginary yawn, "had you not spoken about my brother . . ."

"I am coming to him now, citoyenne. Among the papers there was a letter to Sir Andrew Ffoulkes, written by your brother, St. Just."

"Well? And?"

"That letter shows him to be not only in sympathy with the enemies of France, but actually a helper, if not a member, of the League of the Scarlet Pimpernel."

The blow had been struck at last. All along, Marguerite had been expecting it; she would not show fear, she was determined to seem unconcerned, flippant even. She wished, when the shock came, to be prepared for it, to have all her wits about her—those wits which had been nicknamed the keenest in Europe. Even now she did not flinch. She knew that Chauvelin had spoken the truth; the man was too earnest, too blindly devoted to the misguided cause he had at heart, too proud of his countrymen, of those makers of revolutions, to stoop to low, purposeless falsehoods.

That letter of Armand's—foolish, imprudent Armand—was in Chauvelin's hands. Marguerite knew that as if she had seen the letter with her own eyes; and Chauvelin would hold that letter for purposes of his own, until it suited him to destroy it or to make use of it against Armand. All that she knew, and yet she continued to laugh more gaily, more loudly than she had done before.

"La, man!" she said, speaking over her shoulder and looking him full and squarely in the face, "did I not say it was some imaginary plot. . . . Armand in league with that enigmatic Scarlet Pimpernel! . . . Armand busy helping those French aristocrats whom he despises! . . . Faith, the tale does infinite credit to your imagination!"

"Let me make my point clear, citoyenne," said Chauvelin, with the same unruffled calm, "I must assure you that St. Just is compromised beyond the slightest hope of pardon."

Inside the orchestra box all was silent for a moment or two. Marguerite sat, straight upright, rigid and inert, trying to think, trying to face the situation, to realise what had best be done.

In the house Storace had finished the *aria*, and was even now bowing in her classic garb, but in approved eighteenth-century fashion, to the enthusiastic audience, who cheered her to the echo.

"Chauvelin," said Marguerite Blakeney at last, quietly, and without that touch of bravado which had characterised her attitude all along, "Chauvelin, my friend, shall we try to understand one another. It seems that my wits have become rusty by contact with this damp climate. Now, tell me, you are very anxious to discover the identity of the Scarlet Pimpernel, isn't that so?"

"France's most bitter enemy, citoyenne . . . all the more dangerous, as he works in the dark."

"All the more noble, you mean. . . . Well!—and you would now force me to do some spying work for you in exchange for my brother Armand's safety?—Is that it?"

"Fie! two very ugly words, fair lady," protested Chauvelin, urbanely. "There can be no question of force, and the service which I would ask of you, in the name of France, could never be called by the shocking name of spying."

"At any rate, that is what it is called over here," she said drily. "That is your intention, is it not?"

"My intention is, that you yourself win a free pardon for Armand St. Just by doing me a small service."

"What is it?"

"Only watch for me to-night, Citoyenne St. Just," he said eagerly. "Listen: among the papers which were found about the person of Sir Andrew Ffoulkes there was a tiny note. See!" he added, taking a tiny scrap of paper from his pocket-book and handing it to her.

It was the same scrap of paper which, four days ago, the two young men had been in the act of reading, at the very moment when they were attacked by Chauvelin's minions. Marguerite took it mechanically and stooped to read it. There were only two lines, written in a distorted, evidently disguised, handwriting; she read them half aloud—

> "'Remember we must not meet more often than is strictly necessary. You have all instructions for the 2nd. If you wish to speak to me again, I shall be at G.'s ball.'"

"What does it mean?" she asked.

"Look again, citoyenne, and you will understand."

"There is a device here in the corner, a small red flower . . ."

"Yes."

"The Scarlet Pimpernel," she said eagerly, "and G.'s ball means Grenville's ball. . . . He will be at my Lord Grenville's ball to-night."

"That is how I interpret the note, citoyenne," concluded Chauvelin, blandly. "Lord Antony Dewhurst and Sir Andrew Ffoulkes, after they were pinioned and searched by my spies, were carried by my orders to a lonely house on the Dover Road, which I had rented for the purpose: there they remained close prisoners until this morning. But having found this tiny scrap of paper, my intention was that they should be in London, in time to attend my Lord Grenville's ball. You see, do you not? that they must have a great deal to say to their chief . . . and thus they will have an opportunity of speaking to him to-night, just as he directed them to do. Therefore, this morning, those two young gallants found every bar and bolt open in that lonely house on the Dover Road, their jailers disappeared, and two good horses standing ready saddled and tethered in the yard. I have not seen them yet, but I think we may safely conclude that they did not draw rein until they reached London. Now you see how simple it all is, citoyenne!"

"It does seem simple, doesn't it?" she said, with a final bitter attempt at flippancy, "when you want to kill a chicken . . . you take hold of it . . . then you wring its neck . . . it's only the chicken who does not find it quite so simple. Now you hold a knife at my throat, and a hostage for my obedience. . . . You find it simple. . . . I don't."

"Nay, citoyenne, I offer you a chance of saving the brother you love from the consequences of his own folly."

Marguerite's face softened, her eyes at last grew moist, as she murmured, half to herself:

"The only being in the world who has loved me truly and constantly.[EOL] . . . But what do you want me to do, Chauvelin?" she said, with a world of despair in her tear-choked voice. "In my present position, it is well-nigh impossible!"

"Nay, citoyenne," he said drily and relentlessly, not heeding that despairing, childlike appeal, which might have melted a heart of stone, "as Lady Blakeney, no one suspects you, and with your help to-night I may—who knows?—succeed in finally establishing the identity of the Scarlet Pimpernel. . . . You are going to the ball anon. . . . Watch for me there, citoyenne, watch and listen. . . . You can tell me if you hear a chance word or whisper. . . . You can note everyone to whom Sir Andrew Ffoulkes or Lord Antony Dewhurst will speak. You are absolutely beyond suspicion now. The Scarlet Pimpernel will be at Lord Grenville's ball to-night. Find out who he is, and I will pledge the word of France that your brother shall be safe."

Chauvelin was putting the knife to her throat. Marguerite felt herself entangled in one of those webs, from which she could hope for no escape. A precious hostage was being held for her obedience: for she knew that this man would never make an empty threat. No doubt Armand was already signaled to the Committee of Public Safety as one of the "suspect"; he would not be allowed to leave France again, and would be ruthlessly struck, if she refused to obey Chauvelin. For a moment—woman-like—she still hoped to temporise. She held out her hand to this man, whom she now feared and hated.

"If I promise to help you in this matter, Chauvelin," she said pleasantly, "will you give me that letter of St. Just's?"

"If you render me useful assistance to-night, citoyenne," he replied with a sarcastic smile, "I will give you that letter . . . to-morrow."

"You do not trust me?"

"I trust you absolutely, dear lady, but St. Just's life is forfeit to his country . . . it rests with you to redeem it."

"I may be powerless to help you," she pleaded, "were I ever so willing."

"That would be terrible indeed," he said quietly, "for you . . . and for St. Just."

Marguerite shuddered. She felt that from this man she could expect no mercy. All-powerful, he held the beloved life in the hollow of his hand. She knew him too well not to know that, if he failed in gaining his own ends, he would be pitiless.

She felt cold in spite of the oppressive air of the opera-house. The heart-appealing strains of the music seemed to reach her, as from a distant land. She drew her costly lace scarf up around her shoulders, and sat silently watching the brilliant scene, as if in a dream.

For a moment her thoughts wandered away from the loved one who was in danger, to that other man who also had a claim on her confidence and her affection. She felt lonely, frightened for Armand's sake; she longed to seek comfort and advice from someone who would know how to help and console. Sir Percy Blakeney had loved her once; he was her husband; why should she stand alone through this terrible ordeal? He had very little brains, it is true, but he had plenty of muscle: surely, if she provided the thought, and he the manly energy and pluck, together they could outwit the astute diplomatist, and save the hostage from his vengeful hands, without imperiling the life of the noble leader of that gallant little band of heroes. Sir Percy knew St. Just well—he seemed attached to him—she was sure that he could help.

Chauvelin was taking no further heed of her. He had said his cruel "Either—or—" and left her to decide. He, in his turn now, appeared to be absorbed in the soul-stirring melodies of *Orpheus*, and was beating time to the music with his sharp, ferret-like head.

A discreet rap at the door roused Marguerite from her thoughts. It was Sir Percy Blakeney, tall, sleepy, good-humoured, and wearing that half-shy, half-inane smile, which just now seemed to irritate her every nerve.

"Er . . . your chair is outside . . . m'dear," he said, with his most exasperating drawl, "I suppose you will want to go to that demmed ball.[EOL] . . . Excuse me—er—Monsieur Chauvelin—I had not observed you. . . ."

He extended two slender, white fingers towards Chauvelin, who had risen when Sir Percy entered the box.

"Are you coming, m'dear?"

"Hush! Sh! Sh!" came in angry remonstrance from different parts of the house.

"Demmed impudence," commented Sir Percy with a good-natured smile.

Marguerite sighed impatiently. Her last hope seemed suddenly to have vanished away. She wrapped her cloak round her and without looking at her husband:

"I am ready to go," she said, taking his arm. At the door of the box she turned and looked straight at Chauvelin, who, with his *chapeau-bras* under his arm, and a curious smile round his thin lips, was preparing to follow the strangely ill-assorted couple.

"It is only *au revoir*, Chauvelin," she said pleasantly, "we shall meet at my Lord Grenville's ball, anon."

And in her eyes the astute Frenchman read, no doubt, something which caused him profound satisfaction, for, with a sarcastic smile, he took a delicate pinch of snuff, then, having dusted his dainty lace jabot, he rubbed his thin, bony hands contentedly together.

XI. LORD GRENVILLE'S BALL

The historic ball given by the then Secretary of State for Foreign Affairs—Lord Grenville—was the most brilliant function of the year. Though the autumn season had only just begun, everybody who was anybody had contrived to be in London in time to be present there, and to shine at this ball, to the best of his or her respective ability.

His Royal Highness the Prince of Wales had promised to be present. He was coming on presently from the opera. Lord Grenville himself had listened to the two first acts of *Orpheus*, before preparing to receive his guests. At ten o'clock—an unusually late hour in those days—the grand rooms of the Foreign Office, exquisitely decorated with exotic palms and flowers, were filled to overflowing. One room had been set apart for dancing, and the dainty strains of the minuet made a soft accompaniment to the gay chatter, the merry laughter of the numerous and brilliant company.

In a smaller chamber, facing the top of the fine stairway, the distinguished host stood ready to receive his guests. Distinguished men, beautiful women, notabilities from every European country had already filed past him, had exchanged the elaborate bows and curtsies with him, which the extravagant fashion of the time demanded, and then, laughing and talking, had dispersed in the ball, reception, and card rooms beyond.

Not far from Lord Grenville's elbow, leaning against one of the console tables, Chauvelin, in his irreproachable black costume, was taking a quiet survey of the brilliant throng. He noted that Sir Percy and Lady Blakeney had not yet arrived, and his keen, pale eyes glanced quickly towards the door every time a newcomer appeared.

He stood somewhat isolated: the envoy of the Revolutionary Government of France was not likely to be very popular in England, at a time when the news of the awful September massacres, and of the Reign of Terror and Anarchy, had just begun to filtrate across the Channel.

In his official capacity he had been received courteously by his English colleagues: Mr. Pitt had shaken him by the hand; Lord Grenville had entertained him more than once; but the more intimate circles of London society ignored him altogether; the women openly turned their backs upon him; the men who held no official position refused to shake his hand.

But Chauvelin was not the man to trouble himself about these social amenities, which he called mere incidents in his diplomatic career. He was blindly enthusiastic for the revolutionary cause, he despised all social inequalities, and he had a burning love for his own country: these three sentiments made him supremely indifferent to the snubs he received in this fog-ridden, loyalist, old-fashioned England.

But, above all, Chauvelin had a purpose at heart. He firmly believed that the French aristocrat was the most bitter enemy of France; he would have wished to see every one of them annihilated: he was one of those who, during this awful Reign of Terror, had been the first to utter the historic and ferocious desire "that aristocrats might have but one head between them, so that it might be cut off with a single stroke of the guillotine." And thus he looked upon every French aristocrat, who had succeeded in escaping from France, as so much prey of which the guillotine had been unwarrantably cheated. There is no doubt that those royalist *émigrés*, once they had managed to cross the frontier, did their very best to stir up foreign indignation against France. Plots without end were hatched in England, in Belgium, in Holland, to try and induce some great power to send troops into revolutionary Paris, to free King Louis, and to summarily hang the bloodthirsty leaders of that monster republic.

Small wonder, therefore, that the romantic and mysterious personality of the Scarlet Pimpernel was a source of bitter hatred to Chauvelin. He and the few young jackanapes under his command, well furnished with money, armed with boundless daring, and acute cunning, had succeeded in rescuing hundreds of aristocrats from France. Nine-tenths of the *émigrés*, who were *fêted* at the English court, owed their safety to that man and to his league.

Chauvelin had sworn to his colleagues in Paris that he would discover the identity of that meddlesome Englishman, entice him over to France, and then . . . Chauvelin drew a deep breath of satisfaction at the very thought of seeing that enigmatic head falling under the knife of the guillotine, as easily as that of any other man.

Suddenly there was a great stir on the handsome staircase, all conversation stopped for a moment as the major-domo's voice outside announced,—

"His Royal Highness the Prince of Wales and suite, Sir Percy Blakeney, Lady Blakeney."

Lord Grenville went quickly to the door to receive his exalted guest.

The Prince of Wales, dressed in a magnificent court suit of salmon-coloured velvet richly embroidered with gold, entered with Marguerite Blakeney on his arm; and on his left Sir Percy, in gorgeous shimmering cream satin, cut in the extravagant "Incroyable" style, his fair hair free from powder, priceless lace at his neck and wrists, and the flat *chapeau-bras* under his arm.

After the few conventional words of deferential greeting, Lord Grenville said to his royal guest,—

"Will your Highness permit me to introduce M. Chauvelin, the accredited agent of the French Government?"

Chauvelin, immediately the Prince entered, had stepped forward, expecting this introduction. He bowed very low, whilst the Prince returned his salute with a curt nod of the head.

"Monsieur," said His Royal Highness coldly, "we will try to forget the government that sent you, and look upon you merely as our guest—a private gentleman from France. As such you are welcome, Monsieur."

"Monseigneur," rejoined Chauvelin, bowing once again. "Madame," he added, bowing ceremoniously before Marguerite.

"Ah! my little Chauvelin!" she said with unconcerned gaiety, and extending her tiny hand to him. "Monsieur and I are old friends, your Royal Highness."

"Ah, then," said the Prince, this time very graciously, "you are doubly welcome, Monsieur."

"There is someone else I would crave permission to present to your Royal Highness," here interposed Lord Grenville.

"Ah! who is it?" asked the Prince.

"Madame la Comtesse de Tournay de Basserive and her family, who have but recently come from France."

"By all means!—They are among the lucky ones then!"

Lord Grenville turned in search of the Comtesse, who sat at the further end of the room.

"Lud love me!" whispered His Royal Highness to Marguerite, as soon as he had caught sight of the rigid figure of the old lady; "Lud love me! she looks very virtuous and very melancholy."

"Faith, your Royal Highness," she rejoined with a smile, "virtue is like precious odours, most fragrant when it is crushed."

"Virtue, alas!" sighed the Prince, "is mostly unbecoming to your charming sex, Madame."

"Madame la Comtesse de Tournay de Basserive," said Lord Grenville, introducing the lady.

"This is a pleasure, Madame; my royal father, as you know, is ever glad to welcome those of your compatriots whom France has driven from her shores."

"Your Royal Highness is ever gracious," replied the Comtesse with becoming dignity. Then, indicating her daughter, who stood timidly by her side: "My daughter Suzanne, Monseigneur," she said.

"Ah! charming!—charming!" said the Prince, "and now allow me, Comtesse, to introduce to you, Lady Blakeney, who honours us with her friendship. You and she will have much to say to one another, I vow. Every compatriot of Lady Blakeney's is doubly welcome for her sake . . . her friends are our friends . . . her enemies, the enemies of England."

Marguerite's blue eyes had twinkled with merriment at this gracious speech from her exalted friend. The Comtesse de Tournay, who lately had so flagrantly insulted her, was here receiving a public lesson, at which Marguerite could not help but rejoice. But the Comtesse, for whom respect of royalty amounted almost to a religion, was too well-schooled in courtly etiquette to show the slightest sign of embarrassment, as the two ladies curtsied ceremoniously to one another.

"His Royal Highness is ever gracious, Madame," said Marguerite, demurely, and with a wealth of mischief in her twinkling blue eyes, "but here there is no need for his kind mediation. . . . Your amiable reception of me at our last meeting still dwells pleasantly in my memory."

"We poor exiles, Madame," rejoined the Comtesse, frigidly, "show our gratitude to England by devotion to the wishes of Monseigneur."

"Madame!" said Marguerite, with another ceremonious curtsey.

"Madame," responded the Comtesse with equal dignity.

The Prince in the meanwhile was saying a few gracious words to the young Vicomte.

"I am happy to know you, Monsieur le Vicomte," he said. "I knew your father well when he was ambassador in London."

"Ah, Monseigneur!" replied the Vicomte, "I was a leetle boy then . . . and now I owe the honour of this meeting to our protector, the Scarlet Pimpernel."

"Hush!" said the Prince, earnestly and quickly, as he indicated Chauvelin, who had stood a little on one side throughout the whole of this little scene, watching Marguerite and the Comtesse with an amused, sarcastic little smile around his thin lips.

"Nay, Monseigneur," he said now, as if in direct response to the Prince's challenge, "pray do not check this gentleman's display of gratitude; the name of that interesting red flower is well known to me—and to France."

The Prince looked at him keenly for a moment or two.

"Faith, then, Monsieur," he said, "perhaps you know more about our national hero than we do ourselves . . . perchance you know who he is.[EOL] . . . See!" he added, turning to the groups round the room, "the ladies hang upon your lips . . . you would render yourself popular among the fair sex if you were to gratify their curiosity."

"Ah, Monseigneur," said Chauvelin, significantly, "rumour has it in France that your Highness could—an you would—give the truest account of that enigmatical wayside flower."

He looked quickly and keenly at Marguerite as he spoke; but she betrayed no emotion, and her eyes met his quite fearlessly.

"Nay, man," replied the Prince, "my lips are sealed! and the members of the league jealously guard the secret of their chief . . . so his fair adorers have to be content with worshipping a shadow. Here in England, Monsieur," he added, with wonderful charm and dignity, "we but name the Scarlet Pimpernel, and every fair cheek is suffused with a blush of enthusiasm. None have seen him save his faithful lieutenants. We know not if he be tall or short, fair or dark, handsome or ill-formed; but we know that he is the bravest gentleman in all the world, and we all feel a little proud, Monsieur, when we remember that he is an Englishman."

"Ah, Monsieur Chauvelin," added Marguerite, looking almost with defiance across at the placid, sphinx-like face of the Frenchman, "His Royal Highness should add that we ladies think of him as of a hero of old . . . we worship him . . . we wear his badge . . . we tremble for him when he is in danger, and exult with him in the hour of his victory."

Chauvelin did no more than bow placidly both to the Prince and to Marguerite; he felt that both speeches were intended—each in their way—to convey contempt or defiance. The pleasure-loving, idle Prince he despised; the beautiful woman, who in her golden hair wore a spray of small red flowers composed of rubies and diamonds—her he held in the hollow of his hand: he could afford to remain silent and to await events.

A long, jovial, inane laugh broke the sudden silence which had fallen over everyone.

"And we poor husbands," came in slow, affected accents from gorgeous Sir Percy, "we have to stand by . . . while they worship a demmed shadow."

Everyone laughed—the Prince more loudly than anyone. The tension of subdued excitement was relieved, and the next moment everyone was laughing and chatting merrily as the gay crowd broke up and dispersed in the adjoining rooms.

XII. THE SCRAP OF PAPER

Marguerite suffered intensely. Though she laughed and chatted, though she was more admired, more surrounded, more *fêted* than any woman there, she felt like one condemned to death, living her last day upon this earth.

Her nerves were in a state of painful tension, which had increased a hundredfold during that brief hour which she had spent in her husband's company, between the opera and the ball. The short ray of hope—that she might find in this good-natured, lazy individual a valuable friend and adviser—had vanished as quickly as it had come, the moment she found herself alone with him. The same feeling of good-humoured contempt which one feels for an animal or a faithful servant, made her turn away with a smile from the man who should have been her moral support in this heart-rending crisis through which she was passing: who should have been her cool-headed adviser, when feminine sympathy and sentiment tossed her hither and thither, between her love for her brother, who was far away and in mortal peril, and horror of the awful service which Chauvelin had exacted from her, in exchange for Armand's safety.

There he stood, the moral support, the cool-headed adviser, surrounded by a crowd of brainless, empty-headed young fops, who were even now repeating from mouth to mouth, and with every sign of the keenest enjoyment, a doggerel quatrain which he had just given forth.

Everywhere the absurd, silly words met her: people seemed to have little else to speak about, even the Prince had asked her, with a laugh, whether she appreciated her husband's latest poetic efforts.

BARONESS ORCZY

"All done in the tying of a cravat," Sir Percy had declared to his clique of admirers.

"*We seek him here, we seek him there,
Those Frenchies seek him everywhere.
Is he in heaven? —Is he in hell?
That demmed, elusive Pimpernel?*"

Sir Percy's *bon mot* had gone the round of the brilliant reception-rooms. The Prince was enchanted. He vowed that life without Blakeney would be but a dreary desert. Then, taking him by the arm, had led him to the card-room, and engaged him in a long game of hazard.

Sir Percy, whose chief interest in most social gatherings seemed to centre round the card-table, usually allowed his wife to flirt, dance, to amuse or bore herself as much as she liked. And to-night, having delivered himself of his *bon mot*, he had left Marguerite surrounded by a crowd of admirers of all ages, all anxious and willing to help her to forget that somewhere in the spacious reception-rooms, there was a long, lazy being who had been fool enough to suppose that the cleverest woman in Europe would settle down to the prosaic bonds of English matrimony.

Her still overwrought nerves, her excitement and agitation, lent beautiful Marguerite Blakeney much additional charm: escorted by a veritable bevy of men of all ages and of most nationalities, she called forth many exclamations of admiration from everyone as she passed.

She would not allow herself any more time to think. Her early, somewhat Bohemian training had made her something of a fatalist. She felt that events would shape themselves, that the directing of them was not in her hands. From Chauvelin she knew that she could expect no mercy. He had set a price upon Armand's head, and left it to her to pay or not, as she chose.

Later on in the evening she caught sight of Sir Andrew Ffoulkes and Lord Antony Dewhurst, who seemingly had just arrived. She noticed at once that Sir Andrew immediately made for little Suzanne de Tournay, and that the two young people soon managed to isolate themselves in one of the deep embrasures of the mullioned windows, there to carry on a long conversation, which seemed very earnest and very pleasant on both sides.

Both the young men looked a little haggard and anxious, but otherwise they were irreproachably dressed, and there was not the slightest sign, about their courtly demeanour, of the terrible catastrophe, which they must have felt hovering round them and round their chief.

That the League of the Scarlet Pimpernel had no intention of abandoning its cause, she had gathered through little Suzanne herself, who spoke openly of the assurance she and her mother had had that the Comte de Tournay would be rescued from France by the league, within the next few days. Vaguely she began to wonder, as she looked at the brilliant and fashionable crowd in the gaily-lighted ball-room, which of these worldly men round her was the mysterious "Scarlet Pimpernel," who held the threads of such daring plots, and the fate of valuable lives in his hands.

A burning curiosity seized her to know him: although for months she had heard of him and had accepted his anonymity, as everyone else in society had done; but now she longed to know—quite impersonally, quite apart from Armand, and oh! quite apart from Chauvelin—only for her own sake, for the sake of the enthusiastic admiration she had always bestowed on his bravery and cunning.

He was at the ball, of course, somewhere, since Sir Andrew Ffoulkes and Lord Antony Dewhurst were here, evidently expecting to meet their chief—and perhaps to get a fresh *mot d'ordre* from him.

Marguerite looked round at everyone, at the aristocratic high-typed Norman faces, the squarely-built, fair-haired Saxon, the more gentle, humorous caste of the Celt, wondering which of these betrayed the power, the energy, the cunning which had imposed its will and its leadership upon a number of high-born English gentlemen, among whom rumour asserted was His Royal Highness himself.

Sir Andrew Ffoulkes? Surely not, with his gentle blue eyes, which were looking so tenderly and longingly after little Suzanne, who was being led away from the pleasant *tête-à-tête* by her stern mother. Marguerite watched him across the room, as he finally turned away with a sigh, and seemed to stand, aimless and lonely, now that Suzanne's dainty little figure had disappeared in the crowd.

She watched him as he strolled towards the doorway, which led to a small boudoir beyond, then paused and leaned against the framework of it, looking still anxiously all round him.

Marguerite contrived for the moment to evade her present attentive cavalier, and she skirted the fashionable crowd, drawing nearer to the doorway, against which Sir Andrew was leaning. Why she wished to get closer to him, she could not have said: perhaps she was impelled by an all-powerful fatality, which so often seems to rule the destinies of men.

Suddenly she stopped: her very heart seemed to stand still, her eyes, large and excited, flashed for a moment towards that doorway, then as quickly were turned away again. Sir Andrew Ffoulkes was still in the same listless position by the door, but Marguerite had distinctly seen that Lord Hastings—a young buck, a friend of her husband's and one of the Prince's set—had, as he quickly brushed past him, slipped something into his hand.

For one moment longer—oh! it was the merest flash—Marguerite paused: the next she had, with admirably played unconcern, resumed her walk across the room—but this time more quickly towards that doorway whence Sir Andrew had now disappeared.

All this, from the moment that Marguerite had caught sight of Sir Andrew leaning against the doorway, until she followed him into the little boudoir beyond, had occurred in less than a minute. Fate is usually swift when she deals a blow.

Now Lady Blakeney had suddenly ceased to exist. It was Marguerite St. Just who was there only: Marguerite St. Just who had passed her childhood, her early youth, in the protecting arms of her brother Armand. She had forgotten everything else—her rank, her dignity, her secret enthusiasms—everything save that Armand stood in peril of his life, and that there, not twenty feet away from her, in the small boudoir which was quite deserted, in the very hands of Sir Andrew Ffoulkes, might be the talisman which would save her brother's life.

Barely another thirty seconds had elapsed between the moment when Lord Hastings slipped the mysterious "something" into Sir Andrew's hand, and the one when she, in her turn, reached the deserted boudoir. Sir Andrew was standing with his back to her and close to a table upon which stood a massive silver candelabra. A slip of paper was in his hand, and he was in the very act of perusing its contents.

Unperceived, her soft clinging robe making not the slightest sound upon the heavy carpet, not daring to breathe until she had accomplished her purpose, Marguerite slipped close behind him. . . . At that moment he looked round and saw her; she uttered a groan, passed her hand across her forehead, and murmured faintly,—

"The heat in the room was terrible . . . I felt so faint. . . . Ah! . . ."

She tottered almost as if she would fall, and Sir Andrew, quickly recovering himself, and crumpling in his hand the tiny note he had been reading, was only, apparently, just in time to support her.

"You are ill, Lady Blakeney?" he asked with much concern. "Let me . . ."

"No, no, nothing—" she interrupted quickly. "A chair—quick."

She sank into a chair close to the table, and throwing back her head, closed her eyes.

"There!" she murmured, still faintly; "the giddiness is passing off.[EOL] . . . Do not heed me, Sir Andrew; I assure you I already feel better."

At moments like these there is no doubt—and psychologists actually assert it—that there is in us a sense which has absolutely nothing to do with the other five: it is not that we see, it is not that we hear or touch, yet we seem to do all three at once. Marguerite sat there with her eyes apparently closed. Sir Andrew was immediately behind her, and on her right was the table with the five-armed candelabra upon it. Before her mental vision there was absolutely nothing but Armand's face. Armand, whose life was in the most imminent danger, and who seemed to be looking at her from a background upon which were dimly painted the seething crowd of Paris, the bare walls of the Tribunal of Public Safety, with Foucquier-Tinville, the Public Prosecutor, demanding Armand's life in the name of the people of France, and the lurid guillotine with its stained knife waiting for another victim . . . Armand! . . .

For one moment there was dead silence in the little boudoir. Beyond, from the brilliant ball-room, the sweet notes of the gavotte, the frou-frou of rich dresses, the talk and laughter of a large and merry crowd, came as a strange, weird accompaniment to the drama which was being enacted here.

Sir Andrew had not uttered another word. Then it was that that extra sense became potent in Marguerite Blakeney. She could not see, for her eyes were closed; she could not hear, for the noise from the ball-room drowned the soft rustle of that momentous scrap of paper; nevertheless she knew—as if she had both seen and heard—that Sir Andrew was even now holding the paper to the flame of one of the candles.

At the exact moment that it began to catch fire, she opened her eyes, raised her hand and, with two dainty fingers, had taken the burning scrap of paper from the young man's hand. Then she blew out the flame, and held the paper to her nostril with perfect unconcern.

"How thoughtful of you, Sir Andrew," she said gaily, "surely 'twas your grandmother who taught you that the smell of burnt paper was a sovereign remedy against giddiness."

She sighed with satisfaction, holding the paper tightly between her jeweled fingers; that talisman which perhaps would save her brother Armand's life. Sir Andrew was staring at her, too dazed for the moment to realise what had actually happened; he had been taken so completely by surprise, that he seemed quite unable to grasp the fact that the slip of paper, which she held in her dainty hand, was one perhaps on which the life of his comrade might depend.

Marguerite burst into a long, merry peal of laughter.

"Why do you stare at me like that?" she said playfully. "I assure you I feel much better; your remedy has proved most effectual. This room is most delightfully cool," she added, with the same perfect composure, "and the sound of the gavotte from the ball-room is fascinating and soothing."

She was prattling on in the most unconcerned and pleasant way, whilst Sir Andrew, in an agony of mind, was racking his brains as to the quickest method he could employ to get that bit of paper out of that beautiful woman's hand. Instinctively, vague and tumultuous thoughts rushed through his mind: he suddenly remembered her nationality, and worst of all, recollected that horrible tale anent the Marquis de St. Cyr, which in England no one had credited, for the sake of Sir Percy, as well as for her own.

"What? Still dreaming and staring?" she said, with a merry laugh, "you are most ungallant, Sir Andrew; and now I come to think of it, you seemed more startled than pleased when you saw me just now. I do believe, after all, that it was not concern for my health, nor yet a remedy taught you by your grandmother that caused you to burn this tiny scrap of paper. . . . I vow it must have been your lady love's last cruel epistle you were trying to destroy. Now confess!" she added, playfully holding up the scrap of paper, "does this contain her final *congé*, or a last appeal to kiss and make friends?"

"Whichever it is, Lady Blakeney," said Sir Andrew, who was gradually recovering his self-possession, "this little note is undoubtedly mine, and . . ."

Not caring whether his action was one that would be styled ill-bred towards a lady, the young man had made a bold dash for the note; but Marguerite's thoughts flew quicker than his own; her actions, under pressure of this intense excitement, were swifter and more sure. She was tall and strong; she took a quick step backwards and knocked over the small Sheraton table which was already top-heavy, and which fell down with a crash, together with the massive candelabra upon it.

She gave a quick cry of alarm:

"The candles, Sir Andrew—quick!"

There was not much damage done; one or two of the candles had blown out as the candelabra fell; others had merely sent some grease upon the valuable carpet; one had ignited the paper shade over it. Sir Andrew quickly and dexterously put out the flames and replaced the candelabra upon the table; but this had taken him a few seconds to do, and those seconds had been all that Marguerite needed to cast a quick glance at the paper, and to note its contents—a dozen words in the same distorted handwriting she had seen before, and bearing the same device—a star-shaped flower drawn in red ink.

When Sir Andrew once more looked at her, he only saw on her face alarm at the untoward accident and relief at its happy issue; whilst the tiny and momentous note had apparently fluttered to the ground. Eagerly the young man picked it up, and his face looked much relieved, as his fingers closed tightly over it.

"For shame, Sir Andrew," she said, shaking her head with a playful sigh, "making havoc in the heart of some impressionable duchess, whilst conquering the affections of my sweet little Suzanne. Well, well! I do believe it was Cupid himself who stood by you, and threatened the entire Foreign Office with destruction by fire, just on purpose to make me drop love's message, before it had been polluted by my indiscreet eyes. To think that, a moment longer, and I might have known the secrets of an erring duchess."

"You will forgive me, Lady Blakeney," said Sir Andrew, now as calm as she was herself, "if I resume the interesting occupation which you had interrupted?"

"By all means, Sir Andrew! How should I venture to thwart the love-god again? Perhaps he would mete out some terrible chastisement against my presumption. Burn your love-token, by all means!"

Sir Andrew had already twisted the paper into a long spill, and was once again holding it to the flame of the candle, which had remained alight. He did not notice the strange smile on the face of his fair *vis-à-vis*, so intent was he on the work of destruction; perhaps, had he done so, the look of relief would have faded from his face. He watched the fateful note, as it curled under the flame. Soon the last fragment fell on the floor, and he placed his heel upon the ashes.

"And now, Sir Andrew," said Marguerite Blakeney, with the pretty nonchalance peculiar to herself, and with the most winning of smiles, "will you venture to excite the jealousy of your fair lady by asking me to dance the minuet?"

XIII. EITHER—OR?

The few words which Marguerite Blakeney had managed to read on the half-scorched piece of paper, seemed literally to be the words of Fate. "Start myself to-morrow. . . ." This she had read quite distinctly; then came a blur caused by the smoke of the candle, which obliterated the next few words; but, right at the bottom, there was another sentence, which was now standing clearly and distinctly, like letters of fire, before her mental vision. "If you wish to speak to me again, I shall be in the supper-room at one o'clock precisely." The whole was signed with the hastily-scrawled little device—a tiny star-shaped flower, which had become so familiar to her.

One o'clock precisely! It was now close upon eleven, the last minuet was being danced, with Sir Andrew Ffoulkes and beautiful Lady Blakeney leading the couples, through its delicate and intricate figures.

Close upon eleven! the hands of the handsome Louis XV. clock upon its ormolu bracket seemed to move along with maddening rapidity. Two hours more, and her fate and that of Armand would be sealed. In two hours she must make up her mind whether she will keep the knowledge so cunningly gained to herself, and leave her brother to his fate, or whether she will willfully betray a brave man, whose life was devoted to his fellow-men, who was noble, generous, and above all, unsuspecting. It seemed a horrible thing to do. But then, there was Armand! Armand, too, was noble and brave, Armand, too, was unsuspecting. And Armand loved her, would have willingly trusted his life in her hands, and now, when she could save him from death, she hesitated. Oh! it was monstrous; her brother's kind, gentle face, so full of love for her, seemed to be looking reproachfully at her. "You might have saved me, Margot!" he seemed to say to her, "and you chose the life of a stranger, a man you do not know, whom you have never seen, and preferred that he should be safe, whilst you sent me to the guillotine!"

All these conflicting thoughts raged through Marguerite's brain, while, with a smile upon her lips, she glided through the graceful mazes of the minuet. She noted—with that acute sense of hers—that she had succeeded in completely allaying Sir Andrew's fears.

Her self-control had been absolutely perfect—she was a finer actress at this moment, and throughout the whole of this minuet, than she had ever been upon the boards of the Comédie Française; but then, a beloved brother's life had not depended upon her histrionic powers.

She was too clever to overdo her part, and made no further allusions to the supposed *billet doux*, which had caused Sir Andrew Ffoulkes such an agonizing five minutes. She watched his anxiety melting away under her sunny smile, and soon perceived that, whatever doubt may have crossed his mind at the moment, she had, by the time the last bars of the minuet had been played, succeeded in completely dispelling it; he never realised in what a fever of excitement she was, what effort it cost her to keep up a constant ripple of *banal* conversation.

When the minuet was over, she asked Sir Andrew to take her into the next room.

"I have promised to go down to supper with His Royal Highness," she said, "but before we part, tell me . . . am I forgiven?"

"Forgiven?"

"Yes! Confess, I gave you a fright just now. . . . But, remember, I am not an Englishwoman, and I do not look upon the exchanging of *billet doux* as a crime, and I vow I'll not tell my little Suzanne. But now, tell me, shall I welcome you at my water-party on Wednesday?"

"I am not sure, Lady Blakeney," he replied evasively. "I may have to leave London to-morrow."

"I would not do that, if I were you," she said earnestly; then seeing the anxious look once more reappearing in his eyes, she added gaily; "No one can throw a ball better than you can, Sir Andrew, we should so miss you on the bowling-green."

He had led her across the room, to one beyond, where already His Royal Highness was waiting for the beautiful Lady Blakeney.

"Madame, supper awaits us," said the Prince, offering his arm to Marguerite, "and I am full of hope. The goddess Fortune has frowned so persistently on me at hazard, that I look with confidence for the smiles of the goddess of Beauty."

"Your Highness has been unfortunate at the card tables?" asked Marguerite, as she took the Prince's arm.

"Aye! most unfortunate. Blakeney, not content with being the richest among my father's subjects, has also the most outrageous luck. By the way, where is that inimitable wit? I vow, Madam, that this life would be but a dreary desert without your smiles and his sallies."

XIV. ONE O'CLOCK PRECISELY!

Supper had been extremely gay. All those present declared that never had Lady Blakeney been more adorable, nor that "demmed idiot" Sir Percy more amusing.

His Royal Highness had laughed until the tears streamed down his cheeks at Blakeney's foolish yet funny repartees. His doggerel verse, "We seek him here, we seek him there," etc., was sung to the tune of "Ho! Merry Britons!" and to the accompaniment of glasses knocked loudly against the table. Lord Grenville, moreover, had a most perfect cook—some wags asserted that he was a scion of the old French *noblesse*, who, having lost his fortune, had come to seek it in the *cuisine* of the Foreign Office.

Marguerite Blakeney was in her most brilliant mood, and surely not a soul in that crowded supper-room had even an inkling of the terrible struggle which was raging within her heart.

The clock was ticking so mercilessly on. It was long past midnight, and even the Prince of Wales was thinking of leaving the supper-table. Within the next half-hour the destinies of two brave men would be pitted against one another—the dearly-beloved brother and he, the unknown hero.

Marguerite had not even tried to see Chauvelin during this last hour; she knew that his keen, fox-like eyes would terrify her at once, and incline the balance of her decision towards Armand. Whilst she did not see him, there still lingered in her heart of hearts a vague, undefined hope that "something" would occur, something big, enormous, epoch-making, which would shift from her young, weak shoulders this terrible burden of responsibility, of having to choose between two such cruel alternatives.

But the minutes ticked on with that dull monotony which they invariably seem to assume when our very nerves ache with their incessant ticking.

After supper, dancing was resumed. His Royal Highness had left, and there was general talk of departing among the older guests; the young ones were indefatigable and had started on a new gavotte, which would fill the next quarter of an hour.

Marguerite did not feel equal to another dance; there is a limit to the most enduring self-control. Escorted by a Cabinet Minister, she had once more found her way to the tiny boudoir, still the most deserted among all the rooms. She knew that Chauvelin must be lying in wait for her somewhere, ready to seize the first possible opportunity for a *tête-à-tête*. His eyes had met hers for a moment after the 'fore-supper minuet, and she knew that the keen diplomatist, with those searching pale eyes of his, had divined that her work was accomplished.

Fate had willed it so. Marguerite, torn by the most terrible conflict heart of woman can ever know, had resigned herself to its decrees. But Armand must be saved at any cost; he, first of all, for he was her brother, had been mother, father, friend to her ever since she, a tiny babe, had lost both her parents. To think of Armand dying a traitor's death on the guillotine was too horrible even to dwell upon—impossible, in fact. That could never be, never. . . . As for the stranger, the hero . . . well! there, let Fate decide. Marguerite would redeem her brother's life at the hands of the relentless enemy, then let that cunning Scarlet Pimpernel extricate himself after that.

Perhaps—vaguely—Marguerite hoped that the daring plotter, who for so many months had baffled an army of spies, would still manage to evade Chauvelin and remain immune to the end.

She thought of all this, as she sat listening to the witty discourse of the Cabinet Minister, who, no doubt, felt that he had found in Lady Blakeney a most perfect listener. Suddenly she saw the keen, fox-like face of Chauvelin peeping through the curtained doorway.

"Lord Fancourt," she said to the Minister, "will you do me a service?"

"I am entirely at your ladyship's service," he replied gallantly.

"Will you see if my husband is still in the card-room? And if he is, will you tell him that I am very tired, and would be glad to go home soon."

The commands of a beautiful woman are binding on all mankind, even on Cabinet Ministers. Lord Fancourt prepared to obey instantly.

"I do not like to leave your ladyship alone," he said.

"Never fear. I shall be quite safe here—and, I think, undisturbed . . . but I am really tired. You know Sir Percy will drive back to Richmond. It is a long way, and we shall not —an we do not hurry—get home before daybreak."

Lord Fancourt had perforce to go.

The moment he had disappeared, Chauvelin slipped into the room, and the next instant stood calm and impassive by her side.

"You have news for me?" he said.

An icy mantle seemed to have suddenly settled round Marguerite's shoulders; though her cheeks glowed with fire, she felt chilled and numbed. Oh, Armand! will you ever know the terrible sacrifice of pride, of dignity, of womanliness a devoted sister is making for your sake?

"Nothing of importance," she said, staring mechanically before her, "but it might prove a clue. I contrived—no matter how—to detect Sir Andrew Ffoulkes in the very act of burning a paper at one of these candles, in this very room. That paper I succeeded in holding between my fingers for the space of two minutes, and to cast my eye on it for that of ten seconds."

"Time enough to learn its contents?" asked Chauvelin, quietly.

She nodded. Then she continued in the same even, mechanical tone of voice—

"In the corner of the paper there was the usual rough device of a small star-shaped flower. Above it I read two lines, everything else was scorched and blackened by the flame."

"And what were these two lines?"

Her throat seemed suddenly to have contracted. For an instant she felt that she could not speak the words, which might send a brave man to his death.

"It is lucky that the whole paper was not burned," added Chauvelin, with dry sarcasm, "for it might have fared ill with Armand St. Just. What were the two lines, citoyenne?"

"One was, 'I start myself to-morrow,'" she said quietly; "the other—'If you wish to speak to me, I shall be in the supper-room at one o'clock precisely.'"

Chauvelin looked up at the clock just above the mantelpiece.

"Then I have plenty of time," he said placidly.

"What are you going to do?" she asked.

She was pale as a statue, her hands were icy cold, her head and heart throbbed with the awful strain upon her nerves. Oh, this was cruel! cruel! What had she done to have deserved all this? Her choice was made: had she done a vile action or one that was sublime? The recording angel, who writes in the book of gold, alone could give an answer.

"What are you going to do?" she repeated mechanically.

"Oh, nothing for the present. After that it will depend."

"On what?"

"On whom I shall see in the supper-room at one o'clock precisely."

"You will see the Scarlet Pimpernel, of course. But you do not know him."

"No. But I shall presently."

"Sir Andrew will have warned him."

"I think not. When you parted from him after the minuet he stood and watched you, for a moment or two, with a look which gave me to understand that something had happened between you. It was only natural, was it not? that I should make a shrewd guess as to the nature of that 'something.' I thereupon engaged the young gallant in a long and animated conversation—we discussed Herr Glück's singular success in London—until a lady claimed his arm for supper."

"Since then?"

"I did not lose sight of him through supper. When we all came upstairs again, Lady Portarles buttonholed him and started on the subject of pretty Mlle. Suzanne de Tournay. I knew he would not move until Lady Portarles had exhausted the subject, which will not be for another quarter of an hour at least, and it is five minutes to one now."

He was preparing to go, and went up to the doorway, where, drawing aside the curtain, he stood for a moment pointing out to Marguerite the distant figure of Sir Andrew Ffoulkes in close conversation with Lady Portarles.

"I think," he said, with a triumphant smile, "that I may safely expect to find the person I seek in the dining-room, fair lady."

"There may be more than one."

"Whoever is there, as the clock strikes one, will be shadowed by one of my men; of these, one, or perhaps two, or even three, will leave for France to-morrow. *One* of these will be the 'Scarlet Pimpernel.'"

"Yes?—And?"

"I also, fair lady, will leave for France to-morrow. The papers found at Dover upon the person of Sir Andrew Ffoulkes speak of the neighbourhood of Calais, of an inn which I know well, called 'Le Chat Gris,' of a lonely place somewhere on the coast—the Père Blanchard's hut—which I must endeavour to find. All these places are given as the point where this meddlesome Englishman has bidden the traitor de Tournay and others to meet his emissaries. But it seems that he has decided not to send his emissaries, that 'he will start himself to-morrow.' Now, one of those persons whom I shall see anon in the supper-room, will be journeying to Calais, and I shall follow that person, until I have tracked him to where those fugitive aristocrats await him; for that person, fair lady, will be the man whom I have sought for, for nearly a year, the man whose energy has outdone me, whose ingenuity has baffled me, whose audacity has set me wondering—yes! me!—who have seen a trick or two in my time—the mysterious and elusive Scarlet Pimpernel."

"And Armand?" she pleaded.

"Have I ever broken my word? I promise you that the day the Scarlet Pimpernel and I start for France, I will send you that imprudent letter of his by special courier. More than that, I will pledge you the word of France, that the day I lay hands on that meddlesome Englishman, St. Just will be here in England, safe in the arms of his charming sister."

And with a deep and elaborate bow and another look at the clock, Chauvelin glided out of the room.

It seemed to Marguerite that through all the noise, all the din of music, dancing, and laughter, she could hear his cat-like tread, gliding through the vast reception-rooms; that she could hear him go down the massive staircase, reach the dining-room and open the door. Fate *had* decided, had made her speak, had made her do a vile and abominable thing, for the sake of the brother she loved. She lay back in her chair, passive and still, seeing the figure of her relentless enemy ever present before her aching eyes.

When Chauvelin reached the supper-room it was quite deserted. It had that woebegone, forsaken, tawdry appearance, which reminds one so much of a ball-dress, the morning after.

Half-empty glasses littered the table, unfolded napkins lay about, the chairs—turned towards one another in groups of twos and threes—seemed like the seats of ghosts, in close conversation with one another. There were sets of two chairs—very close to one another—in the far corners of the room, which spoke of recent whispered flirtations, over cold game-pie and champagne; there were sets of three and four chairs, that recalled pleasant, animated discussions over the latest scandals; there were chairs straight up in a row that still looked starchy, critical, acid, like antiquated dowagers; there were a few isolated, single chairs, close to the table, that spoke of gourmands intent on the most *recherché* dishes, and others overturned on the floor, that spoke volumes on the subject of my Lord Grenville's cellars.

It was a ghostlike replica, in fact, of that fashionable gathering upstairs; a ghost that haunts every house where balls and good suppers are given; a picture drawn with white chalk on grey cardboard, dull and colourless, now that the bright silk dresses and gorgeously embroidered coats were no longer there to fill in the foreground, and now that the candles flickered sleepily in their sockets.

Chauvelin smiled benignly, and rubbing his long, thin hands together, he looked round the deserted supper-room, whence even the last flunkey had retired in order to join his friends in the hall below. All was silence in the dimly-lighted room, whilst the sound of the gavotte, the hum of distant talk and laughter, and the rumble of an occasional coach outside, only seemed to reach this palace of the Sleeping Beauty as the murmur of some flitting spooks far away.

It all looked so peaceful, so luxurious, and so still, that the keenest observer—a veritable prophet—could never have guessed that, at this present moment, that deserted supper-room was nothing but a trap laid for the capture of the most cunning and audacious plotter those stirring times had ever seen.

Chauvelin pondered and tried to peer into the immediate future. What would this man be like, whom he and the leaders of a whole revolution had sworn to bring to his death? Everything about him was weird and mysterious; his personality, which he had so cunningly concealed, the power he wielded over nineteen English gentlemen who seemed to obey his every command blindly and enthusiastically, the passionate love and submission he had roused in his little trained band, and, above all, his marvellous audacity, the boundless impudence which had caused him to beard his most implacable enemies, within the very walls of Paris.

No wonder that in France the *sobriquet* of the mysterious Englishman roused in the people a superstitious shudder. Chauvelin himself as he gazed round the deserted room, where presently the weird hero would appear, felt a strange feeling of awe creeping all down his spine.

But his plans were well laid. He felt sure that the Scarlet Pimpernel had not been warned, and felt equally sure that Marguerite Blakeney had not played him false. If she had . . . a cruel look, that would have made her shudder, gleamed in Chauvelin's keen, pale eyes. If she had played him a trick, Armand St. Just would suffer the extreme penalty.

But no, no! of course she had not played him false!

Fortunately the supper-room was deserted: this would make Chauvelin's task all the easier, when presently that unsuspecting enigma would enter it alone. No one was here now save Chauvelin himself.

Stay! as he surveyed with a satisfied smile the solitude of the room, the cunning agent of the French Government became aware of the peaceful, monotonous breathing of some one of my Lord Grenville's guests, who, no doubt, had supped both wisely and well, and was enjoying a quiet sleep, away from the din of the dancing above.

Chauvelin looked round once more, and there in the corner of a sofa, in the dark angle of the room, his mouth open, his eyes shut, the sweet sounds of peaceful slumbers proceeding from his nostrils, reclined the gorgeously-apparelled, long-limbed husband of the cleverest woman in Europe.

Chauvelin looked at him as he lay there, placid, unconscious, at peace with all the world and himself, after the best of suppers, and a smile, that was almost one of pity, softened for a moment the hard lines of the Frenchman's face and the sarcastic twinkle of his pale eyes.

Evidently the slumberer, deep in dreamless sleep, would not interfere with Chauvelin's trap for catching that cunning Scarlet Pimpernel. Again he rubbed his hands together, and, following the example of Sir Percy Blakeney, he, too, stretched himself out in the corner of another sofa, shut his eyes, opened his mouth, gave forth sounds of peaceful breathing, and ... waited!

XV. DOUBT

Marguerite Blakeney had watched the slight sable-clad figure of Chauvelin, as he worked his way through the ball-room. Then perforce she had had to wait, while her nerves tingled with excitement.

Listlessly she sat in the small, still deserted boudoir, looking out through the curtained doorway on the dancing couples beyond: looking at them, yet seeing nothing, hearing the music, yet conscious of naught save a feeling of expectancy, of anxious, weary waiting.

Her mind conjured up before her the vision of what was, perhaps at this very moment, passing downstairs. The half-deserted dining-room, the fateful hour—Chauvelin on the watch!—then, precise to the moment, the entrance of a man, he, the Scarlet Pimpernel, the mysterious leader, who to Marguerite had become almost unreal, so strange, so weird was this hidden identity.

She wished she were in the supper-room, too, at this moment, watching him as he entered; she knew that her woman's penetration would at once recognise in the stranger's face—whoever he might be—that strong individuality which belongs to a leader of men—to a hero: to the mighty, high-soaring eagle, whose daring wings were becoming entangled in the ferret's trap.

Woman-like, she thought of him with unmixed sadness; the irony of that fate seemed so cruel which allowed the fearless lion to succumb to the gnawing of a rat! Ah! had Armand's life not been at stake! . . .

"Faith! your ladyship must have thought me very remiss," said a voice suddenly, close to her elbow. "I had a deal of difficulty in delivering your message, for I could not find Blakeney anywhere at first . . ."

Marguerite had forgotten all about her husband and her message to him; his very name, as spoken by Lord Fancourt, sounded strange and unfamiliar to her, so completely had she in the last five minutes lived her old life in the Rue de Richelieu again, with Armand always near her to love and protect her, to guard her from the many subtle intrigues which were forever raging in Paris in those days.

"I did find him at last," continued Lord Fancourt, "and gave him your message. He said that he would give orders at once for the horses to be put to."

"Ah!" she said, still very absently, "you found my husband, and gave him my message?"

"Yes; he was in the dining-room fast asleep. I could not manage to wake him up at first."

"Thank you very much," she said mechanically, trying to collect her thoughts.

"Will your ladyship honour me with the *contredanse* until your coach is ready?" asked Lord Fancourt.

"No, I thank you, my lord, but—and you will forgive me—I really am too tired, and the heat in the ball-room has become oppressive."

"The conservatory is deliciously cool; let me take you there, and then get you something. You seem ailing, Lady Blakeney."

"I am only very tired," she repeated wearily, as she allowed Lord Fancourt to lead her, where subdued lights and green plants lent coolness to the air. He got her a chair, into which she sank. This long interval of waiting was intolerable. Why did not Chauvelin come and tell her the result of his watch?

Lord Fancourt was very attentive. She scarcely heard what he said, and suddenly startled him by asking abruptly,—

"Lord Fancourt, did you perceive who was in the dining-room just now besides Sir Percy Blakeney?"

"Only the agent of the French Government, M. Chauvelin, equally fast asleep in another corner," he said. "Why does your ladyship ask?"

"I know not . . . I . . . Did you notice the time when you were there?"

"It must have been about five or ten minutes past one. . . . I wonder what your ladyship is thinking about," he added, for evidently the fair lady's thoughts were very far away, and she had not been listening to his intellectual conversation.

But indeed her thoughts were not very far away: only one storey below, in this same house, in the dining-room where sat Chauvelin still on the watch. Had he failed? For one instant that possibility rose before her as a hope—the hope that the Scarlet Pimpernel had been warned by Sir Andrew, and that Chauvelin's trap had failed to catch his bird; but that hope soon gave way to fear. Had he failed? But then—Armand!

Lord Fancourt had given up talking since he found that he had no listener. He wanted an opportunity for slipping away: for sitting opposite to a lady, however fair, who is evidently not heeding the most vigorous efforts made for her entertainment, is not exhilarating, even to a Cabinet Minister.

"Shall I find out if your ladyship's coach is ready," he said at last, tentatively.

"Oh, thank you . . . thank you . . . if you would be so kind . . . I fear I am but sorry company . . . but I am really tired . . . and, perhaps, would be best alone."

She had been longing to be rid of him, for she hoped that, like the fox he so resembled, Chauvelin would be prowling round, thinking to find her alone.

But Lord Fancourt went, and still Chauvelin did not come. Oh! what had happened? She felt Armand's fate trembling in the balance . . . she feared—now with a deadly fear—that Chauvelin *had* failed, and that the mysterious Scarlet Pimpernel had proved elusive once more; then she knew that she need hope for no pity, no mercy, from him.

He had pronounced his "Either—or—" and nothing less would content him: he was very spiteful, and would affect the belief that she had willfully misled him, and having failed to trap the eagle once again, his revengeful mind would be content with the humble prey—Armand!

Yet she had done her best; had strained every nerve for Armand's sake. She could not bear to think that all had failed. She could not sit still; she wanted to go and hear the worst at once; she wondered even that Chauvelin had not come yet, to vent his wrath and satire upon her.

Lord Grenville himself came presently to tell her that her coach was ready, and that Sir Percy was already waiting for her—ribbons in hand. Marguerite said "Farewell" to her distinguished host; many of her friends stopped her, as she crossed the rooms, to talk to her, and exchange pleasant *au revoirs*.

The Minister only took final leave of beautiful Lady Blakeney on the top of the stairs; below, on the landing, a veritable army of gallant gentlemen were waiting to bid "Good-bye" to the queen of beauty and fashion, whilst outside, under the massive portico, Sir Percy's magnificent bays were impatiently pawing the ground.

At the top of the stairs, just after she had taken final leave of her host, she suddenly saw Chauvelin; he was coming up the stairs slowly, and rubbing his thin hands very softly together.

There was a curious look on his mobile face, partly amused and wholly puzzled, and as his keen eyes met Marguerite's they became strangely sarcastic.

"M. Chauvelin," she said, as he stopped on the top of the stairs, bowing elaborately before her, "my coach is outside; may I claim your arm?"

As gallant as ever, he offered her his arm and led her downstairs. The crowd was very great, some of the Minister's guests were departing, others were leaning against the banisters watching the throng as it filed up and down the wide staircase.

"Chauvelin," she said at last desperately, "I must know what has happened."

"What has happened, dear lady?" he said, with affected surprise. "Where? When?"

"You are torturing me, Chauvelin. I have helped you to-night . . . surely I have the right to know. What happened in the dining-room at one o'clock just now?"

She spoke in a whisper, trusting that in the general hubbub of the crowd her words would remain unheeded by all, save the man at her side.

"Quiet and peace reigned supreme, fair lady; at that hour I was asleep in the corner of one sofa and Sir Percy Blakeney in another."

"Nobody came into the room at all?"

"Nobody."

"Then we have failed, you and I? . . ."

"Yes! we have failed—perhaps . . ."

"But Armand?" she pleaded.

"Ah! Armand St. Just's chances hang on a thread . . . pray heaven, dear lady, that that thread may not snap."

"Chauvelin, I worked for you, sincerely, earnestly . . . remember. . . ."

"I remember my promise," he said quietly; "the day that the Scarlet Pimpernel and I meet on French soil, St. Just will be in the arms of his charming sister."

"Which means that a brave man's blood will be on my hands," she said, with a shudder.

"His blood, or that of your brother. Surely at the present moment you must hope, as I do, that the enigmatical Scarlet Pimpernel will start for Calais to-day—"

"I am only conscious of one hope, citoyen."

"And that is?"

"That Satan, your master, will have need of you elsewhere, before the sun rises to-day."

"You flatter me, citoyenne."

She had detained him for a while, midway down the stairs, trying to get at the thoughts which lay beyond that thin, fox-like mask. But Chauvelin remained urbane, sarcastic, mysterious; not a line betrayed to the poor, anxious woman whether she need fear or whether she dared to hope.

Downstairs on the landing she was soon surrounded. Lady Blakeney never stepped from any house into her coach, without an escort of fluttering human moths around the dazzling light of her beauty. But before she finally turned away from Chauvelin, she held out a tiny hand to him, with that pretty gesture of childish appeal which was so essentially her own.

"Give me some hope, my little Chauvelin," she pleaded.

With perfect gallantry he bowed over that tiny hand, which looked so dainty and white through the delicately transparent black lace mitten, and kissing the tips of the rosy fingers:—

"Pray heaven that the thread may not snap," he repeated, with his enigmatic smile.

And stepping aside, he allowed the moths to flutter more closely round the candle, and the brilliant throng of the *jeunesse dorée*, eagerly attentive to Lady Blakeney's every movement, hid the keen, fox-like face from her view.

XVI. RICHMOND

A few minutes later she was sitting, wrapped in costly furs, near Sir Percy Blakeney on the box-seat of his magnificent coach, and the four splendid bays had thundered down the quiet street.

The night was warm in spite of the gentle breeze which fanned Marguerite's burning cheeks. Soon London houses were left behind, and rattling over old Hammersmith Bridge, Sir Percy was driving his bays rapidly towards Richmond.

The river wound in and out in its pretty delicate curves, looking like a silver serpent beneath the glittering rays of the moon. Long shadows from overhanging trees spread occasional deep palls right across the road. The bays were rushing along at breakneck speed, held but slightly back by Sir Percy's strong, unerring hands.

These nightly drives after balls and suppers in London were a source of perpetual delight to Marguerite, and she appreciated her husband's eccentricity keenly, which caused him to adopt this mode of taking her home every night, to their beautiful home by the river, instead of living in a stuffy London house. He loved driving his spirited horses along the lonely, moonlit roads, and she loved to sit on the box-seat, with the soft air of an English late summer's night fanning her face after the hot atmosphere of a ball or supper-party. The drive was not a long one—less than an hour, sometimes, when the bays were very fresh, and Sir Percy gave them full rein.

To-night he seemed to have a very devil in his fingers, and the coach seemed to fly along the road, beside the river. As usual, he did not speak to her, but stared straight in front of him, the ribbons seeming to lie quite loosely in his slender, white hands. Marguerite looked at him tentatively once or twice; she could see his handsome profile, and one lazy eye, with its straight fine brow and drooping heavy lid.

The face in the moonlight looked singularly earnest, and recalled to Marguerite's aching heart those happy days of courtship, before he had become the lazy nincompoop, the effete fop, whose life seemed spent in card and supper rooms.

But now, in the moonlight, she could not catch the expression of the lazy blue eyes; she could only see the outline of the firm chin, the corner of the strong mouth, the well-cut massive shape of the forehead; truly, nature had meant well by Sir Percy; his faults must all be laid at the door of that poor, half-crazy mother, and of the distracted heart-broken father, neither of whom had cared for the young life which was sprouting up between them, and which, perhaps, their very carelessness was already beginning to wreck.

Marguerite suddenly felt intense sympathy for her husband. The moral crisis she had just gone through made her feel indulgent towards the faults, the delinquencies, of others.

How thoroughly a human being can be buffeted and overmastered by Fate, had been borne in upon her with appalling force. Had anyone told her a week ago that she would stoop to spy upon her friends, that she would betray a brave and unsuspecting man into the hands of a relentless enemy, she would have laughed the idea to scorn.

Yet she had done these things; anon, perhaps the death of that brave man would be at her door, just as two years ago the Marquis de St. Cyr had perished through a thoughtless word of hers; but in that case she was morally innocent—she had meant no serious harm—fate merely had stepped in. But this time she had done a thing that obviously was base, had done it deliberately, for a motive which, perhaps, high moralists would not even appreciate.

And as she felt her husband's strong arm beside her, she also felt how much more he would dislike and despise her, if he knew of this night's work. Thus human beings judge of one another, superficially, casually, throwing contempt on one another, with but little reason, and no charity. She despised her husband for his inanities and vulgar, unintellectual occupations; and he, she felt, would despise her still worse, because she had not been strong enough to do right for right's sake, and to sacrifice her brother to the dictates of her conscience.

Buried in her thoughts, Marguerite had found this hour in the breezy summer night all too brief; and it was with a feeling of keen disappointment, that she suddenly realised that the bays had turned into the massive gates of her beautiful English home.

Sir Percy Blakeney's house on the river has become a historic one: palatial in its dimensions, it stands in the midst of exquisitely laid-out gardens, with a picturesque terrace and frontage to the river. Built in Tudor days, the old red brick of the walls looks eminently picturesque in the midst of a bower of green, the beautiful lawn, with its old sun-dial, adding the true note of harmony to its foreground. Great secular trees lent cool shadows to the grounds, and now, on this warm early autumn night, the leaves slightly turned to russets and gold, the old garden looked singularly poetic and peaceful in the moonlight.

With unerring precision, Sir Percy had brought the four bays to a standstill immediately in front of the fine Elizabethan entrance hall; in spite of the lateness of the hour, an army of grooms seemed to have emerged from the very ground, as the coach had thundered up, and were standing respectfully round.

Sir Percy jumped down quickly, then helped Marguerite to alight. She lingered outside for a moment, whilst he gave a few orders to one of his men. She skirted the house, and stepped on to the lawn, looking out dreamily into the silvery landscape. Nature seemed exquisitely at peace, in comparison with the tumultuous emotions she had gone through: she could faintly hear the ripple of the river and the occasional soft and ghostlike fall of a dead leaf from a tree.

All else was quiet round her. She had heard the horses prancing as they were being led away to their distant stables, the hurrying of servants' feet as they had all gone within to rest: the house also was quite still. In two separate suites of apartments, just above the magnificent reception-rooms, lights were still burning; they were her rooms, and his, well divided from each other by the whole width of the house, as far apart as their own lives had become. Involuntarily she sighed—at that moment she could really not have told why.

She was suffering from unconquerable heartache. Deeply and achingly she was sorry for herself. Never had she felt so pitiably lonely, so bitterly in want of comfort and of sympathy. With another sigh she turned away from the river towards the house, vaguely wondering if, after such a night, she could ever find rest and sleep.

Suddenly, before she reached the terrace, she heard a firm step upon the crisp gravel, and the next moment her husband's figure emerged out of the shadow. He, too, had skirted the house, and was wandering along the lawn, towards the river. He still wore his heavy driving coat with the numerous lapels and collars he himself had set in fashion, but he had thrown it well back, burying his hands as was his wont, in the deep pockets of his satin breeches: the gorgeous white costume he had worn at Lord Grenville's ball, with its jabot of priceless lace, looked strangely ghostly against the dark background of the house.

He apparently did not notice her, for, after a few moments' pause, he presently turned back towards the house, and walked straight up to the terrace.

"Sir Percy!"

He already had one foot on the lowest of the terrace steps, but at her voice he started, and paused, then looked searchingly into the shadows whence she had called to him.

She came forward quickly into the moonlight, and, as soon as he saw her, he said, with that air of consummate gallantry he always wore when speaking to her,—

"At your service, Madame!"

But his foot was still on the step, and in his whole attitude there was a remote suggestion, distinctly visible to her, that he wished to go, and had no desire for a midnight interview.

"The air is deliciously cool," she said, "the moonlight peaceful and poetic, and the garden inviting. Will you not stay in it awhile; the hour is not yet late, or is my company so distasteful to you, that you are in a hurry to rid yourself of it?"

"Nay, Madame," he rejoined placidly, "but 'tis on the other foot the shoe happens to be, and I'll warrant you'll find the midnight air more poetic without my company: no doubt the sooner I remove the obstruction the better your ladyship will like it."

He turned once more to go.

"I protest you mistake me, Sir Percy," she said hurriedly, and drawing a little closer to him; "the estrangement, which, alas! has arisen between us, was none of my making, remember."

"Begad! you must pardon me there, Madame!" he protested coldly, "my memory was always of the shortest."

He looked her straight in the eyes, with that lazy nonchalance which had become second nature to him. She returned his gaze for a moment, then her eyes softened, as she came up quite close to him, to the foot of the terrace steps.

"Of the shortest, Sir Percy? Faith! how it must have altered! Was it three years ago or four that you saw me for one hour in Paris, on your way to the East? When you came back two years later you had not forgotten me."

She looked divinely pretty as she stood there in the moonlight, with the fur-cloak sliding off her beautiful shoulders, the gold embroidery on her dress shimmering around her, her childlike blue eyes turned up fully at him.

He stood for a moment, rigid and still, but for the clenching of his hand against the stone balustrade of the terrace.

"You desired my presence, Madame," he said frigidly. "I take it that it was not with a view to indulging in tender reminiscences."

His voice certainly was cold and uncompromising: his attitude before her, stiff and unbending. Womanly decorum would have suggested that Marguerite should return coldness for coldness, and should sweep past him without another word, only with a curt nod of the head: but womanly instinct suggested that she should remain—that keen instinct, which makes a beautiful woman conscious of her powers long to bring to her knees the one man who pays her no homage. She stretched out her hand to him.

"Nay, Sir Percy, why not? the present is not so glorious but that I should not wish to dwell a little in the past."

He bent his tall figure, and taking hold of the extreme tip of the fingers which she still held out to him, he kissed them ceremoniously.

"I' faith, Madame," he said, "then you will pardon me, if my dull wits cannot accompany you there."

Once again he attempted to go, once more her voice, sweet, childlike, almost tender, called him back.

"Sir Percy."

"Your servant, Madame."

"Is it possible that love can die?" she said with sudden, unreasoning vehemence. "Methought that the passion which you once felt for me would outlast the span of human life. Is there nothing left of that love, Percy . . . which might help you . . . to bridge over that sad estrangement?"

His massive figure seemed, while she spoke thus to him, to stiffen still more, the strong mouth hardened, a look of relentless obstinacy crept into the habitually lazy blue eyes.

"With what object, I pray you, Madame?" he asked coldly.

"I do not understand you."

"Yet 'tis simple enough," he said with sudden bitterness, which seemed literally to surge through his words, though he was making visible efforts to suppress it, "I humbly put the question to you, for my slow wits are unable to grasp the cause of this, your ladyship's sudden new mood. Is it that you have the taste to renew the devilish sport which you played so successfully last year? Do you wish to see me once more a love-sick suppliant at your feet, so that you might again have the pleasure of kicking me aside, like a troublesome lap-dog?"

She had succeeded in rousing him for the moment: and again she looked straight at him, for it was thus she remembered him a year ago.

"Percy! I entreat you!" she whispered, "can we not bury the past?"

"Pardon me, Madame, but I understood you to say that your desire was to dwell in it."

"Nay! I spoke not of *that* past, Percy!" she said, while a tone of tenderness crept into her voice. "Rather did I speak of the time when you loved me still! and I . . . oh! I was vain and frivolous; your wealth and position allured me: I married you, hoping in my heart that your great love for me would beget in me a love for you . . . but, alas! . . ."

The moon had sunk low down behind a bank of clouds. In the east a soft grey light was beginning to chase away the heavy mantle of the night. He could only see her graceful outline now, the small queenly head, with its wealth of reddish golden curls, and the glittering gems forming the small, star-shaped, red flower which she wore as a diadem in her hair.

"Twenty-four hours after our marriage, Madame, the Marquis de St. Cyr and all his family perished on the guillotine, and the popular rumour reached me that it was the wife of Sir Percy Blakeney who helped to send them there."

"Nay! I myself told you the truth of that odious tale."

"Not till after it had been recounted to me by strangers, with all its horrible details."

"And you believed them then and there," she said with great vehemence, "without a proof or question—you believed that I, whom you vowed you loved more than life, whom you professed you worshipped, that *I* could do a thing so base as these *strangers* chose to recount. You thought I meant to deceive you about it all—that I ought to have spoken before I married you: yet, had you listened, I would have told you that up to the very morning on which St. Cyr went to the guillotine, I was straining every nerve, using every influence I possessed, to save him and his family. But my pride sealed my lips, when your love seemed to perish, as if under the knife of that same guillotine. Yet I would have told you how I was duped! Aye! I, whom that same popular rumour had endowed with the sharpest wits in France! I was tricked into doing this thing, by men who knew how to play upon my love for an only brother, and my desire for revenge. Was it unnatural?"

Her voice became choked with tears. She paused for a moment or two, trying to regain some sort of composure. She looked appealingly at him, almost as if he were her judge. He had allowed her to speak on in her own vehement, impassioned way, offering no comment, no word of sympathy: and now, while she paused, trying to swallow down the hot tears that gushed to her eyes, he waited, impassive and still. The dim, grey light of early dawn seemed to make his tall form look taller and more rigid. The lazy, good-natured face looked strangely altered. Marguerite, excited, as she was, could see that the eyes were no longer languid, the mouth no longer good-humoured and inane. A curious look of intense passion seemed to glow from beneath his drooping lids, the mouth was tightly closed, the lips compressed, as if the will alone held that surging passion in check.

Marguerite Blakeney was, above all, a woman, with all a woman's fascinating foibles, all a woman's most lovable sins. She knew in a moment that for the past few months she had been mistaken: that this man who stood here before her, cold as a statue, when her musical voice struck upon his ear, loved her, as he had loved her a year ago: that his passion might have been dormant, but that it was there, as strong, as intense, as overwhelming, as when first her lips met his in one long, maddening kiss.

Pride had kept him from her, and, woman-like, she meant to win back that conquest which had been hers before. Suddenly it seemed to her that the only happiness life could ever hold for her again would be in feeling that man's kiss once more upon her lips.

"Listen to the tale, Sir Percy," she said, and her voice now was low, sweet, infinitely tender. "Armand was all in all to me! We had no parents, and brought one another up. He was my little father, and I, his tiny mother; we loved one another so. Then one day—do you mind me, Sir Percy? the Marquis de St. Cyr had my brother Armand thrashed—thrashed by his lacqueys—that brother whom I loved better than all the world! And his offence? That he, a plebeian, had dared to love the daughter of the aristocrat; for that he was waylaid and thrashed . . . thrashed like a dog within an inch of his life! Oh, how I suffered! his humiliation had eaten into my very soul! When the opportunity occurred, and I was able to take my revenge, I took it. But I only thought to bring that proud marquis to trouble and humiliation. He plotted with Austria against his own country. Chance gave me knowledge of this; I spoke of it, but I did not know—how could I guess?—they trapped and duped me. When I realised what I had done, it was too late."

"It is perhaps a little difficult, Madame," said Sir Percy, after a moment of silence between them, "to go back over the past. I have confessed to you that my memory is short, but the thought certainly lingered in my mind that, at the time of the Marquis' death, I entreated you for an explanation of those same noisome popular rumours. If that same memory does not, even now, play me a trick, I fancy that you refused me *all* explanation then, and demanded of my love a humiliating allegiance it was not prepared to give."

"I wished to test your love for me, and it did not bear the test. You used to tell me that you drew the very breath of life but for me, and for love of me."

"And to probe that love, you demanded that I should forfeit mine honour," he said, whilst gradually his impassiveness seemed to leave him, his rigidity to relax; "that I should accept without murmur or question, as a dumb and submissive slave, every action of my mistress. My heart overflowing with love and passion, I *asked* for no explanation—I *waited* for one, not doubting—only hoping. Had you spoken but one word, from you I would have accepted any explanation and believed it. But you left me without a word, beyond a bald confession of the actual horrible facts; proudly you returned to your brother's house, and left me alone . . . for weeks . . . not knowing, now, in whom to believe, since the shrine, which contained my one illusion, lay shattered to earth at my feet."

She need not complain now that he was cold and impassive; his very voice shook with an intensity of passion, which he was making superhuman efforts to keep in check.

"Aye! the madness of my pride!" she said sadly. "Hardly had I gone, already I had repented. But when I returned, I found you, oh, so altered! wearing already that mask of somnolent indifference which you have never laid aside until . . . until now."

She was so close to him that her soft, loose hair was wafted against his cheek; her eyes, glowing with tears, maddened him, the music in her voice sent fire through his veins. But he would not yield to the magic charm of this woman whom he had so deeply loved, and at whose hands his pride had suffered so bitterly. He closed his eyes to shut out the dainty vision of that sweet face, of that snow-white neck and graceful figure, round which the faint rosy light of dawn was just beginning to hover playfully.

"Nay, Madame, it is no mask," he said icily; "I swore to you . . . once, that my life was yours. For months now it has been your plaything . . . it has served its purpose."

But now she knew that that very coldness was a mask. The trouble, the sorrow she had gone through last night, suddenly came back to her mind, but no longer with bitterness, rather with a feeling that this man who loved her, would help her to bear the burden.

"Sir Percy," she said impulsively, "Heaven knows you have been at pains to make the task, which I had set to myself, terribly difficult to accomplish. You spoke of my mood just now; well! we will call it that, if you will. I wished to speak to you . . . because . . . because I was in trouble . . . and had need . . . of your sympathy."

"It is yours to command, Madame."

"How cold you are!" she sighed. "Faith! I can scarce believe that but a few months ago one tear in my eye had set you well-nigh crazy. Now I come to you . . . with a half-broken heart . . . and . . . and . . ."

"I pray you, Madame," he said, whilst his voice shook almost as much as hers, "in what way can I serve you?"

"Percy!—Armand is in deadly danger. A letter of his . . . rash, impetuous, as were all his actions, and written to Sir Andrew Ffoulkes, has fallen into the hands of a fanatic. Armand is hopelessly compromised . . . to-morrow, perhaps he will be arrested . . . after that the guillotine . . . unless . . . unless . . . oh! it is horrible!" . . . she said, with a sudden wail of anguish, as all the events of the past night came rushing back to her mind, "horrible! . . . and you do not understand . . . you cannot . . . and I have no one to whom I can turn . . . for help . . . or even for sympathy. . . ."

Tears now refused to be held back. All her trouble, her struggles, the awful uncertainty of Armand's fate overwhelmed her. She tottered, ready to fall, and leaning against the stone balustrade, she buried her face in her hands and sobbed bitterly.

At first mention of Armand St. Just's name and of the peril in which he stood, Sir Percy's face had become a shade more pale; and the look of determination and obstinacy appeared more marked than ever between his eyes. However, he said nothing for the moment, but watched her, as her delicate frame was shaken with sobs, watched her until unconsciously his face softened, and what looked almost like tears seemed to glisten in his eyes.

"And so," he said with bitter sarcasm, "the murderous dog of the revolution is turning upon the very hands that fed it? . . . Begad, Madame," he added very gently, as Marguerite continued to sob hysterically, "will you dry your tears? . . . I never could bear to see a pretty woman cry, and I . . ."

Instinctively, with sudden, overmastering passion, at sight of her helplessness and of her grief, he stretched out his arms, and the next, would have seized her and held her to him, protected from every evil with his very life, his very heart's blood. . . . But pride had the better of it in this struggle once again; he restrained himself with a tremendous effort of will, and said coldly, though still very gently,—

"Will you not turn to me, Madame, and tell me in what way I may have the honour to serve you?"

She made a violent effort to control herself, and turning her tear-stained face to him, she once more held out her hand, which he kissed with the same punctilious gallantry; but Marguerite's fingers, this time, lingered in his hand for a second or two longer than was absolutely necessary, and this was because she had felt that his hand trembled perceptibly and was burning hot, whilst his lips felt as cold as marble.

"Can you do aught for Armand?" she said sweetly and simply. "You have so much influence at court . . . so many friends . . ."

"Nay, Madame, should you not rather seek the influence of your French friend, M. Chauvelin? His extends, if I mistake not, even as far as the Republican Government of France."

"I cannot ask him, Percy. . . . Oh! I wish I dared to tell you . . . but . . . but . . . he has put a price on my brother's head, which . . ."

She would have given worlds if she had felt the courage then to tell him everything . . . all she had done that night—how she had suffered and how her hand had been forced. But she dared not give way to that impulse . . . not now, when she was just beginning to feel that he still loved her, when she hoped that she could win him back. She dared not make another confession to him. After all, he might not understand; he might not sympathise with her struggles and temptation. His love still dormant might sleep the sleep of death.

Perhaps he divined what was passing in her mind. His whole attitude was one of intense longing—a veritable prayer for that confidence, which her foolish pride withheld from him. When she remained silent he sighed, and said with marked coldness—

"Faith, Madame, since it distresses you, we will not speak of it. . . . As for Armand, I pray you have no fear. I pledge you my word that he shall be safe. Now, have I your permission to go? The hour is getting late, and . . ."

"You will at least accept my gratitude?" she said, as she drew quite close to him, and speaking with real tenderness.

With a quick, almost involuntary effort he would have taken her then in his arms, for her eyes were swimming in tears, which he longed to kiss away; but she had lured him once, just like this, then cast him aside like an ill-fitting glove. He thought this was but a mood, a caprice, and he was too proud to lend himself to it once again.

"It is too soon, Madame!" he said quietly; "I have done nothing as yet. The hour is late, and you must be fatigued. Your women will be waiting for you upstairs."

He stood aside to allow her to pass. She sighed, a quick sigh of disappointment. His pride and her beauty had been in direct conflict, and his pride had remained the conqueror. Perhaps, after all, she had been deceived just now; what she took to be the light of love in his eyes might only have been the passion of pride or, who knows, of hatred instead of love. She stood looking at him for a moment or two longer. He was again as rigid, as impassive, as before. Pride had conquered, and he cared naught for her. The grey of dawn was gradually yielding to the rosy light of the rising sun. Birds began to twitter; Nature awakened, smiling in happy response to the warmth of this glorious

October morning. Only between these two hearts there lay a strong, impassable barrier, built up of pride on both sides, which neither of them cared to be the first to demolish.

He had bent his tall figure in a low ceremonious bow, as she finally, with another bitter little sigh, began to mount the terrace steps.

The long train of her gold-embroidered gown swept the dead leaves off the steps, making a faint harmonious sh—sh—sh as she glided up, with one hand resting on the balustrade, the rosy light of dawn making an aureole of gold round her hair, and causing the rubies on her head and arms to sparkle. She reached the tall glass doors which led into the house. Before entering, she paused once again to look at him, hoping against hope to see his arms stretched out to her, and to hear his voice calling her back. But he had not moved; his massive figure looked the very personification of unbending pride, of fierce obstinacy.

Hot tears again surged to her eyes, and as she would not let him see them, she turned quickly within, and ran as fast as she could up to her own rooms.

Had she but turned back then, and looked out once more on to the rose-lit garden, she would have seen that which would have made her own sufferings seem but light and easy to bear—a strong man, overwhelmed with his own passion and his own despair. Pride had given way at last, obstinacy was gone: the will was powerless. He was but a man madly, blindly, passionately in love, and as soon as her light footsteps had died away within the house, he knelt down upon the terrace steps, and in the very madness of his love he kissed one by one the places where her small foot had trodden, and the stone balustrade there, where her tiny hand had rested last.

XVII. FAREWELL

When Marguerite reached her room, she found her maid terribly anxious about her.

"Your ladyship will be so tired," said the poor woman, whose own eyes were half closed with sleep. "It is past five o'clock."

"Ah, yes, Louise, I daresay I shall be tired presently," said Marguerite, kindly; "but you are very tired now, so go to bed at once. I'll get into bed alone."

"But, my lady . . ."

"Now, don't argue, Louise, but go to bed. Give me a wrap, and leave me alone."

Louise was only too glad to obey. She took off her mistress's gorgeous ball-dress, and wrapped her up in a soft billowy gown.

"Does your ladyship wish for anything else?" she asked, when that was done.

"No, nothing more. Put out the lights as you go out."

"Yes, my lady. Good-night, my lady."

"Good-night, Louise."

When the maid was gone, Marguerite drew aside the curtains and threw open the windows. The garden and the river beyond were flooded with rosy light. Far away to the east, the rays of the rising sun had changed the rose into vivid gold. The lawn was deserted now, and Marguerite looked down upon the terrace where she had stood a few moments ago trying vainly to win back a man's love, which once had been so wholly hers.

It was strange that through all her troubles, all her anxiety for Armand, she was mostly conscious at the present moment of a keen and bitter heartache.

Her very limbs seemed to ache with longing for the love of a man who had spurned her, who had resisted her tenderness, remained cold to her appeals, and had not responded to the glow of passion, which had caused her to feel and hope that those happy olden days in Paris were not all dead and forgotten.

How strange it all was! She loved him still. And now that she looked back upon the last few months of misunderstandings and of loneliness, she realised that she had never ceased to love him; that deep down in her heart she had always vaguely felt that his foolish inanities, his empty laugh, his lazy nonchalance were nothing but a mask; that the real man, strong, passionate, wilful, was there still—the man she had loved, whose intensity had fascinated her, whose personality attracted her, since she always felt that behind his apparently slow wits there was a certain something, which he kept hidden from all the world, and most especially from her.

A woman's heart is such a complex problem—the owner thereof is often most incompetent to find the solution of this puzzle.

Did Marguerite Blakeney, "the cleverest woman in Europe," really love a fool? Was it love that she had felt for him a year ago when she married him? Was it love she felt for him now that she realised that he still loved her, but that he would not become her slave, her passionate, ardent lover once again? Nay! Marguerite herself could not have told that. Not at this moment at any rate; perhaps her pride had sealed her mind against a better understanding of her own heart. But this she did know—that she meant to capture that obstinate heart back again. That she would conquer once more . . . and then, that she would never lose him[EOL] . . . . She would keep him, keep his love, deserve it, and cherish it; for this much was certain, that there was no longer any happiness possible for her without that one man's love.

Thus the most contradictory thoughts and emotions rushed madly through her mind. Absorbed in them, she had allowed time to slip by; perhaps, tired out with long excitement, she had actually closed her eyes and sunk into a troubled sleep, wherein quickly fleeting dreams seemed but the continuation of her anxious thoughts—when suddenly she was roused, from dream or meditation, by the noise of footsteps outside her door.

Nervously she jumped up and listened; the house itself was as still as ever; the footsteps had retreated. Through her wide-open windows the brilliant rays of the morning sun were flooding her room with light. She looked up at the clock; it was half-past six—too early for any of the household to be already astir.

She certainly must have dropped asleep, quite unconsciously. The noise of the footsteps, also of hushed, subdued voices had awakened her—what could they be?

Gently, on tip-toe, she crossed the room and opened the door to listen; not a sound—that peculiar stillness of the early morning when sleep with all mankind is at its heaviest. But the noise had made her nervous, and when, suddenly, at her feet, on the very doorstep, she saw something white lying there—a letter evidently—she hardly dared touch it. It seemed so ghostlike. It certainly was not there when she came upstairs; had Louise dropped it? or was some tantalising spook at play, showing her fairy letters where none existed?

At last she stooped to pick it up, and, amazed, puzzled beyond measure, she saw that the letter was addressed to herself in her husband's large, businesslike-looking hand.

What could he have to say to her, in the middle of the night, which could not be put off until the morning?

She tore open the envelope and read:—

> "A most unforeseen circumstance forces me to leave for the North immediately, so I beg your ladyship's pardon if I do not avail myself of the honour of bidding you good-bye. My business may keep me employed for about a week, so I shall not have the privilege of being present at your ladyship's water-party on Wednesday. I remain your ladyship's most humble and most obedient servant,
> PERCY BLAKENEY."

Marguerite must suddenly have been imbued with her husband's slowness of intellect, for she had perforce to read the few simple lines over and over again, before she could fully grasp their meaning.

She stood on the landing, turning over and over in her hand this curt and mysterious epistle, her mind a blank, her nerves strained with agitation and a presentiment she could not very well have explained.

Sir Percy owned considerable property in the North, certainly, and he had often before gone there alone and stayed away a week at a time; but it seemed so very strange that circumstances should have arisen between five and six o'clock in the morning that compelled him to start in this extreme hurry.

Vainly she tried to shake off an unaccustomed feeling of nervousness: she was trembling from head to foot. A wild, unconquerable desire seized her to see her husband again, at once, if only he had not already started.

Forgetting the fact that she was only very lightly clad in a morning wrap, and that her hair lay loosely about her shoulders, she flew down the stairs, right through the hall towards the front door.

It was as usual barred and bolted, for the indoor servants were not yet up; but her keen ears had detected the sound of voices and the pawing of a horse's hoof against the flag-stones.

With nervous, trembling fingers Marguerite undid the bolts one by one, bruising her hands, hurting her nails, for the locks were heavy and stiff. But she did not care; her whole frame shook with anxiety at the very thought that she might be too late; that he might have gone without her seeing him and bidding him "God-speed!"

At last, she had turned the key and thrown open the door. Her ears had not deceived her. A groom was standing close by holding a couple of horses; one of these was Sultan, Sir Percy's favourite and swiftest horse, saddled ready for a journey.

The next moment Sir Percy himself appeared round the further corner of the house and came quickly towards the horses. He had changed his gorgeous ball costume, but was as usual irreproachably and richly apparelled in a suit of fine cloth, with lace jabot and ruffles, high top-boots, and riding breeches.

Marguerite went forward a few steps. He looked up and saw her. A slight frown appeared between his eyes.

"You are going?" she said quickly and feverishly. "Whither?"

"As I have had the honour of informing your ladyship, urgent, most unexpected business calls me to the North this morning," he said, in his usual cold, drawly manner.

"But . . . your guests to-morrow . . ."

"I have prayed your ladyship to offer my humble excuses to His Royal Highness. You are such a perfect hostess, I do not think that I shall be missed."

"But surely you might have waited for your journey . . . until after our water-party . . ." she said, still speaking quickly and nervously. "Surely the business is not so urgent . . . and you said nothing about it—just now."

"My business, as I had the honour to tell you, Madame, is as unexpected as it is urgent. . . . May I therefore crave your permission to go. . . . Can I do aught for you in town? . . . on my way back?"

"No . . . no . . . thanks . . . nothing. . . . But you will be back soon?"

"Very soon."

"Before the end of the week?"

"I cannot say."

He was evidently trying to get away, whilst she was straining every nerve to keep him back for a moment or two.

"Percy," she said, "will you not tell me why you go to-day? Surely I, as your wife, have the right to know. You have *not* been called away to the North. I know it. There were no letters, no couriers from there before we left for the opera last night, and nothing was waiting for you when we returned from the ball. . . . You are *not* going to the North, I feel convinced. . . . There is some mystery . . . and . . ."

"Nay, there is no mystery, Madame," he replied, with a slight tone of impatience. "My business has to do with Armand . . . there! Now, have I your leave to depart?"

"With Armand? . . . But you will run no danger?"

"Danger? I? . . . Nay, Madame, your solicitude does me honour. As you say, I have some influence; my intention is to exert it before it be too late."

"Will you allow me to thank you at least?"

"Nay, Madame," he said coldly, "there is no need for that. My life is at your service, and I am already more than repaid."

"And mine will be at yours, Sir Percy, if you will but accept it, in exchange for what you do for Armand," she said, as, impulsively, she stretched out both her hands to him. "There! I will not detain you . . . my thoughts go with you . . . Farewell! . . ."

How lovely she looked in this morning sunlight, with her ardent hair streaming around her shoulders. He bowed very low and kissed her hand; she felt the burning kiss and her heart thrilled with joy and hope.

"You will come back?" she said tenderly.

"Very soon!" he replied, looking longingly into her blue eyes.

"And . . . you will remember? . . ." she asked as her eyes, in response to his look, gave him an infinity of promise.

"I will always remember, Madame, that you have honoured me by commanding my services."

The words were cold and formal, but they did not chill her this time. Her woman's heart had read his, beneath the impassive mask his pride still forced him to wear.

He bowed to her again, then begged her leave to depart. She stood on one side whilst he jumped on to Sultan's back, then, as he galloped out of the gates, she waved him a final "Adieu."

A bend in the road soon hid him from view; his confidential groom had some difficulty in keeping pace with him, for Sultan flew along in response to his master's excited mood. Marguerite, with a sigh that was almost a happy one, turned and went within. She went back to her room, for suddenly, like a tired child, she felt quite sleepy.

Her heart seemed all at once to be in complete peace, and, though it still ached with undefined longing, a vague and delicious hope soothed it as with a balm.

She felt no longer anxious about Armand. The man who had just ridden away, bent on helping her brother, inspired her with complete confidence in his strength and in his power. She marveled at herself for having ever looked upon him as an inane fool; of course, *that* was a mask worn to hide the bitter wound she had dealt to his faith and to his love. His passion would have overmastered him, and he would not let her see how much he still cared and how deeply he suffered.

But now all would be well: she would crush her own pride, humble it before him, tell him everything, trust him in everything; and those happy days would come back, when they used to wander off together in the forests of Fontainebleau, when they spoke little—for he was always a silent man—but when she felt that against that strong heart she would always find rest and happiness.

The more she thought of the events of the past night, the less fear had she of Chauvelin and his schemes. He had failed to discover the identity of the Scarlet Pimpernel, of that she felt sure. Both Lord Fancourt and Chauvelin himself had assured her that no one had been in the dining-room at one o'clock except the Frenchman himself and Percy—Yes!—Percy! she might have asked him, had she thought of it! Anyway, she had no fears that the unknown and brave hero would fall in Chauvelin's trap; his death at any rate would not be at her door.

Armand certainly was still in danger, but Percy had pledged his word that Armand would be safe, and somehow, as Marguerite had seen him riding away, the possibility that he could fail in whatever he undertook never even remotely crossed her mind. When Armand was safely over in England she would not allow him to go back to France.

She felt almost happy now, and, drawing the curtains closely together again to shut out the piercing sun, she went to bed at last, laid her head upon the pillow, and, like a wearied child, soon fell into a peaceful and dreamless sleep.

XVIII. THE MYSTERIOUS DEVICE

The day was well advanced when Marguerite woke, refreshed by her long sleep. Louise had brought her some fresh milk and a dish of fruit, and she partook of this frugal breakfast with hearty appetite.

Thoughts crowded thick and fast in her mind as she munched her grapes; most of them went galloping away after the tall, erect figure of her husband, whom she had watched riding out of sight more than five hours ago.

In answer to her eager inquiries, Louise brought back the news that the groom had come home with Sultan, having left Sir Percy in London. The groom thought that his master was about to get on board his schooner, which was lying off just below London Bridge. Sir Percy had ridden thus far, had then met Briggs, the skipper of the *Day Dream*, and had sent the groom back to Richmond with Sultan and the empty saddle.

This news puzzled Marguerite more than ever. Where could Sir Percy be going just now in the *Day Dream*? On Armand's behalf, he had said. Well! Sir Percy had influential friends everywhere. Perhaps he was going to Greenwich, or . . . but Marguerite ceased to conjecture; all would be explained anon: he said that he would come back, and that he would remember.

A long, idle day lay before Marguerite. She was expecting the visit of her old schoolfellow, little Suzanne de Tournay. With all the merry mischief at her command, she had tendered her request for Suzanne's company to the Comtesse in the presence of the Prince of Wales last night. His Royal Highness had loudly applauded the notion, and declared that he would give himself the pleasure of calling on the two ladies in the course of the afternoon. The Comtesse had not dared to refuse, and then and there was entrapped into a promise to send little Suzanne to spend a long and happy day at Richmond with her friend.

Marguerite expected her eagerly; she longed for a chat about old schooldays with the child; she felt that she would prefer Suzanne's company to that of anyone else, and together they would roam through the fine old garden and rich deer park, or stroll along the river.

But Suzanne had not come yet, and Marguerite being dressed, prepared to go downstairs. She looked quite a girl this morning in her simple muslin frock, with a broad blue sash round her slim waist, and the dainty cross-over fichu into which, at her bosom, she had fastened a few late crimson roses.

She crossed the landing outside her own suite of apartments, and stood still for a moment at the head of the fine oak staircase, which led to the lower floor. On her left were her husband's apartments, a suite of rooms which she practically never entered.

They consisted of bedroom, dressing and reception-room, and, at the extreme end of the landing, of a small study, which, when Sir Percy did not use it, was always kept locked. His own special and confidential valet, Frank, had charge of this room. No one was ever allowed to go inside. My lady had never cared to do so, and the other servants had, of course, not dared to break this hard-and-fast rule.

Marguerite had often, with that good-natured contempt which she had recently adopted towards her husband, chaffed him about this secrecy which surrounded his private study. Laughingly she had always declared that he strictly excluded all prying eyes from his sanctum for fear they should detect how very little "study" went on within its four walls: a comfortable arm-chair for Sir Percy's sweet slumbers was, no doubt, its most conspicuous piece of furniture.

Marguerite thought of all this on this bright October morning as she glanced along the corridor. Frank was evidently busy with his master's rooms, for most of the doors stood open, that of the study amongst the others.

A sudden, burning, childish curiosity seized her to have a peep at Sir Percy's sanctum. The restriction, of course, did not apply to her, and Frank would, of course, not dare to oppose her. Still, she hoped that the valet would be busy in one of the other rooms, that she might have that one quick peep in secret, and unmolested.

Gently, on tip-toe, she crossed the landing and, like Blue Beard's wife, trembling half with excitement and wonder, she paused a moment on the threshold, strangely perturbed and irresolute.

The door was ajar, and she could not see anything within. She pushed it open tentatively: there was no sound: Frank was evidently not there, and she walked boldly in.

At once she was struck by the severe simplicity of everything around her: the dark and heavy hangings, the massive oak furniture, the one or two maps on the wall, in no way recalled to her mind the lazy man about town, the lover of race-courses, the dandified leader of fashion, that was the outward representation of Sir Percy Blakeney.

There was no sign here, at any rate, of hurried departure. Everything was in its place, not a scrap of paper littered the floor, not a cupboard or drawer was left open. The curtains were drawn aside, and through the open window the fresh morning air was streaming in.

Facing the window, and well into the centre of the room, stood a ponderous business-like desk, which looked as if it had seen much service. On the wall to the left of the desk, reaching almost from floor to ceiling, was a large full-length portrait of a woman, magnificently framed, exquisitely painted, and signed with the name of Boucher. It was Percy's mother.

Marguerite knew very little about her, except that she had died abroad, ailing in body as well as in mind, when Percy was still a lad. She must have been a very beautiful woman once, when Boucher painted her, and as Marguerite looked at the portrait, she could not but be struck by the extraordinary resemblance which must have existed between mother and son. There was the same low, square forehead, crowned with thick, fair hair, smooth and heavy; the same deep-set, somewhat lazy blue eyes beneath firmly marked, straight brows; and in those eyes there was the same intensity behind that apparent laziness, the same latent passion which used to light up Percy's face in the olden days before his marriage, and which Marguerite had again noted, last night at dawn, when she had come quite close to him, and had allowed a note of tenderness to creep into her voice.

Marguerite studied the portrait, for it interested her: after that she turned and looked again at the ponderous desk. It was covered with a mass of papers, all neatly tied and docketed, which looked like accounts and receipts arrayed with perfect method. It had never before struck Marguerite—nor had she, alas! found it worth while to inquire—as to how Sir Percy, whom all the world had credited with a total lack of brains, administered the vast fortune which his father had left him.

Since she had entered this neat, orderly room, she had been taken so much by surprise, that this obvious proof of her husband's strong business capacities did not cause her more than a passing thought of wonder. But it also strengthened her in the now certain knowledge that, with his worldly inanities, his foppish ways, and foolish talk, he was not only wearing a mask, but was playing a deliberate and studied part.

Marguerite wondered again. Why should he take all this trouble? Why should he—who was obviously a serious, earnest man—wish to appear before his fellow-men as an empty-headed nincompoop?

He may have wished to hide his love for a wife who held him in contempt . . . but surely such an object could have been gained at less sacrifice, and with far less trouble than constant incessant acting of an unnatural part.

She looked round her quite aimlessly now: she was horribly puzzled, and a nameless dread, before all this strange, unaccountable mystery, had begun to seize upon her. She felt cold and uncomfortable suddenly in this severe and dark room. There were no pictures on the wall, save the fine Boucher portrait, only a couple of maps, both of parts of France, one of the North coast and the other of the environs of Paris. What did Sir Percy want with those, she wondered.

Her head began to ache, she turned away from this strange Blue Beard's chamber, which she had entered, and which she did not understand. She did not wish Frank to find her here, and with a last look round, she once more turned to the door. As she did so, her foot knocked against a small object, which had apparently been lying close to the desk, on the carpet, and which now went rolling, right across the room.

She stooped to pick it up. It was a solid gold ring, with a flat shield, on which was engraved a small device.

Marguerite turned it over in her fingers, and then studied the engraving on the shield. It represented a small star-shaped flower, of a shape she had seen so distinctly twice before: once at the opera, and once at Lord Grenville's ball.

XIX. THE SCARLET PIMPERNEL

At what particular moment the strange doubt first crept into Marguerite's mind, she could not herself afterwards have said. With the ring tightly clutched in her hand, she had run out of the room, down the stairs, and out into the garden, where, in complete seclusion, alone with the flowers, and the river and the birds, she could look again at the ring, and study that device more closely.

Stupidly, senselessly, now, sitting beneath the shade of an overhanging sycamore, she was looking at the plain gold shield, with the star-shaped little flower engraved upon it.

Bah! It was ridiculous! she was dreaming! her nerves were overwrought, and she saw signs and mysteries in the most trivial coincidences. Had not everybody about town recently made a point of affecting the device of that mysterious and heroic Scarlet Pimpernel?

Did she not herself wear it embroidered on her gowns? set in gems and enamel in her hair? What was there strange in the fact that Sir Percy should have chosen to use the device as a seal-ring? He might easily have done that . . . yes . . . quite easily . . . and . . . besides . . . what connection could there be between her exquisite dandy of a husband, with his fine clothes and refined, lazy ways, and the daring plotter who rescued French victims from beneath the very eyes of the leaders of a bloodthirsty revolution?

Her thoughts were in a whirl—her mind a blank . . . She did not see anything that was going on around her, and was quite startled when a fresh young voice called to her across the garden.

"*Chérie!—chérie!* where are you?" and little Suzanne, fresh as a rosebud, with eyes dancing with glee, and brown curls fluttering in the soft morning breeze, came running across the lawn.

"They told me you were in the garden," she went on prattling merrily, and throwing herself with pretty, girlish impulse into Marguerite's arms, "so I ran out to give you a surprise. You did not expect me quite so soon, did you, my darling little Margot *chérie?*"

Marguerite, who had hastily concealed the ring in the folds of her kerchief, tried to respond gaily and unconcernedly to the young girl's impulsiveness.

"Indeed, sweet one," she said with a smile, "it is delightful to have you all to myself, and for a nice whole long day. . . . You won't be bored?"

"Oh! bored! Margot, how *can* you say such a wicked thing. Why! when we were in the dear old convent together, we were always happy when we were allowed to be alone together."

"And to talk secrets."

The two young girls had linked their arms in one another's and began wandering round the garden.

"Oh! how lovely your home is, Margot, darling," said little Suzanne, enthusiastically, "and how happy you must be!"

"Aye, indeed! I ought to be happy—oughtn't I, sweet one?" said Marguerite, with a wistful little sigh.

"How sadly you say it, *chérie*. . . . Ah, well, I suppose now that you are a married woman you won't care to talk secrets with me any longer. Oh! what lots and lots of secrets we used to have at school! Do you remember?—some we did not even confide to Sister Theresa of the Holy Angels—though she was such a dear."

"And now you have one all-important secret, eh, little one?" said Marguerite, merrily, "which you are forthwith going to confide to me. Nay, you need not blush, *chérie*," she added, as she saw Suzanne's pretty little face crimson with blushes. "Faith, there's naught to be ashamed of! He is a noble and true man, and one to be proud of as a lover, and . . . as a husband."

"Indeed, *chérie*, I am not ashamed," rejoined Suzanne, softly; "and it makes me very, very proud to hear you speak so well of him. I think maman will consent," she added thoughtfully, "and I shall be—oh! so happy—but, of course, nothing is to be thought of until papa is safe. . . ."

Marguerite started. Suzanne's father! the Comte de Tournay!—one of those whose life would be jeopardised if Chauvelin succeeded in establishing the identity of the Scarlet Pimpernel.

She had understood all along from the Comtesse, and also from one or two of the members of the league, that their mysterious leader had pledged his honour to bring the fugitive Comte de Tournay safely out of France. Whilst little Suzanne—unconscious of all—save her own all-important little secret, went prattling on, Marguerite's thoughts went back to the events of the past night.

Armand's peril, Chauvelin's threat, his cruel "Either—or—" which she had accepted.

And then her own work in the matter, which should have culminated at one o'clock in Lord Grenville's dining-room, when the relentless agent of the French Government would finally learn who was this mysterious Scarlet Pimpernel, who so openly defied an army of spies and placed himself so boldly, and for mere sport, on the side of the enemies of France.

Since then she had heard nothing from Chauvelin. She had concluded that he had failed, and yet, she had not felt anxious about Armand, because her husband had promised her that Armand would be safe.

But now, suddenly, as Suzanne prattled merrily along, an awful horror came upon her for what she had done. Chauvelin had told her nothing, it was true; but she remembered how sarcastic and evil he looked when she took final leave of him after the ball. Had he discovered something then? Had he already laid his plans for catching the daring plotter, red-handed, in France, and sending him to the guillotine without compunction or delay?

Marguerite turned sick with horror, and her hand convulsively clutched the ring in her dress.

"You are not listening, *chérie*," said Suzanne, reproachfully, as she paused in her long, highly interesting narrative.

"Yes, yes, darling—indeed I am," said Marguerite with an effort, forcing herself to smile. "I love to hear you talking . . . and your happiness makes me so very glad. . . . Have no fear, we will manage to propitiate maman. Sir Andrew Ffoulkes is a noble English gentleman; he has money and position, the Comtesse will not refuse her consent. . . . But . . . now, little one . . . tell me . . . what is the latest news about your father?"

"Oh!" said Suzanne, with mad glee, "the best we could possibly hear. My Lord Hastings came to see maman early this morning. He said that all is now well with dear papa, and we may safely expect him here in England in less than four days."

"Yes," said Marguerite, whose glowing eyes were fastened on Suzanne's lips, as she continued merrily:

"Oh, we have no fear now! You don't know, *chérie*, that that great and noble Scarlet Pimpernel himself has gone to save papa. He has gone, *chérie* . . . actually gone . . ." added Suzanne excitedly. "He was in London this morning; he will be in Calais, perhaps, to-morrow . . . where he will meet papa . . . and then . . . and then . . ."

The blow had fallen. She had expected it all along, though she had tried for the last half-hour to delude herself and to cheat her fears. He had gone to Calais, had been in London this morning . . . he . . . the Scarlet Pimpernel . . . Percy Blakeney . . . her husband . . . whom she had betrayed last night to Chauvelin. . . .

Percy . . . Percy . . . her husband . . . the Scarlet Pimpernel. . . . Oh! how could she have been so blind? She understood it now—all at once . . . that part he played—the mask he wore . . . in order to throw dust in everybody's eyes.

And all for sheer sport and devilry of course!—saving men, women and children from death, as other men destroy and kill animals for the excitement, the love of the thing. The idle, rich man wanted some aim in life—he, and the few young bucks he enrolled under his banner, had amused themselves for months in risking their lives for the sake of an innocent few.

Perhaps he had meant to tell her when they were first married; and then the story of the Marquis de St. Cyr had come to his ears, and he had suddenly turned from her, thinking, no doubt, that she might some day betray him and his comrades, who had sworn to follow him; and so he had tricked her, as he tricked all others, whilst hundreds now owed their lives to him, and many families owed him both life and happiness.

The mask of the inane fop had been a good one, and the part consummately well played. No wonder that Chauvelin's spies had failed to detect, in the apparently brainless nincompoop, the man whose reckless daring and resourceful ingenuity had baffled the keenest French spies, both in France and in England. Even last night when Chauvelin went to Lord Grenville's dining-room to seek that daring Scarlet Pimpernel, he only saw that inane Sir Percy Blakeney fast asleep in a corner of the sofa.

Had his astute mind guessed the secret, then? Here lay the whole awful, horrible, amazing puzzle. In betraying a nameless stranger to his fate in order to save her brother, had Marguerite Blakeney sent her husband to his death?

No! no! no! a thousand times no! Surely Fate could not deal a blow like that: Nature itself would rise in revolt: her hand, when it held that tiny scrap of paper last night, would surely have been struck numb ere it committed a deed so appalling and so terrible.

"But what is it, *chérie*?" said little Suzanne, now genuinely alarmed, for Marguerite's colour had become dull and ashen. "Are you ill, Marguerite? What is it?"

"Nothing, nothing, child," she murmured, as in a dream. "Wait a moment . . . let me think . . . think! . . . You said . . . the Scarlet Pimpernel had gone to-day. . . . ?"

"Marguerite, *chérie*, what is it? You frighten me. . . ."

"It is nothing, child, I tell you . . . nothing. . . . I must be alone a minute—and—dear one . . . I may have to curtail our time together to-day. . . . I may have to go away—you'll understand?"

"I understand that something has happened, *chérie*, and that you want to be alone. I won't be a hindrance to you. Don't think of me. My maid, Lucile, has not yet gone . . . we will go back together . . . don't think of me."

She threw her arms impulsively round Marguerite. Child as she was, she felt the poignancy of her friend's grief, and with the infinite tact of her girlish tenderness, she did not try to pry into it, but was ready to efface herself.

She kissed Marguerite again and again, then walked sadly back across the lawn. Marguerite did not move, she remained there, thinking . . . wondering what was to be done.

Just as little Suzanne was about to mount the terrace steps, a groom came running round the house towards his mistress. He carried a sealed letter in his hand. Suzanne instinctively turned back; her heart told her that here perhaps was further ill news for her friend, and she felt that her poor Margot was not in a fit state to bear any more.

The groom stood respectfully beside his mistress, then he handed her the sealed letter.

"What is that?" asked Marguerite.

"Just come by runner, my lady."

Marguerite took the letter mechanically, and turned it over in her trembling fingers.

"Who sent it?" she said.

"The runner said, my lady," replied the groom, "that his orders were to deliver this, and that your ladyship would understand from whom it came."

Marguerite tore open the envelope. Already her instinct had told her what it contained, and her eyes only glanced at it mechanically.

It was a letter written by Armand St. Just to Sir Andrew Ffoulkes—the letter which Chauvelin's spies had stolen at "The Fisherman's Rest," and which Chauvelin had held as a rod over her to enforce her obedience.

Now he had kept his word—he had sent her back St. Just's compromising letter . . . for he was on the track of the Scarlet Pimpernel.

Marguerite's senses reeled, her very soul seemed to be leaving her body; she tottered, and would have fallen but for Suzanne's arm round her waist. With superhuman effort she regained control over herself—there was yet much to be done.

"Bring that runner here to me," she said to the servant, with much calm. "He has not gone?"

"No, my lady."

The groom went, and Marguerite turned to Suzanne.

"And you, child, run within. Tell Lucile to get ready. I fear I must send you home, child. And—stay, tell one of the maids to prepare a travelling dress and cloak for me."

Suzanne made no reply. She kissed Marguerite tenderly, and obeyed without a word; the child was overawed by the terrible, nameless misery in her friend's face.

A minute later the groom returned, followed by the runner who had brought the letter.

"Who gave you this packet?" asked Marguerite.

"A gentleman, my lady," replied the man, "at 'The Rose and Thistle' inn opposite Charing Cross. He said you would understand."

"At 'The Rose and Thistle'? What was he doing?"

"He was waiting for the coach, your ladyship, which he had ordered."

"The coach?"

"Yes, my lady. A special coach he had ordered. I understood from his man that he was posting straight to Dover."

"That's enough. You may go." Then she turned to the groom: "My coach and the four swiftest horses in the stables, to be ready at once."

The groom and runner both went quickly off to obey. Marguerite remained standing for a moment on the lawn quite alone. Her graceful figure was as rigid as a statue, her eyes were fixed, her hands were tightly clasped across her breast; her lips moved as they murmured with pathetic heart-breaking persistence,—

"What's to be done? What's to be done? Where to find him?—Oh, God! grant me light."

But this was not the moment for remorse and despair. She had done—unwittingly—an awful and terrible thing—the very worst crime, in her eyes, that woman ever committed—she saw it in all its horror. Her very blindness in not having guessed her husband's secret seemed now to her another deadly sin. She ought to have known! she ought to have known!

How could she imagine that a man who could love with so much intensity as Percy Blakeney had loved her from the first—how could such a man be the brainless idiot he chose to appear? She, at least, ought to have known that he was wearing a mask, and having found that out, she should have torn it from his face, whenever they were alone together.

Her love for him had been paltry and weak, easily crushed by her own pride; and she, too, had worn a mask in assuming a contempt for him, whilst, as a matter of fact, she completely misunderstood him.

But there was no time now to go over the past. By her own blindness she had sinned; now she must repay, not by empty remorse, but by prompt and useful action.

Percy had started for Calais, utterly unconscious of the fact that his most relentless enemy was on his heels. He had set sail early that morning from London Bridge. Provided he had a favourable wind, he would no doubt be in France within twenty-four hours; no doubt he had reckoned on the wind and chosen this route.

Chauvelin, on the other hand, would post to Dover, charter a vessel there, and undoubtedly reach Calais much about the same time. Once in Calais, Percy would meet all those who were eagerly waiting for the noble and brave Scarlet Pimpernel, who had come to rescue them from horrible and unmerited death. With Chauvelin's eyes now fixed upon his every movement, Percy would thus not only be endangering his own life, but that of Suzanne's father, the old Comte de Tournay, and of those other fugitives who were waiting for him and trusting in him. There was also Armand, who had gone to meet de Tournay, secure in the knowledge that the Scarlet Pimpernel was watching over his safety.

All these lives, and that of her husband, lay in Marguerite's hands; these she must save, if human pluck and ingenuity were equal to the task.

Unfortunately, she could not do all this quite alone. Once in Calais she would not know where to find her husband, whilst Chauvelin, in stealing the papers at Dover, had obtained the whole itinerary. Above everything, she wished to warn Percy.

She knew enough about him by now to understand that he would never abandon those who trusted in him, that he would not turn back from danger, and leave the Comte de Tournay to fall into the bloodthirsty hands that knew of no mercy. But if he were warned, he might form new plans, be more wary, more prudent. Unconsciously, he might fall into a cunning trap, but—once warned—he might yet succeed.

And if he failed—if indeed Fate, and Chauvelin, with all the resources at his command, proved too strong for the daring plotter after all—then at least she would be there by his side, to comfort, love and cherish, to cheat death perhaps at the last by making it seem sweet, if they died both together, locked in each other's arms, with the supreme happiness of knowing that passion had responded to passion, and that all misunderstandings were at an end.

Her whole body stiffened as with a great and firm resolution. This she meant to do, if God gave her wits and strength. Her eyes lost their fixed look; they glowed with inward fire at the thought of meeting him again so soon, in the very midst of most deadly perils; they sparkled with the joy of sharing these dangers with him—of helping him perhaps—of being with him at the last—if she failed.

The childlike sweet face had become hard and set, the curved mouth was closed tightly over her clenched teeth. She meant to do or die, with him and for his sake. A frown, which spoke of an iron will and unbending resolution, appeared between the two straight brows; already her plans were formed. She would go and find Sir Andrew Ffoulkes first; he was Percy's best friend, and Marguerite remembered with a thrill, with what blind enthusiasm the young man always spoke of his mysterious leader.

He would help her where she needed help; her coach was ready. A change of raiment, and a farewell to little Suzanne, and she could be on her way.

Without haste, but without hesitation, she walked quietly into the house.

XX. THE FRIEND

Less than half an hour later, Marguerite, buried in thoughts, sat inside her coach, which was bearing her swiftly to London.

She had taken an affectionate farewell of little Suzanne, and seen the child safely started with her maid, and in her own coach, back to town. She had sent one courier with a respectful letter of excuse to His Royal Highness, begging for a postponement of the august visit on account of pressing and urgent business, and another on ahead to bespeak a fresh relay of horses at Faversham.

Then she had changed her muslin frock for a dark travelling costume and mantle, had provided herself with money—which her husband's lavishness always placed fully at her disposal—and had started on her way.

She did not attempt to delude herself with any vain and futile hopes; the safety of her brother Armand was to have been conditional on the imminent capture of the Scarlet Pimpernel. As Chauvelin had sent her back Armand's compromising letter, there was no doubt that he was quite satisfied in his own mind that Percy Blakeney was the man whose death he had sworn to bring about.

No! there was no room for any fond delusions! Percy, the husband whom she loved with all the ardour which her admiration for his bravery had kindled, was in immediate, deadly peril, through her hand. She had betrayed him to his enemy—unwittingly 'tis true—but she *had* betrayed him, and if Chauvelin succeeded in trapping him, who so far was unaware of his danger, then his death would be at her door. His death! when with her very heart's blood, she would have defended him and given willingly her life for his.

She had ordered her coach to drive her to the "Crown" inn; once there, she told her coachman to give the horses food and rest. Then she ordered a chair, and had herself carried to the house in Pall Mall where Sir Andrew Ffoulkes lived.

Among all Percy's friends who were enrolled under his daring banner, she felt that she would prefer to confide in Sir Andrew Ffoulkes. He had always been her friend, and now his love for little Suzanne had brought him closer to her still. Had he been away from home, gone on the mad errand with Percy, perhaps, then she would have called on Lord Hastings or Lord Tony—for she wanted the help of one of these young men, or she would be indeed powerless to save her husband.

Sir Andrew Ffoulkes, however, was at home, and his servant introduced her ladyship immediately. She went upstairs to the young man's comfortable bachelor's chambers, and was shown into a small, though luxuriously furnished, dining-room. A moment or two later Sir Andrew himself appeared.

He had evidently been much startled when he heard who his lady visitor was, for he looked anxiously—even suspiciously—at Marguerite, whilst performing the elaborate bows before her, which the rigid etiquette of the time demanded.

Marguerite had laid aside every vestige of nervousness; she was perfectly calm, and having returned the young man's elaborate salute, she began very calmly,—

"Sir Andrew, I have no desire to waste valuable time in much talk. You must take certain things I am going to tell you for granted. These will be of no importance. What is important is that your leader and comrade, the Scarlet Pimpernel . . . my husband . . . Percy Blakeney . . . is in deadly peril."

Had she had the remotest doubt of the correctness of her deductions, she would have had them confirmed now, for Sir Andrew, completely taken by surprise, had grown very pale, and was quite incapable of making the slightest attempt at clever parrying.

"No matter how I know this, Sir Andrew," she continued quietly, "thank God that I do, and that perhaps it is not too late to save him. Unfortunately, I cannot do this quite alone, and therefore have come to you for help."

"Lady Blakeney," said the young man, trying to recover himself, "I . . ."

"Will you hear me first?" she interrupted. "This is how the matter stands. When the agent of the French Government stole your papers that night in Dover, he found amongst them certain plans, which you or your leader meant to carry out for the rescue of the Comte de Tournay and others. The Scarlet Pimpernel—Percy, my husband—has gone on this errand himself to-day. Chauvelin knows that the Scarlet Pimpernel and Percy Blakeney are one and the same person. He will follow him to Calais, and there will lay hands on him. You know as well as I do the fate that awaits him at the hands of the Revolutionary Government of France. No interference from England—from King George himself—would save him. Robespierre and his gang would see to it that the interference came too late. But not only that, the much-trusted leader will also have been unconsciously the means of revealing the hiding-place of the Comte de Tournay and of all those who, even now, are placing their hopes in him."

She had spoken quietly, dispassionately, and with firm, unbending resolution. Her purpose was to make that young man trust and help her, for she could do nothing without him.

"I do not understand," he repeated, trying to gain time, to think what was best to be done.

"Aye! but I think you do, Sir Andrew. You must know that I am speaking the truth. Look these facts straight in the face. Percy has sailed for Calais, I presume for some lonely part of the coast, and Chauvelin is on his track. *He* has posted for Dover, and will cross the Channel probably to-night. What do you think will happen?"

The young man was silent.

"Percy will arrive at his destination: unconscious of being followed he will seek out de Tournay and the others—among these is Armand St. Just, my brother—he will seek them out, one after another, probably, not knowing that the sharpest eyes in the world are watching his every movement. When he has thus unconsciously betrayed those who blindly trust in him, when nothing can be gained from him, and he is ready to come back to England, with those whom he has gone so bravely to save, the doors of the trap will close upon him, and he will be sent to end his noble life upon the guillotine."

Still Sir Andrew was silent.

"You do not trust me," she said passionately. "Oh, God! cannot you see that I am in deadly earnest? Man, man," she added, while, with her tiny hands she seized the young man suddenly by the shoulders, forcing him to look straight at her, "tell me, do I look like that vilest thing on earth—a woman who would betray her own husband?"

"God forbid, Lady Blakeney," said the young man at last, "that I should attribute such evil motives to you, but . . ."

"But what? . . . tell me. . . . Quick, man! . . . the very seconds are precious!"

"Will you tell me," he asked resolutely, and looking searchingly into her blue eyes, "whose hand helped to guide M. Chauvelin to the knowledge which you say he possesses?"

"Mine," she said quietly, "I own it—I will not lie to you, for I wish you to trust me absolutely. But I had no idea—how *could* I have?—of the identity of the Scarlet Pimpernel . . . and my brother's safety was to be my prize if I succeeded."

"In helping Chauvelin to track the Scarlet Pimpernel?"

She nodded.

"It is no use telling you how he forced my hand. Armand is more than a brother to me, and . . . and . . . how *could* I guess? . . . But we waste time, Sir Andrew . . . every second is precious . . . in the name of God! . . . my husband is in peril . . . your friend!—your comrade!—Help me to save him."

Sir Andrew felt his position to be a very awkward one. The oath he had taken before his leader and comrade was one of obedience and secrecy; and yet the beautiful woman, who was asking him to trust her, was undoubtedly in earnest; his friend and leader was equally undoubtedly in imminent danger and . . .

"Lady Blakeney," he said at last, "God knows you have perplexed me, so that I do not know which way my duty lies. Tell me what you wish me to do. There are nineteen of us ready to lay down our lives for the Scarlet Pimpernel if he is in danger."

"There is no need for lives just now, my friend," she said drily; "my wits and four swift horses will serve the necessary purpose. But I must know where to find him. See," she added, while her eyes filled with tears, "I have humbled myself before you, I have owned my fault to you; shall I also confess my weakness?—My husband and I have been estranged, because he did not trust me, and because I was too blind to understand. You must confess that the bandage which he put over my eyes was a very thick one. Is it small wonder that I did not see through it? But last night, after I led him unwittingly into such deadly peril, it suddenly fell from my eyes. If you will not help me, Sir Andrew, I would still strive to save my husband. I would still exert every faculty I possess for his sake; but I might be powerless, for I might arrive too late, and nothing would be left for you but lifelong remorse, and . . . and . . . for me, a broken heart."

"But, Lady Blakeney," said the young man, touched by the gentle earnestness of this exquisitely beautiful woman, "do you know that what you propose doing is man's work?—you cannot possibly journey to Calais alone. You would be running the greatest possible risks to yourself, and your chances of finding your husband now—were I to direct you ever so carefully—are infinitely remote."

"Oh, I hope there are risks!" she murmured softly. "I hope there are dangers, too!—I have so much to atone for. But I fear you are mistaken. Chauvelin's eyes are fixed upon you all, he will scarce notice me. Quick, Sir Andrew!—the coach is ready, and there is not a moment to be lost. . . . I *must* get to him! I *must*!" she repeated with almost savage energy, "to warn him that that man is on his track. . . . Can't you see—can't you see, that I *must* get to him . . . even . . . even if it be too late to save him . . . at least . . . to be by his side . . . at the last."

"Faith, Madame, you must command me. Gladly would I or any of my comrades lay down our lives for your husband. If you *will* go yourself . . ."

"Nay, friend, do you not see that I would go mad if I let you go without me?" She stretched out her hand to him. "You *will* trust me?"

"I await your orders," he said simply.

"Listen, then. My coach is ready to take me to Dover. Do you follow me, as swiftly as horses will take you. We meet at nightfall at 'The Fisherman's Rest.' Chauvelin would avoid it, as he is known there, and I think it would be the safest. I will gladly accept your escort to Calais . . . as you say, I might miss Sir Percy were you to direct me ever so carefully. We'll charter a schooner at Dover and cross over during the night. Disguised, if you will agree to it, as my lacquey, you will, I think, escape detection."

"I am entirely at your service, Madame," rejoined the young man earnestly. "I trust to God that you will sight the *Day Dream* before we reach Calais. With Chauvelin at his heels, every step the Scarlet Pimpernel takes on French soil is fraught with danger."

"God grant it, Sir Andrew. But now, farewell. We meet to-night at Dover! It will be a race between Chauvelin and me across the Channel to-night—and the prize—the life of the Scarlet Pimpernel."

He kissed her hand, and then escorted her to her chair. A quarter of an hour later she was back at the "Crown" inn, where her coach and horses were ready and waiting for her. The next moment they thundered along the London streets, and then straight on to the Dover road at maddening speed.

She had no time for despair now. She was up and doing and had no leisure to think. With Sir Andrew Ffoulkes as her companion and ally, hope had once again revived in her heart.

God would be merciful. He would not allow so appalling a crime to be committed, as the death of a brave man, through the hand of a woman who loved him, and worshipped him, and who would gladly have died for his sake.

Marguerite's thoughts flew back to him, the mysterious hero, whom she had always unconsciously loved, when his identity was still unknown to her. Laughingly, in the olden days, she used to call him the shadowy king of her heart, and now she had suddenly found that this enigmatic personality whom she had worshipped, and the man who loved her so passionately, were one and the same: what wonder that one or two happier Visions began to force their way before her mind? She vaguely wondered what she would say to him when first they would stand face to face.

She had had so many anxieties, so much excitement during the past few hours, that she allowed herself the luxury of nursing these few more hopeful, brighter thoughts. Gradually the rumble of the coach wheels, with its incessant monotony, acted soothingly on her nerves: her eyes, aching with fatigue and many shed and unshed tears, closed involuntarily, and she fell into a troubled sleep.

XXI. SUSPENSE

It was late into the night when she at last reached "The Fisherman's Rest." She had done the whole journey in less than eight hours, thanks to innumerable changes of horses at the various coaching stations, for which she always paid lavishly, thus obtaining the very best and swiftest that could be had.

Her coachman, too, had been indefatigable; the promise of special and rich reward had no doubt helped to keep him up, and he had literally burned the ground beneath his mistress' coach wheels.

The arrival of Lady Blakeney in the middle of the night caused a considerable flutter at "The Fisherman's Rest." Sally jumped hastily out of bed, and Mr. Jellyband was at great pains how to make his important guest comfortable.

Both these good folk were far too well drilled in the manners appertaining to innkeepers, to exhibit the slightest surprise at Lady Blakeney's arrival, alone, at this extraordinary hour. No doubt they thought all the more, but Marguerite was far too absorbed in the importance—the deadly earnestness—of her journey, to stop and ponder over trifles of that sort.

The coffee-room—the scene lately of the dastardly outrage on two English gentlemen—was quite deserted. Mr. Jellyband hastily relit the lamp, rekindled a cheerful bit of fire in the great hearth, and then wheeled a comfortable chair by it, into which Marguerite gratefully sank.

"Will your ladyship stay the night?" asked pretty Miss Sally, who was already busy laying a snow-white cloth on the table, preparatory to providing a simple supper for her ladyship.

"No! not the whole night," replied Marguerite. "At any rate, I shall not want any room but this, if I can have it to myself for an hour or two."

"It is at your ladyship's service," said honest Jellyband, whose rubicund face was set in its tightest folds, lest it should betray before "the quality" that boundless astonishment which the worthy fellow had begun to feel.

"I shall be crossing over at the first turn of the tide," said Marguerite, "and in the first schooner I can get. But my coachman and men will stay the night, and probably several days longer, so I hope you will make them comfortable."

"Yes, my lady; I'll look after them. Shall Sally bring your ladyship some supper?"

"Yes, please. Put something cold on the table, and as soon as Sir Andrew Ffoulkes comes, show him in here."

"Yes, my lady."

Honest Jellyband's face now expressed distress in spite of himself. He had great regard for Sir Percy Blakeney, and did not like to see his lady running away with young Sir Andrew. Of course, it was no business of his, and Mr. Jellyband was no gossip. Still, in his heart, he recollected that her ladyship was after all only one of them "furriners"; what wonder that she was immoral like the rest of them?

"Don't sit up, honest Jellyband," continued Marguerite, kindly, "nor you either, Mistress Sally. Sir Andrew may be late."

Jellyband was only too willing that Sally should go to bed. He was beginning not to like these goings-on at all. Still, Lady Blakeney would pay handsomely for the accommodation, and it certainly was no business of his.

Sally arranged a simple supper of cold meat, wine, and fruit on the table, then with a respectful curtsey, she retired, wondering in her little mind why her ladyship looked so serious, when she was about to elope with her gallant.

Then commenced a period of weary waiting for Marguerite. She knew that Sir Andrew—who would have to provide himself with clothes befitting a lacquey—could not possibly reach Dover for at least a couple of hours. He was a splendid horseman of course, and would make light in such an emergency of the seventy odd miles between London and Dover. He would, too, literally burn the ground beneath his horse's hoofs, but he might not always get very good remounts, and in any case, he could not have started from London until at least an hour after she did.

She had seen nothing of Chauvelin on the road. Her coachman, whom she questioned, had not seen anyone answering the description his mistress gave him of the wizened figure of the little Frenchman.

Evidently, therefore, he had been ahead of her all the time. She had not dared to question the people at the various inns, where they had stopped to change horses. She feared that Chauvelin had spies all along the route, who might overhear her questions, then outdistance her and warn her enemy of her approach.

Now she wondered at what inn he might be stopping, or whether he had had the good luck of chartering a vessel already, and was now himself on the way to France. That thought gripped her at the heart as with an iron vice. If indeed she should be too late already!

The loneliness of the room overwhelmed her; everything within was so horribly still;

the ticking of the grandfather's clock—dreadfully slow and measured—was the only sound which broke this awful loneliness.

Marguerite had need of all her energy, all her steadfastness of purpose, to keep up her courage through this weary midnight waiting.

Everyone else in the house but herself must have been asleep. She had heard Sally go upstairs. Mr. Jellyband had gone to see to her coachman and men, and then had returned and taken up a position under the porch outside, just where Marguerite had first met Chauvelin about a week ago. He evidently meant to wait up for Sir Andrew Ffoulkes, but was soon overcome by sweet slumbers, for presently—in addition to the slow ticking of the clock—Marguerite could hear the monotonous and dulcet tones of the worthy fellow's breathing.

For some time now, she had realised that the beautiful warm October's day, so happily begun, had turned into a rough and cold night. She had felt very chilly, and was glad of the cheerful blaze in the hearth: but gradually, as time wore on, the weather became more rough, and the sound of the great breakers against the Admiralty Pier, though some distance from the inn, came to her as the noise of muffled thunder.

The wind was becoming boisterous, rattling the leaded windows and the massive doors of the old-fashioned house: it shook the trees outside and roared down the vast chimney. Marguerite wondered if the wind would be favourable for her journey. She had no fear of the storm, and would have braved worse risks sooner than delay the crossing by an hour.

A sudden commotion outside roused her from her meditations. Evidently it was Sir Andrew Ffoulkes, just arrived in mad haste, for she heard his horse's hoofs thundering on the flag-stones outside, then Mr. Jellyband's sleepy, yet cheerful tones bidding him welcome.

For a moment, then, the awkwardness of her position struck Marguerite; alone at this hour, in a place where she was well known, and having made an assignation with a young cavalier equally well known, and who arrives in disguise! What food for gossip to those mischievously inclined.

The idea struck Marguerite chiefly from its humorous side: there was such quaint contrast between the seriousness of her errand, and the construction which would naturally be put on her actions by honest Mr. Jellyband, that, for the first time since many hours, a little smile began playing round the corners of her childlike mouth, and when, presently, Sir Andrew, almost unrecognisable in his lacquey-like garb, entered the coffee-room, she was able to greet him with quite a merry laugh.

"Faith! Monsieur, my lacquey," she said, "I am satisfied with your appearance!"

Mr. Jellyband had followed Sir Andrew, looking strangely perplexed. The young gallant's disguise had confirmed his worst suspicions. Without a smile upon his jovial face, he drew the cork from the bottle of wine, set the chairs ready, and prepared to wait.

"Thanks, honest friend," said Marguerite, who was still smiling at the thought of what the worthy fellow must be thinking at that very moment, "we shall require nothing more; and here's for all the trouble you have been put to on our account."

She handed two or three gold pieces to Jellyband, who took them respectfully, and with becoming gratitude.

"Stay, Lady Blakeney," interposed Sir Andrew, as Jellyband was about to retire, "I am afraid we shall require something more of my friend Jelly's hospitality. I am sorry to say we cannot cross over to-night."

"Not cross over to-night?" she repeated in amazement. "But we must, Sir Andrew, we must! There can be no question of cannot, and whatever it may cost, we must get a vessel to-night."

But the young man shook his head sadly.

"I am afraid it is not a question of cost, Lady Blakeney. There is a nasty storm blowing from France, the wind is dead against us, we cannot possibly sail until it has changed."

Marguerite became deadly pale. She had not foreseen this. Nature herself was playing her a horrible, cruel trick. Percy was in danger, and she could not go to him, because the wind happened to blow from the coast of France.

"But we must go!—we must!" she repeated with strange, persistent energy, "you know, we must go!—can't you find a way?"

"I have been down to the shore already," he said, "and had a talk to one or two skippers. It is quite impossible to set sail to-night, so every sailor assured me. No one," he added, looking significantly at Marguerite, "*no one* could possibly put out of Dover to-night."

Marguerite at once understood what he meant. *No one* included Chauvelin as well as herself. She nodded pleasantly to Jellyband.

"Well, then, I must resign myself," she said to him. "Have you a room for me?"

"Oh, yes, your ladyship. A nice, bright, airy room. I'll see to it at once. . . . And there is another one for Sir Andrew—both quite ready."

"That's brave now, mine honest Jelly," said Sir Andrew, gaily, and clapping his worthy host vigorously on the back. "You unlock both those rooms, and leave our candles here on the dresser. I vow you are dead with sleep, and her ladyship must have some supper before she retires. There, have no fear, friend of the rueful countenance, her ladyship's visit, though at this unusual hour, is a great honour to thy house, and Sir Percy Blakeney will reward thee doubly, if thou seest well to her privacy and comfort."

Sir Andrew had no doubt guessed the many conflicting doubts and fears which raged in honest Jellyband's head; and, as he was a gallant gentleman, he tried by this brave hint to allay some of the worthy innkeeper's suspicions. He had the satisfaction of seeing that he had partially succeeded. Jellyband's rubicund countenance brightened somewhat, at mention of Sir Percy's name.

"I'll go and see to it at once, sir," he said with alacrity, and with less frigidity in his manner. "Has her ladyship everything she wants for supper?"

"Everything, thanks, honest friend, and as I am famished and dead with fatigue, I pray you see to the rooms."

"Now tell me," she said eagerly, as soon as Jellyband had gone from the room, "tell me all your news."

"There is nothing else much to tell you, Lady Blakeney," replied the young man. "The storm makes it quite impossible for any vessel to put out of Dover this tide. But, what seemed to you at first a terrible calamity is really a blessing in disguise. If we cannot cross over to France to-night, Chauvelin is in the same quandary."

"He may have left before the storm broke out."

"God grant he may," said Sir Andrew, merrily, "for very likely then he'll have been driven out of his course! Who knows? He may now even be lying at the bottom of the sea, for there is a furious storm raging, and it will fare ill with all small craft which happen to be out. But I fear me we cannot build our hopes upon the shipwreck of that cunning devil, and of all his murderous plans. The sailors I spoke to, all assured me that no schooner had put out of Dover for several hours: on the other hand, I ascertained that a stranger had arrived by coach this afternoon, and had, like myself, made some inquiries about crossing over to France."

"Then Chauvelin is still in Dover?"

"Undoubtedly. Shall I go waylay him and run my sword through him? That were indeed the quickest way out of the difficulty."

"Nay! Sir Andrew, do not jest! Alas! I have often since last night caught myself wishing for that fiend's death. But what you suggest is impossible! The laws of this country do not permit of murder! It is only in our beautiful France that wholesale slaughter is done lawfully, in the name of Liberty and of brotherly love."

Sir Andrew had persuaded her to sit down to the table, to partake of some supper and to drink a little wine. This enforced rest of at least twelve hours, until the next tide, was sure to be terribly difficult to bear in the state of intense excitement in which she was. Obedient in these small matters like a child, Marguerite tried to eat and drink.

Sir Andrew, with that profound sympathy born in all those who are in love, made her almost happy by talking to her about her husband. He recounted to her some of the daring escapes the brave Scarlet Pimpernel had contrived for the poor French fugitives, whom a relentless and bloody revolution was driving out of their country. He made her eyes glow with enthusiasm by telling her of his bravery, his ingenuity, his resourcefulness, when it meant snatching the lives of men, women, and even children from beneath the very edge of that murderous, ever-ready guillotine.

He even made her smile quite merrily by telling her of the Scarlet Pimpernel's quaint and many disguises, through which he had baffled the strictest watch set against him at the barricades of Paris. This last time, the escape of the Comtesse de Tournay and her children had been a veritable masterpiece—Blakeney disguised as a hideous old market-woman, in filthy cap and straggling grey locks, was a sight fit to make the gods laugh.

Marguerite laughed heartily as Sir Andrew tried to describe Blakeney's appearance, whose gravest difficulty always consisted in his great height, which in France made disguise doubly difficult.

Thus an hour wore on. There were many more to spend in enforced inactivity in Dover. Marguerite rose from the table with an impatient sigh. She looked forward with dread to the night in the bed upstairs, with terribly anxious thoughts to keep her company, and the howling of the storm to help chase sleep away.

She wondered where Percy was now. The *Day Dream* was a strong, well-built, sea-going yacht. Sir Andrew had expressed the opinion that no doubt she had got in the lee of the wind before the storm broke out, or else perhaps had not ventured into the open at all, but was lying quietly at Gravesend.

Briggs was an expert skipper, and Sir Percy handled a schooner as well as any master mariner. There was no danger for them from the storm.

It was long past midnight when at last Marguerite retired to rest. As she had feared, sleep sedulously avoided her eyes. Her thoughts were of the blackest during these long, weary hours, whilst that incessant storm raged which was keeping her away from Percy. The sound of the distant breakers made her heart ache with melancholy. She was in the mood when the sea has a saddening effect upon the nerves. It is only when we are very happy, that we can bear to gaze merrily upon the vast and limitless expanse of water, rolling on and on with such persistent, irritating monotony, to the accompaniment of our thoughts, whether grave or gay. When they are gay, the waves echo their gaiety; but when they are sad, then every breaker, as it rolls, seems to bring additional sadness, and to speak to us of hopelessness and of the pettiness of all our joys.

XXII. CALAIS

The weariest nights, the longest days, sooner or later must perforce come to an end.

Marguerite had spent over fifteen hours in such acute mental torture as well-nigh drove her crazy. After a sleepless night, she rose early, wild with excitement, dying to start on her journey, terrified lest further obstacles lay in her way. She rose before anyone else in the house was astir, so frightened was she, lest she should miss the one golden opportunity of making a start.

When she came downstairs, she found Sir Andrew Ffoulkes sitting in the coffee-room. He had been out half an hour earlier, and had gone to the Admiralty Pier, only to find that neither the French packet nor any privately chartered vessel could put out of Dover yet. The storm was then at its fullest, and the tide was on the turn. If the wind did not abate or change, they would perforce have to wait another ten or twelve hours until the next tide, before a start could be made. And the storm had not abated, the wind had not changed, and the tide was rapidly drawing out.

Marguerite felt the sickness of despair when she heard this melancholy news. Only the most firm resolution kept her from totally breaking down, and thus adding to the young man's anxiety, which evidently had become very keen.

Though he tried to disguise it, Marguerite could see that Sir Andrew was just as anxious as she was to reach his comrade and friend. This enforced inactivity was terrible to them both.

How they spent that wearisome day at Dover, Marguerite could never afterwards say. She was in terror of showing herself, lest Chauvelin's spies happened to be about, so she had a private sitting-room, and she and Sir Andrew sat there hour after hour, trying to take, at long intervals, some perfunctory meals, which little Sally would bring them, with nothing to do but to think, to conjecture, and only occasionally to hope.

The storm had abated just too late; the tide was by then too far out to allow a vessel to put off to sea. The wind had changed, and was settling down to a comfortable north-westerly breeze—a veritable godsend for a speedy passage across to France.

And there those two waited, wondering if the hour would ever come when they could finally make a start. There had been one happy interval in this long weary day, and that was when Sir Andrew went down once again to the pier, and presently came back to tell Marguerite that he had chartered a quick schooner, whose skipper was ready to put to sea the moment the tide was favourable.

From that moment the hours seemed less wearisome; there was less hopelessness in the waiting; and at last, at five o'clock in the afternoon, Marguerite, closely veiled and followed by Sir Andrew Ffoulkes, who, in the guise of her lacquey, was carrying a number of impedimenta, found her way down to the pier.

Once on board, the keen, fresh sea-air revived her, the breeze was just strong enough to nicely swell the sails of the *Foam Crest*, as she cut her way merrily towards the open.

The sunset was glorious after the storm, and Marguerite, as she watched the white cliffs of Dover gradually disappearing from view, felt more at peace and once more almost hopeful.

Sir Andrew was full of kind attentions, and she felt how lucky she had been to have him by her side in this, her great trouble.

Gradually the grey coast of France began to emerge from the fast-gathering evening mists. One or two lights could be seen flickering, and the spires of several churches to rise out of the surrounding haze.

Half an hour later Marguerite had landed upon French shore. She was back in that country where at this very moment men slaughtered their fellow-creatures by the hundreds, and sent innocent women and children in thousands to the block.

The very aspect of the country and its people, even in this remote sea-coast town, spoke of that seething revolution, three hundred miles away, in beautiful Paris, now rendered hideous by the constant flow of the blood of her noblest sons, by the wailing of the widows, and the cries of fatherless children.

The men all wore red caps—in various stages of cleanliness—but all with the tricolour cockade pinned on the left-hand side. Marguerite noticed with a shudder that, instead of the laughing, merry countenance habitual to her own countrymen, their faces now invariably wore a look of sly distrust.

Every man nowadays was a spy upon his fellows: the most innocent word uttered in jest might at any time be brought up as a proof of aristocratic tendencies, or of treachery against the people. Even the women went about with a curious look of fear and of hate lurking in their brown eyes; and all watched Marguerite as she stepped on shore, followed by Sir Andrew, and murmured as she passed along: "*Sacrés aristos!*" or else "*Sacrés Anglais!*"

Otherwise their presence excited no further comment. Calais, even in those days, was in constant business communication with England, and English merchants were often to be seen on this coast. It was well known that in view of the heavy duties in England, a vast deal of French wines and brandies were smuggled across. This pleased the French *bourgeois* immensely; he liked to see the English Government and the English king, both of whom he hated, cheated out of their revenues; and an English smuggler was always a welcome guest at the tumble-down taverns of Calais and Boulogne.

So, perhaps, as Sir Andrew gradually directed Marguerite through the tortuous streets of Calais, many of the population, who turned with an oath to look at the strangers clad in the English fashion, thought that they were bent on purchasing dutiable articles for their own fog-ridden country, and gave them no more than a passing thought.

Marguerite, however, wondered how her husband's tall, massive figure could have passed through Calais unobserved: she marveled what disguise he assumed to do his noble work, without exciting too much attention.

Without exchanging more than a few words, Sir Andrew was leading her right across the town, to the other side from that where they had landed, and on the way towards Cap Gris Nez. The streets were narrow, tortuous, and mostly evil-smelling, with a mixture of stale fish and damp cellar odours. There had been heavy rain here during the storm last night, and sometimes Marguerite sank ankle-deep in the mud, for the roads were not lighted save by the occasional glimmer from a lamp inside a house.

But she did not heed any of these petty discomforts: "We may meet Blakeney at the 'Chat Gris,'" Sir Andrew had said, when they landed, and she was walking as if on a carpet of rose-leaves, for she was going to meet him almost at once.

At last they reached their destination. Sir Andrew evidently knew the road, for he had walked unerringly in the dark, and had not asked his way from anyone. It was too dark then for Marguerite to notice the outside aspect of this house. The "Chat Gris," as Sir Andrew had called it, was evidently a small wayside inn on the outskirts of Calais, and on the way to Gris Nez. It lay some little distance from the coast, for the sound of the sea seemed to come from afar.

Sir Andrew knocked at the door with the knob of his cane, and from within Marguerite heard a sort of grunt and the muttering of a number of oaths. Sir Andrew knocked again, this time more peremptorily: more oaths were heard, and then shuffling steps seemed to draw near the door. Presently this was thrown open, and Marguerite found herself on the threshold of the most dilapidated, most squalid room she had ever seen in all her life.

The paper, such as it was, was hanging from the walls in strips; there did not seem to be a single piece of furniture in the room that could, by the wildest stretch of imagination, be called "whole." Most of the chairs had broken backs, others had no seats to them, one corner of the table was propped up with a bundle of faggots, there where the fourth leg had been broken.

In one corner of the room there was a huge hearth, over which hung a stock-pot, with a not altogether unpalatable odour of hot soup emanating therefrom. On one side of the room, high up in the wall, there was a species of loft, before which hung a tattered blue-and-white checked curtain. A rickety set of steps led up to this loft.

On the great bare walls, with their colourless paper, all stained with varied filth, there were chalked up at intervals in great bold characters, the words: "Liberté—Egalité—Fraternité."

The whole of this sordid abode was dimly lighted by an evil-smelling oil-lamp, which hung from the rickety rafters of the ceiling. It all looked so horribly squalid, so dirty and uninviting, that Marguerite hardly dared to cross the threshold.

Sir Andrew, however, had stepped unhesitatingly forward.

"English travellers, citoyen!" he said boldly, and speaking in French.

The individual who had come to the door in response to Sir Andrew's knock, and who, presumably, was the owner of this squalid abode, was an elderly, heavily-built peasant, dressed in a dirty blue blouse, heavy sabots, from which wisps of straw protruded all round, shabby blue trousers, and the inevitable red cap with the tricolour cockade, that proclaimed his momentary political views. He carried a short wooden pipe, from which the odour of rank tobacco emanated. He looked with some suspicion and a great deal of contempt at the two travellers, muttered "*Sacrrrés Anglais!*" and spat upon the ground to further show his independence of spirit, but, nevertheless, he stood aside to let them enter, no doubt well aware that these same *sacrrrés Anglais* always had well-filled purses.

"Oh, lud!" said Marguerite, as she advanced into the room, holding her handkerchief to her dainty nose, "what a dreadful hole! Are you sure this is the place?"

"Aye! 'tis the place, sure enough," replied the young man as, with his lace-edged, fashionable handkerchief, he dusted a chair for Marguerite to sit on; "but I vow I never saw a more villainous hole."

"Faith!" she said, looking round with some curiosity and a great deal of horror at the dilapidated walls, the broken chairs, the rickety table, "it certainly does not look inviting."

The landlord of the "Chat Gris"—by name, Brogard—had taken no further notice of his guests; he concluded that presently they would order supper, and in the meanwhile it was not for a free citizen to show deference, or even courtesy, to anyone, however smartly they might be dressed.

By the hearth sat a huddled-up figure clad, seemingly, mostly in rags: that figure was apparently a woman, although even that would have been hard to distinguish, except for the cap, which had once been white, and for what looked like the semblance of a petticoat. She was sitting mumbling to herself, and from time to time stirring the brew in her stock-pot.

"Hey, my friend!" said Sir Andrew at last, "we should like some supper.[EOL] . . . The citoyenne there," he added, pointing to the huddled-up bundle of rags by the hearth, "is concocting some delicious soup, I'll warrant, and my mistress has not tasted food for several hours."

It took Brogard some few moments to consider the question. A free citizen does not respond too readily to the wishes of those who happen to require something of him.

"*Sacrrrés aristos!*" he murmured, and once more spat upon the ground.

Then he went very slowly up to a dresser which stood in a corner of the room; from this he took an old pewter soup-tureen and slowly, and without a word, he handed it to his better-half, who, in the same silence, began filling the tureen with the soup out of her stock-pot.

Marguerite had watched all these preparations with absolute horror; were it not for the earnestness of her purpose, she would incontinently have fled from this abode of dirt and evil smells.

"Faith! our host and hostess are not cheerful people," said Sir Andrew, seeing the look of horror on Marguerite's face. "I would I could offer you a more hearty and more appetising meal . . . but I think you will find the soup eatable and the wine good; these people wallow in dirt, but live well as a rule."

"Nay! I pray you, Sir Andrew," she said gently, "be not anxious about me. My mind is scarce inclined to dwell on thoughts of supper."

Brogard was slowly pursuing his gruesome preparations; he had placed a couple of spoons, also two glasses on the table, both of which Sir Andrew took the precaution of wiping carefully.

Brogard had also produced a bottle of wine and some bread, and Marguerite made an effort to draw her chair to the table and to make some pretence at eating. Sir Andrew, as befitting his *rôle* of lacquey, stood behind her chair.

"Nay, Madame, I pray you," he said, seeing that Marguerite seemed quite unable to eat, "I beg of you to try and swallow some food—remember you have need of all your strength."

The soup certainly was not bad; it smelt and tasted good. Marguerite might have enjoyed it, but for the horrible surroundings. She broke the bread, however, and drank some of the wine.

"Nay, Sir Andrew," she said, "I do not like to see you standing. You have need of food just as much as I have. This creature will only think that I am an eccentric Englishwoman eloping with her lacquey, if you'll sit down and partake of this semblance of supper beside me."

Indeed, Brogard having placed what was strictly necessary upon the table, seemed not to trouble himself any further about his guests. The Mere Brogard had quietly shuffled out of the room, and the man stood and lounged about, smoking his evil-smelling pipe, sometimes under Marguerite's very nose, as any free-born citizen who was anybody's equal should do.

"Confound the brute!" said Sir Andrew, with native British wrath, as Brogard leant up against the table, smoking and looking down superciliously at these two *sacrrrés Anglais*.

"In Heaven's name, man," admonished Marguerite, hurriedly, seeing that Sir Andrew, with British-born instinct, was ominously clenching his fist, "remember that you are in France, and that in this year of grace this is the temper of the people."

"I'd like to scrag the brute!" muttered Sir Andrew, savagely.

He had taken Marguerite's advice and sat next to her at table, and they were both making noble efforts to deceive one another, by pretending to eat and drink.

"I pray you," said Marguerite, "keep the creature in a good temper, so that he may answer the questions we must put to him."

"I'll do my best, but, begad! I'd sooner scrag him than question him. Hey! my friend," he said pleasantly in French, and tapping Brogard lightly on the shoulder, "do you see many of our quality along these parts? Many English travellers, I mean?"

Brogard looked round at him, over his near shoulder, puffed away at his pipe for a moment or two as he was in no hurry, then muttered,—

"Heu!—sometimes!"

"Ah!" said Sir Andrew, carelessly, "English travellers always know where they can get good wine, eh! my friend?—Now, tell me, my lady was desiring to know if by any chance you happen to have seen a great friend of hers, an English gentleman, who often comes to Calais on business; he is tall, and recently was on his way to Paris—my lady hoped to have met him in Calais."

Marguerite tried not to look at Brogard, lest she should betray before him the burning anxiety with which she waited for his reply. But a free-born French citizen is never in any hurry to answer questions: Brogard took his time, then he said very slowly,—

"Tall Englishman?—To-day!—Yes."

"You have seen him?" asked Sir Andrew, carelessly.

"Yes, to-day," muttered Brogard, sullenly. Then he quietly took Sir Andrew's hat from a chair close by, put it on his own head, tugged at his dirty blouse, and generally tried to express in pantomime that the individual in question wore very fine clothes. "*Sacré aristo!*" he muttered, "that tall Englishman!"

Marguerite could scarce repress a scream.

"It's Sir Percy right enough," she murmured, "and not even in disguise!"

She smiled, in the midst of all her anxiety and through her gathering tears, at thought of "the ruling passion strong in death"; of Percy running into the wildest, maddest dangers, with the latest-cut coat upon his back, and the laces of his jabot unruffled.

"Oh! the foolhardiness of it!" she sighed. "Quick, Sir Andrew! ask the man when he went."

"Ah, yes, my friend," said Sir Andrew, addressing Brogard, with the same assumption of carelessness, "my lord always wears beautiful clothes; the tall Englishman you saw, was certainly my lady's friend. And he has gone, you say?"

"He went . . . yes . . . but he's coming back . . . here—he ordered supper . . ."

Sir Andrew put his hand with a quick gesture of warning upon Marguerite's arm; it came none too soon, for the next moment her wild, mad joy would have betrayed her. He was safe and well, was coming back here presently, she would see him in a few moments perhaps. . . . Oh! the wildness of her joy seemed almost more than she could bear.

"Here!" she said to Brogard, who seemed suddenly to have been transformed in her eyes into some heaven-born messenger of bliss. "Here!—did you say the English gentleman was coming back here?"

The heaven-born messenger of bliss spat upon the floor, to express his contempt for all and sundry *aristos*, who chose to haunt the "Chat Gris."

"Heu!" he muttered, "he ordered supper—he will come back. . . . *Sacré Anglais!*" he added, by way of protest against all this fuss for a mere Englishman.

"But where is he now?—Do you know?" she asked eagerly, placing her dainty white hand upon the dirty sleeve of his blue blouse.

"He went to get a horse and cart," said Brogard, laconically, as, with a surly gesture, he shook off from his arm that pretty hand which princes had been proud to kiss.

"At what time did he go?"

But Brogard had evidently had enough of these questionings. He did not think that it was fitting for a citizen—who was the equal of anybody—to be thus catechised by these *sacrés aristos*, even though they were rich English ones. It was distinctly more fitting to his new-born dignity to be as rude as possible; it was a sure sign of servility to meekly reply to civil questions.

"I don't know," he said surlily. "I have said enough, *voyons, les aristos!* . . . He came to-day. He ordered supper. He went out.—He'll come back. *Voilà!*"

And with this parting assertion of his rights as a citizen and a free man, to be as rude as he well pleased, Brogard shuffled out of the room, banging the door after him.

XXIII. HOPE

"Faith, Madame!" said Sir Andrew, seeing that Marguerite seemed desirous to call her surly host back again, "I think we'd better leave him alone. We shall not get anything more out of him, and we might arouse his suspicions. One never knows what spies may be lurking around these God-forsaken places."

"What care I?" she replied lightly, "now I know that my husband is safe, and that I shall see him almost directly!"

"Hush!" he said in genuine alarm, for she had talked quite loudly, in the fulness of her glee, "the very walls have ears in France, these days."

He rose quickly from the table, and walked round the bare, squalid room, listening attentively at the door, through which Brogard had just disappeared, and whence only muttered oaths and shuffling footsteps could be heard. He also ran up the rickety steps that led to the attic, to assure himself that there were no spies of Chauvelin's about the place.

"Are we alone, Monsieur, my lacquey?" said Marguerite, gaily, as the young man once more sat down beside her. "May we talk?"

"As cautiously as possible!" he entreated.

"Faith, man! but you wear a glum face! As for me, I could dance with joy! Surely there is no longer any cause for fear. Our boat is on the beach, the *Foam Crest* not two miles out at sea, and my husband will be here, under this very roof, within the next half hour perhaps. Sure! there is naught to hinder us. Chauvelin and his gang have not yet arrived."

"Nay, madam! that I fear we do not know."

"What do you mean?"

"He was at Dover at the same time that we were."

"Held up by the same storm, which kept us from starting."

"Exactly. But—I did not speak of it before, for I feared to alarm you—I saw him on the beach not five minutes before we embarked. At least, I swore to myself at the time that it was himself; he was disguised as a *curé*, so that Satan, his own guardian, would scarce have known him. But I heard him then, bargaining for a vessel to take him swiftly to Calais; and he must have set sail less than an hour after we did."

Marguerite's face had quickly lost its look of joy. The terrible danger in which Percy stood, now that he was actually on French soil, became suddenly and horribly clear to her. Chauvelin was close upon his heels; here in Calais, the astute diplomatist was all-powerful; a word from him and Percy could be tracked and arrested and . . .

Every drop of blood seemed to freeze in her veins; not even during the moments of her wildest anguish in England had she so completely realised the imminence of the peril in which her husband stood. Chauvelin had sworn to bring the Scarlet Pimpernel to the guillotine, and now the daring plotter, whose anonymity hitherto had been his safeguard, stood revealed through her own hand, to his most bitter, most relentless enemy.

Chauvelin—when he waylaid Lord Tony and Sir Andrew Ffoulkes in the coffee-room of "The Fisherman's Rest"—had obtained possession of all the plans of this latest expedition. Armand St. Just, the Comte de Tournay and other fugitive royalists were to have met the Scarlet Pimpernel—or rather, as it had been originally arranged, two of his emissaries—on this day, the 2nd of October, at a place evidently known to the league, and vaguely alluded to as the "Père Blanchard's hut."

Armand, whose connection with the Scarlet Pimpernel and disavowal of the brutal policy of the Reign of Terror was still unknown to his countrymen, had left England a little more than a week ago, carrying with him the necessary instructions, which would enable him to meet the other fugitives and to convey them to this place of safety.

This much Marguerite had fully understood from the first, and Sir Andrew Ffoulkes had confirmed her surmises. She knew, too, that when Sir Percy realised that his own plans and his directions to his lieutenants had been stolen by Chauvelin, it was too late to communicate with Armand, or to send fresh instructions to the fugitives.

They would, of necessity, be at the appointed time and place, not knowing how grave was the danger which now awaited their brave rescuer.

Blakeney, who as usual had planned and organised the whole expedition, would not allow any of his younger comrades to run the risk of almost certain capture. Hence his hurried note to them at Lord Grenville's ball—"Start myself to-morrow—alone."

And now with his identity known to his most bitter enemy, his every step would be dogged, the moment he set foot in France. He would be tracked by Chauvelin's emissaries, followed until he reached that mysterious hut where the fugitives were waiting for him, and there the trap would be closed on him and on them.

There was but one hour—the hour's start which Marguerite and Sir Andrew had of their enemy—in which to warn Percy of the imminence of his danger, and to persuade him to give up the foolhardy expedition, which could only end in his own death.

But there *was* that one hour.

"Chauvelin knows of this inn, from the papers he stole," said Sir Andrew, earnestly, "and on landing will make straight for it."

"He has not landed yet," she said, "we have an hour's start on him, and Percy will be here directly. We shall be mid-Channel ere Chauvelin has realised that we have slipped through his fingers."

She spoke excitedly and eagerly, wishing to infuse into her young friend some of that buoyant hope which still clung to her heart. But he shook his head sadly.

"Silent again, Sir Andrew?" she said with some impatience. "Why do you shake your head and look so glum?"

"Faith, Madame," he replied, "'tis only because in making your rose-coloured plans, you are forgetting the most important factor."

"What in the world do you mean?—I am forgetting nothing. . . . What factor do you mean?" she added with more impatience.

"It stands six foot odd high," replied Sir Andrew, quietly, "and hath name Percy Blakeney."

"I don't understand," she murmured.

"Do you think that Blakeney would leave Calais without having accomplished what he set out to do?"

"You mean . . . ?"

"There's the old Comte de Tournay . . ."

"The Comte . . . ?" she murmured.

"And St. Just . . . and others . . ."

"My brother!" she said with a heart-broken sob of anguish. "Heaven help me, but I fear I had forgotten."

"Fugitives as they are, these men at this moment await with perfect confidence and unshaken faith the arrival of the Scarlet Pimpernel, who has pledged his honour to take them safely across the Channel."

Indeed, she had forgotten! With the sublime selfishness of a woman who loves with her whole heart, she had in the last twenty-four hours had no thought save for him. His precious, noble life, his danger—he, the loved one, the brave hero, he alone dwelt in her mind.

"My brother!" she murmured, as one by one the heavy tears gathered in her eyes, as memory came back to her of Armand, the companion and darling of her childhood, the man for whom she had committed the deadly sin, which had so hopelessly imperilled her brave husband's life.

"Sir Percy Blakeney would not be the trusted, honoured leader of a score of English gentlemen," said Sir Andrew, proudly, "if he abandoned those who placed their trust in him. As for breaking his word, the very thought is preposterous!"

There was silence for a moment or two. Marguerite had buried her face in her hands, and was letting the tears slowly trickle through her trembling fingers. The young man said nothing; his heart ached for this beautiful woman in her awful grief. All along he had felt the terrible *impasse* in which her own rash act had plunged them all. He knew his friend and leader so well, with his reckless daring, his mad bravery, his worship of his own word of honour. Sir Andrew knew that Blakeney would brave any danger, run the wildest risks sooner than break it, and, with Chauvelin at his very heels, would make a final attempt, however desperate, to rescue those who trusted in him.

"Faith, Sir Andrew," said Marguerite at last, making brave efforts to dry her tears, "you are right, and I would not now shame myself by trying to dissuade him from doing his duty. As you say, I should plead in vain. God grant him strength and ability," she added fervently and resolutely, "to outwit his pursuers. He will not refuse to take you with him, perhaps, when he starts on his noble work; between you, you will have cunning as well as valour! God guard you both! In the meanwhile I think we should lose no time. I still believe that his safety depends upon his knowing that Chauvelin is on his track."

"Undoubtedly. He has wonderful resources at his command. As soon as he is aware of his danger he will exercise more caution: his ingenuity is a veritable miracle."

"Then, what say you to a voyage of reconnaissance in the village whilst I wait here against his coming!—You might come across Percy's track and thus save valuable time. If you find him, tell him to beware!—his bitterest enemy is on his heels!"

"But this is such a villainous hole for you to wait in."

"Nay, that I do not mind!—But you might ask our surly host if he could let me wait in another room, where I could be safer from the prying eyes of any chance traveller. Offer him some ready money, so that he should not fail to give me word the moment the tall Englishman returns."

She spoke quite calmly, even cheerfully now, thinking out her plans, ready for the worst if need be; she would show no more weakness, she would prove herself worthy of him, who was about to give his life for the sake of his fellow-men.

Sir Andrew obeyed her without further comment. Instinctively he felt that hers now was the stronger mind; he was willing to give himself over to her guidance, to become the hand, whilst she was the directing head.

He went to the door of the inner room, through which Brogard and his wife had disappeared before, and knocked; as usual, he was answered by a salvo of muttered oaths.

"Hey! friend Brogard!" said the young man peremptorily, "my lady would wish to rest here awhile. Could you give her the use of another room? She would wish to be alone."

He took some money out of his pocket, and allowed it to jingle significantly in his hand. Brogard had opened the door, and listened, with his usual surly apathy, to the young man's request. At sight of the gold, however, his lazy attitude relaxed slightly; he took his pipe from his mouth and shuffled into the room.

He then pointed over his shoulder at the attic up in the wall.

"She can wait up there!" he said with a grunt. "It's comfortable, and I have no other room."

"Nothing could be better," said Marguerite in English; she at once realised the advantages such a position hidden from view would give her. "Give him the money, Sir Andrew; I shall be quite happy up there, and can see everything without being seen."

She nodded to Brogard, who condescended to go up to the attic, and to shake up the straw that lay on the floor.

"May I entreat you, madam, to do nothing rash," said Sir Andrew, as Marguerite prepared in her turn to ascend the rickety flight of steps. "Remember this place is infested with spies. Do not, I beg of you, reveal yourself to Sir Percy, unless you are absolutely certain that you are alone with him."

Even as he spoke, he felt how unnecessary was this caution: Marguerite was as calm, as clear-headed as any man. There was no fear of her doing anything that was rash.

"Nay," she said with a slight attempt at cheerfulness, "that can I faithfully promise you. I would not jeopardise my husband's life, nor yet his plans, by speaking to him before strangers. Have no fear, I will watch my opportunity, and serve him in the manner I think he needs it most."

Brogard had come down the steps again, and Marguerite was ready to go up to her safe retreat.

"I dare not kiss your hand, madam," said Sir Andrew, as she began to mount the steps, "since I am your lacquey, but I pray you be of good cheer. If I do not come across Blakeney in half an hour, I shall return, expecting to find him here."

"Yes, that will be best. We can afford to wait for half an hour. Chauvelin cannot possibly be here before that. God grant that either you or I may have seen Percy by then. Good luck to you, friend! Have no fear for me."

Lightly she mounted the rickety wooden steps that led to the attic. Brogard was taking no further heed of her. She could make herself comfortable there or not as she chose. Sir Andrew watched her until she had reached the loft and sat down upon the straw. She pulled the tattered curtains across, and the young man noted that she was singularly well placed there, for seeing and hearing, whilst remaining unobserved.

He had paid Brogard well; the surly old innkeeper would have no object in betraying her. Then Sir Andrew prepared to go. At the door he turned once again and looked up at the loft. Through the ragged curtains Marguerite's sweet face was peeping down at him, and the young man rejoiced to see that it looked serene, and even gently smiling. With a final nod of farewell to her, he walked out into the night.

XXIV. THE DEATH-TRAP

The next quarter of an hour went by swiftly and noiselessly. In the room downstairs, Brogard had for a while busied himself with clearing the table, and re-arranging it for another guest.

It was because she watched these preparations that Marguerite found the time slipping by more pleasantly. It was for Percy that this semblance of supper was being got ready. Evidently Brogard had a certain amount of respect for the tall Englishman, as he seemed to take some trouble in making the place look a trifle less uninviting than it had done before.

He even produced, from some hidden recess in the old dresser, what actually looked like a table-cloth; and when he spread it out, and saw it was full of holes, he shook his head dubiously for a while, then was at much pains so to spread it over the table as to hide most of its blemishes.

Then he got out a serviette, also old and ragged, but possessing some measure of cleanliness, and with this he carefully wiped the glasses, spoons and plates, which he put on the table.

Marguerite could not help smiling to herself as she watched all these preparations, which Brogard accomplished to an accompaniment of muttered oaths. Clearly the great height and bulk of the Englishman, or perhaps the weight of his fist, had overawed this free-born citizen of France, or he would never have been at such trouble for any *sacrré aristo*.

When the table was set—such as it was—Brogard surveyed it with evident satisfaction. He then dusted one of the chairs with the corner of his blouse, gave a stir to the stock-pot, threw a fresh bundle of faggots on to the fire, and slouched out of the room.

Marguerite was left alone with her reflections. She had spread her travelling cloak over the straw, and was sitting fairly comfortably, as the straw was fresh, and the evil odours from below came up to her only in a modified form.

But, momentarily, she was almost happy; happy because, when she peeped through the tattered curtains, she could see a rickety chair, a torn table-cloth, a glass, a plate and a spoon; that was all. But those mute and ugly things seemed to say to her that they were waiting for Percy; that soon, very soon, he would be here, that the squalid room being still empty, they would be alone together.

That thought was so heavenly, that Marguerite closed her eyes in order to shut out everything but that. In a few minutes she would be alone with him; she would run down the ladder, and let him see her; then he would take her in his arms, and she would let him see that, after that, she would gladly die for him, and with him, for earth could hold no greater happiness than that.

And then what would happen? She could not even remotely conjecture. She knew, of course, that Sir Andrew was right, that Percy would do everything he had set out to accomplish; that she—now she was here—could do nothing, beyond warning him to be cautious, since Chauvelin himself was on his track. After having cautioned him, she would perforce have to see him go off upon his terrible and daring mission; she could not even with a word or look, attempt to keep him back. She would have to obey, whatever he told her to do, even perhaps have to efface herself, and wait, in indescribable agony, whilst he, perhaps, went to his death.

But even that seemed less terrible to bear than the thought that he should never know how much she loved him—that at any rate would be spared her; the squalid room itself, which seemed to be waiting for him, told her that he would be here soon.

Suddenly her over-sensitive ears caught the sound of distant footsteps drawing near; her heart gave a wild leap of joy! Was it Percy at last? No! the step did not seem quite as long, nor quite as firm as his; she also thought that she could hear two distinct sets of footsteps. Yes! that was it! two men were coming this way. Two strangers perhaps, to get a drink, or . . .

But she had not time to conjecture, for presently there was a peremptory call at the door, and the next moment it was violently thrown open from the outside, whilst a rough, commanding voice shouted,—

"Hey! Citoyen Brogard! Holá!"

Marguerite could not see the newcomers, but, through a hole in one of the curtains, she could observe one portion of the room below.

She heard Brogard's shuffling footsteps, as he came out of the inner room, muttering his usual string of oaths. On seeing the strangers, however, he paused in the middle of the room, well within range of Marguerite's vision, looked at them, with even more withering contempt than he had bestowed upon his former guests, and muttered, "*Sacrrrée soutane!*"

Marguerite's heart seemed all at once to stop beating; her eyes, large and dilated, had fastened on one of the newcomers, who, at this point, had taken a quick step forward towards Brogard. He was dressed in the soutane, broad-brimmed hat and buckled shoes habitual to the French *curé*, but as he stood opposite the innkeeper, he threw open his soutane for a moment, displaying the tricolour scarf of officialism, which sight immediately had the effect of transforming Brogard's attitude of contempt, into one of cringing obsequiousness.

It was the sight of this French *curé*, which seemed to freeze the very blood in Marguerite's veins. She could not see his face, which was shaded by his broad-brimmed hat, but she recognised the thin, bony hands, the slight stoop, the whole gait of the man! It was Chauvelin!

The horror of the situation struck her as with a physical blow; the awful disappointment, the dread of what was to come, made her very senses reel, and she needed almost superhuman effort, not to fall senseless beneath it all.

"A plate of soup and a bottle of wine," said Chauvelin imperiously to Brogard, "then clear out of here—understand? I want to be alone."

Silently, and without any muttering this time, Brogard obeyed. Chauvelin sat down at the table, which had been prepared for the tall Englishman, and the innkeeper busied himself obsequiously round him, dishing up the soup and pouring out the wine. The man who had entered with Chauvelin and whom Marguerite could not see, stood waiting close by the door.

At a brusque sign from Chauvelin, Brogard had hurried back to the inner room, and the former now beckoned to the man who had accompanied him.

In him Marguerite at once recognised Desgas, Chauvelin's secretary and confidential factotum, whom she had often seen in Paris, in the days gone by. He crossed the room, and for a moment or two listened attentively at the Brogards' door.

"Not listening?" asked Chauvelin, curtly.

"No, citoyen."

For a second Marguerite dreaded lest Chauvelin should order Desgas to search the place; what would happen if she were to be discovered, she hardly dared to imagine. Fortunately, however, Chauvelin seemed more impatient to talk to his secretary than afraid of spies, for he called Desgas quickly back to his side.

"The English schooner?" he asked.

"She was lost sight of at sundown, citoyen," replied Desgas, "but was then making west, towards Cap Gris Nez."

"Ah!—good!—" muttered Chauvelin, "and now, about Captain Jutley?—what did he say?"

"He assured me that all the orders you sent him last week have been implicitly obeyed. All the roads which converge to this place have been patrolled night and day ever since: and the beach and cliffs have been most rigorously searched and guarded."

"Does he know where this 'Père Blanchard's hut' is?"

"No, citoyen, nobody seems to know of it by that name. There are any amount of fishermen's huts all along the coast, of course . . . but . . ."

"That'll do. Now about to-night?" interrupted Chauvelin, impatiently.

"The roads and the beach are patrolled as usual, citoyen, and Captain Jutley awaits further orders."

"Go back to him at once, then. Tell him to send reinforcements to the various patrols; and especially to those along the beach—you understand?"

Chauvelin spoke curtly and to the point, and every word he uttered struck at Marguerite's heart like the death-knell of her fondest hopes.

"The men," he continued, "are to keep the sharpest possible look-out for any stranger who may be walking, riding, or driving, along the road or the beach, more especially for a tall stranger, whom I need not describe further, as probably he will be disguised; but he cannot very well conceal his height, except by stooping. You understand?"

"Perfectly, citoyen," replied Desgas.

"As soon as any of the men have sighted a stranger, two of them are to keep him in view. The man who loses sight of the tall stranger, after he is once seen, will pay for his negligence with his life; but one man is to ride straight back here and report to me. Is that clear?"

"Absolutely clear, citoyen."

"Very well, then. Go and see Jutley at once. See the reinforcements start off for the patrol duty, then ask the captain to let you have half-a-dozen more men and bring them here with you. You can be back in ten minutes. Go—"

Desgas saluted and went to the door.

As Marguerite, sick with horror, listened to Chauvelin's directions to his underling, the whole of the plan for the capture of the Scarlet Pimpernel became appallingly clear to her. Chauvelin wished that the fugitives should be left in false security waiting in their hidden retreat until Percy joined them. Then the daring plotter was to be surrounded and caught red-handed, in the very act of aiding and abetting royalists, who were traitors to the republic. Thus, if his capture were noised abroad, even the British Government could not legally protest in his favour; having plotted with the enemies of the French Government, France had the right to put him to death.

Escape for him and them would be impossible. All the roads patrolled and watched, the trap well set, the net, wide at present, but drawing together tighter and tighter, until it closed upon the daring plotter, whose superhuman cunning even could not rescue him from its meshes now.

Desgas was about to go, but Chauvelin once more called him back. Marguerite vaguely wondered what further devilish plans he could have formed, in order to entrap one brave man, alone, against two-score of others. She looked at him as he turned to speak to Desgas; she could just see his face beneath the broad-brimmed *curé's* hat. There was at that moment so much deadly hatred, such fiendish malice in the thin face and pale, small eyes, that Marguerite's last hope died in her heart, for she felt that from this man she could expect no mercy.

"I had forgotten," repeated Chauvelin, with a weird chuckle, as he rubbed his bony, talon-like hands one against the other, with a gesture of fiendish satisfaction. "The tall stranger may show fight. In any case no shooting, remember, except as a last resort. I want that tall stranger alive ... if possible."

He laughed, as Dante has told us that the devils laugh at sight of the torture of the damned. Marguerite had thought that by now she had lived through the whole gamut of horror and anguish that human heart could bear; yet now, when Desgas left the house, and she remained alone in this lonely, squalid room, with that fiend for company, she felt as if all that she had suffered was nothing compared with this. He continued to laugh and chuckle to himself for a while, rubbing his hands together in anticipation of his triumph.

His plans were well laid, and he might well triumph! Not a loophole was left, through which the bravest, the most cunning man might escape. Every road guarded, every corner watched, and in that lonely hut somewhere on the coast, a small band of fugitives waiting for their rescuer, and leading him to his death—nay! to worse than death. That fiend there, in a holy man's garb, was too much of a devil to allow a brave man to die the quick, sudden death of a soldier at the post of duty.

He, above all, longed to have the cunning enemy, who had so long baffled him, helpless in his power; he wished to gloat over him, to enjoy his downfall, to inflict upon him what moral and mental torture a deadly hatred alone can devise. The brave eagle, captured, and with noble wings clipped, was doomed to endure the gnawing of the rat. And she, his wife, who loved him, and who had brought him to this, could do nothing to help him.

Nothing, save to hope for death by his side, and for one brief moment in which to tell him that her love—whole, true and passionate—was entirely his.

Chauvelin was now sitting close to the table; he had taken off his hat, and Marguerite could just see the outline of his thin profile and pointed chin, as he bent over his meagre supper. He was evidently quite contented, and awaited events with perfect calm; he even seemed to enjoy Brogard's unsavoury fare. Marguerite wondered how so much hatred could lurk in one human being against another.

Suddenly, as she watched Chauvelin, a sound caught her ear, which turned her very heart to stone. And yet that sound was not calculated to inspire anyone with horror, for it was merely the cheerful sound of a gay, fresh voice singing lustily, "God save the King!"

XXV. THE EAGLE AND THE FOX

Marguerite's breath stopped short; she seemed to feel her very life standing still momentarily whilst she listened to that voice and to that song. In the singer she had recognised her husband. Chauvelin, too, had heard it, for he darted a quick glance towards the door, then hurriedly took up his broad-brimmed hat and clapped it over his head.

The voice drew nearer; for one brief second the wild desire seized Marguerite to rush down the steps and fly across the room, to stop that song at any cost, to beg the cheerful singer to fly—fly for his life, before it be too late. She checked the impulse just in time.

Chauvelin would stop her before she reached the door, and, moreover, she had no idea if he had any soldiers posted within his call. Her impetuous act might prove the death-signal of the man she would have died to save.

> *"Long to reign over us,*
> *God save the King!"*

sang the voice more lustily than ever. The next moment the door was thrown open and there was dead silence for a second or so.

Marguerite could not see the door: she held her breath, trying to imagine what was happening.

Percy Blakeney on entering had, of course, at once caught sight of the *curé* at the table; his hesitation lasted less than five seconds, the next moment Marguerite saw his tall figure crossing the room, whilst he called in a loud, cheerful voice,—

"Hello, there! no one about? Where's that fool Brogard?"

He wore the magnificent coat and riding-suit which he had on when Marguerite last saw him at Richmond, so many hours ago. As usual, his get-up was absolutely irreproachable, the fine Mechlin lace at his neck and wrists was immaculate in its gossamer daintiness, his hands looked slender and white, his fair hair was carefully brushed, and he carried his eye-glass with his usual affected gesture. In fact, at this moment, Sir Percy Blakeney, Bart., might have been on his way to a garden-party at the Prince of Wales', instead of deliberately, cold-bloodedly running his head in a trap, set for him by his deadliest enemy.

He stood for a moment in the middle of the room, whilst Marguerite, absolutely paralysed with horror, seemed unable even to breathe.

Every moment she expected that Chauvelin would give a signal, that the place would fill with soldiers, that she would rush down and help Percy to sell his life dearly. As he stood there, suavely unconscious, she very nearly screamed out to him,—

"Fly, Percy!—'tis your deadly enemy!—fly before it be too late!"

But she had not time even to do that, for the next moment Blakeney quietly walked to the table, and, jovially clapping the *curé* on the back, said in his own drawly, affected way,—

"Odd's fish! . . . er . . . M. Chauvelin. . . . I vow I never thought of meeting you here."

Chauvelin, who had been in the very act of conveying soup to his mouth, fairly choked. His thin face became absolutely purple, and a violent fit of coughing saved this cunning representative of France from betraying the most boundless surprise he had ever experienced. There was no doubt that this bold move on the part of the enemy had been wholly unexpected, as far as he was concerned: and the daring impudence of it completely nonplussed him for the moment.

Obviously he had not taken the precaution of having the inn surrounded with soldiers. Blakeney had evidently guessed that much, and no doubt his resourceful brain had already formed some plan by which he could turn this unexpected interview to account.

Marguerite up in the loft had not moved. She had made a solemn promise to Sir Andrew not to speak to her husband before strangers, and she had sufficient self-control not to throw herself unreasoningly and impulsively across his plans. To sit still and watch these two men together was a terrible trial of fortitude. Marguerite had heard Chauvelin give the orders for the patrolling of all the roads. She knew that if Percy now left the "Chat Gris"—in whichever direction he happened to go—he could not go far without being sighted by some of Captain Jutley's men on patrol. On the other hand, if he stayed, then Desgas would have time to come back with the half-dozen men Chauvelin had specially ordered.

The trap was closing in, and Marguerite could do nothing but watch and wonder. The two men looked such a strange contrast, and of the two it was Chauvelin who exhibited a slight touch of fear. Marguerite knew him well enough to guess what was passing in his mind. He had no fear for his own person, although he certainly was alone in a lonely inn with a man who was powerfully built, and who was daring and reckless beyond the bounds of probability. She knew that Chauvelin would willingly have braved perilous encounters for the sake of the cause he had at heart, but what he did fear was that this impudent Englishman would, by knocking him down, double his own chances of escape; his underlings might not succeed so well in capturing the Scarlet Pimpernel, when not directed by the cunning hand and the shrewd brain, which had deadly hate for an incentive.

Evidently, however, the representative of the French Government had nothing to fear for the moment, at the hands of his powerful adversary. Blakeney, with his most inane laugh and pleasant good-nature, was solemnly patting him on the back.

"I am so demmed sorry . . ." he was saying cheerfully, "so very sorry . . . I seem to have upset you . . . eating soup, too . . . nasty, awkward thing, soup . . . er . . . Begad!—a friend of mine died once . . . er . . . choked . . . just like you . . . with a spoonful of soup."

And he smiled shyly, good-humouredly, down at Chauvelin.

"Odd's life!" he continued, as soon as the latter had somewhat recovered himself, "beastly hole this . . . ain't it now? La! you don't mind?" he added, apologetically, as he sat down on a chair close to the table and drew the soup tureen towards him. "That fool Brogard seems to be asleep or something."

There was a second plate on the table, and he calmly helped himself to soup, then poured himself out a glass of wine.

For a moment Marguerite wondered what Chauvelin would do. His disguise was so good that perhaps he meant, on recovering himself, to deny his identity: but Chauvelin was too astute to make such an obviously false and childish move, and already he too had stretched out his hand and said pleasantly,—

"I am indeed charmed to see you, Sir Percy. You must excuse me—h'm—I thought you the other side of the Channel. Sudden surprise almost took my breath away."

"La!" said Sir Percy, with a good-humoured grin, "it did that quite, didn't it—er—M. —er—Chaubertin?"

"Pardon me—Chauvelin."

"I beg pardon—a thousand times. Yes—Chauvelin of course. . . . Er . . . I never could cotton to foreign names. . . ."

He was calmly eating his soup, laughing with pleasant good-humour, as if he had come all the way to Calais for the express purpose of enjoying supper at this filthy inn, in the company of his arch-enemy.

For the moment Marguerite wondered why Percy did not knock the little Frenchman down then and there—and no doubt something of the sort must have darted through his mind, for every now and then his lazy eyes seemed to flash ominously, as they rested on the slight figure of Chauvelin, who had now quite recovered himself and was also calmly eating his soup.

But the keen brain, which had planned and carried through so many daring plots, was too far-seeing to take unnecessary risks. This place, after all, might be infested with spies; the innkeeper might be in Chauvelin's pay. One call on Chauvelin's part might bring twenty men about Blakeney's ears for aught he knew, and he might be caught and trapped before he could help or, at least, warn the fugitives. This he would not risk; he meant to help the others, to get *them* safely away; for he had pledged his word to them, and his word he *would* keep. And whilst he ate and chatted, he thought and planned, whilst, up in the loft, the poor, anxious woman racked her brain as to what she should do, and endured agonies of longing to rush down to him, yet not daring to move for fear of upsetting his plans.

"I didn't know," Blakeney was saying jovially, "that you . . . er . . . were in holy orders."

"I . . . er . . . hem . . ." stammered Chauvelin. The calm impudence of his antagonist had evidently thrown him off his usual balance.

"But, la! I should have known you anywhere," continued Sir Percy, placidly, as he poured himself out another glass of wine, "although the wig and hat have changed you a bit."

"Do you think so?"

"Lud! they alter a man so . . . but . . . begad! I hope you don't mind my having made the remark? . . . Demmed bad form making remarks. . . . I hope you don't mind?"

"No, no, not at all—hem! I hope Lady Blakeney is well," said Chauvelin, hurriedly changing the topic of conversation.

Blakeney, with much deliberation, finished his plate of soup, drank his glass of wine, and, momentarily, it seemed to Marguerite as if he glanced quickly all round the room.

"Quite well, thank you," he said at last, drily. There was a pause, during which Marguerite could watch these two antagonists who, evidently in their minds, were measuring themselves against one another. She could see Percy almost full face where he sat at the table not ten yards from where she herself was crouching, puzzled, not knowing what to do, or what she should think. She had quite controlled her impulse by now of rushing down and disclosing herself to her husband. A man capable of acting a part, in the way he was doing at the present moment, did not need a woman's word to warn him to be cautious.

Marguerite indulged in the luxury, dear to every tender woman's heart, of looking at the man she loved. She looked through the tattered curtain, across at the handsome face of her husband, in whose lazy blue eyes, and behind whose inane smile, she could now so plainly see the strength, energy, and resourcefulness which had caused the Scarlet Pimpernel to be reverenced and trusted by his followers. "There are nineteen of us ready to lay down our lives for your husband, Lady Blakeney," Sir Andrew had said to her; and as she looked at the forehead, low, but square and broad, the eyes, blue, yet deep-set and intense, the whole aspect of the man, of indomitable energy, hiding, behind a perfectly acted comedy, his almost superhuman strength of will and marvellous ingenuity, she understood the fascination which he exercised over his followers, for had he not also cast his spells over her heart and her imagination?

Chauvelin, who was trying to conceal his impatience beneath his usual urbane manner, took a quick look at his watch. Desgas should not be long: another two or three minutes, and this impudent Englishman would be secure in the keeping of half a dozen of Captain Jutley's most trusted men.

"You are on your way to Paris, Sir Percy?" he asked carelessly.

"Odd's life, no," replied Blakeney, with a laugh. "Only as far as Lille—not Paris for me . . . beastly uncomfortable place Paris, just now . . . eh, Monsieur Chaubertin . . . beg pardon . . . Chauvelin!"

"Not for an English gentleman like yourself, Sir Percy," rejoined Chauvelin, sarcastically, "who takes no interest in the conflict that is raging there."

"La! you see it's no business of mine, and our demmed government is all on your side of the business. Old Pitt daren't say 'Bo' to a goose. You are in a hurry, sir," he added, as Chauvelin once again took out his watch; "an appointment, perhaps. . . . I pray you take no heed of me.[EOL] . . . My time's my own."

He rose from the table and dragged a chair to the hearth. Once more Marguerite was terribly tempted to go to him, for time was getting on; Desgas might be back at any moment with his men. Percy did not know that and . . . oh! how horrible it all was—and how helpless she felt.

"I am in no hurry," continued Percy, pleasantly, "but, la! I don't want to spend any more time than I can help in this God-forsaken hole! But, begad! sir," he added, as Chauvelin had surreptitiously looked at his watch for the third time, "that watch of yours won't go any faster for all the looking you give it. You are expecting a friend, maybe?"

"Aye—a friend!"

"Not a lady—I trust, Monsieur l'Abbé," laughed Blakeney; "surely the holy Church does not allow? . . . eh? . . . what! But, I say, come by the fire . . . it's getting demmed cold."

He kicked the fire with the heel of his boot, making the logs blaze in the old hearth. He seemed in no hurry to go, and apparently was quite unconscious of his immediate danger. He dragged another chair to the fire, and Chauvelin, whose impatience was by now quite beyond control, sat down beside the hearth, in such a way as to command a view of the door. Desgas had been gone nearly a quarter of an hour. It was quite plain to Marguerite's aching senses that as soon as he arrived, Chauvelin would abandon all his other plans with regard to the fugitives, and capture this impudent Scarlet Pimpernel at once.

"Hey, M. Chauvelin," the latter was saying airily, "tell me, I pray you, is your friend pretty? Demmed smart these little French women sometimes—what? But I protest I need not ask," he added, as he carelessly strode back towards the supper-table. "In matters of taste the Church has never been backward. . . . Eh?"

But Chauvelin was not listening. His every faculty was now concentrated on that door through which presently Desgas would enter. Marguerite's thoughts, too, were centred there, for her ears had suddenly caught, through the stillness of the night, the sound of numerous and measured treads some distance away.

It was Desgas and his men. Another three minutes and they would be here! Another three minutes and the awful thing would have occurred: the brave eagle would have fallen in the ferret's trap! She would have moved now and screamed, but she dared not;

for whilst she heard the soldiers approaching, she was looking at Percy and watching his every movement. He was standing by the table whereon the remnants of the supper, plates, glasses, spoons, salt and pepper-pots were scattered pell-mell. His back was turned to Chauvelin and he was still prattling along in his own affected and inane way, but from his pocket he had taken his snuff-box, and quickly and suddenly he emptied the contents of the pepper-pot into it.

Then he again turned with an inane laugh to Chauvelin,—

"Eh? Did you speak, sir?"

Chauvelin had been too intent on listening to the sound of those approaching footsteps, to notice what his cunning adversary had been doing. He now pulled himself together, trying to look unconcerned in the very midst of his anticipated triumph.

"No," he said presently, "that is—as you were saying, Sir Percy—?"

"I was saying," said Blakeney, going up to Chauvelin, by the fire, "that the Jew in Piccadilly has sold me better snuff this time than I have ever tasted. Will you honour me, Monsieur l'Abbé?"

He stood close to Chauvelin in his own careless, *débonnaire* way, holding out his snuff-box to his arch-enemy.

Chauvelin, who, as he told Marguerite once, had seen a trick or two in his day, had never dreamed of this one. With one ear fixed on those fast-approaching footsteps, one eye turned to that door where Desgas and his men would presently appear, lulled into false security by the impudent Englishman's airy manner, he never even remotely guessed the trick which was being played upon him.

He took a pinch of snuff.

Only he, who has ever by accident sniffed vigorously a dose of pepper, can have the faintest conception of the hopeless condition in which such a sniff would reduce any human being.

Chauvelin felt as if his head would burst—sneeze after sneeze seemed nearly to choke him; he was blind, deaf, and dumb for the moment, and during that moment Blakeney quietly, without the slightest haste, took up his hat, took some money out of his pocket, which he left on the table, then calmly stalked out of the room!

XXVI. THE JEW

It took Marguerite some time to collect her scattered senses; the whole of this last short episode had taken place in less than a minute, and Desgas and the soldiers were still about two hundred yards away from the "Chat Gris."

When she realised what had happened, a curious mixture of joy and wonder filled her heart. It all was so neat, so ingenious. Chauvelin was still absolutely helpless, far more so than he could even have been under a blow from the fist, for now he could neither see, nor hear, nor speak, whilst his cunning adversary had quietly slipped through his fingers.

Blakeney was gone, obviously to try and join the fugitives at the Père Blanchard's hut. For the moment, true, Chauvelin was helpless; for the moment the daring Scarlet Pimpernel had not been caught by Desgas and his men. But all the roads and the beach were patrolled. Every place was watched, and every stranger kept in sight. How far could Percy go, thus arrayed in his gorgeous clothes, without being sighted and followed? [NEW PARAGRAPH] Now she blamed herself terribly for not having gone down to him sooner, and given him that word of warning and of love which, perhaps, after all, he needed. He could not know of the orders which Chauvelin had given for his capture, and even now, perhaps . . .

But before all these horrible thoughts had taken concrete form in her brain, she heard the grounding of arms outside, close to the door, and Desgas' voice shouting "Halt!" to his men.

Chauvelin had partially recovered; his sneezing had become less violent, and he had struggled to his feet. He managed to reach the door just as Desgas' knock was heard on the outside.

Chauvelin threw open the door, and before his secretary could say a word, he had managed to stammer between two sneezes—

"The tall stranger—quick!—did any of you see him?"

"Where, citoyen?" asked Desgas, in surprise.

"Here, man! through that door! not five minutes ago."

"We saw nothing, citoyen! The moon is not yet up, and . . ."

"And you are just five minutes too late, my friend," said Chauvelin, with concentrated fury.

"Citoyen . . . I . . ."

"You did what I ordered you to do," said Chauvelin, with impatience. "I know that, but you were a precious long time about it. Fortunately, there's not much harm done, or it had fared ill with you, Citoyen Desgas."

Desgas turned a little pale. There was so much rage and hatred in his superior's whole attitude.

"The tall stranger, citoyen—" he stammered.

"Was here, in this room, five minutes ago, having supper at that table. Damn his impudence! For obvious reasons, I dared not tackle him alone. Brogard is too big a fool, and that cursed Englishman appears to have the strength of a bullock, and so he slipped away under your very nose."

"He cannot go far without being sighted, citoyen."

"Ah?"

"Captain Jutley sent forty men as reinforcements for the patrol duty: twenty went down to the beach. He again assured me that the watch has been constant all day, and that no stranger could possibly get to the beach, or reach a boat, without being sighted."

"That's good.—Do the men know their work?"

"They have had very clear orders, citoyen: and I myself spoke to those who were about to start. They are to shadow—as secretly as possible—any stranger they may see, especially if he be tall, or stoop as if he would disguise his height."

"In no case to detain such a person, of course," said Chauvelin, eagerly. "That impudent Scarlet Pimpernel would slip through clumsy fingers. We must let him get to the Père Blanchard's hut now; there surround and capture him."

"The men understand that, citoyen, and also that, as soon as a tall stranger has been sighted, he must be shadowed, whilst one man is to turn straight back and report to you."

"That is right," said Chauvelin, rubbing his hands, well pleased.

"I have further news for you, citoyen."

"What is it?"

"A tall Englishman had a long conversation about three-quarters of an hour ago with a Jew, Reuben by name, who lives not ten paces from here."

"Yes—and?" queried Chauvelin, impatiently.

"The conversation was all about a horse and cart, which the tall Englishman wished to hire, and which was to have been ready for him by eleven o'clock."

"It is past that now. Where does that Reuben live?"

"A few minutes' walk from this door."

"Send one of the men to find out if the stranger has driven off in Reuben's cart."

"Yes, citoyen."

Desgas went to give the necessary orders to one of the men. Not a word of this conversation between him and Chauvelin had escaped Marguerite, and every word they had spoken seemed to strike at her heart, with terrible hopelessness and dark foreboding.

She had come all this way, and with such high hopes and firm determination to help her husband, and so far she had been able to do nothing, but to watch, with a heart breaking with anguish, the meshes of the deadly net closing round the daring Scarlet Pimpernel.

He could not now advance many steps, without spying eyes to track and denounce him. Her own helplessness struck her with the terrible sense of utter disappointment. The possibility of being of the slightest use to her husband had become almost *nil*, and her only hope rested in being allowed to share his fate, whatever it might ultimately be.

For the moment, even her chance of ever seeing the man she loved again, had become a remote one. Still, she was determined to keep a close watch over his enemy, and a vague hope filled her heart, that whilst she kept Chauvelin in sight, Percy's fate might still be hanging in the balance.

Desgas had left Chauvelin moodily pacing up and down the room, whilst he himself waited outside for the return of the man whom he had sent in search of Reuben. Thus several minutes went by. Chauvelin was evidently devoured with impatience. Apparently he trusted no one: this last trick played upon him by the daring Scarlet Pimpernel had made him suddenly doubtful of success, unless he himself was there to watch, direct and superintend the capture of this impudent Englishman.

About five minutes later, Desgas returned, followed by an elderly Jew, in a dirty, threadbare gaberdine, worn greasy across the shoulders. His red hair, which he wore after the fashion of the Polish Jews, with the corkscrew curls each side of his face, was plentifully sprinkled with grey—a general coating of grime, about his cheeks and his chin, gave him a peculiarly dirty and loathsome appearance. He had the habitual stoop, those of his race affected in mock humility in past centuries, before the dawn of equality and freedom in matters of faith, and he walked behind Desgas with the peculiar shuffling gait which has remained the characteristic of the Jew trader in continental Europe to this day.

Chauvelin, who had all the Frenchman's prejudice against the despised race, motioned to the fellow to keep at a respectful distance. The group of the three men were standing just underneath the hanging oil-lamp, and Marguerite had a clear view of them all.

"Is this the man?" asked Chauvelin.

"No, citoyen," replied Desgas, "Reuben could not be found, so presumably his cart has gone with the stranger; but this man here seems to know something, which he is willing to sell for a consideration."

"Ah!" said Chauvelin, turning away with disgust from the loathsome specimen of humanity before him.

The Jew, with characteristic patience, stood humbly on one side, leaning on a thick knotted staff, his greasy, broad-brimmed hat casting a deep shadow over his grimy face, waiting for the noble Excellency to deign to put some questions to him.

"The citoyen tells me," said Chauvelin peremptorily to him, "that you know something of my friend, the tall Englishman, whom I desire to meet.[EOL] . . . *Morbleu!* keep your distance, man," he added hurriedly, as the Jew took a quick and eager step forward.

"Yes, your Excellency," replied the Jew, who spoke the language with that peculiar lisp which denotes Eastern origin, "I and Reuben Goldstein met a tall Englishman, on the road, close by here this evening."

"Did you speak to him?"

"He spoke to us, your Excellency. He wanted to know if he could hire a horse and cart to go down along the St. Martin Road, to a place he wanted to reach to-night."

"What did you say?"

"I did not say anything," said the Jew in an injured tone, "Reuben Goldstein, that accursed traitor, that son of Belial . . ."

"Cut that short, man," interrupted Chauvelin, roughly, "and go on with your story."

"He took the words out of my mouth, your Excellency; when I was about to offer the wealthy Englishman my horse and cart, to take him wheresoever he chose, Reuben had already spoken, and offered his half-starved nag, and his broken-down cart."

"And what did the Englishman do?"

"He listened to Reuben Goldstein, your Excellency, and put his hand in his pocket then and there, and took out a handful of gold, which he showed to that descendant of Beelzebub, telling him that all that would be his, if the horse and cart were ready for him by eleven o'clock."

"And, of course, the horse and cart were ready?"

"Well! they were ready in a manner, so to speak, your Excellency. Reuben's nag was lame as usual; she refused to budge at first. It was only after a time and with plenty of kicks, that she at last could be made to move," said the Jew with a malicious chuckle.

"Then they started?"

"Yes, they started about five minutes ago. I was disgusted with that stranger's folly. An Englishman too!—He ought to have known Reuben's nag was not fit to drive."

"But if he had no choice?"

"No choice, your Excellency?" protested the Jew, in a rasping voice, "did I not repeat to him a dozen times, that my horse and cart would take him quicker, and more comfortably than Reuben's bag of bones. He would not listen. Reuben is such a liar, and has such insinuating ways. The stranger was deceived. If he was in a hurry, he would have had better value for his money by taking my cart."

"You have a horse and cart too, then?" asked Chauvelin, peremptorily.

"Aye! that I have, your Excellency, and if your Excellency wants to drive . . ."

"Do you happen to know which way my friend went in Reuben Goldstein's cart?"

Thoughtfully the Jew rubbed his dirty chin. Marguerite's heart was beating well-nigh to bursting. She had heard the peremptory question; she looked anxiously at the Jew, but could not read his face beneath the shadow of his broad-brimmed hat. Vaguely she felt somehow as if he held Percy's fate in his long, dirty hands.

There was a long pause, whilst Chauvelin frowned impatiently at the stooping figure before him: at last the Jew slowly put his hand in his breast pocket, and drew out from its capacious depths a number of silver coins. He gazed at them thoughtfully, then remarked, in a quiet tone of voice,—

"This is what the tall stranger gave me, when he drove away with Reuben, for holding my tongue about him, and his doings."

Chauvelin shrugged his shoulders impatiently.

"How much is there there?" he asked.

"Twenty francs, your Excellency," replied the Jew, "and I have been an honest man all my life."

Chauvelin without further comment took a few pieces of gold out of his own pocket, and leaving them in the palm of his hand, he allowed them to jingle as he held them out towards the Jew.

"How many gold pieces are there in the palm of my hand?" he asked quietly.

Evidently he had no desire to terrorise the man, but to conciliate him, for his own purposes, for his manner was pleasant and suave. No doubt he feared that threats of the guillotine, and various other persuasive methods of that type, might addle the old man's brains, and that he would be more likely to be useful through greed of gain, than through terror of death.

The eyes of the Jew shot a quick, keen glance at the gold in his interlocutor's hand.

"At least five, I should say, your Excellency," he replied obsequiously.

"Enough, do you think, to loosen that honest tongue of yours?"

"What does your Excellency wish to know?"

"Whether your horse and cart can take me to where I can find my friend the tall stranger, who has driven off in Reuben Goldstein's cart?"

"My horse and cart can take your Honour there, where you please."

"To a place called the Père Blanchard's hut?"

"Your Honour has guessed?" said the Jew in astonishment.

"You know the place?"

"I know it, your Honour."

"Which road leads to it?"

"The St. Martin Road, your Honour, then a footpath from there to the cliffs."

"You know the road?" repeated Chauvelin, roughly.

"Every stone, every blade of grass, your Honour," replied the Jew quietly.

Chauvelin without another word threw the five pieces of gold one by one before the Jew, who knelt down, and on his hands and knees struggled to collect them. One rolled away, and he had some trouble to get it, for it had lodged underneath the dresser. Chauvelin quietly waited while the old man scrambled on the floor, to find the piece of gold.

When the Jew was again on his feet, Chauvelin said,—

"How soon can your horse and cart be ready?"

"They are ready now, your Honour."

"Where?"

"Not ten mètres from this door. Will your Excellency deign to look?"

"I don't want to see it. How far can you drive me in it?"

"As far as the Père Blanchard's hut, your Honour, and further than Reuben's nag took your friend. I am sure that, not two leagues from here, we shall come across that wily Reuben, his nag, his cart and the tall stranger all in a heap in the middle of the road."

"How far is the nearest village from here?"

"On the road which the Englishman took, Miquelon is the nearest village, not two leagues from here."

"There he could get fresh conveyance, if he wanted to go further?"

"He could—if he ever got so far."

"Can you?"

"Will your Excellency try?" said the Jew simply.

"That is my intention," said Chauvelin very quietly, "but remember, if you have deceived me, I shall tell off two of my most stalwart soldiers to give you such a beating, that your breath will perhaps leave your ugly body for ever. But if we find my friend the tall Englishman, either on the road or at the Père Blanchard's hut, there will be ten more gold pieces for you. Do you accept the bargain?"

The Jew again thoughtfully rubbed his chin. He looked at the money in his hand, then at his stern interlocutor, and at Desgas, who had stood silently behind him all this while. After a moment's pause, he said deliberately,—

"I accept."

"Go and wait outside then," said Chauvelin, "and remember to stick to your bargain, or by Heaven, I will keep to mine."

With a final, most abject and cringing bow, the old Jew shuffled out of the room. Chauvelin seemed pleased with his interview, for he rubbed his hands together, with that usual gesture of his, of malignant satisfaction.

"My coat and boots," he said to Desgas at last.

Desgas went to the door, and apparently gave the necessary orders, for presently a soldier entered, carrying Chauvelin's coat, boots, and hat.

He took off his soutane, beneath which he was wearing close-fitting breeches and a cloth waistcoat, and began changing his attire.

"You, citoyen, in the meanwhile," he said to Desgas, "go back to Captain Jutley as fast as you can, and tell him to let you have another dozen men, and bring them with you along the St. Martin Road, where I daresay you will soon overtake the Jew's cart with myself in it. There will be hot work presently, if I mistake not, in the Père Blanchard's hut. We shall corner our game there, I'll warrant, for this impudent Scarlet Pimpernel has had the audacity—or the stupidity, I hardly know which—to adhere to his original plans. He has gone to meet de Tournay, St. Just and the other traitors, which for the moment, I thought, perhaps, he did not intend to do. When we find them, there will be a band of desperate men at bay. Some of our men will, I presume, be put *hors de combat*. These royalists are good swordsmen, and the Englishman is devilish cunning, and looks very powerful. Still, we shall be five against one at least. You can follow the cart closely with your men, all along the St. Martin Road, through Miquelon. The Englishman is ahead of us, and not likely to look behind him."

Whilst he gave these curt and concise orders, he had completed his change of attire.

The priest's costume had been laid aside, and he was once more dressed in his usual dark, tight-fitting clothes. At last he took up his hat.

"I shall have an interesting prisoner to deliver into your hands," he said with a chuckle, as with unwonted familiarity he took Desgas' arm, and led him towards the door. "We won't kill him outright, eh, friend Desgas? The Père Blanchard's hut is—an I mistake not—a lonely spot upon the beach, and our men will enjoy a bit of rough sport there with the wounded fox. Choose your men well, friend Desgas . . . of the sort who would enjoy that type of sport—eh? We must see that Scarlet Pimpernel wither a bit—what?—shrink and tremble, eh? . . . before we finally . . ."—he made an expressive gesture, whilst he laughed a low, evil laugh, which filled Marguerite's soul with sickening horror.

"Choose your men well, Citoyen Desgas," he said once more, as he led his secretary finally out of the room.

XXVII. ON THE TRACK

Never for a moment did Marguerite Blakeney hesitate. The last sounds outside the "Chat Gris" had died away in the night. She had heard Desgas giving orders to his men, and then starting off towards the fort, to get a reinforcement of a dozen more men: six were not thought sufficient to capture the cunning Englishman, whose resourceful brain was even more dangerous than his valour and his strength.

Then a few minutes later, she heard the Jew's husky voice again, evidently shouting to his nag, then the rumble of wheels, and noise of a rickety cart bumping over the rough road.

Inside the inn, everything was still. Brogard and his wife, terrified of Chauvelin, had given no sign of life; they hoped to be forgotten, and at any rate to remain unperceived: Marguerite could not even hear their usual volleys of muttered oaths.

She waited a moment or two longer, then she quietly slipped down the broken stairs, wrapped her dark cloak closely round her and slipped out of the inn.

The night was fairly dark, sufficiently so at any rate to hide her dark figure from view, whilst her keen ears kept count of the sound of the cart going on ahead. She hoped by keeping well within the shadow of the ditches which lined the road, that she would not be seen by Desgas' men, when they approached, or by the patrols, which she concluded were still on duty.

Thus she started to do this, the last stage of her weary journey, alone, at night, and on foot. Nearly three leagues to Miquelon, and then on to the Père Blanchard's hut, wherever that fatal spot might be, probably over rough roads: she cared not.

The Jew's nag could not get on very fast, and though she was weary with mental fatigue and nerve strain, she knew that she could easily keep up with it, on a hilly road, where the poor beast, who was sure to be half-starved, would have to be allowed long and frequent rests. The road lay some distance from the sea, bordered on either side by shrubs and stunted trees, sparsely covered with meagre foliage, all turning away from the North, with their branches looking in the semi-darkness, like stiff, ghostly hair, blown by a perpetual wind.

Fortunately, the moon showed no desire to peep between the clouds, and Marguerite hugging the edge of the road, and keeping close to the low line of shrubs, was fairly safe from view. Everything around her was so still: only from far, very far away, there came like a long, soft moan, the sound of the distant sea.

The air was keen and full of brine; after that enforced period of inactivity, inside the evil-smelling, squalid inn, Marguerite would have enjoyed the sweet scent of this autumnal night, and the distant melancholy rumble of the waves; she would have revelled in the calm and stillness of this lonely spot, a calm, broken only at intervals by the strident and mournful cry of some distant gull, and by the creaking of the wheels, some way down the road: she would have loved the cool atmosphere, the peaceful immensity of Nature, in this lonely part of the coast: but her heart was too full of cruel foreboding, of a great ache and longing for a being who had become infinitely dear to her.

Her feet slipped on the grassy bank, for she thought it safest not to walk near the centre of the road, and she found it difficult to keep up a sharp pace along the muddy incline. She even thought it best not to keep too near to the cart; everything was so still, that the rumble of the wheels could not fail to be a safe guide.

The loneliness was absolute. Already the few dim lights of Calais lay far behind, and on this road there was not a sign of human habitation, not even the hut of a fisherman or of a woodcutter anywhere near; far away on her right was the edge of the cliff, below it the rough beach, against which the incoming tide was dashing itself with its constant, distant murmur. And ahead the rumble of the wheels, bearing an implacable enemy to his triumph.

Marguerite wondered at what particular spot, on this lonely coast, Percy could be at this moment. Not very far surely, for he had had less than a quarter of an hour's start of Chauvelin. She wondered if he knew that in this cool, ocean-scented bit of France, there lurked many spies, all eager to sight his tall figure, to track him to where his unsuspecting friends waited for him, and then, to close the net over him and them.

Chauvelin, on ahead, jolted and jostled in the Jew's vehicle, was nursing comfortable thoughts. He rubbed his hands together, with content, as he thought of the web which he had woven, and through which that ubiquitous and daring Englishman could not hope to escape. As the time went on, and the old Jew drove him leisurely but surely along the dark road, he felt more and more eager for the grand finale of this exciting chase after the mysterious Scarlet Pimpernel.

The capture of the audacious plotter would be the finest leaf in Citoyen Chauvelin's wreath of glory. Caught, red-handed, on the spot, in the very act of aiding and abetting the traitors against the Republic of France, the Englishman could claim no protection from his own country. Chauvelin had, in any case, fully made up his mind that all intervention should come too late.

Never for a moment did the slightest remorse enter his heart, as to the terrible position in which he had placed the unfortunate wife, who had unconsciously betrayed her husband. As a matter of fact, Chauvelin had ceased even to think of her: she had been a useful tool, that was all.

The Jew's lean nag did little more than walk. She was going along at a slow jog trot, and her driver had to give her long and frequent halts.

"Are we a long way yet from Miquelon?" asked Chauvelin from time to time.

"Not very far, your Honour," was the uniform placid reply.

"We have not yet come across your friend and mine, lying in a heap in the roadway," was Chauvelin's sarcastic comment.

"Patience, noble Excellency," rejoined the son of Moses, "they are ahead of us. I can see the imprint of the cart wheels, driven by that traitor, that son of the Amalekite."

"You are sure of the road?"

"As sure as I am of the presence of those ten gold pieces in the noble Excellency's pockets, which I trust will presently be mine."

"As soon as I have shaken hands with my friend the tall stranger, they will certainly be yours."

"Hark, what was that?" said the Jew suddenly.

Through the stillness, which had been absolute, there could now be heard distinctly the sound of horses' hoofs on the muddy road.

"They are soldiers," he added in an awed whisper.

"Stop a moment, I want to hear," said Chauvelin.

Marguerite had also heard the sound of galloping hoofs, coming towards the cart, and towards herself. For some time she had been on the alert thinking that Desgas and his squad would soon overtake them, but these came from the opposite direction, presumably from Miquelon. The darkness lent her sufficient cover. She had perceived that the cart had stopped, and with utmost caution, treading noiselessly on the soft road, she crept a little nearer.

Her heart was beating fast, she was trembling in every limb; already she had guessed what news these mounted men would bring. "Every stranger on these roads or on the beach must be shadowed, especially if he be tall or stoops as if he would disguise his height; when sighted a mounted messenger must at once ride back and report." Those had been Chauvelin's orders. Had then the tall stranger been sighted, and was this the mounted messenger, come to bring the great news, that the hunted hare had run its head into the noose at last?

Marguerite, realising that the cart had come to a standstill, managed to slip nearer to it in the darkness; she crept close up, hoping to get within earshot, to hear what the messenger had to say.

She heard the quick words of challenge—

"Liberté, Fraternité, Egalité!" then Chauvelin's quick query:—

"What news?"

Two men on horseback had halted beside the vehicle.

Marguerite could see them silhouetted against the midnight sky. She could hear their voices, and the snorting of their horses, and now, behind her, some little distance off, the regular and measured tread of a body of advancing men: Desgas and his soldiers.

There had been a long pause, during which, no doubt, Chauvelin satisfied the men as to his identity, for presently, questions and answers followed each other in quick succession.

"You have seen the stranger?" asked Chauvelin, eagerly.

"No, citoyen, we have seen no tall stranger; we came by the edge of the cliff."

"Then?"

"Less than a quarter of a league beyond Miquelon, we came across a rough construction of wood, which looked like the hut of a fisherman, where he might keep his tools and nets. When we first sighted it, it seemed to be empty, and at first we thought that there was nothing suspicious about it, until we saw some smoke issuing through an aperture at the side. I dismounted and crept close to it. It was then empty, but in one corner of the hut, there was a charcoal fire, and a couple of stools were also in the hut. I consulted with my comrades, and we decided that they should take cover with the horses, well out of sight, and that I should remain on the watch, which I did."

"Well! and did you see anything?"

"About half an hour later, I heard voices, citoyen, and presently, two men came along towards the edge of the cliff; they seemed to me to have come from the Lille Road. One was young, the other quite old. They were talking in a whisper, to one another, and I could not hear what they said." [NEW PARAGRAPH] One was young, the other quite old. Marguerite's aching heart almost stopped beating as she listened: was the young one Armand?—her brother?—and the old one de Tournay—were they the two fugitives who, unconsciously, were used as a decoy, to entrap their fearless and noble rescuer.

"The two men presently went into the hut," continued the soldier, whilst Marguerite's aching nerves seemed to catch the sound of Chauvelin's triumphant chuckle, "and I crept nearer to it then. The hut is very roughly built, and I caught snatches of their conversation."

"Yes?—Quick!—What did you hear?"

"The old man asked the young one if he were sure that was the right place. 'Oh, yes,' he replied, ''tis the place sure enough,' and by the light of the charcoal fire he showed to his companion a paper, which he carried. 'Here is the plan,' he said, 'which he gave me before I left London. We were to adhere strictly to that plan, unless I had contrary orders, and I have had none. Here is the road we followed, see . . . here the fork . . . here we cut across the St. Martin Road . . . and here is the footpath which brought us to the edge of the cliff.' I must have made a slight noise then, for the young man came to the door of the hut, and peered anxiously all round him. When he again joined his companion, they whispered so low, that I could no longer hear them."

"Well?—and?" asked Chauvelin, impatiently.

"There were six of us altogether, patrolling that part of the beach, so we consulted together, and thought it best that four should remain behind and keep the hut in sight, and I and my comrade rode back at once to make report of what we had seen."

"You saw nothing of the tall stranger?"

"Nothing, citoyen."

"If your comrades see him, what would they do?"

"Not lose sight of him for a moment, and if he showed signs of escape, or any boat came in sight, they would close in on him, and, if necessary, they would shoot: the firing would bring the rest of the patrol to the spot. In any case they would not let the stranger go."

"Aye! but I did not want the stranger hurt—not just yet," murmured Chauvelin, savagely, "but there, you've done your best. The Fates grant that I may not be too late . . ."

"We met half a dozen men just now, who have been patrolling this road for several hours."

"Well?"

"They have seen no stranger either."

"Yet he is on ahead somewhere, in a cart or else . . . . Here! there is not a moment to lose. How far is that hut from here?"

"About a couple of leagues, citoyen."

"You can find it again?—at once?—without hesitation?"

"I have absolutely no doubt, citoyen."

"The footpath, to the edge of the cliff?—Even in the dark?"

"It is not a dark night, citoyen, and I know I can find my way," repeated the soldier firmly.

"Fall in behind then. Let your comrade take both your horses back to Calais. You won't want them. Keep beside the cart, and direct the Jew to drive straight ahead; then stop him, within a quarter of a league of the footpath; see that he takes the most direct road."

Whilst Chauvelin spoke, Desgas and his men were fast approaching, and Marguerite could hear their footsteps within a hundred yards behind her now. She thought it unsafe to stay where she was, and unnecessary too, as she had heard enough. She seemed suddenly to have lost all faculty even for suffering: her heart, her nerves, her brain seemed to have become numb after all these hours of ceaseless anguish, culminating in this awful despair.

For now there was absolutely not the faintest hope. Within two short leagues of this spot, the fugitives were waiting for their brave deliverer. He was on his way, somewhere on this lonely road, and presently he would join them; then the well-laid trap would close, two dozen men, led by one whose hatred was as deadly as his cunning was malicious, would close round the small band of fugitives, and their daring leader. They would all be captured. Armand, according to Chauvelin's pledged word, would be restored to her, but her husband, Percy, whom with every breath she drew she seemed to love and worship more and more, he would fall into the hands of a remorseless enemy, who had no pity for a brave heart, no admiration for the courage of a noble soul, who would show nothing but hatred for the cunning antagonist, who had baffled him so long.

She heard the soldier giving a few brief directions to the Jew, then she retired quickly to the edge of the road, and cowered behind some low shrubs, whilst Desgas and his men came up.

All fell in noiselessly behind the cart, and slowly they all started down the dark road. Marguerite waited until she reckoned that they were well outside the range of earshot, then, she too in the darkness, which suddenly seemed to have become more intense, crept noiselessly along.

XXVIII. THE PÈRE BLANCHARD'S HUT

As in a dream, Marguerite followed on; the web was drawing more and more tightly every moment round the beloved life, which had become dearer than all. To see her husband once again, to tell him how she had suffered, how much she had wronged, and how little understood him, had become now her only aim. She had abandoned all hope of saving him: she saw him gradually hemmed in on all sides, and, in despair, she gazed round her into the darkness, and wondered whence he would presently come, to fall into the death-trap which his relentless enemy had prepared for him.

The distant roar of the waves now made her shudder; the occasional dismal cry of an owl, or a sea-gull, filled her with unspeakable horror. She thought of the ravenous beasts—in human shape—who lay in wait for their prey, and destroyed them, as mercilessly as any hungry wolf, for the satisfaction of their own appetite of hate. Marguerite was not afraid of the darkness, she only feared that man, on ahead, who was sitting at the bottom of a rough wooden cart, nursing thoughts of vengeance, which would have made the very demons in hell chuckle with delight.

Her feet were sore. Her knees shook under her, from sheer bodily fatigue. For days now she had lived in a wild turmoil of excitement; she had not had a quiet rest for three nights; now, she had walked on a slippery road for nearly two hours, and yet her determination never swerved for a moment. She would see her husband, tell him all, and, if he was ready to forgive the crime, which she had committed in her blind ignorance, she would yet have the happiness of dying by his side.

She must have walked on almost in a trance, instinct alone keeping her up, and guiding her in the wake of the enemy, when suddenly her ears, attuned to the slightest sound, by that same blind instinct, told her that the cart had stopped, and that the soldiers had halted. They had come to their destination. No doubt on the right, somewhere close ahead, was the footpath that led to the edge of the cliff and to the hut.

Heedless of any risks, she crept quite close up to where Chauvelin stood, surrounded by his little troop: he had descended from the cart, and was giving some orders to the men. These she wanted to hear: what little chance she yet had, of being useful to Percy, consisted in hearing absolutely every word of his enemy's plans.

The spot where all the party had halted must have lain some eight hundred mètres from the coast; the sound of the sea came only very faintly, as from a distance. Chauvelin and Desgas, followed by the soldiers, had turned off sharply to the right of the road, apparently on to the footpath, which led to the cliffs. The Jew had remained on the road, with his cart and nag.

Marguerite, with infinite caution, and literally crawling on her hands and knees, had also turned off to the right: to accomplish this she had to creep through the rough, low shrubs, trying to make as little noise as possible as she went along, tearing her face and hands against the dry twigs, intent only upon hearing without being seen or heard. Fortunately—as is usual in this part of France—the footpath was bordered by a low, rough hedge, beyond which was a dry ditch, filled with coarse grass. In this Marguerite managed to find shelter; she was quite hidden from view, yet could contrive to get within three yards of where Chauvelin stood, giving orders to his men.

"Now," he was saying in a low and peremptory whisper, "where is the Père Blanchard's hut?"

"About eight hundred mètres from here, along the footpath," said the soldier who had lately been directing the party, "and half-way down the cliff."

"Very good. You shall lead us. Before we begin to descend the cliff, you shall creep down to the hut, as noiselessly as possible, and ascertain if the traitor royalists are there? Do you understand?"

"I understand, citoyen."

"Now listen very attentively, all of you," continued Chauvelin, impressively, and addressing the soldiers collectively, "for after this we may not be able to exchange another word, so remember every syllable I utter, as if your very lives depended on your memory. Perhaps they do," he added drily.

"We listen, citoyen," said Desgas, "and a soldier of the Republic never forgets an order."

"You, who have crept up to the hut, will try to peep inside. If an Englishman is there with those traitors, a man who is tall above the average, or who stoops as if he would disguise his height, then give a sharp, quick whistle as a signal to your comrades. All of you," he added, once more speaking to the soldiers collectively, "then quickly surround and rush into the hut, and each seize one of the men there, before they have time to draw their firearms; if any of them struggle, shoot at their legs or arms, but on no account kill the tall man. Do you understand?"

"We understand, citoyen."

"The man who is tall above the average is probably also strong above the average; it will take four or five of you at least to overpower him."

There was a little pause, then Chauvelin continued,—

"If the royalist traitors are still alone, which is more than likely to be the case, then warn your comrades who are lying in wait there, and all of you creep and take cover behind the rocks and boulders round the hut, and wait there, in dead silence, until the tall Englishman arrives; then only rush the hut, when he is safely within its doors. But remember that you must be as silent as the wolf is at night, when he prowls around the pens. I do not wish those royalists to be on the alert—the firing of a pistol, a shriek or call on their part would be sufficient, perhaps, to warn the tall personage to keep clear of the cliffs, and of the hut, and," he added emphatically, "it is the tall Englishman whom it is your duty to capture to-night."

"You shall be implicitly obeyed, citoyen."

"Then get along as noiselessly as possible, and I will follow you."

"What about the Jew, citoyen?" asked Desgas, as silently like noiseless shadows, one by one the soldiers began to creep along the rough and narrow footpath.

"Ah, yes; I had forgotten the Jew," said Chauvelin, and, turning towards the Jew, he called him peremptorily.

"Here, you . . . Aaron, Moses, Abraham, or whatever your confounded name may be," he said to the old man, who had quietly stood beside his lean nag, as far away from the soldiers as possible.

"Benjamin Rosenbaum, so it please your Honour," he replied humbly.

"It does not please me to hear your voice, but it does please me to give you certain orders, which you will find it wise to obey."

"So it please your Honour . . ."

"Hold your confounded tongue. You shall stay here, do you hear? with your horse and cart until our return. You are on no account to utter the faintest sound, or even to breathe louder than you can help; nor are you, on any consideration whatever, to leave your post, until I give you orders to do so. Do you understand?"

"But your Honour—" protested the Jew pitiably.

"There is no question of 'but' or of any argument," said Chauvelin, in a tone that made the timid old man tremble from head to foot. "If, when I return, I do not find you here, I most solemnly assure you that, wherever you may try to hide yourself, I can find you, and that punishment swift, sure and terrible, will sooner or later overtake you. Do you hear me?"

"But your Excellency . . ."

"I said, do you hear me?"

The soldiers had all crept away; the three men stood alone together in the dark and lonely road, with Marguerite there, behind the hedge, listening to Chauvelin's orders, as she would to her own death sentence.

"I heard your Honour," protested the Jew again, while he tried to draw nearer to Chauvelin, "and I swear by Abraham, Isaac and Jacob that I would obey your Honour most absolutely, and that I would not move from this place until your Honour once more deigned to shed the light of your countenance upon your humble servant; but remember, your Honour, I am a poor old man; my nerves are not as strong as those of a young soldier. If midnight marauders should come prowling round this lonely road, I might scream or run in my fright! And is my life to be forfeit, is some terrible punishment to come on my poor old head for that which I cannot help?"

The Jew seemed in real distress; he was shaking from head to foot. Clearly he was not the man to be left by himself on this lonely road. The man spoke truly; he might unwittingly, in sheer terror, utter the shriek that might prove a warning to the wily Scarlet Pimpernel.

Chauvelin reflected for a moment.

"Will your horse and cart be safe alone, here, do you think?" he asked roughly.

"I fancy, citoyen," here interposed Desgas, "that they will be safer without that dirty, cowardly Jew than with him. There seems no doubt that, if he gets scared, he will either make a bolt of it, or shriek his head off."

"But what am I to do with the brute?"

"Will you send him back to Calais, citoyen?"

"No, for we shall want him to drive back the wounded presently," said Chauvelin, with grim significance.

There was a pause again—Desgas, waiting for the decision of his chief, and the old Jew whining beside his nag.

"Well, you lazy, lumbering old coward," said Chauvelin at last, "you had better shuffle along behind us. Here, Citoyen Desgas, tie this handkerchief tightly round the fellow's mouth."

Chauvelin handed a scarf to Desgas, who solemnly began winding it round the Jew's mouth. Meekly Benjamin Rosenbaum allowed himself to be gagged; he, evidently, preferred this uncomfortable state to that of being left alone, on the dark St. Martin Road. Then the three men fell in line.

"Quick!" said Chauvelin, impatiently, "we have already wasted much valuable time."

And the firm footsteps of Chauvelin and Desgas, the shuffling gait of the old Jew, soon died away along the footpath.

Marguerite had not lost a single one of Chauvelin's words of command. Her every nerve was strained to completely grasp the situation first, then to make a final appeal to those wits which had so often been called the sharpest in Europe, and which alone might be of service now.

Certainly the situation was desperate enough; a tiny band of unsuspecting men, quietly awaiting the arrival of their rescuer, who was equally unconscious of the trap laid for them all. It seemed so horrible, this net, as it were drawn in a circle, at dead of night, on a lonely beach, round a few defenceless men, defenceless because they were tricked and unsuspecting; of these one was the husband she idolized, another the brother she loved. She vaguely wondered who the others were, who were also calmly waiting for the Scarlet Pimpernel, while death lurked behind every boulder of the cliffs.

For the moment she could do nothing but follow the soldiers and Chauvelin. She feared to lose her way, or she would have rushed forward and found that wooden hut, and perhaps been in time to warn the fugitives and their brave deliverer yet.

For a second, the thought flashed through her mind of uttering the piercing shrieks, which Chauvelin seemed to dread, as a possible warning to the Scarlet Pimpernel and his friends—in the wild hope that they would hear, and have yet time to escape before it was too late. But she did not know how far from the edge of the cliff she was; she did not know if her shrieks would reach the ears of the doomed men. Her effort might be premature, and she would never be allowed to make another. Her mouth would be securely gagged, like that of the Jew, and she, a helpless prisoner in the hands of Chauvelin's men.

Like a ghost she flitted noiselessly behind that hedge: she had taken her shoes off, and her stockings were by now torn off her feet. She felt neither soreness nor weariness; indomitable will to reach her husband in spite of adverse Fate, and of a cunning enemy, killed all sense of bodily pain within her, and rendered her instincts doubly acute.

She heard nothing save the soft and measured footsteps of Percy's enemies on in front; she saw nothing but—in her mind's eye—that wooden hut, and he, her husband, walking blindly to his doom.

Suddenly, those same keen instincts within her made her pause in her mad haste, and cower still further within the shadow of the hedge. The moon, which had proved a friend to her by remaining hidden behind a bank of clouds, now emerged in all the glory of an early autumn night, and in a moment flooded the weird and lonely landscape with a rush of brilliant light.

There, not two hundred mètres ahead, was the edge of the cliff, and below, stretching far away to free and happy England, the sea rolled on smoothly and peaceably. Marguerite's gaze rested for an instant on the brilliant, silvery waters; and as she gazed, her heart, which had been numb with pain for all these hours, seemed to soften and distend, and her eyes filled with hot tears: not three miles away, with white sails set, a graceful schooner lay in wait.

Marguerite had guessed rather than recognised her. It was the *Day Dream*, Percy's favourite yacht, with old Briggs, that prince of skippers, aboard, and all her crew of British sailors: her white sails, glistening in the moonlight, seemed to convey a message to Marguerite of joy and hope, which yet she feared could never be. She waited there, out at sea, waited for her master, like a beautiful white bird all ready to take flight, and he would never reach her, never see her smooth deck again, never gaze any more on the white cliffs of England, the land of liberty and of hope.

The sight of the schooner seemed to infuse into the poor, wearied woman the superhuman strength of despair. There was the edge of the cliff, and some way below was the hut, where presently, her husband would meet his death. But the moon was out: she could see her way now: she would see the hut from a distance, run to it, rouse them all, warn them at any rate to be prepared and to sell their lives dearly, rather than be caught like so many rats in a hole.

She stumbled on behind the hedge in the low, thick grass of the ditch. She must have run on very fast, and had outdistanced Chauvelin and Desgas, for presently she reached the edge of the cliff, and heard their footsteps distinctly behind her. But only a very few yards away, and now the moonlight was full upon her, her figure must have been distinctly silhouetted against the silvery background of the sea.

Only for a moment, though; the next she had cowered, like some animal doubled up within itself. She peeped down the great rugged cliffs—the descent would be easy enough, as they were not precipitous, and the great boulders afforded plenty of foothold. Suddenly, as she gazed, she saw at some little distance on her left, and about midway down the cliffs, a rough wooden construction, through the walls of which a tiny red light glimmered like a beacon. Her very heart seemed to stand still, the eagerness of joy was so great that it felt like an awful pain.

She could not gauge how distant the hut was, but without hesitation she began the steep descent, creeping from boulder to boulder, caring nothing for the enemy behind, or for the soldiers, who evidently had all taken cover since the tall Englishman had not yet appeared.

On she pressed, forgetting the deadly foe on her track, running, stumbling, foot-sore, half-dazed, but still on . . . When, suddenly, a crevice, or stone, or slippery bit of rock, threw her violently to the ground. She struggled again to her feet, and started running forward once more to give them that timely warning, to beg them to flee before he came, and to tell him to keep away—away from this death-trap—away from this awful doom. But now she realised that other steps, quicker than her own, were already close at her heels. The next instant a hand dragged at her skirt, and she was down on her knees again, whilst something was wound round her mouth to prevent her uttering a scream.

Bewildered, half frantic with the bitterness of disappointment, she looked round her helplessly, and, bending down quite close to her, she saw through the mist, which seemed to gather round her, a pair of keen, malicious eyes, which appeared to her excited brain to have a weird, supernatural green light in them.

She lay in the shadow of a great boulder; Chauvelin could not see her features, but he passed his thin, white fingers over her face.

"A woman!" he whispered, "by all the Saints in the calendar."

"We cannot let her loose, that's certain," he muttered to himself. "I wonder now . . ."

Suddenly he paused, and after a few seconds of deadly silence, he gave forth a long, low, curious chuckle, while once again Marguerite felt, with a horrible shudder, his thin fingers wandering over her face.

"Dear me! dear me!" he whispered, with affected gallantry, "this is indeed a charming surprise," and Marguerite felt her resistless hand raised to Chauvelin's thin, mocking lips.

The situation was indeed grotesque, had it not been at the same time so fearfully tragic: the poor, weary woman, broken in spirit, and half frantic with the bitterness of her disappointment, receiving on her knees the *banal* gallantries of her deadly enemy.

Her senses were leaving her; half choked with the tight grip round her mouth, she had no strength to move or to utter the faintest sound. The excitement which all along had kept up her delicate body seemed at once to have subsided, and the feeling of blank despair to have completely paralysed her brain and nerves.

Chauvelin must have given some directions, which she was too dazed to hear, for she felt herself lifted from off her feet: the bandage round her mouth was made more secure, and a pair of strong arms carried her towards that tiny, red light, on ahead, which she had looked upon as a beacon and the last faint glimmer of hope.

XXIX. TRAPPED

She did not know how long she was thus carried along, she had lost all notion of time and space, and for a few seconds tired nature, mercifully, deprived her of consciousness.

When she once more realised her state, she felt that she was placed with some degree of comfort upon a man's coat, with her back resting against a fragment of rock. The moon was hidden again behind some clouds, and the darkness seemed in comparison more intense. The sea was roaring some two hundred feet below her, and on looking all round she could no longer see any vestige of the tiny glimmer of red light.

That the end of the journey had been reached, she gathered from the fact that she heard rapid questions and answers spoken in a whisper quite close to her.

"There are four men in there, citoyen; they are sitting by the fire, and seem to be waiting quietly."

"The hour?"

"Nearly two o'clock."

"The tide?"

"Coming in quickly."

"The schooner?"

"Obviously an English one, lying some three kilometres out. But we cannot see her boat."

"Have the men taken cover?"

"Yes, citoyen."

"They will not blunder?"

"They will not stir until the tall Englishman comes, then they will surround and overpower the five men."

"Right. And the lady?"

"Still dazed, I fancy. She's close beside you, citoyen."

"And the Jew?"

"He's gagged, and his legs strapped together. He cannot move or scream."

"Good. Then have your gun ready, in case you want it. Get close to the hut and leave me to look after the lady."

Desgas evidently obeyed, for Marguerite heard him creeping away along the stony cliff, then she felt that a pair of warm, thin, talon-like hands took hold of both her own, and held them in a grip of steel.

"Before that handkerchief is removed from your pretty mouth, fair lady," whispered Chauvelin close to her ear, "I think it right to give you one small word of warning. What has procured me the honour of being followed across the Channel by so charming a companion, I cannot, of course, conceive, but, if I mistake not, the purpose of this flattering attention is not one that would commend itself to my vanity, and I think that I am right in surmising, moreover, that the first sound which your pretty lips would utter, as soon as the cruel gag is removed, would be one that would perhaps prove a warning to the cunning fox, which I have been at such pains to track to his lair."

He paused a moment, while the steel-like grasp seemed to tighten round her wrist; then he resumed in the same hurried whisper:—

"Inside that hut, if again I am not mistaken, your brother, Armand St. Just, waits with that traitor de Tournay, and two other men unknown to you, for the arrival of the mysterious rescuer, whose identity has for so long puzzled our Committee of Public Safety—the audacious Scarlet Pimpernel. No doubt if you scream, if there is a scuffle here, if shots are fired, it is more than likely that the same long legs that brought this scarlet enigma here, will as quickly take him to some place of safety. The purpose then, for which I have travelled all these miles, will remain unaccomplished. On the other hand it only rests with yourself that your brother—Armand—shall be free to go off with you to-night if you like, to England, or any other place of safety."

Marguerite could not utter a sound, as the handkerchief was wound very tightly round her mouth, but Chauvelin was peering through the darkness very closely into her face; no doubt too her hand gave a responsive appeal to his last suggestion, for presently he continued:—

"What I want you to do to ensure Armand's safety is a very simple thing, dear lady."

"What is it?" Marguerite's hand seemed to convey to his, in response.

"To remain—on this spot, without uttering a sound, until I give you leave to speak. Ah! but I think you will obey," he added, with that funny dry chuckle of his as Marguerite's whole figure seemed to stiffen, in defiance of this order, "for let me tell you that if you scream, nay! if you utter one sound, or attempt to move from here, my men—there are thirty of them about—will seize St. Just, de Tournay, and their two friends, and shoot them here—by my orders—before your eyes."

Marguerite had listened to her implacable enemy's speech with ever-increasing terror. Numbed with physical pain, she yet had sufficient mental vitality in her to realise the full horror of this terrible "either—or" he was once more putting before her; an "either—or" ten thousand times more appalling and horrible, than the one he had suggested to her that fatal night at the ball.

This time it meant that she should keep still, and allow the husband she worshipped to walk unconsciously to his death, or that she should, by trying to give him a word of warning, which perhaps might even be unavailing, actually give the signal for her own brother's death, and that of three other unsuspecting men.

She could not see Chauvelin, but she could almost feel those keen, pale eyes of his fixed maliciously upon her helpless form, and his hurried, whispered words reached her ear, as the death-knell of her last faint, lingering hope.

"Nay, fair lady," he added urbanely, "you can have no interest in anyone save in St. Just, and all you need do for his safety is to remain where you are, and to keep silent. My men have strict orders to spare him in every way. As for that enigmatic Scarlet Pimpernel, what is he to you? Believe me, no warning from you could possibly save him. And now dear lady, let me remove this unpleasant coercion, which has been placed before your pretty mouth. You see I wish you to be perfectly free, in the choice which you are about to make."

Her thoughts in a whirl, her temples aching, her nerves paralyzed, her body numb with pain, Marguerite sat there, in the darkness which surrounded her as with a pall. From where she sat she could not see the sea, but she heard the incessant mournful murmur of the incoming tide, which spoke of her dead hopes, her lost love, the husband she had with her own hand betrayed, and sent to his death.

Chauvelin removed the handkerchief from her mouth. She certainly did not scream: at that moment, she had no strength to do anything but barely to hold herself upright, and to force herself to think.

Oh! think! think! think! of what she should do. The minutes flew on; in this awful stillness she could not tell how fast or how slowly; she heard nothing, she saw nothing: she did not feel the sweet-smelling autumn air, scented with the briny odour of the sea, she no longer heard the murmur of the waves, the occasional rattling of a pebble, as it rolled down some steep incline. More and more unreal did the whole situation seem. It was impossible that she, Marguerite Blakeney, the queen of London society, should actually be sitting here on this bit of lonely coast, in the middle of the night, side by side with a most bitter enemy: and oh! it was not possible that somewhere, not many hundred feet away perhaps, from where she stood, the being she had once despised, but who now, in every moment of this weird, dreamlike life, became more and more dear—it was not possible that *he* was unconsciously, even now walking to his doom, whilst she did nothing to save him.

Why did she not with unearthly screams, that would re-echo from one end of the lonely beach to the other, send out a warning to him to desist, to retrace his steps, for death lurked here whilst he advanced? Once or twice the screams rose to her throat—as if by instinct: then, before her eyes there stood the awful alternative: her brother and those three men shot before her eyes, practically by her orders: she their murderer.

Oh! that fiend in human shape, next to her, knew human—female—nature well. He had played upon her feelings as a skillful musician plays upon an instrument. He had gauged her very thoughts to a nicety.

She could not give that signal—for she was weak, and she was a woman. How could she deliberately order Armand to be shot before her eyes, to have his dear blood upon her head, he dying perhaps with a curse on her, upon his lips. And little Suzanne's father, too! he, an old man; and the others!—oh! it was all too, too horrible.

Wait! wait! wait! how long? The early morning hours sped on, and yet it was not dawn: the sea continued its incessant mournful murmur, the autumnal breeze sighed gently in the night: the lonely beach was silent, even as the grave.

Suddenly from somewhere, not very far away, a cheerful, strong voice was heard singing "God save the King!"

XXX. THE SCHOONER

Marguerite's aching heart stood still. She felt, more than she heard, the men on the watch preparing for the fight. Her senses told her that each, with sword in hand, was crouching, ready for the spring.

The voice came nearer and nearer; in the vast immensity of these lonely cliffs, with the loud murmur of the sea below, it was impossible to say how near, or how far, nor yet from which direction came that cheerful singer, who sang to God to save his King, whilst he himself was in such deadly danger. Faint at first, the voice grew louder and louder;

from time to time a small pebble detached itself apparently from beneath the firm tread of the singer, and went rolling down the rocky cliffs to the beach below.

Marguerite as she heard, felt that her very life was slipping away, as if when that voice drew nearer, when that singer became entrapped . . .

She distinctly heard the click of Desgas' gun close to her. . . .

No! no! no! no! Oh, God in heaven! this cannot be! let Armand's blood then be upon her own head! let her be branded as his murderer! let even he, whom she loved, despise and loathe her for this, but God! oh God! save him at any cost!

With a wild shriek, she sprang to her feet, and darted round the rock, against which she had been cowering; she saw the little red gleam through the chinks of the hut; she ran up to it and fell against its wooden walls, which she began to hammer with clenched fists in an almost maniacal frenzy, while she shouted,—

"Armand! Armand! for God's sake fire! your leader is near! he is coming! he is betrayed! Armand! Armand! fire in Heaven's name!"

She was seized and thrown to the ground. She lay there moaning, bruised, not caring, but still half-sobbing, half-shrieking,—

"Percy, my husband, for God's sake fly! Armand! Armand! why don't you fire?"

"One of you stop that woman screaming," hissed Chauvelin, who hardly could refrain from striking her.

Something was thrown over her face; she could not breathe, and perforce she was silent.

The bold singer, too, had become silent, warned, no doubt, of his impending danger by Marguerite's frantic shrieks. The men had sprung to their feet, there was no need for further silence on their part; the very cliffs echoed the poor, heart-broken woman's screams.

Chauvelin, with a muttered oath, which boded no good to her, who had dared to upset his most cherished plans, had hastily shouted the word of command,—

"Into it, my men, and let no one escape from that hut alive!"

The moon had once more emerged from between the clouds: the darkness on the cliffs had gone, giving place once more to brilliant, silvery light. Some of the soldiers had rushed to the rough, wooden door of the hut, whilst one of them kept guard over Marguerite.

The door was partially open; one of the soldiers pushed it further, but within all was darkness, the charcoal fire only lighting with a dim, red light the furthest corner of the hut. The soldiers paused automatically at the door, like machines waiting for further orders.

Chauvelin, who was prepared for a violent onslaught from within, and for a vigorous resistance from the four fugitives, under cover of the darkness, was for the moment paralyzed with astonishment when he saw the soldiers standing there at attention, like sentries on guard, whilst not a sound proceeded from the hut.

Filled with strange, anxious foreboding, he, too, went to the door of the hut, and peering into the gloom, he asked quickly,—

"What is the meaning of this?"

"I think, citoyen, that there is no one there now," replied one of the soldiers imperturbably.

"You have not let those four men go?" thundered Chauvelin, menacingly. "I ordered you to let no man escape alive!—Quick, after them all of you! Quick, in every direction!"

The men, obedient as machines, rushed down the rocky incline towards the beach, some going off to right and left, as fast as their feet could carry them.

"You and your men will pay with your lives for this blunder, citoyen sergeant," said Chauvelin viciously to the sergeant who had been in charge of the men; "and you, too, citoyen," he added, turning with a snarl to Desgas, "for disobeying my orders."

"You ordered us to wait, citoyen, until the tall Englishman arrived and joined the four men in the hut. No one came," said the sergeant sullenly.

"But I ordered you just now, when the woman screamed, to rush in and let no one escape."

"But, citoyen, the four men who were there before had been gone some time, I think . . ."

"You think?—You? . . ." said Chauvelin, almost choking with fury, "and you let them go . . ."

"You ordered us to wait, citoyen," protested the sergeant, "and to implicitly obey your commands on pain of death. We waited."

"I heard the men creep out of the hut, not many minutes after we took cover, and long before the woman screamed," he added, as Chauvelin seemed still quite speechless with rage.

"Hark!" said Desgas suddenly.

In the distance the sound of repeated firing was heard. Chauvelin tried to peer along the beach below, but as luck would have it, the fitful moon once more hid her light behind a bank of clouds, and he could see nothing.

"One of you go into the hut and strike a light," he stammered at last.

Stolidly the sergeant obeyed: he went up to the charcoal fire and lit the small lantern he carried in his belt; it was evident that the hut was quite empty.

"Which way did they go?" asked Chauvelin.

"I could not tell, citoyen," said the sergeant; "they went straight down the cliff first, then disappeared behind some boulders."

"Hush! what was that?"

All three men listened attentively. In the far, very far distance, could be heard faintly echoing and already dying away, the quick, sharp splash of half a dozen oars. Chauvelin took out his handkerchief and wiped the perspiration from his forehead.

"The schooner's boat!" was all he gasped.

Evidently Armand St. Just and his three companions had managed to creep along the side of the cliffs, whilst the men, like true soldiers of the well-drilled Republican army, had with blind obedience, and in fear of their lives, implicitly obeyed Chauvelin's orders —to wait for the tall Englishman, who was the important capture.

They had no doubt reached one of the creeks which jut far out to sea on this coast at intervals; behind this, the boat of the *Day Dream* must have been on the look-out for them, and they were by now safely on board the British schooner.

As if to confirm this last supposition, the dull boom of a gun was heard from out at sea.

"The schooner, citoyen," said Desgas, quietly; "she's off."

It needed all Chauvelin's nerve and presence of mind not to give way to a useless and undignified access of rage. There was no doubt now, that once again, that accursed British head had completely outwitted him. How he had contrived to reach the hut, without being seen by one of the thirty soldiers who guarded the spot, was more than Chauvelin could conceive. That he had done so before the thirty men had arrived on the cliff was, of course, fairly clear, but how he had come over in Reuben Goldstein's cart, all the way from Calais, without being sighted by the various patrols on duty was impossible of explanation. It really seemed as if some potent Fate watched over that daring Scarlet Pimpernel, and his astute enemy almost felt a superstitious shudder pass through him, as he looked round at the towering cliffs, and the loneliness of this outlying coast.

But surely this was reality! and the year of grace 1792: there were no fairies and hobgoblins about. Chauvelin and his thirty men had all heard with their own ears that accursed voice singing "God save the King," fully twenty minutes *after* they had all taken cover around the hut; by that time the four fugitives must have reached the creek, and got into the boat, and the nearest creek was more than a mile from the hut.

Where had that daring singer got to? Unless Satan himself had lent him wings, he could not have covered that mile on a rocky cliff in the space of two minutes; and only two minutes had elapsed between his song and the sound of the boat's oars away at sea. He must have remained behind, and was even now hiding somewhere about the cliffs; the patrols were still about, he would still be sighted, no doubt. Chauvelin felt hopeful once again.

One or two of the men, who had run after the fugitives, were now slowly working their way up the cliff: one of them reached Chauvelin's side, at the very moment that this hope arose in the astute diplomatist's heart.

"We were too late, citoyen," the soldier said, "we reached the beach just before the moon was hidden by that bank of clouds. The boat had undoubtedly been on the lookout behind that first creek, a mile off, but she had shoved off some time ago, when we got to the beach, and was already some way out to sea. We fired after her, but of course, it was no good. She was making straight and quickly for the schooner. We saw her very clearly in the moonlight."

"Yes," said Chauvelin, with eager impatience, "she had shoved off some time ago, you said, and the nearest creek is a mile further on."

"Yes, citoyen! I ran all the way, straight to the beach, though I guessed the boat would have waited somewhere near the creek, as the tide would reach there earliest. The boat must have shoved off some minutes before the woman began to scream."

Some minutes before the woman began to scream! Then Chauvelin's hopes had not deceived him. The Scarlet Pimpernel may have contrived to send the fugitives on ahead by the boat, but he himself had not had time to reach it; he was still on shore, and all the roads were well patrolled. At any rate, all was not yet lost, and would not be, whilst that impudent Britisher was still on French soil.

"Bring the light in here!" he commanded eagerly, as he once more entered the hut.

The sergeant brought his lantern, and together the two men explored the little place: with a rapid glance Chauvelin noted its contents: the cauldron placed close under an aperture in the wall, and containing the last few dying embers of burned charcoal, a couple of stools, overturned as if in the haste of sudden departure, then the fisherman's tools and his nets lying in one corner, and beside them, something small and white.

"Pick that up," said Chauvelin to the sergeant, pointing to this white scrap, "and bring it to me."

It was a crumpled piece of paper, evidently forgotten there by the fugitives, in their hurry to get away. The sergeant, much awed by the citoyen's obvious rage and impatience, picked the paper up and handed it respectfully to Chauvelin.

"Read it, sergeant," said the latter curtly.

"It is almost illegible, citoyen . . . a fearful scrawl. . . ."

"I ordered you to read it," repeated Chauvelin, viciously.

The sergeant, by the light of his lantern, began deciphering the few hastily scrawled words.

> "I cannot quite reach you, without risking your lives and endangering the success of your rescue. When you receive this, wait two minutes, then creep out of the hut one by one, turn to your left sharply, and creep cautiously down the cliff; keep to the left all the time, till you reach the first rock, which you see jutting far out to sea—behind it in the creek the boat is on the look-out for you—give a long, sharp whistle—she will come up—get into her—my men will row you to the schooner, and thence to England and safety—once on board the Day Dream send the boat back for me, tell my men that I shall be at the creek, which is in a direct line opposite the 'Chat Gris' near Calais. They know it. I shall be there as soon as possible—they must wait for me at a safe distance out at sea, till they hear the usual signal. Do not delay—and obey these instructions implicitly."

"Then there is the signature, citoyen," added the sergeant, as he handed the paper back to Chauvelin.

But the latter had not waited an instant. One phrase of the momentous scrawl had caught his ear. "I shall be at the creek which is in a direct line opposite the 'Chat Gris' near Calais": that phrase might yet mean victory for him.

"Which of you knows this coast well?" he shouted to his men who now one by one had all returned from their fruitless run, and were all assembled once more round the hut.

"I do, citoyen," said one of them, "I was born in Calais, and know every stone of these cliffs."

"There is a creek in a direct line from the 'Chat Gris'?"

"There is, citoyen. I know it well."

"The Englishman is hoping to reach that creek. He does *not* know every stone of these cliffs, he may go there by the longest way round, and in any case he will proceed cautiously for fear of the patrols. At any rate, there is a chance to get him yet. A thousand francs to each man who gets to that creek before that long-legged Englishman."

"I know a short cut across the cliffs," said the soldier, and with an enthusiastic shout, he rushed forward, followed closely by his comrades.

Within a few minutes their running footsteps had died away in the distance. Chauvelin listened to them for a moment; the promise of the reward was lending spurs to the soldiers of the Republic. The gleam of hate and anticipated triumph was once more apparent on his face.

Close to him Desgas still stood mute and impassive, waiting for further orders, whilst two soldiers were kneeling beside the prostrate form of Marguerite. Chauvelin gave his secretary a vicious look. His well-laid plan had failed, its sequel was problematical; there was still a great chance now that the Scarlet Pimpernel might yet escape, and Chauvelin, with that unreasoning fury, which sometimes assails a strong nature, was longing to vent his rage on somebody.

The soldiers were holding Marguerite pinioned to the ground, though she, poor soul, was not making the faintest struggle. Overwrought nature had at last peremptorily asserted herself, and she lay there in a dead swoon: her eyes circled by deep purple lines, that told of long, sleepless nights, her hair matted and damp round her forehead, her lips parted in a sharp curve that spoke of physical pain.

The cleverest woman in Europe, the elegant and fashionable Lady Blakeney, who had dazzled London society with her beauty, her wit and her extravagances, presented a very pathetic picture of tired-out, suffering womanhood, which would have appealed to any, but the hard, vengeful heart of her baffled enemy.

"It is no use mounting guard over a woman who is half dead," he said spitefully to the soldiers, "when you have allowed five men who were very much alive to escape."

Obediently the soldiers rose to their feet.

"You'd better try and find that footpath again for me, and that broken-down cart we left on the road."

Then suddenly a bright idea seemed to strike him.

"Ah! by-the-bye! where is the Jew?"

"Close by here, citoyen," said Desgas; "I gagged him and tied his legs together as you commanded."

From the immediate vicinity, a plaintive moan reached Chauvelin's ears. He followed his secretary, who led the way to the other side of the hut, where, fallen into an absolute heap of dejection, with his legs tightly pinioned together and his mouth gagged, lay the unfortunate descendant of Israel.

His face in the silvery light of the moon looked positively ghastly with terror: his eyes were wide open and almost glassy, and his whole body was trembling, as if with ague, while a piteous wail escaped his bloodless lips. The rope which had originally been wound round his shoulders and arms had evidently given way, for it lay in a tangle about his body, but he seemed quite unconscious of this, for he had not made the slightest attempt to move from the place where Desgas had originally put him: like a terrified chicken which looks upon a line of white chalk, drawn on a table, as on a string which paralyzes its movements.

"Bring the cowardly brute here," commanded Chauvelin.

He certainly felt exceedingly vicious, and since he had no reasonable grounds for venting his ill-humour on the soldiers who had but too punctually obeyed his orders, he felt that the son of the despised race would prove an excellent butt. With true French contempt of the Jew, which has survived the lapse of centuries even to this day, he would not go too near him, but said with biting sarcasm, as the wretched old man was brought in full light of the moon by the two soldiers,—

"I suppose now, that being a Jew, you have a good memory for bargains?"

"Answer!" he again commanded, as the Jew with trembling lips seemed too frightened to speak.

"Yes, your Honour," stammered the poor wretch.

"You remember, then, the one you and I made together in Calais, when you undertook to overtake Reuben Goldstein, his nag and my friend the tall stranger? Eh?"

"B . . . b . . . but . . . your Honour . . ."

"There is no 'but.' I said, do you remember?"

"Y . . . y . . . y . . . yes . . . your Honour!"

"What was the bargain?"

There was dead silence. The unfortunate man looked round at the great cliffs, the moon above, the stolid faces of the soldiers, and even at the poor, prostrate, inanimate woman close by, but said nothing.

"Will you speak?" thundered Chauvelin, menacingly.

He did try, poor wretch, but, obviously, he could not. There was no doubt, however, that he knew what to expect from the stern man before him.

"Your Honour . . ." he ventured imploringly.

"Since your terror seems to have paralyzed your tongue," said Chauvelin, sarcastically, "I must needs refresh your memory. It was agreed between us, that if we overtook my friend the tall stranger, before he reached this place, you were to have ten pieces of gold."

A low moan escaped from the Jew's trembling lips.

"But," added Chauvelin, with slow emphasis, "if you deceived me in your promise, you were to have a sound beating, one that would teach you not to tell lies."

"I did not, your Honour; I swear it by Abraham . . ."

"And by all the other patriarchs, I know. Unfortunately, they are still in Hades, I believe, according to your creed, and cannot help you much in your present trouble. Now, you did not fulfil your share of the bargain, but I am ready to fulfil mine. Here," he added, turning to the soldiers, "the buckle-end of your two belts to this confounded Jew."

As the soldiers obediently unbuckled their heavy leather belts, the Jew set up a howl that surely would have been enough to bring all the patriarchs out of Hades and elsewhere, to defend their descendant from the brutality of this French official.

"I think I can rely on you, citoyen soldiers," laughed Chauvelin, maliciously, "to give this old liar the best and soundest beating he has ever experienced. But don't kill him," he added drily.

"We will obey, citoyen," replied the soldiers as imperturbably as ever.

He did not wait to see his orders carried out: he knew that he could trust these soldiers—who were still smarting under his rebuke—not to mince matters, when given a free hand to belabour a third party.

"When that lumbering coward has had his punishment," he said to Desgas, "the men can guide us as far as the cart, and one of them can drive us in it back to Calais. The Jew and the woman can look after each other," he added roughly, "until we can send somebody for them in the morning. They can't run away very far, in their present condition, and we cannot be troubled with them just now."

Chauvelin had not given up all hope. His men, he knew, were spurred on by the hope of the reward. That enigmatic and audacious Scarlet Pimpernel, alone and with thirty men at his heels, could not reasonably be expected to escape a second time.

But he felt less sure now: the Englishman's audacity had baffled him once, whilst the wooden-headed stupidity of the soldiers, and the interference of a woman had turned his hand, which held all the trumps, into a losing one. If Marguerite had not taken up his time, if the soldiers had had a grain of intelligence, if . . . it was a long "if," and

Chauvelin stood for a moment quite still, and enrolled thirty odd people in one long, overwhelming anathema. Nature, poetic, silent, balmy, the bright moon, the calm, silvery sea spoke of beauty and of rest, and Chauvelin cursed nature, cursed man and woman, and, above all, he cursed all long-legged, meddlesome British enigmas with one gigantic curse.

The howls of the Jew behind him, undergoing his punishment, sent a balm through his heart, overburdened as it was with revengeful malice. He smiled. It eased his mind to think that some human being at least was, like himself, not altogether at peace with mankind.

He turned and took a last look at the lonely bit of coast, where stood the wooden hut, now bathed in moonlight, the scene of the greatest discomfiture ever experienced by a leading member of the Committee of Public Safety.

Against a rock, on a hard bed of stone, lay the unconscious figure of Marguerite Blakeney, while some few paces further on, the unfortunate Jew was receiving on his broad back the blows of two stout leather belts, wielded by the stolid arms of two sturdy soldiers of the Republic. The howls of Benjamin Rosenbaum were fit to make the dead rise from their graves. They must have wakened all the gulls from sleep, and made them look down with great interest at the doings of the lords of the creation.

"That will do," commanded Chauvelin, as the Jew's moans became more feeble, and the poor wretch seemed to have fainted away, "we don't want to kill him."

Obediently the soldiers buckled on their belts, one of them viciously kicking the Jew to one side.

"Leave him there," said Chauvelin, "and lead the way now quickly to the cart. I'll follow."

He walked up to where Marguerite lay, and looked down into her face. She had evidently recovered consciousness, and was making feeble efforts to raise herself. Her large, blue eyes were looking at the moonlit scene round her with a scared and terrified look; they rested with a mixture of horror and pity on the Jew, whose luckless fate and wild howls had been the first signs that struck her, with her returning senses; then she caught sight of Chauvelin, in his neat, dark clothes, which seemed hardly crumpled after the stirring events of the last few hours. He was smiling sarcastically, and his pale eyes peered down at her with a look of intense malice.

With mock gallantry, he stooped and raised her icy-cold hand to his lips, which sent a thrill of indescribable loathing through Marguerite's weary frame.

"I much regret, fair lady," he said in his most suave tones, "that circumstances, over which I have no control, compel me to leave you here for the moment. But I go away, secure in the knowledge that I do not leave you unprotected. Our friend Benjamin here, though a trifle the worse for wear at the present moment, will prove a gallant defender of your fair person, I have no doubt. At dawn I will send an escort for you; until then, I feel sure that you will find him devoted, though perhaps a trifle slow."

Marguerite only had the strength to turn her head away. Her heart was broken with cruel anguish. One awful thought had returned to her mind, together with gathering consciousness: "What had become of Percy?—What of Armand?"

She knew nothing of what had happened after she heard the cheerful song, "God save the King," which she believed to be the signal of death.

"I, myself," concluded Chauvelin, "must now very reluctantly leave you. *Au revoir,* fair lady. We meet, I hope, soon in London. Shall I see you at the Prince of Wales' garden party?—No?—Ah, well, *au revoir!*—Remember me, I pray, to Sir Percy Blakeney."

And, with a last ironical smile and bow, he once more kissed her hand, and disappeared down the footpath in the wake of the soldiers, and followed by the imperturbable Desgas.

XXXI. THE ESCAPE

Marguerite listened—half-dazed as she was—to the fast-retreating, firm footsteps of the four men.

All nature was so still that she, lying with her ear close to the ground, could distinctly trace the sound of their tread, as they ultimately turned into the road, and presently the faint echo of the old cart-wheels, the halting gait of the lean nag, told her that her enemy was a quarter of a league away. How long she lay there she knew not. She had lost count of time; dreamily she looked up at the moonlit sky, and listened to the monotonous roll of the waves.

The invigorating scent of the sea was nectar to her wearied body, the immensity of the lonely cliffs was silent and dreamlike. Her brain only remained conscious of its ceaseless, its intolerable torture of uncertainty.

She did not know!—

She did not know whether Percy was even now, at this moment, in the hands of the soldiers of the Republic, enduring—as she had done herself—the gibes and jeers of his malicious enemy. She did not know, on the other hand, whether Armand's lifeless body did not lie there, in the hut, whilst Percy had escaped, only to hear that his wife's hands had guided the human bloodhounds to the murder of Armand and his friends.

The physical pain of utter weariness was so great, that she hoped confidently her tired body could rest here for ever, after all the turmoil, the passion, and the intrigues of the last few days—here, beneath that clear sky, within sound of the sea, and with this balmy autumn breeze whispering to her a last lullaby. All was so solitary, so silent, like unto dreamland. Even the last faint echo of the distant cart had long ago died away, afar.

Suddenly . . . a sound . . . the strangest, undoubtedly, that these lonely cliffs of France had ever heard, broke the silent solemnity of the shore.

So strange a sound was it that the gentle breeze ceased to murmur, the tiny pebbles to roll down the steep incline! So strange, that Marguerite, wearied, overwrought as she was, thought that the beneficial unconsciousness of the approach of death was playing her half-sleeping senses a weird and elusive trick.

It was the sound of a good, solid, absolutely British "Damn!"

The sea-gulls in their nests awoke and looked round in astonishment; a distant and solitary owl set up a midnight hoot, the tall cliffs frowned down majestically at the strange, unheard-of sacrilege.

Marguerite did not trust her ears. Half-raising herself on her hands, she strained every sense to see or hear, to know the meaning of this very earthly sound.

All was still again for the space of a few seconds; the same silence once more fell upon the great and lonely vastness.

Then Marguerite, who had listened as in a trance, who felt she must be dreaming with that cool, magnetic moonlight overhead, heard again; and this time her heart stood still, her eyes large and dilated, looked round her, not daring to trust to her other sense.

"Odd's life! but I wish those demmed fellows had not hit quite so hard!"

This time it was quite unmistakable, only one particular pair of essentially British lips could have uttered those words, in sleepy, drawly, affected tones.

"Damn!" repeated those same British lips, emphatically. "Zounds! but I'm as weak as a rat!"

In a moment Marguerite was on her feet.

Was she dreaming? Were those great, stony cliffs the gates of paradise? Was the fragrant breath of the breeze suddenly caused by the flutter of angels' wings, bringing tidings of unearthly joys to her, after all her suffering, or—faint and ill—was she the prey of delirium?

She listened again, and once again she heard the same very earthly sounds of good, honest British language, not the least akin to whisperings from paradise or flutter of angels' wings.

She looked round her eagerly at the tall cliffs, the lonely hut, the great stretch of rocky beach. Somewhere there, above or below her, behind a boulder or inside a crevice, but still hidden from her longing, feverish eyes, must be the owner of that voice, which once used to irritate her, but which now would make her the happiest woman in Europe, if only she could locate it.

"Percy! Percy!" she shrieked hysterically, tortured between doubt and hope, "I am here! Come to me! Where are you? Percy! Percy! . . ."

"It's all very well calling me, m'dear!" said the same sleepy, drawly voice, "but odd's my life, I cannot come to you: those demmed frog-eaters have trussed me like a goose on a spit, and I am as weak as a mouse . . . I cannot get away."

And still Marguerite did not understand. She did not realise for at least another ten seconds whence came that voice, so drawly, so dear, but alas! with a strange accent of weakness and of suffering. There was no one within sight . . . except by that rock . . . Great God! . . . the Jew! . . . Was she mad or dreaming? . . .

His back was against the pale moonlight, he was half-crouching, trying vainly to raise himself with his arms tightly pinioned. Marguerite ran up to him, took his head in both her hands . . . and looked straight into a pair of blue eyes, good-natured, even a trifle amused—shining out of the weird and distorted mask of the Jew.

"Percy! . . . Percy! . . . my husband!" she gasped, faint with the fulness of her joy. "Thank God! Thank God!"

"La! m'dear," he rejoined good-humouredly, "we will both do that anon, an you think you can loosen these demmed ropes, and release me from my inelegant attitude."

She had no knife, her fingers were numb and weak, but she worked away with her teeth, while great welcome tears poured from her eyes, onto those poor, pinioned hands.

"Odd's life!" he said, when at last, after frantic efforts on her part, the ropes seemed at last to be giving way, "but I marvel whether it has ever happened before, that an English gentleman allowed himself to be licked by a demmed foreigner, and made no attempt to give as good as he got."

It was very obvious that he was exhausted from sheer physical pain, and when at last the rope gave way, he fell in a heap against the rock.

Marguerite looked helplessly round her.

"Oh! for a drop of water on this awful beach!" she cried in agony, seeing that he was ready to faint again.

"Nay, m'dear," he murmured with his good-humoured smile, "personally I should prefer a drop of good French brandy! an you'll dive in the pocket of this dirty old garment, you'll find my flask. . . . I am demmed if I can move."

When he had drunk some brandy, he forced Marguerite to do likewise.

"La! that's better now! Eh! little woman?" he said, with a sigh of satisfaction. "Heigh-ho! but this is a queer rig-up for Sir Percy Blakeney, Bart., to be found in by his lady, and no mistake. Begad!" he added, passing his hand over his chin, "I haven't been shaved for nearly twenty hours: I must look a disgusting object. As for these curls . . ."

And laughingly he took off the disfiguring wig and curls, and stretched out his long limbs, which were cramped from many hours' stooping. Then he bent forward and looked long and searchingly into his wife's blue eyes.

"Percy," she whispered, while a deep blush suffused her delicate cheeks and neck, "if you only knew . . ."

"I do know, dear . . . everything," he said with infinite gentleness.

"And can you ever forgive?"

"I have naught to forgive, sweetheart; your heroism, your devotion, which I, alas! so little deserved, have more than atoned for that unfortunate episode at the ball."

"Then you knew? . . ." she whispered, "all the time . . ."

"Yes!" he replied tenderly, "I knew . . . all the time. . . . But, begad! had I but known what a noble heart yours was, my Margot, I should have trusted you, as you deserved to be trusted, and you would not have had to undergo the terrible sufferings of the past few hours, in order to run after a husband, who has done so much that needs forgiveness."

They were sitting side by side, leaning up against a rock, and he had rested his aching head on her shoulder. She certainly now deserved the name of "the happiest woman in Europe."

"It is a case of the blind leading the lame, sweetheart, is it not?" he said with his good-natured smile of old. "Odd's life! but I do not know which are the more sore, my shoulders or your little feet."

He bent forward to kiss them, for they peeped out through her torn stockings, and bore pathetic witness to her endurance and devotion.

"But Armand . . ." she said, with sudden terror and remorse, as in the midst of her happiness the image of the beloved brother, for whose sake she had so deeply sinned, rose now before her mind.

"Oh! have no fear for Armand, sweetheart," he said tenderly, "did I not pledge you my word that he should be safe? He with de Tournay and the others are even now on board the *Day Dream*."

"But how?" she gasped, "I do not understand."

"Yet, 'tis simple enough, m'dear," he said with that funny, half-shy, half-inane laugh of his, "you see! when I found that that brute Chauvelin meant to stick to me like a leech, I thought the best thing I could do, as I could not shake him off, was to take him along with me. I had to get to Armand and the others somehow, and all the roads were patrolled, and everyone on the look-out for your humble servant. I knew that when I slipped through Chauvelin's fingers at the 'Chat Gris,' that he would lie in wait for me here, whichever way I took. I wanted to keep an eye on him and his doings, and a British head is as good as a French one any day."

Indeed it had proved to be infinitely better, and Marguerite's heart was filled with joy and marvel, as he continued to recount to her the daring manner in which he had snatched the fugitives away, right from under Chauvelin's very nose.

"Dressed as the dirty old Jew," he said gaily, "I knew I should not be recognised. I had met Reuben Goldstein in Calais earlier in the evening. For a few gold pieces he supplied me with this rig-out, and undertook to bury himself out of sight of everybody, whilst he lent me his cart and nag."

"But if Chauvelin had discovered you," she gasped excitedly, "your disguise was good... but he is so sharp."

"Odd's fish!" he rejoined quietly, "then certainly the game would have been up. I could but take the risk. I know human nature pretty well by now," he added, with a note of sadness in his cheery, young voice, "and I know these Frenchmen out and out. They so loathe a Jew, that they never come nearer than a couple of yards of him, and begad! I fancy that I contrived to make myself look about as loathsome an object as it is possible to conceive."

"Yes!—and then?" she asked eagerly.

"Zooks!—then I carried out my little plan: that is to say, at first I only determined to leave everything to chance, but when I heard Chauvelin giving his orders to the soldiers, I thought that Fate and I were going to work together after all. I reckoned on the blind obedience of the soldiers. Chauvelin had ordered them on pain of death not to stir until the tall Englishman came. Desgas had thrown me down in a heap quite close to the hut; the soldiers took no notice of the Jew, who had driven Citoyen Chauvelin to this spot. I managed to free my hands from the ropes, with which the brute had trussed me; I always carry pencil and paper with me wherever I go, and I hastily scrawled a few important instructions on a scrap of paper; then I looked about me. I crawled up to the hut, under the very noses of the soldiers, who lay under cover without stirring, just as Chauvelin had ordered them to do, then I dropped my little note into the hut, through a chink in the wall, and waited. In this note I told the fugitives to walk noiselessly out of the hut, creep down the cliffs, keep to the left until they came to the first creek, to give a certain signal, when the boat of the *Day Dream*, which lay in wait not far out to sea, would pick them up. They obeyed implicitly, fortunately for them and for me. The soldiers who saw them were equally obedient to Chauvelin's orders. They did not stir! I waited for nearly half an hour; when I knew that the fugitives were safe I gave the signal, which caused so much stir."

And that was the whole story. It seemed so simple! and Marguerite could but marvel at the wonderful ingenuity, the boundless pluck and audacity which had evolved and helped to carry out this daring plan.

"But those brutes struck you!" she gasped in horror, at the bare recollection of the fearful indignity.

"Well! that could not be helped," he said gently, "whilst my little wife's fate was so uncertain, I had to remain here by her side. Odd's life!" he added merrily, "never fear! Chauvelin will lose nothing by waiting, I warrant! Wait till I get him back to England!— La! he shall pay for the thrashing he gave me with compound interest, I promise you."

Marguerite laughed. It was so good to be beside him, to hear his cheery voice, to watch that good-humoured twinkle in his blue eyes, as he stretched out his strong arms, in longing for that foe, and anticipation of his well-deserved punishment.

Suddenly, however, she started: the happy blush left her cheek, the light of joy died out of her eyes: she had heard a stealthy footfall overhead, and a stone had rolled down from the top of the cliffs right down to the beach below.

"What's that?" she whispered in horror and alarm.

"Oh! nothing, m'dear," he muttered with a pleasant laugh, "only a trifle you happened to have forgotten . . . my friend, Ffoulkes . . ."

"Sir Andrew!" she gasped.

Indeed, she had wholly forgotten the devoted friend and companion, who had trusted and stood by her during all these hours of anxiety and suffering. She remembered him now, tardily and with a pang of remorse.

"Aye! you had forgotten him, hadn't you, m'dear?" said Sir Percy, merrily. "Fortunately, I met him, not far from the 'Chat Gris,' before I had that interesting supper party, with my friend Chauvelin. . . . Odd's life! but I have a score to settle with that young reprobate!—but in the meanwhile, I told him of a very long, very roundabout road, that would bring him here by a very circuitous road which Chauvelin's men would never suspect, just about the time when we are ready for him, eh, little woman?"

"And he obeyed?" asked Marguerite, in utter astonishment.

"Without word or question. See, here he comes. He was not in the way when I did not want him, and now he arrives in the nick of time. Ah! he will make pretty little Suzanne a most admirable and methodical husband."

In the meanwhile Sir Andrew Ffoulkes had cautiously worked his way down the cliffs: he stopped once or twice, pausing to listen for the whispered words, which would guide him to Blakeney's hiding-place.

"Blakeney!" he ventured to say at last cautiously, "Blakeney! are you there?"

The next moment he rounded the rock against which Sir Percy and Marguerite were leaning, and seeing the weird figure still clad in the long Jew's gaberdine, he paused in sudden, complete bewilderment.

But already Blakeney had struggled to his feet.

"Here I am, friend," he said with his funny, inane laugh, "all alive! though I do look a begad scarecrow in these demmed things."

"Zooks!" ejaculated Sir Andrew in boundless astonishment as he recognised his leader, "of all the . . ."

The young man had seen Marguerite, and happily checked the forcible language that rose to his lips, at sight of the exquisite Sir Percy in this weird and dirty garb.

"Yes!" said Blakeney, calmly, "of all the . . . hem! . . . My friend!—I have not yet had time to ask you what you were doing in France, when I ordered you to remain in London? Insubordination? What? Wait till my shoulders are less sore, and, by Gad, see the punishment you'll get."

"Odd's fish! I'll bear it," said Sir Andrew, with a merry laugh, "seeing that you are alive to give it. . . . Would you have had me allow Lady Blakeney to do the journey alone? But, in the name of heaven, man, where did you get these extraordinary clothes?"

"Lud! they are a bit quaint, ain't they?" laughed Sir Percy, jovially. "But, odd's fish!" he added, with sudden earnestness and authority, "now you are here, Ffoulkes, we must lose no more time: that brute Chauvelin may send some one to look after us."

Marguerite was so happy, she could have stayed here for ever, hearing his voice, asking a hundred questions. But at mention of Chauvelin's name she started in quick alarm, afraid for the dear life she would have died to save.

"But how can we get back?" she gasped; "the roads are full of soldiers between here and Calais, and . . ."

"We are not going back to Calais, sweetheart," he said, "but just the other side of Gris Nez, not half a league from here. The boat of the *Day Dream* will meet us there."

"The boat of the *Day Dream*?"

"Yes!" he said, with a merry laugh; "another little trick of mine. I should have told you before that when I slipped that note into the hut, I also added another for Armand, which I directed him to leave behind, and which has sent Chauvelin and his men running full tilt back to the 'Chat Gris' after me; but the first little note contained my real instructions, including those to old Briggs. He had my orders to go out further to sea, and then towards the west. When well out of sight of Calais, he will send the galley to a little creek he and I know of, just beyond Gris Nez. The men will look out for me—we have a preconcerted signal, and we will all be safely aboard, whilst Chauvelin and his men solemnly sit and watch the creek which is 'just opposite the "Chat Gris."'"

"The other side of Gris Nez? But I . . . I cannot walk, Percy," she moaned helplessly as, trying to struggle to her tired feet, she found herself unable even to stand.

"I will carry you, dear," he said simply; "the blind leading the lame, you know."

Sir Andrew was ready, too, to help with the precious burden, but Sir Percy would not entrust his beloved to any arms but his own.

"When you and she are both safely on board the *Day Dream*," he said to his young comrade, "and I feel that Mlle. Suzanne's eyes will not greet me in England with reproachful looks, then it will be my turn to rest."

And his arms, still vigorous in spite of fatigue and suffering, closed round Marguerite's poor, weary body, and lifted her as gently as if she had been a feather.

Then, as Sir Andrew discreetly kept out of earshot, there were many things said—or rather whispered—which even the autumn breeze did not catch, for it had gone to rest.

All his fatigue was forgotten; his shoulders must have been very sore, for the soldiers had hit hard, but the man's muscles seemed made of steel, and his energy was almost supernatural. It was a weary tramp, half a league along the stony side of the cliffs, but never for a moment did his courage give way or his muscles yield to fatigue. On he tramped, with firm footstep, his vigorous arms encircling the precious burden, and . . . no doubt, as she lay, quiet and happy, at times lulled to momentary drowsiness, at others watching, through the slowly gathering morning light, the pleasant face with the lazy, drooping blue eyes, ever cheerful, ever illumined with a good-humoured smile, she whispered many things, which helped to shorten the weary road, and acted as a soothing balsam to his aching sinews.

The many-hued light of dawn was breaking in the east, when at last they reached the creek beyond Gris Nez. The galley lay in wait: in answer to a signal from Sir Percy, she drew near, and two sturdy British sailors had the honour of carrying my lady into the boat.

Half an hour later, they were on board the *Day Dream*. The crew, who of necessity were in their master's secrets, and who were devoted to him heart and soul, were not surprised to see him arriving in so extraordinary a disguise.

Armand St. Just and the other fugitives were eagerly awaiting the advent of their brave rescuer; he would not stay to hear the expressions of their gratitude, but found his way to his private cabin as quickly as he could, leaving Marguerite quite happy in the arms of her brother.

Everything on board the *Day Dream* was fitted with that exquisite luxury, so dear to Sir Percy Blakeney's heart, and by the time they all landed at Dover he had found time to get into some of the sumptuous clothes which he loved, and of which he always kept a supply on board his yacht.

The difficulty was to provide Marguerite with a pair of shoes, and great was the little middy's joy when my lady found that she could put foot on English shore in his best pair.

The rest is silence!—silence and joy for those who had endured so much suffering, yet found at last a great and lasting happiness.

But it is on record that at the brilliant wedding of Sir Andrew Ffoulkes, Bart., with Mlle. Suzanne de Tournay de Basserive, a function at which H.R.H. the Prince of Wales and all the *élite* of fashionable society were present, the most beautiful woman there was unquestionably Lady Blakeney, whilst the clothes Sir Percy Blakeney wore were the talk of the *jeunesse dorée* of London for many days.

It is also a fact that M. Chauvelin, the accredited agent of the French Republican Government, was not present at that or any other social function in London, after that memorable evening at Lord Grenville's ball.

I WILL REPAY

An Adventure of the Scarlet Pimpernel

I WILL REPAY

PROLOGUE

I. Paris 1783

"Coward! Coward! Coward!"

The words rang out, clear, strident, passionate, in a crescendo of agonised humiliation.

The boy, quivering with rage, had sprung to his feet, and, losing his balance, he fell forward clutching at the table, whilst with a convulsive movement of the lids, he tried in vain to suppress the tears of shame which were blinding him.

"Coward!" He tried to shout the insult so that all might hear, but his parched throat refused him service, his trembling hand sought the scattered cards upon the table, he collected them together, quickly, nervously, fingering them with feverish energy, then he hurled them at the man opposite, whilst with a final effort he still contrived to mutter: "Coward!"

The older men tried to interpose, but the young ones only laughed, quite prepared for the adventure which must inevitably ensue, the only possible ending to a quarrel such as this.

Conciliation or arbitration was out of the question. Déroulède should have known better than to speak disrespectfully of Adèle de Montchéri, when the little Vicomte de Marny's infatuation for the notorious beauty had been the talk of Paris and Versailles these many months past.

Adèle was very lovely and a veritable tower of greed and egotism. The Marnys were rich and the little Vicomte very young, and just now the brightly-plumaged hawk was busy plucking the latest pigeon, newly arrived from its ancestral cote.

The boy was still in the initial stage of his infatuation. To him Adèle was a paragon of all the virtues, and he would have done battle on her behalf against the entire aristocracy of France, in a vain endeavour to justify his own exalted opinion of one of the most dissolute women of the epoch. He was a first-rate swordsman too, and his friends had already learned that it was best to avoid all allusions to Adèle's beauty and weaknesses.

But Déroulède was a noted blunderer. He was little versed in the manners and tones of that high society in which, somehow, he still seemed an intruder. But for his great wealth, no doubt, he never would have been admitted within the intimate circle of aristocratic France. His ancestry was somewhat doubtful and his coat-of-arms unadorned with quarterings.

But little was known of his family or the origin of its wealth; it was only known that his father had suddenly become the late King's dearest friend, and commonly surmised that Déroulède gold had on more than one occasion filled the emptied coffers of the First Gentleman of France.

Déroulède had not sought the present quarrel. He had merely blundered in that clumsy way of his, which was no doubt a part of the inheritance bequeathed to him by his bourgeois ancestry.

He knew nothing of the little Vicomte's private affairs, still less of his relationship with Adèle, but he knew enough of the world and enough of Paris to be acquainted with the lady's reputation. He hated at all times to speak of women. He was not what in those days would be termed a ladies' man, and was even somewhat unpopular with the sex. But in this instance the conversation had drifted in that direction, and when Adèle's name was mentioned, every one became silent, save the little Vicomte, who waxed enthusiastic.

A shrug of the shoulders on Déroulède's part had aroused the boy's ire, then a few casual words, and, without further warning, the insult had been hurled and the cards thrown in the older man's face.

Déroulède did not move from his seat. He sat erect and placid, one knee crossed over the other, his serious, rather swarthy face perhaps a shade paler than usual: otherwise it seemed as if the insult had never reached his ears, or the cards struck his cheek.

He had perceived his blunder, just twenty seconds too late. Now he was sorry for the boy and angered with himself, but it was too late to draw back. To avoid a conflict he would at this moment have sacrificed half his fortune, but not one particle of his dignity.

He knew and respected the old Duc de Marny, a feeble old man now, almost a dotard whose hitherto spotless *blason* , the young Vicomte, his son, was doing his best to besmirch.

When the boy fell forward, blind and drunk with rage, Déroulède leant towards him automatically, quite kindly, and helped him to his feet. He would have asked the lad's pardon for his own thoughtlessness, had that been possible: but the stilted code of so-called honour forbade so logical a proceeding. It would have done no good, and could but imperil his own reputation without averting the traditional sequel.

The panelled walls of the celebrated gaming saloon had often witnessed scenes such as this. All those present acted by routine. The etiquette of dueling prescribed certain formalities, and these were strictly but rapidly adhered to.

The young Vicomte was quickly surrounded by a close circle of friends. His great name, his wealth, his father's influence, had opened for him every door in Versailles and

Paris. At this moment he might have had an army of seconds to support him in the coming conflict.

Déroulède for a while was left alone near the card table, where the unsnuffed candles began smouldering in their sockets. He had risen to his feet, somewhat bewildered at the rapid turn of events. His dark, restless eyes wandered for a moment round the room, as if in quick search for a friend.

But where the Vicomte was at home by right, Déroulède had only been admitted by reason of his wealth. His acquaintances and sycophants were many, but his friends very few.

For the first time this fact was brought home to him. Every one in the room must have known and realised that he had not willfully sought this quarrel, that throughout he had borne himself as any gentleman would, yet now, when the issue was so close at hand, no one came forward to stand by him.

"For form's sake, monsieur, will you choose your seconds?"

It was the young Marquis de Villefranche who spoke, a little haughtily, with a certain ironical condescension towards the rich parvenu, who was about to have the honour of crossing swords with one of the noblest gentlemen in France.

"I pray you, Monsieur le Marquis," rejoined Déroulède coldly, "to make the choice for me. You see, I have few friends in Paris."

The Marquis bowed, and gracefully flourished his lace handkerchief. He was accustomed to being appealed to in all matters pertaining to etiquette, to the toilet, to the latest cut in coats, and the procedure in duels. Good-natured, foppish, and idle, he felt quite happy and in his element thus to be made chief organizer of the tragic farce, about to be enacted on the parquet floor of the gaming saloon.

He looked about the room for a while, scrutinizing the faces of those around him. The gilded youth was crowding round De Marny; a few older men stood in a group at the farther end of the room: to these the Marquis turned, and addressing one of them, an elderly man with a military bearing and a shabby brown coat:

"Mon Colonel," he said, with another flourishing bow; "I am deputed by M. Déroulède to provide him with seconds for this affair of honour, may I call upon you to ..."

"Certainly, certainly," replied the Colonel. "I am not intimately acquainted with M. Déroulède, but since you stand sponsor, M. le Marquis ..."

"Oh!" rejoined the Marquis, lightly, "a mere matter of form, you know. M. Déroulède belongs to the entourage of Her Majesty. He is a man of honour. But I am not his sponsor. Marny is my friend, and if you prefer not to ..."

"Indeed I am entirely at M. Déroulède's service," said the Colonel, who had thrown a quick, scrutinizing glance at the isolated figure near the card table, "if he will accept my services ..."

"He will be very glad to accept, my dear Colonel," whispered the Marquis with an ironical twist of his aristocratic lips. "He has no friends in our set, and if you and De Quettare will honour him, I think he should be grateful."

M. de Quettare, adjutant to M. le Colonel, was ready to follow in the footsteps of his chief, and the two men, after the prescribed salutations to M. le Marquis de Villefranche, went across to speak to Déroulède.

"If you will accept our services, monsieur," began the Colonel abruptly, "mine, and my adjutant's, M. de Quettare, we place ourselves entirely at your disposal."

"I thank you, messieurs," rejoined Déroulède. "The whole thing is a farce, and that young man is a fool; but I have been in the wrong and ..."

"You would wish to apologise?" queried the Colonel icily.

The worthy soldier had heard something of Déroulède's reputed bourgeois ancestry. This suggestion of an apology was no doubt in accordance with the customs of the middle-classes, but the Colonel literally gasped at the unworthiness of the proceeding. An apology? Bah! Disgusting! cowardly! beneath the dignity of any gentleman, however wrong he might be. How could two soldiers of His Majesty's army identify themselves with such doings?

But Déroulède seemed unconscious of the enormity of his suggestion.

"If I could avoid a conflict," he said, "I would tell the Vicomte that I had no knowledge of his admiration for the lady we were discussing and ..."

"Are you so very much afraid of getting a sword scratch, monsieur?" interrupted the Colonel impatiently, whilst M. de Quettare elevated a pair of aristocratic eyebrows in bewilderment at such an extraordinary display of bourgeois cowardice.

"You mean, Monsieur le Colonel?"—queried Déroulède.

"That you must either fight the Vicomte de Marny to-night, or clear out of Paris to-morrow. Your position in our set would become untenable," retorted the Colonel, not unkindly, for in spite of Déroulède's extraordinary attitude, there was nothing in his bearing or his appearance that suggested cowardice or fear.

"I bow to your superior knowledge of your friends, M. le Colonel," responded Déroulède, as he silently drew his sword from its sheath.

The centre of the saloon was quickly cleared. The seconds measured the length of the swords and then stood behind the antagonists, slightly in advance of the groups of spectators, who stood massed all round the room.

They represented the flower of what France had of the best and noblest in name, in lineage, in chivalry, in that year of grace 1783. The storm-cloud which a few years hence was destined to break over their heads, sweeping them from their palaces to the prison and the guillotine, was only gathering very slowly in the dim horizon of squalid, starving Paris: for the next half-dozen years they would still dance and gamble, fight and flirt, surround a tottering throne, and hoodwink a weak monarch. The Fates' avenging sword still rested in its sheath; the relentless, ceaseless wheel still bore them up in their whirl of pleasure; the downward movement had only just begun: the cry of the oppressed children of France had not yet been heard above the din of dance music and lovers' serenades.

The young Duc de Châteaudun was there, he who, nine years later, went to the guillotine on that cold September morning, his hair dressed in the latest fashion, the finest Mechlin lace around his wrists, playing a final game of piquet with his younger brother, as the tumbril bore them along through the hooting, yelling crowd of the half-naked starvelings of Paris.

There was the Vicomte de Mirepoix, who, a few years later, standing on the platform of the guillotine, laid a bet with M. de Miranges that his own blood would flow bluer than that of any other head cut off that day in France. Citizen Samson heard the bet made, and when De Mirepoix's head fell into the basket, the headsman lifted it up for M. de Miranges to see. The latter laughed.

"Mirepoix was always a braggart," he said lightly, as he laid his head upon the block. "Who'll take my bet that my blood turns out to be bluer than his?"

But of all these comedies, these tragico-farces of later years, none who were present on that night, when the Vicomte de Marny fought Paul Déroulède, had as yet any presentiment.

They watched the two men fighting, with the same casual interest, at first, which they would have bestowed on the dancing of a new movement in the minuet.

De Marny came of a race that had wielded the sword of many centuries, but he was hot, excited, not a little addled with wine and rage. Déroulède was lucky; he would come out of the affair with a slight scratch.

A good swordsman too, that wealthy parvenu. It was interesting to watch his swordplay: very quiet at first, no feint or parry, scarcely a riposte, only *en garde,* always *en garde* very carefully, steadily, ready for his antagonist at every turn and in every circumstance.

Gradually the circle round the combatants narrowed. A few discreet exclamations of admiration greeted Déroulède's most successful parry. De Marny was getting more and more excited, the older man more and more sober and reserved.

A thoughtless lunge placed the little Vicomte at his opponent's mercy. The next instant he was disarmed, and the seconds were pressing forward to end the conflict.

Honour was satisfied: the parvenu and the scion of the ancient race had crossed swords over the reputation of one of the most dissolute women in France. Déroulède's moderation was a lesson to all the hot-headed young bloods who toyed with their lives, their honour, their reputation as lightly as they did with their lace-edged handkerchiefs and gold snuff-boxes.

Already Déroulède had drawn back. With the gentle tact peculiar to kindly people, he avoided looking at his disarmed antagonist. But something in the older man's attitude seemed to further nettle the over-stimulated sensibility of the young Vicomte.

"This is no child's play, monsieur," he said excitedly. "I demand full satisfaction."

"And are you not satisfied?" queried Déroulède. "You have borne yourself bravely, you have fought in honour of your liege lady. I, on the other hand ..."

"You," shouted the boy hoarsely, "you shall publicly apologise to a noble and virtuous woman whom you have outraged—now—at—once—on your knees ..."

"You are mad, Vicomte," rejoined Déroulède coldly. "I am willing to ask your forgiveness for my blunder ..."

"An apology—in public—on your knees ..."

The boy had become more and more excited. He had suffered humiliation after humiliation. He was a mere lad, spoilt, adulated, pampered from his boyhood: the wine had got into his head, the intoxication of rage and hatred blinded his saner judgment.

"Coward!" he shouted again and again.

His seconds tried to interpose, but he waved them feverishly aside. He would listen to no one. He saw no one save the man who had insulted Adèle, and who was heaping further insults upon her, by refusing this public acknowledgment of her virtues.

De Marny hated Déroulède at this moment with the most deadly hatred the heart of man can conceive. The older man's calm, his chivalry, his consideration only enhanced the boy's anger and shame.

The hubbub had become general. Everyone seemed carried away with this strange fever of enmity, which was seething in the Vicomte's veins. Most of the young men crowded round De Marny, doing their best to pacify him. The Marquis de Villefranche declared that the matter was getting quite outside the rules.

No one took much notice of Déroulède. In the remote corners of the saloon a few elderly dandies were laying bets as to the ultimate issue of the quarrel.

Déroulède, however, was beginning to lose his temper. He had no friends in that room, and therefore there was no sympathetic observer there, to note the gradual darkening of his eyes, like the gathering of a cloud heavy with the coming storm.

"I pray you, messieurs, let us cease the argument," he said at last, in a loud, impatient voice. "M. le Vicomte de Marny desires a further lesson, and, by God! he shall have it. En garde, M. le Vicomte!"

The crowd quickly drew back. The seconds once more assumed the bearing and imperturbable expression which their important function demanded. The hubbub ceased as the swords began to clash.

Everyone felt that farce was turning to tragedy.

And yet it was obvious from the first that Déroulède merely meant once more to disarm his antagonist, to give him one more lesson, a little more severe perhaps than the last. He was such a brilliant swordsman, and De Marny was so excited, that the advantage was with him from the very first.

How it all happened, nobody afterwards could say. There is no doubt that the little Vicomte's sword-play had become more and more wild: that he uncovered himself in the most reckless way, whilst lunging wildly at his opponent's breast, until at last, in one of these mad, unguarded moments, he seemed literally to throw himself upon Déroulède's weapon.

The latter tried with lightning-swift motion of the wrist to avoid the fatal issue, but it was too late, and without a sigh or groan, scarce a tremor, the Vicomte de Marny fell.

The sword dropped out of his hand, and it was Déroulède himself who caught the boy in his arms.

It had all occurred so quickly and suddenly that no one had realised it all, until it was over, and the lad was lying prone on the ground, his elegant blue satin coat stained with red, and his antagonist bending over him.

There was nothing more to be done. Etiquette demanded that Déroulède should withdraw. He was not allowed to do anything for the boy whom he had so unwillingly sent to his death.

As before, no one took much notice of him. Silence, the awesome silence caused by the presence of the great Master, fell upon all those around. Only in the far corner a shrill voice was heard to say:

"I hold you at five hundred louis, Marquis. The parvenu is a good swordsman."

The groups parted as Déroulède walked out of the room, followed by the Colonel and M. de Quettare, who stood by him to the last. Both were old and proved soldiers, both had chivalry and courage in them, with which to do tribute to the brave man whom they had seconded.

At the door of the establishment, they met the leech who had been summoned some little time ago to hold himself in readiness for any eventuality.

The great eventuality had occurred: it was beyond the leech's learning. In the brilliantly lighted saloon above, the only son of the Duc de Marny was breathing his last, whilst Déroulède, wrapping his mantle closely round him, strode out into the dark street, all alone.

II.

The head of the house of Marny was at this time barely seventy years of age. But he had lived every hour, every minute of his life, from the day when the Grand Monarque gave him his first appointment as gentleman page in waiting when he was a mere lad, barely twelve years of age, to the moment—some ten years ago now—when Nature's relentless hand struck him down in the midst of his pleasures, withered him in a flash as she does a sturdy old oak, and nailed him— a cripple, almost a dotard—to the invalid chair which he would only quit for his last resting place.

Juliette was then a mere slip of a girl, an old man's child, the spoilt darling of his last happy years. She had retained some of the melancholy which had characterised her mother, the gentle lady who had endured so much so patiently, and who had bequeathed this final tender burden—her baby girl—to the brilliant, handsome husband whom she had so deeply loved, and so often forgiven.

When the Duc de Marny entered the final awesome stage of his gilded career, that deathlike life which he dragged on for ten years wearily to the grave, Juliette became his only joy, his one gleam of happiness in the midst of torturing memories.

In her deep, tender eyes he would see mirrored the present, the future for her, and would forget his past, with all its gaieties, its mad, merry years, that meant nothing now but bitter regrets, and endless rosary of the might-have-beens.

And then there was the boy. The little Vicomte, the future Duc de Marny, who would in *his* life and with *his* youth recreate the glory of the family, and make France once more ring with the echo of brave deeds and gallant adventures, which had made the name of Marny so glorious in camp and court.

The Vicomte was not his father's love, but he was his father's pride, and from the depths of his huge, cushioned arm-chair, the old man would listen with delight to stories from Versailles and Paris, the young Queen and the fascinating Lamballe, the latest play and the newest star in the theatrical firmament. His feeble, tottering mind would then take him back, along the paths of memory, to his own youth and his own triumphs, and in the joy and pride in his son, he would forget himself for the sake of the boy.

When they brought the Vicomte home that night, Juliette was the first to wake. She heard the noise outside the great gates, the coach slowly drawing up, the ring for the doorkeeper, and the sound of Matthieu's mutterings, who never liked to be called up in the middle of the night to let anyone through the gates.

Somehow a presentiment of evil at once struck the young girl: the footsteps sounded so heavy and muffled along the flagged courtyard, and up the great oak staircase. It seemed as if they were carrying something heavy, something inert or dead.

She jumped out of bed and hastily wrapped a cloak round her thin girlish shoulders, and slipped her feet into a pair of heelless shoes, then she opened her bedroom door and looked out upon the landing.

Two men, whom she did not know, were walking upstairs abreast, two more were carrying a heavy burden, and Matthieu was behind moaning and crying bitterly.

Juliette did not move. She stood in the doorway rigid as a statue. The little cortège went past her. No one saw her, for the landings in the Hotel de Marny are very wide, and Matthieu's lantern only threw a dim, flickering light upon the floor.

The men stopped outside the Vicomte's room. Matthieu opened it, and then the five men disappeared within, with their heavy burden.

A moment later old Pétronelle, who had been Juliette's nurse, and was now her devoted slave, came to her, all bathed in tears.

She had just heard the news, and she could scarcely speak, but she folded the young girl, her dear pet lamb, in her arms, and rocking herself to and fro she sobbed and eased her aching, motherly heart.

But Juliette did not cry. It was all so sudden, so awful. She, at fourteen years of age, had never dreamed of death; and now there was her brother, her Philippe, in whom she had so much joy, so much pride —he was dead—and her father must be told ...

The awfulness of this task seemed to Juliette like unto the last Judgment Day; a thing so terrible, so appalling, so impossible, that it would take a host of angels to proclaim its inevitableness.

The old cripple, with one foot in the grave, whose whole feeble mind, whose pride, whose final flicker of hope was concentrated in his boy, must be told that the lad had been brought home dead.

"Will you tell him, Pétronelle?" she asked repeatedly, during the brief intervals when the violence of the old nurse's grief subsided somewhat.

"No—no—darling, I cannot—I cannot—" moaned Pétronelle, amidst a renewed shower of sobs.

Juliette's entire soul—a child's soul it was—rose in revolt at thought of what was before her. She felt angered with God for having put such a thing upon her. What right had He to demand a girl of her years to endure so much mental agony?

To lose her brother, and to witness her father's grief! She couldn't! she couldn't! she couldn't! God was evil and unjust!

A distant tinkle of a bell made all her nerves suddenly quiver. Her father was awake then? He had heard the noise, and was ringing his bell to ask for an explanation of the disturbance.

With one quick movement Juliette jerked herself free from the nurse's arms, and before Pétronelle could prevent her, she had run out of the room, straight across the dark landing to a large panelled door opposite.

The old Duc de Marny was sitting on the edge of his bed, with his long, thin legs dangling helplessly to the ground.

Crippled as he was, he had struggled to this upright position, he was making frantic, miserable efforts to raise himself still further. He, too, had heard the dull thud of feet, the shuffling gait of men when carrying a heavy burden.

His mind flew back half-a-century, to the days when he had witnessed scenes wherein he was then merely a half-interested spectator. He knew the cortège composed of valets and friends, with the leech walking beside that precious burden, which anon would be deposited on the bed and left to the tender care of a mourning family.

Who knows what pictures were conjured up before that enfeebled vision? But he guessed. And when Juliette dashed into his room and stood before him, pale, trembling, a world of misery in her great eyes, she knew that he guessed and that she need not tell him. God had already done that for her.

Pierre, the old Duc's devoted valet, dressed him as quickly as he could. M. le Duc insisted on having his *habit de cérémonie*, the rich suit of black velvet with the priceless lace and diamond buttons, which he had worn when they laid le Roi Soleil to his eternal rest.

He put on his orders and buckled on his sword. The gorgeous clothes, which had suited him so well in the prime of his manhood, hung somewhat loosely on his attenuated frame, but he looked a grand and imposing figure, with his white hair tied behind with a great black bow, and the fine jabot of beautiful point d'Angleterre falling in a soft cascade below his chin.

Then holding himself as upright as he could, he sat in his invalid chair, and four flunkeys in full livery carried him to the deathbed of his son.

All the house was astir by now. Torches burned in great sockets in the vast hall and along the massive oak stairway, and hundreds of candles flickered ghostlike in the vast apartments of the princely mansion.

The numerous servants were arrayed on the landing, all dressed in the rich livery of the ducal house.

The death of an heir of the Marnys is an event that history makes a note of.

The old Duc's chair was placed close to the bed, where lay the dead body of the young Vicomte. He made no movement, nor did he utter a word or sigh. Some of those who were present at the time declared that his mind had completely given way, and that he neither felt nor understood the death of his son.

The Marquis de Villefranche, who had followed his friend to the last, took a final leave of the sorrowing house.

Juliette scarcely noticed him. Her eyes were fixed on her father. She would not look at her brother. A childlike fear had seized her, there, suddenly, between these two silent figures: the living and the dead.

But just as the Marquis was leaving the room, the old man spoke for the first time.

"Marquis," he said very quietly, "you forget—you have not yet told me who killed my son."

"It was in a fair fight, M. de Duc," replied the young Marquis, awed in spite of all his frivolity, his light-heartedness, by this strange, almost mysterious tragedy.

"Who killed my son, M. le Marquis?" repeated the old man mechanically. "I have the right to know," he added with sudden, weird energy.

"It was M. Paul Déroulède, M. le Duc," replied the Marquis. "I repeat, it was in fair fight."

The old Duc sighed as if in satisfaction. Then with a courteous gesture of farewell reminiscent of the *grand siècle* he added:

"All thanks from me and mine to you, Marquis, would seem but a mockery. Your devotion to my son is beyond human thanks. I'll not detain you now. Farewell."

Escorted by two lacqueys, the Marquis passed out of the room.

"Dismiss all the servants, Juliette; I have something to say," said the old Duc, and the young girl, silent, obedient, did as her father bade her.

Father and sister were alone with their dead. As soon as the last hushed footsteps of the retreating servants died away in the distance, the Duc de Marny seemed to throw away the lethargy which had enveloped him until now. With a quick, feverish gesture he seized his daughter's wrist, and murmured excitedly:

"His name. You heard his name, Juliette?"

"Yes, father," replied the child.

"Paul Déroulède! Paul Déroulède! You'll not forget it?"

"Never, father!"

"He killed your brother! You understand that? Killed my only son, the hope of my house, the last descendant of the most glorious race that has ever added lustre to the history of France."

"In fair fight, father!" protested the child.

"'Tis not fair for a man to kill a boy," retorted the old man, with furious energy. "Déroulède is thirty: my boy was scarce out of his teens: may the vengeance of God fall upon the murderer!"

Juliette, awed, terrified, was gazing at her father with great, wondering eyes. He seemed unlike himself. His face wore a curious expression of ecstasy and of hatred, also of hope and exultation, whenever he looked steadily at her.

That the final glimmer of a tottering reason was fast leaving the poor, aching head she was too young to realise. Madness was a word that had only a vague meaning for her. Though she did not understand her father at the present moment, though she was half afraid of him, she would have rejected with scorn and horror any suggestion that he was mad.

Therefore when he took her hand and, drawing her nearer to the bed and to himself, placed it upon her dead brother's breast, she recoiled at the touch of the inanimate body, so unlike anything she had ever touched before, but she obeyed her father without any question, and listened to his words as to those of a sage.

"Juliette, you are now fourteen, and able to understand what I am going to ask of you. If I were not chained to this miserable chair, if I were not a hopeless, abject cripple, I would not depute anyone, not even you, my only child, to do that, which God demands that one of us should do."

He paused a moment, then continued earnestly:

"Remember, Juliette, that you are of the house of Marny, that you are a Catholic, and that God hears you now. For you shall swear an oath before Him and me, an oath from which only death can relieve you. Will you swear, my child?"

"If you wish it, father."

"You have been to confession lately, Juliette?"

"Yes, father; also to holy communion, yesterday," replied the child. "It was the Fête-Dieu, you know."

"Then you are in a state of grace, my child?"

"I was yesterday morning, father," replied the young girl naïvely, "but I have committed some little sins since then."

"Then make your confession to God in your heart now. You must be in a state of grace when you speak the oath."

The child closed her eyes, and as the old man watched her, he could see the lips framing the words of her spiritual confession.

Juliette made the sign of the cross, then opened her eyes and looked at her father.

"I am ready, father," she said; "I hope God has forgiven me the little sins of yesterday."

"Will you swear, my child?"

"What, father?"

"That you will avenge your brother's death on his murderer?"

"But, father ..."

"Swear it, my child!"

"How can I fulfil that oath, father?—I don't understand ..."

"God will guide you, my child. When you are older you will understand."

For a moment Juliette still hesitated. She was just on that borderland between childhood and womanhood when all the sensibilities, the nervous system, the emotions, are strung to their highest pitch.

Throughout her short life she had worshipped her father with a whole-hearted, passionate devotion, which had completely blinded her to his weakening faculties and the feebleness of his mind.

She was also in that initial stage of enthusiastic piety which overwhelms every girl of temperament, if she be brought up in the Roman Catholic religion, when she is first initiated into the mysteries of the Sacraments.

Juliette had been to confession and communion. She had been confirmed by Monseigneur, the Archbishop. Her ardent nature had responded to the full to the sensuous and ecstatic expressions of the ancient faith.

And somehow her father's wish, her brother's death, all seemed mingled in her brain with that religion, for which in her juvenile enthusiasm she would willingly have laid down her life.

She thought of all the saints, whose lives she had been reading. Her young heart quivered at the thought of *their* sacrifices, their martyrdoms, their sense of duty.

An exaltation, morbid perhaps, superstitious and overwhelming, took possession of her mind; also, perhaps, far back in the innermost recesses of her heart, a pride in her own importance, her mission in life, her individuality: for she was a girl after all, a mere child, about to become a woman.

But the old Duc was waxing impatient.

"Surely you do not hesitate, Juliette, with your dead brother's body clamouring mutely for revenge? You, the only Marny left now!—for from this day I too shall be as dead."

"No, father," said the young girl in an awed whisper, "I do not hesitate. I will swear, just as you bid me."

"Repeat the words after me, my child."

"Yes, father."

"Before the face of Almighty God, who sees and hears me ..."

"Before the face of Almighty God, who sees and hears me," repeated Juliette firmly.

"I swear that I will seek out Paul Déroulède."

"I swear that I will seek out Paul Déroulède."

"And in any manner which God may dictate to me encompass his death, his ruin or dishonour, in revenge for my brother's death."

"And in any manner which God may dictate to me encompass his death, his ruin or dishonour, in revenge for my brother's death," said Juliette solemnly.

"May my brother's soul remain in torment until the final Judgment Day if I should break my oath, but may it rest in eternal peace the day on which his death is fitly avenged."

"May my brother's soul remain in torment until the final Judgment Day if I should break my oath, but may it rest in eternal peace the day on which his death is fitly avenged."

The child fell upon her knees. The oath was spoken, the old man was satisfied.

He called for his valet, and allowed himself quietly to be put to bed.

One brief hour had transformed a child into a woman. A dangerous transformation when the brain is overburdened with emotions, when the nerves are overstrung and the heart full to breaking.

For the moment, however, the childlike nature reasserted itself for the last time, for Juliette, sobbing, had fled out of the room, to the privacy of her own apartment, and thrown herself passionately into the arms of kind old Pétronelle.

CHAPTER 1. PARIS: 1793. THE OUTRAGE

It would have been very difficult to say why Citizen Déroulède was quite so popular as he was. Still more difficult would it have been to state the reason why he remained immune from the prosecutions, which were being conducted at the rate of several scores a day, now against the moderate Gironde, anon against the fanatic Mountain, until the whole of France was transformed into one gigantic prison, that daily fed the guillotine.

But Déroulède remained unscathed. Even Merlin's law of the suspect had so far failed to touch him. And when, last July, the murder of Marat brought an entire holocaust of victims to the guillotine—from Adam Lux, who would have put up a statue in honour of Charlotte Corday, with the inscription: "Greater than Brutus", to Charlier, who would have had her publicly tortured and burned at the stake for her crime—Déroulède alone said nothing, and was allowed to remain silent.

The most seething time of that seething revolution. No one knew in the morning if his head would still be on his own shoulders in the evening, or if it would be held up by Citizen Samson the headsman, for the sansculottes of Paris to see.

Yet Déroulède was allowed to go his own way. Marat once said of him: "Il n'est pas dangereux." The phrase had been taken up. Within the precincts of the National Convention, Marat was still looked upon as the great protagonist of Liberty, a martyr to his own convictions carried to the extreme, to squalor and dirt, to the downward levelling of man to what is the lowest type in humanity. And his sayings were still treasured up: even the Girondins did not dare to attack his memory. Dead Marat was more powerful than his living presentment had been.

And he had said that Déroulède was not dangerous. Not dangerous to Republicanism, to liberty, to that downward, levelling process, the tearing down of old traditions, and the annihilation of past pretensions.

Déroulède had once been very rich. He had had sufficient prudence to give away in good time that which, undoubtedly, would have been taken away from him later on.

But when he gave willingly, at a time when France needed it most, and before she had learned how to help herself to what she wanted.

And somehow, in this instance, France had not forgotten: an invisible fortress seemed to surround Citizen Déroulède and keep his enemies at bay. They were few, but they existed. The National Convention trusted him. "He was not dangerous" to them. The people looked upon him as one of themselves, who gave whilst he had something to give. Who can gauge that most elusive of all things: *Popularity?*

He lived a quiet life, and had never yielded to the omni-prevalent temptation of writing pamphlets, but lived alone with his mother and Anne Mie, the little orphaned cousin whom old Madame Déroulède had taken care of, ever since the child could toddle.

Everyone knew his house in the Rue Ecole de Médecine, not far from the one wherein Marat lived and died, the only solid, stone house in the midst of a row of hovels, evil-smelling and squalid.

The street was narrow then, as it is now, and whilst Paris was cutting off the heads of her children for the sake of Liberty and Fraternity, she had no time to bother about cleanliness and sanitation.

Rue Ecole de Médecine did little credit to the school after which it was named, and it was a most unattractive crowd that usually thronged its uneven, muddy pavements.

A neat gown, a clean kerchief, were quite an unusual sight down this way, for Anne Mie seldom went out, and old Madame Déroulède hardly ever left her room. A good deal of brandy was being drunk at the two drinking bars, one at each end of the long, narrow street, and by five o'clock in the afternoon it was undoubtedly best for women to remain indoors.

The crowd of disheveled elderly Amazons who stood gossiping at the street corner could hardly be called women now. A ragged petticoat, a greasy red kerchief round the head, a tattered, stained shift—to this pass of squalor and shame had Liberty brought the daughters of France.

And they jeered at any passer-by less filthy, less degraded than themselves.

"Ah! voyons l'aristo!" they shouted every time a man in decent clothes, a woman with tidy cap and apron, passed swiftly down the street.

And the afternoons were very lively. There was always plenty to see: first and foremost, the long procession of tumbrils, winding its way from the prisons to the Place de la Révolution. The forty-four thousand sections of the Committee of Public Safety sent their quota, each in their turn, to the guillotine.

At one time these tumbrils contained royal ladies and gentlemen, *ci-devant* dukes and princesses, aristocrats from every county in France, but now this stock was becoming exhausted. The wretched Queen Marie Antoinette still lingered in the Temple with her son and daughter. Madame Elisabeth was still allowed to say her prayers in peace, but *ci-devant* dukes and counts were getting scarce: those who had not perished at the hand of Citizen Samson were plying some trade in Germany or England.

There were aristocratic joiners, innkeepers, and hairdressers. The proudest names in France were hidden beneath trade signs in London and Hamburg. A good number owed their lives to that mysterious Scarlet Pimpernel, that unknown Englishman who had snatched scores of victims from the clutches of Tinville the Prosecutor, and sent M. Chauvelin, baffled, back to France.

Aristocrats were getting scarce, so it was now the turn of deputies of the National Convention, of men of letters, men of science or of art, men who had sent others to the guillotine a twelvemonth ago, and men who had been loudest in defence of anarchy and its Reign of Terror.

They had revolutionised the Calendar: the Citizen-Deputies, and every good citizen of France, called this 19th day of August 1793 the 2nd Fructidor of the year I. of the New Era.

At six o'clock on that afternoon a young girl suddenly turned the angle of the Rue Ecole de Médecine, and after looking quickly to the right and left she began deliberately walking along the narrow street.

It was crowded just then. Groups of excited women stood jabbering before every doorway. It was the home-coming hour after the usual spectacle on the Place de la Révolution. The men had paused at the various drinking booths, crowding the women out. It would be the turn of these Amazons next, at the brandy bars; for the moment they were left to gossip, and to jeer at the passer-by.

At first the young girl did not seem to heed them. She walked quickly along, looking defiantly before her, carrying her head erect, and stepping carefully from cobblestone to cobblestone, avoiding the mud, which could have dirtied her dainty shoes.

The harridans passed the time of day to her, and the time of day meant some obscene remark unfit for women's ears. The young girl wore a simple grey dress, with fine lawn kerchief neatly folded across her bosom, a large hat with flowing ribbons sat above the fairest face that ever gladdened men's eyes to see.

Fairer still it would have been, but for the look of determination which made it seem hard and old for the girl's years.

She wore the tricolour scarf round her waist, else she had been more seriously molested ere now. But the Republican colours were her safeguard: whilst she walked quietly along, no one could harm her.

Then suddenly a curious impulse seemed to seize her. It was just outside the large stone house belonging to Citizen-Deputy Déroulède. She had so far taken no notice of the groups of women which she had come across. When they obstructed the footway, she had calmly stepped out into the middle of the road.

It was wise and prudent, for she could close her ears to obscene language and need pay no heed to insult.

Suddenly she threw up her head defiantly.

"Will you please let me pass?" she said loudly, as a disheveled Amazon stood before her with arms akimbo, glancing sarcastically at the lace petticoat, which just peeped beneath the young girl's simple grey frock.

"Let her pass? Let her pass? Ho! ho! ho!" laughed the old woman, turning to the nearest group of idlers, and apostrophising them with a loud oath. "Did *you* know, citizeness, that this street had been specially made for aristos to pass along?"

"I am in a hurry, will you let me pass at once?" commanded the young girl, tapping her foot impatiently on the ground.

There was the whole width of the street on her right, plenty of room for her to walk along. It seemed positive madness to provoke a quarrel singlehanded against this noisy group of excited females, just home from the ghastly spectacle around the guillotine.

And yet she seemed to do it willfully, as if coming to the end of her patience, all her proud, aristocratic blood in revolt against this evil-smelling crowd which surrounded her.

Half-tipsy men and noisome, naked urchins seemed to have sprung from everywhere.

"Oho, quelle aristo!" they shouted with ironical astonishment, gazing at the young girl's face, fingering her gown, thrusting begrimed, hate-distorted faces close to her own.

Instinctively she recoiled and backed towards the house immediately on her left. It was adorned with a porch made of stout oak beams, with a tiled roof; an iron lantern descended from this, and there was a stone parapet below, and a few steps, at right angles from the pavement, led up to the massive door.

On these steps the young girl had taken refuge. Proud, defiant, she confronted the howling mob, which she had so willfully provoked.

"Of a truth, Citizeness Margot, that grey dress would become you well!" suggested a young man, whose red cap hung in tatters over an evil and dissolute-looking face.

"And all that fine lace would make a splendid jabot round the aristo's neck when Citizen Samson holds up her head for us to see," added another, as with mock elegance he stooped and with two very grimy fingers slightly raised the young girl's grey frock, displaying the lace-edged petticoat beneath.

A volley of oaths and loud, ironical laughter greeted this sally.

"'Tis mighty fine lace to be thus hidden away," commented an elderly harridan. "Now, would you believe it, my fine madam, but my legs are bare underneath my kirtle?"

"And dirty, too, I'll lay a wager," laughed another. "Soap is dear in Paris just now."

"The lace on the aristo's kerchief would pay the baker's bill of a whole family for a month!" shouted an excited voice.

Heat and brandy further addled the brains of this group of French citizens; hatred gleamed out of every eye. Outrage was imminent. The young girl seemed to know it, but she remained defiant and self-possessed, gradually stepping back and back up the steps, closely followed by her assailants.

"To the Jew with the gewgaw, then!" shouted a thin, haggard female viciously, as she suddenly clutched at the young girl's kerchief, and with a mocking, triumphant laugh tore it from her bosom.

This outrage seemed to be the signal for the breaking down of the final barriers which ordinary decency should have raised. The language and vituperation became such as no chronicler could record.

The girl's dainty white neck, her clear skin, the refined contour of shoulders and bust, seemed to have aroused the deadliest lust of hate in these wretched creatures, rendered bestial by famine and squalor.

It seemed almost as if one would vie with the other in seeking for words which would most offend these small aristocratic ears.

The young girl was now crouching against the doorway, her hands held up to her ears to shut out the awful sounds. She did not seem frightened, only appalled at the terrible volcano which she had provoked.

Suddenly a miserable harridan struck her straight in the face, with hard, grimy fist, and a long shout of exultation greeted this monstrous deed.

Then only did the girl seem to lose her self-control.

"A moi," she shouted loudly, whilst hammering with both hands against the massive doorway. "A moi! Murder! Murder! Citoyen Déroulède, à moi!"

But her terror was greeted with renewed glee by her assailants. They were now roused to the highest point of frenzy: the crowd of brutes would in the next moment have torn the helpless girl from her place of refuge and dragged her into the mire, an outraged prey, for the satisfaction of an ungovernable hate.

But just as half-a-dozen pairs of talon-like hands clutched frantically at her skirts, the door behind her was quickly opened. She felt her arm seized firmly, and herself dragged swiftly within the shelter of the threshold.

Her senses, overwrought by the terrible adventure which she had just gone through, were threatening to reel; she heard the massive door close, shutting out the yells of baffled rage, the ironical laughter, the obscene words, which sounded in her ears like the shrieks of Dante's damned.

She could not see her rescuer, for the hall into which he had hastily dragged her was only dimly lighted. But a peremptory voice said quickly:

"Up the stairs, the room straight in front of you, my mother is there. Go quickly."

She had fallen on her knees, cowering against the heavy oak beam which supported the ceiling, and was straining her eyes to catch sight of the man, to whom at this moment she perhaps owed more than her life: but he was standing against the doorway, with his hand on the latch.

"What are you going to do?" she murmured.

"Prevent their breaking into my house in order to drag you out of it," he replied quietly; "so, I pray you, do as I bid you."

Mechanically she obeyed him, drew herself to her feet, and, turning towards the stairs, began slowly to mount the shallow steps. Her knees were shaking under her, her whole body was trembling with horror at the awesome crisis she had just traversed.

She dared not look back at her rescuer. Her head was bent, and her lips were murmuring half-audible words as she went.

Outside the hooting and yelling was becoming louder and louder. Enraged fists were hammering violently against the stout oak door.

At the top of the stairs, moved by an irresistible impulse, she turned and looked into the hall.

She saw his figure dimly outlined in the gloom, one hand on the latch, his head thrown back to watch her movements.

A door stood ajar immediately in front of her. She pushed it open and went within.

At that moment he too opened the door below. The shrieks of the howling mob once more resounded close to her ears. It seemed as if they had surrounded him. She wondered what was happening, and marvelled how he dared to face that awful crowd alone.

The room into which she had entered was gay and cheerful-looking with its dainty chintz hangings and graceful, elegant pieces of furniture. The young girl looked up, as a kindly voice said to her, from out the depths of a capacious armchair:

"Come in, come in, my dear, and close the door behind you! Did those wretches attack you? Never mind. Paul will speak to them. Come here, my dear, and sit down; there's no cause now for fear."

Without a word the young girl came forward. She seemed now to be walking in a dream, the chintz hangings to be swaying ghostlike around her, the yells and shrieks below to come from the very bowels of the earth.

The old lady continued to prattle on. She had taken the girl's hand in hers, and was gently forcing her down on to a low stool beside her armchair. She was talking about Paul, and said something about Anne Mie, and then about the National Convention, and those beasts and savages, but mostly about Paul.

The noise outside had subsided. The girl felt strangely sick and tired. Her head seemed to be whirling round, the furniture to be dancing round her; the old lady's face looked at her through a swaying veil, and then—and then ...

Tired Nature was having her way at last; she folded the quivering young body in her motherly arms, and wrapped the aching senses beneath her merciful mantle of unconsciousness.

CHAPTER 2. CITIZEN-DEPUTY

When, presently, the young girl awoke, with a delicious feeling of rest and well-being, she had plenty of leisure to think.

So, then, this was his house! She was actually a guest, a rescued protégé, beneath the roof of Citoyen Déroulède.

He had dragged her from the clutches of the howling mob which she had provoked; his mother had made her welcome, a sweet-faced, young girl scarce out of her teens, sad-eyed and slightly deformed, had waited upon her and made her happy and comfortable.

Juliette de Marny was in the house of the man, whom she had sworn before her God and before her father to pursue with hatred and revenge.

Ten years had gone by since then.

Lying upon the sweet-scented bed which the hospitality of the Déroulèdes had provided for her, she seemed to see passing before her the spectres of these past ten years —the first four, after her brother's death, until the old Duc de Marny's body slowly followed his soul to its grave.

After that last glimmer of life beside the deathbed of his son, the old Duc had practically ceased to be. A mute, shrunken figure, he merely existed; his mind vanished, his memory gone, a wreck whom Nature fortunately remembered at last, and finally took away from the invalid chair which had been his world.

Then came those few years at the Convent of the Ursulines. Juliette had hoped that she had a vocation; her whole soul yearned for a secluded, a religious, life, for great barriers of solemn vows and days spent in prayer and contemplation, to interpose between herself and the memory of that awful night when, obedient to her father's will, she had made the solemn oath to avenge her brother's death.

She was only eighteen when she first entered the convent, directly after her father's death, when she felt very lonely—both morally and mentally lonely—and followed by the obsession of that oath.

She never spoke of it to anyone except to her confessor, and he, a simple-minded man of great learning and a total lack of knowledge of the world, was completely at a loss how to advise.

The Archbishop was consulted. He could grant a dispensation, and release her of that most solemn vow.

When first this idea was suggested to her, Juliette was exultant. Her entire nature, which in itself was wholesome, light-hearted, the very reverse of morbid, rebelled against this unnatural task placed upon her young shoulders. It was only religion—the strange, warped religion of that extraordinary age—which kept her to it, which forbade her breaking lightly that most unnatural oath.

The Archbishop was a man of many duties, many engagements. He agreed to give this strange "cas de conscience" his most earnest attention. He would make no promises. But Mademoiselle de Marny was rich: a munificent donation to the poor of Paris, or to some cause dear to the Holy Father himself, might perhaps be more acceptable to God than the fulfilment of a compulsory vow.

Juliette, within the convent walls, was waiting patiently for the Archbishop's decision at the very moment, when the greatest upheaval the world has ever known was beginning to shake the very foundations of France.

The Archbishop had other things now to think about than isolated cases of conscience. He forgot all about Juliette, probably. He was busy consoling a monarch for the loss of his throne, and preparing himself and his royal patron for the scaffold.

The Convent of the Ursulines was scattered during the Terror. Everyone remembers the Thermidor massacres, and the thirty-four nuns, all daughters of ancient families of France, who went so cheerfully to the scaffold.

Juliette was one of those who escaped condemnation. How or why, she herself could not have told. She was very young, and still a postulant; she was allowed to live in retirement with Pétronelle, her old nurse, who had remained faithful through all these years.

Then the Archbishop was prosecuted and imprisoned. Juliette made frantic efforts to see him, but all in vain. When he died, she looked upon her spiritual guide's death as a direct warning from God, that nothing could relieve her of her oath.

She had watched the turmoils of the Revolution through the attic window of her tiny apartment in Paris. Waited upon by faithful Pétronelle, she had been forced to live on the savings of that worthy old soul, as all her property, all the Marny estates, the *dot* she took with her to the convent—everything, in fact—had been seized by the Revolutionary Government, self-appointed to level fortunes, as well as individuals.

From that attic window she had seen beautiful Paris writhing under the pitiless lash of the demon of terror which it had provoked; she had heard the rumble of the tumbrils, dragging day after day their load of victims to the insatiable maker of this Revolution of Fraternity—the Guillotine.

She had seen the gay, light-hearted people of this Star-City turned to howling beasts of prey, its women changed to sexless vultures, with murderous talons implanted in everything that is noble, high or beautiful.

She was not twenty when the feeble, vacillating monarch and his imperious consort were dragged back—a pair of humiliated prisoners—to the capital from which they had tried to flee.

Two years later, she had heard the cries of an entire people exulting over a regicide.

Then the murder of Marat, by a young girl like herself, the pale-faced, large-eyed Charlotte, who had committed a crime for the sake of a conviction. "Greater than Brutus!" some had called her. Greater than Joan of Arc, for it was to a mission of evil and of sin that she was called from the depths of her Breton village, and not to one of glory and triumph.

"Greater than Brutus!"

Juliette followed the trial of Charlotte Corday with all the passionate ardour of her exalted temperament.

Just think what an effect it must have had upon the mind of this young girl, who for nine years—the best of her life—had also lived with the idea of a sublime mission pervading her very soul.

She watched Charlotte Corday at her trial. Conquering her natural repulsion for such scenes, and the crowds which usually watched them, she had forced her way into the foremost rank of the narrow gallery which overlooked the Hall of the Revolutionary Tribunal.

She heard the indictment, heard Tinville's speech and the calling of the witnesses.

"All this is unnecessary. I killed Marat!"

Juliette heard the fresh young voice ringing out clearly above the murmur of voices, the howls of execration; she saw the beautiful young face, clear, calm, impassive.

"I killed Marat!"

And there in the special space allotted to the Citizen-Deputies, sitting among those who represented the party of the Moderate Gironde, was Paul Déroulède, the man whom she had sworn to pursue with a vengeance as great, as complete, as that which guided Charlotte Corday's hand.

She watched him during the trial, and wondered if he had any presentiment of the hatred which dogged him, like unto the one which had dogged Marat.

He was very dark, almost swarthy a son of the South, with brown hair, free from powder, thrown back and revealing the brow of a student rather than that of a legislator. He watched Charlotte Corday earnestly, and Juliette who watched him saw the look of measureless pity, which softened the otherwise hard look of his close-set eyes.

He made an impassioned speech for the defence: a speech which has become historic. It would have cost any other man his head.

Juliette marvelled at his courage; to defend Charlotte Corday was equivalent to acquiescing in the death of Marat: Marat, the friend of the people; Marat, whom his funeral orators had compared to the Great, the Sacred Leveller of Mankind!

But Déroulède's speech was not a defence, it was an appeal. The most eloquent man of that eloquent age, his words seemed to find that hidden bit of sentiment which still lurked in the hearts of these strange protagonists of Hate.

Everyone round Juliette listened as he spoke: "It is Citoyen Déroulède!" whispered the bloodthirsty Amazons, who sat knitting in the gallery.

But there was no further comment. A huge, magnificently-equipped hospital for sick children had been thrown open in Paris that very morning, a gift to the nation from Citoyen Déroulède. Surely he was privileged to talk a little, if it pleased him. His hospital would cover quite a good many defalcations.

Even the rabid Mountain, Danton, Merlin, Santerre, shrugged their shoulders. "It is

Déroulède, let him talk an he list. Murdered Marat said of him that he was not dangerous."

Juliette heard it all. The knitters round her were talking loudly. Even Charlotte was almost forgotten whilst Déroulède talked. He had a fine voice, of strong calibre, which echoed powerfully through the hall.

He was rather short, but broad-shouldered and well knit, with an expressive hand, which looked slender and delicate below the fine lace ruffle.

Charlotte Corday was condemned. All Déroulède's eloquence could not save her.

Juliette left the court in a state of mad exultation. She was very young: the scenes she had witnessed in the past two years could not help but excite the imagination of a young girl, left entirely to her own intellectual and moral resources.

What scenes! Great God!

And now to wait for an opportunity! Charlotte Corday, the half-educated little provincial should not put to shame Mademoiselle de Marny, the daughter of a hundred dukes, of those who had made France before she took to unmaking herself.

But she could not formulate any definite plans. Pétronelle, poor old soul, her only confidante, was not of the stuff that heroines are made of. Juliette felt impelled by duty, and duty at best is not so prompt a counsellor as love or hate.

Her adventure outside Déroulède's house had not been premeditated. Impulse and coincidence had worked their will with her.

She had been in the habit, daily, for the past month, of wandering down the Rue Ecole de Médecine, ostensibly to gaze at Marat's dwelling, as crowds of idlers were wont to do, but really in order to look at Déroulède's house. Once or twice she saw him coming or going from home. Once she caught sight of the inner hall, and of a young girl in a dark kirtle and snow-white kerchief bidding him good-bye at his door. Another time she caught sight of him at the corner of the street, helping that same young girl over the muddy pavement. He had just met her, and she was carrying a basket of provisions: he took it from her and carried it to the house.

Chivalrous—eh?—and innately so, evidently, for the girl was slightly deformed: hardly a hunchback, but weak and unattractive-looking, with melancholy eyes, and a pale, pinched face.

It was the thought of that little act of simple chivalry, witnessed the day before, which caused Juliette to provoke the scene which, but for Déroulède's timely interference, might have ended so fatally. But she reckoned on that interference: the whole thing had occurred to her suddenly, and she had carried it through.

Had not her father said to her that when the time came, God would show her a means to the end?

And now she was inside the house of the man who had murdered her brother and sent her sorrowing father, a poor, senseless maniac, tottering to the grave.

Would God's finger point again, and show her what to do next, how best to accomplish what she had sworn to do?

CHAPTER 3. HOSPITALITY

"Is there anything more I can do for you now, mademoiselle?"

The gentle, timid voice roused Juliette from the contemplation of the past.

She smiled at Anne Mie, and held her hand out towards her.

"You have all been so kind," she said, "I want to get up now and thank you all."

"Don't move unless you feel quite well."

"I am quite well now. Those horrid people frightened me so, that is why I fainted."

"They would have half-killed you, if ..."

"Will you tell me where I am?" asked Juliette.

"In the house of M. Paul Déroulède—I should have said of Citizen-Deputy Déroulède. He rescued you from the mob, and pacified them. He has such a beautiful voice that he can make anyone listen to him, and ..."

"And you are fond of him, mademoiselle?" added Juliette, suddenly feeling a mist of tears rising to her eyes.

"Of course I am fond of him," rejoined the other girl simply, whilst a look of the most tender-hearted devotion seemed to beautify her pale face. "He and Madame Déroulède have brought me up; I never knew my parents. They have cared for me, and he has taught me all I know."

"What do they call you, mademoiselle?"

"My name is Anne Mie."

"And mine, Juliette—Juliette Marny," she added after a slight hesitation. "I have no parents either. My old nurse, Pétronelle, has brought me up, and—But tell me more about M. Déroulède—I owe him so much, I'd like to know him better."

"Will you not let me arrange your hair?" said Anne Mie as if purposely evading a direct reply. "M. Déroulède is in the salon with madame. You can see him then."

Juliette asked no more questions, but allowed Anne Mie to tidy her hair for her, to lend her a fresh kerchief and generally to efface all traces of her terrible adventure. She felt puzzled and tearful. Anne Mie's gentleness seemed somehow to jar on her spirits. She could not understand the girl's position in the Déroulède household. Was she a relative, or a superior servant? In these troublous times she might easily have been both.

In any case she was a childhood's companion of the Citizen-Deputy— whether on an equal or a humbler footing, Juliette would have given much to ascertain.

With the marvelous instinct peculiar to women of temperament, she had already divined Anne Mie's love for Déroulède. The poor young cripple's very soul seemed to quiver magnetically at the bare mention of his name, her whole face became transfigured: Juliette even thought her beautiful then.

She looked at herself critically in the glass, and adjusted a curl, which looked its best when it was rebellious. She scrutinised her own face carefully; why? she could not tell: another of those subtle feminine instincts perhaps.

The becoming simplicity of the prevailing mode suited her to perfection. The waist line, rather high but clearly defined—a precursor of the later more accentuated fashion—gave grace to her long slender limbs, and emphasised the lissomeness of her figure. The kerchief, edged with fine lace, and neatly folded across her bosom, softened the contour of her girlish bust and shoulders.

And her hair was a veritable glory round her dainty, piquant face. Soft, fair, and curly, it emerged in a golden halo from beneath the prettiest little lace cap imaginable.

She turned and faced Anne Mie, ready to follow her out of the room, and the young crippled girl sighed as she smoothed down the folds of her own apron, and gave a final touch to the completion of Juliette's attire.

The time before the evening meal slipped by like a dream-hour for Juliette.

She had lived so much alone, had led such an introspective life, that she had hardly realised and understood all that was going on around her. At the time when the inner vitality of France first asserted itself and then swept away all that hindered its mad progress, she was tied to the invalid chair of her half-demented father; then, after that, the sheltering walls of the Ursuline Convent had hidden from her mental vision the true meaning of the great conflict, between the Old Era and the New.

Déroulède was neither a pedant nor yet a revolutionary: his theories were Utopian and he had an extraordinary overpowering sympathy for his fellow-men.

After the first casual greetings with Juliette, he had continued a discussion with his mother, which the young girl's entrance had interrupted.

He seemed to take but little notice of her, although at times his dark, keen eyes would seek hers, as if challenging her for a reply.

He was talking of the mob of Paris, whom he evidently understood so well. Incidents such as the one which Juliette had provoked, had led to rape and theft, often to murder, before now: but outside Citizen-Deputy Déroulède's house everything was quiet, half-an-hour after Juliette's escape from that howling, brutish crowd.

He had merely spoken to them, for about twenty minutes, and they had gone away quite quietly, without even touching one hair of his head. He seemed to love them: to know how to separate the little good that was in them, from that hard crust of evil, which misery had put around their hearts.

Once he addressed Juliette somewhat abruptly: "Pardon me, mademoiselle, but for your own sake we must guard you a prisoner here awhile. No one would harm you under this roof, but it would not be safe for you to cross the neighbouring streets to-night."

"But I must go, monsieur. Indeed, indeed I must!" she said earnestly. "I am deeply grateful to you, but I could not leave Pétronelle."

"Who is Pétronelle?"

"My dear old nurse, monsieur. She has never left me. Think how anxious and miserable she must be, at my prolonged absence."

"Where does she live?"

"At No. 15 Rue Taitbout, but ..."

"Will you allow me to take her a message?—telling her that you are safe and under my roof, where it is obviously more prudent that you should remain at present."

"If you think it best, monsieur," she replied.

Inwardly she was trembling with excitement. God had not only brought her to this house, but willed that she should stay in it.

"In whose name shall I take the message, mademoiselle?" he asked.

"My name is Juliette Marny."

She watched him keenly as she said it, but there was not the slightest sign in his expressive face, to show that he had recognised the name.

Ten years is a long time, and every one had lived through so much during those years! A wave of intense wrath swept through Juliette's soul, as she realised that he had forgotten. The name meant nothing to him! It did not recall to him the fact that his hand was stained with blood. During ten years she had suffered, she had fought with herself, fought for him as it were, against the Fate which she was destined to mete out to him, whilst he had forgotten, or at least had ceased to think.

He bowed to her and went out of the room.

The wave of wrath subsided, and she was left alone with Madame Déroulède: presently Anne Mie came in.

The three women chatted together, waiting for the return of the master of the house. Juliette felt well and, in spite of herself, almost happy. She had lived so long in the miserable, little attic alone with Pétronelle that she enjoyed the well-being of this refined home. It was not so grand or gorgeous of course as her father's princely palace opposite the Louvre, a wreck now, since it was annexed by the Committee of National Defence, for the housing of soldiery. But the Déroulèdes' home was essentially a refined one. The delicate china on the tall chimney-piece, the few bits of Buhl and Vernis Martin about the room, the vision through the open doorway of the supper-table spread with a fine white cloth, and sparkling with silver, all spoke of fastidious tastes, of habits of luxury and elegance, which the spirit of Equality and Anarchy had not succeeded in eradicating.

When Déroulède came back, he brought an atmosphere of breezy cheerfulness with him.

The street was quiet now, and when walking past the hospital—his own gift to the Nation—he had been loudly cheered. One or two ironical voices had asked him what he had done with the aristo and her lace furbelows, but it remained at that and Mademoiselle Marny need have no fear.

He had brought Pétronelle along with him: his careless, lavish hospitality would have suggested the housing of Juliette's entire domestic establishment, had she possessed one.

As it was, the worthy old soul's deluge of happy tears had melted his kindly heart. He offered her and her young mistress shelter, until the small cloud should have rolled by.

After that he suggested a journey to England. Emigration now was the only real safety, and Mademoiselle Marny had unpleasantly drawn on herself the attention of the Paris rabble. No doubt, within the next few days her name would figure among the "suspect." She would be safest out of the country, and could not do better than place herself under the guidance of that English enthusiast, who had helped so many persecuted Frenchmen to escape from the terrors of the Revolution: the man who was such a thorn in the flesh of the Committee of Public Safety, and who went by the nickname of The Scarlet Pimpernel.

CHAPTER 4. THE FAITHFUL HOUSE-DOG

After supper they talked of Charlotte Corday.

Juliette clung to the vision of that heroine, and liked to talk of her. She appeared as a justification of her own actions, which somehow seemed to require justification.

She loved to hear Paul Déroulède talk; liked to provoke his enthusiasm and to see his stern, dark face light up with the inward fire of the enthusiast.

She had openly avowed herself as the daughter of the Duc de Marny. When she actually named her father, and her brother killed in duel, she saw Déroulède looking long and searchingly at her. Evidently he wondered if she knew everything: but she returned his gaze fearlessly and frankly, and he apparently was satisfied.

Madame Déroulède seemed to know nothing of the circumstances of that duel. Déroulède tried to draw Juliette out, to make her speak of her brother. She replied to his questions quite openly, but there was nothing in what she said, suggestive of the fact that she knew who killed her brother.

She wanted him to know who she was. If he feared an enemy in her, there was yet time enough for him to close his doors against her.

But less than a minute later, he had renewed his warmest offers of hospitality.

"Until we can arrange for your journey to England," he added with a short sigh, as if reluctant to part from her.

To Juliette his attitude seemed one of complete indifference for the wrong he had done to her and to her father: feeling that she was an avenging spirit, with flaming sword in hand, pursuing her brother's murderer like a relentless Nemesis, she would have preferred to see him cowed before her, even afraid of her, though she was only a young and delicate girl.

She did not understand that in the simplicity of his heart, he only wished to make amends. The quarrel with the young Vicomte de Marny had been forced upon him, the fight had been honourable and fair, and on his side fought with every desire to spare the young man. He had merely been the instrument of Fate, but he felt happy that Fate once more used him as her tool, this time to save the sister.

Whilst Déroulède and Juliette talked together Anne Mie cleared the supper-table, then came and sat on a low stool at madame's feet. She took no part in the conversation, but every now and then Juliette felt the girl's melancholy eyes fixed almost reproachfully upon her.

When Juliette had retired with Pétronelle, Déroulède took Anne Mie's hand in his.

"You will be kind to my guest, Anne Mie, won't you? She seems very lonely, and has gone through a great deal."

"Not more than I have," murmured the young girl involuntarily.

"You are not happy, Anne Mie? I thought ..."

"Is a wretched, deformed creature ever happy?" she said with sudden vehemence, as tears of mortification rushed to her eyes, in spite of herself.

"I did not think that you were wretched," he replied with some sadness, "and neither in my eyes, nor in my mother's, are you in any way deformed."

Her mood changed at once. She clung to him, pressing his hand between her own.

"Forgive me! I—I don't know what's the matter with me to-night," she said with a nervous little laugh. "Let me see, you asked me to be kind to Mademoiselle Marny, did you not?"

He nodded with a smile.

"Of course I'll be kind to her. Isn't every one kind to one who is young and beautiful, and has great, appealing eyes, and soft, curly hair? Ah me! how easy is the path in life for some people! What do you want me to do, Paul? Wait on her? Be her little maid? Soothe her nerves or what? I'll do it all, though in her eyes I shall remain both wretched and deformed, a creature to pity, the harmless, necessary house-dog ..."

She paused a moment: said "Good-night" to him, and turned to go, candle in hand, looking pathetic and fragile, with that ugly contour of shoulder, which Déroulède assured her he could not see.

The candle flickered in the draught, illumining the thin, pinched face, the large melancholy eyes of the faithful house-dog.

"Who can watch and bite!" she said half-audibly as she slipped out of the room. "For I do not trust you, my fine madam, and there was something about that comedy this afternoon, which somehow, I don't quite understand."

CHAPTER 5. A DAY IN THE WOODS

But whilst men and women set to work to make the towns of France hideous with their shrieks and their hootings, their mock-trials and bloody guillotines, they could not quite prevent Nature from working her sweet will with the country.

June, July, and August had received new names—they were now called Messidor, Thermidor, and Fructidor, but under these new names they continued to pour forth upon the earth the same old fruits, the same flowers, the same grass in the meadows and leaves upon the trees.

Messidor brought its quota of wild roses in the hedgerows, just as archaic June had done. Thermidor covered the barren cornfields with its flaming mantle of scarlet poppies, and Fructidor, though now called August, still tipped the wild sorrel with dots of crimson, and laid the first wash of tender colour on the pale cheeks of the ripening peaches.

And Juliette—young, girlish, feminine and inconsequent—had sighed for country and sunshine, had longed for a ramble in the woods, the music of the birds, the sight of the meadows sugared with marguerites.

She had left the house early: accompanied by Pétronelle, she had been rowed along the river as far as Suresnes. They had brought some bread and fresh butter, a little wine and fruit in a basket, and from here she meant to wander homewards through the woods.

It was all so peaceful, so remote: even the noise of shrieking, howling Paris did not reach the leafy thickets of Suresnes.

It almost seemed as if this little old-world village had been forgotten by the destroyers of France. It had never been a royal residence, the woods had never been preserved for royal sport: there was no vengeance to be wreaked upon its peaceful glades and sleepy, fragrant meadows.

Juliette spent a happy day; she loved the flowers, the trees, the birds, and Pétronelle was silent and sympathetic. As the afternoon wore on, and it was time to go home, Juliette turned townwards with a sigh.

You all know that road through the woods, which lies to the north-west of Paris: so leafy, so secluded. No large, hundred-year-old trees, no fine oaks or antique elms, but numberless delicate stems of hazel-nut and young ash, covered with honeysuckle at this time of year, sweet-smelling and so peaceful after that awful turmoil of the town.

Obedient to Madame Déroulède's suggestion, Juliette had tied a tricolour scarf round her waist, and a Phrygian cap of crimson cloth, with the inevitable rosette on one side, adorned her curly head.

She had gathered a huge bouquet of poppies, marguerites and blue lupin —Nature's tribute to the national colours—and as she wandered through the sylvan glades she looked like some quaint dweller of the woods—a sprite, mayhap—with old mother Pétronelle trotting behind her, like an attendant witch.

Suddenly she paused, for in the near distance she had perceived the sound of footsteps upon the leafy turf, and the next moment Paul Déroulède emerged from out the thicket and came rapidly towards her.

"We were so anxious about you at home!" he said, almost by way of an apology. "My mother became so restless ..."

"That to quiet her fears you came in search of me!" she retorted with a gay little laugh, the laugh of a young girl, scarce a woman as yet, who feels that she is good to look at, good to talk to, who feels her wings for the first time, the wings with which to soar into that mad, merry, elusive land called Romance. Ay, her wings! but her power also! that sweet, subtle power of the woman: the yoke which men love, rail at, and love again, the yoke that enslaves them and gives them the joy of kings.

How happy the day had been! Yet it had been incomplete!

Pétronelle was somewhat dull, and Juliette was too young to enjoy long companionship with her own thoughts. Now suddenly the day seemed to have become perfect. There was someone there to appreciate the charm of the woods, the beauty of that blue sky peeping though the tangled foliage of the honeysuckle-covered trees. There was some one to talk to, someone to admire the fresh white frock Juliette had put on that morning.

"But how did you know where to find me?" she asked with a quaint touch of immature coquetry.

"I didn't know," he replied quietly. "They told me you had gone to Suresness, and meant to wander homewards through the woods. It frightened me, for you will have to go through the north-west barrier, and ..."

"Well?"

He smiled, and looked earnestly for a moment at the dainty apparition before him.

"Well, you know!" he said gaily, "that tricolour scarf and the red cap are not quite sufficient as a disguise: you look anything but a staunch friend of the people. I guessed that your muslin frock would be clean, and that there would still be some tell-tale lace upon it."

She laughed again, and with delicate fingers lifted her pretty muslin frock, displaying a white frou-frou of flounces beneath the hem.

"How careless and childish!" he said, almost roughly.

"Would you have me coarse and grimy to be a fitting match for your partisans?" she retorted.

His tone of mentor nettled her, his attitude seemed to her priggish and dictatorial, and as the sun disappearing behind a sudden cloud, so her childish merriment quickly gave place to a feeling of unexplainable disappointment.

"I humbly beg your pardon," he said quietly, "And must crave your kind indulgence for my mood: but I have been so anxious ..."

"Why should you be anxious about me?"

She had meant to say this indifferently, as if caring little what the reply might be: but in her effort to seem indifferent her voice became haughty, a reminiscence of the days when she still was the daughter of the Duc de Marny, the richest and most high-born heiress in France.

"Was that presumptuous?" he asked, with a slight touch of irony, in response to her own hauteur.

"It was merely unnecessary," she replied. "I have already laid too many burdens on your shoulders, without wishing to add that of anxiety."

"You have laid no burden on me," he said quietly, "save one of gratitude."

"Gratitude? What have I done?"

"You committed a foolish, thoughtless act outside my door, and gave me the chance of easing my conscience of a heavy load."

"In what way?"

"I had never hoped that the Fates would be so kind as to allow me to render a member of your family a slight service."

"I understand that you saved my life the other day, Monsieur Déroulède. I know that I am still in peril and that I owe my safety to you ..."

"Do you also know that your brother owed his death to me?"

She closed her lips firmly, unable to reply, wrathful with him, for having suddenly and without any warning, placed a clumsy hand upon that hidden sore.

"I always meant to tell you," he continued somewhat hurriedly; "for it almost seemed to me that I have been cheating you, these last few days. I don't suppose that you can quite realise what it means to me to tell you this just now; but I owe it to you, I think. In later years you might find out, and then regret the days you spent under my roof. I called you childish a moment ago, you must forgive me; I know that you are a woman, and hope therefore that you will understand me. I killed your brother in fair fight. He provoked me as no man was ever provoked before ..."

"Is it necessary, M. Déroulède, that you should tell me all this?" she interrupted him with some impatience.

"I thought you ought to know."

"You must know, on the other hand, that I have no means of hearing the history of the quarrel from my brother's point of view now."

The moment the words were out of her lips she had realised how cruelly she had spoken. He did not reply; he was too chivalrous, too gentle, to reproach her. Perhaps he understood for the first time how bitterly she had felt her brother's death, and how deeply she must be suffering, now that she knew herself to be face to face with his murderer.

She stole a quick glance at him, through her tears. She was deeply penitent for what she had said. It almost seemed to her as if a dual nature was at war within her.

The mention of her brother's name, the recollection of that awful night beside his dead body, of those four years whilst she watched her father's moribund reason slowly wandering towards the grave, seemed to rouse in her a spirit of rebellion, and of evil, which she felt was not entirely of herself.

The woods had become quite silent. It was late afternoon, and they had gradually wandered farther and farther away from pretty sylvan Suresness, towards great, anarchic, deathdealing Paris. In this part of the woods the birds had left their homes; the trees, shorn of their lower branches looked like gaunt spectres, raising melancholy heads towards the relentless, silent sky.

In the distance, from behind the barriers, a couple of miles away, the boom of a gun was heard.

"They are closing the barriers," he said quietly after a long pause. "I am glad I was fortunate enough to meet you."

"It was kind of you to seek for me," she said meekly. "I didn't mean what I said just now ..."

"I pray you, say no more about it. I can so well understand. I only wish ..."

"It would be best I should leave your house," she said gently; "I have so ill repaid your hospitality. Pétronelle and I can easily go back to our lodgings."

"You would break my mother's heart if you left her now," he said, almost roughly. "She has become very fond of you, and knows, just as well as I do, the dangers that would beset you outside my house. My coarse and grimy partisans," he added, with a bitter touch of sarcasm, "have that advantage, that they are loyal to me, and would not harm you while under my roof."

"But you ..." she murmured.

She felt somehow that she had wounded him very deeply, and was half angry with herself for her seeming ingratitude, and yet childishly glad to have suppressed in him that attitude of mentorship, which he was beginning to assume over her.

"You need not fear that my presence will offend you much longer, mademoiselle," he said coldly. "I can quite understand how hateful it must be to you, though I would have wished that you could believe at least in my sincerity."

"Are you going away then?"

"Not out of Paris altogether. I have accepted the post of Governor of the Conciergerie."

"Ah!—where the poor Queen ..."

She checked herself suddenly. Those words would have been called treasonable to the people of France.

Instinctively and furtively, as everyone did in these days, she cast a rapid glance behind her.

"You need not be afraid," he said; "there is no one here but Pétronelle."

"And you."

"Oh! I echo your words. Poor Marie Antoinette!"

"You pity her?"

"How can I help it?"

"But you are of that horrible National Convention, who will try her, condemn her, execute her as they did the King."

"I am of the National Convention. But I will not condemn her, nor be a party to another crime. I go as Governor of the Conciergerie, to help her, if I can."

"But your popularity—your life—if you befriend her?"

"As you say, mademoiselle, my life, if I befriend her," he said simply.

She looked at him with renewed curiosity in her gaze.

How strange were men in these days! Paul Déroulède, the republican, the recognised idol of the lawless people of France, was about to risk his life for the woman he had helped to dethrone.

Pity with him did not end with the rabble of Paris; it had reached Charlotte Corday, though it failed to save her, and now it extended to the poor dispossessed Queen. Somehow, in his face this time, she saw either success or death.

"When do you leave?" she asked.

"To-morrow night."

She said nothing more. Strangely enough, a tinge of melancholy had settled over her spirits. No doubt the proximity of the town was the cause of this. She could already hear the familiar noise of muffled drums, the loud, excited shrieking of the mob, who stood round the gates of Paris, at this time of the evening, waiting to witness some important capture, perhaps that of a hated aristocrat striving to escape from the people's revenge.

They had reached the edge of the wood, and gradually, as she walked, the flowers she had gathered fell unheeded out of her listless hands one by one.

First the blue lupins: their bud-laden heads were heavy and they dropped to the ground, followed by the white marguerites, that lay thick behind her now on the grass like a shroud. The red poppies were the lightest, their thin gummy stalks clung to her hands longer than the rest. At last she let them fall too, singly, like great drops of blood, that glistened as her long white gown swept them aside.

Déroulède was absorbed in his thoughts, and seemed not to heed her. At the barrier, however, he roused himself and took out the passes which alone enabled Juliette and Pétronelle to re-enter the town unchallenged. He himself as Citizen-Deputy could come and go as he wished.

Juliette shuddered as the great gates closed behind her with a heavy clank. It seemed to shut out even the memory of this happy day, which for a brief space had been quite perfect.

She did not know Paris very well, and wondered where lay that gloomy Conciergerie, where a dethroned queen was living her last days, in an agonised memory of the past. But as they crossed the bridge she recognised all round her the massive towers of the great city: Notre Dame, the grateful spire of La Sainte Chapelle, the sombre outline of St. Gervais, and behind her the Louvre with its great history and irreclaimable grandeur. How small her own tragedy seemed in the midst of this great sanguinary drama, the last act of which had not yet even begun. Her own revenge, her oath, her tribulations, what were they in comparison with that great flaming Nemesis which had swept away a throne, that vow of retaliation carried out by thousands against other thousands, that long story of degradation, of regicide, of fratricide, the awesome chapters of which were still being unfolded one by one?

She felt small and petty: ashamed of the pleasure she had felt in the woods, ashamed of her high spirits and light-heartedness, ashamed of that feeling of sudden pity and admiration for the man who had done her and her family so deep an injury, which she was too feeble, too vacillating to avenge.

The majestic outline of the Louvre seemed to frown sarcastically on her weakness, the silent river to mock her and her wavering purpose. The man beside her had wronged her and hers far more deeply than the Bourbons had wronged their people. The people of France were taking their revenge, and God had at the close of this last happy day of her life pointed once more to the means for her great end.

CHAPTER 6. THE SCARLET PIMPERNEL

It was some few hours later. The ladies sat in the drawing-room, silent and anxious.

Soon after supper a visitor had called, and had been closeted with Paul Déroulède in the latter's study for the past two hours.

A tall, somewhat lazy-looking figure, he was sitting at a table face to face with the Citizen-Deputy. On a chair beside him lay a heavy caped coat, covered with the dust and the splashings of a long journey, but he himself was attired in clothes that suggested the most fastidious taste, and the most perfect of tailors; he wore with apparent ease the eccentric fashion of the time, the short-waisted coat of many lapels, the double waistcoat and billows of delicate lace. Unlike Déroulède he was of great height, with fair hair and a somewhat lazy expression in his good-natured blue eyes, and as he spoke, there was just a soupçon of foreign accent in the pronunciation of the French vowels, a certain drawl of o's and a's, that would have betrayed the Britisher to an observant ear.

The two men had been talking earnestly for some time, the tall Englishman was watching his friend keenly, whilst an amused, pleasant smile lingered round the corners of his firm mouth and jaw. Déroulède, restless and enthusiastic, was pacing to and fro.

"But I don't understand now, how you managed to reach Paris, my dear Blakeney!" said Déroulède at last, placing an anxious hand on his friend's shoulder. "The government has not forgotten The Scarlet Pimpernel."

"La! I took care of that!" responded Blakeney with his short, pleasant laugh. "I sent Tinville my autograph this morning."

"You are mad, Blakeney!"

"Not altogether, my friend. My faith! 'twas not only foolhardiness caused me to grant that devilish prosecutor another sight of my scarlet device. I knew what you maniacs would be after, so I came across in the *Daydream*, just to see if I couldn't get my share of the fun."

"Fun, you call it?" queried the other bitterly.

"Nay! what would you have me call it? A mad, insane, senseless tragedy, with but one issue?—the guillotine for you all."

"Then why did you come?"

"To—What shall I say, my friend?" rejoined Sir Percy Blakeney, with that inimitable drawl of his. "To give your demmed government something else to think about, whilst you are all busy running your heads into a noose."

"What makes you think we are doing that?"

"Three things, my friend—may I offer you a pinch of snuff—No?—Ah well!..." And with the graceful gesture of an accomplished dandy, Sir Percy flicked off a grain of dust from his immaculate Mechlin ruffles.

"Three things," he continued quietly; "an imprisoned Queen, about to be tried for her life, the temperament of a Frenchman—some of them— and the idiocy of mankind generally. These three things make me think that a certain section of hot-headed Republicans with yourself, my dear Déroulède, *en tête*, are about to attempt the most stupid, senseless, purposeless thing that was ever concocted by the excitable brain of a demmed Frenchman."

Déroulède smiled.

"Does it not seem amusing to you, Blakeney, that you should sit there and condemn anyone for planning mad, insane, senseless things."

"La! I'll not sit, I'll stand!" rejoined Blakeney with a laugh, as he drew himself up to his full height, and stretched his long, lazy limbs. "And now let me tell you, friend, that my League of The Scarlet Pimpernel never attempted the impossible, and to try and drag the Queen out of the clutches of these murderous rascals now, is attempting the unattainable."

"And yet we mean to try."

"I know it. I guessed it, that is why I came: that is also why I sent a pleasant little note to the Committee of Public Safety, signed with the device they know so well: The Scarlet Pimpernel."

"Well?"

"Well! the result is obvious. Robespierre, Danton, Tinville, Merlin, and the whole of the demmed murderous crowd, will be busy looking after me—a needle in a haystack. They'll put the abortive attempt down to me, and you may—*ma foi!* I only suggest that you *may* escape safely out of France—in the *Daydream,* and with the help of your humble servant."

"But in the meanwhile they'll discover you, and they'll not let you escape a second time."

"My friend! if a terrier were to lose his temper, he never would run a rat to earth. Now your Revolutionary Government has lost its temper with me, ever since I slipped through Chauvelin's fingers; they are blind with their own fury, whilst I am perfectly happy and cool as a cucumber. My life has become valuable to me, my friend. There is someone over the water now who weeps when I don't return—No! no! never fear—they'll not get The Scarlet Pimpernel this journey ..."

He laughed, a gay, pleasant laugh, and his strong, firm face seemed to soften at thought of the beautiful wife, over in England, who was waiting anxiously for his safe return.

"And yet you'll not help us to rescue the Queen?" rejoined Déroulède, with some bitterness.

"By every means in my power," replied Blakeney, "save the insane. But I will help to get you all out of the demmed hole, when you have failed."

"We'll not fail," asserted the other hotly.

Sir Percy Blakeney went close up to his friend and placed his long, slender hand, with a touch of almost womanly tenderness upon the latter's shoulder.

"Will you tell me your plans?"

In a moment Déroulède was all fire and enthusiasm.

"There are not many of us in it," he began, "although half France will be in sympathy with us. We have plenty of money, of course, and also the necessary disguise for the royal lady."

"Yes?"

"I, in the meanwhile, have asked for and obtained the post of Governor of the Conciergerie; I go into my new quarters to-morrow. In the meanwhile, I am making arrangements for my mother and—and those dependent upon me to quit France immediately."

Blakeney had perceived the slight hesitation when Déroulède mentioned those dependent upon him. He looked scrutinisingly at his friend, who continued quickly:

"I am still very popular among the people. My family can go about unmolested. I must get them out of France, however, in case—in case ..."

"Of course," rejoined the other simply.

"As soon as I am assured that they are safe, my friends and I can prosecute our plans.

You see the trial of the Queen has not yet been decided on, but I know that it is in the air. We hope to get her away, disguised in one of the uniforms of the National Guard. As you know, it will be my duty to make the final round every evening in the prison, and to see that everything is safe for the night. Two fellows watch all night, in the room next to that occupied by the Queen. Usually they drink and play cards all night long. I want an opportunity to drug their brandy, and thus to render them more loutish and idiotic than usual; then for a blow on the head that will make them senseless. It should be easy, for I have a strong fist, and after that ..."

"Well? After that, friend?" rejoined Sir Percy earnestly, "after that? Shall I fill in the details of the picture?—the guard twenty-five strong outside the Conciergerie, how will you pass them?"

"I as the Governor, followed by one of my guards ..."

"To go whither?"

"I have the right to come and go as I please."

"I' faith! so you have, but 'one of your guards'—eh? Wrapped to the eyes in a long mantle to hide the female figure beneath. I have been in Paris but a few hours, and yet already I have realised that there is not one demmed citizen within its walls, who does not at this moment suspect some other demmed citizen of conniving at the Queen's escape. Even the sparrows on the house-tops are objects of suspicion. No figure wrapped in a mantle will from this day forth leave Paris unchallenged."

"But you yourself, friend?" suggested Déroulède. "You think you can quit Paris unrecognised—then why not the Queen?"

"Because she is a woman, and has been a queen. She has nerves, poor soul, and weaknesses of body and of mind now. Alas for her! Alas for France! who wreaks such idle vengeance on so poor an enemy? Can you take hold of Marie Antoinette by the shoulders, shove her into the bottom of a cart and pile sacks of potatoes on the top of her? I did that to the Comtesse de Tournai and her daughter, as stiff-necked a pair of French aristocrats as ever deserved the guillotine for their insane prejudices. But can you do it to Marie Antoinette? She'd rebuke you publicly, and betray herself and you in a flash, sooner than submit to a loss of dignity."

"But would you leave her to her fate?"

"Ah! there's the trouble, friend. Do you think you need appeal to the sense of chivalry of my league? We are still twenty strong, and heart and soul in sympathy with your mad schemes. The poor, poor Queen! But you are bound to fail, and then who will help you all, if we too are put out of the way?"

"We should succeed if you helped us. At one time you used proudly to say: 'The League of The Scarlet Pimpernel has never failed.'"

"Because it attempted nothing which it could not accomplish. But, la! since you put me on my mettle—Demm it all! I'll have to think about it!"

And he laughed that funny, somewhat inane laugh of his, which had deceived the clever men of two countries as to his real personality.

Déroulède went up to the heavy oak desk which occupied a conspicuous place in the centre of one of the walls. He unlocked it and drew forth a bundle of papers.

"Will you look through these?" he asked, handing them to Sir Percy Blakeney.

"What are they?"

"Different schemes I have drawn up, in case my original plan should not succeed."

"Burn them, my friend," said Blakeney laconically. "Have you not yet learned the lesson of never putting your hand to paper?"

"I can't burn these. You see, I shall not be able to have long conversations with Marie Antoinette. I must give her my suggestions in writing, that she may study them and not fail me, through lack of knowledge of her part."

"Better that than papers in these times, my friend: these papers, if found, would send you, untried, to the guillotine."

"I am careful, and, at present, quite beyond suspicion. Moreover, among the papers is a complete collection of passports, suitable for any character the Queen and her attendant may be forced to assume. It has taken me some months to collect them, so as not to arouse suspicion; I gradually got them together, on one pretence or another: now I am ready for any eventuality ..."

He suddenly paused. A look in his friend's face had given him a swift warning.

He turned, and there in the doorway, holding back the heavy portière, stood Juliette, graceful, smiling, a little pale, this no doubt owing to the flickering light of the unsnuffed candles.

So young and girlish did she look in her soft, white muslin frock that at sight of her the tension in Déroulède's face seemed to relax. Instinctively he had thrown the papers back into the desk, but his look had softened, from the fire of obstinate energy to that of inexpressible tenderness.

Blakeney was quietly watching the young girl as she stood in the doorway, a little bashful and undecided.

"Madame Déroulède sent me," she said hesitatingly, "she says the hour is getting late and she is very anxious. M. Déroulède, would you come and reassure her?"

"In a moment, mademoiselle," he replied lightly, "my friend and I have just finished our talk. May I have the honour to present him?—Sir Percy Blakeney, a traveller from England. Blakeney, this is Mademoiselle Juliette de Marny, my mother's guest."

CHAPTER 7. A WARNING

Sir Percy bowed very low, with all the graceful flourish and elaborate gesture the eccentric customs of the time demanded.

He had not said a word, since the first exclamation of warning, with which he had drawn his friend's attention to the young girl in the doorway.

Noiselessly, as she had come, Juliette glided out of the room again, leaving behind her an atmosphere of wild flowers, of the bouquet she had gathered, then scattered in the woods.

There was silence in the room for awhile. Déroulède was locking up his desk and slipping the keys into his pocket.

"Shall we join my mother for a moment, Blakeney?" he said, moving towards the door.

"I shall be proud to pay my respects," replied Sir Percy; "but before we close the subject, I think I'll change my mind about those papers. If I am to be of service to you I think I had best look through them, and give you my opinion of your schemes."

Déroulède looked at him keenly for a moment.

"Certainly," he said at last, going up to his desk. "I'll stay with you whilst you read them through."

"La! not to-night, my friend," said Sir Percy lightly; "the hour is late, and madame is waiting for us. They'll be quite safe with me, and you'll entrust them to my care."

Déroulède seemed to hesitate. Blakeney had spoken in his usual airy manner, and was even now busy readjusting the set of his perfectly-tailored coat.

"Perhaps you cannot quite trust me?" laughed Sir Percy gaily. "I seemed too lukewarm just now."

"No; it's not that, Blakeney!" said Déroulède quietly at last. "There is no mistrust in me, all the mistrust is on your side."

"Faith!—" began Sir Percy.

"Nay! do not explain. I understand and appreciate your friendship, but I should like to convince you how unjust is your mistrust of one of God's purest angels, that ever walked the earth."

"Oho! that's it, is it, friend Déroulède? Methought you had foresworn the sex altogether, and now you are in love."

"Madly, blindly, stupidly in love, my friend," said Déroulède with a sigh. "Hopelessly, I fear me!"

"Why hopelessly?"

"She is the daughter of the late Duc de Marny, one of the oldest names in France; a Royalist to the backbone ..."

"Hence your overwhelming sympathy for the Queen!"

"Nay! you wrong me there, friend. I'd have tried to save the Queen, even if I had never learned to love Juliette. But you see now how unjust were your suspicions."

"Had I any?"

"Don't deny it. You were loud in urging me to burn those papers a moment ago. You called them useless and dangerous and now ..."

"I still think them useless and dangerous, and by reading them would wish to confirm my opinion and give weight to my arguments."

"If I were to part from them now I would seem to be mistrusting her."

"You are a mad idealist, my dear Déroulède!"

"How can I help it? I have lived under the same roof with her for three weeks now. I have begun to understand what a saint is like."

"And 'twill be when you understand that your idol has feet of clay that you'll learn the real lesson of love," said Blakeney earnestly.

"Is it love to worship a saint in heaven, whom you dare not touch, who hovers above you like a cloud, which floats away from you even as you gaze? To love is to feel one being in the world at one with us, our equal in sin as well as in virtue. To love, for us men, is to clasp one woman with our arms, feeling that she lives and breathes just as we do, suffers as we do, thinks with us, loves with us, and, above all, sins with us. Your mock saint who stands in a niche is not a woman if she have not suffered, still less a woman if she have not sinned. Fall at the feet of your idol an you wish, but drag her down to your level after that—the only level she should ever reach, that of your heart."

Who shall render faithfully a true account of the magnetism which poured forth from this remarkable man as he spoke: this well-dressed, foppish apostle of the greatest love that man has ever known. And as he spoke the whole story of his own great, true love for the woman who once had so deeply wronged him seemed to stand clearly written in the strong, lazy, good-humoured, kindly face glowing with tenderness for her.

Déroulède felt this magnetism, and therefore did not resent the implied suggestion, anent the saint whom he was still content to worship.

A dreamer and an idealist, his mind held spellbound by the great social problems which were causing the upheaval of a whole country, he had not yet had the time to learn the sweet lesson which Nature teaches to her elect—the lesson of a great, a true, human and passionate love. To him, at present, Juliette represented the perfect embodiment of his most idealistic dreams. She stood in his mind so far above him that if she proved unattainable, he would scarce have suffered. It was such a foregone conclusion.

Blakeney's words were the first to stir in his heart a desire for something beyond that quasi-mediaeval worship, something weaker and yet infinitely stronger, something more earthy and yet almost divine.

"And now, shall we join the ladies?" said Blakeney after a long pause, during which the mental workings of his alert brain were almost visible, in the earnest look which he cast at his friend. "You shall keep the papers in your desk, give them into the keeping of your saint, trust her all in all rather than not at all, and if the time should come that your heaven-enthroned ideal fall somewhat heavily to earth, then give me the privilege of being a witness to your happiness."

"You are still mistrustful, Blakeney," said Déroulède lightly. "If you say much more I'll give these papers into Mademoiselle Marny's keeping until to-morrow."

CHAPTER 8. ANNE MIE

That night, when Blakeney, wrapped in his cloak, was walking down the Rue Ecole de Médecine towards his own lodgings, he suddenly felt a timid hand upon his sleeve.

Anne Mie stood beside him, her pale, melancholy face peeping up at the tall Englishman, through the folds of a dark hood closely tied under her chin.

"Monsieur," she said timidly, "do not think me very presumptuous. I— I would wish to have five minutes' talk with you—may I?"

He looked down with great kindness at the quaint, wizened little figure, and the strong face softened at the sight of the poor, deformed shoulder, the hard, pinched look of the young mouth, the general look of pathetic helplessness which appeals so strongly to the chivalrous.

"Indeed, mademoiselle," he said gently, "you make me very proud; and I can serve you in any way, I pray you command me. But," he added, seeing Anne Mie's somewhat scared look, "this street is scarce fit for private conversation. Shall we try and find a better spot?"

Paris had not yet gone to bed. In these times it was really safest to be out in the open streets. There, everybody was more busy, more on the move, on the lookout for suspected houses, leaving the wanderer alone.

Blakeney led Anne Mie towards the Luxembourg Gardens, the great devastated pleasure-ground of the ci-devant tyrants of the people. The beautiful Anne of Austria, and the Medici before her, Louis XIII, and his gallant musketeers—all have given place to the great cannon-forging industry of this besieged Republic. France, attacked on every side, is forcing her sons to defend her: persecuted, martyrised, done to death by her, she is still their Mother: La Patrie, who needs their arms against the foreign foe. England is threatening the north, Prussia and Austria the east. Admiral Hood's flag is flying on Toulon Arsenal.

The siege of the Republic!

And the Republic is fighting for dear life. The Tuileries and Luxembourg Gardens are transformed into a township of gigantic smithies; and Anne Mie, with scared eyes, and clinging to Blakeney's arm, cast furtive, terrified glances at the huge furnaces and the begrimed, darkly scowling faces of the workers within.

"The people of France in arms against tyranny!" Great placards, bearing these inspiring words, are affixed to gallows-shaped posts, and flutter in the evening breeze, rendered scorching by the heat of the furnaces all around.

Farther on, a group of older men, squatting on the ground, are busy making tents, and some women—the same Megaeras who daily shriek round the guillotine—are plying their needles and scissors for the purpose of making clothes for the soldiers.

The soldiers are the entire able-bodied male population of France.

"The people of France in arms against tyranny!"

That is their sign, their trade-mark; one of these placards, fitfully illuminated by a torch of resin, towers above a group of children busy tearing up scraps of old linen—their mothers', their sisters' linen —in order to make lint for the wounded.

Loud curses and suppressed mutterings fill the smoke-laden air.

The people of France, in arms against tyranny, is bending its broad back before the most cruel, the most absolute and brutish slave-driving ever exercised over mankind.

Not even mediaeval Christianity has ever dared such wholesale enforcements of its doctrines, as this constitution of Liberty and Fraternity.

Merlin's "Law of the Suspect" has just been formulated. From now onward each and every citizen of France must watch his words, his looks, his gestures, lest they be suspect. Of what—of treason to the Republic, to the people? Nay, worse! lest they be suspect of being suspect to the great era of Liberty.

Therefore in the smithies and among the groups of tent-makers a moment's negligence, a careless attention to the work, might lead to a brief trial on the morrow and the inevitable guillotine. Negligence is treason to the higher interests of the Republic.

Blakeney dragged Anne Mie away from the sight. These roaring furnaces frightened her; he took her down the Place St Michel, towards the river. It was quieter here.

"What dreadful people they have become," she said, shuddering; "even I can remember how different they used to be."

The houses on the banks of the river were mostly converted into hospitals, preparatory for the great siege. Some hundred mètres lower down, the new children's hospital, endowed by Citizen-Deputy Déroulède, loomed, white, clean, and comfortable-looking, amidst its more squalid fellows.

"I think it would be best not to sit down," suggested Blakeney, "and wiser for you to throw your hood away from your face."

He seemed to have no fears for himself; many had said that he bore a charmed life; and yet ever since Admiral Hood had planted his flag on Toulon Arsenal, the English were more feared than ever, and The Scarlet Pimpernel more hated than most.

"You wished to speak to me about Paul Déroulède," he said kindly, seeing that the young girl was making desperate efforts to say what lay on her mind. "He is my friend, you know."

"Yes; that is why I wished to ask you a question," she replied.

"What is it?"

"Who is Juliette de Marny, and why did she seek an entrance into Paul's house?"

"Did she seek it, then?"

"Yes; I saw the scene from the balcony. At the time it did not strike me as a farce. I merely thought that she had been stupid and foolhardy. But since then I have reflected. She provoked the mob of the street, willfully, just at the very moment when she reached M. Déroulède's door. She meant to appeal to his chivalry, and called for help, well knowing that he would respond."

She spoke rapidly and excitedly now, throwing off all shyness and reserve. Blakeney was forced to check her vehemence, which might have been thought "suspicious" by some idle citizen unpleasantly inclined.

"Well? And now?" he asked, for the young girl had paused, as if ashamed of her excitement.

"And now she stays in the house, on and on, day after day," continued Anne Mie, speaking more quietly, though with no less intensity. "Why does she not go? She is not safe in France. She belongs to the most hated of all the classes—the idle, rich aristocrats of the old régime. Paul has several times suggested plans for her emigration to England. Madame Déroulède, who is an angel, loves her, and would not like to part from her, but it would be obviously wiser for her to go, and yet she stays. Why?"

"Presumably because ..."

"Because she is in love with Paul?" interrupted Anne Mie vehemently. "No, no; she does not love him—at least—Oh! sometimes I don't know. Her eyes light up when he comes, and she is listless when he goes. She always spends a longer time over her toilet, when we expect him home to dinner," she added, with a touch of naïve femininity. "But — if it be love, then that love is strange and unwomanly; it is a love that will not be for his good ..."

"Why should you think that?"

"I don't know," said the girl simply. "Isn't it an instinct?"

"Not a very unerring one in this case, I fear."

"Why?"

"Because your own love for Paul Déroulède has blinded you— Ah! you must pardon me, mademoiselle; you sought this conversation and not I, and I fear me I have wounded you. Yet I would wish you to know how deep is my sympathy with you, and how great my desire to render you a service if I could."

"I was about to ask a service of you, monsieur."

"Then command me, I beg of you."

"You are Paul's friend—persuade him that that woman in his house is a standing danger to his life and liberty."

"He would not listen to me."

"Oh! a man always listens to another."

"Except on one subject—the woman he loves."

He had said the last words very gently but very firmly. He was deeply, tenderly sorry for the poor, deformed, fragile girl, doomed to be a witness of that most heartrending of human tragedies, the passing away of her own scarce-hoped-for happiness. But he felt that at this moment the kindest act would be one of complete truth. He knew that Paul Déroulède's heart was completely given to Juliette de Marny; he too, like Anne Mie, instinctively mistrusted the beautiful girl and her strange, silent ways, but, unlike the poor hunchback, he knew that no sin which Juliette might commit would henceforth tear her from out the heart of his friend; that if, indeed, she turned out to be false, or even treacherous, she would, nevertheless, still hold a place in Déroulède's very soul, which no one else would ever fill.

"You think he loves her?" asked Anne Mie at last.

"I am sure of it."

"And she?"

"Ah! I do not know. I would trust your instinct—a woman's—sooner than my own."

"She is false, I tell you, and is hatching treason against Paul."

"Then all we can do is to wait."

"Wait?"

"And watch carefully, earnestly, all the time. There! shall I pledge you my word that Déroulède shall come to no harm?"

"Pledge me your word that you'll part him from that woman."

"Nay; that is beyond my power. A man like Paul Déroulède only loves once in life, but when he does, it is for always."

Once more she was silent, pressing her lips closely together, as if afraid of what she might say.

He saw that she was bitterly disappointed, and sought for a means of tempering the cruelty of the blow.

"It will be your task to watch over Paul," he said; "with your friendship to guard and protect him, we need have no fear for his safety, I think."

"I will watch," she replied quietly.

Gradually he had led her steps back towards the Rue Ecole de Médecine.

A great melancholy had fallen over his bold, adventurous spirit. How full of tragedies was this great city, in the last throes of its insane and cruel struggle for an unattainable goal. And yet, despite its guillotine and mock trials, its tyrannical laws and overfilled prisons, its very sorrows paled before the dead, dull misery of this deformed girl's heart.

A wild exaltation, a fever of enthusiasm lent glamour to the scenes which were daily enacted on the Place de la Revolution, turning the final acts of the tragedies into glaring, lurid melodrama, almost unreal in its poignant appeal to the sensibilities.

But here there was only this dead, dull misery, an aching heart, a poor, fragile creature in the throes of an agonised struggle for a fast-disappearing happiness.

Anne Mie hardly knew now what she had hoped, when she sought this interview with Sir Percy Blakeney. Drowning in a sea of hopelessness, she had clutched at what might prove a chance of safety. Her reason told her that Paul's friend was right. Déroulède was a man who would love but once in his life. He had never loved—for he had too much pitied—poor, pathetic little Anne Mie.

Nay; why should we say that love and pity are akin?

Love, the great, the strong, the conquering god—Love that subdues a world, and rides roughshod over principle, virtue, tradition, over home, kindred, and religion—what cares he for the easy conquest of the pathetic being, who appeals to his sympathy?

Love means equality—the same height of heroism or of sin. When Love stoops to pity, he has ceased to soar in the boundless space, that rarefied atmosphere wherein man feels himself made at last truly in the image of God.

CHAPTER 9. JEALOUSY

At the door of her home Blakeney parted from Anne Mie, with all the courtesy with which he would have bade adieu to the greatest lady in his own land.

Anne Mie let herself into the house with her own latch-key. She closed the heavy door noiselessly, then glided upstairs like a quaint little ghost.

But on the landing above she met Paul Déroulède.

He had just come out of his room, and was still fully dressed.

"Anne Mie!" he said, with such an obvious cry of pleasure, that the young girl, with beating heart, paused a moment on the top of the stairs, as if hoping to hear that cry again, feeling that indeed he was glad to see her, had been uneasy because of her long absence.

"Have I made you anxious?" she asked at last.

"Anxious!" he exclaimed. "Little one, I have hardly lived this last hour, since I realised that you had gone out so late as this, and all alone."

"How did you know?"

"Mademoiselle de Marny knocked at my door an hour ago. She had gone to your room to see you, and, not finding you there, she searched the house for you, and finally, in her anxiety, came to me. We did not dare to tell my mother. I won't ask you where you have been, Anne Mie, but another time, remember, little one, that the streets of Paris are not safe, and that those who love you suffer deeply, when they know you to be in peril."

"Those who love me!" murmured the girl under her breath.

"Could you not have asked me to come with you?"

"No; I wanted to be alone. The streets were quite safe, and—I wanted to speak with Sir Percy Blakeney."

"With Blakeney?" he exclaimed in boundless astonishment. "Why, what in the world did you want to say him?"

The girl, so unaccustomed to lying, had blurted out the truth, almost against her will.

"I thought he could help me, as I was much perturbed and restless."

"You went to him sooner than to me?" said Déroulède in a tone of gentle reproach, and still puzzled at this extraordinary action on the part of the girl, usually so shy and reserved.

"My anxiety was about you, and you would have mocked me for it."

"Indeed, I should never mock you, Anne Mie. But why should you be anxious about me?"

"Because I see you wandering blindly on the brink of a great danger, and because I see you confiding in those, whom you had best mistrust."

He frowned a little, and bit his lip to check the rough word that was on the tip of his tongue.

"Is Sir Percy Blakeney one of those whom I had best mistrust?" he said lightly.

"No," she answered curtly.

"Then, dear, there is no cause for unrest. He is the only one of my friends whom you have not known intimately. All those who are round me now, you know that you can trust and that you can love," he added earnestly and significantly.

He took her hand; it was trembling with obvious suppressed agitation. She knew that he had guessed what was passing in her mind, and now was deeply ashamed of what she had done. She had been tortured with jealousy for the past three weeks, but at least she had suffered quite alone: no one had been allowed to touch that wound, which more often than not, excites derision rather than pity. Now, by her own actions, two men knew her secret. Both were kind and sympathetic; but Déroulède resented her imputations, and Blakeney had been unable to help her.

A wave of morbid introspection swept over her soul. She realised in a moment how petty and base had been her thoughts and how purposeless her actions. She would have given her life at this moment to eradicate from Déroulède's mind the knowledge of her own jealousy; she hoped that at least he had not guessed her love.

She tried to read his thoughts, but in the dark passage, only dimly lighted by the candles in Déroulède's room beyond, she could not see the expression of his face, but the hand which held hers was warm and tender. She felt herself pitied, and blushed at the thought. With a hasty good-night she fled down the passage, and locked herself in her room, alone with her own thoughts at last.

CHAPTER 10. DENUNCIATION

But what of Juliette?

What of this wild, passionate, romantic creature tortured by a Titanic conflict? She, but a girl, scarcely yet a woman, torn by the greatest antagonistic powers that ever fought for a human soul. On the one side duty, tradition, her dead brother, her father—above all, her religion and the oath she had sworn before God; on the other justice and honour, a case of right and wrong, honesty and pity.

How she fought with these powers now!

She fought with them, struggled with them on her knees. She tried to crush memory, tried to forget that awful midnight scene ten years ago, her brother's dead body, her father's avenging hand holding her own, as he begged her to do that, which he was too feeble, too old to accomplish.

His words rang in her ears from across that long vista of the past.

"Before the face of Almighty God, who sees and hears me, I swear ..."

And she had repeated those words loudly and of her own free will, with her hand resting on her brother's breast, and God Himself looking down upon her, for she had called upon Him to listen.

"I swear that I will seek out Paul Déroulède, and in any manner which God may dictate to me encompass his death, his ruin, or dishonour in revenge for my brother's death. May my brother's soul remain in torment until the final Judgment Day if I should break my oath, but may it rest in eternal peace, the day on which his death is fitly avenged."

Almost it seemed to her as if father and brother were standing by her side, as she knelt and prayed.—Oh! how she prayed!

In many ways she was only a child. All her years had been passed in confinement, either beside her dying father or, later, between the four walls of the Ursuline Convent.

And during those years her soul had been fed on a contemplative, ecstatic religion, a kind of sanctified superstition, which she would have deemed sacrilege to combat.

Her first step into womanhood was taken with that oath upon her lips; since then, with a stoical sense of duty, she had lashed herself into a daily, hourly remembrance of the great mission imposed upon her.

To have neglected it would have been, to her, equal to denying God.

She had but vague ideas of the doctrinal side of religion. Purgatory was to her merely a word, but a word representing a real spiritual state—one of expectancy, of restlessness, of sorrow. And vaguely, yet determinedly, she believed that her brother's soul suffered, because she had been too weak to fulfil her oath.

The Church had not come to her rescue. The ministers of her religion were scattered to the four corners of besieged, agonising France. She had no one to help her, no one to comfort her. That very peaceful, contemplative life she had led in the convent, only served to enhance her feeling of the solemnity of her mission.

It was true, it was inevitable, because it was so hard.

To the few who, throughout those troublous times, had kept a feeling of veneration for their religion, this religion had become one of abnegation and martyrdom.

A spirit of uncompromising Jansenism seemed to call forth sacrifices and renunciation, whereas the happy-go-lucky Catholicism of the past century had only suggested an easy, flowered path, to a comfortable, well-upholstered heaven.

The harder the task seemed which was set before her, the more real it became to Juliette. God, she firmly believed, had at last, after ten years, shown her the way to wreak vengeance upon her brother's murderer. He had brought her to this house, caused her to see and hear part of the conversation between Blakeney and Déroulède, and this at the moment of all others, when even the semblance of a conspiracy against the Republic would bring the one inevitable result in its train: disgrace first, the hasty mock trial, the hall of justice, and the guillotine.

She tried not to hate Déroulède. She wished to judge him coldly and impartially, or rather to indict him before the throne of God, and to punish him for the crime he had committed ten years ago. Her personal feelings must remain out of the question.

Had Charlotte Corday considered her own sensibilities, when with her own hand she put an end to Marat?

Juliette remained on her knees for hours. She heard Anne Mie come home, and Déroulède's voice of welcome on the landing. This was perhaps the most bitter moment of this awful soul conflict, for it brought to her mind the remembrance of those others who would suffer too, and who were innocent—Madame Déroulède and poor, crippled Anne Mie. They had done no wrong, and yet how heavily would they be punished!

And then the saner judgment, the human, material code of ethics gained for a while the upper hand. Juliette would rise from her knees, dry her eyes, prepare quietly to go to bed, and to forget all about the awful, relentless Fate which dragged her to the fulfilment of its will, and then sink back, broken-hearted, murmuring impassioned prayers for forgiveness to her father, her brother, her God.

The soul was young and ardent, and it fought for abnegation, martyrdom, and stern duty; the body was childlike, and it fought for peace, contentment, and quiet reason.

The rational body was conquered by the passionate, powerful soul.

Blame not the child, for in herself she was innocent. She was but another of the many victims of this cruel, mad, hysterical time, that spirit of relentless tyranny, forcing its doctrines upon the weak.

With the first break of dawn Juliette at last finally rose from her knees, bathed her burning eyes and head, tidied her hair and dress, then she sat down at the table, and began to write.

She was a transformed being now, no longer a child, essentially a woman—a Joan of Arc with a mission, a Charlotte Corday going to martyrdom, a human, suffering, erring soul, committing a great crime for the sake of an idea.

She wrote out carefully and with a steady hand the denunciation of Citizen-Deputy Déroulède which has become an historical document, and is preserved in the chronicles of France.

You have all seen it at the Musée Carnavalet in its glass case, its yellow paper and faded ink revealing nothing of the soul conflict of which it was the culminating victory. The cramped, somewhat schoolgirlish writing is the mute, pathetic witness of one of the saddest tragedies, that era of sorrow and crime has ever known:

> *To the Representatives of the People now sitting in Assembly at the National Convention*
> You trust and believe in the Representative of the people: Citizen-Deputy Paul Déroulède. He is false, and a traitor to the Republic. He is planning, and hopes to effect, the release of ci-devant Marie Antoinette, widow of the traitor Louis Capet. Haste! ye representatives of the people! proofs of his assertion, papers and plans, are still in the house of the Citizen-Deputy Déroulède. This statement is made by one who knows.
> *I. The 23rd Fructidor.*

When her letter was written she read it through carefully, made the one or two little corrections, which are still visible in the document, then folded her missive, hid it within the folds of her kerchief, and, wrapping a dark cloak and hood round her, she slipped noiselessly out of her room.

The house was all quiet and still. She shuddered a little as the cool morning air fanned her hot cheeks: it seemed like the breath of ghosts.

She ran quickly down the stairs, and as rapidly as she could, pushed back the heavy bolts of the front door, and slipped out into the street.

Already the city was beginning to stir. There was no time for sleep, when so much had to be done for the safety of the threatened Republic. As Juliette turned her steps towards the river, she met the crowd of workmen, whom France was employing for her defence.

Behind her, in the Luxembourg Gardens, and all along the opposite bank of the river, the furnaces were already ablaze, and the smiths at work forging the guns.

At every step now Juliette came across the great placards, pinned to the tall gallows-shaped posts, which proclaim to every passing citizen, that the people of France are up and in arms.

Right across the Place de l'Institut a procession of market carts, laden with vegetables and a little fruit, wends its way slowly towards the centre of the town. They each carry tiny tricolour flags, with a Pike and Cap of Liberty surmounting the flagstaff.

They are good patriots the market-gardeners, who come in daily to feed the starving mob of Paris, with the few handfuls of watery potatoes, and miserable, vermin-eaten cabbages, which that fraternal Revolution still allows them to grow without hindrance.

Everyone seems busy with their work this early in the morning: the business of killing does not begin until later in the day.

For the moment Juliette can get along quite unmolested: the women and children mostly hurrying on towards the vast encampments in the Tuileries, where lint, and bandages, and coats for the soldiers are manufactured all the day.

The walls of all the houses bear the great patriotic device: "*Liberté, Egalité, Fraternité, sinon La Mort* "; others are more political in their proclamation: "*La République une et indivisible* ."

But on the walls of the Louvre, of the great palace of whilom kings, where the Roi Soleil held his Court, and flirted with the prettiest women in France, there the new and great Republic has affixed its final mandate.

A great poster glued to the wall bears the words: "*La Loi concernan les Suspects* ." Below the poster is a huge wooden box with a slit at the top.

This is the latest invention for securing the safety of this one and indivisible Republic.

Henceforth everyone becomes a traitor at one word of denunciation from an idler or an enemy, and, as in the most tyrannical days of the Spanish Inquisition one-half of the nation was set to spy upon the other, that wooden box, with its slit, is put there ready to receive denunciations from one hand against another.

Had Juliette paused but for the fraction of a second, had she stopped to read the placard setting forth this odious law, had she only reflected, then she would even now have turned back, and fled from that gruesome box of infamies, as she would from a dangerous and noisome reptile or from the pestilence.

But her long vigil, her prayers, her ecstatic visions of heroic martyrs had now completely numbed her faculties. Her vitality, her sensibilities were gone: she had become an automaton gliding to her doom, without a thought or a tremor.

She drew the letter from her bosom, and with a steady hand dropped it into the box. The irreclaimable had now occurred. Nothing she could henceforth say or do, no prayers or agonised vigils, no miracles even, could undo her action or save Paul Déroulède from trial and guillotine.

One or two groups of people hurrying to their work had seen her drop the letter into the box. A couple of small children paused, finger in mouth, gazing at her with inane curiosity; one woman uttered a coarse jest, all of them shrugged their shoulders, and passed on, on their way. Those who habitually crossed this spot were used to such sights.

That wooden box, with its mouthlike slit was like an insatiable monster that was constantly fed, yet was still gaping for more.

Having done the deed Juliette turned, and as rapidly as she had come, so she went back to her temporary home.

A home no more now; she must leave it at once, to-day if possible. This much she knew, that she no longer could touch the bread of the man she had betrayed. She would not appear at breakfast, she could plead a headache, and in the afternoon Pétronelle should pack her things.

She turned into a little shop close by, and asked for a glass of milk and a bit of bread. The woman who served her eyed her with some curiosity, for Juliette just now looked almost out of her mind.

She had not yet begun to think, and she had ceased to suffer.

Both would come presently, and with them the memory of this last irretrievable hour and a just estimate of what she had done.

CHAPTER 11. "VENGEANCE IS MINE."

The pretence of a headache enabled Juliette to keep in her room the greater part of the day. She would have liked to shut herself out from the entire world during those hours which she spent face to face with her own thoughts and her own sufferings.

The sight of Anne Mie's pathetic little face as she brought her food and delicacies and various little comforts, was positive torture to the poor, harrowed soul.

At every sound in the great, silent house she started up, quivering with apprehension and horror. Had the sword of Damocles, which she herself had suspended, already fallen over the heads of those who had shown her nothing but kindness?

She could not think of Madame Déroulède or of Anne Mie without the most agonising, the most torturing shame.

And what of him—the man she had so remorselessly, so ruthlessly betrayed to a tribunal which would know no mercy?

Juliette dared not think of him.

She had never tried to analyse her feelings with regard to him. At the time of Charlotte Corday's trial, when his sonorous voice rang out in its pathetic appeal for the misguided woman, Juliette had given him ungrudging admiration. She remembered now how strongly his magnetic personality had roused in her a feeling of enthusiasm for the poor girl, who had come from the depths of her quiet provincial home, in order to accomplish the horrible deed which would immortalise her name through all the ages to come, and cause her countrymen to proclaim her "greater than Brutus."

Déroulède was pleading for the life of that woman, and it was his very appeal which had aroused Juliette's dormant energy, for the cause which her dead father had enjoined her not to forget. It was Déroulède again whom she had seen but a few weeks ago, standing alone before the mob who would have torn her to pieces, haranguing them on her behalf, speaking to them with that quiet, strong voice of his, ruling them with the rule of love and pity, and turning their wrath to gentleness.

Did she hate him, then?

Surely, surely she hated him for having thrust himself into her life, for having caused her brother's death and covered her father's declining years with sorrow. And, above all, she hated him—indeed, indeed it was hate!—for being the cause of this most hideous action of her life: an action to which she had been driven against her will, one of basest ingratitude and treachery, foreign to every sentiment within her heart, cowardly, abject, the unconscious outcome of this strange magnetism which emanated from him and had cast a spell over her, transforming her individuality and will power, and making of her an unconscious and automatic instrument of Fate.

She would not speak of God's finger again: it was Fate—pagan, devilish Fate!—the weird, shrivelled women who sit and spin their interminable thread. They had decreed; and Juliette, unable to fight, blind and broken by the conflict, had succumbed to the Megaeras and their relentless wheel.

At length silence and loneliness became unendurable. She called Pétronelle, and ordered her to pack her boxes.

"We leave for England to-day", she said curtly.

"For England?" gasped the worthy old soul, who was feeling very happy and comfortable in this hospitable house, and was loth to leave it. "So soon?"

"Why, yes; we had talked of it for some time. We cannot remain here always. My cousins De Crécy are there, and my aunt De Coudremont. We shall be among friends, Pétronelle, if we ever get there."

"If we ever get there!" sighed poor Pétronelle; "we have but very little money, *ma chérie,* and no passports. Have you thought of asking M. Déroulède for them?"

"No, no," rejoined Juliette hastily; "I'll see to the passports somehow, Pétronelle. Sir Percy Blakeney is English; he'll tell me what to do."

"Do you know where he lives, my jewel?"

"Yes; I heard him tell Madame Déroulède last night that he was lodging with a provincial named Brogard at the Sign of the Cruche Cassée. I'll go seek him, Pétronelle; I am sure he will help me. The English are so resourceful and practical. He'll get us our passports, I know, and advise us as to the best way to proceed. Do you stay here and get all our things ready. I'll not be long."

She took up a cloak and hood, and, throwing them over her arm, she slipped out of the room.

Déroulède had left the house earlier in the day. She hoped that he had not yet returned, and ran down the stairs quickly, so that she might go out unperceived.

The house was quite peaceful and still. It seemed strange to Juliette that there did not hang over it some sort of pall-like presentiment of coming evil.

From the kitchen, at some little distance from the hall, Anne Mie's voice was heard singing an old ditty:

> *"De ta tige détachée*
> *Pauvre feuille désséchée*
> *Où vas-tu?"*

Juliette paused a moment. An awful ache had seized her heart; her eyes unconsciously filled with tears, as they roamed round the walls of this house which had sheltered her so hospitably, these three weeks past.

And now whither was she going? Like the poor, dead leaf of the song, she was wastrel, torn from the parent bough, homeless, friendless, having turned against the one hand which, in this great time of peril, had been extended to her in kindness and in love.

Conscience was beginning to rise up against her, and that hydra-headed tyrant Remorse. She closed her eyes to shut out the hideous vision of her crime; she tried to forget this home which her treachery had desecrated.

> *"Je vais où va toute chose*
> *Où va la feuille de rose*
> *Et la feuille de laurier,"*

sang Anne Mie plaintively.

A great sob broke from Juliette's aching heart. The misery of it all was more than she could bear. Ah, pity her if you can! She had fought and striven, and been conquered. A girl's soul is so young, so impressionable; and she had grown up with that one, awful, all-pervading idea of duty to accomplish, a most solemn oath to fulfil, one sworn to her dying father, and on the dead body of her brother. She had begged for guidance, prayed for release, and the voice from above had remained silent. Weak, miserable, cringing, the human soul, when torn with earthly passion, must look at its own strength for the fight.

And now the end had come. That swift, scarce tangible dream of peace, which had flitted through her mind during the past few weeks, had vanished with the dawn, and she was left desolate, alone with her great sin and its lifelong expiation.

Scarce knowing what she did, she fell on her knees, there on that threshold, which she was about to leave for ever. Fate had placed on her young shoulders a burden too heavy for her to bear.

"Juliette!"

At first she did not move. It was his voice coming from the study behind her. Its magic thrilled her, as it had done that day in the Hall of Justice. Strong, passionate, tender, it seemed now to raise every echo of response in her heart. She thought it was a dream, and remained there on her knees lest it should be dispelled.

Then she heard his footsteps on the flagstones of the hall. Anne Mie's plaintive singing had died away in the distance. She started, and jumped to her feet, hastily drying her eyes. The momentary dream was dispelled, and she was ashamed of her weakness. He, the cause of all her sorrows, of her sin, and of her degradation, had no right to see her suffer.

She would have fled out of the house now, but it was too late. He had come out of his study, and, seeing her there on her knees weeping, he came quickly forward, trying, with all the innate chivalry of his upright nature, not to let her see that he had been a witness to her tears.

"You are going out, mademoiselle?" he said courteously, as, wrapping her cloak around her, she was turning towards the door.

"Yes, yes," she replied hastily; "a small errand, I ..."

"Is it anything I can do for you?"

"No."

"If ..." he added, with visible embarrassment, "if your errand would brook a delay, might I crave the honour of your presence in my study for a few moments?"

"My errand brooks of no delay, Citizen Déroulède," she said as composedly as she could, "and perhaps on my return I might ..."

"I am leaving almost directly, mademoiselle, and I would wish to bid you good-bye."

He stood aside to allow her to pass, either out, through the street door or across the hall to his study.

There had been no reproach in his voice towards the guest, who was thus leaving him without a word of farewell. Perhaps if there had been any, Juliette would have rebelled. As it was, an unconquerable magnetism seemed to draw her towards him, and, making an almost imperceptible sign of acquiescence, she glided past him into his room.

The study was dark and cool; for the room faced the west, and the shutters had been closed, in order to keep out the hot August sun. At first Juliette could see nothing, but she felt his presence near her, as he followed her into the room, leaving the door slightly ajar.

"It is kind of you, mademoiselle," he said gently, "to accede to my request, which was perhaps presumptuous. But, you see, I am leaving this house to-day, and I had a selfish longing to hear your voice bidding me farewell."

Juliette's large, burning eyes were gradually piercing the semi-gloom around her. She could see him distinctly now, standing close beside her, in an attitude of the deepest, almost reverential respect.

The study was as usual neat and tidy, denoting the orderly habits of a man of action and energy. On the ground there was a valise, ready strapped as if for a journey, and on the top of it a bulky letter-case of stout pigskin, secured with a small steel lock. Juliette's eyes fastened upon this case with a look of fascination and of horror. Obviously it contained Déroulède's papers, the plans for Marie Antoinette's escape, the passports of which he had spoken the day before to his friend, Sir Percy Blakeney—the proofs, in fact, which she had offered to the representatives of the people, in support of her denunciation of the Citizen-Deputy.

After his request he had said nothing more. He was waiting for her to speak; but her voice felt parched; it seemed to her as if hands of steel were gripping her throat, smothering the words she would have longed to speak.

"Will you not wish me godspeed, mademoiselle?" he repeated gently.

"Godspeed?" Oh! the awful irony of it all! Should God speed him to a mock trial and to the guillotine? He was going thither, though he did not know it, and was even now trying to take the hand which had deliberately sent him there.

At last she made an effort to speak, and in a toneless, even voice she contrived to murmur:

"You are not going for long, Citizen-Deputy?"

"In these times, mademoiselle," he replied, "any farewell might be for ever. But I am actually going for a month to the Conciergerie, to take charge of the unfortunate prisoner there."

"For a month!" she repeated mechanically.

"Oh yes!" he said, with a smile. "You see, our present Government is afraid that poor Marie Antoinette will exercise her fascinations over any lieutenant-governor of her prison, if he remain near her long enough, so a new one is appointed every month. I shall be in charge during this coming Vendémiaire. I shall hope to return before the equinox, but—who can tell?"

"In any case then, Citoyen Déroulède, the farewell I bid you to-night will be a very long one."

"A month will seem a century to me," he said earnestly, "since I must spend it without seeing you, but ..."

He looked long and searchingly at her. He did not understand her in her present mood, so scared and wild did she seem, so unlike that girlish, light-hearted self, which had made the dull old house so bright these past few weeks.

"But I should not dare to hope," he murmured, "that a similar reason would cause you to call that month a long one."

She turned perhaps a trifle paler than she had been hitherto, and her eyes roamed round the room like those of a trapped hare seeking to escape.

"You misunderstand me, Citoyen Déroulède," she said at last hurriedly. "You have all been kind—very kind—but Pétronelle and I can no longer trespass on your hospitality. We have friends in England, and many enemies here ..."

"I know," he interrupted quietly; "it would be the most arrant selfishness on my part to suggest, that you should stay here an hour longer than necessary. I fear that after to-day my roof may no longer prove a sheltering one for you. But will you allow me to arrange for your safety, as I am arranging for that of my mother and Anne Mie? My English friend Sir Percy Blakeney, has a yacht in readiness off the Normandy coast. I have already seen to your passports and to all the arrangements of your journey as far as there, and Sir Percy, or one of his friends, will see you safely on board the English yacht. He has given me his promise that he will do this, and I trust him as I would myself. For the journey through France, my name is a sufficient guarantee that you will be unmolested; and if you will allow it, my mother and Anne Mie will travel in your company. Then ..."

"I pray you stop, Citizen Déroulède," she suddenly interrupted excitedly. "You must forgive me, but I cannot allow thus to make any arrangements for me. Pétronelle and I must do as best we can. All your time and trouble should be spent for the benefit of those who have a claim upon you, whilst I ..."

"You speak unkindly, mademoiselle; there is no question of claim."

"And you have no right to think ..." she continued, with a growing, nervous excitement, drawing her hand hurriedly away, for he had tried to seize it.

"Ah! pardon me," he interrupted earnestly, "there you are wrong. I have the right to think of you and for you—the inalienable right conferred upon me by my great love for you."

"Citizen-Deputy!"

"Nay, Juliette; I know my folly, and I know my presumption. I know the pride of your caste and of your party, and how much you despise the partisan of the squalid mob of France. Have I said that I aspired to gain your love? I wonder if I have ever dreamed it? I only know, Juliette, that you are to me something akin to the angels, something white and ethereal, intangible, and perhaps ununderstandable. Yet, knowing my folly, I glory in it, my dear, and I would not let you go out of my life without telling you of that, which has made every hour of the past few weeks a paradise for me—my love for you, Juliette."

He spoke in that low, impressive voice of his, and with those soft, appealing tones with which she had once heard him pleading for poor Charlotte Corday. Yet now he was not pleading for himself, not for his selfish wish or for his own happiness, only pleading for his love, that she should know of it, and, knowing it, have pity in her heart for him, and let him serve her to the end.

He did not say anything more for a while; he had taken her hand, which she no longer withdrew from him, for there was sweet pleasure in feeling his strong fingers close tremblingly over hers. He pressed his lips upon her hand, upon the soft palm and delicate wrist, his burning kisses bearing witness to the tumultuous passion, which his reverence for her was holding in check.

She tried to tear herself away from him, but he would not let her go:

"Do not go away just yet, Juliette," he pleaded. "Think! I may never see you again; but when you are far from me—in England, perhaps— amongst your own kith and kin, will you try sometimes to think kindly of one who so wildly, so madly worships you?"

She would have stilled, an she could, the beating of her heart, which went out to him at last with all the passionate intensity of her great, pent-up love. Every word he spoke had its echo within her very soul, and she tried not to hear his tender appeal, not to see his dark head bending in worship before her. She tried to forget his presence, not to know that he was there—he, the man whom she had betrayed to serve her own miserable vengeance, whom in her mad, exalted rage she had thought that she hated, but whom she now knew that she loved better than her life, better than her soul, her traditions, or her oath.

Now, at this moment, she made every effort to conjure up the vision of her brother brought home dead upon a stretcher, of her father's declining years, rendered hideous by the mind unhinged through the great sorrow.

She tried to think of the avenging finger of God pointing the way to the fulfilment of her oath, and called to Him to stand by her in this terrible agony of her soul.

And God spoke to her at last; through the eternal vistas of boundless universe, from that heaven which had known no pity, His voice came to her now, clear, awesome, and implacable:

"Vengeance is mine! I will repay!"

CHAPTER 12. THE SWORD OF DAMOCLES

"In the name of the Republic!"

Absorbed in his thoughts, his dreams, his present happiness, Déroulède had heard nothing of what was going on in the house, during the past few seconds.

At first, to Anne Mie, who was still singing her melancholy ditty over her work in the kitchen, there had seemed nothing unusual in the peremptory ring at the front-door bell. She pulled down her sleeves over her thin arms, smoothed down her cooking apron, then only did she run to see who the visitor might be.

As soon as she had opened the door, however, she understood.

Five men were standing before her, four of whom wore the uniform of the National Guard, and the fifth, the tricolour scarf fringed with gold, which denoted service under the Convention.

This man seemed to be in command of the others, and he immediately stepped into the hall, followed by his four companions, who at a sign from him, effectively cut off Anne Mie from what had been her imminent purpose—namely, to run to the study and warn Déroulède of his danger.

That it was danger of the most certain, the most deadly kind she never doubted for one moment. Even had her instinct not warned her, she would have guessed. One glance at the five men had sufficed to tell her: their attitude, their curt word of command, their air of authority as they crossed the hall—everything revealed the purpose of their visit: a domiciliary search in the house of Citizen-Deputy Déroulède.

Merlin's Law of the Suspect was in full operation. Someone had denounced the Citizen-Deputy to the Committee of Public Safety; and in this year of grace, 1793, and I. of the Revolution, men and women were daily sent to the guillotine on suspicion.

Anne Mie would have screamed, had she dared, but instinct such as hers was far too keen, to betray her into so injudicious an act. She felt that, were Paul Déroulède's eyes upon her at this moment, he would wish her to remain calm and outwardly serene.

The foremost man—he with the tricolour scarf—had already crossed the hall, and was standing outside the study door. It was his word of command which first roused Déroulède from his dream:

"In the name of the Republic!"

Déroulède did not immediately drop the small hand, which a moment ago he had been covering with kisses. He held it to his lips once more, very gently, lingering over this last fond caress, as if over an eternal farewell, then he straightened out his broad, well-knit figure, and turned to the door.

He was very pale, but there was neither fear nor even surprise expressed in his earnest, deep-set eyes. They still seemed to be looking afar, gazing upon a heaven-born vision, which the touch of her hand and the avowal of his love had conjured up before him.

"In the name of the Republic!"

Once more, for the third time—according to custom—the words rang out, clear, distinct, peremptory.

In that one fraction of a second, whilst those six words were spoken, Déroulède's eyes wandered swiftly towards the heavy letter-case, which now held his condemnation, and a wild, mad thought—the mere animal desire to escape from danger—surged up in his brain.

The plans for the escape of Marie Antoinette, the various passports, worded in accordance with the possible disguises the unfortunate Queen might assume—all these papers were more than sufficient proof of what would be termed his treason against the Republic.

He could already hear the indictment against him, could see the filthy mob of Paris dancing a wild saraband round the tumbril, which bore him towards the guillotine; he could hear their yells of execration, could feel the insults hurled against him, by those who had most admired, most envied him. And from all this he would have escaped if he could, if it had not been too late.

It was but a second, or less, whilst the words were spoken outside his door, and whilst all other thoughts in him were absorbed in this one mad desire for escape. He even made a movement, as if to snatch up the letter-case and to hide it about his person. But it was heavy and bulky; it would be sure to attract attention, and might bring upon him the additional indignity of being forced to submit to a personal search.

He caught Juliette's eyes fixed upon him with an intensity of gaze which, in that same one mad moment, revealed to him the depths of her love. Then the second's weakness was gone; he was once more quiet, firm, the man of action, accustomed to meet danger boldly, to rule and to subdue the most turgid mob.

With a quiet shrug of the shoulders, he dismissed all thought of the compromising lettercase, and went to the door.

Already, as no reply had come to the third word of command, it had been thrown open from outside, and Déroulède found himself face to face with the five men.

"Citizen Merlin!" he said quietly, as he recognised the foremost among them.

"Himself, Citizen-Deputy," rejoined the latter, with a sneer, "at your service."

Anne Mie, in a remote corner of the hall, had heard the name, and felt her very soul sicken at its sound.

Merlin! Author of that infamous Law of the Suspect which had set man against man, a father against his son, brother against brother, and friend against friend, had made of every human creature a bloodhound on the track of his fellowmen, dogging in order not to be dogged, denouncing, spying, hounding, in order not to be denounced.

And he, Merlin, gloried in this, the most fiendishly evil law ever perpetrated for the degradation of the human race.

There is that sketch of him in the Musée Carnavalet, drawn just before he, in his turn, went to expiate his crimes on that very guillotine, which he had sharpened and wielded so powerfully against his fellows. The artist has well caught the slouchy, slovenly look of his loosely knit figure, his long limbs and narrow head, with the snakelike eyes and slightly receding chin. Like Marat, his model and prototype, Merlin affected dirty, ragged clothes. The real Sanscullottism, the downward levelling of his fellowmen to the lowest rung of the social ladder, pervaded every action of this noted product of the great Revolution.

Even Déroulède, whose entire soul was filled with a great, all-understanding pity for the weaknesses of mankind, recoiled at sight of this incarnation of the spirit of squalor and degradation, of all that was left of the noble Utopian theories of the makers of the Revolution.

Merlin grinned when he saw Déroulède standing there, calm, impassive, well dressed, as if prepared to receive an honoured guest, rather than a summons to submit to the greatest indignity a proud man has ever been called upon to suffer.

Merlin had always hated the popular Citizen-Deputy. Friend and boon-companion of Marat and his gang, he had for over two years now exerted all the influence he possessed in order to bring Déroulède under a cloud of suspicion.

But Déroulède had the ear of the populace. No one understood as he did the tone of a Paris mob; and the National Convention, ever terrified of the volcano it had kindled, felt that a popular member of its assembly was more useful alive than dead.

But now at last Merlin was having his way. An anonymous denunciation against Déroulède had reached the Public Prosecutor that day. Tinville and Merlin were the fastest of friends, so the latter easily obtained the privilege of being the first to proclaim to his hated enemy, the news of his downfall.

He stood facing Déroulède for a moment, enjoying the present situation to its full. The light from the vast hall struck full upon the powerful figure of the Citizen-Deputy and upon his firm, dark face and magnetic, restless eyes. Behind him the study, with its closely-drawn shutters, appeared wrapped in gloom.

Merlin turned to his men, and, still delighted with his position of a cat playing with a mouse, he pointed to Déroulède, with a smile and a shrug of the shoulders.

"*Voyez-moi donc çà,*" he said, with a coarse jest, and expectorating contemptuously upon the floor, "the aristocrat seems not to understand that we are here in the name of the Republic. There is a very good proverb, Citizen-Deputy," he added, once more addressing Déroulède, "which you seem to have forgotten, and that is that the pitcher which goes too often to the well breaks at last. You have conspired against the liberties of the people for the past ten years. Retribution has come to you at last; the people of France have come to their senses. The National Convention wants to know what treason you are hatching between these four walls, and it has deputed me to find out all there is to know."

"At your service, Citizen-Deputy!" said Déroulède, quietly stepping aside, in order to make way for Merlin and his men.

Resistance was useless, and, like all strong, determined natures, he knew when it was best to give in.

During this while, Juliette had neither moved nor uttered a sound. Little more than a minute had elapsed since the moment when the first peremptory order, to open in the name of the Republic, had sounded like the tocsin through the stillness of the house. Déroulède's kisses were still hot upon her hand, his words of love were still ringing in her ears.

And now this awful, deadly peril, which she with her own hand had brought on the man she loved!

If in one moment's anguish the soul be allowed to expiate a lifelong sin, then indeed did Juliette atone during this one terrible second.

Her conscience, her heart, her entire being rose in revolt against her crime. Her oath, her life, her final denunciation appeared before her in all their hideousness.

And now it was too late.

Déroulède stood facing Merlin, his most implacable enemy. The latter was giving orders to his men, preparatory to searching the house, and there, just on the top of the valise, lay the letter-case, obviously containing those papers, to which the day before she had overheard Déroulède making allusion, whilst he spoke to his friend, Sir Percy Blakeney.

An unexplainable instinct seemed to tell her that the papers were in that case. Her eyes were riveted on it, as if fascinated. An awful terror held her enthralled for one second more, whilst her thoughts, her longings, her desires were all centred on the safety of that one thing.

The next instant she had seized it and thrown it upon the sofa. Then seating herself beside it, with the gesture of a queen and the grace of a Parisienne, she had spread the ample folds of her skirts over the compromising case, hiding it entirely from view.

Merlin in the hall was ordering two men to stand one on each side of Déroulède, and two more to follow him into the room. Now he entered it himself, his narrow eyes trying to pierce the semi-obscurity, which was rendered more palpable by the brilliant light in the hall.

He had not seen Juliette's gesture, but he had heard the *frou-frou* of her skirts, as she seated herself upon the sofa.

"You are not alone Citizen-Deputy, I see," he said, with a sneer, as his snakelike eyes lighted upon the young girl.

"My guest, Citizen Merlin," replied Déroulède as calmly as he could— "Citizen Juliette Marny. I know that it is useless, under these circumstances, to ask for consideration for a woman, but I pray you to remember, as far as is possible, that although we are all Republicans, we are also Frenchmen, and all still equal in our sentiment of chivalry towards our mothers, our sisters, or our guests."

Merlin chuckled, and gazed for a moment ironically at Juliette. He had held, between his talon-like fingers, that very morning, a thin scrap of paper, on which a schoolgirlish hand had scrawled the denunciation against Citizen-Deputy Déroulède.

Coarse in nature, and still coarser in thoughts, this representative of the people had very quickly arrived at a conclusion in his mind, with regard to this so-called guest in the Déroulède household.

"A discarded mistress," he muttered to himself. "Just had another scene, I suppose. He's got tired of her, and she's given him away out of spite."

Satisfied with this explanation of the situation, he was quite inclined to be amiable to Juliette. Moreover, he had caught sight of the valise, and almost thought that the young girl's eyes had directed his attention towards it.

"Open those shutters!" he commanded, "this place is like a vault."

One of the men obeyed immediately, and as the brilliant August sun came streaming into the room, Merlin once more turned to Déroulède.

"Information has been laid against you, Citizen-Deputy," he said, "by an anonymous writer, who states that you have just now in your possession correspondence or other papers intended for the Widow Capet: and the Committee of Public Safety has entrusted me and these citizens to seize such correspondence, and make you answerable for its presence in your house."

Déroulède hesitated for one brief fraction of a second. As soon as the shutters had been opened, and the room flooded in daylight, he had at once perceived that his letter-case had disappeared, and guessed, from Juliette's attitude upon the sofa, that she had concealed it about her person. It was this which caused him to hesitate.

His heart was filled with boundless gratitude to her for her noble effort to save him, but he would have given his life at this moment, to undo what she had done.

The Terrorists were no respecters of persons or of sex. A domiciliary search order, in those days, conferred full powers on those in authority, and Juliette might at any moment now be peremptorily ordered to rise. Through her action she had made herself one with the Citizen-Deputy; if the case were found under the folds of her skirts, she would be accused of connivance, or at any rate of the equally grave charge of shielding a traitor.

The manly pride in him rebelled at the thought of owing his immediate safety to a woman, yet he could not now discard her help, without compromising her irretrievably.

He dared not even to look again towards her, for he felt that at this moment her life as well as his own lay in the quiver of an eyelid; and Merlin's keen, narrow eyes were fixed upon him in eager search for a tremor, a flash, which might betray fear or prove an admission of guilt.

Juliette sat there, calm, impassive, disdainful, and she seemed to Déroulède more angelic, more unattainable even than before. He could have worshipped her for her heroism, her resourcefulness, her quiet aloofness from all these coarse creatures who filled the room with the odour of their dirty clothes, with their rough jests, and their noisome suggestions.

"Well, Citizen-Deputy," sneered Merlin after a while, "you do not reply, I notice."

"The insinuation is unworthy of a reply, citizen," replied Déroulède quietly; "my services to the Republic are well known. I should have thought that the Committee of Public Safety would disdain an anonymous denunciation against a faithful servant of the people of France."

"The Committee of Public Safety knows its own business best, Citizen-Deputy," rejoined Merlin roughly. "If the accusation prove a calumny, so much the better for you. I presume," he added with a sneer, "that you do not propose to offer any resistance whilst these citizens and I search your house."

Without another word Déroulède handed a bunch of keys to the man by his side. Every kind of opposition, argument even, would be worse than useless.

Merlin had ordered the valise and desk to be searched, and two men were busy turning out the contents of both on to the floor. But the desk now only contained a few private household accounts, and notes for the various speeches which Déroulède had at various times delivered in the assemblies of the National Convention. Among these, a few pencil jottings for his great defence of Charlotte Corday were eagerly seized upon by Merlin, and his grimy, clawlike hands fastened upon this scrap of paper, as upon a welcome prey.

But there was nothing else of any importance. Déroulède was a man of thought and of action, with all the enthusiasm of real conviction, but none of the carelessness of a fanatic. The papers which were contained in the letter-case, and which he was taking with him to the Conciergerie, he considered were necessary to the success of his plans, otherwise he never would have kept them, and they were the only proofs that could be brought up against him.

The valise itself was only packed with the few necessaries for a month's sojourn at the Conciergerie; and the men, under Merlin's guidance, were vainly trying to find something, anything that might be construed into treasonable correspondence with the unfortunate prisoner there.

Merlin, whilst his men were busy with the search, was sprawling in one of the big leather-covered chairs, on the arms of which his dirty finger-nails were beating an impatient devil's tattoo. He was at no pains to conceal the intense disappointment which he would experience, were his errand to prove fruitless.

His narrow eyes every now and then wandered towards Juliette, as if asking for her help and guidance. She, understanding his frame of mind, responded to the look. Shutting her mentality off from the coarse suggestion of his attitude towards her, she played her part with cunning, and without flinching. With a glance here and there, she directed the men in their search. Déroulède himself could scarcely refrain from looking at her; he was puzzled, and vaguely marvelled at the perfection, with which she carried through her rôle to the end.

Merlin found himself baffled.

He knew quite well that Citizen-Deputy Déroulède was not a man to be lightly dealt with. No mere suspicion or anonymous denunciation would be sufficient in his case, to bring him before the tribunal of the Revolution. Unless there were proofs—positive, irrefutable, damnable proofs—of Paul Déroulède's treachery, the Public Prosecutor would never dare to frame an indictment against him. The mob of Paris would rise to defend its idol; the hideous hags, who plied their knitting at the foot of the scaffold, would tear the guillotine down, before they would allow Déroulède to mount it.

This was Déroulède's stronghold: the people of Paris, whom he had loved through all their infamies, and whom he had succoured and helped in their private need; and above all the women of Paris, whose children he had caused to be tended in the hospitals which he had built for them—this they had not yet forgotten, and Merlin knew it. One day they would forget—soon, perhaps—then they would turn on their former idol, and, howling, send him to his death, amidst cries of rancour and execration. When that day came there would be no need to worry about treason or about proofs. When the populace had forgotten all that he had done, then Déroulède would fall.

But that time was not yet.

The men had finished ransacking the room; every scrap of paper, every portable article had been eagerly seized upon.

Merlin, half blind with fury, had jumped to his feet.

"Search him!" he ordered peremptorily.

Déroulède set his teeth, and made no protest, calling up every fibre of moral strength within him, to aid him in submitting to this indignity. At a coarse jest from Merlin, he buried his nails into the palms of his hand, not to strike the foulmouthed creature in the face. But he submitted, and stood impassive by, whilst the pockets of his coat were turned inside out by the rough hands of the soldiers.

All the while Juliette had remained silent, watching Merlin as any hawk would its prey. But the Terrorist, through the very coarseness of his nature, was in this case completely fooled.

He knew that it was Juliette who had denounced Déroulède, and had satisfied himself as to her motive. Because he was low and brutish and degraded, he never once suspected the truth, never saw in that beautiful young woman, anything of the double nature within her, of that curious, self-torturing, at times morbid sense of religion and of duty, at war with her own upright, innately healthy disposition.

The low-born, self-degraded Terrorist had put his own construction on Juliette's action, and with this he was satisfied, since it answered to his own estimate of the human race, the race which he was doing his best to bring down to the level of the beast.

Therefore Merlin did not interfere with Juliette, but contented himself with insinuating, by jest and action, what her share in this day's work had been. To these hints Déroulède, of course, paid no heed. For him Juliette was as far above political intrigue as the angels. He would as soon have suspected one of the saints enshrined in Notre Dame as this beautiful, almost ethereal creature, who had been sent by Heaven to gladden his heart and to elevate his very thought.

But Juliette understood Merlin's attitude, and guessed that her written denunciation had come into his hands. Her every thought, every living sensation within her, was centred in this one thing: to save the man she loved from the consequences of her own crime against him. And for this, even the shadow of suspicion must be removed from him. Merlin's iniquitous law should not touch him again.

When Déroulède at last had been released, after the outrage to which he had been personally subjected, Merlin was literally, and figuratively too, looking about him for an issue to his present dubious position.

Judging others by his own standard of conduct, he feared now that the popular Citizen-Deputy would incite the mob against him, in revenge for the indignities which he had had to suffer. And with it all the Terrorist was convinced that Déroulède was guilty, that proofs of his treason did exist, if only he knew where to lay hands on them.

He turned to Juliette with an unexpressed query in his adder-like eyes. She shrugged her shoulders, and made a gesture as if pointing towards the door.

"There are other rooms in the house besides this," her gesture seemed to say; "try them. The proofs are there, 'tis for you to find them."

Merlin had been standing between her and Déroulède, so that the latter saw neither query nor reply.

"You are cunning, Citizen-Deputy," said Merlin now, turning towards him, "and no doubt you have been at pains to put your treasonable correspondence out of the way. You must understand that the Committee of Public Safety will not be satisfied with a mere examination of your study," he added, assuming an air of ironical benevolence, "and I presume you will have no objection, if I and these citizen soldiers pay a visit to other portions of your house."

"As you please," responded Déroulède drily.

"You will accompany us, Citizen-Deputy," commanded the other curtly.

The four men of the National Guard formed themselves into line outside the study door; with a peremptory nod, Merlin ordered Déroulède to pass between them, then he too prepared to follow. At the door he turned, and once more faced Juliette.

"As for you, citizeness," he said, with a sudden access of viciousness against her, "if you have brought us here on a fool's errand, it will go ill with you, remember. Do not leave the house until our return. I may have some questions to put to you."

CHAPTER 13. TANGLED MESHES

Juliette waited a moment or two, until the footsteps of the six men died away up the massive oak stairs.

For the first time, since the sword of Damocles had fallen, she was alone with her thoughts.

She had but a few moments at her command in which to devise an issue out of these tangled meshes, which she had woven round the man she loved.

Merlin and his men would return anon. The comedy could not be kept up through another visit from them, and while the compromising letter-case remained in Déroulède's private study he was in imminent danger at the hands of his enemy.

She thought for a moment of concealing the case about her person, but a second's reflection showed her the futility of such a move. She had not seen the papers themselves; any one of them might be an absolute proof of Déroulède's guilt; the correspondence might be in his handwriting.

If Merlin, furious, baffled, vicious, were to order her to be searched! The horror of the indignity made her shudder, but she would have submitted to that, if thereby she could have saved Déroulède. But of this she could not be sure until after she had looked through the papers, and this she had not the time to do.

Her first and greatest idea was to get out of this room, his private study, with the compromising papers. Not a trace of them must be found here, if he were to remain beyond suspicion.

She rose from the sofa, and peeped through the door. The hall was now deserted; from the left wing of the house, on the floor above, the heavy footsteps of the soldiers and Merlin's occasional brutish laugh could be distinctly heard.

Juliette listened for a moment, trying to understand what was happening. Yes; they had all gone to Déroulède's bedroom, which was on the extreme left, at the end of the first-floor landing. There might be just time to accomplish what she had now resolved to do.

As best she could, she hid the bulky leather case in the folds of her skirt. It was literally neck or nothing now. If she were caught on the stairs by one of the men nothing could save her or—possibly— Déroulède.

At any rate, by remaining where she was, by leaving the events to shape themselves, discovery was absolutely certain. She chose to take the risk.

She slipped noiselessly out of the room and up the great oak stairs. Merlin and his men, busy with their search in Déroulède's bedroom, took no heed of what was going on behind them; Juliette arrived on the landing, and turned sharply to her right, running noiselessly along the thick Aubusson carpet, and thence quickly to her own room.

All this had taken less than a minute to accomplish. The very next moment she heard Merlin's voice ordering one of his men to stand at attention on the landing, but by that time she was safe inside her room. She closed the door noiselessly.

Pétronelle, who had been busy all the afternoon packing up her young mistress' things, had fallen asleep in an arm-chair. Unconscious of the terrible events which were rapidly succeeding each other in the house, the worthy old soul was snoring peaceably, with her hands complacently folded on her ample bosom.

Juliette, for the moment, took no notice of her. As quickly and as dexterously as she could, she was tearing open the heavy leather case with a sharp pair of scissors, and very soon its contents were scattered before her on the table.

One glance at them was sufficient to convince her that most of the papers would undoubtedly, if found, send Déroulède to the guillotine. Most of the correspondence was in the Citizen-Deputy's handwriting. She had, of course, no time to examine it more closely, but instinct naturally told her that it was of a highly compromising character.

She gathered the papers up into a heap, tearing some of them up into strips; then she spread them out upon the ash-pan in front of the large earthenware stove, which stood in a corner of the room.

Unfortunately, this was a hot day in August. Her task would have been far easier if she had wished to destroy a bundle of papers in the depth of winter, when there was a good fire burning in the stove.

But her purpose was firm and her incentive, the greatest that has ever spurred mankind to heroism.

Regardless of any consequences to herself, she had but the one object in view, to save Déroulède at all costs.

On the wall facing her bed, and immediately above a velvet-covered prie-dieu, there was a small figure of the Virgin and Child—one of those quaintly pretty devices for holding holy water, which the reverent superstition of the past century rendered a necessary adjunct of every girl's room.

In front of the figure a small lamp was kept perpetually burning. This Juliette now took between her fingers, carefully, lest the tiny flame should die out. First she poured the oil over the fragments of paper in the ash-pan, then with the wick she set fire to the whole compromising correspondence.

The oil helped the paper to burn quickly; the smell, or perhaps the presence of Juliette in the room caused worthy old Pétronelle to wake.

"It's nothing, Pétronelle," said Juliette quietly; "only a few old letters I am burning. But I want to be alone for a few moments—will you go down to the kitchen until I call you?"

Accustomed to do as her young mistress commanded, Pétronelle rose without a word.

"I have finished putting away your few things, my jewel. There, there! why didn't you tell me to burn your papers for you? You have soiled your dear hands, and ..."

"Sh! Sh! Pétronelle!" said Juliette impatiently, and gently pushing the garrulous old woman towards the door. "Run to the kitchen now quickly, and don't come out of it until I call you. And, Pétronelle," she added, "you will see soldiers about the house perhaps."

"Soldiers! The good God have mercy!"

"Don't be frightened, Pétronelle. But they may ask you questions."

"Questions?"

"Yes; about me."

"My treasure, my jewel," exclaimed Pétronelle in alarm, "have those devils ...?"

"No, no; nothing has happened as yet, but, you know, in these times there is always danger."

"Good God! Holy Mary! Mother of God!"

"Nothing 'll happen if you try to keep quite calm and do exactly as I tell you. Go to the kitchen, and wait there until I call you. If the soldiers come in and question you, if they try to frighten you, remember that we have nothing to fear from men, and that our lives are in God's keeping."

All the while that Juliette spoke, she was watching the heap of paper being gradually reduced to ashes. She tried to fan the flames as best she could, but some of the correspondence was on tough paper, and was slow in being consumed. Pétronelle, tearful but obedient, prepared to leave the room. She was overawed by her mistress' air of aloofness, the pale face rendered ethereally beautiful by the sufferings she had gone through. The eyes glowed large and magnetic, as if in presence of spiritual visions beyond mortal ken; the golden hair looked like a saintly halo above the white, immaculate young brow.

Pétronelle made the sign of the cross, as if she were in the presence of a saint.

As she opened the door there was a sudden draught, and the last flickering flame died out in the ash-pan. Juliette, seeing that Pétronelle had gone, hastily turned over the few half burnt fragments of paper that were left. In none of them had the writing remained legible. All that was compromising to Déroulède was effectually reduced to dust. The small wick in the lamp at the foot of the Virgin and Child had burned itself out for want of oil; there was no means for Juliette to strike another light and to destroy what remained. The leather case was, of course, still there, with its sides ripped open, an indestructible thing.

There was nothing to be done about that. Juliette after a second's hesitation threw it among her dresses in the valise.

Then she too went out of the room.

CHAPTER 14. A HAPPY MOMENT

The search in the Citizen-Deputy's bedroom had proved as fruitless as that in his study. Merlin was beginning to have vague doubts as to whether he had been effectively fooled.

His manner towards Déroulède had undergone a change. He had become suave and unctuous, a kind of elephantine irony pervading his laborious attempts at conciliation.

He and the Public Prosecutor would be severely blamed for this day's work, if the popular Deputy, relying upon the support of the people of Paris, chose to take his revenge.

In France, in this glorious year of the Revolution, there was but one step between censure and indictment. And Merlin knew it. Therefore, although he had not given up all hope of finding proofs of Déroulède's treason, although by the latter's attitude he remained quite convinced that such proof did exist, he was already reckoning upon the cat's paw, the sop he would offer to that Cerberus, the Committee of Public Safety, in exchange for his own exculpation in the matter.

This sop would be Juliette, the denunciator instead of Déroulède the denounced.

But he was still seeking for the proofs.

Somewhat changing his tactics, he had allowed Déroulède to join his mother in the living-room, and had betaken himself to the kitchen in search of Anne Mie, whom he had previously caught sight of in the hall. There he also found old Pétronelle, whom he could scare out of her wits to his heart's content, but from whom he was quite unable to extract any useful information. Pétronelle was too stupid to be dangerous, and Anne Mie was too much on the alert.

But, with a vague idea that a cunning man might choose the most unlikely places for the concealment of compromising property, he was ransacking the kitchen from floor to ceiling.

In the living-room Déroulède was doing his best to reassure his mother, who, in her turn, was forcing herself to be brave, and not to show by her tears how deeply she feared for the safety of her son. As soon as Déroulède had been freed from the presence of the soldiers, he had hastened back to his study, only to find that Juliette had gone, and that the letter-case had also disappeared. Not knowing what to think, trembling for the safety of the woman he adored, he was just debating whether he would seek for her in her own room, when she came towards him across the landing.

There seemed a halo around her now. Déroulède felt that she had never been so beautiful and to him so unattainable. Something told him then, that at this moment she was as far away from him, as if she were an inhabitant of another, more ethereal planet.

When she saw him coming towards her, she put a finger to her lips, and whispered:

"Sh! sh! the papers are destroyed, burned."

"And I owe my safety to you!"

He had said it with his whole soul, an infinity of gratitude filled his heart, a joy and pride in that she had cared for his safety.

But at his words she had grown paler than she was before. Her eyes, large, dilated, and dark, were fixed upon him with an intensity of gaze which almost startled him. He thought that she was about to faint, that the emotions of the past half hour had been too much for her overstrung nerves. He took her hand, and gently dragged her into the living-room.

She sank into a chair, as if utterly weary and exhausted, and he, forgetting his danger, forgetting the world and all else besides, knelt at her feet, and held her hands in his.

She sat bolt upright, her great eyes still fixed upon him. At first it seemed as if he could not be satiated with looking at her; he felt as if he had never, never really seen her. She had been a dream of beauty to him ever since that awful afternoon when he had held her, half fainting, in his arms, and had dragged her under the shelter of his roof.

From that hour he had worshipped her: she had cast over him the magic spell of her refinement, her beauty, that aroma of youth and innocence which makes such a strong appeal to the man of sentiment.

He had worshipped her and not tried to understand. He would have deemed it almost sacrilege to pry into the mysteries of her inner self, of that second nature in her which at times made her silent, and almost morose, and cast a lurid gloom over her young beauty.

And though his love for her had grown in intensity, it had remained as heaven born as he deemed her to be—the love of a mortal for a saint, the ecstatic adoration of a St Francis for his Madonna.

Sir Percy Blakeney had called Déroulède an idealist. He was that, in the strictest sense, and Juliette had embodied all that was best in his idealism.

It was for the first time to-day, that he had held her hand just for a moment longer than mere conventionality allowed. The first kiss on her finger-tips had sent the blood rushing wildly to his heart; but he still worshipped her, and gazed upon her as upon a divinity.

She sat bolt upright in the chair, abandoning her small, cold hands to his burning grasp.

His very senses ached with the longing to clasp her in his arms, to draw her to him, and to feel her pulses beat closer against his. It was almost torture now to gaze upon her beauty—that small, oval face, almost like a child's, the large eyes which at times had seemed to be blue but which now appeared to be a deep, unfathomable colour, like the tempestuous sea.

"Juliette!" he murmured at last, as his soul went out to her in a passionate appeal for the first kiss.

A shudder seemed to go through her entire frame, her very lips turned white and cold, and he, not understanding, timorous, chivalrous and humble, thought that she was repelled by his ardour and frightened by a passion to which she was too pure to respond.

Nothing but that one word had been spoken—just her name, an appeal from a strong man, overmastered at last by his boundless love—and she, poor, stricken soul, who had so much loved, so deeply wronged him, shuddered at the thought of what she might have done, had Fate not helped her to save him.

Half ashamed of his passion, he bowed his dark head over her hands, and, once more forcing himself to be calm now, he kissed her finger-tips reverently.

When he looked up again the hard lines in her face had softened, and two tears were slowly trickling down her pale cheeks.

"Will you forgive me, madonna?" he said gently. "I am only a man and you are very beautiful. No—don't take your little hands away. I am quite calm now, and know how one should speak to angels."

Reason, justice, rectitude—everything was urging Juliette to close her ears to the words of love, spoken by the man whom she had betrayed. But who shall blame her for listening to the sweetest sound the ears of a woman can ever hear—the sound of the voice of the loved one in his first declaration of love?

She sat and listened, whilst he whispered to her those soft, endearing words, of which a strong man alone possesses the enchanting secret.

She sat and listened, whilst all around her was still. Madame Déroulède, at the farther end of the room, was softly muttering a few prayers.

They were all alone these two in the mad and beautiful world, which man has created for himself—the world of romance—that world more wonderful than any heaven, where only those may enter who have learned the sweet lesson of love. Déroulède roamed in it at will. He had created his own romance, wherein he was as a humble worshipper, spending his life in the service of his madonna.

And she too forgot the earth, forgot the reality, her oath, her crime and its punishment, and began to think that it was good to live, good to love, and good to have at her feet the one man in all the world whom she could fondly worship.

Who shall tell what he whispered? Enough that she listened and that she smiled; and he, seeing her smile, felt happy.

CHAPTER 15. DETECTED

The opening and shutting of the door roused them both from their dreams.

Anne Mie, pale, trembling, with eyes looking wild and terrified, had glided into the room.

Déroulède had sprung to his feet. In a moment he had thrust his own happiness into the background at sight of the poor child's obvious suffering. He went quickly towards her, and would have spoken to her, but she ran past him up to Madame Déroulède, as if she were beside herself with some unexplainable terror.

"Anne Mie," he said firmly, "what is it? Have those devils dared ..."

In a moment reality had come rushing back upon him with full force, and bitter reproaches surged up in his heart against himself, for having in this moment of selfish joy forgotten those who looked up to him for help and protection.

He knew the temper of the brutes who had been set upon his track, knew that low-minded Merlin and his noisome ways, and blamed himself severely for having left Anne Mie and Pétronelle alone with him even for a few moments.

But Anne Mie quickly reassured him.

"They have not molested us much," she said, speaking with a visible effort and enforced calmness. "Pétronelle and I were together, and they made us open all the cupboards and uncover all the dishes. They then asked us many questions."

"Questions? Of what kind?" asked Déroulède.

"About you, Paul," replied Anne Mie, "and about maman, and also about —about the citizeness, your guest."

Déroulède looked at her closely, vaguely wondering at the strange attitude of the child. She was evidently labouring under some strong excitement, and in her thin, brown little hand she was clutching a piece of paper.

"Anne Mie! Child," he said very gently, "you seem quite upset—as if something terrible had happened. What is that paper you are holding, my dear?"

Anne Mie gazed down upon it. She was obviously making frantic efforts to maintain her self-possession.

Juliette at first sight of Anne Mie seemed literally to have been turned to stone. She sat upright, rigid as a statue, her eyes fixed upon the poor, crippled girl as if upon an inexorable judge, about to pronounce sentence upon her of life or death.

Instinct, that keen sense of coming danger which Nature sometimes gives to her elect, had told her that, within the next few seconds, her doom would be sealed; that Fate would descend upon her, holding the sword of Nemesis; and it was Anne Mie's tiny, half-shrivelled hand which had placed that sword into the grasp of Fate.

"What is that paper? Will you let me see it, Anne Mie?" repeated Déroulède.

"Citizen Merlin gave it to me just now," began Anne Mie more quietly; "he seems very wroth at finding nothing compromising against you, Paul. They were a long time in the kitchen, and now they have gone to search my room and Pétronelle's; but Merlin—oh! that awful man!—he seemed like a beast infuriated with his disappointment."

"Yes, yes."

"I don't know what he hoped to get out of me, for I told him that you never spoke to your mother or to me about your political business, and that I was not in the habit of listening at the keyholes."

"Yes. And ..."

"Then he began to speak of—of our guest—but, of course, there again I could tell him nothing. He seemed to be puzzled as to who had denounced you. He spoke about an anonymous denunciation, which reached the Public Prosecutor early this morning. It was written on a scrap of paper, and thrown into the public box, it seems, and ..."

"It is indeed very strange," said Déroulède, musing over this extraordinary occurrence, and still more over Anne Mie's strange excitement in the telling of it. "I never knew I had a hidden enemy. I wonder if I shall ever find out ..."

"That is just what I said to Citizen Merlin," rejoined Anne Mie.

"What?"

"That I wondered if you, or—or any of us who love you, will ever find out who your hidden enemy might be."

"It was a mistake to talk so fully with such a brute, little one."

"I didn't say much, and I thought it wisest to humour him, as he seemed to wish to talk on that subject."

"Well? And what did he say?"

"He laughed, and asked me if I would very much like to know."

"I hope you said No, Anne Mie?"

"Indeed, indeed, I said Yes," she retorted with sudden energy, her eyes fixed now upon Juliette, who still sat rigid and silent, watching every movement of Anne Mie from the moment in which she began to tell her story.

"Would I not wish to know who is your enemy, Paul—the creature who was base and treacherous enough to attempt to deliver you into the hands of those merciless villains? What wrong had you done to anyone?"

"Sh! Hush, Anne Mie! you are too excited," he said, smiling now, in spite of himself, at the young girl's vehemence over what he thought was but a trifle—the discovery of his own enemy.

"I am sorry, Paul. How can I help being excited," rejoined Anne Mie with quaint, pathetic gentleness, "when I speak of such base treachery, as that which Merlin has suggested?"

"Well? And what did he suggest?"

"He did more than suggest," whispered Anne Mie almost inaudibly; "he gave me this paper—the anonymous denunciation which reached the Public Prosecutor this morning—he thought one of us might recognise the handwriting."

Then she paused, some five steps away from Déroulède, holding out towards him the crumpled paper, which up to now she had clutched determinedly in her hand. Déroulède was about to take it from her, and just before he had turned to do so, his eyes lighted on Juliette.

She said nothing, she had merely risen instinctively, and had reached Anne Mie's side in less than the fraction of a second.

It was all a flash, and there was dead silence in the room, but in that one-hundredth part of a second, Déroulède had read guilt in the face of Juliette.

It was nothing but instinct, a sudden, awful, unexplainable revelation. Her soul seemed suddenly to stand before him in all its misery and in all its sin.

It was as if the fire from heaven had descended in one terrific crash, burying beneath its devastating flames his ideals, his happiness, and his divinity. She was no longer there. His madonna had ceased to be.

There stood before him a beautiful woman, on whom he had lavished all the pent-up treasures of his love, whom he had succoured, sheltered, and protected, and who had repaid him thus.

She had forced an entry into his house; she had spied upon him, dogged him, lied to him. The moment was too sudden, too awful for him to make even a wild guess at her motives. His entire life, his whole past, the present, and the future, were all blotted out in this awful dispersal of his most cherished dream. He had forgotten everything else save her appalling treachery; how could he even remember that once, long ago, in fair fight, he had killed her brother?

She did not even try now to hide her guilt.

A look of appeal, touching in its trustfulness, went out to him, begging him to spare her further shame. Perhaps she felt that love, such as his, could not be killed in a flash.

His entire nature was full of pity, and to that pity she made a final appeal, lest she should be humiliated before Madame Déroulède and Anne Mie.

And he, still under the spell of those magic moments when he had knelt at her feet, understood her prayer, and closing his eyes just for one brief moment in order to shut out for ever that radiant vision of a pure angel whom he had worshipped, turned quietly to Anne Mie.

"Give me that paper, Anne Mie," he said coldly. "I may perhaps recognise the handwriting of my most bitter enemy."

"'Tis unnecessary now," replied Anne Mie slowly, still gazing at the face of Juliette, in which she too had read what she wished to read.

The paper dropped out of her hand.

Déroulède stooped to pick it up. He unfolded it, smoothed it out, and then saw that it was blank.

"There is nothing written on this paper," he said mechanically.

"No," rejoined Anne Mie; "no other words save the story of her treachery."

"What you have done is evil and wicked, Anne Mie."

"Perhaps so; but I had guessed the truth, and I wished to know. God showed me this way, how to do it, and how to let you know as well."

"The less you speak of God just now, Anne Mie, the better, I think. Will you attend to maman? she seems faint and ill."

Madame Déroulède, silent and placid in her arm-chair, had watched the tragic scene before her, almost like a disinterested spectator. All her ideas and all her thoughts had been paralysed, since the moment when the first summons at the front door had warned her of the imminence of the peril to her son.

The final discovery of Juliette's treachery had left her impassive. Since her son was in danger, she cared little as to whence that danger had come.

Obedient to Déroulède's wish, Anne Mie was attending to the old lady's comforts. The poor, crippled girl was already feeling the terrible reaction of her deed.

In her childish mind she had planned this way, in which to bring the traitor to shame. Anne Mie knew nothing, cared nothing, about the motives which had actuated Juliette; all she knew was that a terrible Judas-like deed had been perpetrated against the man, on whom she herself had lavished her pathetic, hopeless love.

All the pent-up jealousy which had tortured her for the past three weeks rose up, and goaded her into unmasking her rival.

Never for a moment did she doubt Juliette's guilt. The god of love may be blind, tradition has so decreed it, but the demon of jealousy has a hundred eyes, more keen than those of the lynx.

Anne Mie, pushed aside by Merlin's men when they forced their way into Déroulède's study, had, nevertheless, followed them to the door. When the curtains were drawn aside and the room filled with light, she had seen Juliette enthroned, apparently calm and placid, upon the sofa.

It was instinct, the instinct born of her own rejected passion, which caused her to read in the beautiful girl's face all that lay hidden behind the pale, impassive mask. That same second sight made her understand Merlin's hints and allusions. She caught every inflection of his voice, heard everything, saw everything.

And in the midst of her anxiety and her terrors for the man she loved, there was the wild, primitive, intensely human joy at the thought of bringing that enthroned idol, who had stolen his love, down to earth at last.

Anne Mie was not clever; she was simple and childish, with no complexity of passions or devious ways of intellect. It was her elemental jealousy which suggested the cunning plan for the unmasking of Juliette. She would make the girl cringe and fear, threaten her with discovery, and through her very terror shame her before Paul Déroulède.

And now it was all done; it had all occurred as she had planned it. Paul knew that his love had been wasted upon a liar and a traitor, and Juliette stood pale, humiliated, a veritable wreck of shamed humanity.

Anne Mie had triumphed, and was profoundly, abjectly wretched in her triumph. Great sobs seemed to tear at her very heart-strings. She had pulled down Paul's idol from her pedestal, but the one look she had cast at his face had shown her that she had also wrecked his life.

He seemed almost old now. The earnest, restless gaze had gone from his eyes; he was staring mutely before him, twisting between nerveless fingers that blank scrap of paper, which had been the means of annihilating his dream.

All energy of attitude, all strength of bearing, which were his chief characteristics, seemed to have gone. There was a look of complete blankness, of hopelessness in his listless gesture.

"How he loved her!" sighed Anne Mie, as she tenderly wrapped the shawl round Madame Déroulède's shoulders.

Juliette had said nothing; it seemed as if her very life had gone out of her. She was a mere statue now, her mind numb, her heart dead, her very existence a fragile piece of mechanism. But she was looking at Déroulède. That one sense in her had remained alive: her sight.

She looked and looked: and saw every passing sign of mental agony on his face: the look of recognition of her guilt, the bewilderment at the appalling crash, and now that hideous deathlike emptiness of his soul and mind.

Never once did she detect horror or loathing. He had tried to save her from being further humiliated before his mother, but there was no hatred or contempt in his eyes, when he realised that she had been unmasked by a trick.

She looked and looked, for there was no hope in her, not even despair. There was nothing in her mind, nothing in her soul, but a great pall-like blank.

Then gradually, as the minutes sped on, she saw the strong soul within him make a sudden fight against the darkness of his despair: the movement of the fingers became less listless; the powerful, energetic figure straightened itself out; remembrance of other matters, other interests than his own began to lift the overwhelming burden of his grief.

He remembered the letter-case containing the compromising papers. A vague wonder arose in him as to Juliette's motives in warding off, through her concealment of it, the inevitable moment of its discovery by Merlin.

The thought that her entire being had undergone a change, and that she now wished to save him, never once entered his mind; if it had, he would have dismissed it as the outcome of maudlin sentimentality, the conceit of the fop, who believes his personality to be irresistible.

His own self-torturing humility pointed but to the one conclusion: that she had fooled him all along; fooled him when she sought his protection; fooled him when she taught him to love her; fooled him, above all, at the moment when, subjugated by the intensity of his passion, he had for one brief second ceased to worship in order to love.

When the bitter remembrance of that moment of sweetest folly rushed back to his aching brain, then at last did he look up at her with one final, agonised look of reproach, so great, so tender, and yet so final, that Anne Mie, who saw it, felt as if her own heart would break with the pity of it all.

But Juliette had caught the look too. The tension of her nerves seemed suddenly to relax. Memory rushed back upon her with tumultuous intensity. Very gradually her knees gave beneath her, and at last she knelt down on the floor before him, her golden head bent under the burden of her guilt and her shame.

CHAPTER 16. UNDER ARREST

Déroulède did not attempt to go to her.

Only presently, when the heavy footsteps of Merlin and his men were once more heard upon the landing, she quietly rose to her feet.

She had accomplished her act of humiliation and repentance, there before them all.

She looked for the last time upon those whom she had so deeply wronged, and in her heart spoke an eternal farewell to that great, and mighty, and holy love which she had called forth and then had so hopelessly crushed.

Now she was ready for the atonement.

Merlin had already swaggered into the room. The long and arduous search throughout the house had not improved either his temper or his personal appearance. He was more covered with grime than he had been before, and his narrow forehead had almost disappeared beneath the tangled mass of his ill-kempt hair, which he had perpetually tugged forward and roughed up in his angry impatience.

One look at his face had already told Juliette what she wished to know. He had searched her room, and found the fragments of burnt paper, which she had purposely left in the ash-pan.

How he would act now was the one thing of importance left for Juliette to ponder over. That she would not escape arrest and condemnation was at once made clear to her. Merlin's look of sneering contempt, when he glanced towards her, had told her that.

Déroulède himself had been conscious of a feeling of intense relief when the men re-entered the room. The tension had become unendurable. When he saw his dethroned madonna kneel in humiliation at his feet, an overwhelming pain had wrenched his very heart-strings.

And yet he could not go to her. The passionate, human nature within him felt a certain proud exultation at seeing her there.

She was not above him now, she was no longer akin to the angels.

He had given no further thought to his own immediate danger. Vaguely he guessed that Merlin would find the leather case. Where it was he could not tell; perhaps Juliette herself had handed it to the soldiers. She had only hidden it for a few moments, out of impulse perhaps, fearing lest, at the first instant of its discovery, Merlin might betray her.

He remembered now those hints and insinuations which had gone out from the Terrorist to Juliette whilst the search was being conducted in the study. At the time he had merely looked upon these as a base attempt at insult, and had tortured himself almost beyond bearing, in the endeavour to refrain from punishing that evilmouthed creature, who dared to bandy words with his madonna.

But now he understood, and felt his very soul writhing with shame at the remembrance of it all.

Oh yes; the return of Merlin and his men, the presence of these grimy, degraded brutes, was welcome now. He would have wished to crowd in the entire world, the universe and its population, between him and his fallen idol.

Merlin's manner towards him had lost nothing of its ironical benevolence. There was even a touch of obsequiousness apparent in the ugly face, as the representative of the people approached the popular Citizen-Deputy.

"Citizen-Deputy," began Merlin, "I have to bring you the welcome news, that we have found nothing in your house that in any way can cast suspicion upon your loyalty to the Republic. My orders, however, were to bring you before the Committee of Public Safety, whether I had found proofs of your guilt or not. I have found none."

He was watching Déroulède keenly, hoping even at this eleventh hour to detect a look or a sign, which would furnish him with the proofs for which he was seeking. The slightest suggestion of relief on Déroulède's part, a sigh of satisfaction, would have been sufficient at this moment, to convince him and the Committee of Public Safety that the Citizen-Deputy was guilty after all.

But Déroulède never moved. He was sufficiently master of himself not to express either surprise or satisfaction. Yet he felt both— satisfaction not for his own safety, but because of his mother and Anne Mie, whom he would immediately send out of the country, out of all danger; and also because of her, of Juliette Marny, his guest, who, whatever she may have done against him, had still a claim on his protection. His feeling of surprise was less keen, and quite transient. Merlin had not found the letter-case. Juliette, stricken with tardy remorse perhaps, had succeeded in concealing it. The matter had practically ceased to interest him. It was equally galling to owe his betrayal or his ultimate safety to her.

He kissed his mother tenderly, bidding her good-bye, and pressed Anne Mie's timid little hand warmly between his own. He did what he could to reassure them, but, for their own sakes, he dared say nothing before Merlin, as to his plans for their safety.

After that he was ready to follow the soldiers.

As he passed close to Juliette he bowed, and almost inaudibly whispered:

"Adieu!"

She heard the whisper, but did not respond. Her look alone gave him the reply to his eternal farewell.

His footsteps and those of his escort were heard echoing down the staircase, then the hall door to open and shut. Through the open window came the sound of hoarse cheering as the popular Citizen-Deputy appeared in the street.

Merlin, with two men beside him, remained under the portico; he told off the other two to escort Déroulède as far as the Hall of Justice, where sat the members of the Committee of Public Safety. The Terrorist had a vague fear that the Citizen-Deputy would speak to the mob.

An unruly crowd of women had evidently been awaiting his appearance. The news had quickly spread along the streets that Merlin, Merlin himself, the ardent, bloodthirsty Jacobin, had made a descent upon Paul Déroulède's house, escorted by four soldiers. Such an indignity, put upon the man they most trusted in the entire assembly of the Convention, had greatly incensed the crowd. The women jeered at the soldiers as soon as they appeared, and Merlin dared not actually forbid Déroulède to speak.

"*A la lanterne, vieux crétin!*" shouted one of the women, thrusting her fist under Merlin's nose.

"Give the word, Citizen-Deputy," rejoined another, "and we'll break his ugly face. *Nous lui casserons la gueule!* "

"*A la lanterne! A la lanterne!*"

One word from Déroulède now would have caused an open riot, and in those days self defence against the mob was construed into enmity against the people.

Merlin's work, too, was not yet accomplished. He had had no intention of escorting Déroulède himself; he had still important business to transact inside the house which he had just quitted, and had merely wished to get the Citizen-Deputy well out of the way, before he went upstairs again.

Moreover, he had expected something of a riot in the streets. The temper of the people of Paris was at fever heat just now. The hatred of the populace against a certain class, and against certain individuals, was only equaled by their enthusiasm in favour of others.

They had worshipped Marat for his squalor and his vices; they worshipped Danton for his energy and Robespierre for his calm; they worshipped Déroulède for his voice, his gentleness and his pity, for his care of their children and the eloquence of his speech.

It was that eloquence which Merlin feared now; but he little knew the type of man he had to deal with.

Déroulède's influence over the most unruly, the most vicious populace the history of the world has ever known, was not obtained through fanning its passions. That popularity, though brilliant, is always ephemeral. The passions of a mob will invariably turn against those who have helped to rouse them. Marat did not live to see the waning of his star; Danton was dragged to the guillotine by those whom he had taught to look upon that instrument of death as the only possible and unanswerable political argument; Robespierre succumbed to the orgies of bloodshed he himself had brought about. But Déroulède remained master of the people of Paris for as long as he chose to exert that mastery. When they listened to him they felt better, nobler, less hopelessly degraded.

He kept up in their poor, misguided hearts that last flickering sense of manhood which their bloodthirsty tyrants, under the guise of Fraternity and Equality, were doing their best to smother.

Even now, when he might have turned the temper of the small crowd outside his door to his own advantage, he preferred to say nothing; he even pacified them with a gesture.

He well knew that those whom he incited against Merlin now would, once their blood was up, probably turn against him in less than half-an-hour.

Merlin, who all along had meant to return to the house, took his opportunity now. He allowed Déroulède and the two men to go on ahead, and beat a hasty retreat back into the house, followed by the jeers of the women.

"*A la lanterne, vieux crétin!*" they shouted as soon as the hall door was once more closed in their faces. A few of them began hammering against the door with their fists; then they realised that their special favourite, Citizen-Deputy Déroulède, was marching along between two soldiers, as if he were a prisoner. The word went round that he was under arrest, and was being taken to the Hall of Justice— a prisoner.

This was not to be. The mob of Paris had been taught that it was the master in the city, and it had learned its lesson well. For the moment it had chosen to take Paul Déroulède under its special protection, and as a guard of honour to him—the women in ragged kirtles, the men with bare legs and stripped to the waist, the children all yelling, hooting, and shrieking—followed him, to see that none dared harm him.

CHAPTER 17. ATONEMENT

Merlin waited a while in the hall, until he heard the noise of the shrieking crowd gradually die away in the distance, then with a grunt of satisfaction he one more mounted the stairs.

All these events outside had occurred during a very few minutes, and Madame Déroulède and Anne Mie had been too anxious as to what was happening in the streets, to take any notice of Juliette.

They had not dared to step out on to the balcony to see what was going on, and, therefore, did not understand what the reopening and shutting of the front door had meant.

The next instant, however, Merlin's heavy, slouching footsteps on the stairs had caused Anne Mie to look round in alarm.

"It is only the soldiers come back for me," said Juliette quietly.

"For you?"

"Yes; they are coming to take me away. I suppose they did not wish to do it in the presence of Mr. Déroulède, for fear ..."

She had no time to say more. Anne Mie was still looking at her in awed and mute surprise, when Merlin entered the room.

In his hand he held a leather case, all torn, and split at one end, and a few tiny scraps of half-charred paper. He walked straight up to Juliette, and roughly thrust the case and papers into her face.

"These are yours?" he said roughly.

"Yes."

"I suppose you know where they were found?"

She nodded quietly in reply.

"What were these papers which you burnt?"

"Love letters."

"You lie!"

She shrugged her shoulders.

"As you please," she said curtly.

"What were these papers?" he repeated, with a loud obscene oath which, however, had not the power to disturb the young girl's serenity.

"I have told you," she said: "love letters, which I wished to burn."

"Who was your lover?" he asked.

Then as she did not reply he indicated the street, where cries of "Déroulède! Vive Déroulède!" still echoed from afar.

"Were the letters from him?"

"No."

"You had more than one lover, then?"

He laughed, and a hideous leer seemed further to distort his ugly countenance.

He thrust his face quite close to hers, and she closed her eyes, sick with the horror of this contact with the degraded wretch. Even Anne Mie had uttered a cry of sympathy at sight of this evil-smelling, squalid creature torturing, with his close proximity, the beautiful, refined girl before him.

With a rough gesture he put his clawlike hand under her delicate chin, forcing her to turn round and to look at him. She shuddered at the loathsome touch, but her quietude never forsook her for a moment.

It was into the power of wretches such as this man, that she had willfully delivered the man she loved. This brutish creature's familiarity put the finishing touch to her own degradation, but it gave her the courage to carry through her purpose to the end.

"You had more than one lover, then?" said Merlin, with a laugh which would have pleased the devil himself. "And you wished to send one of them to the guillotine in order to make way for the other? Was that it?"

"Was that it?" he repeated, suddenly seizing one of her wrists, and giving it a savage twist, so that she almost screamed with the pain.

"Yes," she replied firmly.

"Do you know that you brought me here on a fool's errand?" he asked viciously; "that the Citizen-Deputy Déroulède cannot be sent to the guillotine on mere suspicion, eh? Did you know that, when you wrote out that denunciation?"

"No; I did not know."

"You thought we could arrest him on mere suspicion?"

"Yes."

"You knew he was Innocent?"

"I knew it."

"Why did you burn your love letters?"

"I was afraid that they would be found, and would be brought under the notice of the Citizen-Deputy."

"A splendid combination, *ma foi!*" said Merlin, with an oath, as he turned to the two other women, who sat pale and shrinking in a corner of the room, not understanding what was going on, not knowing what to think or what to believe. They had known nothing of Déroulède's plans for the escape of Marie Antoinette, they didn't know what the letter-case had contained, and yet they both vaguely felt that the beautiful girl, who stood up so calmly before the loathsome Terrorist, was not a wanton, as she tried to make out, but only misguided, mad perhaps—perhaps a martyr.

"Did you know anything of this?" queried Merlin roughly from trembling Anne Mie.

"Nothing," she replied.

"No one knew anything of my private affairs or of my private correspondence," said Juliette coldly; "as you say, it was a splendid combination. I had hoped that it would succeed. But I understand now that Citizen-Deputy Déroulède is a personage of too much importance to be brought to trial on mere suspicion, and my denunciation of him was not based on facts."

"And do you know, my fine aristocrat," sneered Merlin viciously, "that it is not wise either to fool the Committee of Public Safety, or to denounce without cause one of the representatives of the people?"

"I know," she rejoined quietly, "that you, Citizen Merlin, are determined that someone shall pay for this day's blunder. You dare not now attack the Citizen-Deputy, and so you must be content with me."

"Enough of this talk now; I have no time to bandy words with aristos," he said roughly.

"Come now, follow the men quietly. Resistance would only aggravate your case."

"I am quite prepared to follow you. May I speak two words to my friends before I go?"

"No."

"I may never be able to speak to them again."

"I have said No, and I mean No. Now then, forward. March! I have wasted too much time already."

Juliette was too proud to insist any further. She had hoped, by one word, to soften Madame Déroulède's and Anne Mie's heart towards her. She did not know whether they believed that miserable lie which she had been telling to Merlin; she only guessed that for the moment they still thought her the betrayer of Paul Déroulède.

But that one word was not to be spoken. She would have to go forth to her certain trial, to her probable death, under the awful cloud, which she herself had brought over her own life.

She turned quietly, and walked towards the door, where the two men already stood at attention.

Then it was that some heaven-born instinct seemed suddenly to guide Anne Mie. The crippled girl was face to face with a psychological problem, which in itself was far beyond her comprehension, but vaguely she felt that it was a problem. Something in Juliette's face had already caused her to bitterly repent her action towards her, and now, as this beautiful, refined woman was about to pass from under the shelter of this roof, to the cruel publicity and terrible torture of that awful revolutionary tribunal, Anne Mie's whole heart went out to her in boundless sympathy.

Before Merlin or the men could prevent her, she had run up to Juliette, taken her hand, which hung listless and cold, and kissed it tenderly.

Juliette seemed to wake as if from a dream. She looked down at Anne Mie with a glance of hope, almost of joy, and whispered:

"It was an oath—I swore it to my father and my dead brother. Tell him."

Anne Mie could only nod; she could not speak, for her tears were choking her.

"But I'll atone—with my life. Tell him," whispered Juliette.

"Now then," shouted Merlin, "out of the way, hunchback, unless you want to come along too."

"Forgive me," said Anne Mie through her tears.

Then the men pushed her roughly aside. But at the door Juliette turned to her once more, and said:

"Pétronelle—take care of her ..."

And with a firm step she followed the soldiers out of the room.

Presently the front door was heard to open, then to shut with a loud bang, and the house in the Rue Ecole de Médecine was left in silence.

CHAPTER 18. IN THE LUXEMBOURG PRISON

Juliette was alone at last—that is to say, comparatively alone, for there were too many aristocrats, too many criminals and traitors, in the prisons of Paris now, to allow of any seclusion of those who were about to be tried, condemned, and guillotined.

The young girl had been marched through the crowded streets of Paris, followed by a jeering mob, who readily recognised in the gentle, high-bred girl the obvious prey, which the Committee of Public Safety was wont, from time to time to throw to the hungry hydra-headed dog of the Revolution.

Lately the squalid spectators of the noisome spectacle on the Place de la Guillotine had had few of these very welcome sights: an aristocrat —a real, elegant, refined woman, with white hands and proud, pale face—mounting the steps of the same scaffold on which perished the vilest criminals and most degraded brutes.

Madame Guillotine was, above all, catholic in her tastes, her gaunt arms, painted blood red, were open alike to the murderer and the thief, the aristocrats of ancient lineage, and the proletariat from the gutter.

But lately the executions had been almost exclusively of a political character. The Girondins were fighting their last upon the bloody arena of the Revolution. One by one they fell still fighting, still preaching moderation, still foretelling disaster and appealing to that people, whom they had roused from one slavery, in order to throw it headlong under a tyrannical yoke more brutish, more absolute than before.

There were twelve prisons in Paris then, and forty thousand in France, and they were all full. An entire army went round the country recruiting prisoners. There was no room for separate cells, no room for privacy, no cause or desire for the most elementary sense of delicacy.

Women, men, children—all were herded together, for one day, perhaps two, and a night or so, and then death would obliterate the petty annoyances, the womanly blushes caused by this sordid propinquity.

Death levelled all, erased everything.

When Marie Antoinette mounted the guillotine she had forgotten that for six weeks she practically lived day and night in the immediate companionship of a set of degraded soldiery.

Juliette, as she marched through the streets between two men of the National Guard, and followed by Merlin, was hooted and jeered at, insulted, pelted with mud. One woman tried to push past the soldiers, and to strike her in the face—a woman! not thirty! —and who was dragging a pale, squalid little boy by the hand.

"*Crache donc sur l'aristo, voyons!*" the woman said to this poor, miserable little scrap of humanity as the soldiers pushed her roughly aside. "Spit on the aristocrat!" And the child tortured its own small, parched mouth so that, in obedience to its mother, it might defile and bespatter a beautiful, innocent girl.

The soldiers laughed, and improved the occasion with another insulting jest. Even Merlin forgot his vexation, delighted at the incident.

But Juliette had seen nothing of it all.

She was walking as in a dream. The mob did not exist for her; she heard neither insult nor vituperation. She did not see the evil, dirty faces pushed now and then quite close to her; she did not feel the rough hands of the soldiers jostling her through the crowd: she had gone back to her own world of romance, where she dwelt alone now with the man she loved. Instead of the squalid houses of Paris, with their eternal device of Fraternity and Equality, there were beautiful trees and shrubs of laurel and of roses around her, making the air fragrant with their soft, intoxicating perfumes; sweet voices from the land of dreams filled the atmosphere with their tender murmur, whilst overhead a cloudless sky illumined this earthly paradise.

She was happy—supremely, completely happy. She had saved him from the consequences of her own iniquitous crime, and she was about to give her life for him, so that his safety might be more completely assured.

Her love for him he would never know; now he knew only her crime, but presently, when she would be convicted and condemned, confronted with a few scraps of burned paper and a torn letter-case, then he would know that she had stood her trial, self-accused, and meant to die for him.

Therefore the past few moments were now wholly hers. She had the rights to dwell on those few happy seconds when she listened to the avowal of his love. It was ethereal, and perhaps not altogether human, but it was hers. She had been his divinity, his madonna; he had loved in her that, which was her truer, her better self.

What was base in her was not truly her. That awful oath, sworn so solemnly, had been her relentless tyrant; and her religion—a religion of superstition and of false ideals—had blinded her, and dragged her into crime.

She had arrogated to herself that which was God's alone—"Vengeance!" which is not for man.

That through it all she should have known love, and learned its tender secrets, was more than she deserved. That she should have felt his burning kisses on her hand was heavenly compensation for all she would have to suffer.

And so she allowed them to drag her through the sansculotte mob of Paris, who would have torn her to pieces then and there, so as not to delay the pleasure of seeing her die.

They took her to the Luxembourg, once the palace of the Medici, the home of proud "Monsieur" in the days of the Great Monarch, now a loathsome, overfilled prison.

It was then six o'clock in the afternoon, drawing towards the close of this memorable day. She was handed over to the governor of the prison, a short, thick-set man in black trousers and black-shag woollen shirt, and wearing a dirty red cap, with tricolour rosette on the side of his unkempt head.

He eyed her up and down as she passed under the narrow doorway, then murmured one swift query to Merlin:

"Dangerous?"

"Yes," replied Merlin laconically.

"You understand," added the governor; "we are so crowded. We ought to know if individual attention is required."

"Certainly," said Merlin, "you will be personally responsible for this prisoner to the Committee of Public Safety."

"Any visitors allowed?"

"Certainly not, without the special permission of the Public Prosecutor."

Juliette heard this brief exchange of words over her future fate.

No visitor would be allowed to see her. Well, perhaps that would be best. She would have been afraid to meet Déroulède again, afraid to read in his eyes that story of his dead love, which alone might have destroyed her present happiness.

And she wished to see no one. She had a memory to dwell on—a short, heavenly memory. It consisted of a few words, a kiss—the last one— on her hand, and that passionate murmur which had escaped from his lips when he knelt at her feet:

"Juliette!"

CHAPTER 19. COMPLEXITIES

Citizen-Deputy Déroulède had been privately interviewed by the Committee of Public Safety, and temporarily allowed to go free.

The brief proceedings had been quite private, the people of Paris were not to know as yet that their favourite was under a cloud. When he had answered all the questions put to him, and Merlin—just returned from his errand at the Luxembourg Prison—had given his version of the domiciliary visitation in the Citizen-Deputy's house, the latter was briefly told that for the moment the Republic had no grievance against him.

But he knew quite well what that meant. He would be henceforth under suspicion, watched incessantly, as a mouse is by the cat, and pounced upon, the moment time would be considered propitious for his final downfall.

The inevitable waning of his popularity would be noted by keen, jealous eyes; and Déroulède, with his sure knowledge of mankind and of character, knew well enough that his popularity was bound to wane sooner or later, as all such ephemeral things do.

In the meanwhile, during the short respite which his enemies would leave him, his one thought and duty would be to get his mother and Anne Mie safely out of the country.

And also ...

He thought of *her*, and wondered what had happened. As he walked swiftly across the narrow footbridge, and reached the other side of the river, the events of the past few hours rushed upon his memory with terrible, overwhelming force.

A bitter ache filled his heart at the remembrance of her treachery. The baseness of it all was so appalling. He tried to think if he had ever wronged her; wondered if perhaps she loved someone else, and wished *him* out of her way.

But, then, he had been so humble, so unassuming in his love. He had arrogated nothing unto himself, asked for nothing, demanded nothing in virtue of his protecting powers over her.

He was torturing himself with this awful wonderment of why she had treated him thus.

Out of revenge for her brother's death—that was the only explanation he could find, the only palliation for her crime.

He knew nothing of her oath to her father, and, of course, had never heard of the sad history of this young, sensitive girl placed in one terrible moment between her dead brother and her demented father. He only thought of common, sordid revenge for a sin he had been practically forced to commit.

And how he had loved her! Yes, *loved* —for that was in the past now.

She had ceased to be a saint or a madonna; she had fallen from her pedestal so low that he could not find the way to descend and grope after the fragments of his ideal.

At his own door he was met by Anne Mie in tears.

"She has gone," murmured the young girl. "I feel as if I had murdered her."

"Gone? Who? Where?" queried Déroulède rapidly, an icy feeling of terror gripping him by the heart-strings.

"Juliette has gone," replied Anne Mie; "those awful brutes took her away."

"When?"

"Directly after you left. That man Merlin found some ashes and scraps of paper in her room ..."

"Ashes?"

"Yes; and a torn letter-case."

"Great God!"

"She said that they were love letters, which she had been burning for fear you should see them."

"She said so? Anne Mie, Anne Mie, are you quite sure?"

It was all so horrible, and he did not quite understand it all; his brain, which was usually so keen and so active, refused him service at this terrible juncture.

"Yes; I am quite sure," continued Anne Mie, in the midst of her tears. "And oh! that awful Merlin said some dastardly things. But she persisted in her story, that she had— another lover. Oh, Paul, I am sure it is not true. I hated her because—because—you loved her so, and I mistrusted her, but I cannot believe that she was quite as base as that."

"No, no, child," he said in a toneless, miserable voice; "she was not so base as that. Tell me more of what she said."

"She said very little else. But Merlin asked her whether she had denounced you so as to get you out of the way. He hinted that— that ..."

"That I was her lover too?"

"Yes," murmured Anne Mie.

She hardly liked to look at him; the strong face had become hard and set in its misery.

"And she allowed them to say all this?" he asked at last.

"Yes. And she followed them without a murmur, as Merlin said she would have to answer before the Committee of Public Safety, for having fooled the representatives of the people."

"She'll answer for it with her life," murmured Déroulède. "And with mine!" he added half audibly.

Anne Mie did not hear him; her pathetic little soul was filled with a great, an overwhelming pity of Juliette and for Paul.

"Before they took her away," she said, placing her thin, delicate-looking hands on his arm. "I ran to her, and bade her farewell. The soldiers pushed me roughly aside; but I contrived to kiss her—and then she whispered a few words to me."

"Yes? What were they?"

"'It was an oath,' she said. 'I swore it to my father and to my dead brother. Tell him,'" repeated Anne Mie slowly.

An oath!

Now he understood, and oh! how he pitied her. How terribly she must have suffered in her poor, harassed soul when her noble, upright nature fought against this hideous treachery.

That she was true and brave in herself, of that Déroulède had no doubt. And now this awful sin upon her conscience, which must be causing her endless misery.

And, alas! the atonement would never free her from the load of self-condemnation. She had elected to pay with her life for her treason against him and his family. She would be arraigned before a tribunal which would inevitably condemn her. Oh! the pity of it all!

One moment's passionate emotion, a lifelong superstition and mistaken sense of duty, and now this endless misery, this terrible atonement of a wrong that could never be undone.

And she had never loved him!

That was the true, the only sting which he knew now; it rankled more than her sin, more than her falsehood, more than the shattering of his ideal.

With a passionate desire for his safety, she had sacrificed herself in order to atone for the material evil which she had done.

But there was the wreck of his hopes and of his dreams!

Never until now, when he had irretrievably lost her, did Déroulède realise how great had been his hopes; how he had watched day after day for a look in her eyes, a word from her lips, to show him that she too —his unattainable saint—would one day come to earth, and respond to his love.

And now and then, when her beautiful face lighted up at sight of him, when she smiled a greeting to him on his return from his work, when she looked with pride and admiration on him from the public bench in the assemblies of the Convention—then he had begun to hope, to think, to dream.

And it was all a sham! A mask to hide the terrible conflict that was raging within her soul, nothing more.

She did not love him, of that he felt convinced. Man like, he did not understand to the full that great and wonderful enigma, which has puzzled the world since primeval times: a woman's heart.

The eternal contradictions which go to make up the complex nature of an emotional woman were quite incomprehensible to him. Juliette had betrayed him to serve her own sense of what was just and right, her revenge and her oath. Therefore she did not love him.

It was logic, sound common-sense, and, aided by his own diffidence where women were concerned, it seemed to him irrefutable.

To a man like Paul Déroulède, a man of thought, of purpose, and of action, the idea of being false to the thing loved, of hate and love being interchangeable, was absolutely foreign and unbelievable. He had never hated the thing he loved or loved the thing he hated. A man's feelings in these respects are so much less complex, so much less contradictory.

Would a man betray his friend? No—never. He might betray his enemy, the creature he abhorred, whose downfall would cause him joy. But his friend? The very idea was repugnant, impossible to an upright nature.

Juliette's ultimate access of generosity in trying to save him, when she was at last brought face to face with the terrible wrong she had committed, *that* he put down to one of those noble impulses of which he knew her soul to be fully capable, and even then his own diffidence suggested that she did it more for the sake of his mother or for Anne Mie rather than for him.

Therefore what mattered life to him now? She was lost to him for ever, whether he succeeded in snatching her from the guillotine or not. He had but little hope to save her, but he would not owe his life to her.

Anne Mie, seeing him wrapped in his own thoughts, had quietly withdrawn. Her own good sense told her already that Paul Déroulède's first step would be to try and get his mother out of danger, and out of the country, while there was yet time.

So, without waiting for instructions, she began that same evening to pack up her belongings and those of Madame Déroulède.

There was no longer any hatred in her heart against Juliette. Where Paul Déroulède had failed to understand, there Anne Mie had already made a guess. She firmly believed that nothing now could save Juliette from death, and a great feeling of tenderness had crept into her heart, for the woman whom she had looked upon as an enemy and a rival.

She too had learnt in those brief days the great lesson that revenge belongs to God alone.

CHAPTER 20. THE CHEVAL BORGNE

It was close upon midnight.

The place had become suffocatingly hot; the fumes of rank tobacco, of rancid butter, and of raw spirits hung like a vapour in mid-air.

The principal room in the "Auberge du Cheval Borgne" had been used for the past five years now as the chief meeting-place of the ultra-sansculotte party of the Republic.

The house itself was squalid and dirty, up one of those mean streets which, by their narrow way and shelving buildings, shut out sun, air, and light from their miserable inhabitants.

The Cheval Borgne was one of the most wretched-looking dwellings in this street of evil repute. The plaster was cracked, the walls themselves seemed bulging outward, preparatory to a final collapse. The ceilings were low, and supported by beams black with age and dirt.

At one time it had been celebrated for its vast cellarage, which had contained some rare old wines. And in the days of the Grand Monarch young bucks were wont to quit the gay salons of the ladies, in order to repair to the Cheval Borgne for a night's carouse.

In those days the vast cellarage was witness of many a dark encounter, of many a mysterious death; could the slimy walls have told their own tale, it would have been one which would have put to shame the wildest chronicles of M. Vidoq.

Now it was no longer so.

Things were done in broad daylight on the Place de la Révolution: there was no need for dark, mysterious cellars, in which to accomplish deeds of murder and of revenge.

Rats and vermin of all sorts worked their way now in the underground portion of the building. They ate up each other, and held their orgies in the cellars, whilst men did the same sort of thing in the rooms above.

It was a club of Equality and Fraternity. Any passer-by was at liberty to enter and take part in the debates, his only qualification for this temporary membership being an inordinate love for Madame la Guillotine.

It was from the sordid rooms of the Cheval Borgne that most of the denunciations had gone forth which led but to the one inevitable ending—death.

They sat in conclave here, some twoscore or so at first, the rabid patriots of this poor, downtrodden France. They talked of Liberty mostly, with many oaths and curses against the tyrants, and then started a tyranny, an autocracy, ten thousand times more awful than any wielded by the dissolute Bourbons.

And this was the temple of Liberty, this dark, damp, evil-smelling brothel, with is narrow, cracked window-panes, which let in but an infinitesimal fraction of air, and that of the foulest, most unwholesome kind.

The floor was of planks roughly put together; now they were worm-eaten, bare, save for a thick carpet of greasy dust, which deadened the sound of booted feet. The place only boasted of a couple of chairs, both of which had to be propped against the wall lest they should break, and bring the sitter down upon the floor; otherwise a number of empty wine barrels did duty for seats, and rough deal boards on broken trestles for tables.

There had once been a paper on the walls, now it hung down in strips, showing the cracked plaster beneath. The whole place had a tone of yellowish-grey grime all over it, save where, in the centre of the room, on a rough double post, shaped like the guillotine, a scarlet cap of Liberty gave a note of lurid colour to the dismal surroundings.

On the walls here and there the eternal device, so sublime in conception, so sordid in execution, recalled the aims of the so-called club: "Liberté, Fraternité, Egalité, sinon la Mort."

Below the device, in one or two corners of the room, the wall was further adorned with rough charcoal sketches, mostly of an obscene character, the work of one of the members of the club, who had chosen this means of degrading his art.

To-night the assembly had been reduced to less than a score.

Even according to the dictates of these apostles of Fraternity: *"la guillotine va toujours"* —the guillotine goes on always. She had become the most potent factor in the machinery of government, of this great Revolution, and she had been daily, almost hourly fed through the activity of this nameless club, which held its weird and awesome sittings in the dank coffee-room of the Cheval Borgne.

The number of the active members had been reduced. Like the rats in the cellars below, they had done away with one another, swallowed one another up, torn each other to pieces in this wild rage for a Utopian fraternity.

Marat, founder of the organisation, had been murdered by a girl's hand; but Charon, Manuel, Osselin had gone the usual way, denounced by their colleagues, Rabaut, Custine, Bison, who in their turn were sent to the guillotine by those more powerful, perhaps more eloquent, than themselves.

It was merely a case of who could shout the loudest at an assembly of the National Convention.

"La guillotine va toujours!"

After the death of Marat, Merlin became the most prominent member of the club—he and Foucquier-Tinville, his bosom friend, Public Prosecutor, and the most bloodthirsty homicide of this homicidal age.

Bosom friend both, yet they worked against one another, undermining each other's popularity, whispering persistently, one against the other: "He is a traitor!" It had become just a neck-to-neck race between them towards the inevitable goal—the guillotine.

Foucquier-Tinville is in the ascendant for the moment. Merlin had been given a task which he had failed to accomplish. For days now, weeks even, the debates of this noble assembly had been chiefly concerned with the downfall of Citizen-Deputy Déroulède. His popularity, his calm security in the midst of this reign of terror and anarchy, had been a terrible thorn in the flesh of these rabid Jacobins.

And now the climax had been reached. An anonymous denunciation had roused the hopes of these sanguinary patriots. It all sounded perfectly plausible. To try and save that traitor, Marie Antoinette, the widow of Louis Capet, was just the sort of scheme that would originate in the brain of Paul Déroulède.

He had always been at heart an aristocrat, and the feeling of chivalry for a persecuted woman was only the outward signs of his secret adherence to the hated class.

Merlin had been sent to search the Deputy's house for proofs of the latter's guilt.

And Merlin had come back empty-handed.

The arrest of a female aristo—the probable mistress of Déroulède, who obviously had denounced him—was but small compensation for the failure of the more important capture.

As soon as Merlin joined his friends in the low, ill-lit, evil-smelling room he realised at once that there was a feeling of hostility against him.

Tinville, enthroned on one of the few chairs of which the Cheval Borgne could boast, was surrounded by a group of surly adherents.

On the rough trestles a number of glasses, half filled with raw potato-spirit, gave the keynote to the temper of the assembly.

All those present were dressed in the black-shag spencer, the seedy black breeches, and down-at-heel boots, which had become recognised as the distinctive uniform of the sansculotte party. The inevitable Phrygian cap, with its tricolour cockade, appeared on the heads of all those present, in various stages of dirt and decay.

Tinville had chosen to assume a sarcastic tone with regard to his whilom bosom friend, Merlin. Leaning both elbows on the table, he was picking his teeth with a steel fork, and in the intervals of his interesting operation, gave forth his views on the broad principles of patriotism.

Those who sat round him felt that his star was in the ascendant and assumed the position of satellites. Merlin as he entered had grunted a sullen "Good-eve," and sat himself down in a remote corner of the room.

His greeting had been responded to with a few jeers and a good many dark, threatening looks. Tinville himself had bowed to him with mock sarcasm and an unpleasant leer.

One of the patriots, a huge fellow, almost a giant, with heavy, coarse fists and broad shoulders that obviously suggested coal-heaving, had, after a few satirical observations, dragged one of the empty wine barrels to Merlin's table, and sat down opposite him.

"Take care, Citizen Lenoir," said Tinville, with an evil laugh, "Citizen-Deputy Merlin will arrest you instead of Deputy Déroulède, whom he has allowed to slip through his fingers."

"Nay; I've no fear," replied Lenoir, with an oath. "Citizen Merlin is too much of an aristo to hurt anyone; his hands are too clean; he does not care to do the dirty work of the Republic. Isn't that so, Monsieur Merlin?" added the giant, with a mock bow, and emphasizing the appellation which had fallen into complete disuse in these days of equality.

"My patriotism is too well known," said Merlin roughly, "to fear any attacks from jealous enemies; and as for my search in the Citizen-Deputy's house this afternoon, I was told to find proofs against him, and I found none."

Lenoir expectorated on the floor, crossed his dark hairy arms over the table, and said quietly:

"Real patriotism, as the true Jacobin understands it, makes the proofs it wants and leaves nothing to chance."

A chorus of hoarse murmurs of "Vive la Liberté!" greeted this harangue of the burly coal-heaver.

Feeling that he had gained the ear and approval of the gallery, Lenoir seemed, as it were, to spread himself out, to arrogate to himself the leadership of this band of malcontents, who, disappointed in their lust of Déroulède's downfall, were ready to exult over that of Merlin.

"You were a fool, Citizen Merlin," said Lenoir with slow significance, "not to see that the woman was playing her own game."

Merlin had become livid under the grime on his face. With this ill-kempt sansculotte giant in front of him, he almost felt as if he were already arraigned before that awful, merciless tribunal, to which he had dragged so many innocent victims.

Already he felt, as he sat ensconced behind a table in the far corner of the room, that he was a prisoner at the bar, answering for his failure with his life.

His own laws, his own theories now stood in bloody array against him. Was it not he who had framed the indictments against General Custine for having failed to subdue the cities of the south? against General Westerman and Brunet and Beauharnais for having failed and failed and failed?

And now it was his turn.

These bloodthirsty jackals had been cheated of their prey; they would tear him to pieces in compensation of their loss.

"How could I tell?" he murmured roughly, "the woman had denounced him."

A chorus of angry derision greeted this feeble attempt at defence.

"By your own law, Citizen-Deputy Merlin," commented Tinville sarcastically, "it is a crime against the Republic to be suspected of treason. It is evident, however, that it is quite one thing to frame a law and quite another to obey it."

"What could I have done?"

"Hark at the innocent!" rejoined Lenoir, with a sneer. "What could he have done? Patriots, friends, brothers, I ask you, what could he have done?"

The giant had pushed the wine cask aside, it rolled away from under him, and in the fulness of his contempt for Merlin and his impotence, he stood up before them all, strong in his indictment against treasonable incapacity.

"I ask you," he repeated, with a loud oath, "what any patriot would do, what you or I would have done, in the house of a man whom we all *know* is a traitor to the Republic? Brothers, friends, Citizen-Deputy Merlin found a heap of burnt paper in a grate, he found a letter-case which had obviously contained important documents, and he asks us what he could do!"

"Déroulède is too important a man to be tried without proofs. The whole mob of Paris would have turned on us for having arraigned him, for having dared lay hands upon his sacred person."

"Without proofs? Who said there were no proofs?" queried Lenoir.

"I found the burnt papers and torn letter-case in the woman's room. She owned that they were love letters, and that she had denounced Déroulède in order to be rid of him."

"Then let me tell you, Citizen-Deputy Merlin, that a true patriot would have found those papers in Déroulède's, and not the woman's room; that in the hands of a faithful servant of the Republic those documents would not all have been destroyed, for he would have 'found' one letter addressed to the Widow Capet, which would have proved conclusively that Citizen-Deputy Déroulède was a traitor. That is what a true patriot would have done—what I would have done. *Pardi!* Since Déroulède is so important a personage, since we must all put on kid gloves when we lay hands upon him, then let us fight him with other weapons. Are we aristocrats that we should hesitate to play the part of jackal to this cunning fox? Citizen-Deputy Merlin, are you the son of some ci-devant duke or prince that you dared not *forge* a document which would bring a traitor to his doom? Nay; let me tell you, friends, that the Republic has no use for curs, and calls him a traitor who allows one of her enemies to remain inviolate through his cowardice, his terror of that intangible and fleeting shadow—the wrath of a Paris mob."

Thunderous applause greeted this peroration, which had been delivered with an accompaniment of violent gestures and a wealth of obscene epithets, quite beyond the power of the mere chronicler to render. Lenoir had a harsh, strident voice, very high pitched, and he spoke with a broad, provincial accent, somewhat difficult to locate, but quite unlike the hoarse, guttural tones of the low-class Parisian. His enthusiasm made him seem impressive. He looked, in his ragged, dust-stained clothes, the very personification of the squalid herd which had driven culture, art, refinement to the scaffold in order to make way for sordid vice, and satisfied lusts of hate.

CHAPTER 21. A JACOBIN ORATOR

Tinville alone had remained silent during Lenoir's impassioned speech. It seemed to be his turn now to become surly. He sat picking his teeth, and staring moodily at the enthusiastic orator, who had so obviously diverted popular feeling in his own direction. And Tinville brooked popularity only for himself.

"It is easy to talk now, Citizen—er—Lenoir. Is that your name? Well, you are a comparative stranger here, Citizen Lenoir, and have not yet proved to the Republic that you can do ought else but talk."

"If somebody did not talk, Citizen Tinville—is that your name?" rejoined Lenoir, with a sneer—"if somebody didn't talk, nothing would get done. You all sit here, and condemn the Citizen-Deputy Merlin for being a fool, and I must say I am with you there, but ..."

"*Pardi!* tell us your 'but' citizen," said Tinville, for the coal-heaver had paused, as if trying to collect his thoughts. He had dragged a wine barrel to collect his thoughts. He had dragged a wine barrel close to the trestle table, and now sat astride upon it, facing Tinville and the group of Jacobins. The flickering tallow candle behind him threw into bold silhouette his square, massive head, crowned with its Phrygian cap, and the great breadth of his shoulders, with the shabby knitted spencer and low, turned-down collar.

He had long, thin hands, which were covered with successive coats of coal dust, and with these he constantly made weird gestures, as if in the act of gripping some live thing by the throat.

"We all know that the Deputy Déroulède is a traitor, eh?" he said, addressing the company in general.

"We do," came with uniform assent from all those present.

"Then let us put it to the vote. The Ayes mean death, the Noes freedom."

"Ay, ay!" came from every hoarse, parched throat; and twelve gaunt hands were lifted up demanding death for Citizen-Deputy Déroulède.

"The Ayes have it," said Lenoir quietly, "Now all we need do is to decide how best to carry out our purpose."

Merlin, very agreeably surprised to see public attention thus diverted from his own misdeeds, had gradually lost his surly attitude. He too dragged one of the wine barrels, which did duty for chairs, close to the trestle table, and thus the members of the nameless Jacobin club made a compact group, picturesque in its weird horror, its uncompromising, flaunting ugliness.

"I suppose," said Tinville, who was loth to give up his position as leader of these extremists—"I suppose, Citizen Lenoir, that you are in position to furnish me with proofs of the Citizen-Deputy's guilt?"

"If I furnish you with such proofs, Citizen Tinville," retorted the other, "will you, as Public Prosecutor, carry the indictment through?"

"It is my duty to publicly accuse those who are traitors to the Republic."

"And you, Citizen Merlin," queried Lenoir, "will you help the Republic to the best of your ability to be rid of a traitor?"

"My services to the cause of our great Revolution are too well known -" began Merlin.

But Lenoir interrupted him with impatience.

"*Pardi!* but we'll have no rhetoric now, Citizen Merlin. We all know that you have blundered, and that the Republic cares little for those of her sons who have failed, but whilst you are still Minister of Justice the people of France have need of you—for bringing *other* traitors to the guillotine."

He spoke this last phrase slowly and significantly, lingering on the word "other," as if he wished its whole awesome meaning to penetrate well into Merlin's brain.

"What is your advice then, Citizen Lenoir?"

Apparently, by unanimous consent, the coalheaver, from some obscure province of France, had been tacitly acknowledged the leader of the band. Merlin, still in terror for himself, looked to him for advice; even Tinville was ready to be guided by him. All were at one in their desire to rid themselves of Déroulède, who by his clean living, his aloofness from their own hideous orgies and deadly hates, seemed a living reproach to them all; and they all felt that in Lenoir there must exist some secret dislike of the popular Citizen-Deputy, which would give him a clear insight of how best to bring about his downfall.

"What is your advice?" had been Merlin's query, and everyone there listened eagerly for what was to come.

"We are all agreed," commenced Lenoir quietly, "that just at this moment it would be unwise to arraign the Citizen-Deputy without material proof. The mob of Paris worship him, and would turn against those who had tried to dethrone their idol. Now, Citizen Merlin failed to furnish us with proofs of Déroulède's guilt. For the moment he is a free man, and I imagine a wise one; within two days he will have quitted this country, well knowing that, if he stayed long enough to see his popularity wane, he would also outstay his welcome on earth altogether."

"Ay! Ay!" said some of the men approvingly, whilst others laughed hoarsely at the weird jest.

"I propose, therefore," continued Lenoir after a slight pause, "that it shall be Citizen-Deputy Déroulède himself who shall furnish to the people of France proofs of his own treason against the Republic."

"But how? But how?" rapid, loud and excited queries greeted this extraordinary suggestion from the provincial giant.

"By the simplest means imaginable," retorted Lenoir with imperturbable calm. "Isn't there a good proverb which our grandmothers used to quote, that if you only give a man a sufficient length of rope, he is sure to hang himself? We'll give our aristocratic Citizen-Deputy plenty of rope, I'll warrant, if only our present Minister of Justice," he added, indicating Merlin, "will help us in the little comedy which I propose that we should play."

"Yes! Yes! Go on!" said Merlin excitedly.

"The woman who denounced Déroulède—that is our trump card," continued Lenoir, now waxing enthusiastic with his own scheme and his own eloquence. "She denounced him. Ergo, he had been her lover, whom she wished to be rid of—why? Not, as Citizen Merlin supposed, because he had discarded her. No, no; she had another lover—she has admitted that. She wished to be rid of Déroulède to make way for the other, because he was too persistent—ergo, because he loved her."

"Well, and what does that prove?" queried Tinville with dry sarcasm.

"It proves that Déroulède, being in love with the woman, would do much to save her from the guillotine."

"Of course."

"*Pardi!* let him try, say I," rejoined Lenoir placidly. "Give him the rope with which to hang himself."

"What does he mean?" asked one or two of the men, whose dull brains had not quite as yet grasped the full meaning of this monstrous scheme.

"You don't understand what I mean, citizens; you think I am mad, or drunk, or a traitor like Déroulède? *Eh bien!* give me your attention five minutes longer, and you shall see. Let me suppose that we have reached the moment when the woman—what is her name? Oh! ah! yes! Juliette Marny—stands in the Hall of Justice on her trial before the Committee of Public Safety. Citizen Foucquier-Tinville, one of our greatest patriots, reads the indictment against her: the papers surreptitiously burnt, the torn, mysterious letter-case found in her room. If these are presumed, in the indictment, to be treasonable correspondence with the enemies of the Republic, condemnation follows at once, then the guillotine. There is no defence, no respite. The Minister of Justice, according to Article IX of the Law framed by himself, allows no advocate to those directly accused of treason. But," continued the giant, with slow and calm impressiveness, "in the case of ordinary, civil indictments, offences against public morality or matters pertaining to the penal code, the Minister of Justice allows the accused to be publicly defended. Place Juliette Marny in the dock on a treasonable charge, she will be hustled out of the court in a few minutes, amongst a batch of other traitors, dragged back to her own prison, and executed in the early dawn, before Déroulède has had time to frame a plan for her safety or defence. If, then, he tries to move heaven and earth to rescue the woman he loves, the mob of Paris may,—who knows?—take his part warmly. They are mad where Déroulède is concerned; and we all know that two devoted lovers have ere now found favour with the people of France—a curious remnant of sentimentalism, I suppose—and the popular Citizen-Deputy knows better than anyone else on earth, how to play upon the sentimental feelings of the populace. Now, in the case of a penal offence, mark where the difference would be! The woman Juliette Marny, arraigned for wantonness, for an offence against public morals; the burnt correspondence, admitted to be the letters of a lover—her hatred for Déroulède suggesting the false denunciation. Then the Minister of Justice allows an advocate to defend her. She has none in court; but think you Déroulède would not step forward, and bring all the fervour of his eloquence to bear in favour of his mistress? Can you hear his impassioned speech on her behalf?—I can—the rope, I tell you, citizens, with which he'll hang himself. Will he admit in open court that the burnt correspondence was another lover's letters? No!—a thousand times no!—and, in the face of his emphatic denial of the existence of another lover for Juliette, it will be for our clever Public Prosecutor to bring him down to an admission that the correspondence was his, that it was treasonable, that she burnt them to save him."

He paused, exhausted at last, mopping his forehead, then drinking large gulps of brandy to ease his parched throat.

A veritable chorus of enthusiasm greeted the end of his long peroration. The Machiavellian scheme, almost devilish in its cunning, in its subtle knowledge of human nature and of the heart-strings of a noble organisation like Déroulède's, commended itself to these patriots, who were thirsting for the downfall of a superior enemy.

Even Tinville lost his attitude of dry sarcasm; his thin cheeks were glowing with the lust of the fight.

Already for the past few months, the trials before the Committee of Public Safety had been dull, monotonous, uninteresting. Charlotte Corday had been a happy diversion, but otherwise it had been the case of various deputies, who had held views that had become too moderate, or of the generals who had failed to subdue the towns or provinces of the south.

But now this trial on the morrow—the excitement of it all, the trap laid for Déroulède, the pleasure of seeing him take the first step towards his own downfall. Everyone there was eager and enthusiastic for the fray. Lenoir, having spoken at such length, had now become silent, but everyone else talked, and drank brandy, and hugged his own hate and likely triumph.

For several hours, far into the night, the sitting was continued. Each one of the score of members had some comment to make on Lenoir's speech, some suggestion to offer.

Lenoir himself was the first to break up this weird gathering of human jackals, already exulting over their prey. He bad his companions a quiet good-night, then passed out into the dark street.

After he had gone there were a few seconds of complete silence in the dark and sordid room, where men's ugliest passions were holding absolute sway. The giant's heavy footsteps echoed along the ill-paved street, and gradually died away in the distance.

Then at last Foucquier-Tinville, the Public Prosecutor, spoke:

"And who is that man?" he asked, addressing the assembly of patriots.

Most of them did not know.

"A provincial from the north," said one of the men at last; "he has been here several times before now, and last year he was a fairly constant attendant. I believe he is a butcher by trade, and I fancy he comes from Calais. He was originally brought here by Citizen Brogard, who is good patriot enough."

One by one the members of this bond of Fraternity began to file out of the Cheval Borgne. They nodded curt good-nights to each other, and then went to their respective abodes, which surely could not be dignified with the name of home.

Tinville remained one of the last; he and Merlin seemed suddenly to have buried the hatchet, which a few hours ago had threatened to destroy one or the other of these whilom bosom friends.

Two or three of the most ardent of these ardent extremists had gathered round the Public Prosecutor, and Merlin, the framer of the Law of the Suspect.

"What say you, citizens?" said Tinville at last quietly. "That man Lenoir, meseems, is too eloquent—eh?"

"Dangerous," pronounced Merlin, whilst the others nodded approval.

"But his scheme is good," suggested one of the men.

"And we'll avail ourselves of it," assented Tinville, "but afterwards ..."

He paused, and once more everyone nodded approval.

"Yes; he is dangerous. We'll leave him in peace to-morrow, but afterwards ..."

With a gentle hand Tinville caressed the tall double post, which stood in the centre of the room, and which was shaped like the guillotine. An evil look was on his face: the grin of a death-dealing monster, savage and envious. The others laughed in grim content. Merlin grunted a surly approval. He had no cause to love the provincial coal-heaver who had raised a raucous voice to threaten him.

Then, nodding to one another, the last of the patriots, satisfied with this night's work, passed out into the night.

The watchman was making his rounds, carrying his lantern, and shouting his customary cry:

"Inhabitants of Paris, sleep quietly. Everything is in order, everything is at peace."

CHAPTER 22. THE CLOSE OF DAY

Déroulède had spent the whole of this same night in a wild, impassioned search for Juliette.

Earlier in the day, soon after Anne Mie's revelations, he had sought out his English friend, Sir Percy Blakeney, and talked over with him the final arrangements for the removal of Madame Déroulède and Anne Mie from Paris.

Though he was a born idealist and a Utopian, Paul Déroulède had never for a moment had any illusions with regard to his own popularity. He knew that at any time, and for any trivial cause, the love which the mob bore him would readily turn to hate. He had seen Mirabeau's popularity wane, La Fayette's, Desmoulin's—was it likely that *he* alone would survive the inevitable death of so ephemeral a thing?

Therefore, whilst he was in power, whilst he was loved and trusted, he had, figuratively and actually, put his house in order. He had made full preparations for his own inevitable downfall, for that probable flight from Paris of those who were dependent upon him.

He had, as far back as a year ago, provided himself with the necessary passports, and bespoken with his English friend certain measures for the safety of his mother and his crippled little relative. Now it was merely a question of putting these measures into execution.

Within two hours of Juliette Marny's arrest, Madame Déroulède and Anne Mie had quitted the house in the Rue Ecole de Médecine. They had but little luggage with them, and were ostensibly going into the country to visit a sick cousin.

The mother of the popular Citizen-Deputy was free to travel unmolested. The necessary passports which the safety of the Republic demanded were all in perfect order, and Madame Déroulède and Anne Mie passed through the north gate of Paris an hour before sunset, on that 24th day of Fructidor.

Their large travelling chaise took them some distance on the North Road, where they were to meet Lord Hastings and Lord Anthony Dewhurst, two of The Scarlet Pimpernel's most trusted lieutenants, who were to escort them as far as the coast, and thence see them safely aboard the English yacht.

On that score, therefore, Déroulède had no anxiety. His chief duty was to his mother and to Anne Mie, and that was now fully discharged.

Then there was old Pétronelle.

Ever since the arrest of her young mistress the poor old soul had been in a state of mind bordering on frenzy, and no amount of eloquence on Déroulède's part would persuade her to quit Paris without Juliette.

"If my pet lamb is to die," she said amidst heart-broken sobs, "then I have no cause to live. Let those devils take me along too, if they want a useless, old woman like me. But if my darling is allowed to go free, then what would become of her in this awful city without me? She and I have never been separated; she wouldn't know where to turn for a home. And who would cook for her and iron out her kerchiefs, I'd like to know?"

Reason and common sense were, of course, powerless in face of this sublime and heroic childishness. No one had the heart to tell the old woman that the murderous dog of the Revolution seldom loosened its fangs, once they had closed upon a victim.

All Déroulède could do was to convey Pétronelle to the old abode, which Juliette had quitted in order to come to him, and which had never been formally given up. The worthy soul, calmed and refreshed, deluded herself into the idea that she was waiting for the return of her young mistress, and became quite cheerful at sight of the familiar room.

Déroulède had provided her with money and necessaries. He had but few remaining hopes in his heart, but among them was the firmly implanted one that Pétronelle was too insignificant to draw upon herself the terrible attention of the Committee of Public Safety.

By the nightfall he had seen the good woman safely installed. Then only did he feel free.

At last he could devote himself to what seemed to him the one, the only, aim of his life—to find Juliette.

A dozen prisons in this vast Paris!

Over five thousand prisoners on that night, awaiting trial, condemnation and death.

Déroulède at first, strong in his own power, his personality, had thought that the task would be comparatively easy.

At the Palais de Justice they would tell him nothing: the list of new arrests had not yet been handled in by the commandant of Paris, Citizen Santerre, who classified and docketed the miserable herd of aspirants for the next day's guillotine.

The lists, moreover, would not be completed until the next day, when the trials of the new prisoners would already be imminent.

The work of the Committee of Public Safety was done without much delay.

Then began Déroulède's weary quest through those twelve prisons of Paris. From the Temple to the Conciergerie, from Palais Condé to the Luxembourg, he spent hours in the fruitless search.

Everywhere the same shrug of the shoulders, the same indifferent reply to his eager query:

"Juliette Marny? *Inconnue.*"

Unknown! She had not yet been docketed, not yet classified; she was still one of that immense flock of cattle, sent in ever-increasing numbers to the slaughter-house.

Presently, to-morrow, after a trial which might last ten minutes, after a hasty condemnation and quick return to prison, she would be listed as one of the traitors, whom this great and beneficent Republic sent daily to the guillotine.

Vainly did Déroulède try to persuade, to entreat, to bribe. The sullen guardians of these twelve charnel-houses knew nothing of individual prisoners.

But the Citizen-Deputy was allowed to look for himself. He was conducted to the great vaulted rooms of the Temple, to the vast ballrooms of the Palais Condé, where herded the condemned and those still awaiting trial; he was allowed to witness there the grim farcical tragedies, with which the captives beguiled the few hours which separated them from death.

Mock trials were acted there; Tinville was mimicked; then the Place de la Révolution; Samson the headsman, with a couple of inverted chairs to represent the guillotine.

Daughters of dukes and princes, descendants of ancient lineage, acted in these weird and ghastly comedies. The ladies, with hair bound high over their heads, would kneel before the inverted chairs, and place the snowwhite necks beneath this imaginary guillotine. Speeches were delivered to a mock populace, whilst a mock Santerre ordered a mock roll of drums to drown the last flow of eloquence of the supposed victim.

Oh! the horror of it all—the pity, pathos, and misery of this ghastly parody, in the very face of the sublimity of death!

Déroulède shuddered when first he beheld the scene, shuddered at the very thought of finding Juliette amongst these careless, laughing, thoughtless mimes.

His own, his beautiful Juliette, with her proud face and majestic, queen-like gestures; it was a relief not to see her there.

"Juliette Marny? *Inconnue,*" was the final word he heard about her.

No one told him that by Deputy Merlin's strictest orders she had been labelled "dangerous," and placed in a remote wing of the Luxembourg Palace, together with a few, who, like herself, were allowed to see no one, communicate with no one.

Then when the *couvre-feu* had sounded, when all public places were closed, when the night watchman had begun his rounds, Déroulède knew that his quest for that night must remain fruitless.

But he could not rest. In and out the tortuous streets of Paris he roamed during the better part of that night. He was now only awaiting the dawn to publicly demand the right to stand beside Juliette.

A hopeless misery was in his heart, a longing for a cessation of life; only one thing kept his brain active, his mind clear: the hope of saving Juliette.

The dawn was breaking in the far east when, wandering along the banks of the river, he suddenly felt a touch on his arm.

"Come to my hovel," said a pleasant, lazy voice close to his ear, whilst a kindly hand seemed to drag him away from the contemplation of the dark, silent river. "And a demmed, beastly place it is too, but at least we can talk quietly there."

Déroulède, roused from his meditation, looked up, to see his friend, Sir Percy

Blakeney, standing close beside him. Tall, debonair, well-dressed, he seemed by his very presence to dissipate the morbid atmosphere which was beginning to weigh upon Déroulède's active mind.

Déroulède followed him readily enough through the intricate mazes of old Paris, and down the Rue des Arts, until Sir Percy stopped outside a small hostelry, the door of which stood wide open.

"Mine host has nothing to lose from footpads and thieves," explained the Englishman as he guided his friend through the narrow doorway, then up a flight of rickety stairs, to a small room on the floor above. "He leaves all doors open for anyone to walk in, but, la! the interior of the house looks so uninviting that no one is tempted to enter."

"I wonder you care to stay here," remarked Déroulède, with a momentary smile, as he contrasted in his mind the fastidious appearance of his friend with the dinginess and dirt of these surroundings.

Sir Percy deposited his large person in the capacious depths of a creaky chair, stretched his long limbs out before him, and said quietly:

"I am only staying in this demmed hole until the moment when I can drag you out of this murderous city."

Déroulède shook his head.

"You'd best go back to England, then," he said, "for I'll never leave Paris now."

"Not without Juliette Marny, shall we say?" rejoined Sir Percy placidly.

"And I fear me that she has placed herself beyond our reach," said Déroulède sombrely.

"You know that she is in the Luxembourg Prison?" queried the Englishman suddenly.

"I guessed it, but could find no proof."

"And that she will be tried to-morrow?"

"They never keep a prisoner pining too long," replied Déroulède bitterly. "I guessed that too."

"What do you mean to do?"

"Defend her with the last breath in my body."

"You love her still, then?" asked Blakeney, with a smile.

"Still?" The look, the accent, the agony of a hopeless passion conveyed in that one word, told Sir Percy Blakeney all that he wished to know.

"Yet she betrayed you," he said tentatively.

"And to atone for that sin—an oath, mind you, friend, sworn to her father—she is already to give her life for me."

"And you are prepared to forgive?"

"To understand *is* to forgive," rejoined Déroulède simply, "and I love her."

"Your madonna!" said Blakeney, with a gently ironical smile.

"No; the woman I love, with all her weaknesses, all her sins; the woman to gain whom I would give my soul, to save whom I will give my life."

"And she?"

"She does not love me—would she have betrayed me else?"

He sat beside the table, and buried his head in his hands. Not even his dearest friend should see how much he had suffered, how deeply his love had been wounded.

Sir Percy said nothing, a curious, pleasant smile lurked round the corners of his mobile mouth. Through his mind there flitted the vision of beautiful Marguerite, who had so much loved yet so deeply wronged him, and, looking at his friend, he thought that Déroulède too would soon learn all the contradictions, which wage a constant war in the innermost recesses of a feminine heart.

He made a movement as if he would say something more, something of grave import, then seemed to think better of it, and shrugged his broad shoulders, as if to say:

"Let time and chance take their course now."

When Déroulède looked up again Sir Percy was sitting placidly in the arm-chair, with an absolutely blank expression on his face.

"Now that you know how much I love her, my friend," said Déroulède as soon as he had mastered his emotions, "will you look after her when they have condemned me, and save her for my sake?"

A curious, enigmatic smile suddenly illumined Sir Percy's earnest countenance.

"Save her? Do you attribute supernatural powers to me, then, or to The League of The Scarlet Pimpernel?"

"To you, I think," rejoined Déroulède seriously.

Once more it seemed as if Sir Percy were about to reveal something of great importance to his friend, then once more he checked himself. The Scarlet Pimpernel was, above all, far-seeing and practical, a man of action and not of impulse. The glowing eyes of his friend, his nervous, febrile movements, did not suggest that he was in a fit state to be entrusted with plans, the success of which hung on a mere thread.

Therefore Sir Percy only smiled, and said quietly:

"Well, I'll do my best."

CHAPTER 23. JUSTICE

The day had been an unusually busy one.

Five and thirty prisoners, arraigned before the bar of the Committee of Public Safety, had been tried in the last eight hours—an average of rather more than four to the hour; twelve minutes and a half in which to send a human creature, full of life and health, to solve the great enigma which lies hidden beyond the waters of the Styx.

And Citizen-Deputy Foucquier-Tinville, the Public Prosecutor, had surpassed himself. He seemed indefatigable.

Each of these five and thirty prisoners had been arraigned for treason against the Republic, for conspiracy with her enemies, and all had to have irrefutable proofs of their guilt brought before the Committee of Public Safety. Sometimes a few letters, written to friends abroad, and seized at the frontier; a word of condemnation of the measures of the extremists; and expression of horror at the massacres on the Place de la Révolution, where the guillotine creaked incessantly—these were irrefutable proofs; or else perhaps a couple of pistols, or an old family sword seized in the house of a peaceful citizen, would be brought against a prisoner, as an irrefutable proof of his warlike dispositions against the Republic.

Oh! it was not difficult!

Out of five and thirty indictments, Foucquier-Tinville had obtained thirty convictions.

No wonder his friends declared that he had surpassed himself. It had indeed been a glorious day, and the glow of satisfaction as much as the heat, caused the Public

Prosecutors to mop his high, bony cranium before he had adjourned for the much-needed respite for refreshment.

The day's work was not yet done.

The "politicals" had been disposed of, and there had been such an accumulation of them recently that it was difficult to keep pace with the arrests.

And in the meanwhile the criminal record of the great city had not diminished. Because men butchered one another in the name of Equality, there were none the fewer among the Fraternity of thieves and petty pilferers, of ordinary cut-throats and public wantons.

And these too had to be dealt with by law. The guillotine was impartial, and fell with equal velocity on the neck of the proud duke and the gutter-born *fille de joie*, on a descendant of the Bourbons and the wastrel born in a brothel.

The ministerial decrees favoured the proletariat. A crime against the Republic was indefensible, but one against the individual was dealt with, with all the paraphernalia of an elaborate administration of justice. There were citizen judges and citizen advocates, and the rabble, who crowded in to listen to the trials, acted as honorary jury.

It was all thoroughly well done. The citizen criminals were given every chance.

The afternoon of this hot August day, one of the last of glorious Fructidor, had begun to wane, and the shades of evening to slowly creep into the long, bare room where this travesty of justice was being administered.

The Citizen-President sat at the extreme end of the room, on a rough wooden bench, with a desk in front of him littered with papers.

Just above him, on the bare, whitewashed wall, the words: *"La République: une et indivisible,"* and below them the device: *"Liberté, Egalité, Fraternité!"*

To the right and left of the Citizen-President, four clerks were busy making entries in that ponderous ledger, that amazing record of the foulest crimes the world has ever known, the *"Bulletin du Tribunal Révolutionnaire."*

At present no one is speaking, and the grating of the clerks' quill pens against the paper is the only sound which disturbs the silence of the hall.

In front of the President, on a bench lower than his, sits Citizen Foucquier-Tinville, rested and refreshed, ready to take up his occupation, for as many hours as his country demands it of him.

On every desk a tallow candle, smoking and spluttering, throws a weird light, and more weird shadows, on the faces of clerks and President, on blank walls and ominous devices.

In the centre of the room a platform surrounded by an iron railing is ready for the accused. Just in front of it, from the tall, raftered ceiling above, there hangs a small brass lamp, with a green *abat-jour*.

Each side of the long, whitewashed walls there are three rows of benches, beautiful old carved oak pews, snatched from Notre Dame and from the Churches of St Eustache and St Germain l'Auxerrois. Instead of the pious worshippers of mediaeval times, they now accommodate the lookers-on of the grim spectacle of unfortunates, in their brief halt before the scaffold.

The front row of these benches is reserved for those citizen-deputies who desire to be present at the debates of the Tribunal Révolutionnaire. It is their privilege, almost their duty, as representatives of the people, to see that the sittings are properly conducted.

These benches are already well filled. At one end, on the left, Citizen Merlin, Minister of Justice, sits; next to him Citizen-Minister Lebrun; also Citizen Robespierre, still in the height of his ascendancy, and watching the proceedings with those pale, watery eyes of his and that curious, disdainful smile, which have earned for him the nickname of "the sea-green incorruptible."

Other well-known faces are there also, dimly outlined in the fast-gathering gloom. But everyone notes Citizen-Deputy Déroulède, the idol of the people, as he sits on the extreme end of a bench on the right, with arms tightly folded across his chest, the light from the hanging lamp falling straight on his dark head and proud, straight brows, with the large, restless, eager eyes.

Anon the Citizen-President rings a hand-bell, and there is a discordant noise of hoarse laughter and loud curses, some pushing, jolting, and swearing, as the general public is admitted into the hall.

Heaven save us! What a rabble! Has humanity really such a scum?

Women with a single ragged kirtle and shift, through the interstices of which the naked, grime-covered flesh shows shamelessly: with bare legs, and feet thrust into heavy sabots, hair disheveled, and evil, spirit-sodden faces: women without a semblance of womanhood, with shrivelled, barren breasts, and dry, parched lips, that have never known how to kiss. Women without emotion save that of hate, without desire, save for the satisfaction of hunger and thirst, and lust for revenge against their sisters less wretched, less unsexed than themselves. They crowd in, jostling one another, swarming into the front rows of the benches, where they can get a better view of the miserable victims about to be pilloried before them.

And the men without a semblance of manhood. Bent under the heavy care of their own degradation, dead to pity, to love, to chivalry; dead to all save an inordinate longing for the sight of blood.

And God help them all! for there were the children too. Children— save the mark!— with pallid, precocious little faces, pinched with the ravages of starvation, gazing with dim, filmy eyes on this world of rapacity and hideousness. Children who have seen death!

Oh, the horror of it! Not beautiful, peaceful death, a slumber or a dream, a loved parent or fond sister or brother lying all in white amidst a wealth of flowers, but death in its most awesome aspect, violent, lurid, horrible.

And now they stare around them with eager, greedy eyes, awaiting the amusement of the spectacle; gazing at the President, with his tall Phrygian cap; at the clerks wielding their indefatigable quill pens, writing, writing, writing; at the flickering lights, throwing clouds of sooty smoke, up to the dark ceiling above.

Then suddenly the eyes of one little mite—a poor, tiny midget not yet in her teens—alight on Paul Déroulède's face, on the opposite side of the rooms.

"*Tiens!* Papa Déroulède!" she says, pointing an attenuated little finger across at him, and turning eagerly to those around her, her eyes dilating in wishful recollection of a happy afternoon spent in Papa Déroulède's house, with fine white bread to eat in plenty, and great jars of foaming milk.

He rouses himself from his apathy, and his great earnest eyes lose their look of agonised misery, as he responds to the greeting of the little one.

For one moment—oh! a mere fraction of a second—the squalid faces, the miserable, starved expressions of the crowd, soften at sight of him. There is a faint murmur among the women, which perhaps God's recording angel registered as a blessing. Who knows?

Foucquier-Tinville suppresses a sneer, and the Citizen-President impatiently rings his hand-bell again.

"Bring forth the accused!" he commands in stentorian tones.

There is a movement of satisfaction among the crowd, and the angel of God is forced to hide his face again.

CHAPTER 24. THE TRIAL OF JULIETTE

It is all indelibly placed on record in the "Bulletin du Tribunal Révolutionnaire," under date 25th Fructidor, year I. of the Revolution.

Anyone who cares may read, for the Bulletin is in the Archives of the Bibliothèque Nationale of Paris.

One by one the accused had been brought forth, escorted by two men of the National Guard in ragged, stained uniforms of red, white, and blue; they were then conducted to the small raised platform in the centre of the hall, and made to listen to the charge brought against them by Citizen Foucquier-Tinville, the Public Prosecutor.

They were petty charges mostly: pilfering, fraud, theft, occasionally arson or manslaughter. One man, however, was arraigned for murder with highway robbery, and a woman for the most ignoble traffic, which evil feminine ingenuity could invent.

These two were condemned to the guillotine, the others sent to the galleys at Brest or Toulon—the forger along with the petty thief, the housebreaker with the absconding clerk.

There was no room in the prison for ordinary offences against the criminal code; they were overfilled already with so-called traitors against the Republic.

Three women were sent to the penitentiary at the Salpêtrière, and were dragged out of the court shrilly protesting their innocence, and followed by obscene jeers from the spectators on the benches.

Then there was a momentary hush.

Juliette Marny had been brought in.

She was quite calm, and exquisitely beautiful, dressed in a plain grey bodice and kirtle, with a black band round her slim waist and a soft white kerchief folded across her bosom. Beneath the tiny, white cap her golden hair appeared in dainty, curly profusion; her child-like, oval face was very white, but otherwise quite serene.

She seemed absolutely unconscious of her surroundings, and walked with a firm step up to the platform, looking neither to the right nor to the left of her.

Therefore she did not see Déroulède. A great, a wonderful radiance seemed to shine in her large eyes—the radiance of self-sacrifice.

She was offering not only her life, but everything a woman of refinement holds most dear, for the safety of the man she loved.

A feeling that was almost physical pain, so intense was it, overcame Déroulède, when at last he heard her name loudly called by the Public Prosecutor.

All day he had waited for this awful moment, forgetting his own misery, his own agonised feeling of an irretrievable loss, in the horrible thought of what *she* would endure, what *she* would think, when first she realised the terrible indignity, which was to be put upon her.

Yet for the sake of her, of her chances of safety and of ultimate freedom, it was undoubtedly best that it should be so.

Arraigned for conspiracy against the Republic, she was liable to secret trial, to be brought up, condemned, and executed before he could even hear of her whereabouts, before he could throw himself before her judges and take all guilt upon himself.

Those suspected of treason against the Republic forfeited, according to Merlin's most iniquitous Law, their rights of citizenship, in publicity of trial and in defence.

It all might have been finished before Déroulède knew anything of it.

The other way was, of course, more terrible. Brought forth amongst the scum of criminal Paris, on a charge, the horror of which, he could but dimly hope that she was too innocent to fully understand, he dared not even think of what she would suffer.

But undoubtedly it was better so.

The mud thrown at her robes of purity could never cling to her, and at least her trial would be public; he would be there to take all infamy, all disgrace, all opprobrium on himself.

The strength of his appeal would turn her judges' wrath from her to him; and after these few moments of misery, she would be free to leave Paris, France, to be happy, and to forget him and the memory of him.

An overwhelming, all-compelling love filled his entire soul for the beautiful girl, who had so wronged, yet so nobly tried to save him. A longing for her made his very sinews ache; she was no longer madonna, and her beauty thrilled him, with the passionate, almost sensuous desire to give his life for her.

The indictment against Juliette Marny has become history now.

On that day, the 25th Fructidor, at seven o'clock in the evening, it was read out by the Public Prosecutor, and listened to by the accused —so the Bulletin tells us—with complete calm and apparent indifference. She stood up in that same pillory where once stood poor, guilty Charlotte Corday, where presently would stand proud, guiltless Marie Antoinette.

And Déroulède listened to the scurrilous document, with all the outward calm his strength of will could command. He would have liked to rise from his seat then and there, at once, and in mad, purely animal fury have, with a blow of his fist, quashed the words in Foucquier-Tinville's lying throat.

But for her sake he was bound to listen, and, above all, to act quietly, deliberately, according to form and procedure, so as in no way to imperil her cause.

Therefore he listened whilst the Public Prosecutor spoke.

"Juliette Marny, you are hereby accused of having, by a false and malicious denunciation, slandered the person of a representative of the people; you caused the Revolutionary Tribunal, through this same mischievous act, to bring a charge against this representative of the people, to institute a domiciliary search in his house, and to waste valuable time, which otherwise belonged to the service of the Republic. And this you did, not from a misguided sense of duty towards your country, but in wanton and impure spirit, to be rid of the surveillance of one who had your welfare at heart, and who tried to prevent your leading the immoral life which had become a public scandal, and which has now brought you before this court of justice, to answer to a charge of wantonness, impurity, defamation of character, and corruption of public morals. In proof of which I now place before the court your own admission, that more than one citizen of the Republic has been led by you into immoral relationship with yourself; and further, your own admission, that your accusation against Citizen-Deputy Déroulède was false and mischievous; and further, and finally, your immoral and obscene correspondence with some persons unknown, which you vainly tried to destroy. In consideration of which, and in the name of the people of France, whose spokesman I am, I demand that you be taken hence from this Hall of Justice to the Place de la Révolution, in full view of the citizens of Paris and its environs, and clad in a soiled white garment, emblem of the smirch upon your soul, that there you be publicly whipped by the hands of Citizen Samson, the public executioner; after which, that you be taken to the prison of the Salpêtriere, there to be further detained at the discretion of the Committee of Public Safety. And now, Juliette Marny, you have heard the indictment preferred against you, have you anything to say, why the sentence which I have demanded shall not be passed upon you?"

Jeers, shouts, laughter, and curses greeted this speech of the Public Prosecutor.

All that was most vile and most bestial in this miserable, misguided people struggling for Utopia and Liberty, seemed to come to the surface, whilst listening to the reading of this most infamous document.

The delight of seeing this beautiful, ethereal woman, almost unearthly in her proud aloofness, smirched with the vilest mud to which the vituperation of man can contrive to sink, was a veritable treat to the degraded wretches.

The women yelled hoarse approval; the children, not understanding, laughed in mirthless glee; the men, with loud curses, showed their appreciation of Foucquier-Tinville's speech.

As for Déroulède, the mental agony he endured surpassed any torture which the devils, they say, reserve for the damned. His sinews cracked in his frantic efforts to control himself; he dug his finger-nails into his flesh, trying by physical pain to drown the sufferings of his mind.

He thought that his reason was tottering, that he would go mad if he heard another word of this infamy. The hooting and yelling of that filthy mob sounded like the cries of lost souls, shrieking from hell. All his pity for them was gone, his love for humanity, his devotion to the suffering poor.

A great, an immense hatred for this ghastly Revolution and the people it professed to free filled his whole being, together with a mad, hideous desire to see them suffer, starve, die a miserable, loathsome death. The passion of hate, that now overwhelmed his soul, was at least as ugly as theirs. He was, for one brief moment, now at one with them in their inordinate lust for revenge.

Only Juliette throughout all this remained calm, silent, impassive.

She had heard the indictment, heard the loathsome sentence, for her white cheeks had gradually become ashy pale, but never for a moment did she depart from her attitude of proud aloofness.

She never once turned her head towards the mob who insulted her. She waited in complete passiveness until the yelling and shouting had subsided, motionless save for her finger-tips, which beat an impatient tattoo upon the railing in front of her.

The Bulletin says that she took out her handkerchief and wiped her face with it. *Elle s'essuya le front qui fut perlé de sueur.* The heat had become oppressive.

The atmosphere was overcharged with the dank, penetrating odour of steaming, dirty clothes. The room, though vast, was close and suffocating, the tallow candles flickering in the humid, hot air threw the faces of the President and clerks into bold relief, with curious caricature effects of light and shade.

The petrol lamp above the head of the accused had flared up, and begun to smoke, causing the chimney to crack with a sharp report. This diversion effected a momentary silence among the crowd, and the Public Prosecutor was able to repeat his query:

"Juliette Marny, have you anything to say in reply to the charge brought against you, and why the sentence which I have demanded should not be passed against you?"

The sooty smoke from the lamp came down in small, black, greasy particles; Juliette with her slender finger-tips flicked one of these quietly off her sleeve, then she replied:

"No; I have nothing to say."

"Have you instructed an advocate to defend you, according to your rights of citizenship, which the Law allows?" added the Public Prosecutor solemnly.

Juliette would have replied at once; her mouth had already framed the No with which she meant to answer.

But now at last had come Déroulède's hour. For this he had been silent, had suffered and had held his peace, whilst twice twenty-four hours had dragged their weary lengths along, since the arrest of the woman he loved.

In a moment he was on his feet before them all, accustomed to speak, to dominate, to command.

"Citizeness Juliette Marny has entrusted me with her defence," he said, even before the No had escaped Juliette's white lips, "and I am here to refute the charges brought against her, and to demand in the name of the people of France full acquittal and justice for her."

CHAPTER 25. THE DEFENCE

Intense excitement, which found vent in loud applause, greeted Déroulède's statement.

"*Ça ira! ça ira! vas-y Déroulède!*" came from the crowded benches round; and men, women, and children, wearied with the monotony of the past proceedings, settled themselves down for a quarter of an hour's keen enjoyment.

If Déroulède had anything to do with it, the trial was sure to end in excitement. And the people were always ready to listen to their special favourite.

The citizen-deputies, drowsy after the long, oppressive day, seemed to rouse themselves to renewed interest. Lebrun, like a big, shaggy dog, shook himself free from creeping somnolence. Robespierre smiled between his thin lips, and looked across at Merlin to see how the situation affected him. The enmity between the Minister of Justice and Citizen Déroulède was well known, and everyone noted, with added zest, that the former wore a keen look of anticipated triumph.

High up, on one of the topmost benches, sat Citizen Lenoir, the stage-manager of this palpitating drama. He looked down, with obvious satisfaction, at the scene which he himself had suggested last night to the members of the Jacobin Club. Merlin's sharp eyes had tried to pierce the gloom, which wrapped the crowd of spectators, searching vainly to distinguish the broad figure and massive head of the provincial giant.

The light from the petrol lamp shone full on Déroulède's earnest, dark countenance as he looked Juliette's infamous accuser full in the face, but the tallow candles, flickering weirdly on the President's desk, threw Tinville's short, spare figure and large, unkempt head into curious grotesque silhouette.

Juliette apparently had lost none of her calm, and there was no one there sufficiently interested in her personality to note the tinge of delicate colour which, at the first word of Déroulède, had slowly mounted to her pale cheeks.

Tinville waited until the wave of excitement had broken upon the shoals of expectancy.

Then he resumed:

"Then, Citizen Déroulède, what have *you* to say, why sentence should not be passed upon the accused?"

"I have to say that the accused is innocent of every charge brought against her in your indictment," replied Déroulède firmly.

"And how do you substantiate this statement, Citizen-Deputy?" queried Tinville, speaking with mock unctuousness.

"Very simply, Citizen Tinville. The correspondence to which you refer did not belong to the accused, but to me. It consisted of certain communications, which I desired to hold with Marie Antoinette, now a prisoner in the Conciergerie, during my state there as lieutenant-governor. The Citizeness Juliette Marny, by denouncing me, was serving the Republic, for my communications with Marie Antoinette had reference to my own hopes of seeing her quit this country and take refuge in her own native land."

Gradually, as Déroulède spoke, a murmur, like the distant roar of a monstrous breaker, rose among the crowd on the upper benches. As he continued quietly and firmly, so it grew in volume and in intensity, until his last words were drowned in one mighty, thunderous shout of horror and execration.

Déroulède, the friend and idol of the people, the privileged darling of this unruly population, the father of the children, the friend of the women, the sympathizer in all troubles, Papa Déroulède as the little ones called him—he a traitor, self-accused, plotting and planning for an ex-tyrant, a harlot who had called herself a queen, for Marie Antoinette the Austrian, who had desired and worked for the overthrow of France! He, Déroulède, a traitor!

In one moment, as he spoke, the love which in their crude hearts they bore him, that animal primitive love, was turned to sudden, equally irresponsible hate. He had deceived them, laughed at them, tried to bribe them by feeding their little ones!

Bah! the bread of the traitor! It might have choked the children.

Surprise at first had taken their breath away. Already they had marvelled why he should stand up to defend a wanton. And now, probably feeling that he was on the point of being found out, he thought it better to make a clean breast of his own treason, trusting in his popularity, in his power over the people.

Bah!!!

Not one extenuating circumstance did they find in their hardened hearts for him.

He had been their idol, enshrined in their squalid, degraded minds, and now he had fallen, shattered beyond recall, and they hated and loathed him as much as they had loved him before.

And this his enemies noted, and smiled with complete satisfaction.

Merlin heaved a sigh of relief. Tinville nodded his shaggy head, in token of intense delight.

What that provincial coal-heaver had foretold had indeed come to pass.

The populace, that most fickle of all fickle things in this world, had turned all at once against its favourite. This Lenoir had predicted, and the transition had been even more rapid than he had anticipated.

Déroulède had been given a length of rope, and, figuratively speaking, had already hanged himself.

The reality was a mere matter of a few hours now. At dawn to-morrow the guillotine; and the mob of Paris, who yesterday would have torn his detractors limb from limb, would on the morrow be dragging him, with hoots and yells and howls of execration, to the scaffold.

The most shadowy of all footholds, that of the whim of a populace, had already given way under him. His enemies knew it, and were exulting in their triumph. He knew it himself, and stood up, calmly defiant, ready for any event, if only he succeeded in snatching her beautiful head from the ready embrace of the guillotine.

Juliette herself had remained as if entranced. The colour had again fled from her cheeks, leaving them paler, more ashen than before. It seemed as if in this moment she suffered more than human creature could bear, more than any torture she had undergone hitherto.

He would not owe his life to her.

That was the one overwhelming thought in her, which annihilated all others. His love for her was dead, and he would not accept the great sacrifice at her hands.

Thus these two in the supreme moment of their life saw each other, yet did not understand. A word, a touch would have given them both the key to one another's heart, and it now seemed as if death would part them forever, whilst that great enigma remained unsolved.

The Public Prosecutor had been waiting until the noise had somewhat subsided, and his voice could be heard above the din, then he said, with a smile of ill-concealed satisfaction:

"And is the court, then, to understand, Citizen-Deputy Déroulède, that it was you who tried to burn the treasonable correspondence and to destroy the case which contained it?"

"The treasonable correspondence was mine, and it was I who destroyed it."

"But the accused admitted before Citizen Merlin that she herself was trying to burn certain love letters, that would have brought to light her illicit relationship with another man than yourself," argued Tinville suavely. The rope was perhaps not quite long enough; Déroulède must have all that could be given him, ere this memorable sitting was adjourned.

Déroulède, however, instead of directing his reply straight to his enemy, now turned towards the dense crowd of spectators, on the benches opposite to him.

"Citizens, friends, brothers," he said warmly, "the accused is only a girl, young, innocent knowing nothing of peril or of sin. You all have mothers, sisters, daughters—

have you not watched those dear to you in the many moods of which a feminine heart is capable; have you not seen them affectionate, tender, and impulsive? Would you love them so dearly but for the fickleness of their moods? Have you not worshipped them in your hearts, for those sublime impulses which put all man's plans and calculations to shame? Look on the accused, citizens. She loves the Republic, the people of France, and feared that I, an unworthy representative of her sons, was hatching treason against our great mother. That was her first wayward impulse—to stop me before I committed the awful crime, to punish me, or perhaps only to warn me. Does a young girl calculate, citizens? She acts as her heart dictates; her reason but awakes from slumber later on, when the act is done. Then comes repentance sometimes: another impulse of tenderness which we all revere. Would you extract vinegar from rose leaves? Just as readily could you find reason in a young girl's head. Is that a crime? She wished to thwart me in my treason; then, seeing me in peril, the sincere friendship she had for me gained the upper hand once more. She loved my mother, who might be losing a son; she loved my crippled foster-sister; for *their* sakes, not for mine—a traitor's—did she yield to another, a heavenly impulse, that of saving me from the consequences of my own folly. Was *that* a crime, citizens? When you are ailing, do not your mothers, sisters, wives tend you? when you are seriously ill, would they not give their heart's blood to save you? and when, in the dark hours of your lives, some deed which you would not openly avow before the world overweights your soul with its burden of remorse, is it not again your womenkind who come to you, with tender words and soothing voices, trying to ease your aching conscience, bringing solace, comfort, and peace? And so it was with the accused, citizens. She had seen my crime, and longed to punish it; she saw those who had befriended her in sorrow, and she tried to ease their pain by taking *my* guilt upon her shoulders. She has suffered for the noble lie, which she had told on my behalf, as no woman has ever been made to suffer before. She has stood, white and innocent as your new-born children, in the pillory of infamy. She was ready to endure death, and what was ten thousand times worse than death, because of her own warm-hearted affection. But you, citizens of France, who, above all, are noble, true, and chivalrous, you will not allow the sweet impulses of young and tender womanhood to be punished with the ban of felony. To you, women of France, I appeal in the name of your childhood, your girlhood, your motherhood; take her to your hearts, she is worthy of it, worthier now for having blushed before you, worthier than any heroine in the great roll of honour of France."

His magnetic voice went echoing along the rafters of the great, sordid Hall of Justice, filling it with a glory it had never known before. His enthusiasm thrilled his hearers, his appeal to their honour and chivalry roused all the finer feelings within them. Still hating him for his treason, his magical appeal had turned their hearts towards her.

They had listened to him without interruption, and now at last, when he paused, it was very evident, by muttered exclamations and glances cast at Juliette, that popular feeling, which up to the present had practically ignored her, now went out towards her personality with overwhelming sympathy.

Obviously at the present moment, if Juliette's fate had been put to the plebiscite, she would have been unanimously acquitted.

Merlin, as Déroulède spoke, had once or twice tried to read his friend Foucquier-Tinville's enigmatical expression, but the Public Prosecutor, with his face in deep shadow, had not moved a muscle during the Citizen-Deputy's noble peroration. He sat at his desk, chin resting on hand, staring before him with an expression of indifference, almost of boredom.

Now, when Déroulède finished speaking, and the outburst of human enthusiasm had somewhat subsided, he rose slowly to his feet, and said quietly:

"So you maintain, Citizen-Deputy, that the accused is a chaste and innocent girl, unjustly charged with immorality?"

"I do," protested Déroulède loudly.

"And will you tell the court why you are so ready to publicly accuse yourself of treason against the Republic, knowing full well all the consequences of your action?"

"Would any Frenchman care to save his own life at the expense of a woman's honour?" retorted Déroulède proudly.

A murmur of approval greeted these words, and Tinville remarked unctuously:

"Quite so, quite so. We esteem your chivalry, Citizen-Deputy. The same spirit, no doubt, actuates you to maintain that the accused knew nothing of the papers which you say you destroyed?"

"She knew nothing of them. I destroyed them; I did not know that they had been found; on my return to my house I discovered that the Citizeness Juliette Marny had falsely accused herself of having destroyed some papers surreptitiously."

"She said they were love letters."

"It is false."

"You declare her to be pure and chaste?"

"Before the whole world."

"Yet you were in the habit of frequenting the bedroom of this pure and chaste girl, who dwelt under your roof," said Tinville with slow and deliberate sarcasm.

"It is false."

"If it be false, Citizen Déroulède," continued the other with the same unctuous suavity, "then how comes it that the correspondence which you admit was treasonable, and therefore presumably secret—how comes it that it was found, still smouldering, in the chaste young woman's bedroom, and the torn letter-case concealed among her dresses in a valise?"

"It is false."

"The Minister of Justice, Citizen-Deputy Merlin, will answer for the truth of that."

"It is the truth," said Juliette quietly.

Her voice rang out clear, almost triumphant, in the midst of the breathless pause, caused by the previous swift questions and loud answers.

Déroulède now was silent.

This one simple fact he did not know. Anne Mie, in telling him the events in connection with the arrest of Juliette, had omitted to give him the one little detail, that the burnt letters were found in the young girl's bedroom.

Up to the moment when the Public Prosecutor confronted him with it, he had been under the impression that she had destroyed the papers and the letter-case in the study, where she had remained alone after Merlin and his men had left the room. She could easily have burnt them there, as a tiny spirit lamp was always kept alight on a side table for the use of smokers.

This little fact now altered the entire course of events. Tinville had but to frame an indignant ejaculation:

"Citizens of France, see how you are being befooled and hoodwinked!"

Then he turned once more to Déroulède.

"Citizen Déroulède ..." he began.

But in the tumult that ensued he could no longer hear his own voice. The pent-up rage of the entire mob of Paris seemed to find vent for itself in the howls with which the crowd now tried to drown the rest of the proceedings.

As their brutish hearts had been suddenly melted on behalf of Juliette, in response to Déroulède's passionate appeal, so now they swiftly changed their sympathetic attitude to one of horror and execration.

Two people had fooled and deceived them. One of these they had reverenced and trusted, as much as their degraded minds were capable of reverencing anything, therefore *his* sin seemed doubly damnable.

He and that pale-face aristocrat had for weeks now, months, or years perhaps, conspired against the Republic, against the Revolution, which had been made by a people thirsting for liberty. During these months and years *he* had talked to them, and they had listened; he had poured forth treasures of eloquence, cajoled them, as he had done just now.

The noise and hubbub were growing apace. If Tinville and Merlin had desired to infuriate the mob, they had more than succeeded. All that was most bestial, most savage in this awful Parisian populace rose to the surface now in one wild, mad desire for revenge.

The crowd rushed down from the benches, over one another's heads, over children's fallen bodies; they rushed down because they wanted to get at him, their whilom favourite, and at his pale-faced mistress, and tear them to pieces, hit them, scratch out their eyes. They snarled like so many wild beasts, the women shrieked, the children cried, and the men of the National Guard, hurrying forward, had much ado to keep back this flood-tide of hate.

Had any of them broken loose, from behind the barrier of bayonets hastily raised against them, it would have fared ill with Déroulède and Juliette.

The President wildly rang his bell, and his voice, quivering with excitement, was heard once or twice above the din.

"Clear the court! Clear the court!"

But the people refused to be cleared out of court.

"*A la lanterne les traîtres! Mort à Déroulède. A la lanterne! l'aristo!*"

And in the thickest of the crowd, the broad shoulders and massive head of Citizen Lenoir towered above the others.

At first it seemed as if he had been urging on the mob in its fury. His strident voice, with its broad provincial accent, was heard distinctly shouting loud vituperations against the accused.

Then at a given moment, when the tumult was at its height, when the National Guard felt their bayonets giving way before this onrushing tide of human jackals, Lenoir changed his tactics.

"*Tiens! c'est bête!*" he shouted loudly, "we shall do far better with the traitors when we get them outside. What say you, citizens? Shall we leave the judges here to conclude the farce, and arrange for its sequel ourselves outside the 'Tigre Jaune'?"

At first but little heed was paid to his suggestion, and he repeated it once or twice, adding some interesting details:

"One is freer in the streets, where these apes of the National Guard can't get between the people of France and their just revenge. *Ma foi!* " he added, squaring his broad shoulders, and pushing his way through the crowd towards the door, "I for one am going to see where hangs the most suitable *lanterne.* "

Like a flock of sheep the crowd now followed him.

"The nearest *lanterne!* " they shouted. "In the streets—in the streets! *A la lanterne!* The traitors!"

And with many a jeer, many a loathsome curse, and still more loathsome jests, some of the crowd began to file out. A few only remained to see the conclusion of the farce.

CHAPTER 26. SENTENCE OF DEATH

The "Bulletin du Tribunal Révolutionnaire" tells us that both the accused had remained perfectly calm during the turmoil which raged within the bare walls of the Hall of Justice.

Citizen-Deputy Déroulède, however, so the chroniclers aver, though outwardly impassive, was evidently deeply moved. He had very expressive eyes, clear mirrors of the fine, upright soul within, and in them there was a look of intense emotion as he watched the crowd, which he had so often dominated and controlled, now turning in hatred against him.

He seemed actually to be seeing with a spiritual vision, his own popularity wane and die.

But when the thick of the crowd had pushed and jostled itself out of the hall, that transient emotion seemed to disappear, and he allowed himself quietly to be led from the front bench, where he had sat as a privileged member of the National Convention, to a place immediately behind the dock, and between two men of the National Guard.

From that moment he was a prisoner, accused of treason against the Republic, and obviously his mock trial would be hurried through by his triumphant enemies, whilst the temper of the people was at boiling point against him.

Complete silence had succeeded to the raging tumult of the past few moments. Nothing now could be heard in the vast room, save Foucquier-Tinville's hastily whispered instructions to the clerk nearest to him, and the scratch of the latter's quill pen against the paper.

The President was, with equal rapidity, affixing his signature to various papers handed up to him by the other clerks. The few remaining spectators, the deputies, and those among the crowd who had elected to see the close of the debate, were silent and expectant.

Merlin was mopping his forehead as if in intense fatigue after a hard struggle; Robespierre was coolly taking snuff.

From where Déroulède stood, he could see Juliette's graceful figure silhouetted against the light of the petrol lamp. His heart was torn between intense misery at having failed to save her and a curious, exultant joy at thought of dying beside her.

He knew the procedure of this revolutionary tribunal well—knew that within the next few moments he too would be condemned, that they would both be hustled out of the crowd and dragged through the streets of Paris, and finally thrown into the same prison, to herd with those who, like themselves, had but a few hours to live.

And then to-morrow at dawn, death for them both under the guillotine. Death in public, with all its attendant horrors: the packed tumbril; the priest, in civil clothes, appointed by this godless government, muttering conventional prayers and valueless exhortations.

And in his heart there was nothing but love for her—love and an intense pity—for the punishment she was suffering was far greater than her crime. He hoped that in her heart remorse would not be too bitter; and he looked forward with joy to the next few hours, which he would pass near her, during which he could perhaps still console and soothe her.

She was but the victim of an ideal, of Fate stronger than her own will. She stood, an innocent martyr to the great mistake of her life.

But the minutes sped on. Foucquier-Tinville had evidently completed his new indictments.

The one against Juliette Marny was read out first. She was now accused of conspiring with Paul Déroulède against the safety of the Republic, by having cognisance of a treasonable correspondence carried on with the prisoner, Marie Antoinette; by virtue of which accusation the Public Prosecutor asked her if she had anything to say.

"No," she replied loudly and firmly. "I pray to God for the safety and deliverance of our Queen, Marie Antoinette, and for the overthrow of this Reign of Terror and Anarchy."

These words, registered in the "Bulletin du Tribunal Révolutionnaire" were taken as final and irrefutable proofs of her guilt, and she was then summarily condemned to death.

She was then made to step down from the dock and Déroulède to stand in her place.

He listened quietly to the long indictment which Foucquier-Tinville had already framed against him the evening before, in readiness for this contingency. The words "treason against the Republic" occurred conspicuously and repeatedly. The document itself is at one with the thousands of written charges, framed by that odious Foucquier-Tinville during these periods of bloodshed, and which in themselves are the most scathing indictments against the odious travesty of Justice, perpetrated with his help.

Self-accused, and avowedly a traitor, Déroulède was not even asked if he had anything to say; sentence of death was passed on him, with the rapidity and callousness peculiar to these proceedings.

After which Paul Déroulède and Juliette Marny were led forth, under strong escort, into the street.

CHAPTER 27. THE FRUCTIDOR RIOTS

Many accounts, more or less authentic, have been published of the events known to history as the "Fructidor Riots."

But this is how it all happened: at any rate it is the version related some few days later in England to the Prince of Wales by no less a personage than Sir Percy Blakeney; and who indeed should know better than The Scarlet Pimpernel himself?

Déroulède and Juliette Marny were the last of the batch of prisoners who were tried on that memorable day of Fructidor.

There had been such a number of these, that all the covered carts in use for the conveyance of prisoners to and from the Hall of Justice had already been despatched with their weighty human load; thus it was that only a rough wooden cart, hoodless and rickety, was available, and into this Déroulède and Juliette were ordered to mount.

It was now close on nine o'clock in the evening. The streets of Paris, sparsely illuminated here and there with solitary oil lamps swung across from house to house on wires, presented a miserable and squalid appearance. A thin, misty rain had begun to fall, transforming the ill-paved roads into morasses of sticky mud.

The Hall of Justice was surrounded by a howling and shrieking mob, who, having imbibed all the stores of brandy in the neighbouring drinking bars, was now waiting outside in the dripping rain for the express purpose of venting its pent-up, spirit-sodden lust of rage against the man whom it had once worshipped, but whom now it hated. Men, women, and even children swarmed round the principal entrances of the Palais de Justice, along the bank of the river as far as the Pont au Change, and up towards the Luxembourg Palace, now transformed into the prison, to which the condemned would no doubt be conveyed.

Along the river-bank, and immediately facing the Palais de Justice, a row of gallows-shaped posts, at intervals of a hundred yards or more, held each a smoky petrol lamp, at a height of some eight feet from the ground.

One of these lamps had been knocked down, and from the post itself there now hung ominously a length of rope, with a noose at the end.

Around this improvised gallows a group of women sat, or rather squatted, in the mud; their ragged shifts and kirtles, soaked through with the drizzling rain, hung dankly on their emaciated forms; their hair, in some cases grey, and in others dark or straw-coloured, clung matted round their wet faces, on which the dirt and the damp had drawn weird and grotesque lines.

The men were restless and noisy, rushing aimlessly hither and thither, from the corner of the bridge, up the Rue du Palais, fearful lest their prey be conjured away ere their vengeance was satisfied.

Oh, how they hated their former idol now! Citizen Lenoir, with his broad shoulders and powerful, grime-covered head, towered above the throng; his strident voice, with its raucous, provincial accent, could be distinctly heard above the din, egging on the men, shouting to the women, stirring up hatred against the prisoners, wherever it showed signs of abating in intensity.

The coal-heaver, hailing from some distant province, seemed to have set himself the grim task of provoking the infuriated populace to some terrible deed of revenge against Déroulède and Juliette.

The darkness of the street, the fast-falling mist which obscured the light from the meagre oil lamps, seemed to add a certain weirdness to this moving, seething multitude. No one could see his neighbour. In the blackness of the night the muttering or yelling figures moved about like some spectral creatures from hellish regions—the Akous of Brittany who call to those about to die; whilst the women squatting in the oozing mud, beneath that swinging piece of rope, looked like a group of ghostly witches, waiting for the hour of their Sabbath.

As Déroulède emerged into the open, the light from a swinging lantern in the doorway fell upon his face. The foremost of the crowd recognised him; a howl of execration went up to the cloud-covered sky, and a hundred hands were thrust out in deadly menace against him.

It seemed as if they wished to tear him to pieces.

"*A la lanterne! A la lanterne! le traître!*"

He shivered slightly, as if with the sudden blast of cold, humid air, but he stepped quietly into the cart, closely followed by Juliette.

The strong escort of the National Guard, with Commandant Santerre and his two drummers, had much ado to keep back the mob. It was not the policy of the revolutionary government to allow excesses of summary justice in the streets: the public execution of traitors on the Place de la Révolution, the processions in the tumbrils, were thought to be wholesome examples for other would-be traitors to mark and digest.

Citizen Santerre, military commandant of Paris, had ordered his men to use their bayonets ruthlessly, and, to further overawe the populace, he ordered a prolonged roll of drums, lest Déroulède took it into his head to speak to the crowd.

But Déroulède had no such intention: he seemed chiefly concerned in shielding Juliette from the cold; she had been made to sit in the cart beside him, and he had taken off his coat, and was wrapping it round her against the penetrating rain.

The eye-witnesses of these memorable events have declared that, at a given moment, he looked up suddenly with a curious, eager expression in his eyes, and then raised himself in the cart and seemed to be trying to penetrate the gloom round him, as if in search of a face, or perhaps a voice.

"*A la lanterne! A la lanterne!*" was the continual hoarse cry of the mob.

Up to now, flanked in their rear by the outer walls of the Palais de Justice, the soldiers had found it a fairly easy task to keep the crowd at bay. But there came a time when the cart was bound to move out into the open, in order to convey the prisoners along, by the Rue du Palais, up to the Luxembourg Prison.

This task, however, had become more and more difficult every moment. The people of Paris, who for two years had been told by its tyrants that it was supreme lord of the universe, was mad with rage at seeing its desires frustrated by a few soldiers.

The drums had been greeted by terrific yells, which effectually drowned their roll; the first movement of the cart was hailed by a veritable tumult.

Only the women who squatted round the gallows had not moved from their position of vantage; one of these Mægæras was quietly readjusting the rope, which had got out of place.

But all the men and some of the women were literally besieging the cart, and threatening the soldiers, who stood between them and the object of their fury.

It seemed as if nothing now could save Déroulède and Juliette from an immediate and horrible death.

"*A mort! A mort! A la lanterne les traîtres!*"

Santerre himself, who had shouted himself hoarse, was at a loss what to do. He had sent one man to the nearest cavalry barracks, but reinforcements would still be some little time coming; whilst in the meanwhile his men were getting exhausted, and the mob, more and more excited, threatened to break through their line at every moment.

There was not another second to be lost.

Santerre was for letting the mob have its way, and he would willingly have thrown it the prey for which it clamoured; but orders were orders, and in the year I. of the Revolution it was not good to disobey.

At this supreme moment of perplexity he suddenly felt a respectful touch on his arm.

Close behind him a soldier of the National Guard—not one of his own men—was standing at attention, and holding a small, folded paper in his hand.

"Sent to you by the Minister of Justice," whispered the soldier hurriedly. "The citizen-deputies have watched the tumult from the Hall; they say, you must not lose an instant."

Santerre withdrew from the front rank, up against the side of the cart, where a rough stable lantern had been fixed. He took the paper from the soldier's hand, and, hastily tearing it open, he read it by the dim light of the lantern.

As he read, his thick, coarse features expressed the keenest satisfaction.

"You have two more men with you?" he asked quickly.

"Yes, citizen," replied the man, pointing towards his right; "and the Citizen-Minister said you would give me two more."

"You'll take the prisoners quietly across to the Prison of the Temple —you understand that?"

"Yes, citizen; Citizen Merlin has given me full instructions. You can have the cart drawn back a little more under the shadow of the portico, where the prisoners can be made to alight; they can then be given into my charge. You in the meantime are to stay here with your men, round the empty cart, as long as you can. Reinforcements have been sent for, and must soon be here. When they arrive you are to move along with the cart, as if you were making for the Luxembourg Prison. This manoeuvre will give us time to deliver the prisoners safely at the Temple."

The man spoke hurriedly and peremptorily, and Santerre was only too ready to obey. He felt relieved at thought of reinforcements, and glad to be rid of the responsibility of conducting such troublesome prisoners.

The thick mist, which grew more and more dense, favoured the new manoeuvre, and the constant roll of drums drowned the hastily given orders.

The cart was drawn back into the deepest shadow of the great portico, and whilst the mob were howling their loudest, and yelling out frantic demands for the traitors, Déroulède and Juliette were summarily ordered to step out of the cart. No one saw them, for the darkness here was intense.

"Follow quietly!" whispered a raucous voice in their ears as they did so, "or my orders are to shoot you where you stand."

But neither of them had any wish for resistance. Juliette, cold and numb, was clinging to Déroulède, who had placed a protecting arm round her.

Santerre had told off two of his men to join the new escort of the prisoners, and presently the small party, skirting the walls of the Palais de Justice, began to walk rapidly away from the scene of the riot.

Déroulède noted that some half-dozen men seemed to be surrounding him and Juliette, but the drizzling rain blurred every outline. The blackness of the night too had become absolutely dense, and in the distance the cries of the populace grew more and more faint.

CHAPTER 28. THE UNEXPECTED

The small party walked on in silence. It seemed to consist of a very few men of the National Guard, whom Santerre had placed under the command of the soldier who had transmitted to him the orders of the Citizen-Deputies.

Juliette and Déroulède both vaguely wondered whither they were being led; to some other prison mayhap, away from the fury of the populace. They were conscious of a sense of satisfaction at thought of being freed from that pack of raging wild beasts.

Beyond that they cared nothing. Both felt already the shadow of death hovering over them. The supreme moment of their lives had come, and had found them side by side.

What neither fear nor remorse, sorrow nor joy, could do, that the great and mighty Shadow accomplished in a trice.

Juliette, looking death bravely in the face, held out her hand, and sought that of the man she loved.

There was not one word spoken between them, not even a murmur.

Déroulède, with the unerring instinct of his own unselfish passion, understood all that the tiny hand wished to convey to him.

In a moment everything was forgotten save the joy of this touch. Death, or the fear of death, had ceased to exist. Life was beautiful, and in the soul of these two human creatures there was perfect peace, almost perfect happiness.

With one grasp of the hand they had sought and found one another's soul. What mattered the yelling crowd, the noise and tumult of this sordid world? They had found one another, and, hand-in-hand, shoulder-to-shoulder, they had gone off wandering into the land of dreams, where dwelt neither doubt nor treachery, where there was nothing to forgive.

He no longer said: "She does not love me—would she have betrayed me else?" He felt the clinging, trustful touch of her hand, and knew that, with all her faults, her great sin and her lasting sorrow, her woman's heart, Heaven's most priceless treasure, was indeed truly his.

And she knew that he had forgiven—nay, that he had naught to forgive —for Love is sweet and tender, and judges not. Love is Love—whole, trustful, passionate. Love is perfect understanding and perfect peace.

And so they followed their escort whithersoever it chose to lead them.

Their eyes wandered aimlessly over the mist-laden landscape of this portion of deserted Paris. They had turned away from the river now, and were following the Rue des Arts. Close by on the right was the dismal little hostelry, "La Cruche Cassée," where Sir Percy Blakeney lived. Déroulède, as they neared the place, caught himself vaguely wondering what had become of his English friend.

But it would take more than the ingenuity of the Scarlet Pimpernel to get two noted prisoners out of Paris to-day. Even if ...

"Halt!"

The word of command rang out clearly and distinctly through the rain-soaked atmosphere.

Déroulède threw up his head and listened. Something strange and unaccountable in that same word of command had struck his sensitive ear.

Yet the party had halted, and there was a click as of bayonets or muskets levelled ready to fire.

All had happened in less than a few seconds. The next moment there was a loud cry:

"*A moi*, Déroulède! 'tis the Scarlet Pimpernel!"

A vigorous blow from an unseen hand had knocked down and extinguished the nearest street lantern.

Déroulède felt that he and Juliette were being hastily dragged under an adjoining doorway even as the cheery voice echoed along the narrow street.

Half-a-dozen men were struggling below in the mud, and there was a plentiful supply of honest English oaths. It looked as if the men of the National Guard had fallen upon one another, and had it not been for those same English oaths perhaps Déroulède and Juliette would have been slower to understand.

"Well done, Tony! Gadzooks, Ffoulkes, that was a smart bit of work!"

The lazy, pleasant voice was unmistakable, but, God in heaven! where did it come from?

Of one thing there could be no doubt. The two men despatched by Santerne were lying disabled on the ground, whilst three other soldiers were busy pinioning them with ropes.

What did it all mean?

"La, friend Déroulède! you had not thought, I trust, that I would leave Mademoiselle Juliette in such a demmed, uncomfortable hole?"

And there, close beside Déroulède and Juliette, stood the tall figure of the Jacobin orator, the bloodthirsty Citizen Lenoir. The two young people gazed and gazed, then looked again, dumfounded, hardly daring to trust their vision, for through the grime-covered mask of the gigantic coal-heaver a pair of merry blue eyes was regarding them with lazy-amusement.

"La! I do look a miserable object, I know," said the pseudo coal-heaver at last, "but 'twas the only way to get those murderous devils to do what I wanted. A thousand pardons, mademoiselle; 'twas I brought you to such a terrible pass, but la! you are amongst friends now. Will you deign to forgive me?"

Juliette looked up. Her great, earnest eyes, now swimming in tears, sought those of the brave man who had so nobly stood by her and the man she loved.

"Blakeney ..." began Déroulède.

But Sir Percy quickly interrupted him:

"Hush, man! we have but a few moments. Remember you are in Paris still, and the Lord only knows how we shall all get out of this murderous city to-night. I have said that you and mademoiselle are among friends. That is all for the moment. I had to get you together, or I should have failed. I could only succeed by subjecting you and mademoiselle to terrible indignities. Our League could plan but one rescue, and I had to adopt the best means at my command to have you condemned and led away together. Faith!" he added, with a pleasant laugh, "my friend Tinville will not be pleased when he realises that Citizen Lenoir has dragged the Citizen-Deputies by the nose."

Whilst he spoke he had led Déroulède and Juliette into a dark and narrow room on the ground floor of the hostelry, and presently he called loudly for Brogard, the host of this uninviting abode.

"Brogard!" shouted Sir Percy. "Where is that ass Brogard? La! man," he added as

Citizen Brogard, obsequious and fussy, and with pockets stuffed with English gold, came shuffling along, "where do you hide your engaging countenance? Here! another length of rope for the gallant soldiers. Bring them in here, then give them that potion down their throats, as I have prescribed. Demm it! I wish we need not have brought them along, but that devil Santerre might have been suspicious else. They'll come to no harm, though, and can do us no mischief."

He prattled along merrily. Innately kind and chivalrous, he wished to give Déroulède and Juliette time to recover from their dazed surprise.

The transition from dull despair to buoyant hope had been so sudden: it had all happened in less than three minutes.

The scuffle had been short and sudden outside. The two soldiers of Santerne had been taken completely unawares, and the three young lieutenants of the Scarlet Pimpernel had fallen on them with such vigour that they had hardly had time to utter a cry of "Help!"

Moreover, that cry would have been useless. The night was dark and wet, and those citizens who felt ready for excitement were busy mobbing the Hall of Justice, a mile and a half away. One or two heads had appeared at the small windows of the squalid houses opposite, but it was too dark to see anything, and the scuffle had very quickly subsided.

All was silent now in the Rue des Arts, and in the grimy coffee-room of the Cruche Cassée two soldiers of the National Guard were lying bound and gagged, whilst three others were gaily laughing, and wiping their rain-soaked hands and faces.

In the midst of them all stood the tall, athletic figure of the bold adventurer who had planned this impudent coup.

"La! we've got so far, friends, haven't we?" he said cheerily, "and now for the immediate future. We must all be out of Paris to-night, or the guillotine for the lot of us to-morrow."

He spoke gaily, and with that pleasant drawl of his which was so well known in the fashionable assemblies of London; but there was a ring of earnestness in his voice, and his lieutenants looked up at him, ready to obey him in all things, but aware that danger was looming threateningly ahead.

Lord Anthony Dewhurst, Sir Andrew Ffoulkes, and Lord Hastings, dressed as soldiers of the National Guard, had played their part to perfection. Lord Hastings had presented the order to Santerre, and the three young bucks, at the word of command from their chief, had fallen upon and overpowered the two men whom the commandant of Paris had despatched to look after the prisoners.

So far all was well. But how to get out of Paris? Everyone looked to the Scarlet Pimpernel for guidance.

Sir Percy now turned to Juliette, and with the consummate grace which the elaborate etiquette of the times demanded, he made her a courtly bow.

"Mademoiselle de Marny," he said, "allow me to conduct you to a room, which though unworthy of your presence will, nevertheless, enable you to rest quietly for a few minutes, whilst I give my friend Déroulède further advice and instructions. In the room you will find a disguise, which I pray you to don with all haste. La! they are filthy rags, I own, but your life and—and ours depend upon your help."

Gallantly he kissed the tips of her fingers, and opened the door of an adjoining room to enable her to pass through; then he stood aside, so that her final look, as she went, might be for Déroulède.

As soon as the door had closed upon her he once more turned to the men.

"Those uniforms will not do now," he said peremptorily; "there are bundles of abominable clothes here, Tony. Will you all don them as quickly as you can? We must all look as filthy a band of *sansculottes* to-night as ever walked the streets of Paris."

His lazy drawl had deserted him now. He was the man of action and of thought, the bold adventurer who held the lives of his friends in the hollow of his hand.

The four men hastily obeyed. Lord Anthony Dewhurst—one of the most elegant dandies of London society—had brought forth from a dank cupboard a bundle of clothes, mere rags, filthy but useful.

Within ten minutes the change was accomplished, and four dirty, slouchy figures stood confronting their chief.

"That's capital!" said Sir Percy merrily.

"Now for Mademoiselle de Marny."

Hardly had he spoken when the door of the adjoining room was pushed open, and a horrible apparition stood before the men. A woman in filthy bodice and skirt, with face covered in grime, her yellow hair, matted and greasy, thrust under a dirty and crumpled cap.

A shout of rapturous delight greeted this uncanny apparition.

Juliette, like the true woman she was, had found all her energy and spirits now that she felt that she had an important part to play. She woke from her dream to realise that noble friends had risked their lives for the man she loved and for her.

Of herself she did not think; she only remembered that her presence of mind, her physical and mental strength, would be needed to carry the rescue to a successful end.

Therefore with the rags of a Paris *tricotteuse* she had also donned her personality. She played her part valiantly, and one look at the perfection of her disguise was sufficient to assure the leader of this band of heroes that his instructions would be carried through to the letter.

Déroulède too now looked the ragged *sansculotte* to the life, with bare and muddy feet, frayed breeches, and shabby, black-shag spencer. The four men stood waiting together with Juliette, whilst Sir Percy gave them his final instructions.

"We'll mix with the crowd," he said, "and do all that the crowd does. It is for us to see that that unruly crowd does what we want. Mademoiselle de Marny, a thousand congratulations. I entreat you to take hold of my friend Déroulède's hand, and not to let go of it, on any pretext whatever. La! not a difficult task, I ween," he added, with his genial smile; "and yours, Déroulède, is equally easy. I enjoin you to take charge of Mademoiselle Juliette, and on no account to leave her side until we are out of Paris."

"Out of Paris!" echoed Déroulède, with a troubled sigh.

"Aye!" rejoined Sir Percy boldly; "out of Paris! with a howling mob at our heels causing the authorities to take double precautions. And above all remember, friends, that our rallying cry is the shrill call of the sea-mew thrice repeated. Follow it until you are outside the gates of Paris. Once there, listen for it again; it will lead you to freedom and safety at last. Aye! Outside Paris, by the grace of God."

The hearts of his hearers thrilled as they heard him. Who could help but follow this brave and gallant adventurer, with the magic voice and the noble bearing?

"And now *en route*!" said Blakeney finally, "that ass Santerre will have dispersed the pack of yelling hyenas with his cavalry by now. They'll to the Temple prison to find their prey; we'll in their wake. *A moi*, friends! and remember the sea-gull's cry."

Déroulède drew Juliette's hand in his.

"We are ready," he said; "and God bless the Scarlet Pimpernel."

Then the five men, with Juliette in their midst, went out into the street once more.

CHAPTER 29. PÈRE LACHAISE

It was not difficult to guess which way the crowd had gone; yells, hoots, and hoarse cries could be heard from the farther side of the river.

Citizen Santerne had been unable to keep the mob back until the arrival of the cavalry reinforcements. Within five minutes of the abduction of Déroulède and Juliette the crowd had broken through the line of soldiers, and had stormed the cart, only to find it empty, and the prey disappeared.

"They are safe in the Temple by now!" shouted Santerne hoarsely, in savage triumph at seeing them all baffled.

At first it seemed as if the wrath of the infuriated populace, fooled in its lust for vengeance, would vent itself against the commandant of Paris and his soldiers; for a moment even Santerre's ruddy cheeks had paled at the sudden vision of this unlooked for danger.

Then just as suddenly the cry was raised.

"To the Temple!"

"To the Temple! To the Temple!" came in ready response.

The cry was soon taken up by the entire crowd, and in less than two minutes the purlieus of the Hall of Justice were deserted, and the Pont St Michel, then the Cité and the Pont au Change, swarmed with the rioters. Thence along the north bank of the river, and up the Rue du Temple, the people still yelling, muttering, singing the "*Ça ira,*" and shouting: "*A la lanterne! A la lanterne!*"

Sir Percy Blakeney and his little band of followers had found the Pont Neuf and the adjoining streets practically deserted. A few stragglers from the crowd, soaked through with the rain, their enthusiasm damped, and their throats choked with the mist, were sulkily returning to their homes.

The desultory group of six *sansculottes* attracted little or no attention, and Sir Percy boldly challenged every passer-by.

"The way to the Rue du Temple, citizen?" he asked once or twice, or:

"Have they hung the traitor yet? Can you tell me, citizeness?"

A grunt or an oath were the usual replies, but no one took any further notice of the gigantic coal-heaver and his ragged friends.

At the corner of one of the cross streets, between the Rue du Temple and the Rue des Archives, Sir Percy Blakeney suddenly turned to his followers:

"We are close to the rabble now," he said in a whisper, and speaking in English; "do you all follow the nearest stragglers, and get as soon as possible into the thickest of the crowd. We'll meet again outside the prison—and remember the sea-gull's cry."

He did not wait for an answer, and presently disappeared in the mist.

Already a few stragglers, hangers-on of the multitude, were gradually coming into view, and the yells could be distinctly heard. The mob had evidently assembled in the great square outside the prison, and was loudly demanding the object of its wrath.

The moment for cool-headed action was at hand. The Scarlet Pimpernel had planned the whole thing, but it was for his followers and for those, whom he was endeavouring to rescue from certain death, to help him heart and soul.

Déroulède's grasp tightened on Juliette's little hand.

"Are you frightened, my beloved?" he whispered.

"Not whilst you are near me," she murmured in reply.

A few more minutes' walk up the Rue des Archives and they were in the thick of the crowd. Sir Andrew Ffoulkes, Lord Anthony Dewhurst, and Lord Hastings, the three Englishmen, were in front; Déroulède and Juliette immediately behind them.

The mob itself now carried them along. A motley throng they were, soaked through with the rain, drunk with their own baffled rage, and with the brandy which they had imbibed.

Everyone was shouting; the women louder than the rest; one of them was dragging the length of rope, which might still be useful.

"Ça ira! ça ira! A la lanterne! A la lanterne! les traîtres!"

And Déroulède, holding Juliette by the hand, shouted lustily with them:

"Ça ira!"

Sir Andrew Ffoulkes turned, and laughed. It was rare sport for these young bucks, and they all entered into the spirit of the situation. They all shouted *"A la lanterne!"* egging and encouraging those around them.

Déroulède and Juliette felt the intoxication of the adventure. They were drunk with the joy of their reunion, and seized with the wild, mad, passionate desire for freedom and for life ... Life and love!

So they pushed and jostled on in the mud, followed the crowd, sang and yelled louder than any of them. Was not that very crowd the great bulwark of their safety?

As well have sought for the proverbial needle in the haystack, as for two escaped prisoners in this mad, heaving throng.

The large open space in front of the Temple Prison looked like one great, seething, black mass.

The darkness was almost thick here, the ground like a morass, with inches of clayey mud, which stuck to everything, whilst the sparse lanterns, hung to the prison walls and beneath the portico, threw practically no light into the square.

As the little band, composed of the three Englishmen, and of Déroulède, holding Juliette by the hand, emerged into the open space, they heard a strident cry, like that of a sea-mew thrice repeated, and a hoarse voice shouting from out the darkness:

"*Ma foi!* I'll not believe that the prisoners are in the Temple now! It is my belief, friends, citizens, that we have been fooled once more!"

The voice, with its strange, unaccountable accent, which seemed to belong to no province of France, dominated the almost deafening noise; it penetrated through, even into the brandy-soddened minds of the multitude, for the suggestion was received with renewed shouts of the wildest wrath.

Like one great, living, seething mass the crowd literally bore down upon the huge and frowning prison. Pushing, jostling, yelling, the women screaming, the men cursing, it seemed as if that awesome day— the 14th of July—was to have its sanguinary counterpart to-night, as if the Temple were destined to share the fate of the Bastille.

Obedient to their leader's orders the three young Englishmen remained in the thick of the crowd: together with Déroulède they contrived to form a sturdy rampart round Juliette, effectually protecting her against rough buffetings.

On their right, towards the direction of Ménilmontant, the sea-mew's cry at intervals gave the strength and courage.

The foremost rank of the crowd had reached the portico of the building, and, with howls and snatches of their gutter song, were loudly clamouring for the guardian of the grim prison.

No one appeared; the great gates with their massive bars and hinges remained silent and defiant.

The crowd was becoming dangerous: whispers of the victory of the Bastille, five years ago, engendered thoughts of pillage and of arson.

Then the strident voice was heard again:

"*Pardi!* the prisoners are not in the Temple! The dolts have allowed them to escape, and now are afraid of the wrath of the people!"

It was strange how easily the mob assimilated this new idea. Perhaps the dark, frowning block of massive buildings had overawed them with its peaceful strength, perhaps the dripping rain and oozing clay had damped their desire for an immediate storming of the grim citadel; perhaps it was merely the human characteristic of a wish for something new, something unexpected.

Be that as it may, the cry was certainly taken up with marvelous, quick-change rapidity.

"The prisoners have escaped! The prisoners have escaped!"

Some were for proceeding with the storming of the Temple, but they were in the minority. All along, the crowd had been more inclined for private revenge than for martial deeds of valour; the Bastille had been taken by daylight; the effort might not have been so successful on a pitch-black night such as this, when one could not see one's hand before one's eyes, and the drizzling rain went through to the marrow.

"They've got through one of the barriers by now!" suggested the same voice from out the darkness.

"The barriers—the barriers!" came in sheeplike echo from the crowd.

The little group of fugitives and their friends tightened their hold on one another. They had understood at last.

"It is for us to see that the crowd does what we want," the Scarlet Pimpernel had said.

He wanted it to take him and his friends out of Paris, and, by God! he was like to succeed.

Juliette's heart within her beat almost to choking; her strong little hand gripped Déroulède's fingers with the wild strength of a mad exultation.

Next to the man to whom she had given her love and her very soul she admired and looked up to the remarkable and noble adventurer, the high-born and exquisite dandy, who with grime-covered face, and strong limbs encased in filthy clothes, was playing the most glorious part ever enacted upon the stage.

"To the barriers—to the barriers!"

Like a herd of wild horses, driven by the whip of the herdsmen, the mob began to scatter in all directions. Not knowing what it wanted, not knowing what it would find, half forgetting the very cause and object of its wrath, it made one gigantic rush for the gates of the great city through which the prisoners were supposed to have escaped.

The three Englishmen and Déroulède, with Juliette well protected in their midst, had not joined the general onrush as yet. The crowd in the open place was still very thick, the outward-branching streets were very narrow: through these the multitude, scampering, hurrying, scurrying, like a human torrent let out of a whirlpool, rushed down headlong towards the barriers.

Up the Rue Turbigo to the Belleville gate, the Rue des Filles, and the Rue du Chemin Vert, towards Popincourt, they ran, knocking each other down, jostling the weaker ones on one side, trampling others underfoot. They were all rough, coarse creatures, accustomed to these wild bousculades, ready to pick themselves up, again after any number of falls; whilst the mud was slimy and soft to tumble on, and those who did the trampling had no shoes on their feet.

They rushed out from the dark, open place, these creatures of the night, into streets darker still.

On they ran—on! on!—now in thick, heaving masses, anon in loose, straggling groups—some north, some south, some east, some west.

But it was from the east that came the seagull's cry.

The little band ran boldly towards the east. Down the Rue de la République they followed their leader's call. The crowd was very thick here; the Barrière Ménilmontant was close by, and beyond it there was the cemetery of Père Lachaise. It was the nearest gate to the Temple Prison, and the mob wanted to be up and doing, not to spend too much time running along the muddy streets and getting wet and cold, but to repeat the glorious exploits of the 14th of July, and capture the barriers of Paris by force of will rather than force of arms.

In this rushing mob the four men, with Juliette in their midst, remained quite unchallenged, mere units in an unruly crowd.

In a quarter of an hour Ménilmontant was reached.

The great gates of the city were well guarded by detachments of the National Guard, each under command of an officer. Twenty strong at most—what was that against such a throng?

Who had ever dreamed of Paris being stormed from within?

At every gate to the north and east of the city there was now a rabble some four or five thousand strong, wanting it knew not what. Everyone had forgotten what it was that caused him or her to rush on so blindly, so madly, towards the nearest barrier.

But everyone knew that he or she wanted to get through that barrier, to attack the soldiery, to knock down the captain of the Guard.

And with a wild cry every city gate was stormed.

Like one huge wind-tossed wave, the populace on that memorable night of Fructidor, broke against the cordon of soldiery, that vainly tried to keep it back. Men and women, drunk with brandy and exultation, shouted "*Quatorze Juillet!* " and amidst curses and threats demanded the opening of the gates.

The people of France *would* have its will.

Was it not the supreme lord and ruler of the land, the arbiter of the Fate of this great, beautiful, and maddened country?

The National Guard was powerless; the officers in command could offer but feeble resistance.

The desultory fire, which in the darkness and the pouring rain did very little harm, had the effect of further infuriating the mob.

The drizzle had turned to a deluge, a veritable heavy summer downpour, with occasional distant claps of thunder and incessant sheet-lightning, which ever and anon illumined with its weird, fantastic flash this heaving throng, these begrimed faces, crowned with red caps of Liberty, these witchlike female creatures with wet, straggly hair and gaunt, menacing arms.

Within half-an-hour the people of Paris was outside its own gates.

Victory was complete. The Guard did not resist; the officers had surrendered; the great and mighty rabble had had its way.

Exultant, it swarmed around the fortifications and along the *terrains vagues* which it had conquered by its will.

But the downpour was continuous, and with victory came satiety— satiety coupled with wet skins, muddy feet, tired, wearied bodies, and throats parched with continual shouting.

At Ménilmontant, where the crowd had been thickest, the tempers highest, and the yells most strident, there now stretched before this tired, excited throng, the peaceful vastness of the cemetery of Père Lachaise.

The great alleys of sombre monuments, the weird cedars with their fantastic branches, like arms of a hundred ghosts, quelled and awed these hooting masses of degraded humanity.

The silent majesty of this city of the dead seemed to frown with withering scorn on the passions of the sister city.

Instinctively the rabble was cowed. The cemetery looked dark, dismal, and deserted. The flashes of lightning seemed to reveal ghostlike processions of the departed heroes of France, wandering silently amidst the tombs.

And the populace turned with a shudder away from this vast place of eternal peace.

From within the cemetery gates, there was suddenly heard the sound of a sea-mew calling thrice to its mate. And five dark figures, wrapped in cloaks, gradually detached themselves from the throng, and one by one slipped into the grounds of Père Lachaise through that break in the wall, which is quite close to the main entrance.

Once more the sea-gull's cry.

Those in the crowd who heard it, shivered beneath their dripping clothes. They thought it was a soul in pain risen from one of the graves, and some of the women, forgetting the last few years of godlessness, hastily crossed themselves, and muttered an invocation to the Virgin Mary.

Within the gates all was silent and at peace. The sodden earth gave forth no echo of the muffled footsteps, which slowly crept towards the massive block of stone, which covers the graves of the immortal lovers —Abélard and Heloïse.

CHAPTER 30. CONCLUSION

There is but little else to record.

History has told us how, shamefaced, tired, dripping, the great, all-powerful people of Paris quietly slunk back to their homes, even before the first cock-crow in the villages beyond the gates, acclaimed the pale streak of dawn.

But long before that, even before the church bells of the great city had tolled the midnight hour, Sir Percy Blakeney and his little band of followers had reached the little tavern which stands close to the farthest gate of Père Lachaise.

Without a word, like six silent ghosts, they had traversed the vast cemetery, and reached the quiet hostelry, where the sounds of the seething revolution only came, attenuated by their passage through the peaceful city of the dead.

English gold had easily purchased silence and good will from the half-starved keeper of this wayside inn. A huge travelling chaise already stood in readiness, and four good Flanders horses had been pawing the ground impatiently for the past half hour. From the window of the chaise old Pétronelle's face, wet with anxious tears, was peering anxiously.

A cry of joy and surprise escaped Déroulède and Juliette, and both turned, with a feeling akin to awe, towards the wonderful man who had planned and carried through this bold adventure.

"Nay, my friend," said Sir Percy, speaking more especially to Déroulède; "if you only knew how simple it all was! Gold can do so many things, and my only merit seems to be the possession of plenty of that commodity. You told me yourself how you had provided for old Pétronelle. Under the most solemn assurance that she would meet her young mistress here, I got her to leave Paris. She came out most bravely this morning in one of the market carts. She is so obviously a woman of the people, that no one suspected her. As for the worthy couple who keep this wayside hostel, they have been well paid, and money soon procures a chaise and horses. My English friends and I, we have our own passports, and one for Mademoiselle Juliette, who must travel as an English lady, with her old nurse, Pétronelle. There are some decent clothes in readiness for us all in the inn. A quarter of an hour in which to don them and we must on our way. You can use your own passport, of course; your arrest has been so very sudden that it has not yet been cancelled, and we have an eight hours' start of our enemies. They'll wake up to-morrow morning, begad! and find that you have slipped through their fingers."

He spoke with easy carelessness, and that slow drawl of his, as if he were talking airy nothings in a London drawing-room, instead of recounting the most daring, most colossal piece of effrontery the adventurous brain of man could conceive.

Déroulède could say nothing. His own noble heart was too full of gratitude towards his friend to express it all in a few words.

And time, of course, was precious.

Within the prescribed quarter of an hour the little band of heroes had doffed their grimy, ragged clothes, and now appeared dressed as respectable bourgeois of Paris *en route* for the country. Sir Percy Blakeney had donned the livery of a coachman of a well-to-do house, whilst Lord Anthony Dewhurst wore that of an English lacquey.

Five minutes later Déroulède had lifted Juliette into the travelling chaise, and in spite of fatigue, of anxiety, and emotion, it was immeasurable happiness to feel her arm encircling his shoulders in perfect joy and trust.

Sir Andrew Ffoulkes and Lord Hastings joined them inside the chaise; Lord Anthony sat next to Sir Percy on the box.

And whilst the crowd of Paris was still wondering why it had stormed the gates of the city, the escaped prisoners were borne along the muddy roads of France at breakneck speed northward to the coast.

Sir Percy Blakeney held the reins himself. With his noble heart full of joy, the gallant adventurer himself drove his friends to safety.

They had an eight hours' start, and The League of The Scarlet Pimpernel had done its work thoroughly: well provided with passports, and with relays awaiting them at every station of fifty miles or so, the journey, though wearisome was free from further adventure.

At Le Havre the little party embarked on board Sir Percy Blakeney's yacht the *Daydream*, where they met Madame Déroulède and Anne Mie.

The two ladies, acting under the instructions of Sir Percy, had as originally arranged, pursued their journey northwards, to the populous seaport town.

Anne Mie's first meeting with Juliette was intensely pathetic. The poor little cripple had spent the last few days in an agony of remorse, whilst the heavy travelling chaise bore her farther and farther away from Paris.

She thought Juliette dead, and Paul a prey to despair, and her tender soul ached when she remembered that it was she who had given the final deadly stab to the heart of the man she loved.

Hers was the nature born to abnegation: aye! and one destined to find bliss therein. And when one glance in Paul Déroulède's face told her that she was forgiven, her cup of joy at seeing him happy beside his beloved, was unalloyed with any bitterness.

It was in the beautiful, rosy dawn of one of the last days of that memorable Fructidor, when Juliette and Paul Déroulède, standing on the deck of the *Daydream*, saw the shores of France gradually receding from their view.

Déroulède's arm was round his beloved, her golden hair, fanned by the breeze, brushed lightly against his cheek.

"Madonna!" he murmured.

She turned her head to him. It was the first time that they were quite alone, the first time that all thought of danger had become a mere dream.

What had the future in store for them, in that beautiful, strange land to which the graceful yacht was swiftly bearing them?

England, the land of freedom, would shelter their happiness and their joy; and they looked out towards the North, where lay, still hidden in the arms of the distant horizon, the white cliffs of Albion, whilst the mist even now was wrapping in its obliterating embrace the shores of the land where they had both suffered, where they had both learned to love.

He took her in his arms.

"My wife!" he whispered.

The rosy light touched her golden hair; he raised her face to his, and soul met soul in one long, passionate kiss.

THE ELUSIVE PIMPERNEL

THE ELUSIVE PIMPERNEL

CHAPTER I. PARIS: 1793

THERE WAS NOT EVEN A REACTION.

On! ever on! in that wild, surging torrent; sowing the wind of anarchy, of terrorism, of lust of blood and hate, and reaping a hurricane of destruction and of horror.

On! ever on! France, with Paris and all her children still rushes blindly, madly on; defies the powerful coalition,—Austria, England, Spain, Prussia, all joined together to stem the flow of carnage,—defies the Universe and defies God!

Paris this September 1793!—or shall we call it Vendemiaire, Year I. of the Republic?—call it what we will! Paris! a city of bloodshed, of humanity in its lowest, most degraded aspect. France herself a gigantic self-devouring monster, her fairest cities destroyed, Lyons razed to the ground, Toulon, Marseilles, masses of blackened ruins, her bravest sons turned to lustful brutes or to abject cowards seeking safety at the cost of any humiliation.

That is thy reward, oh mighty, holy Revolution! apotheosis of equality and fraternity! grand rival of decadent Christianity.

Five weeks now since Marat, the bloodthirsty Friend of the People, succumbed beneath the sheath-knife of a virgin patriot, a month since his murderess walked proudly, even enthusiastically, to the guillotine! There has been no reaction—only a great sigh!... Not of content or satisfied lust, but a sigh such as the man-eating tiger might heave after his first taste of long-coveted blood.

A sigh for more!

A king on the scaffold; a queen degraded and abased, awaiting death, which lingers on the threshold of her infamous prison; eight hundred scions of ancient houses that have made the history of France; brave generals, Custine, Blanchelande, Houchard, Beauharnais; worthy patriots, noble-hearted women, misguided enthusiasts, all by the score and by the hundred, up the few wooden steps which lead to the guillotine.

An achievement of truth!

And still that sigh for more!

But for the moment,—a few seconds only,—Paris looked round her mighty self, and thought things over!

The man-eating tiger for the space of a sigh licked his powerful jaws and pondered! Something new!—something wonderful!

We have had a new Constitution, a new Justice, new Laws, a new Almanack!

What next?

Why, obviously!—How comes it that great, intellectual, aesthetic Paris never thought of such a wonderful thing before?

A new religion!

Christianity is old and obsolete, priests are aristocrats, wealthy oppressors of the People, the Church but another form of wanton tyranny.

Let us by all means have a new religion.

Already something has been done to destroy the old! To destroy! always to destroy! Churches have been ransacked, altars spoliated, tombs desecrated, priests and curates murdered; but that is not enough.

There must be a new religion; and to attain that there must be a new God.

"Man is a born idol-worshipper."

Very well then! let the People have a new religion and a new God.

Stay!—Not a God this time!—for God means Majesty, Power, Kingship! everything in fact which the mighty hand of the people of France has struggled and fought to destroy.

Not a God, but a goddess.

A goddess! an idol! a toy! since even the man-eating tiger must play sometimes.

Paris wanted a new religion, and a new toy, and grave men, ardent patriots, mad enthusiasts, sat in the Assembly of the Convention and seriously discussed the means of providing her with both these things which she asked for.

Chaumette, I think it was, who first solved the difficulty:—Procureur Chaumette, head of the Paris Municipality, he who had ordered that the cart which bore the dethroned queen to the squalid prison of the Conciergerie should be led slowly past her own late palace of the Tuileries, and should be stopped there just long enough for her to see and to feel in one grand mental vision all that she had been when she dwelt there, and all that she now was by the will of the People.

Chaumette, as you see, was refined, artistic;—the torture of the fallen Queen's heart meant more to him than a blow of the guillotine on her neck.

No wonder, therefore, that it was Procureur Chaumette who first discovered exactly what type of new religion Paris wanted just now.

"Let us have a Goddess of Reason," he said, "typified if you will by the most beautiful woman in Paris. Let us have a feast of the Goddess of Reason, let there be a pyre of all the gew-gaws which for centuries have been flaunted by overbearing priests before the eyes of starving multitudes, let the People rejoice and dance around that funeral pile, and above it all let the new Goddess tower smiling and triumphant. The Goddess of Reason! the only deity our new and regenerate France shall acknowledge throughout the centuries which are to come!"

Loud applause greeted the impassioned speech.

"A new goddess, by all means!" shouted the grave gentlemen of the National Assembly, "the Goddess of Reason!"

They were all eager that the People should have this toy; something to play with and to tease, round which to dance the mad Carmagnole and sing the ever-recurring "Ca ira."

Something to distract the minds of the populace from the consequences of its own deeds, and the helplessness of its legislators.

Procureur Chaumette enlarged upon his original idea; like a true artist who sees the broad effect of a picture at a glance and then fills in the minute details, he was already busy elaborating his scheme.

"The goddess must be beautiful... not too young... Reason can only go hand in hand with the riper age of second youth... she must be decked out in classical draperies, severe yet suggestive... she must be rouged and painted... for she is a mere idol... easily to be appeased with incense, music and laughter."

He was getting deeply interested in his subject, seeking minutiae of detail, with which to render his theme more and more attractive.

But patience was never the characteristic of the Revolutionary Government of France. The National Assembly soon tired of Chaumette's dithyrambic utterances. Up aloft on the Mountain, Danton was yawning like a gigantic leopard.

Soon Henriot was on his feet. He had a far finer scheme than that of the Procureur to place before his colleagues. A grand National fete, semi-religious in character, but of the new religion which destroyed and desecrated and never knelt in worship.

Citizen Chaumette's Goddess of Reason by all means—Henriot conceded that the idea was a good one—but the goddess merely as a figure-head: around her a procession of unfrocked and apostate priests, typifying the destruction of ancient hierarchy, mules carrying loads of sacred vessels, the spoils of ten thousand churches of France, and ballet girls in bacchanalian robes, dancing the Carmagnole around the new deity.

Public Prosecutor Foucquier Tinville thought all these schemes very tame. Why should the People of France be led to think that the era of a new religion would mean an era of milk and water, of pageants and of fireworks? Let every man, woman, and child know that this was an era of blood and again of blood.

"Oh!" he exclaimed in passionate accents, "would that all the traitors in France had but one head, that it might be cut off with one blow of the guillotine!"

He approved of the National fete, but he desired an apotheosis of the guillotine; he undertook to find ten thousand traitors to be beheaded on one grand and glorious day: ten thousand heads to adorn the Place de la Revolution on a great, never-to-be-forgotten evening, after the guillotine had accomplished this record work.

But Collot d'Herbois would also have his say. Collot lately hailed from the South, with a reputation for ferocity unparalleled throughout the whole of this horrible decade. He would not be outdone by Tinville's bloodthirsty schemes.

He was the inventor of the "Noyades," which had been so successful at Lyons and Marseilles. "Why not give the inhabitants of Paris one of these exhilarating spectacles?" he asked with a coarse, brutal laugh.

Then he explained his invention, of which he was inordinately proud. Some two or three hundred traitors, men, women, and children, tied securely together with ropes in great, human bundles and thrown upon a barge in the middle of the river: the barge with a hole in her bottom! not too large! only sufficient to cause her to sink slowly, very slowly, in sight of the crowd of delighted spectators.

The cries of the women and children, and even of the men, as they felt the waters rising and gradually enveloping them, as they felt themselves powerless even for a fruitless struggle, had proved most exhilarating, so Citizen Collot declared, to the hearts of the true patriots of Lyons.

Thus the discussion continued.

This was the era when every man had but one desire, that of outdoing others in ferocity and brutality, and but one care, that of saving his own head by threatening that of his neighbour.

The great duel between the Titanic leaders of these turbulent parties, the conflict between hot-headed Danton on the one side and cold-blooded Robespierre on the other, had only just begun; the great, all-devouring monsters had dug their claws into one another, but the issue of the combat was still at stake.

Neither of these two giants had taken part in these deliberations anent the new religion and the new goddess. Danton gave signs now and then of the greatest impatience, and muttered something about a new form of tyranny, a new kind of oppression.

On the left, Robespierre in immaculate sea-green coat and carefully gauffered linen was quietly polishing the nails of his right hand against the palm of his left.

But nothing escaped him of what was going on. His ferocious egoism, his unbounded ambition was even now calculating what advantages to himself might accrue from this idea of the new religion and of the National fete, what personal aggrandizement he could derive therefrom.

The matter outwardly seemed trivial enough, but already his keen and calculating mind had seen various side issues which might tend to place him—Robespierre—on a yet higher and more unassailable pinnacle.

Surrounded by those who hated him, those who envied and those who feared him, he ruled over them all by the strength of his own cold-blooded savagery, by the resistless power of his merciless cruelty.

He cared about nobody but himself, about nothing but his own exaltation: every action of his career, since he gave up his small practice in a quiet provincial town in order to throw himself into the wild vortex of revolutionary politics, every word he ever uttered had but one aim—Himself.

He saw his colleagues and comrades of the old Jacobin Clubs ruthlessly destroyed around him: friends he had none, and all left him indifferent; and now he had hundreds of enemies in every assembly and club in Paris, and these too one by one were being swept up in that wild whirlpool which they themselves had created.

Impassive, serene, always ready with a calm answer, when passion raged most hotly around him, Robespierre, the most ambitious, most self-seeking demagogue of his time, had acquired the reputation of being incorruptible and selfless, an enthusiastic servant of the Republic.

The sea-green Incorruptible!

And thus whilst others talked and argued, waxed hot over schemes for processions and pageantry, or loudly denounced the whole matter as the work of a traitor, he, of the sea-green coat, sat quietly polishing his nails.

But he had already weighed all these discussions in the balance of his mind, placed them in the crucible of his ambition, and turned them into something that would benefit him and strengthen his position.

Aye! the feast should be brilliant enough! gay or horrible, mad or fearful, but through it all the people of France must be made to feel that there was a guiding hand which ruled the destinies of all, a head which framed the new laws, which consolidated the new religion and established its new goddess: the Goddess of Reason.

Robespierre, her prophet!

CHAPTER II. A RETROSPECT

The room was close and dark, filled with the smoke from a defective chimney.

A tiny boudoir, once the dainty sanctum of imperious Marie Antoinette; a faint and ghostly odour, like unto the perfume of spectres, seemed still to cling to the stained walls, and to the torn Gobelin tapestries.

Everywhere lay the impress of a heavy and destroying hand: that of the great and glorious Revolution.

In the mud-soiled corners of the room a few chairs, with brocaded cushions rudely torn, leant broken and desolate against the walls. A small footstool, once gilt-legged and satin-covered, had been overturned and roughly kicked to one side, and there it lay on its back, like some little animal that had been hurt, stretching its broken limbs upwards, pathetic to behold.

From the delicately wrought Buhl table the silver inlay had been harshly stripped out of its bed of shell.

Across the Lunette, painted by Boucher and representing a chaste Diana surrounded by a bevy of nymphs, an uncouth hand had scribbled in charcoal the device of the Revolution: Liberte, Egalite, Fraternite ou la Mort; whilst, as if to give a crowning point to the work of destruction and to emphasize its motto, someone had decorated the portrait of Marie Antoinette with a scarlet cap, and drawn a red and ominous line across her neck.

And at the table two men were sitting in close and eager conclave.

Between them a solitary tallow candle, unsnuffed and weirdly flickering, threw fantastic shadows upon the walls, and illumined with fitful and uncertain light the faces of the two men.

How different were these in character!

One, high cheek-boned, with coarse, sensuous lips, and hair elaborately and carefully powdered; the other pale and thin-lipped, with the keen eyes of a ferret and a high intellectual forehead, from which the sleek brown hair was smoothly brushed away.

The first of these men was Robespierre, the ruthless and incorruptible demagogue; the other was Citizen Chauvelin, ex-ambassador of the Revolutionary Government at the English Court.

The hour was late, and the noises from the great, seething city preparing for sleep came to this remote little apartment in the now deserted Palace of the Tuileries, merely as a faint and distant echo.

It was two days after the Fructidor Riots. Paul Deroulede and the woman Juliette Marny, both condemned to death, had been literally spirited away out of the cart which was conveying them from the Hall of Justice to the Luxembourg Prison, and news had just been received by the Committee of Public Safety that at Lyons, the Abbe du Mesnil, with the ci-devant Chevalier d'Egremont and the latter's wife and family, had effected a miraculous and wholly incomprehensible escape from the Northern Prison.

But this was not all. When Arras fell into the hands of the Revolutionary army, and a regular cordon was formed round the town, so that not a single royalist traitor might escape, some three score women and children, twelve priests, the old aristocrats Chermeuil, Delleville and Galipaux and many others, managed to pass the barriers and were never recaptured.

Raids were made on the suspected houses: in Paris chiefly where the escaped prisoners might have found refuge, or better still where their helpers and rescuers might still be lurking. Foucquier Tinville, Public Prosecutor, led and conducted these raids, assisted by that bloodthirsty vampire, Merlin. They heard of a house in the Rue de l'Ancienne Comedie where an Englishmen was said to have lodged for two days.

They demanded admittance, and were taken to the rooms where the Englishman had stayed. These were bare and squalid, like hundreds of other rooms in the poorer quarters of Paris. The landlady, toothless and grimy, had not yet tidied up the one where the Englishman had slept: in fact she did not know he had left for good.

He had paid for his room, a week in advance, and came and went as he liked, she explained to Citizen Tinville. She never bothered about him, as he never took a meal in the house, and he was only there two days. She did not know her lodger was English until the day he left. She thought he was a Frenchman from the South, as he certainly had a peculiar accent when he spoke.

"It was the day of the riots," she continued; "he would go out, and I told him I did not think that the streets would be safe for a foreigner like him: for he always wore such very fine clothes, and I made sure that the starving men and women of Paris would strip them off his back when their tempers were roused. But he only laughed. He gave me a bit of paper and told me that if he did not return I might conclude that he had been killed, and if the Committee of Public Safety asked me questions about me, I was just to show the bit of paper and there would be no further trouble."

She had talked volubly, more than a little terrified at Merlin's scowls, and the attitude of Citizen Tinville, who was known to be very severe if anyone committed any blunders.

But the Citizeness—her name was Brogard and her husband's brother kept an inn in the neighbourhood of Calais—the Citizeness Brogard had a clear conscience. She held a license from the Committee of Public Safety for letting apartments, and she had always given due notice to the Committee of the arrival and departure of her lodgers. The only thing was that if any lodger paid her more than ordinarily well for the accommodation and he so desired it, she would send in the notice conveniently late, and conveniently vaguely worded as to the description, status and nationality of her more liberal patrons.

This had occurred in the case of her recent English visitor.

But she did not explain it quite like that to Citizen Foucquier Tinville or to Citizen Merlin.

However, she was rather frightened, and produced the scrap of paper which the Englishman had left with her, together with the assurance that when she showed it there would be no further trouble.

Tinville took it roughly out of her hand, but would not glance at it. He crushed it into a ball and then Merlin snatched it from him with a coarse laugh, smoothed out the creases on his knee and studied it for a moment.

There were two lines of what looked like poetry, written in a language which Merlin did not understand. English, no doubt.

But what was perfectly clear, and easily comprehended by any one, was the little drawing in the corner, done in red ink and representing a small star-shaped flower.

Then Tinville and Merlin both cursed loudly and volubly, and bidding their men follow them, turned away from the house in the Rue de l'Ancienne Comedie and left its toothless landlady on her own doorstep still volubly protesting her patriotism and her desire to serve the government of the Republic.

Tinville and Merlin, however, took the scrap of paper to Citizen Robespierre, who smiled grimly as he in his turn crushed the offensive little document in the palm of his well-washed hands.

Robespierre did not swear. He never wasted either words or oaths, but he slipped the bit of paper inside the double lid of his silver snuff box and then he sent a special messenger to Citizen Chauvelin in the Rue Corneille, bidding him come that same evening after ten o'clock to room No. 16 in the ci-devant Palace of the Tuileries.

It was now half-past ten, and Chauvelin and Robespierre sat opposite one another in the ex-boudoir of Queen Marie Antoinette, and between them on the table, just below the tallow-candle, was a much creased, exceedingly grimy bit of paper.

It had passed through several unclean hands before Citizen Robespierre's immaculately white fingers had smoothed it out and placed it before the eyes of ex-Ambassador Chauvelin.

The latter, however, was not looking at the paper, he was not even looking at the pale, cruel face before him. He had closed his eyes and for a moment had lost sight of the small dark room, of Robespierre's ruthless gaze, of the mud-stained walls and greasy floor. He was seeing, as in a bright and sudden vision, the brilliantly-lighted salons of the Foreign Office in London, with beautiful Marguerite Blakeney gliding queenlike on the arm of the Prince of Wales.

He heard the flutter of many fans, the frou-frou of silk dresses, and above all the din and sound of dance music, he heard an inane laugh and an affected voice repeating the doggerel rhyme that was even now written on that dirty piece of paper which Robespierre had placed before him:

"We seek him here, and we seek him there,
Those Frenchies seek him everywhere!
Is he in heaven, is he in hell,
That demmed elusive Pimpernel?"

It was a mere flash! One of memory's swiftly effaced pictures, when she shows us for the fraction of a second, indelible pictures from out our past. Chauvelin, in that same second, while his own eyes were closed and Robespierre's fixed upon him, also saw the lonely cliffs of Calais, heard the same voice singing: "God save the King!" the volley of musketry, the despairing cries of Marguerite Blakeney; and once again he felt the keen and bitter pang of complete humiliation and defeat.

CHAPTER III. EX-AMBASSADOR CHAUVELIN

Robespierre had quietly waited the while. He was in no hurry: being a night-bird of very pronounced tastes, he was quite ready to sit here until the small hours of the morning watching Citizen Chauvelin mentally writhing in the throes of recollections of the past few months.

There was nothing that delighted the sea-green Incorruptible quite so much as the aspect of a man struggling with a hopeless situation and feeling a net of intrigue drawing gradually tighter and tighter around him.

Even now, when he saw Chauvelin's smooth forehead wrinkled into an anxious frown, and his thin hand nervously clutched upon the table, Robespierre heaved a pleasurable sigh, leaned back in his chair, and said with an amiable smile:

"You do agree with me, then, Citizen, that the situation has become intolerable?"

Then as Chauvelin did not reply, he continued, speaking more sharply:

"And how terribly galling it all is, when we could have had that man under the guillotine by now, if you had not blundered so terribly last year."

His voice had become hard and trenchant like that knife to which he was so ready to make constant allusion. But Chauvelin still remained silent. There was really nothing that he could say.

"Citizen Chauvelin, how you must hate that man!" exclaimed Robespierre at last.

Then only did Chauvelin break the silence which up to now he had appeared to have forced himself to keep.

"I do!" he said with unmistakable fervour.

"Then why do you not make an effort to retrieve the blunders of last year?" queried Robespierre blandly. "The Republic has been unusually patient and long-suffering with you, Citizen Chauvelin. She has taken your many services and well-known patriotism into consideration. But you know," he added significantly, "that she has no use for worthless tools."

Then as Chauvelin seemed to have relapsed into sullen silence, he continued with his original ill-omened blandness:

"Ma foi! Citizen Chauvelin, were I standing in your buckled shoes, I would not lose another hour in trying to avenge mine own humiliation!"

"Have I ever had a chance?" burst out Chauvelin with ill-suppressed vehemence. "What can I do single-handed? Since war has been declared I cannot go to England unless the Government will find some official reason for my doing so. There is much grumbling and wrath over here, and when that damned Scarlet Pimpernel League has been at work, when a score or so of valuable prizes have been snatched from under the very knife of the guillotine, then, there is much gnashing of teeth and useless cursings, but nothing serious or definite is done to smother those accursed English flies which come buzzing about our ears."

"Nay! you forget, Citizen Chauvelin," retorted Robespierre, "that we of the Committee of Public Safety are far more helpless than you. You know the language of these people, we don't. You know their manners and customs, their ways of thought, the methods they are likely to employ: we know none of these things. You have seen and spoken to men in England who are members of that damned League. You have seen the man who is its leader. We have not."

He leant forward on the table and looked more searchingly at the thin, pallid face before him.

"If you named that leader to me now, if you described him, we could go to work more easily. You could name him, and you would, Citizen Chauvelin."

"I cannot," retorted Chauvelin doggedly.

"Ah! but I think you could. But there! I do not blame your silence. You would wish to reap the reward of your own victory, to be the instrument of your own revenge. Passions! I think it natural! But in the name of your own safety, Citizen, do not be too greedy with your secret. If the man is known to you, find him again, find him, lure him to France! We want him—the people want him! And if the people do not get what they want, they will turn on those who have withheld their prey."

"I understand, Citizen, that your own safety and that of your government is involved in this renewed attempt to capture the Scarlet Pimpernel," retorted Chauvelin drily.

"And your head, Citizen Chauvelin," concluded Robespierre.

"Nay! I know that well enough, and you may believe me, and you will, Citizen, when I say that I care but little about that. The question is, if I am to lure that man to France what will you and your government do to help me?"

"Everything," replied Robespierre, "provided you have a definite plan and a definite purpose."

"I have both. But I must go to England in, at least, a semi-official capacity. I can do nothing if I am to hide in disguise in out-of-the-way corners."

"That is easily done. There has been some talk with the British authorities anent the security and welfare of peaceful French subjects settled in England. After a good deal of correspondence they have suggested our sending a semi-official representative over there to look after the interests of our own people commercially and financially. We can easily send you over in that capacity if it would suit your purpose."

"Admirably. I have only need of a cloak. That one will do as well as another."

"Is that all?"

"Not quite. I have several plans in my head, and I must know that I am fully trusted. Above all, I must have power—decisive, absolute, illimitable power."

There was nothing of the weakling about this small, sable-clad man, who looked the redoubtable Jacobin leader straight in the face and brought a firm fist resolutely down upon the table before him. Robespierre paused a while ere he replied; he was eying the other man keenly, trying to read if behind that earnest, frowning brow there did not lurk some selfish, ulterior motive along with that demand for absolute power.

But Chauvelin did not flinch beneath that gaze which could make every cheek in France blanch with unnamed terror, and after that slight moment of hesitation Robespierre said quietly:

"You shall have the complete power of a military dictator in every town or borough of France which you may visit. The Revolutionary Government shall create you, before you start for England, Supreme Head of all the Sub-Committees of Public Safety. This will mean that in the name of the safety of the Republic every order given by you, of whatsoever nature it might be, must be obeyed implicitly under pain of an arraignment for treason."

Chauvelin sighed a quick, sharp sigh of intense satisfaction, which he did not even attempt to disguise before Robespierre.

"I shall want agents," he said, "or shall we say spies? and, of course, money."

"You shall have both. We keep a very efficient secret service in England and they do a great deal of good over there. There is much dissatisfaction in their Midland counties—you remember the Birmingham riots? They were chiefly the work of our own spies. Then you know Candeille, the actress? She had found her way among some of those circles in London who have what they call liberal tendencies. I believe they are called Whigs. Funny name, isn't it? It means perruque, I think. Candeille has given charity performances in aid of our Paris poor, in one or two of these Whig clubs, and incidentally she has been very useful to us."

"A woman is always useful in such cases. I shall seek out the Citizeness Candeille."

"And if she renders you useful assistance, I think I can offer her what should prove a tempting prize. Women are so vain!" he added, contemplating with rapt attention the enamel-like polish on his finger-nails. "There is a vacancy in the Maison Moliere. Or—what might prove more attractive still—in connection with the proposed National fete, and the new religion for the people, we have not yet chosen a Goddess of Reason. That should appeal to any feminine mind. The impersonation of a goddess, with processions, pageants, and the rest... Great importance and prominence given to one personality.... What say you, Citizen? If you really have need of a woman for the furtherance of your plans, you have that at your disposal which may enhance her zeal."

"I thank you, Citizen," rejoined Chauvelin calmly. "I always entertained a hope that some day the Revolutionary Government would call again on my services. I admit that I failed last year. The Englishman is resourceful. He has wits and he is very rich. He would not have succeeded, I think, but for his money—and corruption and bribery are rife in Paris and on our coasts. He slipped through my fingers at the very moment when I thought that I held him most securely. I do admit all that, but I am prepared to redeem my failure of last year, and... there is nothing more to discuss.—I am ready to start."

He looked round for his cloak and hat, and quietly readjusted the set of his neck-tie. But Robespierre detained him a while longer: that born mountebank, born torturer of the souls of men, had not gloated sufficiently yet on the agony of mind of this fellow-man.

Chauvelin had always been trusted and respected. His services in connection with the foreign affairs of the Revolutionary Government had been invaluable, both before and since the beginning of the European War. At one time he formed part of that merciless decemvirate which—with Robespierre at its head—meant to govern France by laws of bloodshed and of unparalleled ferocity.

But the sea-green Incorruptible had since tired of him, then had endeavoured to push him on one side, for Chauvelin was keen and clever, and, moreover, he possessed all those qualities of selfless patriotism which were so conspicuously lacking in Robespierre.

His failure in bringing that interfering Scarlet Pimpernel to justice and the guillotine had completed Chauvelin's downfall. Though not otherwise molested, he had been left to moulder in obscurity during this past year. He would soon enough have been completely forgotten.

Now he was not only to be given one more chance to regain public favour, but he had demanded powers which in consideration of the aim in view, Robespierre himself could not refuse to grant him. But the Incorruptible, ever envious and jealous, would not allow him to exult too soon.

With characteristic blandness he seemed to be entering into all Chauvelin's schemes, to be helping in every way he could, for there was something at the back of his mind which he meant to say to the ex-ambassador, before the latter took his leave: something which would show him that he was but on trial once again, and which would demonstrate to him with perfect clearness that over him there hovered the all-powerful hand of a master.

"You have but to name the sum you want, Citizen Chauvelin," said the Incorruptible, with an encouraging smile, "the government will not stint you, and you shall not fail for lack of authority or for lack of funds."

"It is pleasant to hear that the government has such uncounted wealth," remarked Chauvelin with dry sarcasm.

"Oh! the last few weeks have been very profitable," retorted Robespierre; "we have confiscated money and jewels from emigrant royalists to the tune of several million francs. You remember the traitor Juliette Marny, who escape to England lately? Well! her mother's jewels and quite a good deal of gold were discovered by one of our most able spies to be under the care of a certain Abbe Foucquet, a calotin from Boulogne—devoted to the family, so it seems."

"Yes?" queried Chauvelin indifferently.

"Our men seized the jewels and gold, that is all. We don't know yet what we mean to do with the priest. The fisherfolk of Boulogne like him, and we can lay our hands on him at any time, if we want his old head for the guillotine. But the jewels were worth having. There's a historic necklace worth half a million at least."

"Could I have it?" asked Chauvelin.

Robespierre laughed and shrugged his shoulders.

"You said it belonged to the Marny family," continued the ex-ambassador. "Juliette Marny is in England. I might meet her. I cannot tell what may happen: but I feel that the historic necklace might prove useful. Just as you please," he added with renewed indifference. "It was a thought that flashed through my mind when you spoke—nothing more."

"And to show you how thoroughly the government trusts you, Citizen Chauvelin," replied Robespierre with perfect urbanity, "I will myself direct that the Marny necklace be placed unreservedly in your hands; and a sum of fifty thousand francs for your expenses in England. You see," he added blandly, "we give you no excuse for a second failure."

"I need none," retorted Chauvelin drily, as he finally rose from his seat, with a sigh of satisfaction that this interview was ended at last.

But Robespierre too had risen, and pushing his chair aside he took a step or two towards Chauvelin. He was a much taller man than the ex-ambassador. Spare and gaunt, he had a very upright bearing, and in the uncertain light of the candle he seemed to tower strangely and weirdly above the other man: the pale hue of his coat, his light-coloured hair, the whiteness of his linen, all helped to give to his appearance at that moment a curious spectral effect.

Chauvelin somehow felt an unpleasant shiver running down his spine as Robespierre, perfectly urbane and gentle in his manner, placed a long, bony hand upon his shoulder.

"Citizen Chauvelin," said the Incorruptible, with some degree of dignified solemnity, "meseems that we very quickly understood one another this evening. Your own conscience, no doubt, gave you a premonition of what the purport of my summons to you would be. You say that you always hoped the Revolutionary Government would give you one great chance to redeem your failure of last year. I, for one, always intended that you should have that chance, for I saw, perhaps, just a little deeper into your heart than my colleagues. I saw not only enthusiasm for the cause of the People of France, not only abhorrence for the enemy of your country, I saw a purely personal and deadly hate of an individual man—the unknown and mysterious Englishman who proved too clever for you last year. And because I believe that hatred will prove sharper and more far-seeing than selfless patriotism, therefore I urged the Committee of Public Safety to allow you to work out your own revenge, and thereby to serve your country more effectually than any other—perhaps more pure-minded patriot would do. You go to England well-provided with all that is necessary for the success of your plans, for the accomplishment of your own personal vengeance. The Revolutionary Government will help you with money, passports, safe conducts; it places its spies and agents at your disposal. It gives you practically unlimited power, wherever you may go. It will not enquire into your motives, nor yet your means, so long as these lead to success. But private vengeance or patriotism, whatever may actuate you, we here in France demand you deliver into our hands the man who is known in two countries as the Scarlet Pimpernel! We want him alive if possible, or dead if it must be so, and we want as many of his henchmen as will follow him to the guillotine. Get them to France, and we'll know how to deal with them, and let the whole of Europe be damned."

He paused for a while, his hand still resting on Chauvelin's shoulder, his pale green eyes holding those of the other man as if in a trance. But Chauvelin neither stirred nor spoke. His triumph left him quite calm; his fertile brain was already busy with his plans. There was no room for fear in his heart, and it was without the slightest tremor that he waited for the conclusion of Robespierre's oration.

"Perhaps, Citizen Chauvelin," said the latter at last, "you have already guessed what there is left for me to say. But lest there should remain in your mind one faint glimmer of doubt or of hope, let me tell you this. The Revolutionary Government gives you this chance of redeeming your failure, but this one only; if you fail again, your outraged country will know neither pardon nor mercy. Whether you return to France or remain in England, whether you travel North, South, East or West, cross the Oceans, or traverse the Alps, the hand of an avenging People will be upon you. Your second failure will be punished by death, wherever you may be, either by the guillotine, if you are in France, or if you seek refuge elsewhere, then by the hand of an assassin.

"Look to it, Citizen Chauvelin! for there will be no escape this time, not even if the mightiest tyrant on earth tried to protect you, not even if you succeeded in building up an empire and placing yourself upon a throne."

His thin, strident voice echoed weirdly in the small, close boudoir. Chauvelin made no reply. There was nothing that he could say. All that Robespierre had put so emphatically before him, he had fully realised, even whilst he was forming his most daring plans.

It was an "either—or" this time, uttered to HIM now. He thought again of Marguerite Blakeney, and the terrible alternative he had put before HER less than a year ago.

Well! he was prepared to take the risk. He would not fail again. He was going to

England under more favourable conditions this time. He knew who the man was, whom he was bidden to lure to France and to death.

And he returned Robespierre's threatening gaze boldly and unflinchingly; then he prepared to go. He took up his hat and cloak, opened the door and peered for a moment into the dark corridor, wherein, in the far distance, the steps of a solitary sentinel could be faintly heard: he put on his hat, turned to look once more into the room where Robespierre stood quietly watching him, and went his way.

CHAPTER IV. THE RICHMOND GALA

It was perhaps the most brilliant September ever known in England, where the last days of dying summer are nearly always golden and beautiful.

Strange that in this country, where that same season is so peculiarly radiant with a glory all its own, there should be no special expression in the language with which to accurately name it.

So we needs must call it "fin d'ete": the ending of the summer; not the absolute end, nor yet the ultimate departure, but the tender lingering of a friend obliged to leave us anon, yet who fain would steal a day here and there, a week or so in which to stay with us: who would make that last pathetic farewell of his endure a little while longer still, and brings forth in gorgeous array for our final gaze all that he has which is most luxuriant, most desirable, most worthy of regret.

And in this year of grace 1793, departing summer had lavished the treasures of her palette upon woodland and river banks; had tinged the once crude green of larch and elm with a tender hue of gold, had brushed the oaks with tones of warm russet, and put patches of sienna and crimson on the beech.

In the gardens the roses were still in bloom, not the delicate blush or lemon ones of June, nor yet the pale Banksias and climbers, but the full-blooded red roses of late summer, and deep-coloured apricot ones, with crinkled outside leaves faintly kissed by the frosty dew. In sheltered spots the purple clematis still lingered, whilst the dahlias, brilliant of hue, seemed overbearing in their gorgeous insolence, flaunting their crudely colored petals against sober backgrounds of mellow leaves, or the dull, mossy tones of ancient, encircling walls.

The Gala had always been held about the end of September. The weather, on the riverside, was most dependable then, and there was always sufficient sunshine as an excuse for bringing out Madam's last new muslin gown, or her pale-coloured quilted petticoat. Then the ground was dry and hard, good alike for walking and for setting up tents and booths. And of these there was of a truth a most goodly array this year: mountebanks and jugglers from every corner of the world, so it seemed, for there was a man with a face as black as my lord's tricorne, and another with such flat yellow cheeks as made one think of batter pudding, and spring aconite, of eggs and other very yellow things.

There was a tent wherein dogs—all sorts of dogs, big, little, black, white or tan—did things which no Christian with respect for his own backbone would have dared to perform, and another where a weird-faced old man made bean-stalks and walking sticks, coins of the realm and lace kerchiefs vanish into thin air.

And as it was nice and hot one could sit out upon the green and listen to the strains of the band, which discoursed sweet music, and watch the young people tread a measure on the sward.

The quality had not yet arrived: for humbler folk had partaken of very early dinner so as to get plenty of fun, and long hours of delight for the sixpenny toll demanded at the gates.

There was so much to see and so much to do: games of bowls on the green, and a beautiful Aunt Sally, there was a skittle alley, and two merry-go-rounds: there were performing monkeys and dancing bears, a woman so fat that three men with arms outstretched could not get round her, and a man so thin that he could put a lady's bracelet round his neck and her garter around his waist.

There were some funny little dwarfs with pinched faces and a knowing manner, and a giant come all the way from Russia—so 'twas said.

The mechanical toys too were a great attraction. You dropped a penny into a little slit in a box and a doll would begin to dance and play the fiddle: and there was the Magic Mill, where for another modest copper a row of tiny figures, wrinkled and old and dressed in the shabbiest of rags, marched in weary procession up a flight of steps into the Mill, only to emerge again the next moment at a further door of this wonderful building looking young and gay, dressed in gorgeous finery and tripping a dance measure as they descended some steps and were finally lost to view.

But what was most wonderful of all and collected the goodliest crowd of gazers and the largest amount of coins, was a miniature representation of what was going on in France even at this very moment.

And you could not help but be convinced of the truth of it all, so cleverly was it done. There was a background of houses and a very red-looking sky. "Too red!" some people said, but were immediately quashed by the dictum of the wise, that the sky represented a sunset, as anyone who looked could see. Then there were a number of little figures, no taller than your hand, but with little wooden faces and arms and legs, just beautifully made little dolls, and these were dressed in kirtles and breeches—all rags mostly—and little coats and wooden shoes. They were massed together in groups with their arms all turned upwards.

And in the center of this little stage on an elevated platform there were miniature wooden posts close together, and with a long flat board at right angles at the foot of the posts, and all painted a bright red. At the further end of the boards was a miniature basket, and between the two posts, at the top, was a miniature knife which ran up and down in a groove and was drawn by a miniature pulley. Folk who knew said that this was a model of a guillotine.

And lo and behold! when you dropped a penny into a slot just below the wooden stage, the crowd of little figures started waving their arms up and down, and another little doll would ascend the elevated platform and lie down on the red board at the foot of the wooden posts. Then a figure dressed in brilliant scarlet put out an arm presumably to touch the pulley, and the tiny knife would rattle down on to the poor little reclining doll's neck, and its head would roll off into the basket beyond.

Then there was a loud whirr of wheels, a buzz of internal mechanism, and all the little figures would stop dead with arms outstretched, whilst the beheaded doll rolled off the board and was lost to view, no doubt preparatory to going through the same gruesome pantomime again.

It was very thrilling, and very terrible: a certain air of hushed awe reigned in the booth where this mechanical wonder was displayed.

The booth itself stood in a secluded portion of the grounds, far from the toll gates, and the band stand and the noise of the merry-go-round, and there were great texts, written in red letters on a black ground, pinned all along the walls.

"Please spare a copper for the starving poor of Paris."

A lady, dressed in grey quilted petticoat and pretty grey and black striped paniers, could be seen walking in the booth from time to time, then disappearing through a partition beyond. She would emerge again presently carrying an embroidered reticule, and would wander round among the crowd, holding out the bag by its chain, and repeating in tones of somewhat monotonous appeal: "For the starving poor of Paris, if you please!"

She had fine, dark eyes, rather narrow and tending upwards at the outer corners, which gave her face a not altogether pleasant expression. Still, they were fine eyes, and when she went round soliciting alms, most of the men put a hand into their breeches pocket and dropped a coin into her embroidered reticule.

She said the word "poor" in rather a funny way, rolling the "r" at the end, and she also said "please" as if it were spelt with a long line of "e's," and so it was concluded that she was French and was begging for her poorer sisters. At stated intervals during the day, the mechanical toy was rolled into a corner, and the lady in grey stood up on a platform and sang queer little songs, the words of which nobody could understand.

"Il etait une bergere et ron et ron, petit patapon...."

But it all left an impression of sadness and of suppressed awe upon the minds and susceptibilities of the worthy Richmond yokels come with their wives or sweethearts to enjoy the fun of the fair, and gladly did everyone emerge out of that melancholy booth into the sunshine, the brightness and the noise.

"Lud! but she do give me the creeps," said Mistress Polly, the pretty barmaid from the Bell Inn, down by the river. "And I must say that I don't see why we English folk should send our hard-earned pennies to those murdering ruffians over the water. Bein' starving so to speak, don't make a murderer a better man if he goes on murdering," she added with undisputable if ungrammatical logic. "Come, let's look at something more cheerful now."

And without waiting for anyone else's assent, she turned towards the more lively portion of the grounds, closely followed by a ruddy-faced, somewhat sheepish-looking youth, who very obviously was her attendant swain.

It was getting on for three o-clock now, and the quality were beginning to arrive. Lord Anthony Dewhurst was already there, chucking every pretty girl under the chin, to the annoyance of her beau. Ladies were arriving all the time, and the humbler feminine hearts were constantly set a-flutter at sight of rich brocaded gowns, and the new Charlottes, all crinkled velvet and soft marabout, which were so becoming to the pretty faces beneath.

There was incessant and loud talking and chattering, with here and there the shriller tones of a French voice being distinctly noticeable in the din. There were a good many French ladies and gentlemen present, easily recognisable, even in the distance, for their clothes were of more sober hue and of lesser richness than those of their English compeers.

But they were great lords and ladies, nevertheless, Dukes and Duchesses and Countesses, come to England for fear of being murdered by those devils in their own country. Richmond was full of them just now, as they were made right welcome both at the Palace and at the magnificent home of Sir Percy and Lady Blakeney.

Ah! here comes Sir Andrew Ffoulkes with his lady! so pretty and dainty does she look, like a little china doll, in her new-fashioned short-waisted gown: her brown hair in soft waves above her smooth forehead, her great, hazel eyes fixed in unaffected admiration on the gallant husband by her side.

"No wonder she dotes on him!" sighed pretty Mistress Polly after she had bobbed her curtsy to my lady. "The brave deeds he did for love of her! Rescued her from those murderers over in France and brought her to England safe and sound, having fought no end of them single-handed, so I've heard it said. Have you not, Master Thomas Jezzard?"

And she looked defiantly at her meek-looking cavalier.

"Bah!" replied Master Thomas with quite unusual vehemence in response to the disparaging look in her brown eyes, "'Tis not he who did it all, as you well know, Mistress Polly. Sir Andrew Ffoulkes is a gallant gentleman, you may take your Bible oath on that, but he that fights the murdering frogeaters single-handed is he whom they call The Scarlet Pimpernel: the bravest gentleman in all the world."

Then, as at mention of the national hero, he thought that he detected in Mistress Polly's eyes an enthusiasm which he could not very well ascribe to his own individuality, he added with some pique:

"But they do say that this same Scarlet Pimpernel is mightily ill-favoured, and that's why no one ever sees him. They say he is fit to scare the crows away and that no Frenchy can look twice at his face, for it's so ugly, and so they let him get out of the country, rather than look at him again."

"Then they do say a mighty lot of nonsense," retorted Mistress Polly, with a shrug of her pretty shoulders, "and if that be so, then why don't you go over to France and join hands with the Scarlet Pimpernel? I'll warrant no Frenchman'll want to look twice at your face."

A chorus of laughter greeted this sally, for the two young people had in the meanwhile been joined by several of their friends, and now formed part of a merry group near the band, some sitting, others standing, but all bent on seeing as much as there was to see in Richmond Gala this day. There was Johnny Cullen, the grocer's apprentice from Twickenham, and Ursula Quekett, the baker's daughter, and several "young 'uns" from the neighbourhood, as well as some older folk.

And all of them enjoyed a joke when they heard one and thought Mistress Polly's retort mightily smart. But then Mistress Polly was possessed of two hundred pounds, all her own, left to her by her grandmother, and on the strength of this extensive fortune had acquired a reputation for beauty and wit not easily accorded to a wench that had been penniless.

But Mistress Polly was also very kind-hearted. She loved to tease Master Jezzard, who was an indefatigable hanger-on at her pretty skirts, and whose easy conquest had rendered her somewhat contemptuous, but at the look of perplexed annoyance and bewildered distress in the lad's face, her better nature soon got the upper hand. She realized that her remark had been unwarrantably spiteful, and wishing to make atonement, she said with a touch of coquetry which quickly spread balm over the honest yokel's injured vanity:

"La! Master Jezzard, you do seem to make a body say some queer things. But there! you must own 'tis mighty funny about that Scarlet Pimpernel!" she added, appealing to the company in general, just as if Master Jezzard had been disputing the fact. "Why won't he let anyone see who he is? And those who know him won't tell. Now I have it for a fact from my lady's own maid Lucy, that the young lady as is stopping at Lady Blakeney's house has actually spoken to the man. She came over from France, come a fortnight to-morrow; she and the gentleman they call Mossoo Deroulede. They both saw the Scarlet Pimpernel and spoke to him. He brought them over from France. Then why won't they say?"

"Say what?" commented Johnny Cullen, the apprentice.

"Who this mysterious Scarlet Pimpernel is."

"Perhaps he isn't," said old Clutterbuck, who was clerk of the vestry at the church of St. John's the Evangelist.

"Yes!" he added sententiously, for he was fond of his own sayings and usually liked to repeat them before he had quite done with them, "that's it, you may be sure. Perhaps he isn't."

"What do you mean, Master Clutterbuck?" asked Ursula Quekett, for she knew the old man liked to explain his wise saws, and as she wanted to marry his son, she indulged him whenever she could. "What do you mean? He isn't what?"

"He isn't. That's all," explained Clutterbuck with vague solemnity.

Then seeing that he had gained the attention of the little party round him, he condescended to come to more logical phraseology.

"I mean, that perhaps we must not ask, 'who IS this mysterious Scarlet Pimpernel?' but 'who WAS that poor and unfortunate gentleman?'"

"Then you think..." suggested Mistress Polly, who felt unaccountably low-spirited at this oratorical pronouncement.

"I have it for a fact," said Mr. Clutterbuck solemnly, "that he whom they call the Scarlet Pimpernel no longer exists now: that he was collared by the Frenchies, as far back as last fall, and in the language of the poets, has never been heard of no more."

Mr. Clutterbuck was very fond of quoting from the works of certain writers whose names he never mentioned, but who went by the poetical generality of "the poets." Whenever he made use of phrases which he was supposed to derive from these great and unnamed authors, he solemnly and mechanically raised his hat, as a tribute of respect to these giant minds.

"You think that The Scarlet Pimpernel is dead, Mr. Clutterbuck? That those horrible Frenchies murdered him? Surely you don't mean that?" sighed Mistress Polly ruefully.

Mr. Clutterbuck put his hand up to his hat, preparatory no doubt to making another appeal to the mysterious poets, but was interrupted in the very act of uttering great thoughts by a loud and prolonged laugh which came echoing from a distant corner of the grounds.

"Lud! but I'd know that laugh anywhere," said Mistress Quekett, whilst all eyes were turned in the direction whence the merry noise had come.

Half a head taller than any of his friends around him, his lazy blue eyes scanning from beneath their drooping lids the motley throng around him, stood Sir Percy

Blakeney, the centre of a gaily-dressed little group which seemingly had just crossed the toll-gate.

"A fine specimen of a man, for sure," remarked Johnnie Cullen, the apprentice.

"Aye! you may take your Bible oath on that!" sighed Mistress Polly, who was inclined to be sentimental.

"Speakin' as the poets," pronounced Mr. Clutterbuck sententiously, "inches don't make a man."

"Nor fine clothes neither," added Master Jezzard, who did not approve of Mistress Polly's sentimental sigh.

"There's my lady!" gasped Miss Barbara suddenly, clutching Master Clutterbuck's arm vigorously. "Lud! but she is beautiful to-day!"

Beautiful indeed, and radiant with youth and happiness, Marguerite Blakeney had just gone through the gates and was walking along the sward towards the band stand. She was dressed in clinging robes of shimmery green texture, the new-fashioned high-waisted effect suiting her graceful figure to perfection. The large Charlotte, made of velvet to match the gown, cast a deep shadow over the upper part of her face, and gave a peculiar softness to the outline of her forehead and cheeks.

Long lace mittens covered her arms and hands and a scarf of diaphanous material edged with dull gold hung loosely around her shoulders.

Yes! she was beautiful! No captious chronicler has ever denied that! and no one who knew her before, and who saw her again on this late summer's afternoon, could fail to mark the additional charm of her magnetic personality. There was a tenderness in her face as she turned her head to and fro, a joy of living in her eyes that was quite irresistibly fascinating.

Just now she was talking animatedly with the young girl who was walking beside her, and laughing merrily the while:

"Nay! we'll find your Paul, never fear! Lud! child, have you forgotten he is in England now, and that there's no fear of his being kidnapped here on the green in broad daylight."

The young girl gave a slight shudder and her child-like face became a shade paler than before. Marguerite took her hand and gave it a kindly pressure. Juliette Marny, but lately come to England, saved from under the very knife of the guillotine, by a timely and daring rescue, could scarcely believe as yet that she and the man she loved were really out of danger.

"There is Monsieur Deroulede," said Marguerite after a slight pause, giving the young girl time to recover herself and pointing to a group of men close by. "He is among friends, as you see."

They made such a pretty picture, these two women, as they stood together for a moment on the green with the brilliant September sun throwing golden reflections and luminous shadows on their slender forms. Marguerite, tall and queen-like in her rich gown, and costly jewels, wearing with glorious pride the invisible crown of happy wifehood: Juliette, slim and girlish, dressed all in white, with a soft, straw hat on her fair curls, and bearing on an otherwise young and child-like face, the hard imprint of the terrible sufferings she had undergone, of the deathly moral battle her tender soul had had to fight.

Soon a group of friends joined them. Paul Deroulede among these, also Sir Andrew and Lady Ffoulkes, and strolling slowly towards them, his hands buried in the pockets of his fine cloth breeches, his broad shoulders set to advantage in a coat of immaculate cut, priceless lace ruffles at neck and wrist, came the inimitable Sir Percy.

CHAPTER V. SIR PERCY AND HIS LADY

To all appearances he had not changed since those early days of matrimony, when his young wife dazzled London society by her wit and by her beauty, and he was one of the many satellites that helped to bring into bold relief the brilliance of her presence, of her sallies and of her smiles.

His friends alone, mayhap—and of these only an intimate few—had understood that beneath that self-same lazy manner, those shy and awkward ways, that half-inane, half-cynical laugh, there now lurked an undercurrent of tender and passionate happiness.

That Lady Blakeney was in love with her own husband, nobody could fail to see, and in the more frivolous cliques of fashionable London this extraordinary phenomenon had oft been eagerly discussed.

"A monstrous thing, of a truth, for a woman of fashion to adore her own husband!" was the universal pronouncement of the gaily-decked little world that centred around Carlton House and Ranelagh.

Not that Sir Percy Blakeney was unpopular with the fair sex. Far be it from the veracious chronicler's mind even to suggest such a thing. The ladies would have voted any gathering dull if Sir Percy's witty sallies did not ring from end to end of the dancing hall, if his new satin coat and 'broidered waistcoat did not call for comment or admiration.

But that was the frivolous set, to which Lady Blakeney had never belonged.

It was well known that she had always viewed her good-natured husband as the most willing and most natural butt for her caustic wit; she still was fond of aiming a shaft or two at him, and he was still equally ready to let the shaft glance harmlessly against the flawless shield of his own imperturbable good humour, but now, contrary to all precedent, to all usages and customs of London society, Marguerite seldom was seen at routs or at the opera without her husband; she accompanied him to all the races, and even one night—oh horror!—had danced the gavotte with him.

Society shuddered and wondered! tried to put Lady Blakeney's sudden infatuation down to foreign eccentricity, and finally consoled itself with the thought that after all this nonsense could not last, and that she was too clever a woman and he too perfect a gentleman to keep up this abnormal state of things for any length of time.

In the meanwhile, the ladies averred that this matrimonial love was a very one-sided affair. No one could assert that Sir Percy was anything but politely indifferent to his wife's obvious attentions. His lazy eyes never once lighted up when she entered a ball-room, and there were those who knew for a fact that her ladyship spent many lonely days in her beautiful home at Richmond whilst her lord and master absented himself with persistent if unchivalrous regularity.

His presence at the Gala had been a surprise to everyone, for all thought him still away, fishing in Scotland or shooting in Yorkshire, anywhere save close to the apron strings of his doting wife. He himself seemed conscious of the fact that he had not been expected at this end-of-summer fete, for as he strolled forward to meet his wife and

Juliette Marny, and acknowledge with a bow here and a nod there the many greetings from subordinates and friends, there was quite an apologetic air about his good-looking face, and an obvious shyness in his smile.

But Marguerite gave a happy little laugh when she saw him coming towards her.

"Oh, Sir Percy!" she said gaily, "and pray have you seen the show? I vow 'tis the maddest, merriest throng I've seen for many a day. Nay! but for the sighs and shudders of my poor little Juliette, I should be enjoying one of the liveliest days of my life."

She patted Juliette's arm affectionately.

"Do not shame me before Sir Percy," murmured the young girl, casting shy glances at the elegant cavalier before her, vainly trying to find in the indolent, foppish personality of this society butterfly, some trace of the daring man of action, the bold adventurer who had snatched her and her lover from out the very tumbril that bore them both to death.

"I know I ought to be gay," she continued with an attempt at a smile, "I ought to forget everything, save what I owe to..."

Sir Percy's laugh broke in on her half-finished sentence.

"Lud! and to think of all that I ought not to forget!" he said loudly. "Tony here has been clamouring for iced punch this last half-hour, and I promised to find a booth wherein the noble liquid is properly dispensed. Within half an hour from now His Royal Highness will be here. I assure you, Mlle. Juliette, that from that time onwards I have to endure the qualms of the damned, for the heir to Great Britain's throne always contrives to be thirsty when I am satiated, which is Tantalus' torture magnified a thousandfold, or to be satiated when my parched palate most requires solace; in either case I am a most pitiable man."

"In either case you contrive to talk a deal of nonsense, Sir Percy," said Marguerite gaily.

"What else would your ladyship have me do this lazy, hot afternoon?"

"Come and view the booths with me," she said. "I am dying for a sight of the fat woman and the lean man, the pig-faced child, the dwarfs and the giants. There! Monsieur Deroulede," she added, turning to the young Frenchman who was standing close beside her, "take Mlle. Juliette to hear the clavecin players. I vow she is tired of my company."

The gaily-dressed group was breaking up. Juliette and Paul Deroulede were only too ready to stroll off arm-in-arm together, and Sir Andrew Ffoulkes was ever in attendance on his young wife.

For one moment Marguerite caught her husband's eye. No one was within earshot.

"Percy," she said.

"Yes, m'dear."

"When did you return?"

"Early this morning."

"You crossed over from Calais?"

"From Boulogne."

"Why did you not let me know sooner?"

"I could not, dear. I arrived at my lodgings in town, looking a disgusting object.... I could not appear before you until I had washed some of the French mud from off my person. Then His Royal Highness demanded my presence. He wanted news of the Duchesse de Verneuil, whom I had the honour of escorting over from France. By the time

I had told him all that he wished to hear, there was no chance of finding you at home, and I thought I should see you here."

Marguerite said nothing for a moment, but her foot impatiently tapped the ground, and her fingers were fidgeting with the gold fringe of her scarf. The look of joy, of exquisite happiness, seemed to have suddenly vanished from her face; there was a deep furrow between her brows.

She sighed a short, sharp sigh, and cast a rapid upward glance at her husband.

He was looking down at her, smiling good-naturedly, a trifle sarcastically perhaps, and the frown on her face deepened.

"Percy," she said abruptly.

"Yes, m'dear."

"These anxieties are terrible to bear. You have been twice over to France within the last month, dealing with your life as lightly as if it did not now belong to me. When will you give up these mad adventures, and leave others to fight their own battles and to save their own lives as best they may?"

She had spoken with increased vehemence, although her voice was scarce raised above a whisper. Even in her sudden, passionate anger she was on her guard not to betray his secret. He did not reply immediately, but seemed to be studying the beautiful face on which heartbroken anxiety was now distinctly imprinted.

Then he turned and looked at the solitary booth in the distance, across the frontal of which a large placard had been recently affixed, bearing the words: "Come and see the true representation of the guillotine!"

In front of the booth a man dressed in ragged breeches, with Phrygian cap on his head, adorned with a tri-colour cockade, was vigorously beating a drum, shouting volubly the while:

"Come in and see, come in and see! the only realistic presentation of the original guillotine. Hundreds perish in Paris every day! Come and see! Come and see! the perfectly vivid performance of what goes on hourly in Paris at the present moment."

Marguerite had followed the direction of Sir Percy's eyes. She too was looking at the booth, she heard the man's monotonous, raucous cries. She gave a slight shudder and once more looked imploringly at her husband. His face—though outwardly as lazy and calm as before—had a strange set look about the mouth and firm jaw, and his slender hand, the hand of a dandy accustomed to handle cards and dice and to play lightly with the foils, was clutched tightly beneath the folds of the priceless Mechlin frills.

It was but a momentary stiffening of the whole powerful frame, an instant's flash of the ruling passion hidden within that very secretive soul. Then he once more turned towards her, the rigid lines of his face relaxed, he broke into a pleasant laugh, and with the most elaborate and most courtly bow he took her hand in his and raising her fingers to his lips, he gave the answer to her questions:

"When your ladyship has ceased to be the most admired woman in Europe, namely, when I am in my grave."

CHAPTER VI. FOR THE POOR OF PARIS

There was no time to say more then. For the laughing, chatting groups of friends had once more closed up round Marguerite and her husband, and she, ever on the alert, gave neither look nor sign that any serious conversation had taken place between Sir Percy and herself.

Whatever she might feel or dread with regard to the foolhardy adventures in which he still persistently embarked, no member of the League ever guarded the secret of his chief more loyally than did Marguerite Blakeney.

Though her heart overflowed with a passionate pride in her husband, she was clever enough to conceal every emotion save that which Nature had insisted on imprinting in her face, her present radiant happiness and her irresistible love. And thus before the world she kept up that bantering way with him, which had characterized her earlier matrimonial life, that good-natured, easy contempt which he had so readily accepted in those days, and which their entourage would have missed and would have enquired after, if she had changed her manner towards him too suddenly.

In her heart she knew full well that within Percy Blakeney's soul she had a great and powerful rival: his wild, mad, passionate love of adventure. For it he would sacrifice everything, even his life; she dared not ask herself if he would sacrifice his love.

Twice in a few weeks he had been over to France: every time he went she could not know if she would ever see him again. She could not imagine how the French Committee of Public Safety could so clumsily allow the hated Scarlet Pimpernel to slip through its fingers. But she never attempted either to warn him or to beg him not to go. When he brought Paul Deroulede and Juliette Marny over from France, her heart went out to the two young people in sheer gladness and pride because of his precious life, which he had risked for them.

She loved Juliette for the dangers Percy had passed, for the anxieties she herself had endured; only to-day, in the midst of this beautiful sunshine, this joy of the earth, of summer and of the sky, she had suddenly felt a mad, overpowering anxiety, a deadly hatred of the wild adventurous life, which took him so often away from her side. His pleasant, bantering reply precluded her following up the subject, whilst the merry chatter of people round her warned her to keep her words and looks under control.

But she seemed now to feel the want of being alone, and, somehow, that distant booth with its flaring placard, and the crier in the Phrygian cap, exercised a weird fascination over her.

Instinctively she bent her steps thither, and equally instinctively the idle throng of her friends followed her. Sir Percy alone had halted in order to converse with Lord Hastings, who had just arrived.

"Surely, Lady Blakeney, you have no thought of patronising that gruesome spectacle?" said Lord Anthony Dewhurst, as Marguerite almost mechanically had paused within a few yards of the solitary booth.

"I don't know," she said, with enforced gaiety, "the place seems to attract me. And I need not look at the spectacle," she added significantly, as she pointed to a roughly-scribbled notice at the entrance of the tent: "In aid of the starving poor of Paris."

"There's a good-looking woman who sings, and a hideous mechanical toy that moves," said one of the young men in the crowd. "It is very dark and close inside the tent. I was lured in there for my sins, and was in a mighty hurry to come out again."

"Then it must be my sins that are helping to lure me too at the present moment," said Marguerite lightly. "I pray you all to let me go in there. I want to hear the good-looking woman sing, even if I do not see the hideous toy on the move."

"May I escort you then, Lady Blakeney?" said Lord Tony.

"Nay! I would rather go in alone," she replied a trifle impatiently. "I beg of you not to heed my whim, and to await my return, there, where the music is at its merriest."

It had been bad manners to insist. Marguerite, with a little comprehensive nod to all her friends, left the young cavaliers still protesting and quickly passed beneath the roughly constructed doorway that gave access into the booth.

A man, dressed in theatrical rags and wearing the characteristic scarlet cap, stood immediately within the entrance, and ostentatiously rattled a money box at regular intervals.

"For the starving poor of Paris," he drawled out in nasal monotonous tones the moment he caught sight of Marguerite and of her rich gown. She dropped some gold into the box and then passed on.

The interior of the booth was dark and lonely-looking after the glare of the hot September sun and the noisy crowd that thronged the sward outside. Evidently a performance had just taken place on the elevated platform beyond, for a few yokels seemed to be lingering in a desultory manner as if preparatory to going out.

A few disjointed comments reached Marguerite's ears as she approached, and the small groups parted to allow her to pass. One or two women gaped in astonishment at her beautiful dress, whilst others bobbed a respectful curtsey.

The mechanical toy arrested her attention immediately. She did not find it as gruesome as she expected, only singularly grotesque, with all those wooden little figures in their quaint, arrested action.

She drew nearer to have a better look, and the yokels who had lingered behind, paused, wondering if she would make any remark.

"Her ladyship was born in France," murmured one of the men, close to her, "she would know if the thing really looks like that."

"She do seem interested," quoth another in a whisper.

"Lud love us all!" said a buxom wench, who was clinging to the arm of a nervous-looking youth, "I believe they're coming for more money."

On the elevated platform at the further end of the tent, a slim figure had just made its appearance, that of a young woman dressed in peculiarly sombre colours, and with a black lace hood thrown lightly over her head.

Marguerite thought that the face seemed familiar to her, and she also noticed that the woman carried a large embroidered reticule in her bemittened hand.

There was a general exodus the moment she appeared. The Richmond yokels did not like the look of that reticule. They felt that sufficient demand had already been made upon their scant purses, considering the meagerness of the entertainment, and they dreaded being lured to further extravagance.

When Marguerite turned away from the mechanical toy, the last of the little crowd had disappeared, and she was alone in the booth with the woman in the dark kirtle and black lace hood.

"For the poor of Paris, Madame," said the latter mechanically, holding out her reticule.

Marguerite was looking at her intently. The face certainly seemed familiar, recalling to her mind the far-off days in Paris, before she married. Some young actress no doubt driven out of France by that terrible turmoil which had caused so much sorrow and so much suffering. The face was pretty, the figure slim and elegant, and the look of obvious sadness in the dark, almond-shaped eyes was calculated to inspire sympathy and pity.

Yet, strangely enough, Lady Blakeney felt repelled and chilled by this sombrely-dressed young person: an instinct, which she could not have explained and which she felt had no justification, warned her that somehow or other, the sadness was not quite genuine, the appeal for the poor not quite heartfelt.

Nevertheless, she took out her purse, and dropping some few sovereigns into the capacious reticule, she said very kindly:

"I hope that you are satisfied with your day's work, Madame; I fear me our British country folk hold the strings of their purses somewhat tightly these times."

The woman sighed and shrugged her shoulders.

"Oh, Madame!" she said with a tone of great dejection, "one does what one can for one's starving countrymen, but it is very hard to elicit sympathy over here for them, poor dears!"

"You are a Frenchwoman, of course," rejoined Marguerite, who had noted that though the woman spoke English with a very pronounced foreign accent, she had nevertheless expressed herself with wonderful fluency and correctness.

"Just like Lady Blakeney herself," replied the other.

"You know who I am?"

"Who could come to Richmond and not know Lady Blakeney by sight."

"But what made you come to Richmond on this philanthropic errand of yours?"

"I go where I think there is a chance of earning a little money for the cause which I have at heart," replied the Frenchwoman with the same gentle simplicity, the same tone of mournful dejection.

What she said was undoubtedly noble and selfless. Lady Blakeney felt in her heart that her keenest sympathy should have gone out to this young woman—pretty, dainty, hardly more than a girl—who seemed to be devoting her young life in a purely philanthropic and unselfish cause. And yet in spite of herself, Marguerite seemed unable to shake off that curious sense of mistrust which had assailed her from the first, nor that feeling of unreality and staginess with which the Frenchwoman's attitude had originally struck her.

Yet she tried to be kind and to be cordial, tried to hide that coldness in her manner which she felt was unjustified.

"It is all very praiseworthy on your part, Madame," she said somewhat lamely. "Madame...?" she added interrogatively.

"My name is Candeille—Desiree Candeille," replied the Frenchwoman.

"Candeille?" exclaimed Marguerite with sudden alacrity, "Candeille... surely..."

"Yes... of the Varietes."

"Ah! then I know why your face from the first seemed familiar to me," said Marguerite, this time with unaffected cordiality. "I must have applauded you many a time in the olden days. I am an ex-colleague, you know. My name was St. Just before I married, and I was of the Maison Moliere."

"I knew that," said Desiree Candeille, "and half hoped that you would remember me."

"Nay! who could forget Demoiselle Candeille, the most popular star in the theatrical firmament?"

"Oh! that was so long ago."

"Only four years."

"A fallen star is soon lost out of sight."

"Why fallen?"

"It was a choice for me between exile from France and the guillotine," rejoined Candeille simply.

"Surely not?" queried Marguerite with a touch of genuine sympathy. With characteristic impulsiveness, she had now cast aside her former misgivings: she had conquered her mistrust, at any rate had relegated it to the background of her mind. This woman was a colleague: she had suffered and was in distress; she had every claim, therefore, on a compatriot's help and friendship. She stretched out her hand and took Desiree Candeille's in her own; she forced herself to feel nothing but admiration for this young woman, whose whole attitude spoke of sorrows nobly borne, of misfortunes proudly endured.

"I don't know why I should sadden you with my story," rejoined Desiree Candeille after a slight pause, during which she seemed to be waging war against her own emotion. "It is not a very interesting one. Hundreds have suffered as I did. I had enemies in Paris. God knows how that happened. I had never harmed anyone, but someone must have hated me and must have wished me ill. Evil is so easily wrought in France these days. A denunciation—a perquisition—an accusation—then the flight from Paris... the forged passports... the disguise... the bribe... the hardships... the squalid hiding places.... Oh! I have gone through it all... tasted every kind of humiliation... endured every kind of insult.... Remember! that I was not a noble aristocrat... a Duchess or an impoverished Countess..." she added with marked bitterness, "or perhaps the English cavaliers whom the popular voice has called the League of the Scarlet Pimpernel would have taken some interest in me. I was only a poor actress and had to find my way out of France alone, or else perish on the guillotine."

"I am so sorry!" said Marguerite simply.

"Tell me how you got on, once you were in England," she continued after a while, seeing that Desiree Candeille seemed absorbed in thought.

"I had a few engagements at first," replied the Frenchwoman. "I played at Sadler's Wells and with Mrs. Jordan at Covent Garden, but the Aliens' Bill put an end to my chances of livelihood. No manager cared to give me a part, and so..."

"And so?"

"Oh! I had a few jewels and I sold them.... A little money and I live on that.... But when I played at Covent Garden I contrived to send part of my salary over to some of the poorer clubs of Paris. My heart aches for those that are starving.... Poor wretches, they are misguided and misled by self-seeking demagogues.... It hurts me to feel that I can do nothing more to help them... and eases my self-respect if, by singing at public fairs, I can still send a few francs to those who are poorer than myself."

She had spoken with ever-increasing passion and vehemence. Marguerite, with eyes fixed into vacancy, seeing neither the speaker nor her surroundings, seeing only visions of those same poor wreckages of humanity, who had been goaded into thirst for blood, when their shrunken bodies should have been clamouring for healthy food,—Marguerite thus absorbed, had totally forgotten her earlier prejudices and now completely failed to note all that was unreal, stagy, theatrical, in the oratorical declamations of the ex-actress from the Varietes.

Pre-eminently true and loyal herself in spite of the many deceptions and treacheries which she had witnessed in her life, she never looked for falsehood or for cant in others. Even now she only saw before her a woman who had been wrongfully persecuted, who had suffered and had forgiven those who had caused her to suffer. She bitterly accused herself for her original mistrust of this noble-hearted, unselfish woman, who was content to tramp around in an alien country, bartering her talents for a few coins, in order that some of those, who were the originators of her sorrows, might have bread to eat and a bed in which to sleep.

"Mademoiselle," she said warmly, "truly you shame me, who am also French-born, with the many sacrifices you so nobly make for those who should have first claim on my own sympathy. Believe me, if I have not done as much as duty demanded of me in the cause of my starving compatriots, it has not been for lack of good-will. Is there any way now," she added eagerly, "in which I can help you? Putting aside the question of money, wherein I pray you to command my assistance, what can I do to be of useful service to you?"

"You are very kind, Lady Blakeney..." said the other hesitatingly.

"Well? What is it? I see there is something in your mind..."

"It is perhaps difficult to express... but people say I have a good voice... I sing some French ditties... they are a novelty in England, I think.... If I could sing them in fashionable salons... I might perhaps..."

"Nay! you shall sing in fashionable salons," exclaimed Marguerite eagerly, "you shall become the fashion, and I'll swear the Prince of Wales himself shall bid you sing at Carlton House... and you shall name your own fee, Mademoiselle... and London society shall vie with the elite of Bath, as to which shall lure you to its most frequented routs.... There! there! you shall make a fortune for the Paris poor... and to prove to you that I mean every word I say, you shall begin your triumphant career in my own salon to-morrow night. His Royal Highness will be present. You shall sing your most engaging songs... and for your fee you must accept a hundred guineas, which you shall send to the poorest workman's club in Paris in the name of Sir Percy and Lady Blakeney."

"I thank your ladyship, but..."

"You'll not refuse?"

"I'll accept gladly... but... you will understand... I am not very old," said Candeille quaintly, "I... I am only an actress... but if a young actress is unprotected... then..."

"I understand," replied Marguerite gently, "that you are far too pretty to frequent the world all alone, and that you have a mother, a sister or a friend... which?... whom you would wish to escort you to-morrow. Is that it?"

"Nay," rejoined the actress, with marked bitterness, "I have neither mother, nor sister, but our Revolutionary Government, with tardy compassion for those it has so relentlessly driven out of France, has deputed a representative of theirs in England to look after the interests of French subjects over here!"

"Yes?"

"They have realised over in Paris that my life here has been devoted to the welfare of the poor people of France. The representative whom the government has sent to England is specially interested in me and in my work. He is a stand-by for me in case of trouble...

in case of insults... A woman alone is oft subject to those, even at the hands of so-called gentlemen... and the official representative of my own country becomes in such cases my most natural protector."

"I understand."

"You will receive him?"

"Certainly."

"Then may I present him to your ladyship?"

"Whenever you like."

"Now, and it please you."

"Now?"

"Yes. Here he comes, at your ladyship's service."

Desiree Candeille's almond-shaped eyes were fixed upon a distant part of the tent, behind Lady Blakeney in the direction of the main entrance to the booth. There was a slight pause after she had spoken and then Marguerite slowly turned in order to see who this official representative of France was, whom at the young actress' request she had just agreed to receive in her house. In the doorway of the tent, framed by its gaudy draperies, and with the streaming sunshine as a brilliant background behind him, stood the sable-clad figure of Chauvelin.

CHAPTER VII. PREMONITION

Marguerite neither moved nor spoke. She felt two pairs of eyes fixed upon her, and with all the strength of will at her command she forced the very blood in her veins not to quit her cheeks, forced her eyelids not to betray by a single quiver the icy pang of a deadly premonition which at sight of Chauvelin seemed to have chilled her entire soul.

There he stood before her, dressed in his usual somber garments, a look almost of humility in those keen grey eyes of his, which a year ago on the cliffs of Calais had peered down at her with such relentless hate.

Strange that at this moment she should have felt an instinct of fear. What cause had she to throw more than a pitiful glance at the man who had tried so cruelly to wrong her, and who had so signally failed?

Having bowed very low and very respectfully, Chauvelin advanced towards her, with all the airs of a disgraced courtier craving audience from his queen.

As he approached she instinctively drew back.

"Would you prefer not to speak to me, Lady Blakeney?" he said humbly.

She could scarcely believe her ears, or trust her eyes. It seemed impossible that a man could have so changed in a few months. He even looked shorter than last year, more shrunken within himself. His hair, which he wore free from powder, was perceptibly tinged with grey.

"Shall I withdraw?" he added after a pause, seeing that Marguerite made no movement to return his salutation.

"It would be best, perhaps," she replied coldly. "You and I, Monsieur Chauvelin, have so little to say to one another."

"Very little indeed," he rejoined quietly; "the triumphant and happy have ever very little to say to the humiliated and the defeated. But I had hoped that Lady Blakeney in the midst of her victory would have spared one thought of pity and one of pardon."

"I did not know that you had need of either from me, Monsieur."

"Pity perhaps not, but forgiveness certainly."

"You have that, if you so desire it."

"Since I failed, you might try to forget."

"That is beyond my power. But believe me, I have ceased to think of the infinite wrong which you tried to do to me."

"But I failed," he insisted, "and I meant no harm to YOU."

"To those I care for, Monsieur Chauvelin."

"I had to serve my country as best I could. I meant no harm to your brother. He is safe in England now. And the Scarlet Pimpernel was nothing to you."

She tried to read his face, tried to discover in those inscrutable eyes of his, some hidden meaning to his words. Instinct had warned her of course that this man could be nothing but an enemy, always and at all times. But he seemed so broken, so abject now, that contempt for his dejected attitude, and for the defeat which had been inflicted on him, chased the last remnant of fear from her heart.

"I did not even succeed in harming that enigmatical personage," continued Chauvelin with the same self-abasement. "Sir Percy Blakeney, you remember, threw himself across my plans, quite innocently of course. I failed where you succeeded. Luck has deserted me. Our government offered me a humble post, away from France. I look after the interests of French subjects settled in England. My days of power are over. My failure is complete. I do not complain, for I failed in a combat of wits... but I failed... I failed... I failed... I am almost a fugitive and I am quite disgraced. That is my present history, Lady Blakeney," he concluded, taking once more a step towards her, "and you will understand that it would be a solace if you extended your hand to me just once more, and let me feel that although you would never willingly look upon my face again, you have enough womanly tenderness in you to force your heart to forgiveness and mayhap to pity."

Marguerite hesitated. He held out his hand and her warm, impulsive nature prompted her to be kind. But instinct would not be gainsaid: a curious instinct to which she refused to respond. What had she to fear from this miserable and cringing little worm who had not even in him the pride of defeat? What harm could he do to her, or to those whom she loved? Her brother was in England! Her husband! Bah! not the enmity of the entire world could make her fear for him!

Nay! That instinct, which caused her to draw away from Chauvelin, as she would from a venomous asp, was certainly not fear. It was hate! She hated this man! Hated him for all that she had suffered because of him; for that terrible night on the cliffs of Calais! The peril to her husband who had become so infinitely dear! The humiliations and self-reproaches which he had endured.

Yes! it was hate! and hate was of all emotions the one she most despised.

Hate? Does one hate a slimy but harmless toad or a stinging fly? It seemed ridiculous, contemptible and pitiable to think of hate in connection with the melancholy figure of this discomfited intriguer, this fallen leader of revolutionary France.

He was holding out his hand to her. If she placed even the tips of her fingers upon it, she would be making the compact of mercy and forgiveness which he was asking of her. The woman Desiree Candeille roused within her the last lingering vestige of her slumbering wrath. False, theatrical and stagy—as Marguerite had originally suspected—

she appeared to have been in league with Chauvelin to bring about this undesirable meeting.

Lady Blakeney turned from one to another, trying to conceal her contempt beneath a mask of passionless indifference. Candeille was standing close by, looking obviously distressed and not a little puzzled. An instant's reflection was sufficient to convince Marguerite that the whilom actress of the Varietes Theatre was obviously ignorant of the events to which Chauvelin had been alluding: she was, therefore, of no serious consequence, a mere tool, mayhap, in the ex-ambassador's hands. At the present moment she looked like a silly child who does not understand the conversation of the "grown-ups."

Marguerite had promised her help and protection, had invited her to her house, and offered her a munificent gift in aid of a deserving cause. She was too proud to go back now on that promise, to rescind the contract because of an unexplainable fear. With regard to Chauvelin, the matter stood differently: she had made him no direct offer of hospitality: she had agreed to receive in her house the official chaperone of an unprotected girl, but she was not called upon to show cordiality to her own and her husband's most deadly enemy.

She was ready to dismiss him out of her life with a cursory word of pardon and a half-expressed promise of oblivion: on that understanding and that only she was ready to let her hand rest for the space of one second in his.

She had looked upon her fallen enemy, seen his discomfiture and his humiliation! Very well! Now let him pass out of her life, all the more easily, since the last vision of him would be one of such utter abjection as would even be unworthy of hate.

All these thoughts, feelings and struggles passed through her mind with great rapidity. Her hesitation had lasted less than five seconds: Chauvelin still wore the look of doubting entreaty with which he had first begged permission to take her hand in his. With an impulsive toss of the head, she had turned straight towards him, ready with the phrase with which she meant to dismiss him from her sight now and forever, when suddenly a well-known laugh broke in upon her ear, and a lazy, drawly voice said pleasantly:

"La! I vow the air is fit to poison you! Your Royal Highness, I entreat, let us turn our backs upon these gates of Inferno, where lost souls would feel more at home than doth your humble servant."

The next moment His Royal Highness the Prince of Wales had entered the tent, closely followed by Sir Percy Blakeney.

CHAPTER VIII. THE INVITATION

It was in truth a strange situation, this chance meeting between Percy Blakeney and ex-Ambassador Chauvelin.

Marguerite looked up at her husband. She saw him shrug his broad shoulders as he first caught sight of Chauvelin, and glance down in his usual lazy, good-humoured manner at the shrunken figure of the silent Frenchman. The words she meant to say never crossed her lips; she was waiting to hear what the two men would say to one another.

The instinct of the grande dame in her, the fashionable lady accustomed to the exigencies of society, just gave her sufficient presence of mind to make the requisite low curtsey before His Royal Highness. But the Prince, forgetting his accustomed gallantry, was also absorbed in the little scene before him. He, too, was looking from the sable-clad figure of Chauvelin to that of gorgeously arrayed Sir Percy. He, too, like Marguerite, was wondering what was passing behind the low, smooth forehead of that inimitable dandy, what behind the inscrutably good-humoured expression of those sleepy eyes.

Of the five persons thus present in the dark and stuffy booth, certainly Sir Percy Blakeney seemed the least perturbed. He had paused just long enough to allow Chauvelin to become fully conscious of a feeling of supreme irritation and annoyance, then he strolled up to the ex-ambassador, with hand outstretched and the most engaging of smiles.

"Ha!" he said, with his usual half-shy, half-pleasant-tempered smile, "my engaging friend from France! I hope, sir, that our demmed climate doth find you well and hearty to-day."

The cheerful voice seemed to ease the tension. Marguerite sighed a sigh of relief. After all, what was more natural than that Percy with his amazing fund of pleasant irresponsibility should thus greet the man who had once vowed to bring him to the guillotine? Chauvelin, himself, accustomed by now to the audacious coolness of his enemy, was scarcely taken by surprise. He bowed low to His Highness, who, vastly amused at Blakeney's sally, was inclined to be gracious to everyone, even though the personality of Chauvelin as a well-known leader of the regicide government was inherently distasteful to him. But the Prince saw in the wizened little figure before him an obvious butt for his friend Blakeney's impertinent shafts, and although historians have been unable to assert positively whether or no George Prince of Wales knew aught of Sir Percy's dual life, yet there is no doubt that he was always ready to enjoy a situation which brought about the discomfiture of any of the Scarlet Pimpernel's avowed enemies.

"I, too, have not met M. Chauvelin for many a long month," said His Royal Highness with an obvious show of irony. "And I mistake not, sir, you left my father's court somewhat abruptly last year."

"Nay, your Royal Highness," said Percy gaily, "my friend Monsieur... er... Chaubertin and I had serious business to discuss, which could only be dealt with in France.... Am I not right, Monsieur?"

"Quite right, Sir Percy," replied Chauvelin curtly.

"We had to discuss abominable soup in Calais, had we not?" continued Blakeney in the same tone of easy banter, "and wine that I vowed was vinegar. Monsieur... er... Chaubertin... no, no, I beg pardon... Chauvelin... Monsieur Chauvelin and I quite agreed upon that point. The only matter on which we were not quite at one was the question of snuff."

"Snuff?" laughed His Royal Highness, who seemed vastly amused.

"Yes, your Royal Highness... snuff... Monsieur Chauvelin here had—if I may be allowed to say so—so vitiated a taste in snuff that he prefers it with an admixture of pepper... Is that not so, Monsieur... er... Chaubertin?"

"Chauvelin, Sir Percy," remarked the ex-ambassador drily.

He was determined not to lose his temper and looked urbane and pleasant, whilst his impudent enemy was enjoying a joke at his expense. Marguerite the while had not taken her eyes off the keen, shrewd face. Whilst the three men talked, she seemed suddenly to have lost her sense of the reality of things. The present situation appeared to her strangely familiar, like a dream which she had dreamt oft times before.

Suddenly it became absolutely clear to her that the whole scene had been arranged and planned: the booth with its flaring placard, Demoiselle Candeille soliciting her patronage, her invitation to the young actress, Chauvelin's sudden appearance, all, all had been concocted and arranged, not here, not in England at all, but out there in Paris, in some dark gathering of blood-thirsty ruffians, who had invented a final trap for the destruction of the bold adventurer, who went by the name of the Scarlet Pimpernel.

And she also was only a puppet, enacting a part which had been written for her: she had acted just as THEY had anticipated, had spoken the very words they had meant her to say: and when she looked at Percy, he seemed supremely ignorant of it all, unconscious of this trap of the existence of which everyone here present was aware, save indeed himself. She would have fought against this weird feeling of obsession, of being a mechanical toy would up to do certain things, but this she could not do; her will appeared paralysed, her tongue even refused her service.

As in a dream she heard His Royal Highness ask for the name of the young actress who was soliciting alms for the poor of Paris.

That also had been prearranged. His Royal Highness for the moment was also a puppet, made to dance, to speak and to act as Chauvelin and his colleagues over in France had decided that he should. Quite mechanically Marguerite introduced Demoiselle Candeille to the Prince's gracious notice.

"If your Highness will permit," she said, "Mademoiselle Candeille will give us some of her charming old French songs at my rout to-morrow."

"By all means! By all means!" said the Prince. "I used to know some in my childhood days. Charming and poetic.... I know.... I know.... We shall be delighted to hear Mademoiselle sing, eh, Blakeney?" he added good-humouredly, "and for your rout to-morrow will you not also invite M. Chauvelin?"

"Nay! but that goes without saying, your Royal Highness," responded Sir Percy, with hospitable alacrity and a most approved bow directed at his arch-enemy. "We shall expect M. Chauvelin. He and I have not met for so long, and he shall be made right welcome at Blakeney Manor."

CHAPTER IX. DEMOISELLE CANDEILLE

Her origin was of the humblest, for her mother—so it was said—had been kitchen-maid in the household of the Duc de Marny, but Desiree had received some kind of education, and though she began life as a dresser in one of the minor theatres of Paris, she became ultimately one of its most popular stars.

She was small and dark, dainty in her manner and ways, and with a graceful little figure, peculiarly supple and sinuous. Her humble origin certainly did not betray itself in her hands and feet, which were exquisite in shape and lilliputian in size.

Her hair was soft and glossy, always free from powder, and cunningly arranged so as to slightly overshadow the upper part of her face.

The chin was small and round, the mouth extraordinarily red, the neck slender and long. But she was not pretty: so said all the women. Her skin was rather coarse in texture and darkish in colour, her eyes were narrow and slightly turned upwards at the corners; no! she was distinctly not pretty.

Yet she pleased the men! Perhaps because she was so artlessly determined to please them. The women said that Demoiselle Candeille never left a man alone until she had succeeded in captivating his fancy if only for five minutes; an interval in a dance... the time to cross a muddy road.

But for five minutes she was determined to hold any man's complete attention, and to exact his admiration. And she nearly always succeeded.

Therefore the women hated her. The men were amused. It is extremely pleasant to have one's admiration compelled, one's attention so determinedly sought after.

And Candeille could be extremely amusing, and as Magdelon in Moliere's "Les Precieuses" was quite inimitable.

This, however, was in the olden days, just before Paris went quite mad, before the Reign of Terror had set in, and ci-devant Louis the King had been executed.

Candeille had taken it into her frolicsome little head that she would like to go to London. The idea was of course in the nature of an experiment. Those dull English people over the water knew so little of what good acting really meant. Tragedy? Well! passons! Their heavy, large-boned actresses might manage one or two big scenes where a commanding presence and a powerful voice would not come amiss, and where prominent teeth would pass unnoticed in the agony of a dramatic climax.

But Comedy!

Ah! ca non, par example! Demoiselle Candeille had seen several English gentlemen and ladies in those same olden days at the Tuileries, but she really could not imagine any of them enacting the piquant scenes of Moliere or Beaumarchais.

Demoiselle Candeille thought of every English-born individual as having very large teeth. Now large teeth do not lend themselves to well-spoken comedy scenes, to smiles, or to double entendre.

Her own teeth were exceptionally small and white, and very sharp, like those of a kitten.

Yes! Demoiselle Candeille thought it would be extremely interesting to go to London and to show to a nation of shopkeepers how daintily one can be amused in a theatre.

Permission to depart from Paris was easy to obtain. In fact the fair lady had never really found it difficult to obtain anything she very much wanted.

In this case she had plenty of friends in high places. Marat was still alive and a great lover of the theatre. Tallien was a personal admirer of hers, Deputy Dupont would do anything she asked.

She wanted to act in London, at a theatre called Drury Lane. She wanted to play Moliere in England in French, and had already spoken with several of her colleagues, who were ready to join her. They would give public representations in aid of the starving population of France; there were plenty of Socialistic clubs in London quite Jacobin and Revolutionary in tendency: their members would give her full support.

She would be serving her country and her countrymen and incidentally see something of the world, and amuse herself. She was bored in Paris.

Then she thought of Marguerite St. Just, once of the Maison Moliere, who had captivated an English milor of enormous wealth. Demoiselle Candeille had never been of the Maison Moliere; she had been the leading star of one of the minor—yet much-frequented—theatres of Paris, but she felt herself quite able and ready to captivate some other unattached milor, who would load her with English money and incidentally bestow an English name upon her.

So she went to London.

The experiment, however, had not proved an unmitigated success. At first she and her company did obtain a few engagements at one or two of the minor theatres, to give representations of some of the French classical comedies in the original language.

But these never quite became the fashion. The feeling against France and all her doings was far too keen in that very set, which Demoiselle Candeille had desired to captivate with her talents, to allow of the English jeunesse doree to flock and see Moliere played in French, by a French troupe, whilst Candeille's own compatriots resident in England had given her but scant support.

One section of these—the aristocrats and emigres—looked upon the actress who was a friend of all the Jacobins in Paris as nothing better than canaille. They sedulously ignored her presence in this country, and snubbed her whenever they had an opportunity.

The other section—chiefly consisting of agents and spies of the Revolutionary Government—she would gladly have ignored. They had at first made a constant demand on her purse, her talents and her time: then she grew tired of them, and felt more and more chary of being identified with a set which was in such ill-odour with that very same jeunesse doree whom Candeille had desired to please.

In her own country she was and always had been a good republican: Marat had given her her first start in life by his violent praises of her talent in his widely-circulated paper; she had been associated in Paris with the whole coterie of artists and actors: every one of them republican to a man. But in London, although one might be snubbed by the emigres and aristocrats—it did not do to be mixed up with the sans-culotte journalists and pamphleteers who haunted the Socialistic clubs of the English capital, and who were the prime organizers of all those seditious gatherings and treasonable unions that caused Mr. Pitt and his colleagues so much trouble and anxiety.

One by one, Desiree Candeille's comrades, male and female, who had accompanied her to England, returned to their own country. When war was declared, some of them were actually sent back under the provisions of the Aliens Bill.

But Desiree had stayed on.

Her old friends in Paris had managed to advise her that she would not be very welcome there just now. The sans-culotte journalists of England, the agents and spies of the Revolutionary Government, had taken their revenge of the frequent snubs inflicted upon them by the young actress, and in those days the fact of being unwelcome in France was apt to have a more lurid and more dangerous significance.

Candeille did not dare return: at any rate not for the present.

She trusted to her own powers of intrigue, and her well-known fascinations, to reconquer the friendship of the Jacobin clique, and she once more turned her attention to the affiliated Socialistic clubs of England. But between the proverbial two stools, Demoiselle Candeille soon came to the ground. Her machinations became known in official quarters, her connection with all the seditious clubs of London was soon bruited abroad, and one evening Desiree found herself confronted with a document addressed to her: "From the Office of His Majesty's Privy Seal," wherein it was set forth that, pursuant to the statute 33 George III. cap. 5, she, Desiree Candeille, a French subject now resident in England, was required to leave this kingdom by order of His Majesty within seven days, and that in the event of the said Desiree Candeille refusing to comply with this order, she would be liable to commitment, brought to trial and sentenced to imprisonment for a month, and afterwards to removal within a limited time under pain of transportation for life.

This meant that Demoiselle Candeille had exactly seven days in which to make complete her reconciliation with her former friends who now ruled Paris and France with a relentless and perpetually bloodstained hand. No wonder that during the night which followed the receipt of this momentous document, Demoiselle Candeille suffered gravely from insomnia.

She dared not go back to France, she was ordered out of England! What was to become of her?

This was just three days before the eventful afternoon of the Richmond Gala, and twenty-four hours after ex-Ambassador Chauvelin had landed in England. Candeille and Chauvelin had since then met at the "Cercle des Jacobins Francais" in Soho Street, and now fair Desiree found herself in lodgings in Richmond, the evening of the day following the Gala, feeling that her luck had not altogether deserted her.

One conversation with Citizen Chauvelin had brought the fickle jade back to Demoiselle Candeilles' service. Nay, more, the young actress saw before her visions of intrigue, of dramatic situations, of pleasant little bits of revenge;—all of which was meat and drink and air to breathe for Mademoiselle Desiree.

She was to sing in one of the most fashionable salons in England: that was very pleasant. The Prince of Wales would hear and see her! that opened out a vista of delightful possibilities! And all she had to do was to act a part dictated to her by Citizen Chauvelin, to behave as he directed, to move in the way he wished! Well! that was easy enough, since the part which she would have to play was one peculiarly suited to her talents.

She looked at herself critically in the glass. Her maid Fanchon—a little French waif picked up in the slums of Soho—helped to readjust a stray curl which had rebelled against the comb.

"Now for the necklace, Mademoiselle," said Fanchon with suppressed excitement.

It had just arrived by messenger: a large morocco case, which now lay open on the dressing table, displaying its dazzling contents.

Candeille scarcely dared to touch it, and yet it was for her. Citizen Chauvelin had sent a note with it.

"Citizeness Candeille will please accept this gift from the government of France in acknowledgment of useful services past and to come."

The note was signed with Robespierre's own name, followed by that of Citizen Chauvelin. The morocco case contained a necklace of diamonds worth the ransom of a king.

"For useful services past and to come!" and there were promises of still further rewards, a complete pardon for all defalcations, a place within the charmed circle of the Comedie Francaise, a grand pageant and apotheosis with Citizeness Candeille impersonating the Goddess of Reason, in the midst of a grand national fete, and the acclamations of excited Paris: and all in exchange for the enactment of a part—simple and easy—outlined for her by Chauvelin!...

How strange! how inexplicable! Candeille took the necklace up in her trembling fingers and gazed musingly at the priceless gems. She had seen the jewels before, long, long ago! round the neck of the Duchesse de Marny, in whose service her own mother had been. She—as a child—had often gazed at and admired the great lady, who seemed like a wonderful fairy from an altogether different world, to the poor little kitchen slut.

How wonderful are the vagaries of fortune! Desiree Candeille, the kitchen-maid's daughter, now wearing her ex-mistress' jewels. She supposed that these had been confiscated when the last of the Marnys—the girl, Juliette—had escaped from France! confiscated and now sent to her—Candeille—as a reward or as a bribe!

In either case they were welcome. The actress' vanity was soothed. She knew Juliette Marny was in England, and that she would meet her to-night at Lady Blakeney's. After the many snubs which she had endured from French aristocrats settled in England, the actress felt that she was about to enjoy an evening of triumph.

The intrigue excited her. She did not quite know what schemes Chauvelin was aiming at, what ultimate end he had had in view when he commanded her services and taught her the part which he wished her to play.

That the schemes were vast and the end mighty, she could not doubt. The reward she had received was proof enough of that.

Little Fanchon stood there in speechless admiration, whilst her mistress still fondly fingered the magnificent necklace.

"Mademoiselle will wear the diamond to-night?" she asked with evident anxiety: she would have been bitterly disappointed to have seen the beautiful thing once more relegated to its dark morocco case.

"Oh, yes, Fanchon!" said Candeille with a sigh of great satisfaction; "see that they are fastened quite securely, my girl."

She put the necklace round her shapely neck and Fanchon looked to see that the clasp was quite secure.

There came the sound of loud knocking at the street door.

"That is M. Chauvelin come to fetch me with the chaise. Am I quite ready, Fanchon?" asked Desiree Candeille.

"Oh yes, Mademoiselle!" sighed the little maid; "and Mademoiselle looks very beautiful to-night."

"Lady Blakeney is very beautiful too, Fanchon," rejoined the actress naively, "but I wonder if she will wear anything as fine as the Marny necklace?"

The knocking at the street door was repeated. Candeille took a final, satisfied survey of herself in the glass. She knew her part and felt that she had dressed well for it. She gave a final, affectionate little tap to the diamonds round her neck, took her cloak and hood from Fanchon, and was ready to go.

CHAPTER X. LADY BLAKENEY'S ROUT

There are several accounts extant, in the fashionable chronicles of the time, of the gorgeous reception given that autumn by Lady Blakeney in her magnificent riverside home.

Never had the spacious apartments of Blakeney Manor looked more resplendent than on this memorable occasion—memorable because of the events which brought the brilliant evening to a close.

The Prince of Wales had come over by water from Carlton House; the Royal Princesses came early, and all fashionable London was there, chattering and laughing, displaying elaborate gowns and priceless jewels, dancing, flirting, listening to the strains of the string band, or strolling listlessly in the gardens, where the late roses and clumps of heliotrope threw soft fragrance on the balmy air.

But Marguerite was nervous and agitated. Strive how she might, she could not throw off that foreboding of something evil to come, which had assailed her from the first moment when she met Chauvelin face to face.

That unaccountable feeling of unreality was still upon her, that sense that she, and the woman Candeille, Percy and even His Royal Highness were, for the time being, the actors in a play written and stage-managed by Chauvelin. The ex-ambassador's humility, his offers of friendship, his quietude under Sir Percy's good-humoured banter, everything was a sham. Marguerite knew it; her womanly instinct, her passionate love, all cried out to her in warning: but there was that in her husband's nature which rendered her powerless in the face of such dangers, as, she felt sure, were now threatening him.

Just before her guests had begun to assemble, she had been alone with him for a few minutes. She had entered the room in which he sat, looking radiantly beautiful in a shimmering gown of white and silver, with diamonds in her golden hair and round her exquisite neck.

Moments like this, when she was alone with him, were the joy of her life. Then and then only did she see him as he really was, with that wistful tenderness in his deep-set eyes, that occasional flash of passion from beneath the lazily-drooping lids. For a few minutes—seconds, mayhap—the spirit of the reckless adventurer was laid to rest, relegated into the furthermost background of his senses by the powerful emotions of the lover.

Then he would seize her in his arms, and hold her to him, with a strange longing to tear from out his heart all other thoughts, feelings and passions save those which made him a slave to her beauty and her smiles.

"Percy!" she whispered to him to-night when freeing herself from his embrace. She looked up at him, and for this one heavenly second felt him all her own. "Percy, you will do nothing rash, nothing foolhardy to-night. That man had planned all that took place yesterday. He hates you, and ..."

In a moment his face and attitude had changed, the heavy lids drooped over the eyes, the rigidity of the mouth relaxed, and that quaint, half-shy, half-inane smile played around the firm lips.

"Of course he does, m'dear," he said in his usual affected, drawly tones, "of course he does, but that is so demmed amusing. He does not really know what or how much he knows, or what I know.... In fact... er... we none of us know anything... just at present...."

He laughed lightly and carelessly, then deliberately readjusted the set of his lace tie.

"Percy!" she said reproachfully.

"Yes, m'dear."

"Lately when you brought Deroulede and Juliette Marny to England... I endured agonies of anxiety... and..."

He sighed, a quick, short, wistful sigh, and said very gently:

"I know you did, m'dear, and that is where the trouble lies. I know that you are fretting, so I have to be so demmed quick about the business, so as not to keep you in suspense too long.... And now I can't take Ffoulkes away from his young wife, and Tony and the others are so mighty slow."

"Percy!" she said once more with tender earnestness.

"I know, I know," he said with a slight frown of self-reproach. "La! but I don't deserve your solicitude. Heavens know what a brute I was for years, whilst I neglected you, and ignored the noble devotion which I, alas! do even now so little to deserve."

She would have said something more, but was interrupted by the entrance of Juliette Marny into the room.

"Some of your guests have arrived, Lady Blakeney," said the young girl, apologising for her seeming intrusion. "I thought you would wish to know."

Juliette looked very young and girlish in a simple white gown, without a single jewel on her arms or neck. Marguerite regarded her with unaffected approval.

"You look charming to-night, Mademoiselle, does she not, Sir Percy?"

"Thanks to your bounty," smiled Juliette, a trifle sadly. "Whilst I dressed to-night, I felt how I should have loved to wear my dear mother's jewels, of which she used to be so proud."

"We must hope that you will recover them, dear, some day," said Marguerite vaguely, as she led the young girl out of the small study towards the larger reception rooms.

"Indeed I hope so," sighed Juliette. "When times became so troublous in France after my dear father's death, his confessor and friend, the Abbe Foucquet, took charge of all my mother's jewels for me. He said they would be safe with the ornaments of his own little church at Boulogne. He feared no sacrilege, and thought they would be most effectually hidden there, for no one would dream of looking for the Marny diamonds in the crypt of a country church."

Marguerite said nothing in reply. Whatever her own doubts might be upon such a subject, it could serve no purpose to disturb the young girl's serenity.

"Dear Abbe Foucquet," said Juliette after a while, "his is the kind of devotion which I feel sure will never be found under the new regimes of anarchy and of so-called equality. He would have laid down his life for my father or for me. And I know that he would never part with the jewels which I entrusted to his care, whilst he had breath and strength to defend them."

Marguerite would have wished to pursue the subject a little further. It was very pathetic to witness poor Juliette's hopes and confidences, which she felt sure would never be realised.

Lady Blakeney knew so much of what was going on in France just now: spoliations, confiscations, official thefts, open robberies, all in the name of equality, of fraternity and of patriotism. She knew nothing, of course, of the Abbe Foucquet, but the tender little picture of the devoted old man, painted by Juliette's words, had appealed strongly to her sympathetic heart.

Instinct and knowledge of the political aspect of France told her that by entrusting valuable family jewels to the old Abbe, Juliette had most unwittingly placed the man she so much trusted in danger of persecution at the hands of a government which did not even admit the legality of family possessions. However, there was neither time nor opportunity now to enlarge upon the subject. Marguerite resolved to recur to it a little later, when she would be alone with Mlle. de Marny, and above all when she could take counsel with her husband as to the best means of recovering the young girl's property for her, whilst relieving a devoted old man from the dangerous responsibility which he had so selflessly undertaken.

In the meanwhile the two women had reached the first of the long line of state apartments wherein the brilliant fete was to take place. The staircase and the hall below were already filled with the early arrivals. Bidding Juliette to remain in the ballroom, Lady Blakeney now took up her stand on the exquisitely decorated landing, ready to greet her guests. She had a smile and a pleasant word for all, as, in a constant stream, the elite of London fashionable society began to file past her, exchanging the elaborate greetings which the stilted mode of the day prescribed to this butterfly-world.

The lacqueys in the hall shouted the names of the guests as they passed up the stairs: names celebrated in politics, in worlds of sport, of science or of art, great historic names, humble, newly-made ones, noble illustrious titles. The spacious rooms were filling fast. His Royal Highness, so 'twas said, had just stepped out of his barge. The noise of laughter and chatter was incessant, like unto a crowd of gaily-plumaged birds. Huge bunches of apricot-coloured roses in silver vases made the air heavy with their subtle perfume. Fans began to flutter. The string band struck the preliminary cords of the gavotte.

At that moment the lacqueys at the foot of the stairs called out in stentorian tones:

"Mademoiselle Desiree Candeille! and Monsieur Chauvelin!"

Marguerite's heart gave a slight flutter; she felt a sudden tightening of the throat. She did not see Candeille at first, only the slight figure of Chauvelin dressed all in black, as usual, with head bent and hands clasped behind his back; he was slowly mounting the wide staircase, between a double row of brilliantly attired men and women, who looked with no small measure of curiosity at the ex-ambassador from revolutionary France.

Demoiselle Candeille was leading the way up the stairs. She paused on the landing in order to make before her hostess a most perfect and most elaborate curtsey. She looked smiling and radiant, beautifully dressed, a small wreath of wrought gold leaves in her hair, her only jewel an absolutely regal one, a magnificent necklace of diamonds round her shapely throat.

CHAPTER XI. THE CHALLENGE

It all occurred just before midnight, in one of the smaller rooms, which lead in enfilade from the principal ballroom.

Dancing had been going on for some time, but the evening was close, and there seemed to be a growing desire on the part of Lady Blakeney's guests to wander desultorily through the gardens and glasshouses, or sit about where some measure of coolness could be obtained.

There was a rumour that a new and charming French artiste was to sing a few peculiarly ravishing songs, unheard in England before. Close to the main ballroom was the octagon music-room which was brilliantly illuminated, and in which a large number of chairs had been obviously disposed for the comfort of an audience. Into this room many of the guests had already assembled. It was quite clear that a chamber-concert—select and attractive as were all Lady Blakeney's entertainments—was in contemplation.

Marguerite herself, released for a moment from her constant duties near her royal guests, had strolled through the smaller rooms, accompanied by Juliette, in order to search for Mademoiselle Candeille and to suggest the commencement of the improvised concert.

Desiree Candeille had kept herself very much aloof throughout the evening, only talking to the one or two gentlemen whom her hostess had presented to her on her arrival, and with M. Chauvelin always in close attendance upon her every movement.

Presently, when dancing began, she retired to a small boudoir, and there sat down, demurely waiting, until Lady Blakeney should require her services.

When Marguerite and Juliette Marny entered the little room, she rose and came forward a few steps.

"I am ready, Madame," she said pleasantly, "whenever you wish me to begin. I have thought out a short programme,—shall I start with the gay or the sentimental songs?"

But before Marguerite had time to utter a reply, she felt her arm nervously clutched by a hot and trembling hand.

"Who... who is this woman?" murmured Juliette Marny close to her ear.

The young girl looked pale and very agitated, and her large eyes were fixed in unmistakable wrath upon the French actress before her. A little startled, not understanding Juliette's attitude, Marguerite tried to reply lightly:

"This is Mademoiselle Candeille, Juliette dear," she said, affecting the usual formal introduction, "of the Varietes Theatre of Paris—Mademoiselle Desiree Candeille, who will sing some charming French ditties for us to-night."

While she spoke she kept a restraining hand on Juliette's quivering arm. Already, with the keen intuition which had been on the qui-vive the whole evening, she scented some mystery in this sudden outburst on the part of her young protegee.

But Juliette did not heed her: she felt surging up in her young, overburdened heart all the wrath and the contempt of the persecuted, fugitive aristocrat against the triumphant usurper. She had suffered so much from that particular class of the risen kitchen-wench of which the woman before her was so typical an example: years of sorrow, of poverty were behind her: loss of fortune, of kindred, of friends—she, even now a pauper, living on the bounty of strangers.

And all this through no fault of her own: the fault of her class mayhap! but not hers!

She had suffered much, and was still overwrought and nerve-strung: for some reason she could not afterwards have explained, she felt spiteful and uncontrolled, goaded into stupid fury by the look of insolence and of triumph with which Candeille calmly regarded her.

Afterwards she would willingly have bitten out her tongue for her vehemence, but for the moment she was absolutely incapable of checking the torrent of her own emotions.

"Mademoiselle Candeille, indeed?" she said in wrathful scorn, "Desiree Candeille, you mean, Lady Blakeney! my mother's kitchen-maid, flaunting shamelessly my dear mother's jewels which she has stolen mayhap..."

The young girl was trembling from head to foot, tears of anger obscured her eyes; her voice, which fortunately remained low—not much above a whisper—was thick and husky.

"Juliette! Juliette! I entreat you," admonished Marguerite, "you must control yourself, you must, indeed you must. Mademoiselle Candeille, I beg of you to retire...."

But Candeille—well-schooled in the part she had to play—had no intention of quitting the field of battle. The more wrathful and excited Mademoiselle de Marny became the more insolent and triumphant waxed the young actress' whole attitude. An ironical smile played round the corners of her mouth, her almond-shaped eyes were half-closed, regarding through dropping lashes the trembling figure of the young impoverished aristocrat. Her head was thrown well back, in obvious defiance of the social conventions, which should have forbidden a fracas in Lady Blakeney's hospitable house, and her fingers provocatively toyed with the diamond necklace which glittered and sparkled round her throat.

She had no need to repeat the words of a well-learnt part: her own wit, her own emotions and feelings helped her to act just as her employer would have wished her to do. Her native vulgarity helped her to assume the very bearing which he would have desired. In fact, at this moment Desiree Candeille had forgotten everything save the immediate present: a more than contemptuous snub from one of those penniless aristocrats, who had rendered her own sojourn in London so unpleasant and unsuccessful.

She had suffered from these snubs before, but had never had the chance of forcing an esclandre, as a result of her own humiliation. That spirit of hatred for the rich and idle classes, which was so characteristic of revolutionary France, was alive and hot within her: she had never had an opportunity—she, the humble fugitive actress from a minor Paris theatre—to retort with forcible taunts to the ironical remarks made at and before her by the various poverty-stricken but haughty emigres who swarmed in those very same circles of London society into which she herself had vainly striven to penetrate.

Now at last, one of this same hated class, provoked beyond self-control, was allowing childish and unreasoning fury to outstrip the usual calm irony of aristocratic rebuffs.

Juliette had paused awhile, in order to check the wrathful tears which, much against her will, were choking the words in her throat and blinding her eyes.

"Hoity! toity!" laughed Candeille, "hark at the young baggage!"

But Juliette had turned to Marguerite and began explaining volubly:

"My mother's jewels!" she said in the midst of her tears, "ask her how she came by them. When I was obliged to leave the home of my fathers,—stolen from me by the Revolutionary Government—I contrived to retain my mother's jewels... you remember, I told you just now.... The Abbe Foucquet—dear old man! Saved them for me... that and a little money which I had... he took charge of them... he said he would place them in safety with the ornaments of his church, and now I see them round that woman's neck... I know that he would not have parted with them save with his life."

All the while that the young girl spoke in a voice half-choked with sobs, Marguerite tried with all the physical and mental will at her command to drag her out of the room and thus to put a summary ending to this unpleasant scene. She ought to have felt angry with Juliette for this childish and senseless outburst, were it not for the fact that somehow she knew within her innermost heart that all this had been arranged and preordained: not by Fate—not by a Higher Hand, but by the most skillful intriguer present-day France had ever known.

And even now, as she was half succeeding in turning Juliette away from the sight of Candeille, she was not the least surprised or startled at seeing Chauvelin standing in the very doorway through which she had hoped to pass. One glance at his face had made her fears tangible and real: there was a look of satisfaction and triumph in his pale, narrow eyes, a flash in them of approbation directed at the insolent attitude of the French actress: he looked like the stage-manager of a play, content with the effect his own well-arranged scenes were producing.

What he hoped to gain by this—somewhat vulgar—quarrel between the two women, Marguerite of course could not guess: that something was lurking in his mind, inimical to herself and to her husband, she did not for a moment doubt, and at this moment she felt that she would have given her very life to induce Candeille and Juliette to cease this passage of arms, without further provocation on either side.

But though Juliette might have been ready to yield to Lady Blakeney's persuasion, Desiree Candeille, under Chauvelin's eye, and fired by her own desire to further humiliate this overbearing aristocrat, did not wish the little scene to end so tamely just yet.

"Your old calotin was made to part with his booty, m'dear," she said, with a contemptuous shrug of her bare shoulders. "Paris and France have been starving these many years past: a paternal government seized all it could with which to reward those that served it well, whilst all that would have been brought, bread and meat for the poor, was being greedily stowed away by shameless traitors!"

Juliette winced at the insult.

"Oh!" she moaned, as she buried her flaming face in her hands.

Too late now did she realise that she had deliberately stirred up a mud-heap and sent noisome insects buzzing about her ears.

"Mademoiselle," said Marguerite authoritatively, "I must ask you to remember that Mlle. de Marny is my friend and that you are a guest in my house."

"Aye! I try not to forget it," rejoined Candeille lightly, "but of a truth you must admit, Citizeness, that it would require the patience of a saint to put up with the insolence of a penniless baggage, who but lately has had to stand her trial in her own country for impurity of conduct."

There was a moment's silence, whilst Marguerite distinctly heard a short sigh of satisfaction escaping from the lips of Chauvelin. Then a pleasant laugh broke upon the ears of the four actors who were enacting the dramatic little scene, and Sir Percy Blakeney, immaculate in his rich white satin coat and filmy lace ruffles, exquisite in manners and courtesy, entered the little boudoir, and with his long back slightly bent, his arm outstretched in a graceful and well-studied curve, he approached Mademoiselle Desiree Candeille.

"May I have the honour," he said with his most elaborate air of courtly deference, "of conducting Mademoiselle to her chaise?"

In the doorway just behind him stood His Royal Highness the Prince of Wales chatting with apparent carelessness to Sir Andrew Ffoulkes and Lord Anthony Dewhurst. A curtain beyond the open door was partially drawn aside, disclosing one or two brilliantly dressed groups, strolling desultorily through the further rooms.

The four persons assembled in the little boudoir had been so absorbed by their own passionate emotions and the violence of their quarrel that they had not noticed the approach of Sir Percy Blakeney and of his friends. Juliette and Marguerite certainly were startled and Candeille was evidently taken unawares. Chauvelin alone seemed quite indifferent and stood back a little when Sir Percy advanced, in order to allow him to pass.

But Candeille recovered quickly enough from her surprise: without heeding Blakeney's proffered arm, she turned with all the airs of an insulted tragedy queen towards Marguerite.

"So 'tis I," she said with affected calm, "who am to bear every insult in a house in which I was bidden as a guest. I am turned out like some intrusive and importunate beggar, and I, the stranger in this land, am destined to find that amidst all these brilliant English gentlemen there is not one man of honour.

"M. Chauvelin," she added loudly, "our beautiful country has, meseems, deputed you to guard the honour as well as the worldly goods of your unprotected compatriots. I call upon you, in the name of France, to avenge the insults offered to me to-night."

She looked round defiantly from one to the other of the several faces which were now turned towards her, but no one, for the moment, spoke or stirred. Juliette, silent and ashamed, had taken Marguerite's hand in hers, and was clinging to it as if wishing to draw strength of character and firmness of purpose through the pores of the other woman's delicate skin.

Sir Percy with backbone still bent in a sweeping curve had not relaxed his attitude of uttermost deference. The Prince of Wales and his friends were viewing the scene with slightly amused aloofness.

For a moment—seconds at most—there was dead silence in the room, during which time it almost seemed as if the beating of several hearts could be distinctly heard.

Then Chauvelin, courtly and urbane, stepped calmly forward.

"Believe me, Citizeness," he said, addressing Candeille directly and with marked emphasis, "I am entirely at your command, but am I not helpless, seeing that those who have so grossly insulted you are of your own irresponsible, if charming, sex?"

Like a great dog after a nap, Sir Percy Blakeney straightened his long back and stretched it out to its full length.

"La!" he said pleasantly, "my ever engaging friend from Calais. Sir, your servant. Meseems we are ever destined to discuss amiable matters, in an amiable spirit.... A glass of punch, Monsieur... er... Chauvelin?"

"I must ask you, Sir Percy," rejoined Chauvelin sternly, "to view this matter with becoming seriousness."

"Seriousness is never becoming, sir," said Blakeney, politely smothering a slight yawn, "and it is vastly unbecoming in the presence of ladies."

"Am I to understand then, Sir Percy," said Chauvelin, "that you are prepared to apologize to Mademoiselle Candeille for this insult offered to her by Lady Blakeney?"

Sir Percy again tried to smother that tiresome little yawn, which seemed most distressing, when he desired to be most polite. Then he flicked off a grain of dust from his immaculate lace ruffle and buried his long, slender hands in the capacious pockets of his white satin breeches; finally he said with the most good-natured of smiles:

"Sir, have you seen the latest fashion in cravats? I would wish to draw your attention to the novel way in which we in England tie a Mechlin-edged bow."

"Sir Percy," retorted Chauvelin firmly, "since you will not offer Mademoiselle Candeille the apology which she has the right to expect from you, are you prepared that you and I should cross swords like honourable gentlemen?"

Blakeney laughed his usual pleasant, somewhat shy laugh, shook his powerful frame and looked from his altitude of six feet three inches down on the small, sable-clad figure of ex-Ambassador Chauvelin.

"The question is, sir," he said slowly, "should we then be two honourable gentlemen crossing swords?"

"Sir Percy..."

"Sir?"

Chauvelin, who for one moment had seemed ready to lose his temper, now made a sudden effort to resume a calm and easy attitude and said quietly:

"Of course, if one of us is coward enough to shirk the contest..."

He did not complete the sentence, but shrugged his shoulders expressive of contempt. The other side of the curtained doorway a little crowd had gradually assembled, attracted hither by the loud and angry voices which came from that small boudoir. Host and hostess had been missed from the reception rooms for some time, His Royal Highness, too, had not been seen for the quarter of an hour: like flies attracted by the light, one by one, or in small isolated groups, some of Lady Blakeney's guests had found their way to the room adjoining the royal presence.

As His Highness was standing in the doorway itself, no one could of course cross the threshold, but everyone could see into the room, and could take stock of the various actors in the little comedy. They were witnessing a quarrel between the French envoy and Sir Percy Blakeney wherein the former was evidently in deadly earnest and the latter merely politely bored. Amused comments flew to and fro: laughter and a babel of irresponsible chatter made an incessant chirruping accompaniment to the duologue between the two men.

But at this stage, the Prince of Wales, who hitherto had seemingly kept aloof from the quarrel, suddenly stepped forward and abruptly interposed the weight of his authority and of his social position between the bickering adversaries.

"Tush, man!" he said impatiently, turning more especially towards Chauvelin, "you talk at random. Sir Percy Blakeney is an English gentleman, and the laws of this country do not admit of duelling, as you understand it in France; and I for one certainly could not allow..."

"Pardon, your Royal Highness," interrupted Sir Percy with irresistible bonhomie, "your Highness does not understand the situation. My engaging friend here does not propose that I should transgress the laws of this country, but that I should go over to France with him, and fight him there, where duelling and... er... other little matters of that sort are allowed."

"Yes! quite so!" rejoined the Prince, "I understand M. Chauvelin's desire. ... But what about you, Blakeney?"

"Oh!" replied Sir Percy lightly, "I have accepted his challenge, of course!"

CHAPTER XII. TIME—PLACE—CONDITIONS

It would be very difficult indeed to say why—at Blakeney's lightly spoken words—an immediate silence should have fallen upon all those present. All the actors in the little drawing-room drama, who had played their respective parts so unerringly up to now, had paused a while, just as if an invisible curtain had come down, marking the end of a scene, and the interval during which the players might recover strength and energy to resume their roles. The Prince of Wales as foremost spectator said nothing for the moment, and beyond the doorway, the audience there assembled seemed suddenly to be holding its breath, waiting—eager, expectant, palpitation—for what would follow now.

Only here and there the gentle frou-frou of a silk skirt, the rhythmic flutter of a fan, broke those few seconds' deadly, stony silence.

Yet it was all simple enough. A fracas between two ladies, the gentlemen interposing, a few words of angry expostulation, then the inevitable suggestion of Belgium or of some other country where the childish and barbarous custom of settling such matters with a couple of swords had not been as yet systematically stamped out.

The whole scene—with but slight variations—had occurred scores of times in London drawing-rooms, English gentlemen had scores of times crossed the Channel for the purpose of settling similar quarrels in continental fashion.

Why should the present situation appear so abnormal? Sir Percy Blakeney—an accomplished gentleman—was past master in the art of fence, and looked more than a match in strength and dexterity for the meagre, sable-clad little opponent who had so summarily challenged him to cross over to France, in order to fight a duel.

But somehow everyone had a feeling at this moment that this proposed duel would be unlike any other combat ever fought between two antagonists. Perhaps it was the white, absolutely stony and unexpressive face of Marguerite which suggested a latent tragedy: perhaps it was the look of unmistakable horror in Juliette's eyes, or that of triumph in those of Chauvelin, or even that certain something in His Royal Highness' face, which seemed to imply that the Prince, careless man of the world as he was, would have given much to prevent this particular meeting from taking place.

Be that as it may, there is no doubt that a certain wave of electrical excitement swept over the little crowd assembled there, the while the chief actor in the little drama, the inimitable dandy, Sir Percy Blakeney himself, appeared deeply engrossed in removing a speck of powder from the wide black satin ribbon which held his gold-rimmed eyeglass.

"Gentlemen!" said His Royal Highness suddenly, "we are forgetting the ladies. My lord Hastings," he added, turning to one of the gentlemen who stood close to him, "I pray you to remedy this unpardonable neglect. Men's quarrels are not fit for ladies' dainty ears."

Sir Percy looked up from his absorbing occupation. His eyes met those of his wife; she was like a marble statue, hardly conscious of what was going on round her. But he, who knew every emotion which swayed that ardent and passionate nature, guessed that beneath that stony calm there lay a mad, almost unconquerable impulse: and that was to shout to all these puppets here, the truth, the awful, the unanswerable truth, to tell them what this challenge really meant; a trap wherein one man consumed with hatred and desire for revenge hoped to entice a brave and fearless foe into a death-dealing snare.

Full well did Percy Blakeney guess that for the space of one second his most cherished secret hovered upon his wife's lips, one turn of the balance of Fate, one breath from the mouth of an unseen sprite, and Marguerite was ready to shout:

"Do not allow this monstrous thing to be! The Scarlet Pimpernel, whom you all admire for his bravery, and love for his daring, stands before you now, face to face with his deadliest enemy, who is here to lure him to his doom!"

For that momentous second therefore Percy Blakeney held his wife's gaze with the magnetism of his own; all there was in him of love, of entreaty, of trust, and of command went out to her through that look with which he kept her eyes riveted upon his face.

Then he saw the rigidity of her attitude relax. She closed her eyes in order to shut out the whole world from her suffering soul. She seemed to be gathering all the mental force of which her brain was capable, for one great effort of self-control. Then she took Juliette's hand in hers, and turned to go out of the room; the gentlemen bowed as she swept past them, her rich silken gown making a soft hush-sh-sh as she went. She nodded to some, curtseyed to the Prince, and had at the last moment the supreme courage and pride to turn her head once more towards her husband, in order to reassure him finally that his secret was as safe with her now, in this hour of danger, as it had been in the time of triumph.

She smiled and passed out of his sight, preceded by Desiree Candeille, who, escorted by one of the gentlemen, had become singularly silent and subdued.

In the little room now there only remained a few men. Sir Andrew Ffoulkes had taken the precaution of closing the door after the ladies had gone.

Then His Royal Highness turned once more to Monsieur Chauvelin and said with an obvious show of indifference:

"Faith, Monsieur! meseems we are all enacting a farce, which can have no final act. I vow that I cannot allow my friend Blakeney to go over to France at your bidding. Your government now will not allow my father's subjects to land on your shores without a special passport, and then only for a specific purpose."

"La, your Royal Highness," interposed Sir Percy, "I pray you have no fear for me on that score. My engaging friend here has—an I mistake not—a passport ready for me in the pocket of his sable-hued coat, and as we are hoping effectually to spit one another over there... gadzooks! but there's the specific purpose.... Is it not true, sir," he added, turning once more to Chauvelin, "that in the pocket of that exquisitely cut coat of yours, you have a passport—name in blank perhaps—which you had specially designed for me?"

It was so carelessly, so pleasantly said, that no one save Chauvelin guessed the real import of Sir Percy's words. Chauvelin, of course, knew their inner meaning: he understood that Blakeney wished to convey to him the fact that he was well aware that the whole scene to-night had been prearranged, and that it was willingly and with eyes wide open that he walked into the trap which the revolutionary patriot had so carefully laid for him.

"The passport will be forthcoming in due course, sir," retorted Chauvelin evasively, "when our seconds have arranged all formalities."

"Seconds be demmed, sir," rejoined Sir Percy placidly, "you do not propose, I trust, that we travel a whole caravan to France."

"Time, place and conditions must be settled, Sir Percy," replied Chauvelin; "you are too accomplished a cavalier, I feel sure, to wish to arrange such formalities yourself."

"Nay! neither you nor I, Monsieur... er... Chauvelin," quoth Sir Percy blandly, "could, I own, settle such things with persistent good-humour; and good-humour in such cases is the most important of all formalities. Is it not so?"

"Certainly, Sir Percy."

"As for seconds? Perish the thought. One second only, I entreat, and that one a lady—the most adorable—the most detestable—the most true—the most fickle amidst all her charming sex.... Do you agree, sir?"

"You have not told me her name, Sir Percy?"

"Chance, Monsieur, Chance.... With His Royal Highness' permission let the wilful jade decide."

"I do not understand."

"Three throws of the dice, Monsieur.... Time... Place... Conditions, you said—three throws and the winner names them.... Do you agree?"

Chauvelin hesitated. Sir Percy's bantering mood did not quite fit in with his own elaborate plans, moreover the ex-ambassador feared a pitfall of some sort, and did not quite like to trust to this arbitration of the dice-box.

He turned, quite involuntarily, in appeal to the Prince of Wales and the other gentlemen present.

But the Englishman of those days was a born gambler. He lived with the dice-box in one pocket and a pack of cards in the other. The Prince himself was no exception to this rule, and the first gentleman in England was the most avowed worshipper of Hazard in the land.

"Chance, by all means," quoth His Highness gaily.

"Chance! Chance!" repeated the others eagerly.

In the midst of so hostile a crowd, Chauvelin felt it unwise to resist. Moreover, one second's reflection had already assured him that this throwing of the dice could not seriously interfere with the success of his plans. If the meeting took place at all—and Sir Percy now had gone too far to draw back—then of necessity it would have to take place in France.

The question of time and conditions of the fight, which at best would be only a farce —only a means to an end—could not be of paramount importance.

Therefore he shrugged his shoulders with well-marked indifference, and said lightly:

"As you please."

There was a small table in the centre of the room with a settee and two or three chairs arranged close to it. Around this table now an eager little group had congregated: the Prince of Wales in the forefront, unwilling to interfere, scarce knowing what madcap plans were floating through Blakeney's adventurous brain, but excited in spite of himself at this momentous game of hazard the issues of which seemed so nebulous, so vaguely fraught with dangers. Close to him were Sir Andrew Ffoulkes, Lord Anthony Dewhurst, Lord Grenville and perhaps a half score gentlemen, young men about town mostly, gay and giddy butterflies of fashion, who did not even attempt to seek in this strange game of chance any hidden meaning save that it was one of Blakeney's irresponsible pranks.

And in the centre of the compact group, Sir Percy Blakeney in his gorgeous suit of shimmering white satin, one knee bent upon a chair, and leaning with easy grace—dice-box in hand—across the small gilt-legged table; beside him ex-Ambassador Chauvelin, standing with arms folded behind his back, watching every movement of his brilliant adversary like some dark-plumaged hawk hovering near a bird of paradise.

"Place first, Monsieur?" suggested Sir Percy.

"As you will, sir," assented Chauvelin.

He took up a dice-box which one of the gentlemen handed to him and the two men threw.

"'Tis mine, Monsieur," said Blakeney carelessly, "mine to name the place where shall occur this historic encounter, 'twixt the busiest man in France and the most idle fop that e'er disgraced these three kingdoms.... Just for the sake of argument, sir, what place would you suggest?"

"Oh! the exact spot is immaterial, Sir Percy," replied Chauvelin coldly, "the whole of France stands at your disposal."

"Aye! I thought as much, but could not be quite sure of such boundless hospitality," retorted Blakeney imperturbably.

"Do you care for the woods around Paris, sir?"

"Too far from the coast, sir. I might be sea-sick crossing over the Channel, and glad to get the business over as soon as possible.... No, not Paris, sir—rather let us say Boulogne.... Pretty little place, Boulogne... do you not think so...?"

"Undoubtedly, Sir Percy."

"Then Boulogne it is... the ramparts, an you will, on the south side of the town."

"As you please," rejoined Chauvelin drily. "Shall we throw again?"

A murmur of merriment had accompanied this brief colloquy between the adversaries, and Blakeney's bland sallies were received with shouts of laughter. Now the dice rattled again and once more the two men threw.

"'Tis yours this time, Monsieur Chauvelin," said Blakeney, after a rapid glance at the dice. "See how evenly Chance favours us both. Mine, the choice of place... admirably done you'll confess.... Now yours the choice of time. I wait upon your pleasure, sir.... The southern ramparts at Boulogne—when?"

"The fourth day from this, sir, at the hour when the Cathedral bell chimes the evening Angelus," came Chauvelin's ready reply.

"Nay! but methought that your demmed government had abolished Cathedrals, and bells and chimes.... The people of France have now to go to hell their own way... for the way to heaven has been barred by the National Convention.... Is that not so?... Methought the Angelus was forbidden to be rung."

"Not at Boulogne, I think, Sir Percy," retorted Chauvelin drily, "and I'll pledge you my word that the evening Angelus shall be rung that night."

"At what hour is that, sir?"

"One hour after sundown."

"But why four days after this? Why not two or three?"

"I might have asked, why the southern ramparts, Sir Percy; why not the western? I chose the fourth day—does it not suit you?" asked Chauvelin ironically.

"Suit me! Why, sir, nothing could suit me better," rejoined Blakeney with his pleasant laugh. "Zounds! but I call it marvellous... demmed marvellous... I wonder now," he added blandly, "what made you think of the Angelus?"

Everyone laughed at this, a little irrelevantly perhaps.

"Ah!" continued Blakeney gaily, "I remember now.... Faith! to think that I was nigh forgetting that when last you and I met, sir, you had just taken or were about to take Holy Orders.... Ah! how well the thought of the Angelus fits in with your clerical garb.... I recollect that the latter was mightily becoming to you, sir..."

"Shall we proceed to settle the conditions of the fight, Sir Percy?" said Chauvelin, interrupting the flow of his antagonist's gibes, and trying to disguise his irritation beneath a mask of impassive reserve.

"The choice of weapons you mean," here interposed His Royal Highness, "but I thought that swords had already been decided on."

"Quite so, your Highness," assented Blakeney, "but there are various little matters in connection with this momentous encounter which are of vast importance.... Am I not right, Monsieur?... Gentlemen, I appeal to you.... Faith! one never knows... my engaging opponent here might desire that I should fight him in green socks, and I that he should wear a scarlet flower in his coat."

"The Scarlet Pimpernel, Sir Percy?"

"Why not, Monsieur? It would look so well in your buttonhole, against the black of the clerical coat, which I understand you sometime affect in France... and when it is withered and quite dead you would find that it would leave an overpowering odour in your nostrils, far stronger than that of incense."

There was general laughter after this. The hatred which every member of the French revolutionary government—including, of course, ex-Ambassador Chauvelin—bore to the national hero was well known.

"The conditions then, Sir Percy," said Chauvelin, without seeming to notice the taunt conveyed in Blakeney's last words. "Shall we throw again?"

"After you, sir," acquiesced Sir Percy.

For the third and last time the two opponents rattled the dice-box and threw. Chauvelin was now absolutely unmoved. These minor details quite failed to interest him. What mattered the conditions of the fight which was only intended as a bait with which to lure his enemy in the open? The hour and place were decided on and Sir Percy would not fail to come. Chauvelin knew enough of his opponent's boldly adventurous spirit not to feel in the least doubtful on that point. Even now, as he gazed with grudging admiration at the massive, well-knit figure of his arch-enemy, noted the thin nervy hands and square jaw, the low, broad forehead and deep-set, half-veiled eyes, he knew that in this matter wherein Percy Blakeney was obviously playing with his very life, the only emotion that really swayed him at this moment was his passionate love of adventure.

The ruling passion strong in death!

Yes! Sir Percy would be on the southern ramparts of Boulogne one hour after sunset on the day named, trusting, no doubt, in his usual marvellous good-fortune, his own presence of mind and his great physical and mental strength, to escape from the trap into which he was so ready to walk.

That remained beyond a doubt! Therefore what mattered details?

But even at this moment, Chauvelin had already resolved on one great thing: namely, that on that eventful day, nothing whatever should be left to Chance; he would meet his cunning enemy not only with cunning, but also with power, and if the entire force of the republican army then available in the north of France had to be requisitioned for the purpose, the ramparts of Boulogne would be surrounded and no chance of escape left for the daring Scarlet Pimpernel.

His wave of meditation, however, was here abruptly stemmed by Blakeney's pleasant voice.

"Lud! Monsieur Chauvelin," he said, "I fear me your luck has deserted you. Chance, as you see, has turned to me once more."

"Then it is for you, Sir Percy," rejoined the Frenchman, "to name the conditions under which we are to fight."

"Ah! that is so, is it not, Monsieur?" quoth Sir Percy lightly. "By my faith! I'll not plague you with formalities.... We'll fight with our coats on if it be cold, in our shirtsleeves if it be sultry.... I'll not demand either green socks or scarlet ornaments. I'll even try and be serious for the space of two minutes, sir, and confine my whole attention —the product of my infinitesimal brain—to thinking out some pleasant detail for this duel, which might be acceptable to you. Thus, sir, the thought of weapons springs to my mind.... Swords you said, I think. Sir! I will e'en restrict my choice of conditions to that of the actual weapons with which we are to fight.... Ffoulkes, I pray you," he added, turning to his friend, "the pair of swords which lie across the top of my desk at this moment....

"We'll not ask a menial to fetch them, eh, Monsieur?" he continued gaily, as Sir Andrew Ffoulkes at a sign from him had quickly left the room. "What need to bruit our pleasant quarrel abroad? You will like the weapons, sir, and you shall have your own choice from the pair.... You are a fine fencer, I feel sure... and you shall decide if a scratch or two or a more serious wound shall be sufficient to avenge Mademoiselle Candeille's wounded vanity."

Whilst he prattled so gaily on, there was dead silence among all those present. The Prince had his shrewd eyes steadily fixed upon him, obviously wondering what this seemingly irresponsible adventurer held at the back of his mind. There is no doubt that everyone felt oppressed, and that a strange murmur of anticipatory excitement went round the little room, when, a few seconds later, Sir Andrew Ffoulkes returned, with two sheathed swords in his hand.

Blakeney took them from his friend and placed them on the little table in front of ex-Ambassador Chauvelin. The spectators strained their necks to look at the two weapons. They were exactly similar one to the other: both encased in plain black leather sheaths, with steel ferrules polished to shine like silver; the handles too were of plain steel, with just the grip fashioned in a twisted basket pattern of the same highly-tempered metal.

"What think you of these weapons, Monsieur?" asked Blakeney, who was carelessly leaning against the back of a chair.

Chauvelin took up one of the two swords and slowly drew it from out its scabbard, carefully examining the brilliant, narrow steel blade as he did so.

"A little old-fashioned in style and make, Sir Percy," he said, closely imitating his opponent's easy demeanour, "a trifle heavier, perhaps, than we in France have been accustomed to lately, but, nevertheless, a beautifully tempered piece of steel."

"Of a truth there's not much the matter with the tempering, Monsieur," quoth Blakeney, "the blades were fashioned at Toledo just two hundred years ago."

"Ah! here I see an inscription," said Chauvelin, holding the sword close to his eyes, the better to see the minute letters engraved in the steel.

"The name of the original owner. I myself bought them—when I travelled in Italy—from one of his descendants."

"Lorenzo Giovanni Cenci," said Chauvelin, spelling the Italian names quite slowly.

"The greatest blackguard that ever trod this earth. You, no doubt, Monsieur, know his history better than we do. Rapine, theft, murder, nothing came amiss to Signor Lorenzo... neither the deadly drug in the cup nor the poisoned dagger."

He had spoken lightly, carelessly, with that same tone of easy banter which he had not forsaken throughout the evening, and the same drawly manner which was habitual to him. But at these last words of his, Chauvelin gave a visible start, and then abruptly replaced the sword—which he had been examining—upon the table.

He threw a quick, suspicious glance at Blakeney, who, leaning back against the chair and one knee resting on the cushioned seat, was idly toying with the other blade, the exact pair to the one which the ex-ambassador had so suddenly put down.

"Well, Monsieur," quoth Sir Percy after a slight pause, and meeting with a swift glance of lazy irony his opponent's fixed gaze. "Are you satisfied with the weapons? Which of the two shall be yours, and which mine?"

"Of a truth, Sir Percy..." murmured Chauvelin, still hesitating.

"Nay, Monsieur," interrupted Blakeney with pleasant bonhomie, "I know what you would say... of a truth, there is no choice between this pair of perfect twins: one is as exquisite as the other.... And yet you must take one and I the other... this or that, whichever you prefer.... You shall take it home with you to-night and practise thrusting at a haystack or at a bobbin, as you please... The sword is yours to command until you have used it against my unworthy person... yours until you bring it out four days hence —on the southern ramparts of Boulogne, when the cathedral bells chime the evening Angelus; then you shall cross it against its faithless twin.... There, Monsieur—they are of equal length... of equal strength and temper... a perfect pair... Yet I pray you choose."

He took up both the swords in his hands and carefully balancing them by the extreme tip of their steel-bound scabbards, he held them out towards the Frenchman. Chauvelin's eyes were fixed upon him, and he from his towering height was looking down at the little sable-clad figure before him.

The Terrorist seemed uncertain what to do. Though he was one of those men whom by the force of their intellect, the strength of their enthusiasm, the power of their cruelty, had built a new anarchical France, had overturned a throne and murdered a king, yet now, face to face with this affected fop, this lazy and debonair adventurer, he hesitated— trying in vain to read what was going on behind that low, smooth forehead or within the depth of those lazy, blue eyes.

He would have given several years of his life at this moment for one short glimpse into the innermost brain cells of this daring mind, to see the man start, quiver but for the fraction of a second, betray himself by a tremor of the eyelid. What counterplan was lurking in Percy Blakeney's head, as he offered to his opponent the two swords which had once belonged to Lorenzo Cenci?

Did any thought of foul play, of dark and deadly poisonings linger in the fastidious mind of this accomplished gentleman?

Surely not!

Chauvelin tried to chide himself for such fears. It seemed madness even to think of Italian poisons, of the Cencis or the Borgias in the midst of this brilliantly lighted English drawing-room.

But because he was above all a diplomatist, a fencer with words and with looks, the envoy of France determined to know, to probe and to read. He forced himself once more to careless laughter and nonchalance of manner and schooled his lips to smile up with gentle irony at the good-humoured face of his arch-enemy.

He tapped one of the swords with his long pointed finger.

"Is this the one you choose, sir?" asked Blakeney.

"Nay! which do you advise, Sir Percy," replied Chauvelin lightly. "Which of those two blades think you is most like to hold after two hundred years the poison of the Cenci?"

But Blakeney neither started nor winced. He broke into a laugh, his own usual pleasant laugh, half shy and somewhat inane, then said in tones of lively astonishment:

"Zounds! sir, but you are full of surprises.... Faith! I never would have thought of that....Marvellous, I call it... demmed marvellous.... What say you, gentlemen?... Your Royal Highness, what think you?... Is not my engaging friend here of a most original turn of mind.... Will you have this sword or that, Monsieur?... Nay, I must insist—else we shall weary our friends if we hesitate too long.... This one then, sir, since you have chosen it," he continued, as Chauvelin finally took one of the swords in his hand. "And now for a bowl of punch.... Nay, Monsieur, 'twas demmed smart what you said just now... I must insist on your joining us in a bowl.... Such wit as yours, Monsieur, must need whetting at times. ... I pray you repeat that same sally again..."

Then finally turning to the Prince and to his friends, he added:

"And after that bowl, gentlemen, shall we rejoin the ladies?"

CHAPTER XIII. REFLECTIONS

It seemed indeed as if the incident were finally closed, the chief actors in the drama having deliberately vacated the centre of the stage.

The little crowd which had stood in a compact mass round the table, began to break up into sundry small groups: laughter and desultory talk, checked for a moment by that oppressive sense of unknown danger, which had weighed on the spirits of those present, once more became general. Blakeney's light-heartedness had put everyone into good-humour; since he evidently did not look upon the challenge as a matter of serious moment, why then, no one else had any cause for anxiety, and the younger men were right glad to join in that bowl of punch which their genial host had offered with so merry a grace.

Lacqueys appeared, throwing open the doors. From a distance the sound of dance music once more broke upon the ear.

A few of the men only remained silent, deliberately holding aloof from the renewed mirthfulness. Foremost amongst these was His Royal Highness, who was looking distinctly troubled, and who had taken Sir Percy by the arm, and was talking to him with obvious earnestness. Lord Anthony Dewhurst and Lord Hastings were holding converse in a secluded corner of the room, whilst Sir Andrew Ffoulkes, as being the host's most intimate friend, felt it incumbent on him to say a few words to ex-Ambassador Chauvelin.

The latter was desirous of effecting a retreat. Blakeney's invitation to join in the friendly bowl of punch could not be taken seriously, and the Terrorist wanted to be alone, in order to think out the events of the past hour.

A lacquey waited on him, took the momentous sword from his hand, found his hat and cloak and called his coach for him: Chauvelin having taken formal leave of his host and acquaintances, quickly worked his way to the staircase and hall, through the less frequented apartments.

He sincerely wished to avoid meeting Lady Blakeney face to face. Not that the slightest twinge of remorse disturbed his mind, but he feared some impulsive action on her part, which indirectly might interfere with his future plans. Fortunately no one took much heed of the darkly-clad, insignificant little figure that glided so swiftly by, obviously determined to escape attention.

In the hall he found Demoiselle Candeille waiting for him. She, too, had evidently been desirous of leaving Blakeney Manor as soon as possible. He saw her to her chaise; then escorted her as far as her lodgings, which were close by: there were still one or two things which he wished to discuss with her, one or two final instructions which he desired to give.

One the whole, he was satisfied with his evening's work: the young actress had well supported him, and had played her part so far with marvellous sang-froid and skill. Sir Percy, whether willingly or blindly, had seemed only too ready to walk into the trap which was being set for him.

This fact alone disturbed Chauvelin not a little, and as half an hour or so later, having taken final leave of his ally, he sat alone in the coach, which was conveying him back to town, the sword of Lorenzo Cenci close to his hand, he pondered very seriously over it.

That the adventurous Scarlet Pimpernel should have guessed all along, that sooner or later the French Revolutionary Government—whom he had defrauded of some of its most important victims,—would desire to be even with him, and to bring him to the scaffold, was not to be wondered at. But that he should be so blind as to imagine that Chauvelin's challenge was anything else but a lure to induce him to go to France, could not possibly be supposed. So bold an adventurer, so keen an intriguer was sure to have scented the trap immediately, and if he appeared ready to fall into it, it was because there had already sprung up in his resourceful mind some bold coup or subtle counterplan, with which he hoped to gratify his own passionate love of sport, whilst once more bringing his enemies to discomfiture and humiliation.

Undoubtedly Sir Percy Blakeney, as an accomplished gentleman of the period, could not very well under the circumstances which had been so carefully stage-managed and arranged by Chauvelin, refuse the latter's challenge to fight him on the other side of the Channel. Any hesitation on the part of the leader of that daring Scarlet Pimpernel League would have covered him with a faint suspicion of pusillanimity, and a subtle breath of ridicule, and in a moment the prestige of the unknown and elusive hero would have vanished forever.

But apart from the necessity of the fight, Blakeney seemed to enter into the spirit of the plot directed against his own life, with such light-hearted merriment, such zest and joy, that Chauvelin could not help but be convinced that the capture of the Scarlet Pimpernel at Boulogne or elsewhere would not prove quite so easy a matter as he had at first anticipated.

That same night he wrote a long and circumstantial letter to his colleague, Citizen Robespierre, shifting thereby, as it were, some of the responsibility of coming events from his own shoulders on to the executive of the Committee of Public Safety.

"I guarantee to you, Citizen Robespierre," he wrote, "and to the members of the Revolutionary Government who have entrusted me with the delicate mission, that four days from this date at one hour after sunset, the man who goes by the mysterious name of the Scarlet Pimpernel, will be on the ramparts of Boulogne on the south side of the town. I have done what has been asked of me. On that day and at that hour, I shall have brought the enemy of the Revolution, the intriguer against the policy of the republic, within the power of the government which he has flouted and outraged. Now look to it, citizens all, that the fruits of my diplomacy and of my skill be not lost to France again. The man will be there at my bidding, 'tis for you to see that he does not escape this time."

This letter he sent by special courier which the National Convention had placed at his disposal in case of emergency. Having sealed it and entrusted it to the man, Chauvelin felt at peace with the world and with himself. Although he was not so sure of success as he would have wished, he yet could not see *how* failure could possibly come about: and the only regret which he felt to-night, when he finally in the early dawn sought a few hours' troubled rest, was that that momentous fourth day was still so very far distant.

CHAPTER XIV. THE RULING PASSION

In the meanwhile silence had fallen over the beautiful old manorial house. One by one the guests had departed, leaving that peaceful sense of complete calm and isolation which follows the noisy chatter of any great throng bent chiefly on enjoyment.

The evening had been universally acknowledged to have been brilliantly successful. True, the much talked of French artiste had not sung the promised ditties, but in the midst of the whirl and excitement of dances, of the inspiring tunes of the string band, the elaborate supper and recherche wines, no one had paid much heed to this change in the programme of entertainments.

And everyone had agreed that never had Lady Blakeney looked more radiantly beautiful than on this night. She seemed absolutely indefatigable; a perfect hostess, full of charming little attentions towards every one, although more than ordinarily absorbed by her duties towards her many royal guests.

The dramatic incidents which had taken place in the small boudoir had not been much bruited abroad. It was always considered bad form in those courtly days to discuss men's quarrels before ladies, and in this instance, those who were present when it all occurred instinctively felt that their discretion would be appreciated in high circles, and held their tongues accordingly.

Thus the brilliant evening was brought to a happy conclusion without a single cloud to mar the enjoyment of the guests. Marguerite performed a veritable miracle of fortitude, forcing her very smiles to seem natural and gay, chatting pleasantly, even wittily, upon every known fashionable topic of the day, laughing merrily the while her poor, aching heart was filled with unspeakable misery.

Now, when everybody had gone, when the last of her guests had bobbed before her the prescribed curtsey, to which she had invariably responded with the same air of easy self-possession, now at last she felt free to give rein to her thoughts, to indulge in the luxury of looking her own anxiety straight in the face and to let the tension of her nerves relax.

Sir Andrew Ffoulkes had been the last to leave and Percy had strolled out with him as far as the garden gate, for Lady Ffoulkes had left in her chaise some time ago, and Sir Andrew meant to walk to his home, not many yards distant from Blakeney Manor.

In spite of herself Marguerite felt her heartstrings tighten as she thought of this young couple so lately wedded. People smiled a little when Sir Andrew Ffoulkes' name was mentioned, some called him effeminate, others uxorious, his fond attachment for his pretty little wife was thought to pass the bounds of decorum. There was no doubt that since his marriage the young man had greatly changed. His love of sport and adventure seemed to have died out completely, yielding evidently to the great, more overpowering love, that for his young wife.

Suzanne was nervous for her husband's safety. She had sufficient influence over him to keep him at home, when other members of the brave little League of The Scarlet Pimpernel followed their leader with mad zest, on some bold adventure.

Marguerite too at first had smiled in kindly derision when Suzanne Ffoulkes, her large eyes filled with tears, had used her wiles to keep Sir Andrew tied to her own dainty apronstrings. But somehow, lately, with that gentle contempt which she felt for the weaker man, there had mingled a half-acknowledged sense of envy.

How different 'twixt her and her husband.

Percy loved her truly and with a depth of passion proportionate to his own curious dual personality: it were sacrilege, almost, to doubt the intensity of his love. But nevertheless she had at all times a feeling as if he were holding himself and his emotions in check, as if his love, as if she, Marguerite, his wife, were but secondary matters in his life; as if her anxieties, her sorrow when he left her, her fears for his safety were but small episodes in the great book of life which he had planned out and conceived for himself.

Then she would hate herself for such thoughts: they seemed like doubts of him. Did any man ever love a woman, she asked herself, as Percy loved her? He was difficult to understand, and perhaps—oh! that was an awful "perhaps"—perhaps there lurked somewhere in his mind a slight mistrust of her. She had betrayed him once! unwittingly 'tis true! did he fear she might do so again?

And to-night after her guests had gone she threw open the great windows that gave on the beautiful terrace, with its marble steps leading down to the cool river beyond. Everything now seemed so peaceful and still; the scent of the heliotrope made the midnight air swoon with its intoxicating fragrance: the rhythmic murmur of the waters came gently echoing from below, and from far away there came the melancholy cry of a night-bird on the prowl.

That cry made Marguerite shudder: her thoughts flew back to the episodes of this night and to Chauvelin, the dark bird of prey with his mysterious death-dealing plans, his subtle intrigues which all tended towards the destruction of one man: his enemy, the husband whom Marguerite loved.

Oh! how she hated these wild adventures which took Percy away from her side. Is not a woman who loves—be it husband or child—the most truly selfish, the most cruelly callous creature in the world, there, where the safety and the well-being of the loved one is in direct conflict with the safety and well-being of others.

She would right gladly have closed her eyes to every horror perpetrated in France, she would not have known what went on in Paris, she wanted her husband! And yet month after month, with but short intervals, she saw him risk that precious life of his, which was the very essence of her own soul, for others! for others! always for others!

And she! she! Marguerite, his wife, was powerless to hold him back! powerless to keep him beside her, when that mad fit of passion seized him to go on one of those wild quests, wherefrom she always feared he could not return alive: and this, although she might use every noble artifice, every tender wile of which a loving and beautiful wife is capable.

At times like those her own proud heart was filled with hatred and with envy towards everything that took him away from her: and to-night all these passionate feelings which she felt were quite unworthy of her and of him seemed to surge within her soul more tumultuously than ever. She was longing to throw herself in his arms, to pour out into his loving ear all that she suffered, in fear and anxiety, and to make one more appeal to his tenderness and to that passion which had so often made him forget the world at her feet.

And so instinctively she walked along the terrace towards that more secluded part of the garden just above the river bank, where she had so oft wandered hand in hand with him, in the honeymoon of their love. There great clumps of old-fashioned cabbage roses grew in untidy splendour, and belated lilies sent intoxicating odours into the air, whilst the heavy masses of Egyptian and Michaelmas daisies looked like ghostly constellations in the gloom.

She thought Percy must soon be coming this way. Though it was so late, she knew that he would not go to bed. After the events of the night, his ruling passion, strong in death, would be holding him in its thrall.

She too felt wide awake and unconscious of fatigue; when she reached the secluded path beside the river, she peered eagerly up and down, and listened for a sound.

Presently it seemed to her that above the gentle clapper of the waters she could hear a rustle and the scrunching of the fine gravel under carefully measured footsteps. She waited a while. The footsteps seemed to draw nearer, and soon, although the starlit night was very dark, she perceived a cloaked and hooded figure approaching cautiously toward her.

"Who goes there?" she called suddenly.

The figure paused: then came rapidly forward, and a voice said timidly:

"Ah! Lady Blakeney!"

"Who are you?" asked Marguerite peremptorily.

"It is I... Desiree Candeille," replied the midnight prowler.

"Demoiselle Candeille!" ejaculated Marguerite, wholly taken by surprise. "What are you doing here? alone? and at this hour?"

"Sh-sh-sh..." whispered Candeille eagerly, as she approached quite close to Marguerite and drew her hood still lower over her eyes. "I am all alone ... I wanted to see someone—you if possible, Lady Blakeney... for I could not rest... I wanted to know what had happened."

"What had happened? When? I don't understand."

"What happened between Citizen Chauvelin and your husband?" asked Candeille.

"What is that to you?" replied Marguerite haughtily.

"I pray you do not misunderstand me..." pleaded Candeille eagerly. "I know my presence in your house... the quarrel which I provoked must have filled your heart with hatred and suspicion towards me... but oh! how can I persuade you?... I acted unwillingly... will you not believe me?... I was that man's tool... and... Oh God!" she added with sudden, wild vehemence, "if only you could know what tyranny that accursed government of France exercises over poor helpless women or men who happen to have fallen within reach of its relentless clutches..."

Her voice broke down in a sob. Marguerite hardly knew what to say or think. She had always mistrusted this woman with her theatrical ways and stagy airs, from the very first moment she saw her in the tent on the green: and she did not wish to run counter against her instinct, in anything pertaining to the present crisis. And yet in spite of her mistrust the actress' vehement words found an echo in the depths of her own heart. How well she knew that tyranny of which Candeille spoke with such bitterness! Had she not suffered from it, endured terrible sorrow and humiliation, when under the ban of that same appalling tyranny she had betrayed the identity—then unknown to her—of the Scarlet Pimpernel?

Therefore when Candeille paused after those last excited words, she said with more gentleness than she had shown hitherto, though still quite coldly:

"But you have not yet told me why you came back here to-night? If Citizen Chauvelin was your taskmaster, then you must know all that has occurred."

"I had a vague hope that I might see you."

"For what purpose?"

"To warn you if I could."

"I need no warning."

"Or are too proud to take one.... Do you know, Lady Blakeney, that Citizen Chauvelin has a personal hatred against your husband?"

"How do you know that?" asked Marguerite, with her suspicions once more on the qui-vive. She could not understand Candeille's attitude. This midnight visit, the vehemence of her language, the strange mixture of knowledge and ignorance which she displayed. What did this woman know of Chauvelin's secret plans? Was she his open ally, or his helpless tool? And was she even now playing a part taught her or commanded her by that prince of intriguers?

Candeille, however, seemed quite unaware of the spirit of antagonism and mistrust which Marguerite took but little pains now to disguise. She clasped her hands together, and her voice shook with the earnestness of her entreaty.

"Oh!" she said eagerly, "have I not seen that look of hatred in Chauvelin's cruel eyes?... He hates your husband, I tell you.... Why I know not... but he hates him.. and means that great harm shall come to Sir Percy through this absurd duel.... Oh! Lady Blakeney, do not let him go... I entreat you, do not let him go!"

But Marguerite proudly drew back a step or two, away from the reach of those hands, stretched out towards her in such vehement appeal.

"You are overwrought, Mademoiselle," she said coldly. "Believe me, I have no need either of your entreaties or of your warning.... I should like you to think that I have no wish to be ungrateful... that I appreciate any kind thought you may have harboured for me in your mind.... But beyond that... please forgive me if I say it somewhat crudely—I do not feel that the matter concerns you in the least.... The hour is late," she added more gently, as if desiring to attenuate the harshness of her last words. "Shall I send my maid to escort you home? She is devoted and discreet..."

"Nay!" retorted the other in tones of quiet sadness, "there is no need of discretion... I am not ashamed of my visit to you to-night.... You are very proud, and for your sake I will pray to God that sorrow and humiliation may not come to you, as I feared.... We are never likely to meet again, Lady Blakeney... you will not wish it, and I shall have passed out of your life as swiftly as I had entered into it.... But there was another thought lurking in my mind when I came to-night.... In case Sir Percy goes to France... the duel is to take place in or near Boulogne... this much I do know... would you not wish to go with him?"

"Truly, Mademoiselle, I must repeat to you..."

"That 'tis no concern of mine... I know... I own that.... But, you see when I came back here to-night in the silence and the darkness—I had not guessed that you would be so proud... I thought that I, a woman, would know how to touch your womanly heart.... I was clumsy, I suppose.... I made so sure that you would wish to go with your husband, in case... in case he insisted on running his head into the noose, which I feel sure Chauvelin has prepared for him.... I myself start for France shortly. Citizen Chauvelin has provided me with the necessary passport for myself and my maid, who was to have accompanied me.... Then, just now, when I was all alone... and thought over all the mischief which that fiend had forced me to do for him, it seemed to me that perhaps..."

She broke off abruptly, and tried to read the other woman's face in the gloom. But Marguerite, who was taller than the Frenchwoman, was standing, very stiff and erect, giving the young actress neither discouragement nor confidence. She did not interrupt Candeille's long and voluble explanation: vaguely she wondered what it was all about, and even now when the Frenchwoman paused, Marguerite said nothing, but watched her quietly as she took a folded paper from the capacious pocket of her cloak and then held it out with a look of timidity towards Lady Blakeney.

"My maid need not come with me," said Desiree Candeille humbly. "I would far rather travel alone... this is her passport and... Oh! you need not take it out of my hand," she added in tones of bitter self-deprecation, as Marguerite made no sign of taking the paper from her. "See! I will leave it here among the roses!... You mistrust me now... it is only natural... presently, perhaps, calmer reflection will come... you will see that my purpose now is selfless... that I only wish to serve you and him."

She stooped and placed the folded paper in the midst of a great clump of centifolium roses, and then without another word she turned and went her way. For a few moments, whilst Marguerite still stood there, puzzled and vaguely moved, she could hear the gentle frou-frou of the other woman's skirts against the soft sand of the path, and then a long-drawn sigh that sounded like a sob.

Then all was still again. The gentle midnight breeze caressed the tops of the ancient oaks and elms behind her, drawing murmurs from their dying leaves like unto the whisperings of ghosts.

Marguerite shuddered with a slight sense of cold. Before her, amongst the dark clump of leaves and the roses, invisible in the gloom, there fluttered with a curious, melancholy flapping, the folded paper placed there by Candeille. She watched it for awhile, as, disturbed by the wind, it seemed ready to take its flight towards the river. Anon it fell to the ground, and Marguerite with sudden overpowering impulse, stooped and picked it up. Then clutching it nervously in her hand, she walked rapidly back towards the house.

CHAPTER XV. FAREWELL

As she neared the terrace, she became conscious of several forms moving about at the foot of the steps, some few feet below where she was standing. Soon she saw the glimmer of lanthorns, heard whispering voices, and the lapping of the water against the side of a boat.

Anon a figure, laden with cloaks and sundry packages, passed down the steps close beside her. Even in the darkness Marguerite recognized Benyon, her husband's confidential valet. Without a moment's hesitation, she flew along the terrace towards the wing of the house occupied by Sir Percy. She had not gone far before she discerned his tall figure walking leisurely along the path which here skirted part of the house.

He had on his large caped coat, which was thrown open in front, displaying a grey travelling suit of fine cloth; his hands were as usual buried in the pockets of his breeches, and on his head he wore the folding chapeau-bras which he habitually affected.

Before she had time to think, or to realize that he was going, before she could utter one single word, she was in his arms, clinging to him with passionate intensity, trying in the gloom to catch every expression of his eyes, every quiver of the face now bent down so close to her.

"Percy, you cannot go... you cannot go!..." she pleaded.

She had felt his strong arms closing round her, his lips seeking hers, her eyes, her hair, her clinging hands, which dragged at his shoulders in a wild agony of despair.

"If you really loved me, Percy," she murmured, "you would not go, you would not go..."

He would not trust himself to speak; it well-nigh seemed as if his sinews cracked with the violent effort at self-control. Oh! how she loved him, when she felt in him the passionate lover, the wild, untamed creature that he was at heart, on whom the frigid courtliness of manner sat but as a thin veneer. This was his own real personality, and there was little now of the elegant and accomplished gentleman of fashion, schooled to hold every emotion in check, to hide every thought, every desire save that for amusement or for display.

She—feeling her power and his weakness now—gave herself wholly to his embrace, not grudging one single, passionate caress, yielding her lips to him, the while she murmured:

"You cannot go... you cannot... why should you go?... It is madness to leave me... I cannot let you go..."

Her arms clung tenderly round him, her voice was warm and faintly shaken with suppressed tears, and as he wildly murmured: "Don't! for pity's sake!" she almost felt that her love would be triumphant.

"For pity's sake, I'll go on pleading, Percy!" she whispered. "Oh! my love, my dear! do not leave me!... we have scarce had time to savour our happiness.. we have such arrears of joy to make up.... Do not go, Percy... there's so much I want to say to you.... Nay! you shall not! you shall not!" she added with sudden vehemence. "Look me straight in the eyes, my dear, and tell me if you can leave now?"

He did not reply, but, almost roughly, he placed his hand over her tear-dimmed eyes, which were turned up to his, in an agony of tender appeal. Thus he blindfolded her with that wild caress. She should not see—no, not even she!—that for the space of a few seconds stern manhood was well-nigh vanquished by the magic of her love.

All that was most human in him, all that was weak in this strong and untamed nature, cried aloud for peace and luxury and idleness: for long summer afternoons spent in lazy content, for the companionship of horses and dogs and of flowers, with no thought or cares save those for the next evening's gavotte, no graver occupation save that of sitting at HER feet.

And during these few seconds, whilst his hand lay across her eyes, the lazy, idle fop of fashionable London was fighting a hand-to-hand fight with the bold leader of a band of adventurers: and his own passionate love for his wife ranged itself with fervent intensity on the side of his weaker self. Forgotten were the horrors of the guillotine, the calls of the innocent, the appeal of the helpless; forgotten the daring adventures, the excitements, the hair's-breadth escapes; for those few seconds, heavenly in themselves, he only remembered her—his wife—her beauty and her tender appeal to him.

She would have pleaded again, for she felt that she was winning in this fight: her instinct—that unerring instinct of the woman who loves and feels herself beloved—told her that for the space of an infinitesimal fraction of time, his iron will was inclined to bend; but he checked her pleading with a kiss.

Then there came a change.

Like a gigantic wave carried inwards by the tide, his turbulent emotion seemed suddenly to shatter itself against a rock of self-control. Was it a call from the boatmen below? a distant scrunching of feet upon the gravel?—who knows, perhaps only a sigh in the midnight air, a ghostly summons from the land of dreams that recalled him to himself.

Even as Marguerite was still clinging to him, with the ardent fervour of her own passion, she felt the rigid tension of his arms relax, the power of his embrace weaken, the wild love-light become dim in his eyes.

He kissed her fondly, tenderly, and with infinite gentleness smoothed away the little damp curls from her brow. There was a wistfulness now in his caress, and in his kiss there was the finality of a long farewell.

"'Tis time I went," he said, "or we shall miss the tide."

These were the first coherent words he had spoken since first she had met him here in this lonely part of the garden, and his voice was perfectly steady, conventional and cold. An icy pang shot through Marguerite's heart. It was as if she had been abruptly wakened from a beautiful dream.

"You are not going, Percy!" she murmured, and her own voice now sounded hollow and forced. "Oh! if you loved me you would not go!"

"If I love you!"

Nay! in this at least there was no dream! no coldness in his voice when he repeated those words with such a sigh of tenderness, such a world of longing, that the bitterness of her great pain vanished, giving place to tears. He took her hand in his. The passion was momentarily conquered, forced within his innermost soul, by his own alter ego, that second personality in him, the cold-blooded and coolly-calculating adventurer who juggled with his life and tossed it recklessly upon the sea of chance 'twixt a doggerel and a smile. But the tender love lingered on, fighting the enemy a while longer, the wistful desire was there for her kiss, the tired longing for the exquisite repose of her embrace.

He took her hand in his, and bent his lips to it, and with the warmth of his kiss upon it, she felt a moisture like a tear.

"I must go, dear," he said, after a little while.

"Why? Why?" she repeated obstinately. "Am I nothing then? Is my life of no account? My sorrows? My fears? My misery? Oh!" she added with vehement bitterness, "why should it always be others? What are others to you and to me, Percy?... Are we not happy here?... Have you not fulfilled to its uttermost that self-imposed duty to people who can be nothing to us?... Is not your life ten thousand times more precious to me than the lives of ten thousand others?"

Even through the darkness, and because his face was so close to hers, she could see a quaint little smile playing round the corners of his mouth.

"Nay, m'dear," he said gently, "'tis not ten thousand lives that call to me to-day... only one at best.... Don't you hate to think of that poor little old cure sitting in the midst of his ruined pride and hopes: the jewels so confidently entrusted to his care, stolen from him, he waiting, perhaps, in his little presbytery for the day when those brutes will march him to prison and to death.... Nay! I think a little sea voyage and English country air would suit the Abbe Foucquet, m'dear, and I only mean to ask him to cross the Channel with me!..."

"Percy!" she pleaded.

"Oh! I know! I know!" he rejoined with that short deprecatory sigh of his, which seemed always to close any discussion between them on that point, "you are thinking of that absurd duel..." He laughed lightly, good-humouredly, and his eyes gleamed with merriment.

"La, m'dear!" he said gaily, "will you not reflect a moment? Could I refuse the challenge before His Royal Highness and the ladies? I couldn't. ... Faith! that was it.... Just a case of couldn't.... Fate did it all... the quarrel... my interference... the challenge.... HE had planned it all of course.... Let us own that he is a brave man, seeing that he and I are not even yet, for that beating he gave me on the Calais cliffs."

"Yes! he has planned it all," she retorted vehemently. "The quarrel to-night, your journey to France, your meeting with him face to face at a given hour and place where he can most readily, most easily close the death-trap upon you."

This time he broke into a laugh. A good, hearty laugh, full of the joy of living, of the madness and intoxication of a bold adventure, a laugh that had not one particle of anxiety or of tremor in it.

"Nay! m'dear!" he said, "but your ladyship is astonishing.... Close a death-trap upon your humble servant?... Nay! the governing citizens of France will have to be very active and mighty wide-awake ere they succeed in stealing a march on me.... Zounds! but we'll give them an exciting chase this time.... Nay! little woman, do not fear!" he said with sudden infinite gentleness, "those demmed murderers have not got me yet."

Oh! how often she had fought with him thus: with him, the adventurer, the part of his dual nature that was her bitter enemy, and which took him, the lover, away from her side. She knew so well the finality of it all, the amazing hold which that unconquerable desire for these mad adventures had upon him. Impulsive, ardent as she was, Marguerite felt in her very soul an overwhelming fury against herself for her own weakness, her own powerlessness in the face of that which forever threatened to ruin her life and her happiness.

Yes! and his also! for he loved her! he loved her! he loved her! the thought went on hammering in her mind, for she knew of its great truth! He loved her and went away! And she, poor, puny weakling, was unable to hold him back; the tendrils which fastened his soul to hers were not so tenacious as those which made him cling to suffering humanity, over there in France, where men and women were in fear of death and torture, and looked upon the elusive and mysterious Scarlet Pimpernel as a heaven-born hero sent to save them from their doom. To them at these times his very heartstrings seemed to turn with unconquerable force, and when, with all the ardour of her own passion, she tried to play upon the cords of his love for her, he could not respond, for they—the strangers—had the stronger claim.

And yet through it all she knew that this love of humanity, this mad desire to serve and to help, in no way detracted from his love for her. Nay, it intensified it, made it purer and better, adding to the joy of perfect intercourse the poetic and subtle fragrance of ever-recurring pain.

But now at last she felt weary of the fight: her heart was aching, bruised and sore. An infinite fatigue seemed to weigh like lead upon her very soul. This seemed so different to any other parting, that had perforce been during the past year. The presence of Chauvelin in her house, the obvious planning of this departure for France, had filled her with a foreboding, nay, almost a certitude of a gigantic and deadly cataclysm.

Her senses began to reel; she seemed not to see anything very distinctly: even the loved form took on a strange and ghostlike shape. He now looked preternaturally tall, and there was a mist between her and him.

She thought that he spoke to her again, but she was not quite sure, for his voice sounded like some weird and mysterious echo. A bosquet of climbing heliotrope close by threw a fragrance into the evening air, which turned her giddy with its overpowering sweetness.

She closed her eyes, for she felt as if she must die, if she held them open any longer; and as she closed them it seemed to her as if he folded her in one last, long, heavenly embrace.

He felt her graceful figure swaying in his arms like a tall and slender lily bending to the wind. He saw that she was but half-conscious, and thanked heaven for this kindly solace to his heart-breaking farewell.

There was a sloping, mossy bank close by, there where the marble terrace yielded to the encroaching shrubbery: a tangle of pale pink monthly roses made a bower overhead. She was just sufficiently conscious to enable him to lead her to this soft green couch. There he laid her amongst the roses, kissed the dear, tired eyes, her hands, her lips, her tiny feet, and went.

CHAPTER XVI. THE PASSPORT

The rhythmic clapper of oars roused Marguerite from this trance-like swoon.

In a moment she was on her feet, all her fatigue gone, her numbness of soul and body vanished as in a flash. She was fully conscious now! conscious that he had gone! that according to every probability under heaven and every machination concocted in hell, he would never return from France alive, and that she had failed to hear the last words which he spoke to her, had failed to glean his last look or to savour his final kiss.

Though the night was starlit and balmy it was singularly dark, and vainly did Marguerite strain her eyes to catch sight of that boat which was bearing him away so swiftly now: she strained her ears, vaguely hoping to catch one last, lingering echo of his voice. But all was silence, save that monotonous clapper, which seemed to beat against her heart like a rhythmic knell of death.

She could hear the oars distinctly: there were six or eight, she thought: certainly no fewer. Eight oarsmen probably, which meant the larger boat, and undoubtedly the longer journey... not to London only with a view to posting to Dover, but to Tilbury Fort, where the "Day Dream" would be in readiness to start with a favourable tide.

Thought was returning to her, slowly and coherently: the pain of the last farewell was still there, bruising her very senses with its dull and heavy weight, but it had become numb and dead, leaving her, herself, her heart and soul, stunned and apathetic, whilst her brain was gradually resuming its activity.

And the more she thought it over, the more certain she grew that her husband was going as far as Tilbury by river and would embark on the "Day Dream" there. Of course he would go to Boulogne at once. The duel was to take place there, Candeille had told her that... adding that she thought she, Marguerite, would wish to go with him.

To go with him!

Heavens above! was not that the only real, tangible thought in that whirling chaos which was raging in her mind?

To go with him! Surely there must be some means of reaching him yet! Fate, Nature, God Himself would never permit so monstrous a thing as this: that she should be parted from her husband, now when his life was not only in danger, but forfeited already... lost... a precious thing all but gone from this world.

Percy was going to Boulogne... she must go too. By posting at once to Dover, she could get the tidal boat on the morrow and reach the French coast quite as soon as the "Day Dream." Once at Boulogne, she would have no difficulty in finding her husband, of that she felt sure. She would have but to dog Chauvelin's footsteps, find out something of his plans, of the orders he gave to troops or to spies,—oh! she would find him! of that she was never for a moment in doubt!

How well she remembered her journey to Calais just a year ago, in company with Sir Andrew Ffoulkes! Chance had favoured her then, had enabled her to be of service to her husband if only by distracting Chauvelin's attention for awhile to herself. Heaven knows! she had but little hope of being of use to him now: an aching sense was in her that fate had at last been too strong! that the daring adventurer had staked once too often, had cast the die and had lost.

In the bosom of her dress she felt the sharp edge of the paper left for her by Desiree Candeille among the roses in the park. She had picked it up almost mechanically then, and tucked it away, hardly heeding what she was doing. Whatever the motive of the French actress had been in placing the passport at her disposal, Marguerite blessed her in her heart for it. To the woman she had mistrusted, she would owe the last supreme happiness of her life.

Her resolution never once wavered. Percy would not take her with him: that was understandable. She could neither expect it nor think it. But she, on the other hand, could not stay in England, at Blakeney Manor, whilst any day, any hour, the death-trap set by Chauvelin for the Scarlet Pimpernel might be closing upon the man whom she worshipped. She would go mad if she stayed. As there could be no chance of escape for Percy now, as he had agreed to meet his deadly enemy face to face at a given place, and a given hour, she could not be a hindrance to him: and she knew enough subterfuge, enough machinations and disguises by now, to escape Chauvelin's observation, unless... unless Percy wanted her, and then she would be there.

No! she could not be a hindrance. She had a passport in her pocket, everything en regle, nobody could harm her, and she could come and go as she pleased. There were plenty of swift horses in the stables, plenty of devoted servants to do her bidding quickly and discreetly: moreover, at moments like these, conventionalities and the possible conjectures and surmises of others became of infinitesimally small importance. The household of Blakeney Manor were accustomed to the master's sudden journeys and absences of several days, presumably on some shooting or other sporting expeditions, with no one in attendance on him, save Benyon, his favourite valet. These passed without any comments now! Bah! let everyone marvel for once at her ladyship's sudden desire to go to Dover, and let it all be a nine days' wonder; she certainly did not care. Skirting the house, she reached the stables beyond. One or two men were astir. To these she gave the necessary orders for her coach and four, then she found her way back to the house.

Walking along the corridor, she went past the room occupied by Juliette de Marny. For a moment she hesitated, then she turned and knocked at the door.

Juliette was not yet in bed, for she went to the door herself and opened it. Obviously she had been quite unable to rest, her hair was falling loosely over her shoulders, and there was a look of grave anxiety on her young face.

"Juliette," said Marguerite in a hurried whisper, the moment she had closed the door behind her and she and the young girl were alone, "I am going to France to be near my husband. He has gone to meet that fiend in a duel which is nothing but a trap, set to capture him, and lead him to his death. I want you to be of help to me, here in my house, in my absence."

"I would give my life for you, Lady Blakeney," said Juliette simply, "is it not HIS since he saved it?"

"It is only a little presence of mind, a little coolness and patience, which I will ask of you, dear," said Marguerite. "You of course know who your rescuer was, therefore you will understand my fears. Until to-night, I had vague doubts as to how much Chauvelin really knew, but now these doubts have naturally vanished. He and the French Revolutionary Government know that the Scarlet Pimpernel and Percy Blakeney are one and the same. The whole scene to-night was prearranged: you and I and all the spectators, and that woman Candeille—we were all puppets piping to that devil's tune. The duel, too, was prearranged!... that woman wearing your mother's jewels!... Had you not provoked her, a quarrel between her and me, or one of my guests would have been forced somehow... I wanted to tell you this, lest you should fret, and think that you were in any way responsible for what has happened.... You were not.... He had arranged it all.... You were only the tool... just as I was. ... You must understand and believe that.... Percy would hate to think that you felt yourself to blame... you are not that, in any way.... The challenge was bound to come.... Chauvelin had arranged that it should come, and if you had failed him as a tool, he soon would have found another! Do you believe that?"

"I believe that you are an angel of goodness, Lady Blakeney," replied Juliette, struggling with her tears, "and that you are the only woman in the world worthy to be his wife."

"But," insisted Marguerite firmly, as the young girl took her cold hand in her own, and gently fondling it, covered it with grateful kisses, "but if... if anything happens... anon... you will believe firmly that you were in no way responsible?... that you were innocent.. and merely a blind tool?..."

"God bless you for that!"

"You will believe it?"

"I will."

"And now for my request," rejoined Lady Blakeney in a more quiet, more matter-of-fact tone of voice. "You must represent me, here, when I am gone: explain as casually and as naturally as you can, that I have gone to join my husband on his yacht for a few days. Lucie, my maid, is devoted and a tower of secrecy; she will stand between you and the rest of the household, in concocting some plausible story. To every friend who calls, to anyone of our world whom you may meet, you must tell the same tale, and if you note an air of incredulity in anyone, if you hear whispers of there being some mystery, well! let the world wag its busy tongue—I care less than naught: it will soon tire of me and my doings, and having torn my reputation to shreds will quickly leave me in peace. But to Sir Andrew Ffoulkes," she added earnestly, "tell the whole truth from me. He will understand and do as he thinks right."

"I will do all you ask, Lady Blakeney, and am proud to think that I shall be serving you, even in so humble and easy a capacity. When do you start?"

"At once. Good-bye, Juliette."

She bent down to the young girl and kissed her tenderly on the forehead, then she glided out of the room as rapidly as she had come. Juliette, of course, did not try to detain her, or to force her help of companionship on her when obviously she would wish to be alone.

Marguerite quickly reached her room. Her maid Lucie was already waiting for her. Devoted and silent as she was, one glance at her mistress' face told her that trouble—grave and imminent—had reached Blakeney Manor.

Marguerite, whilst Lucie undressed her, took up the passport and carefully perused the personal description of one, Celine Dumont, maid to Citizeness Desiree Candeille, which was given therein: tall, blue eyes, light hair, age about twenty-five. It all might have been vaguely meant for her. She had a dark cloth gown, and long black cloak with hood to come well over the head. These she now donned, with some thick shoes, and a dark-coloured handkerchief tied over her head under the hood, so as to hide the golden glory of her hair.

She was quite calm and in no haste. She made Lucie pack a small hand valise with some necessaries for the journey, and provided herself plentifully with money—French and English notes—which she tucked well away inside her dress.

Then she bade her maid, who was struggling with her tears, a kindly farewell, and quickly went down to her coach.

CHAPTER XVII. BOULOGNE

During the journey Marguerite had not much leisure to think. The discomforts and petty miseries incidental on cheap travelling had the very welcome effect of making her forget, for the time being, the soul-rendering crisis through which she was now passing.

For, of necessity, she had to travel at the cheap rate, among the crowd of poorer passengers who were herded aft the packet boat, leaning up against one another, sitting on bundles and packages of all kinds; that part of the deck, reeking with the smell of tar and sea-water, damp, squally and stuffy, was an abomination of hideous discomfort to the dainty, fastidious lady of fashion, yet she almost welcomed the intolerable propinquity, the cold douches of salt water, which every now and then wetted her through and through, for it was the consequent sense of physical wretchedness that helped her to forget the intolerable anguish of her mind.

And among these poorer travellers she felt secure from observation. No one took much notice of her. She looked just like one of the herd, and in the huddled-up little figure, in the dark bedraggled clothes, no one would for a moment have recognized the dazzling personality of Lady Blakeney.

Drawing her hood well over her head, she sat in a secluded corner of the deck, upon the little black valise which contained the few belongings she had brought with her. Her cloak and dress, now mud-stained and dank with splashings of salt-water, attracted no one's attention. There was a keen northeasterly breeze, cold and penetrating, but favourable to a rapid crossing. Marguerite, who had gone through several hours of weary travelling by coach, before she had embarked at Dover in the late afternoon, was unspeakably tired. She had watched the golden sunset out at sea until her eyes were burning with pain, and as the dazzling crimson and orange and purple gave place to the soft grey tones of evening, she descried the round cupola of the church of Our Lady of Boulogne against the dull background of the sky.

After that her mind became a blank. A sort of torpor fell over her sense: she was wakeful and yet half-asleep, unconscious of everything around her, seeing nothing but the distant massive towers of old Boulogne churches gradually detaching themselves one by one from out the fast gathering gloom.

The town seemed like a dream city, a creation of some morbid imagination, presented to her mind's eye as the city of sorrow and death.

When the boat finally scraped her sides along the rough wooden jetty, Marguerite felt as if she were forcibly awakened. She was numb and stiff and thought she must have fallen asleep during the last half hour of the journey. Everything round her was dark. The sky was overcast, and the night seemed unusually sombre. Figures were moving all around her, there was noise and confusion of voices, and a general pushing and shouting which seemed strangely weird in this gloom. Here among the poorer passengers, there had not been thought any necessity for a light, one solitary lantern fixed to a mast only enhanced the intense blackness of everything around. Now and then a face would come within range of this meagre streak of yellow light, looking strangely distorted, with great, elongated shadows across the brow and chin, a grotesque, ghostly apparition which quickly vanished again, scurrying off like some frightened gnome, giving place other forms, other figures all equally grotesque and equally weird.

Marguerite watched them all half stupidly and motionlessly for awhile. She did not quite know what she ought to do, and did not like to ask any questions: she was dazed and the darkness blinded her. Then gradually things began to detach themselves more clearly. On looking straight before her, she began to discern the landing place, the little wooden bridge across which the passengers walked one by one from the boat onto the jetty. The first-class passengers were evidently all alighting now: the crowd of which Marguerite formed a unit, had been pushed back in a more compact herd, out of the way for the moment, so that their betters might get along more comfortably.

Beyond the landing stage a little booth had been erected, a kind of tent, open in front and lighted up within by a couple of lanthorns. Under this tent there was a table, behind which sat a man dressed in some sort of official looking clothes, and wearing the tricolour scarf across his chest.

All the passengers from the boat had apparently to file past this tent. Marguerite could see them now quite distinctly, the profiles of the various faces, as they paused for a moment in front of the table, being brilliantly illuminated by one of the lanterns. Two sentinels wearing the uniform of the National Guard stood each side of the table. The passengers one by one took out their passport as they went by, handed it to the man in the official dress, who examined it carefully, very lengthily, then signed it and returned the paper to its owner: but at times, he appeared doubtful, folded the passport and put it down in front of him: the passenger would protest; Marguerite could not hear what was said, but she could see that some argument was attempted, quickly dismissed by a peremptory order from the official. The doubtful passport was obviously put on one side for further examination, and the unfortunate owner thereof detained, until he or she had been able to give more satisfactory references to the representatives of the Committee of Public Safety, stationed at Boulogne.

This process of examination necessarily took a long time. Marguerite was getting horribly tired, her feet ached and she scarcely could hold herself upright: yet she watched all these people mechanically, making absurd little guesses in her weary mind as to whose passport would find favour in the eyes of the official, and whose would be found suspect and inadequate.

Suspect! a terrible word these times! since Merlin's terrible law decreed now that every man, woman or child, who was suspected by the Republic of being a traitor was a traitor in fact.

How sorry she felt for those whose passports were detained: who tried to argue—so needlessly!—and who were finally led off by a soldier, who had stepped out from somewhere in the dark, and had to await further examination, probably imprisonment and often death.

As to herself, she felt quite safe: the passport given to her by Chauvelin's own accomplice was sure to be quite en regle.

Then suddenly her heart seemed to give a sudden leap and then to stop in its beating for a second or two. In one of the passengers, a man who was just passing in front of the tent, she had recognized the form and profile of Chauvelin.

He had no passport to show, but evidently the official knew who he was, for he stood up and saluted, and listened deferentially whilst the ex-ambassador apparently gave him a few instructions. It seemed to Marguerite that these instructions related to two women who were close behind Chauvelin at the time, and who presently seemed to file past without going through the usual formalities of showing their passports. But of this she could not be quite sure. The women were closely hooded and veiled and her own attention had been completely absorbed by this sudden appearance of her deadly enemy.

Yet what more natural than that Chauvelin should be here now? His object accomplished, he had no doubt posted to Dover, just as she had done. There was no difficulty in that, and a man of his type and importance would always have unlimited means and money at his command to accomplish any journey he might desire to undertake.

There was nothing strange or even unexpected in the man's presence here; and yet somehow it had made the whole, awful reality more tangible, more wholly unforgettable. Marguerite remembered his abject words to her, when first she had seen him at the Richmond fete: he said that he had fallen into disgrace, that, having failed in his service to the Republic, he had been relegated to a subordinate position, pushed aside with contumely to make room for better, abler men.

Well! all that was a lie, of course, a cunning method of gaining access into her house; of that she had already been convinced, when Candeille provoked the esclandre which led to the challenge.

That on French soil he seemed in anything but a subsidiary position, that he appeared to rule rather than to obey, could in no way appear to Marguerite in the nature of surprise.

As the actress had been a willing tool in the cunning hands of Chauvelin, so were probably all these people around her. Where others cringed in the face of officialism, the ex-ambassador had stepped forth as a master: he had shown a badge, spoken a word mayhap, and the man in the tent who had made other people tremble, stood up deferentially and obeyed all commands.

It was all very simple and very obvious: but Marguerite's mind had been asleep, and it was the sight of the sable-clad little figure which had roused it from its happy torpor.

In a moment now her brain was active and alert, and presently it seemed to her as if another figure—taller than those around—had crossed the barrier immediately in the wake of Chauvelin. Then she chided herself for her fancies!

It could not be her husband. Not yet! He had gone by water, and would scarce be in Boulogne before the morning!

Ah! now at last came the turn of the second-class passengers! There was a general bousculade and the human bundle began to move. Marguerite lost sight of the tent and its awe-inspiring appurtenances: she was a mere unit again in this herd on the move. She too progressed along slowly, one step at a time; it was wearisome and she was deadly tired. She was beginning to form plans now that she had arrived in France. All along she had made up her mind that she would begin by seeking out the Abbe Foucquet, for he would prove a link 'twixt her husband and herself. She knew that Percy would communicate with the abbe; had he not told her that the rescue of the devoted old man from the clutches of the Terrorists would be one of the chief objects of his journey? It had never occurred to her what she would do if she found the Abbe Foucquet gone from Boulogne.

"He! la mere! your passport!"

The rough words roused her from her meditations. She had moved forward, quite mechanically, her mind elsewhere, her thoughts not following the aim of her feet. Thus she must have crossed the bridge along with some of the crowd, must have landed on the jetty, and reached the front of the tent, without really knowing what she was doing.

Ah yes! her passport! She had quite forgotten that! But she had it by her, quite in order, given to her in a fit of tardy remorse by Demoiselle Candeille, the intimate friend of one of the most influential members of the Revolutionary Government of France.

She took the passport from the bosom of her dress and handed it to the man in the official dress.

"Your name?" he asked peremptorily.

"Celine Dumont," she replied unhesitatingly, for had she not rehearsed all this in her mind dozens of times, until her tongue could rattle off the borrowed name as easily as it could her own; "servitor to Citizeness Desiree Candeille!"

The man who had very carefully been examining the paper the while, placed it down on the table deliberately in front of him, and said:

"Celine Dumont! Eh! la mere! what tricks are you up to now?"

"Tricks? I don't understand!" she said quietly, for she was not afraid. The passport was en regle: she knew she had nothing to fear.

"Oh! but I think you do!" retorted the official with a sneer, "and 'tis a mighty clever one, I'll allow. Celine Dumont, ma foi! Not badly imagined, ma petite mere: and all would have passed off splendidly; unfortunately, Celine Dumont, servitor to Citizeness Desiree Candeille, passed through these barriers along with her mistress not half an hour ago."

And with long, grimy finger he pointed to an entry in the large book which lay open before him, and wherein he had apparently been busy making notes of the various passengers who had filed past him.

Then he looked up with a triumphant leer at the calm face of Marguerite. She still did not feel really frightened, only puzzled and perturbed; but all the blood had rushed away from her face, leaving her cheeks ashen white, and pressing against her heart, until it almost choked her.

"You are making a mistake, Citizen," she said very quietly. "I am Citizeness Candeille's maid. She gave me the passport herself, just before I left for England; if you will ask her the question, she will confirm what I say, and she assured me that it was quite en regle."

But the man only shrugged his shoulders and laughed derisively. The incident evidently amused him, yet he must have seen many of the same sort; in the far corner of the tent Marguerite seemed to discern a few moving forms, soldiers, she thought, for she caught sight of a glint like that of steel. One or two men stood close behind the official at the desk, and the sentinels were to the right and left of the tent.

With an instinctive sense of appeal, Marguerite looked round from one face to the other: but each looked absolutely impassive and stolid, quite uninterested in this little scene, the exact counterpart of a dozen others, enacted on this very spot within the last hour.

"He! la! la! petite mere!" said the official in the same tone of easy persiflage which he had adopted all along, "but we do know how to concoct a pretty lie, aye! and so circumstantially too! Unfortunately it was Citizeness Desiree Candeille herself who happened to be standing just where you are at the present moment, along with her maid, Celine Dumont, both of whom were specially signed for and recommended as perfectly trustworthy, by no less a person than Citoyen Chauvelin of the Committee of Public Safety."

"But I assure you that there is a mistake," pleaded Marguerite earnestly, "'Tis the other woman who lied, I have my passport and…"

"A truce on this," retorted the man peremptorily. "If everything is as you say, and if you have nothing to hide, you'll be at liberty to continue your journey to-morrow, after you have explained yourself before the citizen governor. Next one now, quick!"

Marguerite tried another protest, just as those others had done, whom she had watched so mechanically before. But already she knew that that would be useless, for she had felt that a heavy hand was being placed on her shoulder, and that she was being roughly led away.

In a flash she had understood and seen the whole sequel of the awful trap which had all along been destined to engulf her as well as her husband.

What a clumsy, blind fool she had been!

What a miserable antagonist the subtle schemes of a past master of intrigue as was Chauvelin. To have enticed the Scarlet Pimpernel to France was a great thing! The challenge was clever, the acceptance of it by the bold adventurer a forgone conclusion, but the master stroke of the whole plan was done, when she, the wife, was enticed over too with the story of Candeille's remorse and the offer of the passport.

Fool! fool that she was!

And how well did Chauvelin know feminine nature! How cleverly he had divined her thoughts, her feelings, the impulsive way in which she would act; how easily he had guessed that, knowing her husband's danger, she, Marguerite, would immediately follow him.

Now the trap had closed on her—and she saw it all, when it was too late.

Percy Blakeney in France! His wife a prisoner! Her freedom and safety in exchange for his life!

The hopelessness of it all struck her with appalling force, and her senses reeled with the awful finality of the disaster.

Yet instinct in her still struggled for freedom. Ahead of her, and all around, beyond the tent and in the far distance there was a provocative alluring darkness: if she only could get away, only could reach the shelter of that remote and sombre distance, she would hide, and wait, not blunder again, oh no! she would be prudent and wary, if only she could get away!

One woman's struggles, against five men! It was pitiable, sublime, absolutely useless.

The man in the tent seemed to be watching her with much amusement for a moment or two, as her whole graceful body stiffened for that absurd and unequal physical contest. He seemed vastly entertained at the sight of this good-looking young woman striving to pit her strength against five sturdy soldiers of the Republic.

"Allons! that will do now!" he said at last roughly. "We have no time to waste! Get the jade away, and let her cool her temper in No. 6, until the citizen governor gives further orders.

"Take her away!" he shouted more loudly, banging a grimy fist down on the table before him, as Marguerite still struggled on with the blind madness of despair. "Pardi! can none of you rid us of that turbulent baggage?"

The crowd behind were pushing forward: the guard within the tent were jeering at those who were striving to drag Marguerite away: these latter were cursing loudly and volubly, until one of them, tired out, furious and brutal, raised his heavy fist and with an obscene oath brought it crashing down upon the unfortunate woman's head.

Perhaps, though it was the work of a savage and cruel creature, the blow proved more merciful than it had been intended: it had caught Marguerite full between the eyes; her aching senses, wearied and reeling already, gave way beneath this terrible violence; her useless struggles ceased, her arms fell inert by her side: and losing consciousness completely, her proud, unbendable spirit was spared the humiliating knowledge of her final removal by the rough soldiers, and of the complete wreckage of her last, lingering hopes.

CHAPTER XVIII. NO. 6

Consciousness returned very slowly, very painfully.

It was night when last Marguerite had clearly known what was going on around her; it was daylight before she realized that she still lived, that she still knew and suffered.

Her head ached intolerably: that was the first conscious sensation which came to her; then she vaguely perceived a pale ray of sunshine, very hazy and narrow, which came from somewhere in front of her and struck her in the face. She kept her eyes tightly shut, for that filmy light caused her an increase of pain.

She seemed to be lying on her back, and her fingers wandering restlessly around felt a hard paillasse, beneath their touch, then a rough pillow, and her own cloak laid over her: thought had not yet returned, only the sensation of great suffering and of infinite fatigue.

Anon she ventured to open her eyes, and gradually one or two objects detached themselves from out the haze which still obscured her vision.

Firstly, the narrow aperture—scarcely a window—filled in with tiny squares of coarse, unwashed glass, through which the rays of the morning sun were making kindly efforts to penetrate, then the cloud of dust illumined by those same rays, and made up—so it seemed to the poor tired brain that strove to perceive—of myriads of abnormally large molecules, over-abundant, and over-active, for they appeared to be dancing a kind of wild saraband before Marguerite's aching eyes, advancing and retreating, forming themselves into groups and taking on funny shapes of weird masques and grotesque faces which grinned at the unconscious figure lying helpless on the rough paillasse.

Through and beyond them Marguerite gradually became aware of three walls of a narrow room, dank and grey, half covered with whitewash and half with greenish mildew! Yes! and there, opposite to her and immediately beneath that semblance of a window, was another paillasse, and on it something dark, that moved.

The words: "Liberte, Egalite, Fraternite ou la Mort!" stared out at her from somewhere beyond those active molecules of dust, but she also saw just above the other paillasse the vague outline of a dark crucifix.

It seemed a terrible effort to co-ordinate all these things, and to try and realize what the room was, and what the meaning of the paillasse, the narrow window and the stained walls, too much altogether for the aching head to take in save very slowly, very gradually.

Marguerite was content to wait and to let memory creep back as reluctantly as it would.

"Do you think, my child, you could drink a little of this now?"

It was a gentle, rather tremulous voice which struck upon her ear. She opened her eyes, and noticed that the dark something which had previously been on the opposite paillasse was no longer there, and that there appeared to be a presence close to her only vaguely defined, someone kindly and tender who had spoken to her in French, with that soft sing-song accent peculiar to the Normandy peasants, and who now seemed to be pressing something cool and soothing to her lips.

"They gave me this for you!" continued the tremulous voice close to her ear. "I think it would do you good, if you tried to take it."

A hand and arm was thrust underneath the rough pillow, causing her to raise her head a little. A glass was held to her lips and she drank.

The hand that held the glass was all wrinkled, brown and dry, and trembled slightly, but the arm which supported her head was firm and very kind.

"There! I am sure you feel better now. Close your eyes and try to go to sleep."

She did as she was bid, and was ready enough to close her eyes. It seemed to her presently as if something had been interposed between her aching head and that trying ray of white September sun.

Perhaps she slept peacefully for a little while after that, for though her head was still very painful, her mouth and throat felt less parched and dry. Through this sleep or semblance of sleep, she was conscious of the same pleasant voice softly droning Paters and Aves close to her ear.

Thus she lay, during the greater part of the day. Not quite fully conscious, not quite awake to the awful memories which anon would crowd upon her thick and fast.

From time to time the same kind and trembling hands would with gentle pressure force a little liquid food through her unwilling lips: some warm soup, or anon a glass of milk. Beyond the pain in her head, she was conscious of no physical ill; she felt at perfect peace, and an extraordinary sense of quiet and repose seemed to pervade this small room, with its narrow window through which the rays of the sun came gradually in more golden splendour as the day drew towards noon, and then they vanished altogether.

The drony voice close beside her acted as a soporific upon her nerves. In the afternoon she fell into a real and beneficent sleep....

But after that, she woke to full consciousness!

Oh! the horror, the folly of it all!

It came back to her with all the inexorable force of an appalling certainty.

She was a prisoner in the hands of those who long ago had sworn to bring The Scarlet Pimpernel to death!

She! his wife, a hostage in their hands! her freedom and safety offered to him as the price of his own! Here there was no question of dreams or of nightmares: no illusions as to the ultimate intentions of her husband's enemies. It was all a reality, and even now, before she had the strength fully to grasp the whole nature of this horrible situation, she knew that by her own act of mad and passionate impulse, she had hopelessly jeopardized the life of the man she loved.

For with that sublime confidence in him begotten of her love, she never for a moment doubted which of the two alternatives he would choose, when once they were placed before him. He would sacrifice himself for her; he would prefer to die a thousand deaths so long as they set her free.

For herself, her own sufferings, her danger or humiliation she cared nothing! Nay! at this very moment she was conscious of a wild passionate desire for death.... In this sudden onrush of memory and of thought she wished with all her soul and heart and mind to die here suddenly, on this hard paillasse, in this lonely and dark prison... so that she should be out of the way once and for all... so that she should NOT be the hostage to be bartered against his precious life and freedom.

He would suffer acutely, terribly at her loss, because he loved her above everything else on earth, he would suffer in every fibre of his passionate and ardent nature, but he would not then have to endure the humiliations, the awful alternatives, the galling impotence and miserable death, the relentless "either—or" which his enemies were even now preparing for him.

And then came a revulsion of feeling. Marguerite's was essentially a buoyant and active nature, a keen brain which worked and schemed and planned, rather than one ready to accept the inevitable.

Hardly had these thoughts of despair and of death formulated themselves in her mind, than with brilliant swiftness, a new train of ideas began to take root.

What if matters were not so hopeless after all?

Already her mind had flown instinctively to thoughts of escape. Had she the right to despair? She, the wife and intimate companion of the man who had astonished the world with his daring, his prowess, his amazing good luck, she to imagine for a moment that in this all-supreme moment of adventurous life the Scarlet Pimpernel would fail!

Was not English society peopled with men, women and children whom his ingenuity had rescued from plights quite as seemingly hopeless as her own, and would not all the resources of that inventive brain be brought to bear upon this rescue which touched him nearer and more deeply than any which he had attempted hitherto.

Now Marguerite was chiding herself for her doubts and for her fears. Already she remembered that amongst the crowd on the landing stage she had perceived a figure—unusually tall—following in the wake of Chauvelin and his companions. Awakened hope had already assured her that she had not been mistaken, that Percy, contrary to her own surmises, had reached Boulogne last night: he always acted so differently to what anyone might expect, that it was quite possible that he had crossed over in the packet-boat after all unbeknown to Marguerite as well as to his enemies.

Oh yes! the more she thought about it all, the more sure was she that Percy was already in Boulogne, and that he knew of her capture and her danger.

What right had she to doubt even for a moment that he would know how to reach her, how—when the time came—to save himself and her?

A warm glow began to fill her veins, she felt excited and alert, absolutely unconscious now of pain or fatigue, in this radiant joy of reawakened hope.

She raised herself slightly, leaning on her elbow: she was still very weak and the slight movement had made her giddy, but soon she would be strong and well... she must be strong and well and ready to do his bidding when the time for escape would have come.

"Ah! you are better, my child, I see..." said that quaint, tremulous voice again, with its soft sing-song accent, "but you must not be so venturesome, you know. The physician said that you had received a cruel blow. The brain has been rudely shaken... and you must lie quite still all to-day, or your poor little head will begin to ache again."

Marguerite turned to look at the speaker, and in spite of her excitement, of her sorrow and of her anxieties, she could not help smiling at the whimsical little figure which sat opposite to her, on a very rickety chair, solemnly striving with slow and measured movement of hand and arm, and a large supply of breath, to get up a polish on the worn-out surface of an ancient pair of buckled shoes.

The figure was slender and almost wizened, the thin shoulders round with an habitual stoop, the lean shanks were encased in a pair of much-darned, coarse black stockings. It was the figure of an old man, with a gentle, clear-cut face furrowed by a forest of wrinkles, and surmounted by scanty white locks above a smooth forehead which looked yellow and polished like an ancient piece of ivory.

He had looked across at Marguerite as he spoke, and a pair of innately kind and mild blue eyes were fixed with tender reproach upon her. Marguerite thought that she had never seen quite so much goodness and simple-heartedness portrayed on any face before. It literally beamed out of those pale blue eyes, which seemed quite full of unshed tears.

The old man wore a tattered garment, a miracle of shining cleanliness, which had once been a soutane of smooth black cloth, but was now a mass of patches and threadbare at shoulders and knees. He seemed deeply intent in the task of polishing his shoes, and having delivered himself of his little admonition, he very solemnly and earnestly resumed his work.

Marguerite's first and most natural instinct had, of course, been one of dislike and mistrust of anyone who appeared to be in some way on guard over her. But when she took in every detail of the quaint figure of the old man, his scrupulous tidiness of apparel, the resigned stoop of his shoulders, and met in full the gaze of those moist eyes, she felt that the whole aspect of the man, as he sat there polishing his shoes, was infinitely pathetic and, in its simplicity, commanding of respect.

"Who are you?" asked Lady Blakeney at last, for the old man after looking at her with a kind of appealing wonder, seemed to be waiting for her to speak.

"A priest of the good God, my dear child," replied the old man with a deep sigh and a shake of his scanty locks, "who is not allowed to serve his divine Master any longer. A poor old fellow, very harmless and very helpless, who had been set here to watch over you.

"You must not look upon me as a jailer because of what I say, my child," he added with a quaint air of deference and apology. "I am very old and very small, and only take up a very little room. I can make myself very scarce; you shall hardly know that I am here. They forced me to it much against my will.... But they are strong and I am weak, how could I deny them since they put me here. After all," he concluded naively, "perhaps it is the will of le bon Dieu, and He knows best, my child, He knows best."

The shoes evidently refused to respond any further to the old man's efforts at polishing them. He contemplated them now, with a whimsical look of regret on his furrowed face, then set them down on the floor and slipped his stockinged feet into them.

Marguerite was silently watching him, still leaning on her elbow. Evidently her brain was still numb and fatigued, for she did not seem able to grasp all that the old man said. She smiled to herself too as she watched him. How could she look upon him as a jailer? He did not seem at all like a Jacobin or a Terrorist, there was nothing of the dissatisfied democrat, of the snarling anarchist ready to lend his hand to any act of ferocity directed against a so-called aristocrat, about this pathetic little figure in the ragged soutane and worn shoes.

He seemed singularly bashful too and ill at ease, and loath to meet Marguerite's great, ardent eyes, which were fixed questioningly upon him.

"You must forgive me, my daughter," he said shyly, "for concluding my toilet before you. I had hoped to be quite ready before you woke, but I had some trouble with my shoes; except for a little water and soap the prison authorities will not provide us poor captives with any means of cleanliness and tidiness, and le bon Dieu does love a tidy body as well as a clean soul.

"But there, there," he added fussily, "I must not continue to gossip like this. You would like to get up, I know, and refresh your face and hands with a little water. Oh! you will see how well I have thought it out. I need not interfere with you at all, and when you make your little bit of toilette, you will feel quite alone... just as if the old man was not there."

He began busying himself about the room, dragging the rickety, rush-bottomed chairs forward. There were four of these in the room, and he began forming a kind of bulwark with them, placing two side by side, then piling the two others up above.

"You will see, my child, you will see!" he kept repeating at intervals as the work of construction progressed. It was no easy matter, for he was of low stature, and his hands were unsteady from apparently uncontrollable nervousness.

Marguerite, leaning slightly forward, her chin resting in her hand, was too puzzled and anxious to grasp the humour of this comical situation. She certainly did not understand. This old man had in some sort of way, and for a hitherto unexplained reason, been set as a guard over her; it was not an unusual device on the part of the inhuman wretches who now ruled France, to add to the miseries and terrors of captivity, where a woman of refinement was concerned, the galling outrage of never leaving her alone for a moment.

That peculiar form of mental torture, surely the invention of brains rendered mad by their own ferocious cruelty, was even now being inflicted on the hapless, dethroned Queen of France. Marguerite, in far-off England, had shuddered when she heard of it, and in her heart had prayed, as indeed every pure-minded woman did then, that proud, unfortunate Marie Antoinette might soon find release from such torments in death.

There was evidently some similar intention with regard to Marguerite herself in the minds of those who now held her prisoner. But this old man seemed so feeble and so helpless, his very delicacy of thought as he built up a screen to divide the squalid room in two, proved him to be singularly inefficient for the task of a watchful jailer.

When the four chairs appeared fairly steady, and in comparatively little danger of toppling, he dragged the paillasse forward and propped it up against the chairs. Finally he drew the table along, which held the cracked ewer and basin, and placed it against this improvised partition: then he surveyed the whole construction with evident gratification and delight.

"There now!" he said, turning a face beaming with satisfaction to Marguerite, "I can continue my prayers on the other side of the fortress. Oh! it is quite safe..." he added, as with a fearsome hand he touched his engineering feat with gingerly pride, "and you will be quite private.... Try and forget that the old abbe is in the room.... He does not count... really he does not count... he has ceased to be of any moment these many months now that Saint Joseph is closed and he may no longer say Mass."

He was obviously prattling on in order to hide his nervous bashfulness. He ensconced himself behind his own finely constructed bulwark, drew a breviary from his pocket and having found a narrow ledge on one of the chairs, on which he could sit, without much danger of bringing the elaborate screen onto the top of his head, he soon became absorbed in his orisons.

Marguerite watched him for a little while longer: he was evidently endeavouring to make her think that he had become oblivious of her presence, and his transparent little manoeuvers amused and puzzled her not a little.

He looked so comical with his fussy and shy ways, yet withal so gentle and so kindly that she felt completely reassured and quite calm.

She tried to raise herself still further and found the process astonishingly easy. Her limbs still ached and the violent, intermittent pain in her head certainly made her feel sick and giddy at times, but otherwise she was not ill. She sat up on the paillasse, then put her feet to the ground and presently walked up to the improvised dressing-room and bathed her face and hands. The rest had done her good, and she felt quite capable of co-ordinating her thoughts, of moving about without too much pain, and of preparing herself both mentally and physically for the grave events which she knew must be imminent.

While she busied herself with her toilet her thoughts dwelt on the one all-absorbing theme: Percy was in Boulogne, he knew that she was here, in prison, he would reach her without fail, in fact he might communicate with her at any moment now, and had without a doubt already evolved a plan of escape for her, more daring and ingenious than any which he had conceived hitherto; therefore, she must be ready, and prepared for any eventuality, she must be strong and eager, in no way despondent, for if he were here, would he not chide her for her want of faith?

By the time she had smoothed her hair and tidied her dress, Marguerite caught herself singing quite cheerfully to herself.

So full of buoyant hope was she.

CHAPTER XIX. THE STRENGTH OF THE WEAK

"M. L'Abbe!..." said Marguerite gravely.

"Yes, mon enfant."

The old man looked up from his breviary, and saw Marguerite's great earnest eyes fixed with obvious calm and trust upon him. She had finished her toilet as well as she could, had shaken up and tidied the paillasse, and was now sitting on the edge of it, her hands clasped between her knees. There was something which still puzzled her, and impatient and impulsive as she was, she had watched the abbe as he calmly went on reading the Latin prayers for the last five minutes, and now she could contain her questionings no longer.

"You said just now that they set you to watch over me..."

"So they did, my child, so they did..." he replied with a sigh, as he quietly closed his book and slipped it back into his pocket. "Ah! they are very cunning... and we must remember that they have the power. No doubt," added the old man, with his own, quaint philosophy, "no doubt le bon Dieu meant them to have the power, or they would not have it, would they?"

"By 'they' you mean the Terrorists and Anarchists of France, M. L'Abbe.... The Committee of Public Safety who pillage and murder, outrage women, and desecrate religion.... Is that not so?"

"Alas! my child!" he sighed.

"And it is 'they' who have set you to watch over me?... I confess I don't understand..."

She laughed, quite involuntarily indeed, for in spite of the reassurance in her heart her brain was still in a whirl of passionate anxiety.

"You don't look at all like one of 'them,' M. l'Abbe," she said.

"The good God forbid!" ejaculated the old man, raising protesting hands up toward the very distant, quite invisible sky. "How could I, a humble priest of the Lord, range myself with those who would flout and defy Him."

"Yet I am a prisoner of the Republic and you are my jailer, M. l'Abbe."

"Ah, yes!" he sighed. "But I am very helpless. This was my cell. I had been here with Francois and Felicite, my sister's children, you know. Innocent lambs, whom those fiends would lead to slaughter. Last night," he continued, speaking volubly, "the soldiers came in and dragged Francois and Felicite out of this room, where, in spite of the danger before us, in spite of what we suffered, we had contrived to be quite happy together. I could read the Mass, and the dear children would say their prayers night and morning at my knee."

He paused awhile. The unshed tears in his mild blue eyes struggled for freedom now, and one or two flowed slowly down his wrinkled cheek. Marguerite, though heartsore and full of agonizing sorrow herself, felt her whole noble soul go out to this kind old man, so pathetic, so high and simple-minded in his grief.

She said nothing, however, and the Abbe continued after a few seconds' silence.

"When the children had gone, they brought you in here, mon enfant, and laid you on the paillasse where Felicite used to sleep. You looked very white, and stricken down, like one of God's lambs attacked by the ravening wolf. Your eyes were closed and you were blissfully unconscious. I was taken before the governor of the prison, and he told me that you would share the cell with me for a time, and that I was to watch you night and day, because..."

The old man paused again. Evidently what he had to say was very difficult to put into words. He groped in his pockets and brought out a large bandana handkerchief, red and yellow and green, with which he began to mop his moist forehead. The quaver in his voice and the trembling of his hands became more apparent and pronounced.

"Yes, M. l'Abbe? Because?..." queried Marguerite gently.

"They said that if I guarded you well, Felicite and Francois would be set free," replied the old man after a while, during which he made vigorous efforts to overcome his nervousness, "and that if you escaped the children and I would be guillotined the very next day."

There was silence in the little room now. The Abbe was sitting quite still, clasping his trembling fingers, and Marguerite neither moved nor spoke. What the old man had just said was very slowly finding its way to the innermost cells of her brain. Until her mind had thoroughly grasped the meaning of it all, she could not trust herself to make a single comment.

It was some seconds before she fully understood it all, before she realized what it meant not only to her, but indirectly to her husband. Until now she had not been fully conscious of the enormous wave of hope which almost in spite of herself had risen triumphant above the dull, grey sea of her former despair; only now when it had been shattered against this deadly rock of almost superhuman devilry and cunning did she understand what she had hoped, and what she must now completely forswear.

No bolts and bars, no fortified towers or inaccessible fortresses could prove so effectual a prison for Marguerite Blakeney as the dictum which morally bound her to her cell.

"If you escape the children and I would be guillotined the very next day."

This meant that even if Percy knew, even if he could reach her, he could never set her free, since her safety meant death to two innocent children and to this simple hearted man.

It would require more than the ingenuity of the Scarlet Pimpernel himself to untie this Gordian knot.

"I don't mind for myself, of course," the old man went on with gentle philosophy. "I have lived my life. What matters if I die to-morrow, or if I linger on until my earthly span is legitimately run out? I am ready to go home whenever my Father calls me. But it is the children, you see. I have to think of them. Francois is his mother's only son, the bread-winner of the household, a good lad and studious too, and Felicite has always been very delicate. She is blind from birth and..."

"Oh! don't... for pity's sake, don't..." moaned Marguerite in an agony of helplessness. "I understand... you need not fear for your children, M. l'Abbe: no harm shall come to them through me."

"It is as the good God wills!" replied the old man quietly.

Then, as Marguerite had once more relapsed into silence, he fumbled for his beads, and his gentle voice began droning the Paters and Aves wherein no doubt his child-like heart found peace and solace.

He understood that the poor woman would not wish to speak, he knew as well as she did the overpowering strength of his helpless appeal. Thus the minutes sped on, the jailer and the captive, tied to one another by the strongest bonds that hand of man could forge, had nothing to say to one another: he, the old priest, imbued with the traditions of his calling, could pray and resign himself to the will of the Almighty, but she was young and ardent and passionate, she loved and was beloved, and an impassable barrier was built up between her and the man she worshipped!

A barrier fashioned by the weak hands of children, one of whom was delicate and blind. Outside was air and freedom, reunion with her husband, an agony of happy remorse, a kiss from his dear lips, and trembling held her back from it all, because of Francois who was the bread-winner and of Felicite who was blind.

Mechanically now Marguerite rose again, and like an automaton—lifeless and thoughtless—she began putting the dingy, squalid room to rights. The Abbe helped her demolish the improvised screen; with the same gentle delicacy of thought which had caused him to build it up, he refrained from speaking to her now: he would not intrude himself on her grief and her despair.

Later on, she forced herself to speak again, and asked the old man his name.

"My name is Foucquet," he replied, "Jean Baptiste Marie Foucquet, late parish priest of the Church of Saint Joseph, the patron saint of Boulogne."

Foucquet! This was l'Abbe Foucquet! the faithful friend and servant of the de Marny family.

Marguerite gazed at him with great, questioning eyes.

What a wealth of memories crowded in on her mind at sound of that name! Her beautiful home at Richmond, her brilliant array of servants and guests, His Royal Highness at her side! life in free, joyous happy England—how infinitely remote it now seemed. Her ears were filled with the sound of a voice, drawly and quaint and gentle, a voice and a laugh half shy, wholly mirthful, and oh! so infinitely dear:

"I think a little sea voyage and English country air would suit the Abbe Foucquet, m'dear, and I only mean to ask him to cross the Channel with me..."

Oh! the joy and confidence expressed in those words! the daring, the ambition! the pride! and the soft, languorous air of the old-world garden round her then, the passion of his embrace! the heavy scent of late roses and of heliotrope, which caused her to swoon in his arms!

And now a narrow prison cell, and that pathetic, tender little creature there, with trembling hands and tear-dimmed eyes, the most powerful and most relentless jailer which the ferocious cunning of her deadly enemies could possibly have devised.

Then she talked to him of Juliette Marny.

The Abbe did not know that Mlle. de Marny had succeeded in reaching England safely and was overjoyed to hear it.

He recounted to Marguerite the story of the Marny jewels: how he had put them safely away in the crypt of his little church, until the Assembly of the Convention had ordered the closing of the churches, and placed before every minister of le bon Dieu the alternative of apostasy or death.

"With me it has only been prison so far," continued the old man simply, "but prison has rendered me just as helpless as the guillotine would have done, for the enemies of le bon Dieu have ransacked the Church of Saint Joseph and stolen the jewels which I should have guarded with my life."

But it was obvious joy for the Abbe to talk of Juliette Marny's happiness. Vaguely, in his remote little provincial cure, he had heard of the prowess and daring of the Scarlet Pimpernel and liked to think that Juliette owed her safety to him.

"The good God will reward him and those whom he cares for," added Abbe Foucquet with that earnest belief in divine interference which seemed so strangely pathetic under these present circumstances.

Marguerite sighed, and for the first time in this terrible soul-stirring crisis through which she was passing so bravely, she felt a beneficent moisture in her eyes: the awful tension of her nerves relaxed. She went up to the old man took his wrinkled hand in hers and falling on her knees beside him she eased her overburdened heart in a flood of tears.

CHAPTER XX. TRIUMPH

The day that Citizen Chauvelin's letter was received by the members of the Committee of Public Safety was indeed one of great rejoicing.

The Moniteur tells us that in the Seance of September 22nd, 1793, or Vendemiaire 1st of the Year I. it was decreed that sixty prisoners, not absolutely proved guilty of treason against the Republic—only suspected—were to be set free.

Sixty!... at the mere news of the possible capture of the Scarlet Pimpernel.

The Committee was inclined to be magnanimous. Ferocity yielded for the moment to the elusive joy of anticipatory triumph.

A glorious prize was about to fall into the hands of those who had the welfare of the people at heart.

Robespierre and his decemvirs rejoiced, and sixty persons had cause to rejoice with them. So be it! There were plans evolved already as to national fetes and wholesale pardons when that impudent and meddlesome Englishman at last got his deserts.

Wholesale pardons which could easily be rescinded afterwards. Even with those sixty it was a mere respite. Those of le Salut Public only loosened their hold for a while, were nobly magnanimous for a day, quite prepared to be doubly ferocious the next.

In the meanwhile let us heartily rejoice!

The Scarlet Pimpernel is in France or will be very soon, and on an appointed day he will present himself conveniently to the soldiers of the Republic for capture and for subsequent guillotine. England is at war with us, there is nothing therefore further to fear from her. We might hang every Englishman we can lay hands on, and England could do no more than she is doing at the present moment: bombard our ports, bluster and threaten, join hands with Flanders, and Austria and Sardinia, and the devil if she choose.

Allons! vogue la galere! The Scarlet Pimpernel is perhaps on our shores at this very moment! Our most stinging, most irritating foe is about to be delivered into our hands.

Citizen Chauvelin's letter is very categorical:

"I guarantee to you, Citizen Robespierre, and to the Members of the Revolutionary Government who have entrusted me with the delicate mission..."

Robespierre's sensuous lips curl into a sarcastic smile. Citizen Chauvelin's pen was ever florid in its style: "entrusted me with the delicate mission," is hardly the way to describe an order given under penalty of death.

But let it pass.

"... that four days from this date, at one hour after sunset, the man who goes by the mysterious name of the Scarlet Pimpernel will be on the southern ramparts of Boulogne, at the extreme southern corner of the town."

"Four days from this date..." and Citizen Chauvelin's letter is dated the nineteenth of September, 1793.

"Too much of an aristocrat—Monsieur le Marquis Chauvelin..." sneers Merlin, the Jacobin. "He does not know that all good citizens had called that date the 28th Fructidor, Year I. of the Republic."

"No matter," retorts Robespierre with impatient frigidity, "whatever we may call the day it was forty-eight hours ago, and in forty-eight hours more that damned Englishman will have run his head into a noose, from which, an I mistake not, he'll not find it easy to extricate himself."

"And you believe in Citizen Chauvelin's assertion," commented Danton with a lazy shrug of the shoulders.

"Only because he asks for help from us," quoth Robespierre drily; "he is sure that the man will be there, but not sure if he can tackle him."

But many were inclined to think that Chauvelin's letter was an idle boast. They knew nothing of the circumstances which had caused that letter to be written: they could not conjecture how it was that the ex-ambassador could be so precise in naming the day and hour when the enemy of France would be at the mercy of those whom he had outraged and flouted.

Nevertheless Citizen Chauvelin asks for help, and help must not be denied him. There must be no shadow of blame upon the actions of the Committee of Public Safety.

Chauvelin had been weak once, had allowed the prize to slip through his fingers; it must not occur again. He has a wonderful head for devising plans, but he needs a powerful hand to aid him, so that he may not fail again.

Collot d'Herbois, just home from Lyons and Tours, is the right man in an emergency like this. Citizen Collot is full of ideas; the inventor of the "Noyades" is sure to find a means of converting Boulogne into one gigantic prison out of which the mysterious English adventurer will find it impossible to escape.

And whilst the deliberations go on, whilst this committee of butchers are busy slaughtering in imagination the game they have not yet succeeded in bringing down, there comes another messenger from Citizen Chauvelin.

He must have ridden hard on the other one's heels, and something very unexpected and very sudden must have occurred to cause the Citizen to send this second note.

This time it is curt and to the point. Robespierre unfolds it and reads it to his colleagues.

"We have caught the woman—his wife—there may be murder attempted against my person, send me some one at once who will carry out my instructions in case of my sudden death."

Robespierre's lips curl in satisfaction, showing a row of yellowish teeth, long and sharp like the fangs of a wolf. A murmur like unto the snarl of a pack of hyenas rises round the table, as Chauvelin's letter is handed round.

Everyone has guessed the importance of this preliminary capture: "the woman—his wife." Chauvelin evidently thinks much of it, for he anticipates an attempt against his life, nay! he is quite prepared for it, ready to sacrifice it for the sake of his revenge.

Who had accused him of weakness?

He only thinks of his duty, not of his life; he does not fear for himself, only that the fruits of his skill might be jeopardized through assassination.

Well! this English adventurer is capable of any act of desperation to save his wife and himself, and Citizen Chauvelin must not be left in the lurch.

Thus, Citizen Collot d'Herbois is despatched forthwith to Boulogne to be a helpmeet and counsellor to Citizen Chauvelin.

Everything that can humanly be devised must be done to keep the woman secure and to set the trap for that elusive Pimpernel.

Once he is caught the whole of France shall rejoice, and Boulogne, who had been instrumental in running the quarry to earth, must be specially privileged on that day.

A general amnesty for all prisoners the day the Scarlet Pimpernel is captured. A public holiday and a pardon for all natives of Boulogne who are under sentence of death: they shall be allowed to find their way to the various English boats—trading and smuggling craft—that always lie at anchor in the roads there.

The Committee of Public Safety feel amazingly magnanimous towards Boulogne; a proclamation embodying the amnesty and the pardon is at once drawn up and signed by Robespierre and his bloodthirsty Council of Ten, it is entrusted to Citizen Collot d'Herbois to be read out at every corner of the ramparts as an inducement to the little town to do its level best. The Englishman and his wife—captured in Boulogne—will both be subsequently brought to Paris, formally tried on a charge of conspiring against the Republic and guillotined as English spies, but Boulogne shall have the greater glory and shall reap the first and richest reward.

And armed with the magnanimous proclamation, the orders for general rejoicings and a grand local fete, armed also with any and every power over the entire city, its municipality, its garrisons, its forts, for himself and his colleague Chauvelin, Citizen Collot d'Herbois starts for Boulogne forthwith.

Needless to tell him not to let the grass grow under his horse's hoofs. The capture of the Scarlet Pimpernel, though not absolutely an accomplished fact, is nevertheless a practical certainty, and no one rejoices over this great event more than the man who is to be present and see all the fun.

Riding and driving, getting what relays of horses or waggons from roadside farms that he can, Collot is not likely to waste much time on the way.

It is 157 miles to Boulogne by road, and Collot, burning with ambition to be in at the death, rides or drives as no messenger of good tidings has ever ridden or driven before.

He does not stop to eat, but munches chunks of bread and cheese in the recess of the lumbering chaise or waggon that bears him along whenever his limbs refuse him service and he cannot mount a horse.

The chronicles tell us that twenty-four hours after he left Paris, half-dazed with fatigue, but ferocious and eager still, he is borne to the gates of Boulogne by an old cart horse requisitioned from some distant farm, and which falls down, dead, at the Porte Gayole, whilst its rider, with a last effort, loudly clamours for admittance into the town "in the name of the Republic."

CHAPTER XXI. SUSPENSE

In his memorable interview with Robespierre, the day before he left for England, Chauvelin had asked that absolute power be given him, in order that he might carry out the plans for the capture of the Scarlet Pimpernel, which he had in his mind. Now that he was back in France he had no cause to complain that the revolutionary government had grudged him this power for which he had asked.

Implicit obedience had followed whenever he had commanded.

As soon as he heard that a woman had been arrested in the act of uttering a passport in the name of Celine Dumont, he guessed at once that Marguerite Blakeney had, with characteristic impulse, fallen into the trap which, with the aid of the woman Candeille, he had succeeded in laying for her.

He was not the least surprised at that. He knew human nature, feminine nature, far too well, ever to have been in doubt for a moment that Marguerite would follow her husband without calculating either costs or risks.

Ye gods! the irony of it all! Had she not been called the cleverest woman in Europe at one time? Chauvelin himself had thus acclaimed her, in those olden days, before she and he became such mortal enemies, and when he was one of the many satellites that revolved round brilliant Marguerite St. Just. And to-night, when a sergeant of the town guards brought him news of her capture, he smiled grimly to himself; the cleverest woman in Europe had failed to perceive the trap laid temptingly open for her.

Once more she had betrayed her husband into the hands of those who would not let him escape a second time. And now she had done it with her eyes open, with loving, passionate heart which ached for self-sacrifice, and only succeeded in imperilling the loved one more hopelessly than before.

The sergeant was waiting for orders. Citizen Chauvelin had come to Boulogne, armed with more full and more autocratic powers than any servant of the new republic had ever been endowed with before. The governor of the town, the captain of the guard, the fort and municipality were all as abject slaves before him.

As soon as he had taken possession of the quarters organized for him in the Town Hall, he had asked for a list of prisoners who for one cause or another were being detained pending further investigations.

The list was long and contained many names which were of not the slightest interest to Chauvelin: he passed them over impatiently.

"To be released at once," he said curtly.

He did not want the guard to be burdened with unnecessary duties, nor the prisons of the little sea-port town to be inconveniently encumbered. He wanted room, space, air, the force and intelligence of the entire town at his command for the one capture which meant life and revenge to him.

"A woman—name unknown—found in possession of a forged passport in the name of Celine Dumont, maid to the Citizeness Desiree Candeille—attempted to land—was interrogated and failed to give satisfactory explanation of herself—detained in room No. 6 of the Gayole prison."

This was one of the last names on the list, the only one of any importance to Citizen Chauvelin. When he read it he nearly drove his nails into the palms of his hands, so desperate an effort did he make not to betray before the sergeant by look or sigh the exultation which he felt.

For a moment he shaded his eyes against the glare of the lamp, but it was not long before he had formulated a plan and was ready to give his orders.

He asked for a list of prisoners already detained in the various forts. The name of l'Abbe Foucquet with those of his niece and nephew attracted his immediate attention. He asked for further information respecting these people, heard that the boy was a widow's only son, the sole supporter of his mother's declining years: the girl was ailing, suffering from incipient phthisis, and was blind.

Pardi! the very thing! L'Abbe himself, the friend of Juliette Marny, the pathetic personality around which this final adventure of the Scarlet Pimpernel was intended to revolve! and these two young people! his sister's children! one of them blind and ill, the other full of vigour and manhood.

Citizen Chauvelin had soon made up his mind.

A few quick orders to the sergeant of the guard, and l'Abbe Foucquet, weak, helpless and gentle, became the relentless jailer who would guard Marguerite more securely than a whole regiment of loyal soldiers could have done.

Then, having despatched a messenger to the Committee of Public Safety, Chauvelin laid himself down to rest. Fate had not deceived him. He had thought and schemed and planned, and events had shaped themselves exactly as foreseen, and the fact that Marguerite Blakeney was at the present moment a prisoner in his hands was merely the result of his own calculations.

As for the Scarlet Pimpernel, Chauvelin could not very well conceive what he would do under these present circumstances. The duel on the southern ramparts had of course become a farce, not likely to be enacted now that Marguerite's life was at stake. The daring adventurer was caught in a network at last, from which all his ingenuity, all his wit, his impudence and his amazing luck could never extricate him.

And in Chauvelin's mind there was still something more. Revenge was the sweetest emotion his bruised and humbled pride could know: he had not yet tasted its complete intoxicating joy: but every hour now his cup of delight became more and more full: in a few days it would overflow.

In the meanwhile he was content to wait. The hours sped by and there was no news yet of that elusive Pimpernel. Of Marguerite he knew nothing save that she was well guarded; the sentry who passed up and down outside room No. 6 had heard her voice and that of the Abbe Foucquet, in the course of the afternoon.

Chauvelin had asked the Committee of Public Safety for aid in his difficult task, but forty-eight hours at least must elapse before such aid could reach him. Forty-eight hours, during which the hand of an assassin might be lurking for him, and might even reach him ere his vengeance was fully accomplished.

That was the only thought which really troubled him. He did not want to die before he had seen the Scarlet Pimpernel a withered abject creature, crushed in fame and honour, too debased to find glorification even in death.

At this moment he only cared for his life because it was needed for the complete success of his schemes. No one else he knew would have that note of personal hatred towards the enemy of France which was necessary now in order to carry out successfully the plans which he had formed.

Robespierre and all the others only desired the destruction of a man who had intrigued against the reign of terror which they had established; his death on the guillotine, even if it were surrounded with the halo of martyrdom, would have satisfied them completely. Chauvelin looked further than that. He hated the man! He had suffered humiliation through him individually. He wished to see him as an object of contempt rather than of pity. And because of the anticipation of this joy, he was careful of his life, and throughout those two days which elapsed between the capture of Marguerite and the arrival of Collot d'Herbois at Boulogne, Chauvelin never left his quarters at the Hotel de Ville, and requisitioned a special escort consisting of proved soldiers of the town guard to attend his every footstep.

On the evening of the 22nd, after the arrival of Citizen Collot in Boulogne, he gave orders that the woman from No. 6 cell be brought before him in the ground floor room of the Fort Gayole.

CHAPTER XXII. NOT DEATH

Two days of agonizing suspense, of alternate hope and despair, had told heavily on Marguerite Blakeney.

Her courage was still indomitable, her purpose firm and her faith secure, but she was without the slightest vestige of news, entirely shut off from the outside world, left to conjecture, to scheme, to expect and to despond alone.

The Abbe Foucquet had tried in his gentle way to be of comfort to her, and she in her turn did her very best not to render his position more cruel than it already was.

A message came to him twice during those forty-eight hours from Francois and Felicite, a little note scribbled by the boy, or a token sent by the blind girl, to tell the Abbe that the children were safe and well, that they would be safe and well so long as the Citizeness with the name unknown remained closely guarded by him in room No. 6.

When these messages came, the old man would sigh and murmur something about the good God: and hope, which perhaps had faintly risen in Marguerite's heart within the last hour or so, would once more sink back into the abyss of uttermost despair.

Outside the monotonous walk of the sentry sounded like the perpetual thud of a hammer beating upon her bruised temples.

"What's to be done? My God? what's to be done?"

Where was Percy now?

"How to reach him!... Oh, God! grant me light!"

The one real terror which she felt was that she would go mad. Nay! that she was in a measure mad already. For hours now,—or was it days?... or years?... she had heard nothing save that rhythmic walk of the sentinel, and the kindly, tremulous voice of the Abbe whispering consolations, or murmuring prayers in her ears, she had seen nothing save that prison door, of rough deal, painted a dull grey, with great old-fashioned lock, and hinges rusty with the damp of ages.

She had kept her eyes fixed on that door until they burned and ached with well-nigh intolerable pain; yet she felt that she could not look elsewhere, lest she missed the golden moment when the bolts would be drawn, and that dull, grey door would swing slowly on its rusty hinges.

Surely, surely, that was the commencement of madness!

Yet for Percy's sake, because he might want her, because he might have need of her courage and of her presence of mind, she tried to keep her wits about her. But it was difficult! oh! terribly difficult! especially when the shade of evening began to gather in, and peopled the squalid, whitewashed room with innumerable threatening ghouls.

Then when the moon came up, a silver ray crept in through the tiny window and struck full upon that grey door, making it look weird and spectral like the entrance to a house of ghosts.

Even now as there was a distinct sound of the pushing of bolts and bars, Marguerite thought that she was the prey of hallucinations. The Abbe Foucquet was sitting in the remote and darkest corner of the room, quietly telling his beads. His serene philosophy and gentle placidity could in no way be disturbed by the opening or shutting of a door, or by the bearer of good or evil tidings.

The room now seemed strangely gloomy and cavernous, with those deep, black shadows all around and that white ray of the moon which struck so weirdly on the door.

Marguerite shuddered with one of those unaccountable premonitions of something evil about to come, which ofttimes assail those who have a nervous and passionate temperament.

The door swung slowly open upon its hinges: there was a quick word of command, and the light of a small oil lamp struck full into the gloom. Vaguely Marguerite discerned a group of men, soldiers no doubt, for there was a glint of arms and the suggestion of tricolour cockades and scarves. One of the men was holding the lamp aloft, another took a few steps forward into the room. He turned to Marguerite, entirely ignoring the presence of the old priest, and addressed her peremptorily.

"Your presence is desired by the citizen governor," he said curtly; "stand up and follow me."

"Whither am I to go?" she asked.

"To where my men will take you. Now then, quick's the word. The citizen governor does not like to wait."

At a word of command from him, two more soldiers now entered the room and placed themselves one on each side of Marguerite, who, knowing that resistance was useless, had already risen and was prepared to go.

The Abbe tried to utter a word of protest and came quickly forward towards Marguerite, but he was summarily and very roughly pushed aside.

"Now then, calotin," said the first soldier with an oath, "this is none of your business. Forward! march!" he added, addressing his men, "and you, Citizeness, will find it wiser to come quietly along and not to attempt any tricks with me, or the gag and manacles will have to be used."

But Marguerite had no intention of resisting. She was too tired even to wonder as to what they meant to do with her or whither they were going; she moved as in a dream and felt a hope within her that she was being led to death: summary executions were the order of the day, she knew that, and sighed for this simple solution of the awful problem which had been harassing her these past two days.

She was being led along a passage, stumbling ever and anon as she walked, for it was but dimly lighted by the same little oil lamp, which one of the soldiers was carrying in front, holding it high up above his head: then they went down a narrow flight of stone steps, until she and her escort reached a heavy oak door.

A halt was ordered at this point: and the man in command of the little party pushed the door open and walked in. Marguerite caught sight of a room beyond, dark and gloomy-looking, as was her own prison cell. Somewhere on the left there was obviously a window; she could not see it but guessed that it was there because the moon struck full upon the floor, ghost-like and spectral, well fitting in with the dream-like state in which Marguerite felt herself to be.

In the centre of the room she could discern a table with a chair close beside it, also a couple of tallow candles, which flickered in the draught caused no doubt by that open window which she could not see.

All these little details impressed themselves on Marguerite's mind, as she stood there, placidly waiting until she should once more be told to move along. The table, the chair, that unseen window, trivial objects though they were, assumed before her overwrought fancy an utterly disproportionate importance. She caught herself presently counting up the number of boards visible on the floor, and watching the smoke of the tallow-candles rising up towards the grimy ceiling.

After a few minutes' weary waiting which seemed endless to Marguerite, there came a short word of command from within and she was roughly pushed forward into the room by one of the men. The cool air of a late September's evening gently fanned her burning temples. She looked round her and now perceived that someone was sitting at the table, the other side of the tallow-candles—a man, with head bent over a bundle of papers and shading his face against the light with his hand.

He rose as she approached, and the flickering flame of the candles played weirdly upon the slight, sable-clad figure, illumining the keen, ferret-like face, and throwing fitful gleams across the deep-set eyes and the narrow, cruel mouth.

It was Chauvelin.

Mechanically Marguerite took the chair which the soldier drew towards her, ordering her curtly to sit down. She seemed to have but little power to move. Though all her faculties had suddenly become preternaturally alert at sight of this man, whose very life now was spent in doing her the most grievous wrong that one human being can do to another, yet all these faculties were forcefully centred in the one mighty effort not to flinch before him, not to let him see for a moment that she was afraid.

She compelled her eyes to look at him fully and squarely, her lips not to tremble, her very heart to stop its wild, excited beating. She felt his keen eyes fixed intently upon her, but more in curiosity than in hatred or satisfied vengeance.

When she had sat down he came round the table and moved towards her. When he drew quite near, she instinctively recoiled. It had been an almost imperceptible action on her part and certainly an involuntary one, for she did not wish to betray a single thought or emotion, until she knew what he wished to say.

But he had noted her movement—a sort of drawing up and stiffening of her whole person as he approached. He seemed pleased to see it, for he smiled sarcastically but with evident satisfaction, and—as if his purpose was now accomplished—he immediately withdrew and went back to his former seat on the other side of the table. After that he ordered the soldiers to go.

"But remain at attention outside, you and your men," he added, "ready to enter if I call."

It was Marguerite's turn to smile at this obvious sign of a lurking fear on Chauvelin's part, and a line of sarcasm and contempt curled her full lips.

The soldiers having obeyed and the oak door having closed upon them, Marguerite was now alone with the man whom she hated and loathed beyond every living thing on earth.

She wondered when he would begin to speak and why he had sent for her. But he seemed in no hurry to begin. Still shading his face with his hand, he was watching her with utmost attention: she, on the other hand, was looking through and beyond him, with contemptuous indifference, as if his presence here did not interest her in the least.

She would give him no opening for this conversation which he had sought and which she felt would prove either purposeless or else deeply wounding to her heart and to her pride. She sat, therefore, quite still with the flickering and yellow light fully illumining her delicate face, with its child-like curves, and delicate features, the noble, straight brow, the great blue eyes and halo of golden hair.

"My desire to see you here to-night, must seem strange to you, Lady Blakeney," said Chauvelin at last.

Then, as she did not reply, he continued, speaking quite gently, almost deferentially:

"There are various matters of grave importance, which the events of the next twenty-four hours will reveal to your ladyship: and believe me that I am actuated by motives of pure friendship towards you in this my effort to mitigate the unpleasantness of such news as you might hear to-morrow perhaps, by giving you due warning of what its nature might be."

She turned great questioning eyes upon him, and in their expression she tried to put all the contempt which she felt, all the bitterness, all the defiance and the pride.

He quietly shrugged his shoulders.

"Ah! I fear me," he said, "that your ladyship, as usual doth me grievous wrong. It is but natural that you should misjudge me, yet believe me..."

"A truce on this foolery, M. Chauvelin," she broke in, with sudden impatient vehemence, "pray leave your protestations of friendship and courtesy alone, there is no one here to hear them. I pray you proceed with what you have to say."

"Ah!" It was a sigh of satisfaction on the part of Chauvelin. Her anger and impatience even at this early stage of the interview proved sufficiently that her icy restraint was only on the surface.

And Chauvelin always knew how to deal with vehemence. He loved to play with the emotions of a passionate fellow-creature: it was only the imperturbable calm of a certain enemy of his that was wont to shake his own impenetrable armour of reserve.

"As your ladyship desires," he said, with a slight and ironical bow of the head. "But before proceeding according to your wish, I am compelled to ask your ladyship just one question."

"And that is?"

"Have you reflected what your present position means to that inimitable prince of dandies, Sir Percy Blakeney?"

"Is it necessary for your present purpose, Monsieur, that you should mention my husband's name at all?" she asked.

"It is indispensable, fair lady," he replied suavely, "for is not the fate of your husband so closely intertwined with yours, that his actions will inevitably be largely influenced by your own."

Marguerite gave a start of surprise, and as Chauvelin had paused she tried to read what hidden meaning lay behind these last words of his. Was it his intention then to propose some bargain, one of those terrible "either-or's" of which he seemed to possess the malignant secret? Oh! if that was so, if indeed he had sent for her in order to suggest one of those terrible alternatives of his, then—be it what it may, be it the wildest conception which the insane brain of a fiend could invent, she would accept it, so long as the man she loved were given one single chance of escape.

Therefore she turned to her arch-enemy in a more conciliatory spirit now, and even endeavoured to match her own diplomatic cunning against his.

"I do not understand," she said tentatively. "How can my actions influence those of my husband? I am a prisoner in Boulogne: he probably is not aware of that fact yet and..."

"Sir Percy Blakeney may be in Boulogne at any moment now," he interrupted quietly.

"An I mistake not, few places can offer such great attractions to that peerless gentleman of fashion than doth this humble provincial town of France just at this present.... Hath it not the honour of harbouring Lady Blakeney within its gates?... And your ladyship may indeed believe me when I say that the day that Sir Percy lands in our hospitable port, two hundred pairs of eyes will be fixed upon him, lest he should wish to quit it again."

"And if there were two thousand, sir," she said impulsively, "they would not stop his coming or going as he pleased."

"Nay, fair lady," he said, with a smile, "are you then endowing Sir Percy Blakeney with the attributes which, as popular fancy has it, belong exclusively to that mysterious English hero, the Scarlet Pimpernel?"

"A truce to your diplomacy, Monsieur Chauvelin," she retorted, goaded by his sarcasm, "why should we try to fence with one another? What was the object of your journey to England? of the farce which you enacted in my house, with the help of the woman Candeille? of that duel and that challenge, save that you desired to entice Sir Percy Blakeney to France?"

"And also his charming wife," he added with an ironical bow.

She bit her lip, and made no comment.

"Shall we say that I succeeded admirably?" he continued, speaking with persistent urbanity and calm, "and that I have strong cause to hope that the elusive Pimpernel will soon be a guest on our friendly shores?... There! you see I too have laid down the foils.... As you say, why should we fence? Your ladyship is now in Boulogne, soon Sir Percy will come to try and take you away from us, but believe me, fair lady, that it would take more than the ingenuity and the daring of the Scarlet Pimpernel magnified a thousandfold to get him back to England again... unless..."

"Unless?..."

Marguerite held her breath. She felt now as if the whole universe must stand still during the next supreme moment, until she had heard what Chauvelin's next words would be.

There was to be an "unless" then? An "either-or" more terrible no doubt than the one he had formulated before her just a year ago.

Chauvelin, she knew, was past master in the art of putting a knife at his victim's throat and of giving it just the necessary twist with his cruel and relentless "unless"!

But she felt quite calm, because her purpose was resolute. There is no doubt that during this agonizing moment of suspense she was absolutely firm in her determination to accept any and every condition which Chauvelin would put before her as the price of her husband's safety. After all, these conditions, since he placed them before HER, could resolve themselves into questions of her own life against her husband's.

With that unreasoning impulse which was one of her most salient characteristics, she never paused to think that, to Chauvelin, her own life or death were only the means to the great end which he had in view: the complete annihilation of the Scarlet Pimpernel.

That end could only be reached by Percy Blakeney's death—not by her own.

Even now as she was watching him with eyes glowing and lips tightly closed, lest a cry of impatient agony should escape her throat, he,—like a snail that has shown its slimy horns too soon, and is not ready to face the enemy as yet,—seemed suddenly to withdraw within his former shell of careless suavity. The earnestness of his tone vanished, giving place to light and easy conversation, just as if he were discussing social topics with a woman of fashion in a Paris drawing-room.

"Nay!" he said pleasantly, "is not your ladyship taking this matter in too serious a spirit? Of a truth you repeated my innocent word 'unless' even as if I were putting knife at your dainty throat. Yet I meant naught that need disturb you yet. Have I not said that I am your friend? Let me try and prove it to you."

"You will find that a difficult task, Monsieur," she said drily.

"Difficult tasks always have had a great fascination for your humble servant. May I try?"

"Certainly."

"Shall we then touch at the root of this delicate matter? Your ladyship, so I understand, is at this moment under the impression that I desire to encompass—shall I say?—the death of an English gentleman for whom, believe me, I have the greatest respect. That is so, is it not?"

"What is so, M. Chauvelin?" she asked almost stupidly, for truly she had not even begun to grasp his meaning. "I do not understand."

"You think that I am at this moment taking measures for sending the Scarlet Pimpernel to the guillotine? Eh?"

"I do."

"Never was so great an error committed by a clever woman. Your ladyship must believe me when I say that the guillotine is the very last place in the world where I would wish to see that enigmatic and elusive personage."

"Are you trying to fool me, M. Chauvelin? If so, for what purpose? And why do you lie to me like that?"

"On my honour, 'tis the truth. The death of Sir Percy Blakeney—I may call him that, may I not?—would ill suit the purpose which I have in view."

"What purpose? You must pardon me, Monsieur Chauvelin," she added with a quick, impatient sigh, "but of a truth I am getting confused, and my wits must have become dull in the past few days. I pray to you to add to your many protestations of friendship a little more clearness in your speech and, if possible, a little more brevity. What then is the purpose which you had in view when you enticed my husband to come over to France?"

"My purpose was the destruction of the Scarlet Pimpernel, not the death of Sir Percy Blakeney. Believe me, I have a great regard for Sir Percy. He is a most accomplished gentleman, witty, brilliant, an inimitable dandy. Why should he not grace with his presence the drawing-rooms of London or of Brighton for many years to come?"

She looked at him with puzzled inquiry. For one moment the thought flashed through her mind that, after all, Chauvelin might be still in doubt as to the identity of the Scarlet Pimpernel.... But no! that hope was madness.... It was preposterous and impossible.... But then, why? why? why?... Oh God! for a little more patience!

"What I have just said may seem a little enigmatic to your ladyship," he continued blandly, "but surely so clever a woman as yourself, so great a lady as is the wife of Sir Percy Blakeney, Baronet, will be aware that there are other means of destroying an enemy than the taking of his life."

"For instance, Monsieur Chauvelin?"

"There is the destruction of his honour," he replied slowly.

A long, bitter laugh, almost hysterical in its loud outburst, broke from the very depths of Marguerite's convulsed heart.

"The destruction of his honour!... ha! ha! ha! ha!... of a truth, Monsieur Chauvelin, your inventive powers have led you beyond the bounds of dreamland!... Ha! ha! ha! ha!... It is in the land of madness that you are wandering, sir, when you talk in one breath of Sir Percy Blakeney and the possible destruction of his honour!"

But he remained apparently quite unruffled, and when her laughter had somewhat subsided, he said placidly:

"Perhaps!..."

Then he rose from his chair, and once more approached her. This time she did not shrink from him. The suggestion which he had made just now, this talk of attacking her husband's honour rather than his life, seemed so wild and preposterous—the conception truly of a mind unhinged—that she looked upon it as a sign of extreme weakness on his part, almost as an acknowledgement of impotence.

But she watched him as he moved round the table more in curiosity now than in fright. He puzzled her, and she still had a feeling at the back of her mind that there must be something more definite and more evil lurking at the back of that tortuous brain.

"Will your ladyship allow me to conduct you to yonder window?" he said, "the air is cool, and what I have to say can best be done in sight of yonder sleeping city."

His tone was one of perfect courtesy, even of respectful deference through which not the slightest trace of sarcasm could be discerned, and she, still actuated by curiosity and interest, not in any way by fear, quietly rose to obey him. Though she ignored the hand which he was holding out towards her, she followed him readily enough as he walked up to the window.

All through this agonizing and soul-stirring interview she had felt heavily oppressed by the close atmosphere of the room, rendered nauseous by the evil smell of the smoky tallow-candles which were left to spread their grease and smoke abroad unchecked. Once or twice she had gazed longingly towards the suggestion of pure air outside.

Chauvelin evidently had still much to say to her: the torturing, mental rack to which she was being subjected had not yet fully done its work. It still was capable of one or two turns, a twist or so which might succeed in crushing her pride and her defiance. Well! so be it! she was in the man's power: had placed herself therein through her own unreasoning impulse. This interview was but one of the many soul-agonies which she had been called upon to endure, and if by submitting to it all she could in a measure mitigate her own faults and be of help to the man she loved, she would find the sacrifice small and the mental torture easy to bear.

Therefore when Chauvelin beckoned to her to draw near, she went up to the window, and leaning her head against the deep stone embrasure, she looked out into the night.

CHAPTER XXIII. THE HOSTAGE

Chauvelin, without speaking, extended his hand out towards the city as if to invite Marguerite to gaze upon it.

She was quite unconscious what hour of the night it might be, but it must have been late, for the little town, encircled by the stony arms of its forts, seemed asleep. The moon, now slowly sinking in the west, edged the towers and spires with filmy lines of silver. To the right Marguerite caught sight of the frowning Beffroi, which even as she gazed out began tolling its heavy bell. It sounded like the tocsin, dull and muffled. After ten strokes it was still.

Ten o'clock! At this hour in far-off England, in fashionable London, the play was just over, crowds of gaily dressed men and women poured out of the open gates of the theatres calling loudly for attendant or chaise. Thence to balls or routs, gaily fluttering like so many butterflies, brilliant and irresponsible....

And in England also, in the beautiful gardens of her Richmond home, ofttimes at ten o'clock she had wandered alone with Percy, when he was at home, and the spirit of adventure in him momentarily laid to rest. Then, when the night was very dark and the air heavy with the scent of roses and lilies, she lay quiescent in his arms in that little arbour beside the river. The rhythmic lapping of the waves was the only sound that stirred the balmy air. He seldom spoke then, for his voice would shake whenever he uttered a word: but his impenetrable armour of flippancy was pierced through and he did not speak because his lips were pressed to hers, and his love had soared beyond the domain of speech.

A shudder of intense mental pain went through her now as she gazed on the sleeping city, and sweet memories of the past turned to bitterness in this agonizing present. One by one as the moon gradually disappeared behind a bank of clouds, the towers of Boulogne were merged in the gloom. In front of her far, far away, beyond the flat sand dunes, the sea seemed to be calling to her with a ghostly and melancholy moan.

The window was on the ground floor of the Fort, and gave direct onto the wide and shady walk which runs along the crest of the city walls; from where she stood Marguerite was looking straight along the ramparts, some thirty metres wide at this point, flanked on either side by the granite balustrade, and adorned with a double row of ancient elms stunted and twisted into grotesque shapes by the persistent action of the wind.

"These wide ramparts are a peculiarity of this city..." said a voice close to her ear, "at times of peace they form an agreeable promenade under the shade of the trees, and a delightful meeting-place for lovers... or enemies...."

The sound brought her back to the ugly realities of the present: the rose-scented garden at Richmond, the lazily flowing river, the tender memories which for that brief moment had confronted her from out a happy past, suddenly vanished from her ken. Instead of these the brine-laden sea-air struck her quivering nostrils, the echo of the old Beffroi died away in her ear, and now from out one of the streets or open places of the sleeping city there came the sound of a raucous voice, shooting in monotonous tones a string of words, the meaning of which failed to reach her brain.

Not many feet below the window, the southern ramparts of the town stretched away into the darkness. She felt unaccountably cold suddenly as she looked down upon them and, with aching eyes, tried to pierce the gloom. She was shivering in spite of the mildness of this early autumnal night: her overwrought fancy was peopling the lonely walls with unearthly shapes strolling along, discussing in spectral language a strange duel which was to take place here between a noted butcher of men and a mad Englishman overfond of adventure.

The ghouls seemed to pass and repass along in front of her and to be laughing audibly because that mad Englishman had been offered his life in exchange for his honour. They laughed and laughed, no doubt because he refused the bargain—Englishmen were always eccentric, and in these days of equality and other devices of a free and glorious revolution, honour was such a very marketable commodity that it seemed ridiculous to prize it quite so highly. Then they strolled away again and disappeared, whilst Marguerite distinctly heard the scrunching of the path beneath their feet. She leant forward to peer still further into the darkness, for this sound had seemed so absolutely real, but immediately a detaining hand was place upon her arm and a sarcastic voice murmured at her elbow:

"The result, fair lady, would only be a broken leg or arm; the height is not great enough for picturesque suicides, and believe me these ramparts are only haunted by ghosts."

She drew back as if a viper had stung her; for the moment she had become oblivious of Chauvelin's presence. However, she would not take notice of his taunt, and, after a slight pause, he asked her if she could hear the town crier over in the public streets.

"Yes," she replied.

"What he says at this present moment is of vast importance to your ladyship," he remarked drily.

"How so?"

"Your ladyship is a precious hostage. We are taking measures to guard our valuable property securely."

Marguerite thought of the Abbe Foucquet, who no doubt was still quietly telling his beads, even if in his heart he had begun to wonder what had become of her. She thought of Francois, who was the breadwinner, and of Felicite, who was blind.

"Methinks you and your colleagues have done that already," she said.

"Not as completely as we would wish. We know the daring of the Scarlet Pimpernel. We are not even ashamed to admit that we fear his luck, his impudence and his marvellous ingenuity.... Have I not told you that I have the greatest possible respect for that mysterious English hero.... An old priest and two young children might be spirited away by that enigmatical adventurer, even whilst Lady Blakeney herself is made to vanish from our sight.

"Ah! I see your ladyship is taking my simple words as a confession of weakness," he continued, noting the swift sigh of hope which had involuntarily escaped her lips. "Nay! and it please you, you shall despise me for it. But a confession of weakness is the first sign of strength. The Scarlet Pimpernel is still at large, and whilst we guard our hostage securely, he is bound to fall into our hands."

"Aye! still at large!" she retorted with impulsive defiance. "Think you that all your bolts and bars, the ingenuity of yourself and your colleagues, the collaboration of the devil himself, would succeed in outwitting the Scarlet Pimpernel, now that his purpose will be to try and drag ME from out your clutches."

She felt hopeful and proud. Now that she had the pure air of heaven in her lungs, that from afar she could smell the sea, and could feel that perhaps in a straight line of vision from where she stood, the "Day-Dream" with Sir Percy on board, might be lying out there in the roads, it seemed impossible that he should fail in freeing her and those poor people—an old man and two children—whose lives depended on her own.

But Chauvelin only laughed a dry, sarcastic laugh and said:

"Hm! perhaps not!... It of course will depend on you and your personality... your feelings in such matters... and whether an English gentleman likes to save his own skin at the expense of others."

Marguerite shivered as if from cold.

"Ah! I see," resumed Chauvelin quietly, "that your ladyship has not quite grasped the position. That public crier is a long way off: the words have lingered on the evening breeze and have failed to reach your brain. Do you suppose that I and my colleagues do not know that all the ingenuity of which the Scarlet Pimpernel is capable will now be directed in piloting Lady Blakeney, and incidentally the Abbe Foucquet with his nephew and niece, safely across the Channel! Four people!... Bah! a bagatelle, for this mighty conspirator, who but lately snatched twenty aristocrats from the prisons of Lyons.... Nay! nay! two children and an old man were not enough to guard our precious hostage, and I was not thinking of either the Abbe Foucquet or of the two children, when I said that an English gentleman would not save himself at the expense of others."

"Of whom then were you thinking, Monsieur Chauvelin? Whom else have you set to guard the prize which you value so highly?"

"The whole city of Boulogne," he replied simply.

"I do not understand."

"Let me make my point clear. My colleague, Citizen Collot d'Herbois, rode over from Paris yesterday; like myself he is a member of the Committee of Public Safety whose duty it is to look after the welfare of France by punishing all those who conspire against her laws and the liberties of the people. Chief among these conspirators, whom it is our duty to punish is, of course, that impudent adventurer who calls himself the Scarlet Pimpernel. He has given the government of France a great deal of trouble through his attempts—mostly successful, as I have already admitted,—at frustrating the just vengeance which an oppressed country has the right to wreak on those who have proved themselves to be tyrants and traitors."

"Is it necessary to recapitulate all this, Monsieur Chauvelin?" she asked impatiently.

"I think so," he replied blandly. "You see, my point is this. We feel that in a measure now the Scarlet Pimpernel is in our power. Within the next few hours he will land at Boulogne... Boulogne, where he has agreed to fight a duel with me... Boulogne, where Lady Blakeney happens to be at this present moment... as you see, Boulogne has a great responsibility to bear: just now she is to a certain extent the proudest city in France, since she holds within her gates a hostage for the appearance on our shores of her country's most bitter enemy. But she must not fall from that high estate. Her double duty is clear before her: she must guard Lady Blakeney and capture the Scarlet Pimpernel; if she fail in the former she must be punished, if she succeed in the latter she shall be rewarded."

He paused and leaned out of the window again, whilst she watched him, breathless and terrified. She was beginning to understand.

"Hark!" he said, looking straight at her. "Do you hear the crier now? He is proclaiming the punishment and the reward. He is making it clear to the citizens of Boulogne that on the day when the Scarlet Pimpernel falls into the hands of the Committee of Public Safety a general amnesty will be granted to all natives of Boulogne who are under arrest at the present time, and a free pardon to all those who, born within these city walls, are to-day under sentence of death.... A noble reward, eh? well-deserved you'll admit.... Should you wonder then if the whole town of Boulogne were engaged just now in finding that mysterious hero, and delivering him into our hands?... How many mothers, sisters, wives, think you, at the present moment, would fail to lay hands on the English adventurer, if a husband's or a son's life or freedom happened to be at stake?... I have some records there," he continued, pointing in the direction of the table, "which tell me that there are five and thirty natives of Boulogne in the local prisons, a dozen more in the prisons of Paris; of these at least twenty have been tried already and are condemned to death. Every hour that the Scarlet Pimpernel succeeds in evading his captors so many deaths lie at his door. If he succeeds in once more reaching England safely three score lives mayhap will be the price of his escape.... Nay! but I see your ladyship is shivering with cold..." he added with a dry little laugh, "shall I close the window? or do you wish to hear what punishment will be meted out to Boulogne, if on the day that the Scarlet Pimpernel is captured, Lady Blakeney happens to have left the shelter of these city walls?"

"I pray you proceed, Monsieur," she rejoined with perfect calm.

"The Committee of Public Safety," he resumed, "would look upon this city as a nest of traitors if on the day that the Scarlet Pimpernel becomes our prisoner Lady Blakeney herself, the wife of that notorious English spy, had already quitted Boulogne. The whole town knows by now that you are in our hands—you, the most precious hostage we can hold for the ultimate capture of the man whom we all fear and detest. Virtually the town-crier is at the present moment proclaiming to the inhabitants of this city: 'We want that man, but we already have his wife, see to it, citizens, that she does not escape! for if she do, we shall summarily shoot the breadwinner in every family in the town!'"

A cry of horror escaped Marguerite's parched lips.

"Are you devils then, all of you," she gasped, "that you should think of such things?"

"Aye! some of us are devils, no doubt," said Chauvelin drily; "but why should you honour us in this case with so flattering an epithet? We are mere men striving to guard our property and mean no harm to the citizens of Boulogne. We have threatened them, true! but is it not for you and that elusive Pimpernel to see that the threat is never put into execution?"

"You would not do it!" she repeated, horror-stricken.

"Nay! I pray you, fair lady, do not deceive yourself. At present the proclamation sounds like a mere threat, I'll allow, but let me assure you that if we fail to capture the Scarlet Pimpernel and if you on the other hand are spirited out of this fortress by that mysterious adventurer we shall undoubtedly shoot or guillotine every able-bodied man and woman in this town."

He had spoken quietly and emphatically, neither with bombast, nor with rage, and Marguerite saw in his face nothing but a calm and ferocious determination, the determination of an entire nation embodied in this one man, to be revenged at any cost. She would not let him see the depth of her despair, nor would she let him read in her face the unutterable hopelessness which filled her soul. It were useless to make an appeal to him: she knew full well that from him she could obtain neither gentleness nor mercy.

"I hope at last I have made the situation quite clear to your ladyship?" he was asking quite pleasantly now. "See how easy is your position: you have but to remain quiescent in room No. 6, and if any chance of escape be offered you ere the Scarlet Pimpernel is captured, you need but to think of all the families of Boulogne, who would be deprived of their breadwinner—fathers and sons mostly, but there are girls too, who support their mothers or sisters; the fish curers of Boulogne are mostly women, and there are the net-makers and the seamstresses, all would suffer if your ladyship were no longer to be found in No. 6 room of this ancient fort, whilst all would be included in the amnesty if the Scarlet Pimpernel fell into our hands..."

He gave a low, satisfied chuckle which made Marguerite think of the evil spirits in hell exulting over the torments of unhappy lost souls.

"I think, Lady Blakeney," he added drily and making her an ironical bow, "that your humble servant hath outwitted the elusive hero at last."

Quietly he turned on his heel and went back into the room, Marguerite remaining motionless beside the open window, where the soft, brine-laden air, the distant murmur of the sea, the occasional cry of a sea-mew, all seemed to mock her agonizing despair.

The voice of the town-crier came nearer and nearer now: she could hear the words he spoke quite distinctly: something about "amnesty" and pardon, the reward for the capture of the Scarlet Pimpernel, the lives of men, women and children in exchange for his.

Oh! she knew what all that meant! that Percy would not hesitate one single instant to throw his life into the hands of his enemies, in exchange for that of others. Others! others! always others! this sigh that had made her heart ache so often in England, what terrible significance it bore now!

And how he would suffer in his heart and in his pride, because of her whom he could not even attempt to save since it would mean the death of others! of others, always of others!

She wondered if he had already landed in Boulogne! Again she remembered the vision on the landing stage: his massive figure, the glimpse she had of the loved form, in the midst of the crowd!

The moment he entered the town he would hear the proclamation read, see it posted up no doubt on every public building, and realize that she had been foolish enough to follow him, that she was a prisoner and that he could do nothing to save her.

What would he do? Marguerite at the thought instinctively pressed her hands to her heart, the agony of it all had become physically painful. She hoped that perhaps this pain meant approaching death! oh! how easy would this simple solution be!

The moon peered out from beneath the bank of clouds which had obscured her for so long; smiling, she drew her pencilled silver lines along the edge of towers and pinnacles, the frowning Beffroi and those stony walls which seemed to Marguerite as if they encircled a gigantic graveyard.

The town-crier had evidently ceased to read the proclamation. One by one the windows in the public square were lighted up from within. The citizens of Boulogne wanted to think over the strange events which had occurred without their knowledge, yet which were apparently to have such direful or such joyous consequences for them.

A man to be captured! the mysterious English adventurer of whom they had all heard, but whom nobody had seen. And a woman—his wife—to be guarded until the man was safely under lock and key.

Marguerite felt as if she could almost hear them talking it over and vowing that she should not escape, and that the Scarlet Pimpernel should soon be captured.

A gentle wind stirred the old gnarled trees on the southern ramparts, a wind that sounded like the sigh of swiftly dying hope.

What could Percy do now? His hands were tied, and he was inevitably destined to endure the awful agony of seeing the woman he loved die a terrible death beside him.

Having captured him, they would not keep him long; no necessity for a trial, for detention, for formalities of any kind. A summary execution at dawn on the public place, a roll of drums, a public holiday to mark the joyful event, and a brave man will have ceased to live, a noble heart have stilled its beatings forever, whilst a whole nation gloried over the deed.

"Sleep, citizens of Boulogne! all is still!"

The night watchman had replaced the town-crier. All was quiet within the city walls: the inhabitants could sleep in peace, a beneficent government was wakeful and guarding their rest.

But many of the windows of the town remained lighted up, and at a little distance below her, round the corner so that she could not see it, a small crowd must have collected in front of the gateway which led into the courtyard of the Gayole Fort. Marguerite could hear a persistent murmur of voices, mostly angry and threatening, and once there were loud cries of: "English spies," and "a la lanterne!"

"The citizens of Boulogne are guarding the treasures of France!" commented Chauvelin drily, as he laughed again, that cruel, mirthless laugh of his.

Then she roused herself from her torpor: she did not know how long she had stood beside the open window, but the fear seized her that that man must have seen and gloated over the agony of her mind. She straightened her graceful figure, threw back her proud head defiantly, and quietly walked up to the table, where Chauvelin seemed once more absorbed in the perusal of his papers.

"Is this interview over?" she asked quietly, and without the slightest tremor in her voice. "May I go now?"

"As soon as you wish," he replied with gentle irony.

He regarded her with obvious delight, for truly she was beautiful: grand in this attitude of defiant despair. The man, who had spent the last half-hour in martyrizing her, gloried over the misery which he had wrought, and which all her strength of will could not entirely banish from her face.

"Will you believe me, Lady Blakeney?" he added, "that there is no personal animosity in my heart towards you or your husband? Have I not told you that I do not wish to compass his death?"

"Yet you propose to send him to the guillotine as soon as you have laid hands on him."

"I have explained to you the measures which I have taken in order to make sure that we DO lay hands on the Scarlet Pimpernel. Once he is in our power, it will rest with him to walk to the guillotine or to embark with you on board his yacht."

"You propose to place an alternative before Sir Percy Blakeney?"

"Certainly."

"To offer him his life?"

"And that of his charming wife."

"In exchange for what?"

"His honour."

"He will refuse, Monsieur."

"We shall see."

Then he touched a handbell which stood on the table, and within a few seconds the door was opened and the soldier who had led Marguerite hither, re-entered the room.

The interview was at an end. It had served its purpose. Marguerite knew now that she must not even think of escape for herself, or hope for safety for the man she loved. Of Chauvelin's talk of a bargain which would touch Percy's honour she would not even think: and she was too proud to ask anything further from him.

Chauvelin stood up and made her a deep bow, as she crossed the room and finally went out of the door. The little company of soldiers closed in around her and she was once more led along the dark passages, back to her own prison cell.

CHAPTER XXIV. COLLEAGUES

As soon as the door had closed behind Marguerite, there came from somewhere in the room the sound of a yawn, a grunt and a volley of oaths.

The flickering light of the tallow candles had failed to penetrate into all the corners, and now from out one of these dark depths, a certain something began to detach itself, and to move forward towards the table at which Chauvelin had once more resumed his seat.

"Has the damned aristocrat gone at last?" queried a hoarse voice, as a burly body clad in loose-fitting coat and mud-stained boots and breeches appeared within the narrow circle of light.

"Yes," replied Chauvelin curtly.

"And a cursed long time you have been with the baggage," grunted the other surlily. "Another five minutes and I'd have taken the matter in my own hands.

"An assumption of authority," commented Chauvelin quietly, "to which your position here does not entitle you, Citizen Collot."

Collot d'Herbois lounged lazily forward, and presently he threw his ill-knit figure into the chair lately vacated by Marguerite. His heavy, square face bore distinct traces of the fatigue endured in the past twenty-four hours on horseback or in jolting market waggons. His temper too appeared to have suffered on the way, and, at Chauvelin's curt and dictatorial replies, he looked as surly as a chained dog.

"You were wasting your breath over that woman," he muttered, bringing a large and grimy fist heavily down on the table, "and your measures are not quite so sound as your fondly imagine, Citizen Chauvelin."

"They were mostly of your imagining, Citizen Collot," rejoined the other quietly, "and of your suggestion."

"I added a touch of strength and determination to your mild milk-and-water notions, Citizen," snarled Collot spitefully. "I'd have knocked that intriguing woman's brains out at the very first possible opportunity, had I been consulted earlier than this."

"Quite regardless of the fact that such violent measures would completely damn all our chances of success as far as the capture of the Scarlet Pimpernel is concerned," remarked Chauvelin drily, with a contemptuous shrug of the shoulders. "Once his wife is dead, the Englishman will never run his head into the noose which I have so carefully prepared for him."

"So you say, Chauvelin; and therefore I suggested to you certain measures to prevent the woman escaping which you will find adequate, I hope."

"You need have no fear, Citizen Collot," said Chauvelin curtly, "this woman will make no attempt at escape now."

"If she does..." and Collot d'Herbois swore an obscene oath.

"I think she understands that we mean to put our threat in execution."

"Threat?... It was no empty threat, Citizen.... Sacre tonnerre! if that woman escapes now, by all the devils in hell I swear that I'll wield the guillotine myself and cut off the head of every able-bodied man or woman in Boulogne, with my own hands."

As he said this his face assumed such an expression of inhuman cruelty, such a desire to kill, such a savage lust for blood, that instinctively Chauvelin shuddered and shrank away from his colleague. All through his career there is no doubt that this man, who was of gentle birth, of gentle breeding, and who had once been called M. le Marquis de Chauvelin, must have suffered in his susceptibilities and in his pride when in contact with the revolutionaries with whom he had chosen to cast his lot. He could not have thrown off all his old ideas of refinement quite so easily, as to feel happy in the presence of such men as Collot d'Herbois, or Marat in his day—men who had become brute beasts, more ferocious far than any wild animal, more scientifically cruel than any feline prowler in jungle or desert.

One look in Collot's distorted face was sufficient at this moment to convince Chauvelin that it were useless for him to view the proclamation against the citizens of Boulogne merely as an idle threat, even if he had wished to do so. That Marguerite would not, under the circumstances, attempt to escape, that Sir Percy Blakeney himself would be forced to give up all thoughts of rescuing her, was a foregone conclusion in Chauvelin's mind, but if this high-born English gentleman had not happened to be the selfless hero that he was, if Marguerite Blakeney were cast in a different, a rougher mould—if, in short, the Scarlet Pimpernel in the face of the proclamation did succeed in dragging his wife out of the clutches of the Terrorists, then it was equally certain that Collot d'Herbois would carry out his rabid and cruel reprisals to the full. And if in the course of the wholesale butchery of the able-bodied and wage-earning inhabitants of Boulogne, the headsman should sink worn out, then would this ferocious sucker of blood put his own hand to the guillotine, with the same joy and lust which he had felt when he ordered one hundred and thirty-eight women of Nantes to be stripped naked by the soldiery before they were flung helter-skelter into the river.

A touch of strength and determination! Aye! Citizen Collot d'Herbois had plenty of that. Was it he, or Carriere who at Arras commanded mothers to stand by while their children were being guillotined? And surely it was Maignet, Collot's friend and colleague, who at Bedouin, because the Red Flag of the Republic had been mysteriously torn down over night, burnt the entire little village down to the last hovel and guillotined every one of the three hundred and fifty inhabitants.

And Chauvelin knew all that. Nay, more! he was himself a member of that so-called government which had countenanced these butcheries, by giving unlimited powers to men like Collot, like Maignet and Carriere. He was at one with them in their republican ideas and he believed in the regeneration and the purification of France, through the medium of the guillotine, but he propounded his theories and carried out his most bloodthirsty schemes with physically clean hands and in an immaculately cut coat.

Even now when Collot d'Herbois lounged before him, with mud-bespattered legs stretched out before him, with dubious linen at neck and wrists, and an odour of rank tobacco and stale, cheap wine pervading his whole personality, the more fastidious man of the world, who had consorted with the dandies of London and Brighton, winced at the enforced proximity.

But it was the joint characteristic of all these men who had turned France into a vast butchery and charnel-house, that they all feared and hated one another, even more whole-heartedly than they hated the aristocrats and so-called traitors whom they sent to the guillotine. Citizen Lebon is said to have dipped his sword into the blood which flowed from the guillotine, whilst exclaiming: "Comme je l'aime ce sang coule de traitre!" but he and Collot and Danton and Robespierre, all of them in fact would have regarded with more delight still the blood of any one of their colleagues.

At this very moment Collot d'Herbois and Chauvelin would with utmost satisfaction have denounced, one the other, to the tender mercies of the Public Prosecutor. Collot made no secret of his hatred for Chauvelin, and the latter disguised it but thinly under the veneer of contemptuous indifference.

"As for that dammed Englishman," added Collot now, after a slight pause, and with another savage oath, "if 'tis my good fortune to lay hands on him, I'd shoot him then and there like a mad dog, and rid France once and forever of this accursed spy."

"And think you, Citizen Collot," rejoined Chauvelin with a shrug of the shoulders, "that France would be rid of all English adventurers by the summary death of this one man?"

"He is the ringleader, at any rate..."

"And has at least nineteen disciples to continue his traditions of conspiracy and intrigue. None perhaps so ingenuous as himself, none with the same daring and good luck perhaps, but still a number of ardent fools only too ready to follow in the footsteps of their chief. Then there's the halo of martyrdom around the murdered hero, the enthusiasm created by his noble death... Nay! nay, Citizen, you have not lived among these English people, you do not understand them, or you would not talk of sending their popular hero to an honoured grave."

But Collot d'Herbois only shook his powerful frame like some big, sulky dog, and spat upon the floor to express his contempt of this wild talk which seemed to have no real tangible purpose.

"You have not caught your Scarlet Pimpernel yet, Citizen," he said with a snort.

"No, but I will, after sundown to-morrow."

"How do you know?"

"I have ordered the Angelus to be rung at one of the closed churches, and he agreed to fight a duel with me on the southern ramparts at that hour and on that day," said Chauvelin simply.

"You take him for a fool?" sneered Collot.

"No, only for a foolhardy adventurer."

"You imagine that with his wife as hostage in our hands, and the whole city of Boulogne on the lookout for him for the sake of the amnesty, that the man would be fool enough to walk on those ramparts at a given hour, for the express purpose of getting himself caught by you and your men?"

"I am quite sure that if we do not lay hands on him before that given hour, that he will be on the ramparts at the Angelus to-morrow," said Chauvelin emphatically.

Collot shrugged his broad shoulders.

"Is the man mad?" he asked with an incredulous laugh.

"Yes, I think so," rejoined the other with a smile.

"And having caught your hare," queried Collot, "how do you propose to cook him?"

"Twelve picked men will be on the ramparts ready to seize him the moment he appears."

"And to shoot him at sight, I hope."

"Only as a last resource, for the Englishman is powerful and may cause our half-famished men a good deal of trouble. But I want him alive, if possible..."

"Why? a dead lion is safer than a live one any day."

"Oh! we'll kill him right enough, Citizen. I pray you have no fear. I hold a weapon ready for that meddlesome Scarlet Pimpernel, which will be a thousand times more deadly and more effectual than a chance shot, or even a guillotine."

"What weapon is that, Citizen Chauvelin?"

Chauvelin leaned forward across the table and rested his chin in his hands; instinctively Collot too leaned towards him, and both men peered furtively round them as if wondering if prying eyes happened to be lurking round. It was Chauvelin's pale eyes which now gleamed with hatred and with an insatiable lust for revenge at least as powerful as Collot's lust for blood; the unsteady light of the tallow candles threw grotesque shadows across his brows, and his mouth was set in such rigid lines of implacable cruelty that the brutish sot beside him gazed on him amazed, vaguely scenting here a depth of feeling which was beyond his power to comprehend. He repeated his question under his breath:

"What weapon do you mean to use against that accursed spy, Citizen Chauvelin?"

"Dishonour and ridicule!" replied the other quietly.

"Bah!"

"In exchange for his life and that of his wife."

"As the woman told you just now... he will refuse."

"We shall see, Citizen."

"You are mad to think such things, Citizen, and ill serve the Republic by sparing her bitterest foe."

A long, sarcastic laugh broke from Chauvelin's parted lips.

"Spare him?—spare the Scarlet Pimpernel!..." he ejaculated. "Nay, Citizen, you need have no fear of that. But believe me, I have schemes in my head by which the man whom we all hate will be more truly destroyed than your guillotine could ever accomplish: schemes, whereby the hero who is now worshipped in England as a demi-god will suddenly become an object of loathing and of contempt.... Ah! I see you understand me now... I wish to so cover him with ridicule that the very name of the small wayside flower will become a term of derision and of scorn. Only then shall we be rid of these pestilential English spies, only then will the entire League of the Scarlet Pimpernel become a thing of the past when its whilom leader, now thought akin to a god, will have found refuge in a suicide's grave, from the withering contempt of the entire world."

Chauvelin had spoken low, hardly above a whisper, and the echo of his last words died away in the great, squalid room like a long-drawn-out sigh. There was dead silence for a while save for the murmur in the wind outside and from the floor above the measured tread of the sentinel guarding the precious hostage in No. 6.

Both men were staring straight in front of them. Collot d'Herbois incredulous, half-contemptuous, did not altogether approve of these schemes which seemed to him wild and uncanny: he liked the direct simplicity of a summary trial, of the guillotine, or of his own well stage-managed "Noyades." He did not feel that any ridicule or dishonour would necessarily paralyze a man in his efforts at intrigue, and would have liked to set Chauvelin's authority aside, to behead the woman upstairs and then to take his chances of capturing the man later on.

But the orders of the Committee of Public Safety had been peremptory: he was to be Chauvelin's help—not his master, and to obey in all things. He did not dare to take any initiative in the matter, for in that case, if he failed, the reprisals against him would indeed be terrible.

He was fairly satisfied now that Chauvelin had accepted his suggestion of summarily sending to the guillotine one member of every family resident in Boulogne, if Marguerite succeeded in effecting an escape, and, of a truth, Chauvelin had hailed the fiendish suggestion with delight. The old abbe with his nephew and niece were undoubtedly not sufficient deterrents against the daring schemes of the Scarlet Pimpernel, who, as a matter of fact, could spirit them out of Boulogne just as easily as he would his own wife.

Collot's plan tied Marguerite to her own prison cell more completely than any other measure could have done, more so indeed than the originator thereof knew or believed.... A man like this d'Herbois—born in the gutter, imbued with every brutish tradition, which generations of jail-birds had bequeathed to him,—would not perhaps fully realize the fact that neither Sir Percy nor Marguerite Blakeney would ever save themselves at the expense of others. He had merely made the suggestion, because he felt that Chauvelin's plans were complicated and obscure, and above all insufficient, and that perhaps after all the English adventurer and his wife would succeed in once more outwitting him, when there would remain the grand and bloody compensation of a wholesale butchery in Boulogne.

But Chauvelin was quite satisfied. He knew that under present circumstances neither Sir Percy nor Marguerite would make any attempt to escape. The ex-ambassador had lived in England: he understood the class to which these two belonged, and was quite convinced that no attempt would be made on either side to get Lady Blakeney away whilst the present ferocious order against the bread-winner of every family in the town held good.

Aye! the measures were sound enough. Chauvelin was easy in his mind about that. In another twenty-four hours he would hold the man completely in his power who had so boldly outwitted him last year; to-night he would sleep in peace: an entire city was guarding the precious hostage.

"We'll go to bed now, Citizen," he said to Collot, who, tired and sulky, was moodily fingering the papers on the table. The scraping sound which he made thereby grated on Chauvelin's overstrung nerves. He wanted to be alone, and the sleepy brute's presence here jarred on his own solemn mood.

To his satisfaction, Collot grunted a surly assent. Very leisurely he rose from his chair, stretched out his loose limbs, shook himself like a shaggy cur, and without uttering another word he gave his colleague a curt nod, and slowly lounged out of the room.

CHAPTER XXV. THE UNEXPECTED

Chauvelin heaved a deep sigh of satisfaction when Collot d'Herbois finally left him to himself. He listened for awhile until the heavy footsteps died away in the distance, then leaning back in his chair, he gave himself over to the delights of the present situation.

Marguerite in his power. Sir Percy Blakeney compelled to treat for her rescue if he did not wish to see her die a miserable death.

"Aye! my elusive hero," he muttered to himself, "methinks that we shall be able to cry quits at last."

Outside everything had become still. Even the wind in the trees out there on the ramparts had ceased their melancholy moaning. The man was alone with his thoughts. He felt secure and at peace, sure of victory, content to await the events of the next twenty-four hours. The other side of the door the guard which he had picked out from amongst the more feeble and ill-fed garrison of the little city for attendance on his own person were ranged ready to respond to his call.

"Dishonour and ridicule! Derision and scorn!" he murmured, gloating over the very sound of these words, which expressed all that he hoped to accomplish, "utter abjections, then perhaps a suicide's grave..."

He loved the silence around him, for he could murmur these words and hear them echoing against the bare stone walls like the whisperings of all the spirits of hate which were waiting to lend him their aid.

How long he had remained thus absorbed in his meditations, he could not afterwards have said; a minute or two perhaps at most, whilst he leaned back in his chair with eyes closed, savouring the sweets of his own thoughts, when suddenly the silence was interrupted by a loud and pleasant laugh and a drawly voice speaking in merry accents:

"The lud live you, Monsieur Chaubertin, and pray how do you propose to accomplish all these pleasant things?"

In a moment Chauvelin was on his feet and with eyes dilated, lips parted in awed bewilderment, he was gazing towards the open window, where astride upon the sill, one leg inside the room, the other out, and with the moon shining full on his suit of delicate-coloured cloth, his wide caped coat and elegant chapeau-bras, sat the imperturbable Sir Percy.

"I heard you muttering such pleasant words, Monsieur," continued Blakeney calmly, "that the temptation seized me to join in the conversation. A man talking to himself is ever in a sorry plight... he is either a mad man or a fool..."

He laughed his own quaint and inane laugh and added apologetically:

"Far be if from me, sir, to apply either epithet to you... demmed bad form calling another fellow names... just when he does not quite feel himself, eh?... You don't feel quite yourself, I fancy just now... eh, Monsieur Chaubertin... er... beg pardon, Chauvelin..."

He sat there quite comfortably, one slender hand resting on the gracefully-fashioned hilt of his sword—the sword of Lorenzo Cenci,—the other holding up the gold-rimmed eyeglass through which he was regarding his avowed enemy; he was dressed as for a ball, and his perpetually amiable smile lurked round the corners of his firm lips.

Chauvelin had undoubtedly for the moment lost his presence of mind. He did not even think of calling to his picked guard, so completely taken aback was he by this unforeseen move on the part of Sir Percy. Yet, obviously, he should have been ready for this eventuality. Had he not caused the town-crier to loudly proclaim throughout the city that if ONE female prisoner escaped from Fort Gayole the entire able-bodied population of Boulogne would suffer?

The moment Sir Percy entered the gates of the town, he could not help but hear the proclamation, and hear at the same time that this one female prisoner who was so precious a charge, was the wife of the English spy: the Scarlet Pimpernel.

Moreover, was it not a fact that whenever or wherever the Scarlet Pimpernel was least expected there and then would he surely appear? Having once realized that it was his wife who was incarcerated in Fort Gayole, was it not natural that he would go and prowl around the prison, and along the avenue on the summit of the southern ramparts, which was accessible to every passer-by? No doubt he had lain in hiding among the trees, had perhaps caught snatches of Chauvelin's recent talk with Collot.

Aye! it was all so natural, so simple! Strange that it should have been so unexpected!

Furious at himself for his momentary stupor, he now made a vigorous effort to face his impudent enemy with the same sang-froid of which the latter had so inexhaustible a fund.

He walked quietly towards the window, compelling his nerves to perfect calm and his mood to indifference. The situation had ceased to astonish him; already his keen mind had seen its possibilities, its grimness and its humour, and he was quite prepared to enjoy these to the full.

Sir Percy now was dusting the sleeve of his coat with a lace-edged handkerchief, but just as Chauvelin was about to come near him, he stretched out one leg, turning the point of a dainty boot towards the ex-ambassador.

"Would you like to take hold of me by the leg, Monsieur Chaubertin?" he said gaily. "'Tis more effectual than a shoulder, and your picked guard of six stalwart fellows can have the other leg.... Nay! I pray you, sir, do not look at me like that.... I vow that it is myself and not my ghost.... But if you still doubt me, I pray you call the guard... ere I fly out again towards that fitful moon..."

"Nay, Sir Percy," said Chauvelin, with a steady voice, "I have no thought that you will take flight just yet.... Methinks you desire conversation with me, or you had not paid me so unexpected a visit."

"Nay, sir, the air is too oppressive for lengthy conversation... I was strolling along these ramparts, thinking of our pleasant encounter at the hour of the Angelus tomorrow... when this light attracted me.... feared I had lost my way and climbed the window to obtain information."

"As to your way to the nearest prison cell, Sir Percy?" queried Chauvelin drily.

"As to anywhere, where I could sit more comfortably than on this demmed sill.... It must be very dusty, and I vow 'tis terribly hard..."

"I presume, Sir Percy, that you did my colleague and myself the honour of listening to our conversation?"

"An you desired to talk secrets, Monsieur... er... Chaubertin... you should have shut this window... and closed this avenue of trees against the chance passer-by."

"What we said was no secret, Sir Percy. It is all over the town to-night."

"Quite so... you were only telling the devil your mind... eh?"

"I had also been having conversation with Lady Blakeney.... Pray did you hear any of that, sir?"

But Sir Percy had evidently not heard the question, for he seemed quite absorbed in the task of removing a speck of dust from his immaculate chapeau-bras.

"These hats are all the rage in England just now," he said airily, "but they have had their day, do you not think so, Monsieur? When I return to town, I shall have to devote my whole mind to the invention of a new headgear..."

"When will you return to England, Sir Percy?" queried Chauvelin with good-natured sarcasm.

"At the turn of the tide to-morrow eve, Monsieur," replied Blakeney.

"In company with Lady Blakeney?"

"Certainly, sir... and yours if you will honour us with your company."

"If you return to England to-morrow, Sir Percy, Lady Blakeney, I fear me, cannot accompany you."

"You astonish me, sir," rejoined Blakeney with an exclamation of genuine and unaffected surprise. "I wonder now what would prevent her?"

"All those whose death would be the result of her flight, if she succeeded in escaping from Boulogne..."

But Sir Percy was staring at him, with wide open eyes expressive of utmost amazement.

"Dear, dear, dear.... Lud! but that sounds most unfortunate..."

"You have not heard of the measures which I have taken to prevent Lady Blakeney quitting this city without our leave?"

"No, Monsieur Chaubertin... no... I have heard nothing..." rejoined Sir Percy blandly. "I lead a very retired life when I come abroad and..."

"Would you wish to hear them now?"

"Quite unnecessary, sir, I assure you... and the hour is getting late..."

"Sir Percy, are you aware of the fact that unless you listen to what I have to say, your wife will be dragged before the Committee of Public Safety in Paris within the next twenty-four hours?" said Chauvelin firmly.

"What swift horses you must have, sir," quoth Blakeney pleasantly. "Lud! to think of it!... I always heard that these demmed French horses would never beat ours across country."

But Chauvelin now would not allow himself to be ruffled by Sir Percy's apparent indifference. Keen reader of emotions as he was, he had not failed to note a distinct change in the drawly voice, a sound of something hard and trenchant in the flippant laugh, ever since Marguerite's name was first mentioned. Blakeney's attitude was apparently as careless, as audacious as before, but Chauvelin's keen eyes had not missed the almost imperceptible tightening of the jaw and the rapid clenching of one hand on the sword hilt even whilst the other toyed in graceful idleness with the filmy Mechlin lace cravat.

Sir Percy's head was well thrown back, and the pale rays of the moon caught the edge of the clear-cut profile, the low massive brow, the drooping lids through which the audacious plotter was lazily regarding the man who held not only his own life, but that of the woman who was infinitely dear to him, in the hollow of his hand.

"I am afraid, Sir Percy," continued Chauvelin drily, "that you are under the impression that bolts and bars will yield to your usual good luck, now that so precious a life is at stake as that of Lady Blakeney."

"I am a greater believer in impressions, Monsieur Chauvelin."

"I told her just now that if she quitted Boulogne ere the Scarlet Pimpernel is in our hands, we should summarily shoot one member of every family in the town—the breadwinner."

"A pleasant conceit, Monsieur... and one that does infinite credit to your inventive faculties."

"Lady Blakeney, therefore, we hold safely enough," continued Chauvelin, who no longer heeded the mocking observations of his enemy; "as for the Scarlet Pimpernel..."

"You have but to ring a bell, to raise a voice, and he too will be under lock and key within the next two minutes, eh?... Passons, Monsieur... you are dying to say something further... I pray you proceed... your engaging countenance is becoming quite interesting in its seriousness."

"What I wish to say to you, Sir Percy, is in the nature of a proposed bargain."

"Indeed?... Monsieur, you are full of surprises... like a pretty woman.... And pray what are the terms of this proposed bargain?"

"Your side of the bargain, Sir Percy, or mine? Which will you hear first?"

"Oh yours, Monsieur... yours, I pray you.... Have I not said that you are like a pretty woman?... Place aux dames, sir! always!"

"My share of the bargain, sir, is simple enough: Lady Blakeney, escorted by yourself and any of your friends who might be in this city at the time, shall leave Boulogne harbour at sunset to-morrow, free and unmolested, if you on the other hand will do your share..."

"I don't yet know what my share in this interesting bargain is to be, sir... but for the sake of argument let us suppose that I do not carry it out.... What then?..."

"Then, Sir Percy... putting aside for the moment the question of the Scarlet Pimpernel altogether... then, Lady Blakeney will be taken to Paris, and will be incarcerated in the prison of the Temple lately vacated by Marie Antoinette—there she will be treated in exactly the same way as the ex-queen is now being treated in the Conciergerie.... Do you know what that means, Sir Percy?... It does not mean a summary trial and a speedy death, with the halo and glory of martyrdom thrown in... it means days, weeks, nay, months, perhaps, of misery and humiliation... it means, that like Marie Antoinette, she will never be allowed solitude for one single instant of the day or night... it means the constant proximity of soldiers, drunk with cruelty and with hate... the insults, the shame..."

"You hound!... you dog!... you cur!... do you not see that I must strangle you for this!..."

The attack had been so sudden and so violent that Chauvelin had not the time to utter the slightest call for help. But a second ago, Sir Percy Blakeney had been sitting on the window-sill, outwardly listening with perfect calm to what his enemy had to say; now he was at the latter's throat, pressing with long and slender hands the breath out of the Frenchman's body, his usually placid face distorted into a mask of hate.

"You cur!... you cur!..." he repeated, "am I to kill you or will you unsay those words?"

Then suddenly he relaxed his grip. The habits of a lifetime would not be gainsaid even now. A second ago his face had been livid with rage and hate, now a quick flush overspread it, as if he were ashamed of this loss of self-control. He threw the little Frenchman away from him like he would a beast which had snarled, and passed his hand across his brow.

"Lud forgive me!" he said quaintly, "I had almost lost my temper."

Chauvelin was not slow in recovering himself. He was plucky and alert, and his hatred for this man was so great that he had actually ceased to fear him. Now he quietly readjusted his cravat, made a vigorous effort to re-conquer his breath, and said firmly as soon as he could contrive to speak at all:

"And if you did strangle me, Sir Percy, you would do yourself no good. The fate which I have mapped out for Lady Blakeney, would then irrevocably be hers, for she is in our power and none of my colleagues are disposed to offer you a means of saving her from it, as I am ready to do."

Blakeney was now standing in the middle of the room, with his hands buried in the pockets of his breeches, his manner and attitude once more calm, debonair, expressive of lofty self-possession and of absolute indifference. He came quite close to the meagre little figure of his exultant enemy, thereby forcing the latter to look up at him.

"Oh!... ah!... yes!" he said airily, "I had nigh forgotten... you were talking of a bargain... my share of it... eh?... Is it me you want?... Do you wish to see me in your Paris prisons?... I assure you, sir, that the propinquity of drunken soldiers may disgust me, but it would in no way disturb the equanimity of my temper."

"I am quite sure of that, Sir Percy—and I can but repeat what I had the honour of saying to Lady Blakeney just now—I do not desire the death of so accomplished a gentleman as yourself."

"Strange, Monsieur," retorted Blakeney, with a return of his accustomed flippancy. "Now I do desire your death very strongly indeed—there would be so much less vermin on the face of the earth.... But pardon me—I was interrupting you.... Will you be so kind as to proceed?"

Chauvelin had not winced at the insult. His enemy's attitude now left him completely indifferent. He had seen that self-possessed man of the world, that dainty and fastidious dandy, in the throes of an overmastering passion. He had very nearly paid with his life for the joy of having roused that supercilious and dormant lion. In fact he was ready to welcome any insults from Sir Percy Blakeney now, since these would be only additional evidences that the Englishman's temper was not yet under control.

"I will try to be brief, Sir Percy," he said, setting himself the task of imitating his antagonist's affected manner. "Will you not sit down?... We must try and discuss these matters like two men of the world.... As for me, I am always happiest beside a board littered with papers.... I am not an athlete, Sir Percy... and serve my country with my pen rather than with my fists."

Whilst he spoke he had reached the table and once more took the chair whereon he had been sitting lately, when he dreamed the dreams which were so near realization now. He pointed with a graceful gesture to the other vacant chair, which Blakeney took without a word.

"Ah!" said Chauvelin with a sigh of satisfaction, "I see that we are about to understand one another.... I have always felt it was a pity, Sir Percy, that you and I could not discuss certain matters pleasantly with one another.... Now, about this unfortunate incident of Lady Blakeney's incarceration, I would like you to believe that I had no part in the arrangements which have been made for her detention in Paris. My colleagues have arranged it all... and I have vainly tried to protest against the rigorous measures which are to be enforced against her in the Temple prison.... But these are answering so completely in the case of the ex-queen, they have so completely broken her spirit and her pride, that my colleagues felt that they would prove equally useful in order to bring the Scarlet Pimpernel—through his wife—to an humbler frame of mind."

He paused a moment, distinctly pleased with his peroration, satisfied that his voice had been without a tremor and his face impassive, and wondering what effect this somewhat lengthy preamble had upon Sir Percy, who through it all had remained singularly quiet. Chauvelin was preparing himself for the next effect which he hoped to produce, and was vaguely seeking for the best words with which to fully express his meaning, when he was suddenly startled by a sound as unexpected as it was disconcerting.

It was the sound of a loud and prolonged snore. He pushed the candle aside, which somewhat obstructed his line of vision, and casting a rapid glance at the enemy, with whose life he was toying even as a cat doth with that of a mouse, he saw that the aforesaid mouse was calmly and unmistakably asleep.

An impatient oath escaped Chauvelin's lips, and he brought his fist heavily down on the table, making the metal candlesticks rattle and causing Sir Percy to open one sleepy eye.

"A thousand pardons, sir," said Blakeney with a slight yawn. "I am so demmed fatigued, and your preface was unduly long.... Beastly bad form, I know, going to sleep during a sermon... but I haven't had a wink of sleep all day.... I pray you to excuse me..."

"Will you condescend to listen, Sir Percy?" queried Chauvelin peremptorily, "or shall I call the guard and give up all thoughts of treating with you?"

"Just whichever you demmed well prefer, sir," rejoined Blakeney impatiently.

And once more stretching out his long limbs, he buried his hands in the pockets of his breeches and apparently prepared himself for another quiet sleep. Chauvelin looked at him for a moment, vaguely wondering what to do next. He felt strangely irritated at what he firmly believed was mere affectation on Blakeney's part, and although he was burning with impatience to place the terms of the proposed bargain before this man, yet he would have preferred to be interrogated, to deliver his "either-or" with becoming sternness and decision, rather than to take the initiative in this discussion, where he should have been calm and indifferent, whilst his enemy should have been nervous and disturbed.

Sir Percy's attitude had disconcerted him, a touch of the grotesque had been given to what should have been a tense moment, and it was terribly galling to the pride of the ex-diplomatist that with this elusive enemy and in spite of his own preparedness for any eventuality, it was invariably the unforeseen that happened.

After a moment's reflection, however, he decided upon a fresh course of action. He rose and crossed the room, keeping as much as possible an eye upon Sir Percy, but the latter sat placid and dormant and evidently in no hurry to move. Chauvelin having reached the door, opened it noiselessly, and to the sergeant in command of his bodyguard who stood at attention outside, he whispered hurriedly:

"The prisoner from No. 6.... Let two of the men bring her hither back to me at once."

CHAPTER XXVI. THE TERMS OF THE BARGAIN

Less than three minutes later, there came to Chauvelin's expectant ears the soft sound made by a woman's skirts against the stone floor. During those three minutes, which had seemed an eternity to his impatience, he had sat silently watching the slumber—affected or real—of his enemy.

Directly he heard the word: "Halt!" outside the door, he jumped to his feet. The next moment Marguerite had entered the room.

Hardly had her foot crossed the threshold than Sir Percy rose, quietly and without haste but evidently fully awake, and turning towards her, made her a low obeisance.

She, poor woman, had of course caught sight of him at once. His presence here, Chauvelin's demand for her reappearance, the soldiers in a small compact group outside the door, all these were unmistakable proofs that the awful cataclysm had at last occurred.

The Scarlet Pimpernel, Percy Blakeney, her husband, was in the hands of the Terrorists of France, and though face to face with her now, with an open window close to him, and an apparently helpless enemy under his hand, he could not—owing to the fiendish measures taken by Chauvelin—raise a finger to save himself and her.

Mercifully for her, nature—in the face of this appalling tragedy—deprived her of the full measure of her senses. She could move and speak and see, she could hear and in a measure understand what was said, but she was really an automaton or a sleep-walker, moving and speaking mechanically and without due comprehension.

Possibly, if she had then and there fully realized all that the future meant, she would have gone mad with the horror of it all.

"Lady Blakeney," began Chauvelin after he had quickly dismissed the soldiers from the room, "when you and I parted from one another just now, I had no idea that I should so soon have the pleasure of a personal conversation with Sir Percy.... There is no occasion yet, believe me, for sorrow or fear.... Another twenty-four hours at most, and you will be on board the 'Day-Dream' outward bound for England. Sir Percy himself might perhaps accompany you; he does not desire that you should journey to Paris, and I may safely say, that in his mind, he has already accepted certain little conditions which I have been forced to impose upon him ere I sign the order for your absolute release."

"Conditions?" she repeated vaguely and stupidly, looking in bewilderment from one to the other.

"You are tired, m'dear," said Sir Percy quietly, "will you not sit down?"

He held the chair gallantly for her. She tried to read his face, but could not catch even a flash from beneath the heavy lids which obstinately veiled his eyes.

"Oh! it is a mere matter of exchanging signatures," continued Chauvelin in response to her inquiring glance and toying with the papers which were scattered on the table. "Here you see is the order to allow Sir Percy Blakeney and his wife, nee Marguerite St. Just, to quit the town of Boulogne unmolested."

He held a paper out towards Marguerite, inviting her to look at it. She caught sight of an official-looking document, bearing the motto and seal of the Republic of France, and of her own name and Percy's written thereon in full.

"It is perfectly en regle, I assure you," continued Chauvelin, "and only awaits my signature."

He now took up another paper which looked like a long closely-written letter. Marguerite watched his every movement, for instinct told her that the supreme moment had come. There was a look of almost superhuman cruelty and malice in the little Frenchman's eyes as he fixed them on the impassive figure of Sir Percy, the while with slightly trembling hands he fingered that piece of paper and smoothed out its creases with loving care.

"I am quite prepared to sign the order for your release, Lady Blakeney," he said, keeping his gaze still keenly fixed upon Sir Percy. "When it is signed you will understand that our measures against the citizens of Boulogne will no longer hold good, and that on the contrary, the general amnesty and free pardon will come into force."

"Yes, I understand that," she replied.

"And all that will come to pass, Lady Blakeney, the moment Sir Percy will write me in his own hand a letter, in accordance with the draft which I have prepared, and sign it with his name."

"Shall I read it to you?" he asked.

"If you please."

"You will see how simple it all is.... A mere matter of form.... I pray you do not look upon it with terror, but only as the prelude to that general amnesty and free pardon, which I feel sure will satisfy the philanthropic heart of the noble Scarlet Pimpernel, since three score at least of the inhabitants of Boulogne will owe their life and freedom to him."

"I am listening, Monsieur," she said calmly.

"As I have already had the honour of explaining, this little document is in the form of a letter addressed personally to me and of course in French," he said finally, and then he looked down on the paper and began to read:

Citizen Chauvelin—

In consideration of a further sum of one million francs and on the understanding that this ridiculous charge brought against me of conspiring against the Republic of France is immediately withdrawn, and I am allowed to return to England unmolested, I am quite prepared to acquaint you with the names and whereabouts of certain persons who under the guise of the League of the Scarlet Pimpernel are even now conspiring to free the woman Marie Antoinette and her son from prison and to place the latter upon the throne of France. You are quite well aware that under the pretence of being the leader of a gang of English adventurers, who never did the Republic of France and her people any real harm, I have actually been the means of unmasking many a royalist plot before you, and of bringing many persistent conspirators to the guillotine. I am surprised that you should cavil at the price I am asking this time for the very important information with which I am able to furnish you, whilst you have often paid me similar sums for work which was a great deal less difficult to do. In order to serve your government effectually, both in England and in France, I must have a sufficiency of money, to enable me to live in a costly style befitting a gentleman of my rank. Were I to alter my mode of life I could not continue to mix in that same social milieu to which all my friends belong and wherein, as you are well aware, most of the royalist plots are hatched.

Trusting therefore to receive a favourable reply to my just demands within the next twenty-four hours, whereupon the names in question shall be furnished you forthwith,

I have the honour to remain, Citizen,

Your humble and obedient servant,

When he had finished reading, Chauvelin quietly folded the paper up again, and then only did he look at the man and the woman before him.

Marguerite sat very erect, her head thrown back, her face very pale and her hands tightly clutched in her lap. She had not stirred whilst Chauvelin read out the infamous document, with which he desired to brand a brave man with the ineradicable stigma of dishonour and of shame. After she heard the first words, she looked up swiftly and questioningly at her husband, but he stood at some little distance from her, right out of the flickering circle of yellowish light made by the burning tallow-candle. He was as rigid as a statue, standing in his usual attitude with legs apart and hands buried in his breeches pockets.

She could not see his face.

Whatever she may have felt with regard to the letter, as the meaning of it gradually penetrated into her brain, she was, of course, convinced of one thing, and that was that never for a moment would Percy dream of purchasing his life or even hers at such a price. But she would have liked some sign from him, some look by which she could be guided as to her immediate conduct: as, however, he gave neither look nor sign, she preferred to assume an attitude of silent contempt.

But even before Chauvelin had had time to look from one face to the other, a prolonged and merry laugh echoed across the squalid room.

Sir Percy, with head thrown back, was laughing whole-heartedly.

"A magnificent epistle, sir," he said gaily, "Lud love you, where did you wield the pen so gracefully?... I vow that if I signed this interesting document no one will believe I could have expressed myself with perfect ease.. and in French too..."

"Nay, Sir Percy," rejoined Chauvelin drily, "I have thought of all that, and lest in the future there should be any doubt as to whether your own hand had or had not penned the whole of this letter, I also make it a condition that you write out every word of it yourself, and sign it here in this very room, in the presence of Lady Blakeney, of myself, of my colleagues and of at least half a dozen other persons whom I will select."

"It is indeed admirably thought out, Monsieur," rejoined Sir Percy, "and what is to become of the charming epistle, may I ask, after I have written and signed it?... Pardon my curiosity.... I take a natural interest in the matter... and truly your ingenuity passes belief..."

"Oh! the fate of this letter will be as simple as was the writing thereof.... A copy of it will be published in our 'Gazette de Paris' as a bait for enterprising English journalists.... They will not be backward in getting hold of so much interesting matter.... Can you not see the attractive headlines in 'The London Gazette,' Sir Percy? 'The League of the Scarlet Pimpernel unmasked! A gigantic hoax! The origin of the Blakeney millions!'... I believe that journalism in England has reached a high standard of excellence... and even the 'Gazette de Paris' is greatly read in certain towns of your charming country.... His Royal Highness the Prince of Wales, and various other influential gentlemen in London, will, on the other hand, be granted a private view of the original through the kind offices of certain devoted friends whom we possess in England.... I don't think that you need have any fear, Sir Percy, that your caligraphy will sink into oblivion. It will be our business to see that it obtains the full measure of publicity which it deserves..."

He paused a moment, then his manner suddenly changed: the sarcastic tone died out of his voice, and there came back into his face that look of hatred and cruelty which Blakeney's persiflage had always the power to evoke.

"You may rest assured of one thing, Sir Percy," he said with a harsh laugh, "that enough mud will be thrown at that erstwhile glorious Scarlet Pimpernel... some of it will be bound to stick..."

"Nay, Monsieur... er... Chaubertin," quoth Blakeney lightly, "I have no doubt that you and your colleagues are past masters in the graceful art of mud-throwing.... But pardon me... er.... I was interrupting you.... Continue, Monsieur... continue, I pray. 'Pon my honour, the matter is vastly diverting."

"Nay, sir, after the publication of this diverting epistle, meseems your honour will ceased to be a marketable commodity."

"Undoubtedly, sir," rejoined Sir Percy, apparently quite unruffled, "pardon a slip of the tongue... we are so much the creatures of habit.... As you were saying...?"

"I have but little more to say, sir.... But lest there should even now be lurking in your mind a vague hope that, having written this letter, you could easily in the future deny its authorship, let me tell you this: my measures are well taken, there will be witnesses to your writing of it.... You will sit here in this room, unfettered, uncoerced in any way, and the money spoken of in the letter will be handed over to you by my colleague, after a few suitable words spoken by him, and you will take the money from him, Sir Percy... and the witnesses will see you take it after having seen you write the letter... they will understand that you are being PAID by the French government for giving information anent royalist plots in this country and in England... they will understand that your identity as the leader of that so-called band is not only known to me and to my colleague, but that it also covers your real character and profession as the paid spy of France."

"Marvellous, I call it... demmed marvellous," quoth Sir Percy blandly.

Chauvelin had paused, half-choked by his own emotion, his hatred and prospective revenge. He passed his handkerchief over his forehead, which was streaming with perspiration.

"Warm work, this sort of thing... eh... Monsieur... er... Chaubertin?..." queried his imperturbable enemy.

Marguerite said nothing; the whole thing was too horrible for words, but she kept her large eyes fixed upon her husband's face... waiting for that look, that sign from him which would have eased the agonizing anxiety in her heart, and which never came.

With a great effort now, Chauvelin pulled himself together and, though his voice still trembled, he managed to speak with a certain amount of calm:

"Probably, Sir Percy, you know," he said, "that throughout the whole of France we are inaugurating a series of national fetes, in honour of the new religion which the people are about to adopt.... Demoiselle Desiree Candeille, whom you know, will at these festivals impersonate the Goddess of Reason, the only deity whom we admit now in France.... She has been specially chosen for this honour, owing to the services which she has rendered us recently... and as Boulogne happens to be the lucky city in which we have succeeded in bringing the Scarlet Pimpernel to justice, the national fete will begin within these city walls, with Demoiselle Candeille as the thrice-honoured goddess."

"And you will be very merry here in Boulogne, I dare swear..."

"Aye, merry, sir," said Chauvelin with an involuntary and savage snarl, as he placed a long claw-like finger upon the momentous paper before him, "merry, for we here in Boulogne will see that which will fill the heart of every patriot in France with gladness.... Nay! 'twas not the death of the Scarlet Pimpernel we wanted... not the noble martyrdom of England's chosen hero... but his humiliation and defeat... derision and scorn... contumely and contempt. You asked me airily just now, Sir Percy, how I proposed to accomplish this object... Well! you know it now—by forcing you... aye, forcing—to write and sign a letter and to take money from my hands which will brand you forever as a liar and informer, and cover you with the thick and slimy mud of irreclaimable infamy..."

"Lud! sir," said Sir Percy pleasantly, "what a wonderful command you have of our language.... I wish I could speak French half as well..."

Marguerite had risen like an automaton from her chair. She felt that she could no longer sit still, she wanted to scream out at the top of her voice, all the horror she felt for this dastardly plot, which surely must have had its origin in the brain of devils. She could not understand Percy. This was one of those awful moments, which she had been destined to experience once or twice before, when the whole personality of her husband seemed to become shadowy before her, to slip, as it were, past her comprehension, leaving her indescribably lonely and wretched, trusting yet terrified.

She thought that long ere this he would have flung back every insult in his opponent's teeth; she did not know what inducements Chauvelin had held out in exchange for the infamous letter, what threats he had used. That her own life and freedom were at stake, was, of course, evident, but she cared nothing for life, and he should know that certainly she would care still less if such a price had to be paid for it.

She longed to tell him all that was in her heart, longed to tell him how little she valued her life, how highly she prized his honour! but how could she, before this fiend who snarled and sneered in his anticipated triumph, and surely, surely Percy knew!

And knowing all that, why did he not speak? Why did he not tear that infamous paper from out that devil's hands and fling it in his face? Yet, though her loving ear caught every intonation of her husband's voice, she could not detect the slightest harshness in his airy laugh; his tone was perfectly natural and he seemed to be, indeed, just as he appeared—vastly amused.

Then she thought that perhaps he would wish her to go now, that he felt desire to be alone with this man, who had outraged him in everything that he held most holy and most dear, his honour and his wife... that perhaps, knowing that his own temper was no longer under control, he did not wish her to witness the rough and ready chastisement which he was intending to mete out to this dastardly intriguer.

Yes! that was it no doubt! Herein she could not be mistaken; she knew his fastidious notions of what was due and proper in the presence of a woman, and that even at a moment like this, he would wish the manners of London drawing-rooms to govern his every action.

Therefore she rose to go, and as she did so, once more tried to read the expression in his face... to guess what was passing in his mind.

"Nay, Madam," he said, whilst he bowed gracefully before her, "I fear me this lengthy conversation hath somewhat fatigued you.... This merry jest 'twixt my engaging friend and myself should not have been prolonged so far into the night.... Monsieur, I pray you, will you not give orders that her ladyship be escorted back to her room?"

He was still standing outside the circle of light, and Marguerite instinctively went up to him. For this one second she was oblivious of Chauvelin's presence, she forgot her well-schooled pride, her firm determination to be silent and to be brave: she could no longer restrain the wild beatings of her heart, the agony of her soul, and with sudden impulse she murmured in a voice broken with intense love and subdued, passionate appeal:

"Percy!"

He drew back a step further into the gloom: this made her realize the mistake she had made in allowing her husband's most bitter enemy to get this brief glimpse into her soul. Chauvelin's thin lips curled with satisfaction, the brief glimpse had been sufficient for him, the rapidly whispered name, the broken accent had told him what he had not known hitherto: namely, that between this man and woman there was a bond far more powerful that that which usually existed between husband and wife, and merely made up of chivalry on the one side and trustful reliance on the other.

Marguerite having realized her mistake, ashamed of having betrayed her feelings even for a moment, threw back her proud head and gave her exultant foe a look of defiance and of scorn. He responded with one of pity, not altogether unmixed with deference. There was something almost unearthly and sublime in this beautiful woman's agonizing despair.

He lowered his head and made her a deep obeisance, lest she should see the satisfaction and triumph which shone through his pity.

As usual Sir Percy remained quite imperturbable, and now it was he, who, with characteristic impudence, touched the hand-bell on the table:

"Excuse this intrusion, Monsieur," he said lightly, "her ladyship is overfatigued and would be best in her room."

Marguerite threw him a grateful look. After all she was only a woman and was afraid of breaking down. In her mind there was no issue to the present deadlock save in death. For this she was prepared and had but one great hope that she could lie in her husband's arms just once again before she died. Now, since she could not speak to him, scarcely dared to look into the loved face, she was quite ready to go.

In answer to the bell, the soldier had entered.

"If Lady Blakeney desires to go..." said Chauvelin.

She nodded and Chauvelin gave the necessary orders: two soldiers stood at attention ready to escort Marguerite back to her prison cell. As she went towards the door she came to within a couple of steps from where her husband was standing, bowing to her as she passed. She stretched out an icy cold hand towards him, and he, in the most approved London fashion, with the courtly grace of a perfect English gentleman, took the little hand in his and stooping very low kissed the delicate finger-tips.

Then only did she notice that the strong, nervy hand which held hers trembled perceptibly, and that his lips—which for an instant rested on her fingers—were burning hot.

CHAPTER XXVII. THE DECISION

Once more the two men were alone.

As far as Chauvelin was concerned he felt that everything was not yet settled, and until a moment ago he had been in doubt as to whether Sir Percy would accept the infamous conditions which had been put before him, or allow his pride and temper to get the better of him and throw the deadly insults back into his adversary's teeth.

But now a new secret had been revealed to the astute diplomatist. A name, softly murmured by a broken-hearted woman, had told him a tale of love and passion, which he had not even suspected before.

Since he had made this discovery he knew that the ultimate issue was no longer in doubt. Sir Percy Blakeney, the bold adventurer, ever ready for a gamble where lives were at stake, might have demurred before he subscribed to his own dishonour, in order to save his wife from humiliation and the shame of the terrible fate that had been mapped out for her. But the same man passionately in love with such a woman as Marguerite Blakeney would count the world well lost for her sake.

One sudden fear alone had shot through Chauvelin's heart when he stood face to face with the two people whom he had so deeply and cruelly wronged, and that was that Blakeney, throwing aside all thought of the scores of innocent lives that were at stake, might forget everything, risk everything, dare everything, in order to get his wife away there and then.

For the space of a few seconds Chauvelin had felt that his own life was in jeopardy, and that the Scarlet Pimpernel would indeed make a desperate effort to save himself and his wife. But the fear was short-lived: Marguerite—as he had well foreseen—would never save herself at the expense of others, and she was tied! tied! tied! That was his triumph and his joy!

When Marguerite finally left the room, Sir Percy made no motion to follow her, but turned once more quietly to his antagonist.

"As you were saying, Monsieur?..." he queried lightly.

"Oh! there is nothing more to say, Sir Percy," rejoined Chauvelin; "my conditions are clear to you, are they not? Lady Blakeney's and your own immediate release in exchange for a letter written to me by your own hand, and signed here by you—in this room—in my presence and that of sundry other persons whom I need not name just now. Also certain money passing from my hand to yours. Failing the letter, a long, hideously humiliating sojourn in the Temple prison for your wife, a prolonged trial and the guillotine as a happy release!... I would add, the same thing for yourself, only that I will do you the justice to admit that you probably do not care."

"Nay! a grave mistake, Monsieur.... I do care... vastly care, I assure you ... and would seriously object to ending my life on your demmed guillotine... a nasty, uncomfortable thing, I should say... and I am told that an inexperienced barber is deputed to cut one's hair.... Brrr!... Now, on the other hand, I like the idea of a national fete... that pretty wench Candeille, dressed as a goddess... the boom of the cannon when your amnesty comes into force.... You WILL boom the cannon, will you not, Monsieur?... Cannon are demmed noisy, but they are effective sometimes, do you not think so, Monsieur?"

"Very effective certainly, Sir Percy," sneered Chauvelin, "and we will certainly boom the cannon from this very fort, an it so please you...."

"At what hour, Monsieur, is my letter to be ready?"

"Why! at any hour you please, Sir Percy."

"The 'Day-Dream' could weigh anchor at eight o'clock... would an hour before that be convenient to yourself?"

"Certainly, Sir Percy... if you will honour me by accepting my hospitality in these uncomfortable quarters until seven o'clock to-morrow eve?..."

"I thank you, Monsieur..."

"Then am I to understand, Sir Percy, that..."

A loud and ringing laugh broke from Blakeney's lips.

"That I accept your bargain, man!... Zounds! I tell you I accept... I'll write the letter, I'll sign it... an you have our free passes ready for us in exchange.... At seven o'clock to-morrow eve, did you say?... Man! do not look so astonished.... The letter, the signature, the money... all your witnesses... have everything ready.... I accept, I say.... And now, in the name of all the evil spirits in hell, let me have some supper and a bed, for I vow that I am demmed fatigued."

And without more ado Sir Percy once more rang the handbell, laughing boisterously the while: then suddenly, with quick transition of mood, his laugh was lost in a gigantic yawn, and throwing his long body onto a chair, he stretched out his legs, buried his hands in his pockets, and the next moment was peacefully asleep.

CHAPTER XXVIII. THE MIDNIGHT WATCH

Boulogne had gone through many phases, in its own languid and sleepy way, whilst the great upheaval of a gigantic revolution shook other cities of France to their very foundations.

At first the little town had held somnolently aloof, and whilst Lyons and Tours conspired and rebelled, whilst Marseilles and Toulon opened their ports to the English and Dunkirk was ready to surrender to the allied forces, she had gazed through half-closed eyes at all the turmoil, and then quietly turned over and gone to sleep again.

Boulogne fished and mended nets, built boats and manufactured boots with placid content, whilst France murdered her king and butchered her citizens.

The initial noise of the great revolution was only wafted on the southerly breezes from Paris to the little seaport towns of Northern France, and lost much of its volume and power in this aerial transit: the fisher folk were too poor to worry about the dethronement of kings: the struggle for daily existence, the perils and hardships of deep-sea fishing engrossed all the faculties they possessed.

As for the burghers and merchants of the town, they were at first content with reading an occasional article in the "Gazette de Paris" or the "Gazette des Tribunaux," brought hither by one or other of the many travellers who crossed the city on their way to the harbour. They were interested in these articles, at times even comfortably horrified at the doings in Paris, the executions and the tumbrils, but on the whole they liked the idea that the country was in future to be governed by duly chosen representatives of the people, rather than be a prey to the despotism of kings, and they were really quite pleased to see the tricolour flag hoisted on the old Beffroi, there where the snow-white standard of the Bourbons had erstwhile flaunted its golden fleur-de-lis in the glare of the midday sun.

The worthy burgesses of Boulogne were ready to shout: "Vive la Republique!" with the same cheerful and raucous Normandy accent as they had lately shouted "Dieu protege le Roi!"

The first awakening from this happy torpor came when that tent was put up on the landing stage in the harbour. Officials, dressed in shabby uniforms and wearing tricolour cockades and scarves, were now quartered in the Town Hall, and repaired daily to that roughly erected tent, accompanied by so many soldiers from the garrison.

There installed, they busied themselves with examining carefully the passports of all those who desired to leave or enter Boulogne. Fisher-folk who had dwelt in the city—father and son and grandfather and many generations before that—and had come and gone in and out of their own boats as they pleased, were now stopped as they beached their craft and made to give an account of themselves to these officials from Paris.

It was, of a truth, more than ridiculous, that these strangers should ask of Jean-Marie who he was, or of Pierre what was his business, or of Desire Francois whither he was going, when Jean-Marie and Pierre and Desire Francois had plied their nets in the roads outside Boulogne harbour for more years than they would care to count.

It also caused no small measure of annoyance that fishermen were ordered to wear tricolour cockades on their caps. They had no special ill-feeling against tricolour cockades, but they did not care about them. Jean-Marie flatly refused to have one pinned on, and being admonished somewhat severely by one of the Paris officials, he became obstinate about the whole thing and threw the cockade violently on the ground and spat upon it, not from any sentiment of anti-republicanism, but just from a feeling of Norman doggedness.

He was arrested, shut up in Fort Gayole, tried as a traitor and publicly guillotined.

The consternation in Boulogne was appalling.

The one little spark had found its way to a barrel of blasting powder and caused a terrible explosion. Within twenty-four hours of Jean-Marie's execution the whole town was in the throes of the Revolution. What the death of King Louis, the arrest of Marie Antoinette, the massacres of September had failed to do, that the arrest and execution of an elderly fisherman accomplished in a trice.

People began to take sides in politics. Some families realized that they came from ancient lineage, and that their ancestors had helped to build up the throne of the Bourbons. Others looked up ancient archives and remembered past oppressions at the hands of the aristocrats.

Thus some burghers of Boulogne became ardent reactionaries, whilst others secretly nursed enthusiastic royalist convictions: some were ready to throw in their lot with the anarchists, to deny the religion of their fathers, to scorn the priests and close the places of worship; others adhered strictly still to the usages and practices of the Church.

Arrest became frequent: the guillotine, erected in the Place de la Senechaussee, had plenty of work to do. Soon the cathedral was closed, the priests thrown into prison, whilst scores of families hoped to escape a similar fate by summary flight.

Vague rumours of a band of English adventurers soon reached the little sea-port town. The Scarlet Pimpernel—English spy or hero, as he was alternately called—had helped many a family with pronounced royalist tendencies to escape the fury of the blood-thirsty Terrorists.

Thus gradually the anti-revolutionaries had been weeded out of the city: some by death and imprisonment, others by flight. Boulogne became the hotbed of anarchism: the idlers and loafers, inseparable from any town where there is a garrison and a harbour, practically ruled the city now. Denunciations were the order of the day. Everyone who owned any money, or lived with any comfort was accused of being a traitor and suspected of conspiracy. The fisher folk wandered about the city, surly and discontented: their trade was at a standstill, but there was a trifle to be earned by giving information: information which meant the arrest, ofttimes the death of men, women and even children who had tried to seek safety in flight, and to denounce whom—as they were trying to hire a boat anywhere along the coast—meant a good square meal for a starving family.

Then came the awful cataclysm.

A woman—a stranger—had been arrested and imprisoned in the Fort Gayole and the town-crier publicly proclaimed that if she escaped from jail, one member of every family in the town—rich or poor, republican or royalist, Catholic or free-thinker—would be summarily guillotined.

That member, the bread-winner!

"Why, then, with the Duvals it would be young Francois-Auguste. He keeps his old mother with his boot-making..."

"And it would be Marie Lebon, she has her blind father dependent on her net-mending."

"And old Mother Laferriere, whose grandchildren were left penniless... she keeps them from starvation by her wash-tub."

"But Francois-Auguste is a real Republican; he belongs to the Jacobin Club."

"And look at Pierre, who never meets a calotin but he must needs spit on him."

"Is there no safety anywhere?... are we to be butchered like so many cattle?..."

Somebody makes the suggestion:

"It is a threat... they would not dare!..."

"Would not dare?..."

'Tis old Andre Lemoine who has spoken, and he spits vigorously on the ground. Andre Lemoine has been a soldier; he was in La Vendee. He was wounded at Tours... and he knows!

"Would not dare?..." he says in a whisper. "I tell you, friends, that there's nothing the present government would not dare. There was the Plaine Saint Mauve... Did you ever hear about that?... little children fusilladed by the score... little ones, I say, and women with babies at their breasts ... weren't they innocent?... Five hundred innocent people butchered in La Vendee... until the Headsman sank—worn not... I could tell worse than that... for I know.... There's nothing they would not dare!..."

Consternation was so great that the matter could not even be discussed.

"We'll go to Gayole and see this woman at any rate."

Angry, sullen crowds assembled in the streets. The proclamation had been read just as the men were leaving the public houses, preparing to go home for the night.

They brought the news to the women, who, at home, were setting the soup and bread on the table for their husbands' supper. There was no thought of going to bed or of sleeping that night. The bread-winner in every family and all those dependent on him for daily sustenance were trembling for their lives.

Resistance to the barbarous order would have been worse than useless, nor did the thought of it enter the heads of these humble and ignorant fisher folk, wearied out with the miserable struggle for existence. There was not sufficient spirit left in this half-starved population of a small provincial city to suggest open rebellion. A regiment of soldiers come up from the South were quartered in the Chateau, and the natives of

Boulogne could not have mustered more than a score of disused blunderbusses between them.

Then they remembered tales which Andre Lemoine had told, the fate of Lyons, razed to the ground, of Toulon burnt to ashes, and they did not dare rebel.

But brothers, fathers, sons trooped out towards Gayole, in order to have a good look at the frowning pile, which held the hostage for their safety. It looked dark and gloomy enough, save for one window which gave on the southern ramparts. This window was wide open and a feeble light flickered from the room beyond, and as the men stood about, gazing at the walls in sulky silence, they suddenly caught the sound of a loud laugh proceeding from within, and of a pleasant voice speaking quite gaily in a language which they did not understand, but which sounded like English.

Against the heavy oaken gateway, leading to the courtyard of the prison, the proclamation written on stout parchment had been pinned up. Beside it hung a tiny lantern, the dim light of which flickered in the evening breeze, and brought at times into sudden relief the bold writing and heavy signature, which stood out, stern and grim, against the yellowish background of the paper, like black signs of approaching death.

Facing the gateway and the proclamation, the crowd of men took its stand. The moon, from behind them, cast fitful, silvery glances at the weary heads bent in anxiety and watchful expectancy: on old heads and young heads, dark, curly heads and heads grizzled with age, on backs bent with toil, and hands rough and gnarled like seasoned timber.

All night the men stood and watched.

Sentinels from the town guard were stationed at the gates, but these might prove inattentive or insufficient, they had not the same price at stake, so the entire able-bodied population of Boulogne watched the gloomy prison that night, lest anyone escaped by wall or window.

They were guarding the precious hostage whose safety was the stipulation for their own.

There was dead silence among them, and dead silence all around, save for that monotonous tok-tok-tok of the parchment flapping in the breeze. The moon, who all along had been capricious and chary of her light, made a final retreat behind a gathering bank of clouds, and the crowd, the soldiers and the great grim walls were all equally wrapped in gloom.

Only the little lantern on the gateway now made a ruddy patch of light, and tinged that fluttering parchment with the colour of blood. Every now and then an isolated figure would detach itself from out the watching throng, and go up to the heavy, oaken door, in order to gaze at the proclamation. Then the light of the lantern illumined a dark head or a grey one, for a moment or two: black or white locks were stirred gently in the wind, and a sigh of puzzlement and disappointment would be distinctly heard.

At times a group of three or four would stand there for awhile, not speaking, only sighing and casting eager questioning glances at one another, whilst trying vainly to find some hopeful word, some turn of phrase of meaning that would be less direful, in that grim and ferocious proclamation. Then a rough word from the sentinel, a push from the butt-end of a bayonet would disperse the little group and send the men, sullen and silent, back into the crowd.

Thus they watched for hours whilst the bell of the Beffroi tolled all the hours of that tedious night. A thin rain began to fall in the small hours of the morning, a wetting, soaking drizzle which chilled the weary watchers to the bone.

But they did not care.

"We must not sleep, for the woman might escape."

Some of them squatted down in the muddy road, the luckier ones managed to lean their backs against the slimy walls.

Twice before the hour of midnight they heard that same quaint and merry laugh proceeding from the lighted room, through the open window. Once it sounded very low and very prolonged, as if in response to a delightful joke.

Anon the heavy gateway of Gayole was opened from within, and half a dozen soldiers came walking out of the courtyard. They were dressed in the uniform of the town-guard, but had evidently been picked out of the rank and file, for all six were exceptionally tall and stalwart, and towered above the sentinel, who saluted and presented arms as they marched out of the gate.

In the midst of them walked a slight, dark figure, clad entirely in black, save for the tricolour scarf round his waist.

The crowd of watchers gazed on the little party with suddenly awakened interest.

"Who is it?" whispered some of the men.

"The citizen-governor," suggested one.

"The new public executioner," ventured another.

"No! no!" quoth Pierre Maxime, the doyen of Boulogne fishermen, and a great authority on every matter public or private with the town; "no, no he is the man who has come down from Paris, the friend of Robespierre. He makes the laws now, the citizen-governor even must obey him. 'Tis he who made the law that if the woman up yonder should escape..."

"Hush!... sh!... sh!..." came in frightened accents from the crowd.

"Hush, Pierre Maxine!... the Citizen might hear thee," whispered the man who stood closest to the old fisherman; "the Citizen might hear thee, and think that we rebelled...."

"What are these people doing here?' queried Chauvelin as he passed out into the street.

"They are watching the prison, Citizen," replied the sentinel, whom he had thus addressed, "lest the female prisoner should attempt to escape."

With a satisfied smile, Chauvelin turned toward the Town Hall, closely surrounded by his escort. The crowd watched him and the soldiers as they quickly disappeared in the gloom, then they resumed the stolid, wearisome vigil of the night.

The old Beffroi now tolled the midnight hour, the one solitary light in the old Fort was extinguished, and after that the frowning pile remained dark and still.

CHAPTER XXIX. THE NATIONAL FETE

"Citizens of Boulogne, awake!"

They had not slept, only some of them had fallen into drowsy somnolence, heavy and nerve-racking, worse indeed than any wakefulness.

Within the houses, the women too had kept the tedious vigil, listening for every sound, dreading every bit of news, which the wind might waft in through the small, open windows.

If one prisoner escaped, every family in Boulogne would be deprived of the bread-winner. Therefore the women wept, and tried to remember those Paters and Aves which the tyranny of liberty, fraternity and equality had ordered them to forget.

Broken rosaries were fetched out from neglected corners, and knees stiff with endless, thankless toil were bent once more in prayer.

"Oh God! Good God! Do not allow that woman to flee!"

"Holy Virgin! Mother of God! Make that she should not escape!"

Some of the women went out in the early dawn to take hot soup and coffee to their men who were watching outside the prison.

"Has anything been seen?"

"Have ye seen the woman?"

"Which room is she in?"

"Why won't they let us see her?"

"Are you sure she hath not already escaped?"

Questions and surmises went round in muffled whispers as the steaming cans were passed round. No one had a definite answer to give, although Desire Melun declared that he had, once during the night, caught sight of a woman's face at one of the windows above: but as he could not describe the woman's face, nor locate with any degree of precision the particular window at which she was supposed to have appeared, it was unanimously decided that Desire must have been dreaming.

"Citizens of Boulogne, awake!"

The cry came first from the Town Hall, and therefore from behind the crowd of men and women, whose faces had been so resolutely set for all these past hours towards the Gayole prison.

They were all awake! but too tired and cramped to move as yet, and to turn in the direction whence arose that cry.

"Citizens of Boulogne, awake!"

It was just the voice of Auguste Moleux, the town-crier of Boulogne, who, bell in hand, was trudging his way along the Rue Daumont, closely followed by two fellows of the municipal guard.

Auguste was in the very midst of the sullen crowd, before the men even troubled about his presence here, but now with many a vigorous "Allons donc!" and "Voyez-moi ca, fais donc place, voyons!" he elbowed his way through the throng.

He was neither tired nor cramped; he served the Republic in comfort and ease, and had slept soundly on his paillasse in the little garret allotted to him in the Town Hall.

The crowd parted in silence, to allow him to pass. Auguste was lean and powerful, the scanty and meagre food, doled out to him by a paternal government, had increased his muscular strength whilst reducing his fat. He had very hard elbows, and soon he managed, by dint of pushing and cursing to reach the gateway of Gayole.

"Voyons! enlevez-moi ca," he commanded in stentorian tones, pointing to the proclamation.

The fellows of the municipal guard fell to and tore the parchment away from the door whilst the crowd looked on with stupid amazement.

What did it all mean?

Then Auguste Moleux turned and faced the men.

"Mes enfants," he said, "my little cabbages! wake up! the government of the Republic has decreed that to-day is to be a day of gaiety and public rejoicings!"

"Gaiety?... Public rejoicings forsooth, when the bread-winner of every family..."

"Hush! Hush! Be silent, all of you," quoth Auguste impatiently, "you do not understand!... All that is at an end... There is no fear that the woman shall escape.... You are all to dance and rejoice.... The Scarlet Pimpernel has been captured in Boulogne, last night..."

"Qui ca the Scarlet Pimpernel?"

"Mais! 'tis that mysterious English adventurer who rescued people from the guillotine!"

"A hero? quoi?"

"No! no! only an English spy, a friend of aristocrats... he would have cared nothing for the bread-winners of Boulogne..."

"He would not have raised a finger to save them."

"Who knows?" sighed a feminine voice, "perhaps he came to Boulogne to help them."

"And he has been caught anyway," concluded Auguste Moleux sententiously, "and, my little cabbages, remember this, that so great is the pleasure of the all-powerful Committee of Public Safety at this capture, that because he has been caught in Boulogne, therefore Boulogne is to be specially rewarded!"

"Holy Virgin, who'd have thought it?"

"Sh... Jeanette, dost not know that there's no Holy Virgin now?"

"And dost know, Auguste, how we are to be rewarded?"

It is a difficult matter for the human mind to turn very quickly from despair to hope, and the fishermen of Boulogne had not yet grasped the fact that they were to make merry and that thoughts of anxiety must be abandoned for those of gaiety.

Auguste Moleux took out a parchment from the capacious pocket of his coat; he put on his most solemn air of officialdom, and pointing with extended forefinger to the parchment, he said:

"A general amnesty to all natives of Boulogne who are under arrest at the present moment: a free pardon to all natives of Boulogne who are under sentence of death: permission to all natives of Boulogne to quit the town with their families, to embark on any vessel they please, in or out of the harbour, and to go whithersoever they choose, without passports, formalities or questions of any kind."

Dead silence followed this announcement. Hope was just beginning to crowd anxiety and sullenness out of the way.

"Then poor Andre Legrand will be pardoned," whispered a voice suddenly; "he was to have been guillotined to-day."

"And Denise Latour! she was innocent enough, the gentle pigeon."

"And they'll let poor Abbe Foucquet out of prison too."

"And Francois!"

"And poor Felicite, who is blind!"

"M. l'Abbe would be wise to leave Boulogne with the children."

"He will too: thou canst be sure of that!"

"It is not good to be a priest just now!"

"Bah! calotins are best dead than alive."

But some in the crowd were silent, others whispered eagerly.

"Thinkest thou it would be safer for us to get out of the country whilst we can?" said one of the men in a muffled tone, and clutching nervously at a woman's wrist.

"Aye! aye! it might leak out about that boat we procured for..."

"Sh!... I was thinking of that..."

"We can go to my aunt Lebrun in Belgium..."

Others talked in whispers of England or the New Land across the seas: they were those who had something to hide, money received from refugee aristocrats, boats sold to would-be emigres, information withheld, denunciations shirked: the amnesty would not last long, 'twas best to be safely out of the way.

"In the meanwhile, my cabbages," quoth Auguste sententiously, "are you not grateful to Citizen Robespierre, who has sent this order specially down from Paris?"

"Aye! aye!" assented the crowd cheerfully.

"Hurrah for Citizen Robespierre!"

"Viva la Republique!"

"And you will enjoy yourselves to-day?"

"That we will!"

"Processions?"

"Aye! with music and dancing."

Out there, far away, beyond the harbour, the grey light of dawn was yielding to the crimson glow of morning. The rain had ceased and heavy slaty clouds parted here and there, displaying glints of delicate turquoise sky, and tiny ethereal vapours in the dim and remote distance of infinity, flecked with touches of rose and gold.

The towers and pinnacles of old Boulogne detached themselves one by one from the misty gloom of night. The old bell of the Beffroi tolled the hour of six. Soon the massive cupola of Notre Dame was clothed in purple hues, and the gilt cross on St. Joseph threw back across the square a blinding ray of gold.

The town sparrows began to twitter, and from far out at sea in the direction of Dunkirk there came the muffled boom of cannon.

"And remember, my pigeons," admonished Auguste Moleux solemnly, "that in this order which Robespierre has sent from Paris, it also says that from to-day onwards le bon Dieu has ceased to be!"

Many faces were turned towards the East just then, for the rising sun, tearing with one gigantic sweep the banks of cloud asunder, now displayed his magnificence in a gorgeous immensity of flaming crimson. The sea, in response, turned to liquid fire beneath the glow, whilst the whole sky was irradiated with the first blush of morning.

Le bon Dieu has ceased to be!

"There is only one religion in France now," explained Auguste Moleux, "the religion of Reason! We are all citizens! We are all free and all able to think for ourselves. Citizen Robespierre has decreed that there is no good God. Le bon Dieu was a tyrant and an aristocrat, and, like all tyrants and aristocrats, He has been deposed. There is no good God, there is no Holy Virgin and no Saints, only Reason, who is a goddess and whom we all honour."

And the townsfolk of Boulogne, with eyes still fixed on the gorgeous East, shouted with sullen obedience:

"Hurrah! for the Goddess of Reason!"

"Hurrah for Robespierre!"

Only the women, trying to escape the town-crier's prying eyes, or the soldiers' stern gaze, hastily crossed themselves behind their husbands' backs, terrified lest le bon Dieu had, after all, not altogether ceased to exist at the bidding of Citizen Robespierre.

Thus the worthy natives of Boulogne, forgetting their anxieties and fears, were ready enough to enjoy the national fete ordained for them by the Committee of Public Safety, in honour of the capture of the Scarlet Pimpernel. They were even willing to accept this new religion which Robespierre had invented: a religion which was only a mockery, with an actress to represent its supreme deity.

Mais, que voulez-vous? Boulogne had long ago ceased to have faith in God: the terrors of the Revolution, which culminated in that agonizing watch of last night, had smothered all thoughts of worship and of prayer.

The Scarlet Pimpernel must indeed be a dangerous spy that his arrest should cause so much joy in Paris!

Even Boulogne had learned by experience that the Committee of Public Safety did not readily give up a prey, once its vulture-like claws had closed upon it. The proportion of condemnations as against acquittals was as a hundred to one.

But because this one man was taken, scores to-day were to be set free!

In the evening at a given hour—seven o'clock as Auguste Moleux, the town-crier, understood—the boom of the cannon would be heard, the gates of the town would be opened, the harbour would become a free port.

The inhabitants of Boulogne were ready to shout:

"Vive the Scarlet Pimpernel!"

Whatever he was—hero or spy—he was undoubtedly the primary cause of all their joy.

By the time Auguste Moleux had cried out the news throughout the town, and pinned the new proclamation of mercy up on every public building, all traces of fatigue and anxiety had vanished. In spite of the fact that wearisome vigils had been kept in every home that night, and that hundreds of men and women had stood about for hours in the vicinity of the Gayole Fort, no sooner was the joyful news known, than all lassitude was forgotten and everyone set to with a right merry will to make the great fete-day a complete success.

There is in every native of Normandy, be he peasant or gentleman, an infinite capacity for enjoyment, and at the same time a marvellous faculty for co-ordinating and systematizing his pleasures.

In a trice the surly crowds had vanished. Instead of these, there were groups of gaily-visaged men pleasantly chattering outside every eating and drinking place in the town. The national holiday had come upon these people quite unawares, so the early part of it had to be spent in thinking out a satisfactory programme for it. Sipping their beer or coffee, or munching their cherries a l'eau-de-vie, the townsfolk of Boulogne, so lately threatened with death, were quietly organizing processions.

There was to be a grand muster on the Place de la Senechaussee, then a torchlight and lanthorn-light march, right round the Ramparts, culminating in a gigantic assembly outside the Town Hall, where the Citizen Chauvelin, representing the Committee of Public Safety, would receive an address of welcome from the entire population of Boulogne.

The procession was to be in costume! There were to be Pierrots and Pierettes, Harlequins and English clowns, aristocrats and goddesses! All day the women and girls were busy contriving travesties of all sorts, and the little tumbledown shops in the Rue de Chateau and the Rue Frederic Sauvage—kept chiefly by Jews and English traders—were ransacked for old bits of finery, and for remnants of costumes, worn in the days when Boulogne was still a gay city and Carnivals were held every year.

And then, of course, there would be the Goddess of Reason, in her triumphal car! the apotheosis of the new religion, which was to make everybody happy, rich and free.

Forgotten were the anxieties of the night, the fears of death, the great and glorious Revolution, which for this one day would cease her perpetual demand for the toll of blood.

Nothing was remembered save the pleasures and joys of the moment, and at times the name of that Englishman—spy, hero or adventurer—the cause of all this bounty: the Scarlet Pimpernel.

CHAPTER XXX. THE PROCESSION

The grandfathers of the present generation of Boulonnese remembered the great day of the National Fete, when all Boulogne, for twenty-four hours, went crazy with joy. So many families had fathers, brothers, sons, languishing in prison under some charge of treason, real or imaginary; so many had dear ones for whom already the guillotine loomed ahead, that the feast on this memorable day of September, 1793, was one of never-to-be-forgotten relief and thanksgiving.

The weather all day had been exceptionally fine. After that glorious sunrise, the sky had remained all day clad in its gorgeous mantle of blue and the sun had continued to smile benignly on the many varied doings of this gay, little seaport town. When it began to sink slowly towards the West a few little fluffy clouds appeared on the horizon, and from a distance, although the sky remained clear and blue, the sea looked quite dark and slaty against the brilliance of the firmament.

Gradually, as the splendour of the sunset gave place to the delicate purple and grey tints of evening, the little fluffy clouds merged themselves into denser masses, and these too soon became absorbed in the great, billowy banks which the southwesterly wind was blowing seawards.

By the time that the last grey streak of dusk vanished in the West, the whole sky looked heavy with clouds, and the evening set in, threatening and dark.

But this by no means mitigated the anticipation of pleasure to come. On the contrary, the fast-gathering gloom was hailed with delight, since it would surely help to show off the coloured lights of the lanthorns, and give additional value to the glow of the torches.

Of a truth 'twas a motley throng which began to assemble on the Place de la Senechaussee, just as the old bell of the Beffroi tolled the hour of six. Men, women and children in ragged finery, Pierrots with neck frills and floured faces, hideous masks of impossible beasts roughly besmeared in crude colours. There were gaily-coloured dominoes, blue, green, pink and purple, harlequins combining all the colours of the rainbow in one tight-fitting garment, and Columbines with short, tarlatan skirts, beneath which peeped bare feet and ankles. There were judges' perruques, and soldiers' helmets of past generations, tall Normandy caps adorned with hundreds of streaming ribbons, and powdered headgear which recalled the glories of Versailles.

Everything was torn and dirty, the dominoes were in rags, the Pierrot frills, mostly made up of paper, already hung in strips over the wearers' shoulders. But what mattered that?

The crowd pushed and jolted, shouted and laughed, the girls screamed as the men snatched a kiss here and there from willing or unwilling lips, or stole an arm round a gaily accoutred waist. The spirit of Old King Carnival was in the evening air—a spirit just awakened from a long Rip van Winkle-like sleep.

In the centre of the Place stood the guillotine, grim and gaunt with long, thin arms stretched out towards the sky, the last glimmer of waning light striking the triangular knife, there, where it was not rusty with stains of blood.

For weeks now Madame Guillotine had been much occupied plying her gruesome trade; she now stood there in the gloom, passive and immovable, seeming to wait placidly for the end of this holiday, ready to begin her work again on the morrow. She towered above these merrymakers, hoisted up on the platform whereon many an innocent foot had trodden, the tattered basket beside her, into which many an innocent head had rolled.

What cared they to-night for Madame Guillotine and the horrors of which she told? A crowd of Pierrots with floured faces and tattered neck-frills had just swarmed up the wooden steps, shouting and laughing, chasing each other round and round on the platform, until one of them lost his footing and fell into the basket, covering himself with bran and staining his clothes with blood.

"Ah! vogue la galere! We must be merry to-night!"

And all these people who for weeks past had been staring death and the guillotine in the face, had denounced each other with savage callousness in order to save themselves, or hidden for days in dark cellars to escape apprehension, now laughed, and danced and shrieked with gladness in a sudden, hysterical outburst of joy.

Close beside the guillotine stood the triumphal car of the Goddess of Reason, the special feature of this great national fete. It was only a rough market cart, painted by an unpractised hand with bright, crimson paint and adorned with huge clusters of autumn-tinted leaves, and the scarlet berries of mountain ash and rowan, culled from the town gardens, or the country side outside the city walls.

In the cart the goddess reclined on a crimson-draped seat, she, herself, swathed in white, and wearing a gorgeous necklace around her neck. Desiree Candeille, a little pale, a little apprehensive of all this noise, had obeyed the final dictates of her taskmaster. She had been the means of bringing the Scarlet Pimpernel to France and vengeance, she was to be honoured therefore above every other woman in France.

She sat in the car, vaguely thinking over the events of the past few days, whilst watching the throng of rowdy merrymakers seething around her. She thought of the noble-hearted, proud woman whom she had helped to bring from her beautiful English home to sorrow and humiliation in a dank French prison, she thought of the gallant English gentleman with his pleasant voice and courtly, debonair manners.

Chauvelin had roughly told her, only this morning, that both were now under arrest as English spies, and that their fate no longer concerned her. Later on the governor of the city had come to tell her that Citizen Chauvelin desired her to take part in the procession and the national fete, as the Goddess of Reason, and that the people of Boulogne were ready to welcome her as such. This had pleased Candeille's vanity, and all day, whilst arranging the finery which she meant to wear for the occasion, she had ceased to think of England and of Lady Blakeney.

But now, when she arrived on the Place de la Senechaussee, and mounting her car, found herself on a level with the platform of the guillotine, her memory flew back to England, to the lavish hospitality of Blakeney Manor, Marguerite's gentle voice, the pleasing grace of Sir Percy's manners, and she shuddered a little when that cruel glint of evening light caused the knife of the guillotine to glisten from out the gloom.

But anon her reflections were suddenly interrupted by loud and prolonged shouts of joy. A whole throng of Pierrots had swarmed into the Place from every side, carrying lighted torches and tall staves, on which were hung lanthorns with many-coloured lights.

The procession was ready to start. A stentorian voice shouted out in resonant accents:
"En avant, la grosse caisse!"

A man now, portly and gorgeous in scarlet and blue, detached himself from out the crowd. His head was hidden beneath the monstrous mask of a cardboard lion, roughly painted in brown and yellow, with crimson for the widely open jaws and the corners of the eyes, to make them seem ferocious and bloodshot. His coat was of bright crimson cloth, with cuts and slashings in it, through which bunches of bright blue paper were made to protrude, in imitation of the costume of mediaeval times.

He had blue stockings on and bright scarlet slippers, and behind him floated a large strip of scarlet flannel, on which moons and suns and stars of gold had been showered in plenty.

Upon his portly figure in front he was supporting the big drum, which was securely strapped round his shoulders with tarred cordages, the spoil of some fishing vessel.

There was a merciful slit in the jaw of the cardboard lion, through which the portly drummer puffed and spluttered as he shouted lustily:
"En avant!"

And wielding the heavy drumstick with a powerful arm, he brought it crashing down against the side of the mighty instrument.

"Hurrah! Hurrah! en avant les trompettes!"

A fanfare of brass instruments followed, lustily blown by twelve young men in motley coats of green, and tall, peaked hats adorned with feathers.

The drummer had begun to march, closely followed by the trumpeters. Behind them a bevy of Columbines in many-coloured tarlatan skirts and hair flying wildly in the breeze, giggling, pushing, exchanging ribald jokes with the men behind, and getting kissed or slapped for their pains.

Then the triumphal car of the goddess, with Demoiselle Candeille standing straight up in it, a tall gold wand in one hand, the other resting in a mass of scarlet berries. All round the car, helter-skelter, tumbling, pushing, came Pierrots and Pierrettes, carrying lanthorns, and Harlequins bearing the torches.

And after the car the long line of more sober folk, the older fishermen, the women in caps and many-hued skirts, the serious townfolk who had scorned the travesty, yet would not be left out of the procession. They all began to march, to the tune of those noisy brass trumpets which were thundering forth snatches from the newly composed "Marseillaise."

Above the sky became more heavy with clouds. Anon a few drops of rain began to fall, making the torches sizzle and splutter, and scatter grease and tar around and wetting the lightly-covered shoulders of tarlatan-clad Columbines. But no one cared! The glow of so much merrymaking kept the blood warm and the skin dry.

The flour all came off the Pierrots' faces, the blue paper slashings of the drummer-in-chief hung in pulpy lumps against his gorgeous scarlet cloak. The trumpeters' feathers became streaky and bedraggled.

But in the name of that good God who had ceased to exist, who in the world or out of it cared if it rained, or thundered and stormed! This was a national holiday, for an English spy was captured, and all natives of Boulogne were free of the guillotine to-night.

The revellers were making the circuit of the town, with lanthorns fluttering in the wind, and flickering torches held up aloft illumining laughing faces, red with the glow of a drunken joy, young faces that only enjoyed the moment's pleasure, serious ones that withheld a frown at thought of the morrow. The fitful light played on the grotesque masques of beasts and reptiles, on the diamond necklace of a very earthly goddess, on God's glorious spoils from gardens and country-side, on smothered anxiety and repressed cruelty.

The crowd had turned its back on the guillotine, and the trumpets now changed the inspiriting tune of the "Marseillaise" to the ribald vulgarity of the "Ca ira!"

Everyone yelled and shouted. Girls with flowing hair produced broomsticks, and astride on these, broke from the ranks and danced a mad and obscene saraband, a dance of witches in the weird glow of sizzling torches, to the accompaniment of raucous laughter and of coarse jokes.

Thus the procession passed on, a sight to gladden the eyes of those who had desired to smother all thought of the Infinite, of Eternity and of God in the minds of those to whom they had nothing to offer in return. A threat of death yesterday, misery, starvation and squalor! all the hideousness of a destroying anarchy, that had nothing to give save a national fete, a tinsel goddess, some shallow laughter and momentary intoxication, a travesty of clothes and of religion and a dance on the ashes of the past.

And there along the ramparts where the massive walls of the city encircled the frowning prisons of Gayole and the old Chateau, dark groups were crouching, huddled together in compact masses, which in the gloom seemed to vibrate with fear. Like hunted quarry seeking for shelter, sombre figures flattened themselves in the angles of the dank walls, as the noisy carousers drew nigh. Then as the torches and lanthorns detached themselves from out the evening shadows, hand would clutch hand and hearts would beat with agonized suspense, whilst the dark and shapeless forms would try to appear smaller, flatter, less noticeable than before.

And when the crowd had passed noisily along, leaving behind it a trail of torn finery, of glittering tinsel and of scarlet berries, when the boom of the big drum and the grating noise of the brass trumpets had somewhat died away, wan faces, pale with anxiety, would peer from out the darkness, and nervous hands would grasp with trembling fingers the small bundles of poor belongings tied up hastily in view of flight.

At seven o'clock, so 'twas said, the cannon would boom from the old Beffroi. The guard would throw open the prison gates, and those who had something or somebody to hide, and those who had a great deal to fear, would be free to go whithersoever they chose.

And mothers, sisters, sweethearts stood watching by the gates, for loved ones tonight would be set free, all along of the capture of that English spy, the Scarlet Pimpernel.

CHAPTER XXXI. FINAL DISPOSITIONS

To Chauvelin the day had been one of restless inquietude and nervous apprehension.

Collot d'Herbois harassed him with questions and complaints intermixed with threats but thinly veiled. At his suggestion Gayole had been transformed into a fully-manned, well-garrisoned fortress. Troops were to be seen everywhere, on the stairs and in the passages, the guard-rooms and offices: picked men from the municipal guard, and the company which had been sent down from Paris some time ago.

Chauvelin had not resisted these orders given by his colleague. He knew quite well that Marguerite would make no attempt at escape, but he had long ago given up all hope of persuading a man of the type of Collot d'Herbois that a woman of her temperament would never think of saving her own life at the expense of others, and that Sir Percy Blakeney, in spite of his adoration for his wife, would sooner see her die before him, than allow the lives of innocent men and women to be the price of hers.

Collot was one of those brutish sots—not by any means infrequent among the Terrorists of that time—who, born in the gutter, still loved to wallow in his native element, and who measured all his fellow-creatures by the same standard which he had always found good enough for himself. In this man there was neither the enthusiastic patriotism of a Chauvelin, nor the ardent selflessness of a Danton. He served the revolution and fostered the anarchical spirit of the times only because these brought him a competence and a notoriety, which an orderly and fastidious government would obviously have never offered him.

History shows no more despicable personality than that of Collot d'Herbois, one of the most hideous products of that utopian Revolution, whose grandly conceived theories of a universal levelling of mankind only succeeded in dragging into prominence a number of half-brutish creatures who, revelling in their own abasement, would otherwise have remained content in inglorious obscurity.

Chauvelin tolerated and half feared Collot, knowing full well that if now the Scarlet Pimpernel escaped from his hands, he could expect no mercy from his colleagues.

The scheme by which he hoped to destroy not only the heroic leader but the entire League by bringing opprobrium and ridicule upon them, was wonderfully subtle in its refined cruelty, and Chauvelin, knowing by now something of Sir Percy Blakeney's curiously blended character, was never for a moment in doubt but that he would write the infamous letter, save his wife by sacrificing his honour, and then seek oblivion and peace in suicide.

With so much disgrace, so much mud cast upon their chief, the League of the Scarlet Pimpernel would cease to be. THAT had been Chauvelin's plan all along. For this end he had schemed and thought and planned, from the moment that Robespierre had given him the opportunity of redeeming his failure of last year. He had built up the edifice of his intrigue, bit by bit, from the introduction of his tool, Candeille, to Marguerite at the

Richmond gala, to the arrest of Lady Blakeney in Boulogne. All that remained for him to see now, would be the attitude of Sir Percy Blakeney to-night, when, in exchange for the stipulated letter, he would see his wife set free.

All day Chauvelin had wondered how it would all go off. He had stage-managed everything, but he did not know how the chief actor would play his part.

From time to time, when his feeling of restlessness became quite unendurable, the ex-ambassador would wander round Fort Gayole and on some pretext or other demand to see one or the other of his prisoners. Marguerite, however, observed complete silence in his presence: she acknowledged his greeting with a slight inclination of the head, and in reply to certain perfunctory queries of his—which he put to her in order to justify his appearance—she either nodded or gave curt monosyllabic answers through partially closed lips.

"I trust that everything is arranged for your comfort, Lady Blakeney."

"I thank you, sir."

"You will be rejoining the 'Day-Dream' to-night. Can I send a messenger over to the yacht for you?"

"I thank you. No."

"Sir Percy is well. He is fast asleep, and hath not asked for your ladyship. Shall I let him know that you are well?"

A nod of acquiescence from Marguerite and Chauvelin's string of queries was at an end. He marvelled at her quietude and thought that she should have been as restless as himself.

Later on in the day, and egged on by Collot d'Herbois and by his own fears, he had caused Marguerite to be removed from No. 6.

This change he heralded by another brief visit to her, and his attitude this time was one of deferential apology.

"A matter of expediency, Lady Blakeney," he explained, "and I trust that the change will be for your comfort."

Again the same curt nod of acquiescence on her part, and a brief:

"As you command, Monsieur!"

But when he had gone, she turned with a sudden passionate outburst towards the Abbe Foucquet, her faithful companion through the past long, weary hours. She fell on her knees beside him and sobbed in an agony of grief.

"Oh! if I could only know... if I could only see him!... for a minute... a second!... if I could only know!..."

She felt as if the awful uncertainty would drive her mad.

If she could only know! If she could only know what he meant to do.

"The good God knows!" said the old man, with his usual simple philosophy, "and perhaps it is all for the best."

The room which Chauvelin had now destined for Marguerite was one which gave from the larger one, wherein last night he had had his momentous interview with her and with Sir Percy.

It was small, square and dark, with no window in it: only a small ventilating hole high up in the wall and heavily grated. Chauvelin, who desired to prove to her that there was no wish on his part to add physical discomfort to her mental tortures, had given orders that the little place should be made as habitable as possible. A thick, soft carpet had been laid on the ground; there was an easy chair and a comfortable-looking couch with a couple of pillows and a rug upon it, and oh, marvel! on the round central table, a vase with a huge bunch of many-coloured dahlias which seemed to throw a note as if of gladness into this strange and gloomy little room.

At the furthest corner, too, a construction of iron uprights and crossway bars had been hastily contrived and fitted with curtains, forming a small recess, behind which was a tidy washstand, fine clean towels and plenty of fresh water. Evidently the shops of Boulogne had been commandeered in order to render Marguerite's sojourn here outwardly agreeable.

But as the place was innocent of window, so was it innocent of doors. The one that gave into the large room had been taken out of its hinges, leaving only the frame, on each side of which stood a man from the municipal guard with fixed bayonet.

Chauvelin himself had conducted Marguerite to her new prison. She followed him—silent and apathetic—with not a trace of that awful torrent of emotion which had overwhelmed her but half-an-hour ago when she had fallen on her knees beside the old priest and sobbed her heart out in a passionate fit of weeping. Even the sight of the soldiers left her outwardly indifferent. As she stepped across the threshold she noticed that the door itself had been taken away: then she gave another quick glance at the soldiers, whose presence there would control her every movement.

The thought of Queen Marie Antoinette in the Conciergerie prison with the daily, hourly humiliation and shame which this constant watch imposed upon her womanly pride and modesty, flashed suddenly across Marguerite's mind, and a deep blush of horror rapidly suffused her pale cheeks, whilst an almost imperceptible shudder shook her delicate frame.

Perhaps, as in a flash, she had at this moment received an inkling of what the nature of that terrible "either—or" might be, with which Chauvelin was trying to force an English gentleman to dishonour. Sir Percy Blakeney's wife had been threatened with Marie Antoinette's fate.

"You see, Madame," said her cruel enemy's unctuous voice close to her ear, "that we have tried our humble best to make your brief sojourn here as agreeable as possible. May I express a hope that you will be quite comfortable in this room, until the time when Sir Percy will be ready to accompany you to the 'Day-Dream.'"

"I thank you, sir," she replied quietly.

"And if there is anything you require, I pray you to call. I shall be in the next room all day and entirely at your service."

A young orderly now entered bearing a small collation—eggs, bread, milk and wine —which he set on the central table. Chauvelin bowed low before Marguerite and withdrew. Anon he ordered the two sentinels to stand the other side of the doorway, against the wall of his own room, and well out of sight of Marguerite, so that, as she moved about her own narrow prison, if she ate or slept, she might have the illusion that she was unwatched.

The sight of the soldiers had had the desired effect on her. Chauvelin had seen her shudder and knew that she understood or that she guessed. He was now satisfied and really had no wish to harass her beyond endurance.

Moreover, there was always the proclamation which threatened the bread-winners of Boulogne with death if Marguerite Blakeney escaped, and which would be in full force until Sir Percy had written, signed and delivered into Chauvelin's hands the letter which was to be the signal for the general amnesty.

Chauvelin had indeed cause to be satisfied with his measures. There was no fear that his prisoners would attempt to escape.

Even Collot d'Herbois had to admit everything was well done. He had read the draft of the proposed letter and was satisfied with its contents. Gradually now into his loutish brain there had filtrated the conviction that Citizen Chauvelin was right, that that accursed Scarlet Pimpernel and his brood of English spies would be more effectually annihilated by all the dishonour and ridicule which such a letter written by the mysterious hero would heap upon them all, than they could ever be through the relentless work of the guillotine. His only anxiety now was whether the Englishman would write that letter.

"Bah! he'll do it," he would say whenever he thought the whole matter over: "Sacre tonnerre! but 'tis an easy means to save his own skin."

"You would sign such a letter without hesitation, eh, Citizen Collot," said Chauvelin, with well-concealed sarcasm, on one occasion when his colleague discussed the all-absorbing topic with him; "you would show no hesitation, if your life were at stake, and you were given the choice between writing that letter and... the guillotine?"

"Parbleu!" responded Collot with conviction.

"More especially," continued Chauvelin drily, "if a million francs were promised you as well?"

"Sacre Anglais!" swore Collot angrily, "you don't propose giving him that money, do you?"

"We'll place it ready to his hand, at any rate, so that it should appear as if he had actually taken it."

Collot looked up at his colleague in ungrudging admiration. Chauvelin had indeed left nothing undone, had thought everything out in this strangely conceived scheme for the destruction of the enemy of France.

"But in the name of all the dwellers in hell, Citizen," admonished Collot, "guard that letter well, once it is in your hands."

"I'll do better than that," said Chauvelin, "I will hand it over to you, Citizen Collot, and you shall ride with it to Paris at once."

"To-night!" assented Collot with a shout of triumph, as he brought his grimy fist crashing down on the table, "I'll have a horse ready saddled at this very gate, and an escort of mounted men... we'll ride like hell's own furies and not pause to breathe until that letter is in Citizen Robespierre's hands."

"Well thought of, Citizen," said Chauvelin approvingly. "I pray you give the necessary orders, that the horses be ready saddled, and the men booted and spurred, and waiting at the Gayole gate, at seven o'clock this evening."

"I wish the letter were written and safely in our hands by now."

"Nay! the Englishman will have it ready by this evening, never fear. The tide is high at half-past seven, and he will be in haste for his wife to be aboard his yacht, ere the turn, even if he..."

He paused, savouring the thoughts which had suddenly flashed across his mind, and a look of intense hatred and cruel satisfaction for a moment chased away the studied impassiveness of his face.

"What do you mean, Citizen?" queried Collot anxiously, "even if he... what?..."

"Oh! nothing, nothing! I was only trying to make vague guesses as to what the Englishman will do AFTER he has written the letter," quoth Chauvelin reflectively.

"Morbleu! he'll return to his own accursed country... glad enough to have escaped with his skin.... I suppose," added Collot with sudden anxiety, "you have no fear that he will refuse at the last moment to write that letter?"

The two men were sitting in the large room, out of which opened the one which was now occupied by Marguerite. They were talking at the further end of it, close to the window, and though Chauvelin had mostly spoken in a whisper, Collot had ofttimes shouted, and the ex-ambassador was wondering how much Marguerite had heard.

Now at Collot's anxious query he gave a quick furtive glance in the direction of the further room wherein she sat, so silent and so still, that it seemed almost as if she must be sleeping.

"You don't think that the Englishman will refuse to write the letter?" insisted Collot with angry impatience.

"No!" replied Chauvelin quietly.

"But if he does?" persisted the other.

"If he does, I send the woman to Paris to-night and have him hanged as a spy in this prison yard without further formality or trial..." replied Chauvelin firmly; "so either way, you see, Citizen," he added in a whisper, "the Scarlet Pimpernel is done for.... But I think that he will write the letter."

"Parbleu! so do I!..." rejoined Collot with a coarse laugh.

CHAPTER XXXII. THE LETTER

Later on, when his colleague left him in order to see to the horses and to his escort for to-night, Chauvelin called Sergeant Hebert, his old and trusted familiar, to him and gave him some final orders.

"The Angelus must be rung at the proper hour, friend Hebert," he began with a grim smile.

"The Angelus, Citizen?" quoth the Sergeant, with complete stupefaction, "'tis months now since it has been rung. It was forbidden by a decree of the Convention, and I doubt me if any of our men would know how to set about it."

Chauvelin's eyes were fixed before him in apparent vacancy, while the same grim smile still hovered round his thin lips. Something of that irresponsible spirit of adventure which was the mainspring of all Sir Percy Blakeney's actions, must for the moment have pervaded the mind of his deadly enemy.

Chauvelin had thought out this idea of having the Angelus rung to-night, and was thoroughly pleased with the notion. This was the day when the duel was to have been fought; seven o'clock would have been the very hour, and the sound of the Angelus to have been the signal for combat, and there was something very satisfying in the thought, that that same Angelus should be rung, as a signal that the Scarlet Pimpernel was withered and broken at last.

In answer to Hebert's look of bewilderment Chauvelin said quietly:

"We must have some signal between ourselves and the guard at the different gates, also with the harbour officials: at a given moment the general amnesty must take effect and the harbour become a free port. I have a fancy that the signal shall be the ringing of the Angelus: the cannons at the gates and the harbour can boom in response; then the prisons can be thrown open and prisoners can either participate in the evening fete or leave the city immediately, as they choose. The Committee of Public Safety has promised the amnesty: it will carry out its promise to the full, and when Citizen Collot d'Herbois arrives in Paris with the joyful news, all natives of Boulogne in the prisons there will participate in the free pardon too."

"I understand all that, Citizen," said Hebert, still somewhat bewildered, "but not the Angelus."

"A fancy, friend Hebert, and I mean to have it."

"But who is to ring it, Citizen?"

"Morbleu! haven't you one calotin left in Boulogne whom you can press into doing this service?"

"Aye! calotins enough! there's the Abbe Foucquet in this very building... in No. 6 cell..."

"Sacre tonnerre!" ejaculated Chauvelin exultingly, "the very man! I know his dossier well! Once he is free, he will make straightway for England... he and his family... and will help to spread the glorious news of the dishonour and disgrace of the much-vaunted Scarlet Pimpernel!... The very man, friend Hebert!... Let him be stationed here... to see the letter written... to see the money handed over—for we will go through with that farce—and make him understand that the moment I give him the order, he can run over to his old church St. Joseph and ring the Angelus. ... The old fool will be delighted... more especially when he knows that he will thereby be giving the very signal which will set his own sister's children free.... You understand?..."

"I understand, Citizen."

"And you can make the old calotin understand?"

"I think so, Citizen.... You want him in this room.... At what time?"

"A quarter before seven."

"Yes. I'll bring him along myself, and stand over him, lest he play any pranks."

"Oh! he'll not trouble you," sneered Chauvelin, "he'll be deeply interested in the proceedings. The woman will be here too, remember," he added with a jerky movement of the hand in the direction of Marguerite's room, "the two might be made to stand together, with four of your fellows round them."

"I understand, Citizen. Are any of us to escort the Citizen Foucquet when he goes to St. Joseph?"

"Aye! two men had best go with him. There will be a crowd in the streets by then... How far is it from here to the church?"

"Less than five minutes."

"Good. See to it that the doors are opened and the bell ropes easy of access."

"It shall be seen to, Citizen. How many men will you have inside this room to-night?"

"Let the walls be lined with men whom you can trust. I anticipate neither trouble nor resistance. The whole thing is a simple formality to which the Englishman has already intimated his readiness to submit. If he changes his mind at the last moment there will be no Angelus rung, no booming of the cannons or opening of the prison doors: there will be no amnesty, and no free pardon. The woman will be at once conveyed to Paris, and...

But he'll not change his mind, friend Hebert," he concluded in suddenly altered tones, and speaking quite lightly, "he'll not change his mind."

The conversation between Chauvelin and his familiar had been carried on in whispers: not that the Terrorist cared whether Marguerite overheard or not, but whispering had become a habit with this man, whose tortuous ways and subtle intrigues did not lend themselves to discussion in a loud voice.

Chauvelin was sitting at the central table, just where he had been last night when Sir Percy Blakeney's sudden advent broke in on his meditations. The table had been cleared of the litter of multitudinous papers which had encumbered it before. On it now there were only a couple of heavy pewter candlesticks, with the tallow candles fixed ready in them, a leather-pad, an ink-well, a sand-box and two or three quill pens: everything disposed, in fact, for the writing and signing of the letter.

Already in imagination, Chauvelin saw his impudent enemy, the bold and daring adventurer, standing there beside that table and putting his name to the consummation of his own infamy. The mental picture thus evoked brought a gleam of cruel satisfaction and of satiated lust into the keen, ferret-like face, and a smile of intense joy lit up the narrow, pale-coloured eyes.

He looked round the room where the great scene would be enacted: two soldiers were standing guard outside Marguerite's prison, two more at attention near the door which gave on the passage: his own half-dozen picked men were waiting his commands in the corridor. Presently the whole room would be lined with troops, himself and Collot standing with eyes fixed on the principal actor of the drama! Hebert with specially selected troopers standing on guard over Marguerite!

No, no! he had left nothing to chance this time, and down below the horses would be ready saddled, that were to convey Collot and the precious document to Paris.

No! nothing was left to chance, and in either case he was bound to win. Sir Percy Blakeney would either write the letter in order to save his wife, and heap dishonour on himself, or he would shrink from the terrible ordeal at the last moment and let Chauvelin and the Committee of Public Safety work their will with her and him.

"In that case the pillory as a spy and summary hanging for you, my friend," concluded Chauvelin in his mind, "and for your wife... Bah, once you are out of the way, even she will cease to matter."

He left Hebert on guard in the room. An irresistible desire seized him to go and have a look at his discomfited enemy, and from the latter's attitude make a shrewd guess as to what he meant to do to-night.

Sir Percy had been given a room on one of the upper floors of the old prison. He had in no way been closely guarded, and the room itself had been made as comfortable as may be. He had seemed quite happy and contented when he had been conducted hither by Chauvelin, the evening before.

"I hope you quite understand, Sir Percy, that you are my guest here to-night," Chauvelin had said suavely, "and that you are free to come and go, just as you please."

"Lud love you, sir," Sir Percy had replied gaily, "but I verily believe that I am."

"It is only Lady Blakeney whom we have cause to watch until to-morrow," added Chauvelin with quiet significance. "Is that not so, Sir Percy?"

But Sir Percy seemed, whenever his wife's name was mentioned, to lapse into irresistible somnolence. He yawned now with his usual affectation, and asked at what hour gentlemen in France were wont to breakfast.

Since then Chauvelin had not seen him. He had repeatedly asked how the English prisoner was faring, and whether he seemed to be sleeping and eating heartily. The orderly in charge invariably reported that the Englishman seemed well, but did not eat much. On the other hand, he had ordered, and lavishly paid for, measure after measure of brandy and bottle after bottle of wine.

"Hm! how strange these Englishmen are!" mused Chauvelin; "this so-called hero is nothing but a wine-sodden brute, who seeks to nerve himself for a trying ordeal by drowning his faculties in brandy... Perhaps after all he doesn't care!..."

But the wish to have a look at that strangely complex creature—hero, adventurer or mere lucky fool—was irresistible, and Chauvelin in the latter part of the afternoon went up to the room which had been allotted to Sir Percy Blakeney.

He never moved now without his escort, and this time also two of his favourite bodyguards accompanied him to the upper floor. He knocked at the door, but received no answer, and after a second or two he bade his men wait in the corridor and, gently turning the latch, walked in.

There was an odour of brandy in the air; on the table two or three empty bottles of wine and a glass half filled with cognac testified to the truth of what the orderly had said, whilst sprawling across the camp bedstead, which obviously was too small for his long limbs, his head thrown back, his mouth open for a vigorous snore, lay the imperturbable Sir Percy fast asleep.

Chauvelin went up to the bedstead and looked down upon the reclining figure of the man who had oft been called the most dangerous enemy of Republican France.

Of a truth, a fine figure of a man, Chauvelin was ready enough to admit that; the long, hard limbs, the wide chest, and slender, white hands, all bespoke the man of birth, breeding and energy: the face too looked strong and clearly-cut in repose, now that the perpetually inane smile did not play round the firm lips, nor the lazy, indolent expression mar the seriousness of the straight brow. For one moment—it was a mere flash—Chauvelin felt almost sorry that so interesting a career should be thus ignominiously brought to a close.

The Terrorist felt that if his own future, his own honour and integrity were about to be so hopelessly crushed, he would have wandered up and down this narrow room like a caged beast, eating out his heart with self-reproach and remorse, and racking his nerves and brain for an issue out of the terrible alternative which meant dishonour or death.

But this man drank and slept.

"Perhaps he doesn't care!"

And as if in answer to Chauvelin's puzzled musing a deep snore escaped the sleeping adventurer's parted lips.

Chauvelin sighed, perplexed and troubled. He looked round the little room, then went up to a small side table which stood against the wall and on which were two or three quill pens and an ink-well, also some loosely scattered sheets of paper. These he turned over with a careless hand and presently came across a closely written page. ——

"Citizen Chauvelin:—In consideration of a further sum of one million francs..."

It was the beginning of the letter!... only a few words so far... with several corrections of misspelt words... and a line left out here and there which confused the meaning... a beginning made by the unsteady hand of that drunken fool... an attempt only at present....

But still... a beginning.

Close by was the draft of it as written out by Chauvelin, and which Sir Percy had evidently begun to copy.

He had made up his mind then.... He meant to subscribe with his own hand to his lasting dishonour... and meaning it, he slept!

Chauvelin felt the paper trembling in his hand. He felt strangely agitated and nervous, now that the issue was so near... so sure!...

"There's no demmed hurry for that, is there... er... Monsieur Chaubertin?..." came from the slowly wakening Sir Percy in somewhat thick, heavy accents, accompanied by a prolonged yawn. "I haven't got the demmed thing quite ready..."

Chauvelin had been so startled that the paper dropped from his hand. He stooped to pick it up.

"Nay! why should you be so scared, sir?" continued Sir Percy lazily, "did you think I was drunk?... I assure you, sir, on my honour, I am not so drunk as you think I am."

"I have no doubt, Sir Percy," replied Chauvelin ironically, "that you have all your marvellous faculties entirely at your command.... I must apologize for disturbing your papers," he added, replacing the half-written page on the table, "I thought perhaps that if the letter was ready ..."

"It will be, sir... it will be... for I am not drunk, I assure you.... and can write with a steady hand... and do honour to my signature...."

"When will you have the letter ready, Sir Percy?"

"The 'Day-Dream' must leave the harbour at the turn of the tide," quoth Sir Percy thickly. "It'll be demmed well time by then... won't it, sir?..."

"About sundown, Sir Percy... not later..."

"About sundown... not later..." muttered Blakeney, as he once more stretched his long limbs along the narrow bed.

He gave a loud and hearty yawn.

"I'll not fail you..." he murmured, as he closed his eyes, and gave a final struggle to get his head at a comfortable angle, "the letter will be written in my best cali... calig.... Lud! but I'm not so drunk as you think I am. ..."

But as if to belie his own oft-repeated assertion, hardly was the last word out of his mouth than his stertorous and even breathing proclaimed the fact that he was once more fast asleep.

With a shrug of the shoulders and a look of unutterable contempt at his broken-down enemy, Chauvelin turned on his heel and went out of the room.

But outside in the corridor he called the orderly to him and gave strict commands that no more wine or brandy was to be served to the Englishman under any circumstances whatever.

"He has two hours in which to sleep off the effects of all that brandy which he had consumed," he mused as he finally went back to his own quarters, "and by that time he will be able to write with a steady hand."

CHAPTER XXXIII. THE ENGLISH SPY

And now at last the shades of evening were drawing in thick and fast. Within the walls of Fort Gayole the last rays of the setting sun had long ago ceased to shed their dying radiance, and through the thick stone embrasures and the dusty panes of glass, the grey light of dusk soon failed to penetrate.

In the large ground-floor room with its window opened upon the wide promenade of the southern ramparts, a silence reigned which was oppressive. The air was heavy with the fumes of the two tallow candles on the table, which smoked persistently.

Against the walls a row of figures in dark blue uniforms with scarlet facings, drab breeches and heavy riding boots, silent and immovable, with fixed bayonets like so many automatons lining the room all round; at some little distance from the central table and out of the immediate circle of light, a small group composed of five soldiers in the same blue and scarlet uniforms. One of these was Sergeant Hebert. In the centre of this group two persons were sitting: a woman and an old man.

The Abbe Foucquet had been brought down from his prison cell a few minutes ago, and told to watch what would go on around him, after which he would be allowed to go to his old church of St. Joseph and ring the Angelus once more before he and his family left Boulogne forever.

The Angelus would be the signal for the opening of all the prison gates in the town. Everyone to-night could come and go as they pleased, and having rung the Angelus, the abbe would be at liberty to join Francois and Felicite and their old mother, his sister, outside the purlieus of the town.

The Abbe Foucquet did not quite understand all this, which was very rapidly and roughly explained to him. It was such a very little while ago that he had expected to see the innocent children mounting up those awful steps which lead to the guillotine, whilst he himself was looking death quite near in the face, that all this talk of amnesty and of pardon had not quite fully reached his brain.

But he was quite content that it had all been ordained by le bon Dieu, and very happy at the thought of ringing the dearly-loved Angelus in his own old church once again. So when he was peremptorily pushed into the room and found himself close to Marguerite, with four or five soldiers standing round them, he quietly pulled his old rosary from his pocket and began murmuring gentle "Paters" and "Aves" under his breath.

Beside him sat Marguerite, rigid as a statue: her cloak thrown over her shoulders, so that its hood might hide her face. She could not now have said how that awful day had passed, how she had managed to survive the terrible, nerve-racking suspense, the agonizing doubt as to what was going to happen. But above all, what she had found most unendurable was the torturing thought that in this same grim and frowning building her husband was there... somewhere... how far or how near she could not say... but she knew that she was parted from him and perhaps would not see him again, not even at the hour of death.

That Percy would never write that infamous letter and LIVE, she knew. That he might write it in order to save her, she feared was possible, whilst the look of triumph on Chauvelin's face had aroused her most agonizing terrors.

When she was summarily ordered to go into the next room, she realized at once that all hope now was more than futile. The walls lined with troops, the attitude of her enemies, and above all that table with paper, ink and pens ready as it were for the accomplishment of the hideous and monstrous deed, all made her very heart numb, as if it were held within the chill embrace of death.

"If the woman moves, speaks or screams, gag her at once!" said Collot roughly the moment she sat down, and Sergeant Hebert stood over her, gag and cloth in hand, whilst two soldiers placed heavy hands on her shoulders.

But she neither moved nor spoke, not even presently when a loud and cheerful voice came echoing from a distant corridor, and anon the door opened and her husband came in, accompanied by Chauvelin.

The ex-ambassador was very obviously in a state of acute nervous tension; his hands were tightly clasped behind his back, and his movements were curiously irresponsible and jerky. But Sir Percy Blakeney looked a picture of calm unconcern: the lace bow at his throat was tied with scrupulous care, his eyeglass upheld at quite the correct angle, and his delicate-coloured caped coat was thrown back just sufficiently to afford a glimpse of the dainty cloth suit and exquisitely embroidered waistcoat beneath.

He was the perfect presentation of a London dandy, and might have been entering a royal drawing-room in company with an honoured guest. Marguerite's eyes were riveted on him as he came well within the circle of light projected by the candles, but not even with that acute sixth sense of a passionate and loving woman could she detect the slightest tremor in the aristocratic hands which held the gold-rimmed eyeglass, nor the faintest quiver of the firmly moulded lips.

This had occurred just as the bell of the old Beffroi chimed three-quarters after six. Now it was close on seven, and in the centre of the room and with his face and figure well lighted up by the candles, at the table pen in hand sat Sir Percy writing.

At his elbow just behind him stood Chauvelin on the one side and Collot d'Herbois on the other, both watching with fixed and burning eyes the writing of that letter.

Sir Percy seemed in no hurry. He wrote slowly and deliberately, carefully copying the draft of the letter which was propped up in front of him. The spelling of some of the French words seemed to have troubled him at first, for when he began he made many facetious and self-deprecatory remarks anent his own want of education, and carelessness in youth in acquiring the gentle art of speaking so elegant a language.

Presently, however, he appeared more at his ease, or perhaps less inclined to talk, since he only received curt monosyllabic answers to his pleasant sallies. Five minutes had gone by without any other sound, save the spasmodic creak of Sir Percy's pen upon the paper, the while Chauvelin and Collot watched every word he wrote.

But gradually from afar there had arisen in the stillness of evening a distant, rolling noise like that of surf breaking against the cliffs. Nearer and louder it grew, and as it increased in volume, so it gained now in diversity. The monotonous, roll-like, far-off thunder was just as continuous as before, but now shriller notes broke out from amongst the more remote sounds, a loud laugh seemed ever and anon to pierce the distance and to rise above the persistent hubbub, which became the mere accompaniment to these isolated tones.

The merrymakers of Boulogne, having started from the Place de la Senechaussee, were making the round of the town by the wide avenue which tops the ramparts. They were coming past the Fort Gayole, shouting, singing, brass trumpets in front, big drum ahead, drenched, hot, and hoarse, but supremely happy.

Sir Percy looked up for a moment as the noise drew nearer, then turned to Chauvelin and pointing to the letter, he said:

"I have nearly finished!"

The suspense in the smoke-laden atmosphere of this room was becoming unendurable, and four hearts at least were beating wildly with overpowering anxiety. Marguerite's eyes were fixed with tender intensity on the man she so passionately loved. She did not understand his actions or his motives, but she felt a wild longing in her, to drink in every line of that loved face, as if with this last, long look she was bidding an eternal farewell to all hopes of future earthly happiness.

The old priest had ceased to tell his beads. Feeling in his kindly heart the echo of the appalling tragedy which was being enacted before him, he had put out a fatherly, tentative hand towards Marguerite, and given her icy fingers a comforting pressure.

And in the hearts of Chauvelin and his colleague there was satisfied revenge, eager, exultant triumph and that terrible nerve-tension which immediately precedes the long-expected climax.

But who can say what went on within the heart of that bold adventurer, about to be brought to the lowest depths of humiliation which it is in the power of man to endure? What behind that smooth unruffled brow still bent laboriously over the page of writing?

The crowd was now on the Place Daumont; some of the foremost in the ranks were ascending the stone steps which lead to the southern ramparts. The noise had become incessant: Pierrots and Pierrettes, Harlequins and Columbines had worked themselves up into a veritable intoxication of shouts and laughter.

Now as they all swarmed up the steps and caught sight of the open window almost on a level with the ground, and of the large dimly-lighted room, they gave forth one terrific and voluminous "Hurrah!" for the paternal government up in Paris, who had given them cause for all this joy. Then they recollected how the amnesty, the pardon, the national fete, this brilliant procession had come about, and somebody in the crowd shouted:

"Allons! les us have a look at that English spy!..."

"Let us see the Scarlet Pimpernel!"

"Yes! yes! let us see what he is like!"

They shouted and stamped and swarmed round the open window, swinging their lanthorns and demanding in a loud tone of voice that the English spy be shown to them.

Faces wet with rain and perspiration tried to peep in at the window. Collot gave brief orders to the soldiers to close the shutters at once and to push away the crowd, but the crowd would not be pushed. It would not be gainsaid, and when the soldiers tried to close the window, twenty angry fists broke the panes of glass.

"I can't finish this writing in your lingo, sir, whilst this demmed row is going on," said Sir Percy placidly.

"You have not much more to write, Sir Percy," urged Chauvelin with nervous impatience, "I pray you, finish the matter now, and get you gone from out this city."

"Send that demmed lot away, then," rejoined Sir Percy calmly.

"They won't go.... They want to see you..."

Sir Percy paused a moment, pen in hand, as if in deep reflection.

"They want to see me," he said with a laugh. "Why, demn it all... then, why not let em?..."

And with a few rapid strokes of the pen, he quickly finished the letter, adding his signature with a bold flourish, whilst the crowd, pushing, jostling, shouting and cursing the soldiers, still loudly demanded to see the Scarlet Pimpernel.

Chauvelin felt as if his heart would veritably burst with the wildness of its beating.

Then Sir Percy, with one hand lightly pressed on the letter, pushed his chair away and with his pleasant ringing voice, said once again:

"Well! demn it... let 'em see me!..."

With that he sprang to his feet and up to his full height, and as he did so he seized the two massive pewter candlesticks, one in each hand, and with powerful arms well outstretched he held them high above his head.

"The letter..." murmured Chauvelin in a hoarse whisper.

But even as he was quickly reaching out a hand, which shook with the intensity of his excitement, towards the letter on the table, Blakeney, with one loud and sudden shout, threw the heavy candlesticks onto the floor. They rattled down with a terrific crash, the lights were extinguished, and the whole room was immediately plunged in utter darkness.

The crowd gave a wild yell of fear: they had only caught sight for one instant of that gigantic figure—which, with arms outstretched had seemed supernaturally tall—weirdly illuminated by the flickering light of the tallow candles and the next moment disappearing into utter darkness before their very gaze. Overcome with sudden superstitious fear, Pierrots and Pierrettes, drummer and trumpeters turned and fled in every direction.

Within the room all was wild confusion. The soldiers had heard a cry:

"La fenetre! La fenetre!"

Who gave it no one knew, no one could afterwards recollect: certain it is that with one accord the majority of the men made a rush for the open window, driven thither partly by the wild instinct of the chase after an escaping enemy, and partly by the same superstitious terror which had caused the crowd to flee. They clambered over the sill and dropped down on to the ramparts below, then started in wild pursuit.

But when the crash came, Chauvelin had given one frantic shout:

"The letter!!!... Collot!!... A moi.... In his hand.... The letter!..."

There was the sound of a heavy thud, of a terrible scuffle there on the floor in the darkness and then a yell of victory from Collot d'Herbois.

"I have the letter! A Paris!"

"Victory!" echoed Chauvelin, exultant and panting, "victory!! The Angelus, friend Hebert! Take the calotin to ring the Angelus!!!"

It was instinct which caused Collot d'Herbois to find the door; he tore it open, letting in a feeble ray of light from the corridor. He stood in the doorway one moment, his slouchy, ungainly form distinctly outlined against the lighter background beyond, a look of exultant and malicious triumph, of deadly hate and cruelty distinctly imprinted on his face and with upraised hand wildly flourishing the precious document, the brand of dishonour for the enemy of France.

"A Paris!" shouted Chauvelin to him excitedly. "Into Robespierre's hands. ... The letter!..."

Then he fell back panting, exhausted on the nearest chair.

Collot, without looking again behind him, called wildly for the men who were to escort him to Paris. They were picked troopers, stalwart veterans from the old municipal guard. They had not broken their ranks throughout the turmoil, and fell into line in perfect order as they followed Citizen Collot out of the room.

Less than five minutes later there was the noise of stamping and champing of bits in the courtyard below, a shout from Collot, and the sound of a cavalcade galloping at break-neck speed towards the distant Paris gate.

CHAPTER XXXIV. THE ANGELUS

And gradually all noises died away around the old Fort Gayole. The shouts and laugher of the merrymakers, who had quickly recovered from their fright, now came only as the muffled rumble of a distant storm, broken here and there by the shrill note of a girl's loud laughter, or a vigorous fanfare from the brass trumpets.

The room where so much turmoil had taken place, where so many hearts had beaten with torrent-like emotions, where the awesome tragedy of revenge and hate, of love and passion had been consummated, was now silent and at peace.

The soldiers had gone: some in pursuit of the revellers, some with Collot d'Herbois, others with Hebert and the calotin who was to ring the Angelus.

Chauvelin, overcome with the intensity of his exultation and the agony of the suspense which he had endured, sat, vaguely dreaming, hardly conscious, but wholly happy and content. Fearless, too, for his triumph was complete, and he cared not now if he lived or died.

He had lived long enough to see the complete annihilation and dishonour of his enemy.

What had happened to Sir Percy Blakeney now, what to Marguerite, he neither knew nor cared. No doubt the Englishman had picked himself up and got away through the window or the door: he would be anxious to get his wife out of the town as quickly as possible. The Angelus would ring directly, the gates would be opened, the harbour made free to everyone....

And Collot was a league outside Boulogne by now... a league nearer to Paris.

So what mattered the humbled wayside English flower?—the damaged and withered Scarlet Pimpernel?...

A slight noise suddenly caused him to start. He had been dreaming, no doubt, having fallen into some kind of torpor, akin to sleep, after the deadly and restless fatigue of the past four days. He certainly had been unconscious of everything around him, of time and of place. But now he felt fully awake.

And again he heard that slight noise, as if something or someone was moving in the room.

He tried to peer into the darkness, but could distinguish nothing. He rose and went to the door. It was still open, and close behind it against the wall a small oil lamp was fixed which lit up the corridor.

Chauvelin detached the lamp and came back with it into the room. Just as he did so there came to his ears the first sound of the little church bell ringing the Angelus.

He stepped into the room holding the lamp high above his head; its feeble rays fell full upon the brilliant figure of Sir Percy Blakeney.

He was smiling pleasantly, bowing slightly towards Chauvelin, and in his hand he held the sheathed sword, the blade of which had been fashioned in Toledo for Lorenzo Cenci, and the fellow of which was lying now—Chauvelin himself knew not where.

"The day and hour, Monsieur, I think," said Sir Percy with courtly grace, "when you and I are to cross swords together; those are the southern ramparts, meseems. Will you precede, sir? and I will follow."

At sight of this man, of his impudence and of his daring, Chauvelin felt an icy grip on his heart. His cheeks became ashen white, his thin lips closed with a snap, and the hand which held the lamp aloft trembled visibly. Sir Percy stood before him, still smiling and with a graceful gesture pointing towards the ramparts.

From the Church of St. Joseph the gentle, melancholy tones of the Angelus sounding the second Ave Maria came faintly echoing in the evening air.

With a violent effort Chauvelin forced himself to self-control, and tried to shake off the strange feeling of obsession which had overwhelmed him in the presence of this extraordinary man. He walked quite quietly up to the table and placed the lamp upon it. As in a flash recollection had come back to him.. the past few minutes!... the letter! and Collot well on his way to Paris!

Bah! he had nothing to fear now, save perhaps death at the hand of this adventurer turned assassin in his misery and humiliation!

"A truce on this folly, Sir Percy," he said roughly, "as you well know, I had never any intention of fighting you with these poisoned swords of yours and..."

"I knew that, M. Chauvelin.... But do YOU know that I have the intention of killing you now... as you stand... like a dog!..."

And throwing down the sword with one of those uncontrolled outbursts of almost animal passion, which for one instant revealed the real, inner man, he went up to Chauvelin and towering above him like a great avenging giant, he savoured for one second the joy of looking down on that puny, slender figure which he could crush with sheer brute force, with one blow from his powerful hands.

But Chauvelin at this moment was beyond fear.

"And if you killed me now, Sir Percy," he said quietly and looking the man whom he so hated fully in the eyes, "you could not destroy that letter which my colleague is taking to Paris at this very moment."

As he had anticipated, his words seemed to change Sir Percy's mood in an instant. The passion in the handsome, aristocratic face faded in a trice, the hard lines round the jaw and lips relaxed, the fire of revenge died out from the lazy blue eyes, and the next moment a long, loud, merry laugh raised the dormant echoes of the old fort.

"Nay, Monsieur Chaubertin," said Sir Percy gaily, "but this is marvellous... demmed marvellous... do you hear that, m'dear?... Gadzooks! but 'tis the best joke I have heard this past twelve-months.... Monsieur here thinks... Lud! but I shall die of laughing.... Monsieur here thinks... that 'twas that demmed letter which went to Paris... and that an English gentleman lay scuffling on the floor and allowed a letter to be filched from him..."

"Sir Percy!..." gasped Chauvelin, as an awful thought seemed suddenly to flash across his fevered brain.

"Lud, sir, you are astonishing!" said Sir Percy, taking a very much crumpled sheet of paper from the capacious pocket of his elegant caped coat, and holding it close to Chauvelin's horror-stricken gaze. "THIS is the letter which I wrote at that table yonder in order to gain time and in order to fool you.... But, by the Lord, you are a bigger demmed fool than ever I took you to be, if you thought it would serve any other purpose save that of my hitting you in the face with it."

And with a quick and violent gesture he struck Chauvelin full in the face with the paper.

"You would like to know, Monsieur Chaubertin, would you not?..." he added pleasantly, "what letter it is that your friend, Citizen Collot, is taking in such hot haste to Paris for you.... Well! the letter is not long and 'tis written in verse.... I wrote it myself upstairs to-day whilst you thought me sodden with brandy and three-parts asleep. But brandy is easily flung out of the window.... Did you think I drank it all?... Nay! as you remember, I told you that I was not so drunk as you thought?... Aye! the letter is writ in English verse, Monsieur, and it reads thus:

"We seek him here! we seek him there! Those Frenchies seek him everywhere! Is he in heaven? is he in hell? That demmed elusive Pimpernel?

"A neat rhyme, I fancy, Monsieur, and one which will, if rightly translated, greatly please your friend and ruler, Citizen Robespierre.... Your colleague Citizen Collot is well on his way to Paris with it by now. ... No, no, Monsieur... as you rightly said just now... I really could not kill you... God having blessed me with the saving sense of humour..."

Even as he spoke the third Ave Maria of the Angelus died away on the morning air. From the harbour and the old Chateau there came the loud boom of cannon.

The hour of the opening of the gates, of the general amnesty and free harbour was announced throughout Boulogne.

Chauvelin was livid with rage, fear and baffled revenge. He made a sudden rush for the door in a blind desire to call for help, but Sir Percy had toyed long enough with his prey. The hour was speeding on: Hebert and some of the soldiers might return, and it was time to think of safety and of flight. Quick as a hunted panther, he had interposed his tall figure between his enemy and the latter's chance of calling for aid, then, seizing the little man by the shoulders, he pushed him back into that portion of the room where Marguerite and the Abbe Foucquet had been lately sitting.

The gag, with cloth and cord, which had been intended for a woman were lying on the ground close by, just where Hebert had dropped them, when he marched the old Abbe off to the Church.

With quick and dexterous hands, Sir Percy soon reduced Chauvelin to an impotent and silent bundle. The ex-ambassador after four days of harrowing nerve-tension, followed by so awful a climax, was weakened physically and mentally, whilst Blakeney, powerful, athletic and always absolutely unperturbed, was fresh in body and spirit. He had slept calmly all the afternoon, having quietly thought out all his plans, left nothing to chance, and acted methodically and quickly, and invariably with perfect repose.

Having fully assured himself that the cords were well fastened, the gag secure and Chauvelin completely helpless, he took the now inert mass up in his arms and carried it into the adjoining room, where Marguerite for twelve hours had endured a terrible martyrdom.

He laid his enemy's helpless form upon the couch, and for one moment looked down on it with a strange feeling of pity quite unmixed with contempt. The light from the lamp in the further room struck vaguely upon the prostrate figure of Chauvelin. He seemed to have lost consciousness, for the eyes were closed, only the hands, which were tied securely to his body, had a spasmodic, nervous twitch in them.

With a good-natured shrug of the shoulders the imperturbable Sir Percy turned to go, but just before he did so, he took a scrap of paper from his waistcoat pocket, and slipped it between Chauvelin's trembling fingers. On the paper were scribbled the four lines of verse which in the next four and twenty hours Robespierre himself and his colleagues would read.

Then Blakeney finally went out of the room.

CHAPTER XXXV. MARGUERITE

As he re-entered the large room, she was standing beside the table, with one dainty hand resting against the back of the chair, her whole graceful figure bent forward as if in an agony of ardent expectation.

Never for an instant, in that supreme moment when his precious life was at stake, did she waver in courage or presence of mind. From the moment that he jumped up and took the candlesticks in his hands, her sixth sense showed her as in a flash what he meant to do and how he would wish her to act.

When the room was plunged in darkness she stood absolutely still; when she heard the scuffle on the floor she never trembled, for her passionate heart had already told her that he never meant to deliver that infamous letter into his enemies' hands. Then, when there was the general scramble, when the soldiers rushed away, when the room became empty and Chauvelin alone remained, she shrank quietly into the darkest corner of the room, hardly breathing, only waiting.... Waiting for a sign from him!

She could not see him, but she felt the beloved presence there, somewhere close to her, and she knew that he would wish her to wait.... She watched him silently... ready to help if he called... equally ready to remain still and to wait.

Only when the helpless body of her deadly enemy was well out of the way did she come from out the darkness, and now she stood with the full light of the lamp illuminating her ruddy golden hair, the delicate blush on her cheek, the flame of love dancing in her glorious eyes.

Thus he saw her as he re-entered the room, and for one second he paused at the door, for the joy of seeing her there seemed greater than he could bear.

Forgotten was the agony of mind which he had endured, the humiliations and the dangers which still threatened: he only remembered that she loved him and that he worshipped her.

The next moment she lay clasped in his arms. All was still around them, save for the gentle patter-patter of the rain on the trees of the ramparts: and from very far away the echo of laughter and music from the distant revellers.

And then the cry of the sea-mew thrice repeated from just beneath the window.

Blakeney and Marguerite awoke from their brief dream: once more the passionate lover gave place to the man of action.

"'Tis Tony, an I mistake not," he said hurriedly, as with loving fingers still slightly trembling with suppressed passion, he readjusted the hood over her head.

"Lord Tony?" she murmured.

"Aye! with Hastings and one or two others. I told them to be ready for us to-night as soon as the place was quiet."

"You were so sure of success then, Percy?" she asked in wonderment.

"So sure," he replied simply.

Then he led her to the window, and lifted her onto the sill. It was not high from the ground and two pairs of willing arms were there ready to help her down.

Then he, too, followed, and quietly the little party turned to walk toward the gate. The ramparts themselves now looked strangely still and silent: the merrymakers were far away, only one or two passers-by hurried swiftly past here and there, carrying bundles, evidently bent on making use of that welcome permission to leave this dangerous soil.

The little party walked on in silence, Marguerite's small hand resting on her husband's arm. Anon they came upon a group of soldiers who were standing somewhat perfunctorily and irresolutely close by the open gate of the Fort.

"Tiens c'est l'Anglais!" said one.

"Morbleu! he is on his way back to England," commented another lazily.

The gates of Boulogne had been thrown open to everyone when the Angelus was rung and the cannon boomed. The general amnesty had been proclaimed, everyone had the right to come and go as they pleased, the sentinels had been ordered to challenge no one and to let everyone pass.

No one knew that the great and glorious plans for the complete annihilation of the Scarlet Pimpernel and his League had come to naught, that Collot was taking a mighty hoax to Paris, and that the man who had thought out and nearly carried through the most fiendishly cruel plan ever conceived for the destruction of an enemy, lay helpless, bound and gagged, within his own stronghold.

And so the little party, consisting of Sir Percy and Marguerite, Lord Anthony Dewhurst and my Lord Hastings, passed unchallenged through the gates of Boulogne.

Outside the precincts of the town they met my Lord Everingham and Sir Philip Glynde, who had met the Abbe Foucquet outside his little church and escorted him safely out of the city, whilst Francois and Felicite with their old mother had been under the charge of other members of the League.

"We were all in the procession, dressed up in all sorts of ragged finery, until the last moment," explained Lord Tony to Marguerite as the entire party now quickly made its way to the harbour. "We did not know what was going to happen.... All we knew was that we should be wanted about this time—the hour when the duel was to have been fought—and somewhere near here on the southern ramparts... and we always have strict orders to mix with the crowd if there happens to be one. When we saw Blakeney raise the candlesticks we guessed what was coming, and we each went to our respective posts. It was all quite simple."

The young man spoke gaily and lightly, but through the easy banter of his tone, there pierced the enthusiasm and pride of the soldier in the glory and daring of his chief.

Between the city walls and the harbour there was much bustle and agitation. The English packet-boat would lift anchor at the turn of the tide, and as every one was free to get aboard without leave or passport, there were a very large number of passengers, bound for the land of freedom.

Two boats from the "Day-Dream" were waiting in readiness for Sir Percy and my lady and those whom they would bring with them.

Silently the party embarked, and as the boats pushed off and the sailors from Sir Percy's yacht bent to their oars, the old Abbe Foucquet began gently droning a Pater and Ave to the accompaniment of his beads.

He accepted joy, happiness and safety with the same gentle philosophy as he would have accepted death, but Marguerite's keen and loving ears caught at the end of each "Pater" a gently murmured request to le bon Dieu to bless and protect our English rescuer.

Only once did Marguerite make allusion to that terrible time which had become the past.

They were wandering together down the chestnut alley in the beautiful garden at Richmond. It was evening, and the air was heavy with the rich odour of wet earth, of belated roses and dying mignonette. She had paused in the alley, and placed a trembling hand upon his arm, whilst raising her eyes filled with tears of tender passion up to his face.

"Percy!" she murmured, "have you forgiven me?"

"What, m'dear?"

"That awful evening in Boulogne... what that fiend demanded... his awful 'either—or'... I brought it all upon you... it was all my fault."

"Nay, my dear, for that 'tis I should thank you..."

"Thank me?"

"Aye," he said, whilst in the fast-gathering dusk she could only just perceive the sudden hardening of his face, the look of wild passion in his eyes, "but for that evening in Boulogne, but for that alternative which that devil placed before me, I might never have known how much you meant to me."

Even the recollection of all the sorrow, the anxiety, the torturing humiliations of that night seemed completely to change him; the voice became trenchant, the hands were tightly clenched. But Marguerite drew nearer to him; her two hands were on his breast; she murmured gently:

"And now?..."

He folded her in his arms, with an agony of joy, and said earnestly:

"Now I know."

THE LEAGUE OF THE SCARLET PIMPERNEL

THE LEAGUE OF THE SCARLET PIMPERNEL

CHAPTER I. SIR PERCY EXPLAINS

I.

IT WAS NOT, Heaven help us all! a very uncommon occurrence these days: a woman almost unsexed by misery, starvation, and the abnormal excitement engendered by daily spectacles of revenge and of cruelty. They were to be met with every day, round every street corner, these harridans, more terrible far than were the men.

This one was still comparatively young, thirty at most; would have been good-looking too, for the features were really delicate, the nose chiseled, the brow straight, the chin round and small. But the mouth! Heavens, what a mouth! Hard and cruel and thin-lipped; and those eyes! sunken and rimmed with purple; eyes that told tales of sorrow and, yes! of degradation. The crowd stood round her, sullen and apathetic; poor, miserable wretches like herself, staring at her antics with lack-lustre eyes and an ever-recurrent contemptuous shrug of the shoulders.

The woman was dancing, contorting her body in the small circle of light formed by a flickering lanthorn which was hung across the street from house to house, striking the muddy pavement with her shoeless feet, all to the sound of a be-ribboned tambourine which she struck now and again with her small, grimy hand. From time to time she paused, held out the tambourine at arm's length, and went the round of the spectators, asking for alms. But at her approach the crowd at once seemed to disintegrate, to melt into the humid evening air; it was but rarely that a greasy token fell into the outstretched tambourine. Then as the woman started again to dance the crowd gradually reassembled, and stood, hands in pockets, lips still sullen and contemptuous, but eyes watchful of the spectacle. There were such few spectacles these days, other than the monotonous processions of tumbrils with their load of aristocrats for the guillotine!

So the crowd watched, and the woman danced. The lanthorn overhead threw a weird light on red caps and tricolour cockades, on the sullen faces of the men and the shoulders of the women, on the dancer's weird antics and her flying, tattered skirts. She was obviously tired, as a poor, performing cur might be, or a bear prodded along to uncongenial buffoonery. Every time that she paused and solicited alms with her tambourine the crowd dispersed, and some of them laughed because she insisted.

"Voyons," she said with a weird attempt at gaiety, "a couple of sous for the entertainment, citizen! You have stood here half an hour. You can't have it all for nothing, what?"

The man—young, square-shouldered, thick-lipped, with the look of a bully about his well-clad person—retorted with a coarse insult, which the woman resented. There were high words; the crowd for the most part ranged itself on the side of the bully. The woman backed against the wall nearest to her, held feeble, emaciated hands up to her ears in a vain endeavour to shut out the hideous jeers and ribald jokes which were the natural weapons of this untamed crowd.

Soon blows began to rain; not a few fell upon the unfortunate woman. She screamed, and the more she screamed the louder did the crowd jeer, the uglier became its temper. Then suddenly it was all over. How it happened the woman could not tell. She had closed her eyes, feeling sick and dizzy; but she had heard a loud call, words spoken in English (a language which she understood), a pleasant laugh, and a brief but violent scuffle. After that the hurrying retreat of many feet, the click of sabots on the uneven pavement and patter of shoeless feet, and then silence.

She had fallen on her knees and was cowering against the wall, had lost consciousness probably for a minute or two. Then she heard that pleasant laugh again and the soft drawl of the English tongue.

"I love to see those beggars scuttling off, like so many rats to their burrows, don't you, Ffoulkes?"

"They didn't put up much fight, the cowards!" came from another voice, also in English. "A dozen of them against this wretched woman. What had best be done with her?"

"I'll see to her," rejoined the first speaker. "You and Tony had best find the others. Tell them I shall be round directly."

It all seemed like a dream. The woman dared not open her eyes lest reality—hideous and brutal—once more confronted her. Then all at once she felt that her poor, weak body, encircled by strong arms, was lifted off the ground, and that she was being carried down the street, away from the light projected by the lanthorn overhead, into the sheltering darkness of a yawning porte cochere. But she was not then fully conscious.

II.

When she reopened her eyes she was in what appeared to be the lodge of a concierge. She was lying on a horsehair sofa. There was a sense of warmth and of security around her. No wonder that it still seemed like a dream. Before her stood a man, tall and straight, surely a being from another world—or so he appeared to the poor wretch who, since uncountable time, had set eyes on none but the most miserable dregs of struggling humanity, who had seen little else but rags, and faces either cruel or wretched. This man was clad in a huge caped coat, which made his powerful figure seem preternaturally large. His hair was fair and slightly curly above his low, square brow; the eyes beneath their heavy lids looked down on her with unmistakable kindness.

The poor woman struggled to her feet. With a quick and pathetically humble gesture she drew her ragged, muddy skirts over her ankles and her tattered kerchief across her breast.

"I had best go now, Monsieur ... citizen," she murmured, while a hot flush rose to the roots of her unkempt hair. "I must not stop here.... I—"

"You are not going, Madame," he broke in, speaking now in perfect French and with a great air of authority, as one who is accustomed to being implicitly obeyed, "until you have told me how, a lady of culture and of refinement, comes to be masquerading as a street-dancer. The game is a dangerous one, as you have experienced to-night."

"It is no game, Monsieur ... citizen," she stammered; "nor yet a masquerade. I have been a street-dancer all my life, and—"

By way of an answer he took her hand, always with that air of authority which she never thought to resent.

"This is not a street-dancer's hand; Madame," he said quietly. "Nor is your speech that of the people."

She drew her hand away quickly, and the flush on her haggard face deepened.

"If you will honour me with your confidence, Madame," he insisted.

The kindly words, the courtesy of the man, went to the poor creature's heart. She fell back upon the sofa and with her face buried in her arms she sobbed out her heart for a minute or two. The man waited quite patiently. He had seen many women weep these days, and had dried many a tear through deeds of valour and of self-sacrifice, which were for ever recorded in the hearts of those whom he had succoured.

When this poor woman had succeeded in recovering some semblance of self-control, she turned her wan, tear-stained face to him and said simply:

"My name is Madeleine Lannoy, Monsieur. My husband was killed during the emeutes at Versailles, whilst defending the persons of the Queen and of the royal children against the fury of the mob. When I was a girl I had the misfortune to attract the attentions of a young doctor named Jean Paul Marat. You have heard of him, Monsieur?"

The other nodded.

"You know him, perhaps," she continued, "for what he is: the most cruel and revengeful of men. A few years ago he threw up his lucrative appointment as Court physician to Monseigneur le Comte d'Artois, and gave up the profession of medicine for that of journalist and politician. Politician! Heaven help him! He belongs to the most bloodthirsty section of revolutionary brigands. His creed is pillage, murder, and revenge; and he chooses to declare that it is I who, by rejecting his love, drove him to these foul extremities. May God forgive him that abominable lie! The evil we do, Monsieur, is within us; it does not come from circumstance. I, in the meanwhile, was a happy wife. My husband, M. de Lannoy, who was an officer in the army, idolised me. We had one child, a boy—"

She paused, with another catch in her throat. Then she resumed, with calmness that, in view of the tale she told, sounded strangely weird:

"In June last year my child was stolen from me—stolen by Marat in hideous revenge for the supposed wrong which I had done him. The details of that execrable outrage are of no importance. I was decoyed from home one day through the agency of a forged message purporting to come from a very dear friend whom I knew to be in grave trouble at the time. Oh! the whole thing was thoroughly well thought out, I can assure you!" she continued, with a harsh laugh which ended in a heartrending sob. "The forged message, the suborned servant, the threats of terrible reprisals if anyone in the village gave me the slightest warning or clue. When the whole miserable business was accomplished, I was just like a trapped animal inside a cage, held captive by immovable bars of obstinate silence and cruel indifference. No one would help me. No one ostensibly knew anything; no one had seen anything, heard anything. The child was gone! My servants, the people in the village—some of whom I could have sworn were true and sympathetic—only shrugged their shoulders. 'Que voulez-vous, Madame? Children of bourgeois as well as of aristos were often taken up by the State to be brought up as true patriots and no longer pampered like so many lap-dogs.'

"Three days later I received a letter from that inhuman monster, Jean Paul Marat. He told me that he had taken my child away from me, not from any idea of revenge for my disdain in the past, but from a spirit of pure patriotism. My boy, he said, should not be brought up with the same ideas of bourgeois effeteness and love of luxury which had disgraced the nation for centuries. No! he should be reared amongst men who had realised the true value of fraternity and equality and the ideal of complete liberty for the individual to lead his own life, unfettered by senseless prejudices of education and refinement. Which means, Monsieur," the poor woman went on with passionate misery, "that my child is to be reared up in the company of all that is most vile and most degraded in the disease-haunted slums of indigent Paris; that, with the connivance of that execrable fiend Marat, my only son will, mayhap, come back to me one day a potential thief, a criminal probably, a drink-sodden reprobate at best. Such things are done every day in this glorious Revolution of ours—done in the sacred name of France and of Liberty. And the moral murder of my child is to be my punishment for daring to turn a deaf ear to the indign passion of a brute!"

Once more she paused, and when the melancholy echo of her broken voice had died away in the narrow room, not another murmur broke the stillness of this far-away corner of the great city.

The man did not move. He stood looking down upon the poor woman before him, a world of pity expressed in his deep-set eyes. Through the absolute silence around there came the sound as of a gentle flutter, the current of cold air, mayhap, sighing through the ill-fitting shutters, or the soft, weird soughing made by unseen things. The man's heart was full of pity, and it seemed as if the Angel of Compassion had come at his bidding and enfolded the sorrowing woman with his wings.

A moment or two later she was able to finish her pathetic narrative.

"Do you marvel, Monsieur," she said, "that I am still sane—still alive? But I only live to find my child. I try and keep my reason in order to fight the devilish cunning of a brute on his own ground. Up to now all my inquiries have been in vain. At first I squandered money, tried judicial means, set an army of sleuth-hounds on the track. I tried bribery, corruption. I went to the wretch himself and abased myself in the dust before him. He only laughed at me and told me that his love for me had died long ago; he now was lavishing its treasures upon the faithful friend and companion—that awful woman, Simonne Evrard—who had stood by him in the darkest hours of his misfortunes. Then it was that I decided to adopt different tactics. Since my child was to be reared in the midst of murderers and thieves, I, too, would haunt their abodes. I became a street-singer, dancer, what you will. I wear rags now and solicit alms. I haunt the most disreputable cabarets in the lowest slums of Paris. I listen and I spy; I question every man, woman, and child who might afford some clue, give me some indication. There is hardly a house in these parts that I have not visited and whence I have not been kicked out as an importunate beggar or worse. Gradually I am narrowing the circle of my investigations. Presently I shall get a clue. I shall! I know I shall! God cannot allow this monstrous thing to go on!"

Again there was silence. The poor woman had completely broken down. Shame, humiliation, passionate grief, had made of her a mere miserable wreckage of humanity.

The man waited awhile until she was composed, then he said simply:

"You have suffered terribly, Madame; but chiefly, I think, because you have been alone in your grief. You have brooded over it until it has threatened your reason. Now, if you will allow me to act as your friend, I will pledge you my word that I will find your son for you. Will you trust me sufficiently to give up your present methods and place yourself entirely in my hands? There are more than a dozen gallant gentlemen, who are my friends, and who will help me in my search. But for this I must have a free hand, and only help from you when I require it. I can find you lodgings where you will be quite safe under the protection of my wife, who is as like an angel as any man or woman I have ever met on this earth. When your son is once more in your arms, you will, I hope, accompany us to England, where so many of your friends have already found a refuge. If this meets with your approval, Madame, you may command me, for with your permission I mean to be your most devoted servant."

Dante, in his wild imaginations of hell and of purgatory and fleeting glimpses of paradise, never put before us the picture of a soul that was lost and found heaven, after a cycle of despair. Nor could Madeleine Lannoy ever explain her feelings at that moment, even to herself. To begin with, she could not quite grasp the reality of this ray of hope, which came to her at the darkest hour of her misery. She stared at the man before her as she would on an ethereal vision; she fell on her knees and buried her face in her hands.

What happened afterwards she hardly knew; she was in a state of semi-consciousness. When she once more woke to reality, she was in comfortable lodgings; she moved and talked and ate and lived like a human being. She was no longer a pariah, an outcast, a poor, half-demented creature, insentient save for an infinite capacity for suffering. She suffered still, but she no longer despaired. There had been such marvelous power and confidence in that man's voice when he said: "I pledge you my word." Madeleine Lannoy lived now in hope and a sweet sense of perfect mental and bodily security. Around her there was an influence, too, a presence which she did not often see, but always felt to be there: a woman, tall and graceful and sympathetic, who was always ready to cheer, to comfort, and to help. Her name was Marguerite. Madame Lannoy never knew her by any other. The man had spoken of her as being as like an angel as could be met on this earth, and poor Madeleine Lannoy fully agreed with him.

III.

Even that bloodthirsty tiger, Jean Paul Marat, has had his apologists. His friends have called him a martyr, a selfless and incorruptible exponent of social and political ideals. We may take it that Simonne Evrard loved him, for a more impassioned obituary speech was, mayhap, never spoken than the one which she delivered before the National Assembly in honour of that sinister demagogue, whose writings and activities will for ever sully some of the really fine pages of that revolutionary era.

But with those apologists we have naught to do. History has talked its fill of the inhuman monster. With the more intimate biographers alone has this true chronicle any concern. It is one of these who tells us that on or about the eighteenth day of Messidor, in the year I of the Republic (a date which corresponds with the sixth of July, 1793, of our own calendar), Jean Paul Marat took an additional man into his service, at the instance of Jeannette Marechal, his cook and maid-of-all-work. Marat was at this time a martyr to an unpleasant form of skin disease, brought on by the terrible privations which he had endured during the few years preceding his association with Simonne Evrard, the faithful friend and housekeeper, whose small fortune subsequently provided him with some degree of comfort.

The man whom Jeannette Marechal, the cook, introduced into the household of No. 30, Rue des Cordeliers, that worthy woman had literally picked one day out of the gutter where he was grabbing for scraps of food like some wretched starving cur. He appeared to be known to the police of the section, his identity book proclaiming him to be one Paul Mole, who had served his time in gaol for larceny. He professed himself willing to do any work required of him, for the merest pittance and some kind of roof over his head. Simonne Evrard allowed Jeannette to take him in, partly out of compassion and partly with a view to easing the woman's own burden, the only other domestic in the house—a man named Bas—being more interested in politics and the meetings of the Club des Jacobins than he was in his master's ailments. The man Mole, moreover, appeared to know something of medicine and of herbs and how to prepare the warm baths which alone eased the unfortunate Marat from pain. He was powerfully built, too, and though he muttered and grumbled a great deal, and indulged in prolonged fits of sulkiness, when he would not open his mouth to anyone, he was, on the whole, helpful and good-tempered.

There must also have been something about his whole wretched personality which made a strong appeal to the "Friend of the People," for it is quite evident that within a few days Paul Mole had won no small measure of his master's confidence.

Marat, sick, fretful, and worried, had taken an unreasoning dislike to his servant Bas. He was thankful to have a stranger about him, a man who was as miserable as he himself had been a very little while ago; who, like himself, had lived in cellars and in underground burrows, and lived on the scraps of food which even street-curs had disdained.

On the seventh day following Mole's entry into the household, and while the latter was preparing his employer's bath, Marat said abruptly to him:

"You'll go as far as the Chemin de Pantin to-day for me, citizen. You know your way?"

"I can find it, what?" muttered Mole, who appeared to be in one of his surly moods.

"You will have to go very circumspectly," Marat went on, in his cracked and feeble voice. "And see to it that no one spies upon your movements. I have many enemies, citizen ... one especially ... a woman.... She is always prying and spying on me.... So beware of any woman you see lurking about at your heels."

Mole gave a half-audible grunt in reply.

"You had best go after dark," the other rejoined after awhile. "Come back to me after nine o'clock. It is not far to the Chemin de Pantin—just where it intersects the Route de Meaux. You can get there and back before midnight. The people will admit you. I will give you a ring—the only thing I possess.... It has little or no value," he added with a harsh, grating laugh. "It will not be worth your while to steal it. You will have to see a brat and report to me on his condition—his appearance, what?... Talk to him a bit.... See what he says and let me know. It is not difficult."

"No, citizen."

Mole helped the suffering wretch into his bath. Not a movement, not a quiver of the eyelid betrayed one single emotion which he may have felt—neither loathing nor sympathy, only placid indifference. He was just a half-starved menial, thankful to accomplish any task for the sake of satisfying a craving stomach. Marat stretched out his shrunken limbs in the herbal water with a sigh of well-being.

"And the ring, citizen?" Mole suggested presently.

The demagogue held up his left hand—it was emaciated and disfigured by disease. A cheap-looking metal ring, set with a false stone, glistened upon the fourth finger.

"Take it off," he said curtly.

The ring must have all along been too small for the bony hand of the once famous Court physician. Even now it appeared embedded in the flabby skin and refused to slide over the knuckle.

"The water will loosen it," remarked Mole quietly.

Marat dipped his hand back into the water, and the other stood beside him, silent and stolid, his broad shoulders bent, his face naught but a mask, void and expressionless beneath its coating of grime.

One or two seconds went by. The air was heavy with steam and a medley of evil-smelling fumes, which hung in the close atmosphere of the narrow room. The sick man appeared to be drowsy, his head rolled over to one side, his eyes closed. He had evidently forgotten all about the ring.

A woman's voice, shrill and peremptory, broke the silence which had become oppressive:

"Here, citizen Mole, I want you! There's not a bit of wood chopped up for my fire, and how am I to make the coffee without firing, I should like to know?"

"The ring, citizen," Mole urged gruffly.

Marat had been roused by the woman's sharp voice. He cursed her for a noisy harridan; then he said fretfully:

"It will do presently—when you are ready to start. I said nine o'clock ... it is only four now. I am tired. Tell citizeness Evrard to bring me some hot coffee in an hour's time.... You can go and fetch me the Moniteur now, and take back these proofs to citizen Dufour. You will find him at the 'Cordeliers,' or else at the printing works.... Come back at nine o'clock.... I am tired now ... too tired to tell you where to find the house which is off the Chemin de Pantin. Presently will do...."

Even while he spoke he appeared to drop into a fitful sleep. His two hands were hidden under the sheet which covered the bath. Mole watched him in silence for a moment or two, then he turned on his heel and shuffled off through the ante-room into the kitchen beyond, where presently he sat down, squatting in an angle by the stove, and started with his usual stolidness to chop wood for the citizeness' fire.

When this task was done, and he had received a chunk of sour bread for his reward from Jeannette Marechal, the cook, he shuffled out of the place and into the street, to do his employer's errands.

IV.

Paul Mole had been to the offices of the Moniteur and to the printing works of L'Ami du Peuple. He had seen the citizen Dufour at the Club and, presumably, had spent the rest of his time wandering idly about the streets of the quartier, for he did not return to the Rue des Cordeliers until nearly nine o'clock.

As soon as he came to the top of the street, he fell in with the crowd which had collected outside No. 30. With his habitual slouchy gait and the steady pressure of his powerful elbows, he pushed his way to the door, whilst gleaning whisperings and rumours on his way.

"The citizen Marat has been assassinated."

"By a woman."

"A mere girl."

"A wench from Caen. Her name is Corday."

"The people nearly tore her to pieces awhile ago."

"She is as much as guillotined already."

The latter remark went off with a loud guffaw and many a ribald joke.

Mole, despite his great height, succeeded in getting through unperceived. He was of no account, and he knew his way inside the house. It was full of people: journalists, gaffers, women and men—the usual crowd that come to gape. The citizen Marat was a great personage. The Friend of the People. An Incorruptible, if ever there was one. Just look at the simplicity, almost the poverty, in which he lived! Only the aristos hated him, and the fat bourgeois who battened on the people. Citizen Marat had sent hundreds of them to the guillotine with a stroke of his pen or a denunciation from his fearless tongue.

Mole did not pause to listen to these comments. He pushed his way through the throng up the stairs, to his late employer's lodgings on the first floor.

The anteroom was crowded, so were the other rooms; but the greatest pressure was around the door immediately facing him, the one which gave on the bathroom. In the kitchen on his right, where awhile ago he had been chopping wood under a flood of abuse from Jeannette Marechal, he caught sight of this woman, cowering by the hearth, her filthy apron thrown over her head, and crying—yes! crying for the loathsome creature, who had expiated some of his abominable crimes at the hands of a poor, misguided girl, whom an infuriated mob was even now threatening to tear to pieces in its rage.

The parlour and even Simonne's room were also filled with people: men, most of whom Mole knew by sight; friends or enemies of the ranting demagogue who lay murdered in the very bath which his casual servant had prepared for him. Every one was discussing the details of the murder, the punishment of the youthful assassin. Simonne Evrard was being loudly blamed for having admitted the girl into citizen Marat's room. But the wench had looked so simple, so innocent, and she said she was the bearer of a message from Caen. She had called twice during the day, and in the evening the citizen himself said that he would see her. Simonne had been for sending her away. But the citizen was peremptory. And he was so helpless ... in his bath ... name of a name, the pitiable affair!

No one paid much attention to Mole. He listened for a while to Simonne's impassioned voice, giving her version of the affair; then he worked his way stolidly into the bathroom.

It was some time before he succeeded in reaching the side of that awful bath wherein lay the dead body of Jean Paul Marat. The small room was densely packed—not with friends, for there was not a man or woman living, except Simonne Evrard and her sisters, whom the bloodthirsty demagogue would have called "friend"; but his powerful personality had been a menace to many, and now they came in crowds to see that he was really dead, that a girl's feeble hand had actually done the deed which they themselves had only contemplated. They stood about whispering, their heads averted from the ghastly spectacle of this miserable creature, to whom even death had failed to lend his usual attribute of tranquil dignity.

The tiny room was inexpressibly hot and stuffy. Hardly a breath of outside air came in through the narrow window, which only gave on the bedroom beyond. An evil-smelling oil-lamp swung from the low ceiling and shed its feeble light on the upturned face of the murdered man.

Mole stood for a moment or two, silent and pensive, beside that hideous form. There was the bath, just as he had prepared it: the board spread over with a sheet and laid across the bath, above which only the head and shoulders emerged, livid and stained. One hand, the left, grasped the edge of the board with the last convulsive clutch of supreme agony.

On the fourth finger of that hand glistened the shoddy ring which Marat had said was not worth stealing. Yet, apparently, it roused the cupidity of the poor wretch who had served him faithfully for these last few days, and who now would once more be thrown, starving and friendless, upon the streets of Paris.

Mole threw a quick, furtive glance around him. The crowd which had come to gloat over the murdered Terrorist stood about whispering, with heads averted, engrossed in their own affairs. He slid his hand surreptitiously over that of the dead man. With dexterous manipulation he lifted the finger round which glistened the metal ring. Death appeared to have shrivelled the flesh still more upon the bones, to have contracted the knuckles and shrunk the tendons. The ring slid off quite easily. Mole had it in his hand, when suddenly a rough blow struck him on the shoulder.

"Trying to rob the dead?" a stern voice shouted in his ear. "Are you a disguised aristo, or what?"

At once the whispering ceased. A wave of excitement went round the room. Some people shouted, others pressed forward to gaze on the abandoned wretch who had been caught in the act of committing a gruesome deed.

"Robbing the dead!"

They were experts in evil, most of these men here. Their hands were indelibly stained with some of the foulest crimes ever recorded in history. But there was something ghoulish in this attempt to plunder that awful thing lying there, helpless, in the water. There was also a great relief to nerve-tension in shouting Horror and Anathema with self-righteous indignation; and additional excitement in the suggested "aristo in disguise."

Mole struggled vigorously. He was powerful and his fists were heavy. But he was soon surrounded, held fast by both arms, whilst half a dozen hands tore at his tattered clothes, searched him to his very skin, for the booty which he was thought to have taken from the dead.

"Leave me alone, curse you!" he shouted, louder than his aggressors. "My name is Paul Mole, I tell you. Ask the citizeness Evrard. I waited on citizen Marat. I prepared his bath. I was the only friend who did not turn away from him in his sickness and his poverty. Leave me alone, I say! Why," he added, with a hoarse laugh, "Jean Paul in his bath was as naked as on the day he was born!"

"'Tis true," said one of those who had been most active in rummaging through Mole's grimy rags. "There's nothing to be found on him."

But suspicion once aroused was not easily allayed. Mole's protestations became more and more vigorous and emphatic. His papers were all in order, he vowed. He had them on him: his own identity papers, clear for anyone to see. Someone had dragged them out of his pocket; they were dank and covered with splashes of mud—hardly legible. They were handed over to a man who stood in the immediate circle of light projected by the lamp. He seized them and examined them carefully. This man was short and slight, was dressed in well-made cloth clothes; his hair was held in at the nape of the next in a modish manner with a black taffeta bow. His hands were clean, slender, and claw-like, and he wore the tricolour scarf of office round his waist which proclaimed him to be a member of one of the numerous Committees which tyrannised over the people.

The papers appeared to be in order, and proclaimed the bearer to be Paul Mole, a native of Besancon, a carpenter by trade. The identity book had recently been signed by Jean Paul Marat, the man's latest employer, and been counter-signed by the Commissary of the section.

The man in the tricolour scarf turned with some acerbity on the crowd who was still pressing round the prisoner.

"Which of you here," he queried roughly, "levelled an unjust accusation against an honest citizen?"

But, as usual in such cases, no one replied directly to the charge. It was not safe these days to come into conflict with men like Mole. The Committees were all on their side, against the bourgeois as well as against the aristos. This was the reign of the proletariat, and the sans-culotte always emerged triumphant in a conflict against the well-to-do. Nor was it good to rouse the ire of citizen Chauvelin, one of the most powerful, as he was the most pitiless members of the Committee of Public Safety. Quiet, sarcastic rather than aggressive, something of the aristo, too, in his clean linen and well-cut clothes, he had not even yielded to the defunct Marat in cruelty and relentless persecution of aristocrats.

Evidently his sympathies now were all with Mole, the out-at-elbows, miserable servant of an equally miserable master. His pale-coloured, deep-set eyes challenged the crowd, which gave way before him, slunk back into the corners, away from his coldly threatening glance. Thus he found himself suddenly face to face with Mole, somewhat isolated from the rest, and close to the tin bath with its grim contents. Chauvelin had the papers in his hand.

"Take these, citizen," he said curtly to the other. "They are all in order."

He looked up at Mole as he said this, for the latter, though his shoulders were bent, was unusually tall, and Mole took the papers from him. Thus for the space of a few seconds the two men looked into one another's face, eyes to eyes—and suddenly Chauvelin felt an icy sweat coursing down his spine. The eyes into which he gazed had a strange, ironical twinkle in them, a kind of good-humoured arrogance, whilst through the firm, clear-cut lips, half hidden by a dirty and ill-kempt beard, there came the sound —oh! a mere echo—of a quaint and inane laugh.

The whole thing—it seemed like a vision—was over in a second. Chauvelin, sick and faint with the sudden rush of blood to his head, closed his eyes for one brief instant. The next, the crowd had closed round him; anxious inquiries reached his re-awakened senses.

But he uttered one quick, hoarse cry:

"Hebert! A moi! Are you there?"

"Present, citizen!" came in immediate response. And a tall figure in the tattered uniform affected by the revolutionary guard stepped briskly out of the crowd. Chauvelin's claw-like hand was shaking visibly.

"The man Mole," he called in a voice husky with excitement. "Seize him at once! And, name of a dog! do not allow a living soul in or out of the house!"

Hebert turned on his heel. The next moment his harsh voice was heard above the din and the general hubbub around:

"Quite safe, citizen!" he called to his chief. "We have the rogue right enough!"

There was much shouting and much cursing, a great deal of bustle and confusion, as the men of the Surete closed the doors of the defunct demagogue's lodgings. Some two score men, a dozen or so women, were locked in, inside the few rooms which reeked of dirt and of disease. They jostled and pushed, screamed and protested. For two or three minutes the din was quite deafening. Simonne Evrard pushed her way up to the forefront of the crowd.

"What is this I hear?" she queried peremptorily. "Who is accusing citizen Mole? And of what, I should like to know? I am responsible for everyone inside these apartments ... and if citizen Marat were still alive—"

Chauvelin appeared unaware of all the confusion and of the woman's protestations. He pushed his way through the crowd to the corner of the anteroom where Mole stood, crouching and hunched up, his grimy hands idly fingering the papers which Chauvelin had returned to him a moment ago. Otherwise he did not move.

He stood, silent and sullen; and when Chauvelin, who had succeeded in mastering his emotion, gave the peremptory command: "Take this man to the depot at once. And do not allow him one instant out of your sight!" he made no attempt at escape.

He allowed Hebert and the men to seize him, to lead him away. He followed without a word, without a struggle. His massive figure was hunched up like that of an old man; his hands, which still clung to his identity papers, trembled slightly like those of a man who is very frightened and very helpless. The men of the Surete handled him very roughly, but he made no protest. The woman Evrard did all the protesting, vowing that the people would not long tolerate such tyranny. She even forced her way up to Hebert.

With a gesture of fury she tried to strike him in the face, and continued, with a loud voice, her insults and objurgations, until, with a movement of his bayonet, he pushed her roughly out of the way.

After that Paul Mole, surrounded by the guard, was led without ceremony out of the house. Chauvelin gazed after him as if he had been brought face to face with a ghoul.

V.

Chauvelin hurried to the depot. After those few seconds wherein he had felt dazed, incredulous, almost under a spell, he had quickly regained the mastery of his nerves, and regained, too, that intense joy which anticipated triumph is wont to give.

In the out-at-elbows, half-starved servant of the murdered Terrorist, citizen Chauvelin, of the Committee of Public Safety, had recognised his arch enemy, that meddlesome and adventurous Englishman who chose to hide his identity under the pseudonym of the Scarlet Pimpernel. He knew that he could reckon on Hebert; his orders not to allow the prisoner one moment out of sight would of a certainty be strictly obeyed.

Hebert, indeed, a few moments later, greeted his chief outside the doors of the depot with the welcome news that Paul Mole was safely under lock and key.

"You had no trouble with him?" Chauvelin queried, with ill-concealed eagerness.

"No, no! citizen, no trouble," was Hebert's quick reply. "He seems to be a well-known rogue in these parts," he continued with a complacent guffaw; "and some of his friends tried to hustle us at the corner of the Rue de Tourraine; no doubt with a view to getting the prisoner away. But we were too strong for them, and Paul Mole is now sulking in his cell and still protesting that his arrest is an outrage against the liberty of the people."

Chauvelin made no further remark. He was obviously too excited to speak.

Pushing past Hebert and the men of the Surete who stood about the dark
and narrow passages of the depot, he sought the Commissary of the
Section in the latter's office.

It was now close upon ten o'clock. The citizen Commissary Cuisinier had finished his work for the day and was preparing to go home and to bed. He was a family man, had been a respectable bourgeois in his day, and though he was a rank opportunist and had sacrificed not only his political convictions but also his conscience to the exigencies of the time, he still nourished in his innermost heart a secret contempt for the revolutionary brigands who ruled over France at this hour.

To any other man than citizen Chauvelin, the citizen Commissary would, no doubt, have given a curt refusal to a request to see a prisoner at this late hour of the evening. But Chauvelin was not a man to be denied, and whilst muttering various objections in his ill-kempt beard, Cuisinier, nevertheless, gave orders that the citizen was to be conducted at once to the cells.

Paul Mole had in truth turned sulky. The turnkey vowed that the prisoner had hardly stirred since first he had been locked up in the common cell. He sat in a corner at the end of the bench, with his face turned to the wall, and paid no heed either to his fellow-prisoners or to the facetious remarks of the warder.

Chauvelin went up to him, made some curt remark. Mole kept an obstinate shoulder turned towards him—a grimy shoulder, which showed naked through a wide rent in his blouse. This portion of the cell was well-nigh in total darkness; the feeble shaft of light which came through the open door hardly penetrated to this remote angle of the squalid burrow. The same sense of mystery and unreality overcame Chauvelin again as he looked on the miserable creature in whom, an hour ago, he had recognised the super-exquisite Sir Percy Blakeney. Now he could only see a vague outline in the gloom: the stooping shoulders, the long limbs, that naked piece of shoulder which caught a feeble reflex from the distant light. Nor did any amount of none too gentle prodding on the part of the warder induce him to change his position.

"Leave him alone," said Chauvelin curly at last. "I have seen all that I wished to see."

The cell was insufferably hot and stuffy. Chauvelin, finical and queasy, turned away with a shudder of disgust. There was nothing to be got now out of a prolonged interview with his captured foe. He had seen him: that was sufficient. He had seen the super-exquisite Sir Percy Blakeney locked up in a common cell with some of the most scrubby and abject rogues which the slums of indigent Paris could yield, having apparently failed in some undertaking which had demanded for its fulfilment not only tattered clothes and grimy hands, but menial service with a beggarly and disease-ridden employer, whose very propinquity must have been positive torture to the fastidious dandy.

Of a truth this was sufficient for the gratification of any revenge. Chauvelin felt that he could now go contentedly to rest after an evening's work excellently done.

He gave order that Mole should be put in a separate cell, denied all intercourse with anyone outside or in the depot, and that he should be guarded on sight day and night. After that he went his way.

VI.

The following morning citizen Chauvelin, of the Committee of Public Safety, gave due notice to citizen Fouquier-Tinville, the Public Prosecutor, that the dangerous English spy, known to the world as the Scarlet Pimpernel, was now safely under lock and key, and that he must be transferred to the Abbaye prison forthwith and to the guillotine as quickly as might be. No one was to take any risks this time; there must be no question either of discrediting his famous League or of obtaining other more valuable information out of him. Such methods had proved disastrous in the past.

There were no safe Englishmen these days, except the dead ones, and it would not take citizen Fouquier-Tinville much thought or time to frame an indictment against the notorious Scarlet Pimpernel, which would do away with the necessity of a prolonged trial. The revolutionary government was at war with England now, and short work could be made of all poisonous spies.

By order, therefore, of the Committee of Public Safety, the prisoner, Paul Mole, was taken out of the cells of the depot and conveyed in a closed carriage to the Abbaye prison. Chauvelin had the pleasure of watching this gratifying spectacle from the windows of the Commissariat. When he saw the closed carriage drive away, with Hebert and two men inside and two others on the box, he turned to citizen Commissary Cuisinier with a sigh of intense satisfaction.

"There goes the most dangerous enemy our glorious revolution has had," he said, with an accent of triumph which he did not attempt to disguise.

Cuisinier shrugged his shoulders.

"Possibly," he retorted curtly. "He did not seem to me to be very dangerous and his papers were quite in order."

To this assertion Chauvelin made no reply. Indeed, how could he explain to this stolid official the subtle workings of an intriguing brain? Had he himself not had many a proof of how little the forging of identity papers or of passports troubled the members of that accursed League? Had he not seen the Scarlet Pimpernel, that exquisite Sir Percy Blakeney, under disguises that were so grimy and so loathsome that they would have repelled the most abject, suborned spy?

Indeed, all that was wanted now was the assurance that Hebert—who himself had a deadly and personal grudge against the Scarlet Pimpernel—would not allow him for one moment out of his sight.

Fortunately as to this, there was no fear. One hint to Hebert and the man was as keen, as determined, as Chauvelin himself.

"Set your mind at rest, citizen," he said with a rough oath. "I guessed how matters stood the moment you gave me the order. I knew you would not take all that trouble for a real Paul Mole. But have no fear! That accursed Englishman has not been one second out of my sight, from the moment I arrested him in the late citizen Marat's lodgings, and by Satan! he shall not be either, until I have seen his impudent head fall under the guillotine."

He himself, he added, had seen to the arrangements for the disposal of the prisoner in the Abbaye: an inner cell, partially partitioned off in one of the guard-rooms, with no egress of its own, and only a tiny grated air-hole high up in the wall, which gave on an outside corridor, and through which not even a cat could manage to slip. Oh! the prisoner was well guarded! The citizen Representative need, of a truth, have no fear! Three or four men—of the best and most trustworthy—had not left the guard-room since the morning. He himself (Hebert) had kept the accursed Englishman in sight all night, had personally conveyed him to the Abbaye, and had only left the guard-room a moment ago in order to speak with the citizen Representative. He was going back now at once, and would not move until the order came for the prisoner to be conveyed to the Court of Justice and thence to summary execution.

For the nonce, Hebert concluded with a complacent chuckle, the Englishman was still crouching dejectedly in a corner of his new cell, with little of him visible save that naked shoulder through his torn shirt, which, in the process of transference from one prison to another, had become a shade more grimy than before.

Chauvelin nodded, well satisfied. He commended Hebert for his zeal, rejoiced with him over the inevitable triumph. It would be well to avenge that awful humiliation at Calais last September. Nevertheless, he felt anxious and nervy; he could not comprehend the apathy assumed by the factitious Mole. That the apathy was assumed Chauvelin was keen enough to guess. What it portended he could not conjecture. But that the Englishman would make a desperate attempt at escape was, of course, a foregone conclusion. It rested with Hebert and a guard that could neither be bribed nor fooled into treachery, to see that such an attempt remained abortive.

What, however, had puzzled citizen Chauvelin all along was the motive which had induced Sir Percy Blakeney to play the role of menial to Jean Paul Marat. Behind it there lay, undoubtedly, one of those subtle intrigues for which that insolent Scarlet Pimpernel was famous; and with it was associated an attempt at theft upon the murdered body of the demagogue ... an attempt which had failed, seeing that the supposititious Paul Mole had been searched and nothing suspicious been found upon his person.

Nevertheless, thoughts of that attempted theft disturbed Chauvelin's equanimity. The old legend of the crumpled roseleaf was applicable in his case. Something of his intense satisfaction would pale if this final enterprise of the audacious adventurer were to be brought to a triumphant close in the end.

VII.

That same forenoon, on his return from the Abbaye and the depot, Chauvelin found that a visitor was waiting for him. A woman, who gave her name as Jeannette Marechal, desired to speak with the citizen Representative. Chauvelin knew the woman as his colleague Marat's maid-of-all-work, and he gave orders that she should be admitted at once.

Jeannette Marechal, tearful and not a little frightened, assured the citizen Representative that her errand was urgent. Her late employer had so few friends; she did not know to whom to turn until she bethought herself of citizen Chauvelin. It took him some little time to disentangle the tangible facts out of the woman's voluble narrative. At first the words: "Child ... Chemin de Pantin ... Leridan," were only a medley of sounds which conveyed no meaning to his ear. But when occasion demanded, citizen Chauvelin was capable of infinite patience. Gradually he understood what the woman was driving at.

"The child, citizen!" she reiterated excitedly. "What's to be done about him? I know that citizen Marat would have wished—"

"Never mind now what citizen Marat would have wished," Chauvelin broke in quietly. "Tell me first who this child is."

"I do not know, citizen," she replied.

"How do you mean, you do not know? Then I pray you, citizeness, what is all this pother about?"

"About the child, citizen," reiterated Jeannette obstinately.

"What child?"

"The child whom citizen Marat adopted last year and kept at that awful house on the Chemin de Pantin."

"I did not know citizen Marat had adopted a child," remarked Chauvelin thoughtfully.

"No one knew," she rejoined. "Not even citizeness Evrard. I was the only one who knew. I had to go and see the child once every month. It was a wretched, miserable brat," the woman went on, her shrivelled old breast vaguely stirred, mayhap, by some atrophied feeling of motherhood. "More than half-starved ... and the look in its eyes, citizen! It was enough to make you cry! I could see by his poor little emaciated body and his nice little hands and feet that he ought never to have been put in that awful house, where—"

She paused, and that quick look of furtive terror, which was so often to be met with in the eyes of the timid these days, crept into her wrinkled face.

"Well, citizeness," Chauvelin rejoined quietly, "why don't you proceed? That awful house, you were saying. Where and what is that awful house of which you speak?"

"The place kept by citizen Leridan, just by Bassin de l'Ourcq," the woman murmured. "You know it, citizen."

Chauvelin nodded. He was beginning to understand.

"Well, now, tell me," he said, with that bland patience which had so oft served him in good stead in his unavowable profession. "Tell me. Last year citizen Marat adopted—we'll say adopted—a child, whom he placed in the Leridans' house on the Pantin road. Is that correct?"

"That is just how it is, citizen. And I—"

"One moment," he broke in somewhat more sternly, as the woman's garrulity was getting on his nerves. "As you say, I know the Leridans' house. I have had cause to send children there myself. Children of aristos or of fat bourgeois, whom it was our duty to turn into good citizens. They are not pampered there, I imagine," he went on drily; "and if citizen Marat sent his—er—adopted son there, it was not with a view to having him brought up as an aristo, what?"

"The child was not to be brought up at all," the woman said gruffly. "I have often heard citizen Marat say that he hoped the brat would prove a thief when he grew up, and would take to alcoholism like a duck takes to water."

"And you know nothing of the child's parents?"

"Nothing, citizen. I had to go to Pantin once a month and have a look at him and report to citizen Marat. But I always had the same tale to tell. The child was looking more and more like a young reprobate every time I saw him."

"Did citizen Marat pay the Leridans for keeping the child?"

"Oh, no, citizen! The Leridans make a trade of the children by sending them out to beg. But this one was not to be allowed out yet. Citizen Marat's orders were very stern, and he was wont to terrify the Leridans with awful threats of the guillotine if they ever allowed the child out of their sight."

Chauvelin sat silent for a while. A ray of light had traversed the dark and tortuous ways of his subtle brain. While he mused the woman became impatient. She continued to talk on with the volubility peculiar to her kind. He paid no heed to her, until one phrase struck his ear.

"So now," Jeannette Marechal was saying, "I don't know what to do. The ring has disappeared, and the Leridans are suspicious."

"The ring?" queried Chauvelin curtly. "What ring?"

"As I was telling you, citizen," she replied querulously, "when I went to see the child, the citizen Marat always gave me this ring to show to the Leridans. Without I brought the ring they would not admit me inside their door. They were so terrified with all the citizen's threats of the guillotine."

"And now you say the ring has disappeared. Since when?"

"Well, citizen," replied Jeannette blandly, "since you took poor Paul Mole into custody."

"What do you mean?" Chauvelin riposted. "What had Paul Mole to do with the child and the ring?"

"Only this, citizen, that he was to have gone to Pantin last night instead of me. And thankful I was not to have to go. Citizen Marat gave the ring to Mole, I suppose. I know he intended to give it to him. He spoke to me about it just before that execrable woman came and murdered him. Anyway, the ring has gone and Mole too. So I imagine that

Mole has the ring and—"

"That's enough!" Chauvelin broke in roughly. "You can go!"

"But, citizen—"

"You can go, I said," he reiterated sharply. "The matter of the child and the Leridans and the ring no longer concerns you. You understand?"

"Y—y—yes, citizen," murmured Jeannette, vaguely terrified.

And of a truth the change in citizen Chauvelin's demeanour was enough to scare any timid creature. Not that he raved or ranted or screamed. Those were not his ways. He still sat beside his desk as he had done before, and his slender hand, so like the talons of a vulture, was clenched upon the arm of his chair. But there was such a look of inward fury and of triumph in his pale, deep-set eyes, such lines of cruelty around his thin, closed lips, that Jeannette Marechal, even with the picture before her mind of Jean Paul Marat in his maddest moods, fled, with the unreasoning terror of her kind, before the sternly controlled, fierce passion of this man.

Chauvelin never noticed that she went. He sat for a long time, silent and immovable. Now he understood. Thank all the Powers of Hate and Revenge, no thought of disappointment was destined to embitter the overflowing cup of his triumph. He had not only brought his arch-enemy to his knees, but had foiled one of his audacious ventures. How clear the whole thing was! The false Paul Mole, the newly acquired menial in the household of Marat, had wormed himself into the confidence of his employer in order to wrest from him the secret of the aristo's child. Bravo! bravo! my gallant Scarlet Pimpernel! Chauvelin now could see it all. Tragedies such as that which had placed an aristo's child in the power of a cunning demon like Marat were not rare these days, and Chauvelin had been fitted by nature and by temperament to understand and appreciate an execrable monster of the type of Jean Paul Marat.

And Paul Mole, the grimy, degraded servant of the indigent demagogue, the loathsome mask which hid the fastidious personality of Sir Percy Blakeney, had made a final and desperate effort to possess himself of the ring which would deliver the child into his power. Now, having failed in his machinations, he was safe under lock and key —guarded on sight. The next twenty-four hours would see him unmasked, awaiting his trial and condemnation under the scathing indictment prepared by Fouquier-Tinville, the unerring Public Prosecutor. The day after that, the tumbril and the guillotine for that execrable English spy, and the boundless sense of satisfaction that his last intrigue had aborted in such a signal and miserable manner.

Of a truth Chauvelin at this hour had every cause to be thankful, and it was with a light heart that he set out to interview the Leridans.

VIII.

The Leridans, anxious, obsequious, terrified, were only too ready to obey the citizen Representative in all things.

They explained with much complacency that, even though they were personally acquainted with Jeannette Marechal, when the citizeness presented herself this very morning without the ring they had refused her permission to see the brat.

Chauvelin, who in his own mind had already reconstructed the whole tragedy of the stolen child, was satisfied that Marat could not have chosen more efficient tools for the execution of his satanic revenge than these two hideous products of revolutionary Paris.

Grasping, cowardly, and avaricious, the Leridans would lend themselves to any abomination for a sufficiency of money; but no money on earth would induce them to risk their own necks in the process. Marat had obviously held them by threats of the guillotine. They knew the power of the "Friend of the People," and feared him accordingly. Chauvelin's scarf of office, his curt, authoritative manner, had an equally awe-inspiring effect upon the two miserable creatures. They became absolutely abject, cringing, maudlin in their protestations of good-will and loyalty. No one, they vowed, should as much as see the child—ring or no ring—save the citizen Representative himself. Chauvelin, however, had no wish to see the child. He was satisfied that its name was Lannoy—for the child had remembered it when first he had been brought to the Leridans. Since then he had apparently forgotten it, even though he often cried after his "Maman!"

Chauvelin listened to all these explanations with some impatience. The child was nothing to him, but the Scarlet Pimpernel had desired to rescue it from out of the clutches of the Leridans; had risked his all—and lost it—in order to effect that rescue! That in itself was a sufficient inducement for Chauvelin to interest himself in the execution of Marat's vengeance, whatever its original mainspring may have been.

At any rate, now he felt satisfied that the child was safe, and that the Leridans were impervious to threats or bribes which might land them on the guillotine.

All that they would own to was to being afraid.

"Afraid of what?" queried Chauvelin sharply.

That the brat may be kidnapped ... stolen. Oh! he could not be decoyed ... they were too watchful for that! But apparently there were mysterious agencies at work....

"Mysterious agencies!" Chauvelin laughed aloud at the suggestion. The "mysterious agency" was even now rotting in an obscure cell at the Abbaye. What other powers could be at work on behalf of the brat?

Well, the Leridans had had a warning!

What warning?

"A letter," the man said gruffly. "But as neither my wife nor I can read—"

"Why did you not speak of this before?" broke in Chauvelin roughly. "Let me see the letter."

The woman produced a soiled and dank scrap of paper from beneath her apron. Of a truth she could not read its contents, for they were writ in English in the form of a doggerel rhyme which caused Chauvelin to utter a savage oath.

"When did this come?" he asked. "And how?"

"This morning, citizen," the woman mumbled in reply. "I found it outside the door, with a stone on it to prevent the wind from blowing it away. What does it mean, citizen?" she went on, her voice shaking with terror, for of a truth the citizen Representative looked as if he had seen some weird and unearthly apparition.

He gave no reply for a moment or two, and the two catiffs had no conception of the tremendous effort at self-control which was hidden behind the pale, rigid mask of the redoubtable man.

"It probably means nothing that you need fear," Chauvelin said quietly at last. "But I will see the Commissary of the Section myself, and tell him to send a dozen men of the

Sureté along to watch your house and be at your beck and call if need be. Then you will feel quite safe, I hope."

"Oh, yes! quite safe, citizen!" the woman replied with a sigh of genuine relief. Then only did Chauvelin turn on his heel and go his way.

IX.

But that crumpled and soiled scrap of paper given to him by the woman Leridan still lay in his clenched hand as he strode back rapidly citywards. It seemed to scorch his palm. Even before he had glanced at the contents he knew what they were. That atrocious English doggerel, the signature—a five-petalled flower traced in crimson! How well he knew them!

"We seek him here, we seek him there!"

The most humiliating moments in Chauvelin's career were associated with that silly rhyme, and now here it was, mocking him even when he knew that his bitter enemy lay fettered and helpless, caught in a trap, out of which there was no escape possible; even though he knew for a positive certainty that the mocking voice which had spoken those rhymes on that far-off day last September would soon be stilled for ever.

No doubt one of that army of abominable English spies had placed this warning outside the Leridans' door. No doubt they had done that with a view to throwing dust in the eyes of the Public Prosecutor and causing a confusion in his mind with regard to the identity of the prisoner at the Abbaye, all to the advantage of their chief.

The thought that such a confusion might exist, that Fouquier-Tinville might be deluded into doubting the real personality of Paul Mole, brought an icy sweat all down Chauvelin's spine. He hurried along the interminably long Chemin de Pantin, only paused at the Barriere du Combat in order to interview the Commissary of the Section on the matter of sending men to watch over the Leridans' house. Then, when he felt satisfied that this would be effectively and quickly done, an unconquerable feeling of restlessness prompted him to hurry round to the lodgings of the Public Prosecutor in the Rue Blanche—just to see him, to speak with him, to make quite sure.

Oh! he must be sure that no doubts, no pusillanimity on the part of any official would be allowed to stand in the way of the consummation of all his most cherished dreams. Papers or no papers, testimony or no testimony, the incarcerated Paul Mole was the Scarlet Pimpernel—of this Chauvelin was as certain as that he was alive. His every sense had testified to it when he stood in the narrow room of the Rue des Cordeliers, face to face—eyes gazing into eyes—with his sworn enemy.

Unluckily, however, he found the Public Prosecutor in a surly and obstinate mood, following on an interview which he had just had with citizen Commissary Cuisinier on the matter of the prisoner Paul Mole.

"His papers are all in order, I tell you," he said impatiently, in answer to Chauvelin's insistence. "It is as much as my head is worth to demand a summary execution."

"But I tell you that, those papers of his are forged," urged Chauvelin forcefully.

"They are not," retorted the other. "The Commissary swears to his own signature on the identity book. The concierge at the Abbaye swears that he knows Mole, so do all the men of the Sureté who have seen him. The Commissary has known him as an indigent, good-for-nothing lubbard who has begged his way in the streets of Paris ever since he was released from gaol some months ago, after he had served a term for larceny. Even your own man Hebert admits to feeling doubtful on the point. You have had the nightmare, citizen," concluded Fouquier-Tinville with a harsh laugh.

"But, name of a dog!" broke in Chauvelin savagely. "You are not proposing to let the man go?"

"What else can I do?" the other rejoined fretfully. "We shall get into terrible trouble if we interfere with a man like Paul Mole. You know yourself how it is these days. We should have the whole of the rabble of Paris clamouring for our blood. If, after we have guillotined him, he is proved to be a good patriot, it will be my turn next. No! I thank you!"

"I tell you, man," retorted Chauvelin desperately, "that the man is not Paul Mole—that he is the English spy whom we all know as the Scarlet Pimpernel."

"EH BIEN!" riposted Fouquier-Tinville. "Bring me more tangible proof that our prisoner is not Paul Mole and I'll deal with him quickly enough, never fear. But if by to-morrow morning you do not satisfy me on the point ... I must let him go his way."

A savage oath rose to Chauvelin's lips. He felt like a man who has been running, panting to reach a goal, who sees that goal within easy distance of him, and is then suddenly captured, caught in invisible meshes which hold him tightly, and against which he is powerless to struggle. For the moment he hated Fouquier-Tinville with a deadly hatred, would have tortured and threatened him until he wrung a consent, an admission, out of him.

Name of a name! when that damnable English spy was actually in his power, the man was a pusillanimous fool to allow the rich prize to slip from his grasp! Chauvelin felt as if he were choking; his slender fingers worked nervily around his cravat; beads of perspiration trickled unheeded down his pallid forehead.

Then suddenly he had an inspiration—nothing less! It almost seemed as if Satan, his friend, had whispered insinuating words into his ear. That scrap of paper! He had thrust it awhile ago into the breast pocket of his coat. It was still there, and the Public Prosecutor wanted a tangible proof.... Then, why not....?

Slowly, his thoughts still in the process of gradual coordination, Chauvelin drew that soiled scrap of paper out of his pocket. Fouquier-Tinville, surly and ill-humoured, had his back half-turned towards him, was moodily picking at his teeth. Chauvelin had all the leisure which he required. He smoothed out the creases in the paper and spread it out carefully upon the desk close to the other man's elbow. Fouquier-Tinville looked down on it, over his shoulder.

"What is that?" he queried.

"As you see, citizen," was Chauvelin's bland reply. "A message, such as you yourself have oft received, methinks, from our mutual enemy, the Scarlet Pimpernel."

But already the Public Prosecutor had seized upon the paper, and of a truth Chauvelin had no longer cause to complain of his colleague's indifference. That doggerel rhyme, no less than the signature, had the power to rouse Fouquier-Tinville's ire, as it had that of disturbing Chauvelin's well-studied calm.

"What is it?" reiterated the Public Prosecutor, white now to the lips.

"I have told you, citizen," rejoined Chauvelin imperturbably. "A message from that

English spy. It is also the proof which you have demanded of me—the tangible proof that the prisoner, Paul Mole, is none other than the Scarlet Pimpernel."

"But," ejaculated the other hoarsely, "where did you get this?"

"It was found in the cell which Paul Mole occupied in the depot of the Rue de Tourraine, where he was first incarcerated. I picked it up there after he was removed ... the ink was scarcely dry upon it."

The lie came quite glibly to Chauvelin's tongue. Was not every method good, every device allowable, which would lead to so glorious an end?

"Why did you not tell me of this before?" queried Fouquier-Tinville, with a sudden gleam of suspicion in his deep-set eyes.

"You had not asked me for a tangible proof before," replied Chauvelin blandly. "I myself was so firmly convinced of what I averred that I had well-nigh forgotten the existence of this damning scrap of paper."

Damning indeed! Fouquier-Tinville had seen such scraps of paper before. He had learnt the doggerel rhyme by heart, even though the English tongue was quite unfamiliar to him. He loathed the English—the entire nation—with all that deadly hatred which a divergence of political aims will arouse in times of acute crises. He hated the English government, Pitt and Burke and even Fox, the happy-go-lucky apologist of the young Revolution. But, above all, he hated that League of English spies—as he was pleased to call them—whose courage, resourcefulness, as well as reckless daring, had more than once baffled his own hideous schemes of murder, of pillage, and of rape.

Thank Beelzebub and his horde of evil spirits, citizen Chauvelin had been clear-sighted enough to detect that elusive Pimpernel under the disguise of Paul Mole.

"You have deserved well of your country," said Tinville with lusty fervour, and gave Chauvelin a vigorous slap on the shoulder. "But for you I should have allowed that abominable spy to slip through our fingers."

"I have succeeded in convincing you, citizen?" Chauvelin retorted dryly.

"Absolutely!" rejoined the other. "You may now leave the matter to me. And 'twill be friend Mole who will be surprised to-morrow," he added with a harsh guffaw, "when he finds himself face to face with me, before a Court of Justice."

He was all eagerness, of course. Such a triumph for him! The indictment of the notorious Scarlet Pimpernel on a charge of espionage would be the crowning glory of his career! Let other men look to their laurels! Those who brought that dangerous enemy of revolution to the guillotine would for ever be proclaimed as the saviours of France.

"A short indictment," he said, when Chauvelin, after a lengthy discussion on various points, finally rose to take his leave, "but a scathing one! I tell you, citizen Chauvelin, that to-morrow you will be the first to congratulate me on an unprecedented triumph."

He had been arguing in favour of a sensational trial and no less sensational execution. Chauvelin, with his memory harking back on many mysterious abductions at the very foot of the guillotine, would have liked to see his elusive enemy quietly put to death amongst a batch of traitors, who would help to mask his personality until after the guillotine had fallen, when the whole of Paris should ring with the triumph of this final punishment of the hated spy.

In the end, the two friends agreed upon a compromise, and parted well pleased with the turn of events which a kind Fate had ordered for their own special benefit.

X.

Thus satisfied, Chauvelin returned to the Abbaye. Hebert was safe and trustworthy, but Hebert, too, had been assailed with the same doubts which had well-nigh wrecked Chauvelin's triumph, and with such doubts in his mind he might slacken his vigilance.

Name of a name! every man in charge of that damnable Scarlet Pimpernel should have three pairs of eyes wherewith to watch his movements. He should have the alert brain of a Robespierre, the physical strength of a Danton, the relentlessness of a Marat. He should be a giant in sheer brute force, a tiger in caution, an elephant in weight, and a mouse in stealthiness!

Name of a name! but 'twas only hate that could give such powers to any man!

Hebert, in the guard-room, owned to his doubts. His comrades, too, admitted that after twenty-four hours spent on the watch, their minds were in a whirl. The Citizen Commissary had been so sure—so was the chief concierge of the Abbaye even now; and the men of the Surete!... they themselves had seen the real Mole more than once ... and this man in the cell.... Well, would the citizen Representative have a final good look at him?

"You seem to forget Calais, citizen Hebert," Chauvelin said sharply, "and the deadly humiliation you suffered then at the hands of this man who is now your prisoner. Surely your eyes should have been, at least, as keen as mine own."

Anxious, irritable, his nerves well-nigh on the rack, he nevertheless crossed the guard-room with a firm step and entered the cell where the prisoner was still lying upon the palliasse, as he had been all along, and still presenting that naked piece of shoulder through the hole in his shirt.

"He has been like this the best part of the day," Hebert said with a shrug of the shoulders. "We put his bread and water right under his nose. He ate and he drank, and I suppose he slept. But except for a good deal of swearing, he has not spoken to any of us."

He had followed his chief into the cell, and now stood beside the palliasse, holding a small dark lantern in his hand. At a sign from Chauvelin he flashed the light upon the prisoner's averted head.

Mole cursed for awhile, and muttered something about "good patriots" and about "retribution." Then, worried by the light, he turned slowly round, and with fish-like, bleary eyes looked upon his visitor.

The words of stinging irony and triumphant sarcasm, all fully prepared, froze on Chauvelin's lips. He gazed upon the prisoner, and a weird sense of something unfathomable and mysterious came over him as he gazed. He himself could not have defined that feeling: the very next moment he was prepared to ridicule his own cowardice—yes, cowardice! because for a second or two he had felt positively afraid.

Afraid of what, forsooth? The man who crouched here in the cell was his arch-enemy, the Scarlet Pimpernel—the man whom he hated most bitterly in all the world, the man whose death he desired more than that of any other living creature. He had been apprehended by the very side of the murdered man whose confidence he had all but gained. He himself (Chauvelin) had at that fateful moment looked into the factitious Mole's eyes, had seen the mockery in them, the lazy insouciance which was the chief attribute of

Sir Percy Blakeney. He had heard a faint echo of that inane laugh which grated upon his nerves. Hebert had then laid hands upon this very same man; agents of the Surete had barred every ingress and egress to the house, had conducted their prisoner straightway to the depot and thence to the Abbaye, had since that moment guarded him on sight, by day and by night. Hebert and the other men as well as the chief warder, all swore to that!

No, no! There could be no doubt! There was no doubt! The days of magic were over! A man could not assume a personality other than his own; he could not fly out of that personality like a bird out of its cage. There on the palliasse in the miserable cell were the same long limbs, the broad shoulders, the grimy face with the three days' growth of stubbly beard—the whole wretched personality of Paul Mole, in fact, which hid the exquisite one of Sir Percy Blakeney, Bart. And yet!...

A cold sweat ran down Chauvelin's spine as he gazed, mute and immovable, into those fish-like, bleary eyes, which were not—no! they were not those of the real Scarlet Pimpernel.

The whole situation became dreamlike, almost absurd. Chauvelin was not the man for such a mock-heroic, melodramatic situation. Commonsense, reason, his own cool powers of deliberation, would soon reassert themselves. But for the moment he was dazed. He had worked too hard, no doubt; had yielded too much to excitement, to triumph, and to hate. He turned to Hebert, who was standing stolidly by, gave him a few curt orders in a clear and well-pitched voice. Then he walked out of the cell, without bestowing another look on the prisoner.

Mole had once more turned over on his palliasse and, apparently, had gone to sleep. Hebert, with a strange and puzzled laugh, followed his chief out of the cell.

XI.

At first Chauvelin had the wish to go back and see the Public Prosecutor—to speak with him—to tell him—what? Yes, what? That he, Chauvelin, had all of a sudden been assailed with the same doubts which already had worried Hebert and the others?—that he had told a deliberate lie when he stated that the incriminating doggerel rhyme had been found in Mole's cell? No, no! Such an admission would not only be foolish, it would be dangerous now, whilst he himself was scarce prepared to trust to his own senses. After all, Fouquier-Tinville was in the right frame of mind for the moment. Paul Mole, whoever he was, was safely under lock and key.

The only danger lay in the direction of the house on the Chemin de Pantin. At the thought Chauvelin felt giddy and faint. But he would allow himself no rest. Indeed, he could not have rested until something approaching certainty had once more taken possession of his soul. He could not—would not—believe that he had been deceived. He was still prepared to stake his very life on the identity of the prisoner at the Abbaye. Tricks of light, the flash of the lantern, the perfection of the disguise, had caused a momentary illusion—nothing more.

Nevertheless, that awful feeling of restlessness which had possessed him during the last twenty-four hours once more drove him to activity. And although commonsense and reason both pulled one way, an eerie sense of superstition whispered in his ear the ominous words, "If, after all!"

At any rate, he would see the Leridans, and once more make sure of them; and, late as was the hour, he set out for the lonely house on the Pantin Road.

Just inside the Barriere du Combat was the Poste de Section, where Commissary Burban was under orders to provide a dozen men of the Surete, who were to be on the watch round and about the house of the Leridans. Chauvelin called in on the Commissary, who assured him that the men were at their post.

Thus satisfied, he crossed the Barriere and started at a brisk walk down the long stretch of the Chemin de Pantin. The night was dark. The rolling clouds overhead hid the face of the moon and presaged the storm. On the right, the irregular heights of the Buttes Chaumont loomed out dense and dark against the heavy sky, whilst to the left, on ahead, a faintly glimmering, greyish streak of reflected light revealed the proximity of the canal.

Close to the spot where the main Route de Meux intersects the Chemin de Pantin, Chauvelin slackened his pace. The house of the Leridans now lay immediately on his left; from it a small, feeble ray of light, finding its way no doubt through an ill-closed shutter, pierced the surrounding gloom. Chauvelin, without hesitation, turned up a narrow track which led up to the house across a field of stubble. The next moment a peremptory challenge brought him to a halt.

"Who goes there?"

"Public Safety," replied Chauvelin. "Who are you?"

"Of the Surete," was the counter reply. "There are a dozen of us about here."

"When did you arrive?"

"Some two hours ago. We marched out directly after you left the orders at the Commissariat."

"You are prepared to remain on the watch all night?"

"Those are our orders, citizen," replied the man.

"You had best close up round the house, then. And, name of a dog!" he added, with a threatening ring in his voice. "Let there be no slackening of vigilance this night. No one to go in or out of that house, no one to approach it under any circumstances whatever. Is that understood?"

"Those were our orders from the first, citizen," said the man simply.

"And all has been well up to now?"

"We have seen no one, citizen."

The little party closed in around their chief and together they marched up to the house. Chauvelin, on tenterhooks, walked quicker than the others. He was the first to reach the door. Unable to find the bell-pull in the dark, he knocked vigorously.

The house appeared silent and wrapped in sleep. No light showed from within save that one tiny speck through the cracks of an ill-fitting shutter, in a room immediately overhead.

In response to Chauvelin's repeated summons, there came anon the sound of someone moving in one of the upstairs rooms, and presently the light overhead disappeared, whilst a door above was heard to open and to close and shuffling footsteps to come slowly down the creaking stairs.

A moment or two later the bolts and bars of the front door were unfastened, a key grated in the rusty lock, a chain rattled in its socket, and then the door was opened slowly and cautiously.

The woman Leridan appeared in the doorway. She held a guttering tallow candle high above her head. Its flickering light illumined Chauvelin's slender figure.

"Ah! the citizen Representative!" the woman ejaculated, as soon as she recognised him. "We did not expect you again to-day, and at this late hour, too. I'll tell my man—"

"Never mind your man," broke in Chauvelin impatiently, and pushed without ceremony past the woman inside the house. "The child? Is it safe?"

He could scarcely control his excitement. There was a buzzing, as of an angry sea, in his ears. The next second, until the woman spoke, seemed like a cycle of years.

"Quite safe, citizen," she said placidly. "Everything is quite safe. We were so thankful for those men of the Sureté. We had been afraid before, as I told the citizen Representative, and my man and I could not rest for anxiety. It was only after they came that we dared go to bed."

A deep sigh of intense relief came from the depths of Chauvelin's heart. He had not realised himself until this moment how desperately anxious he had been. The woman's reassuring words appeared to lift a crushing weight from his mind. He turned to the man behind him.

"You did not tell me," he said, "that some of you had been here already."

"We have not been here before," the sergeant in charge of the little platoon said in reply. "I do not know what the woman means."

"Some of your men came about three hours ago," the woman retorted; "less than an hour after the citizen Representative was here. I remember that my man and I marvelled how quickly they did come, but they said that they had been on duty at the Barriere du Combat when the citizen arrived, and that he had dispatched them off at once. They said they had run all the way. But even so, we thought it was quick work—"

The words were smothered in her throat in a cry of pain, for, with an almost brutal gesture, Chauvelin had seized her by the shoulders.

"Where are those men?" he queried hoarsely. "Answer!"

"In there, and in there," the woman stammered, well-nigh faint with terror as she pointed to two doors, one on each side of the passage. "Three in each room. They are asleep now, I should say, as they seem so quiet. But they were an immense comfort to us, citizen ... we were so thankful to have them in the house...."

But Chauvelin had snatched the candle from her hand. Holding it high above his head, he strode to the door on the right of the passage. It was ajar. He pushed it open with a vicious kick. The room beyond was in total darkness.

"Is anyone here?" he queried sharply.

Nothing but silence answered him. For a moment he remained there on the threshold, silent and immovable as a figure carved in stone. He had just a sufficiency of presence of mind and of will power not to drop the candle, to stand there motionless, with his back turned to the woman and to the men who had crowded in, in his wake. He would not let them see the despair, the rage and grave superstitious fear, which distorted every line of his pallid face.

He did not ask about the child. He would not trust himself to speak, for he had realised already how completely he had been baffled. Those abominable English spies had watched their opportunity, had worked on the credulity and the fears of the Leridans and, playing the game at which they and their audacious chief were such unconquerable experts, they had made their way into the house under a clever ruse.

The men of the Sureté, not quite understanding the situation, were questioning the Leridans. The man, too, corroborated his wife's story. Their anxiety had been worked upon at the moment that it was most acute. After the citizen Representative left them, earlier in the evening, they had received another mysterious message which they had been unable to read, but which had greatly increased their alarm. Then, when the men of the Sureté came.... Ah! they had no cause to doubt that they were men of the Sureté!... their clothes, their speech, their appearance ... figure to yourself, even their uniforms! They spoke so nicely, so reassuringly. The Leridans were so thankful to see them! Then they made themselves happy in the two rooms below, and for additional safety the Lannoy child was brought down from its attic and put to sleep in the one room with the men of the Sureté.

After that the Leridans went to bed. Name of a dog! how were they to blame? Those men and the child had disappeared, but they (the Leridans) would go to the guillotine swearing that they were not to blame.

Whether Chauvelin heard all these jeremiads, he could not afterwards have told you. But he did not need to be told how it had all been done. It had all been so simple, so ingenious, so like the methods usually adopted by that astute Scarlet Pimpernel! He saw it all so clearly before him. Nobody was to blame really, save he himself—he, who alone knew and understood the adversary with whom he had to deal.

But these people here should not have the gratuitous spectacle of a man enduring the torments of disappointment and of baffled revenge. Whatever Chauvelin was suffering now would for ever remain the secret of his own soul. Anon, when the Leridans' rasping voices died away in one of the more distant portions of the house and the men of the Sureté were busy accepting refreshment and gratuity from the two terrified wretches, he had put down the candle with a steady hand and then walked with a firm step out of the house.

Soon the slender figure was swallowed up in the gloom as he strode back rapidly towards the city.

XII.

Citizen Fouquier-Tinville had returned home from the Palais at a very late hour that same evening. His household in his simple lodgings in the Place Dauphine was already abed: his wife and the twins were asleep. He himself had sat down for a moment in the living-room, in dressing-gown and slippers, and with the late edition of the Moniteur in his hand, too tired to read.

It was half-past ten when there came a ring at the front door bell. Fouquier-Tinville, half expecting citizen Chauvelin to pay him a final visit, shuffled to the door and opened it.

A visitor, tall, well-dressed, exceedingly polite and urbane, requested a few minutes' conversation with citizen Fouquier-Tinville.

Before the Public Prosecutor had made up his mind whether to introduce such a late-comer into his rooms, the latter had pushed his way through the door into the ante-chamber, and with a movement as swift as it was unexpected, had thrown a scarf round Fouquier-Tinville's neck and wound it round his mouth, so that the unfortunate man's call for help was smothered in his throat.

So dexterously and so rapidly indeed had the miscreant acted, that his victim had hardly realised the assault before he found himself securely gagged and bound to a chair in his own ante-room, whilst that dare-devil stood before him, perfectly at his ease, his hands buried in the capacious pockets of his huge caped coat, and murmuring a few casual words of apology.

"I entreat you to forgive, citizen," he was saying in an even and pleasant voice, "this necessary violence on my part towards you. But my errand is urgent, and I could not allow your neighbours or your household to disturb the few minutes' conversation which I am obliged to have with you. My friend Paul Mole," he went on, after a slight pause, "is in grave danger of his life owing to a hallucination on the part of our mutual friend citizen Chauvelin; and I feel confident that you yourself are too deeply enamoured of your own neck to risk it willfully by sending an innocent and honest patriot to the guillotine."

Once more he paused and looked down upon his unwilling interlocutor, who, with muscles straining against the cords that held him, and with eyes nearly starting out of their sockets in an access of fear and of rage, was indeed presenting a pitiful spectacle.

"I dare say that by now, citizen," the brigand continued imperturbably, "you will have guessed who I am. You and I have oft crossed invisible swords before; but this, methinks, is the first time that we have met face to face. I pray you, tell my dear friend M. Chauvelin that you have seen me. Also that there were two facts which he left entirely out of his calculations, perfect though these were. The one fact was that there were two Paul Moles—one real and one factitious. Tell him that, I pray you. It was the factitious Paul Mole who stole the ring and who stood for one moment gazing into clever citizen Chauvelin's eyes. But that same factitious Paul Mole had disappeared in the crowd even before your colleague had recovered his presence of mind. Tell him, I pray you, that the elusive Pimpernel whom he knows so well never assumes a fanciful disguise. He discovered the real Paul Mole first, studied him, learned his personality, until his own became a perfect replica of the miserable caitiff. It was the false Paul Mole who induced Jeannette Marechal to introduce him originally into the household of citizen Marat. It was he who gained the confidence of his employer; he, for a consideration, borrowed the identity papers of his real prototype. He again who for a few francs induced the real Paul Mole to follow him into the house of the murdered demagogue and to mingle there with the throng. He who thrust the identity papers back into the hands of their rightful owner whilst he himself was swallowed up by the crowd. But it was the real Paul Mole who was finally arrested and who is now lingering in the Abbaye prison, whence you, citizen Fouquier-Tinville, must free him on the instant, on pain of suffering yourself for the nightmares of your friend."

"The second fact," he went on with the same good-humoured pleasantry, "which our friend citizen Chauvelin had forgotten was that, though I happen to have aroused his unconquerable ire, I am but one man amongst a league of gallant English gentlemen. Their chief, I am proud to say; but without them, I should be powerless. Without one of them near me, by the side of the murdered Marat, I could not have rid myself of the ring in time, before other rough hands searched me to my skin. Without them, I could not have taken Madeleine Lannoy's child from out that terrible hell, to which a miscreant's lustful revenge had condemned the poor innocent. But while citizen Chauvelin, racked with triumph as well as with anxiety, was rushing from the Leridans' house to yours, and thence to the Abbaye prison, to gloat over his captive enemy, the League of the Scarlet Pimpernel carefully laid and carried out its plans at leisure. Disguised as men of the Sureté, we took advantage of the Leridans' terror to obtain access into the house. Frightened to death by our warnings, as well as by citizen Chauvelin's threats, they not only admitted us into their house, but actually placed Madeleine Lannoy's child in our charge. Then they went contentedly to bed, and we, before the real men of the Sureté arrived upon the scene, were already safely out of the way. My gallant English friends are some way out of Paris by now, escorting Madeleine Lannoy and her child into safety. They will return to Paris, citizen," continued the audacious adventurer, with a laugh full of joy and of unconquerable vitality, "and be my henchmen as before in many an adventure which will cause you and citizen Chauvelin to gnash your teeth with rage. But I myself will remain in Paris," he concluded lightly. "Yes, in Paris; under your very nose, and entirely at your service!"

The next second he was gone, and Fouquier-Tinville was left to marvel if the whole apparition had not been a hideous dream. Only there was no doubt that he was gagged and tied to a chair with cords: and here his wife found him, an hour later, when she woke from her first sleep, anxious because he had not yet come to bed.

CHAPTER II. A QUESTION OF PASSPORTS

Bibot was very sure of himself. There never was, never had been, there never would be again another such patriotic citizen of the Republic as was citizen Bibot of the Town Guard.

And because his patriotism was so well known among the members of the Committee of Public Safety, and his uncompromising hatred of the aristocrats so highly appreciated, citizen Bibot had been given the most important military post within the city of Paris.

He was in command of the Porte Montmartre, which goes to prove how highly he was esteemed, for, believe me, more treachery had been going on inside and out of the Porte Montmartre than in any other quarter of Paris. The last commandant there, citizen Ferney, was guillotined for having allowed a whole batch of aristocrats—traitors to the Republic, all of them—to slip through the Porte Montmartre and to find safety outside the walls of Paris. Ferney pleaded in his defense that these traitors had been spirited away from under his very nose by the devil's agency, for surely that meddlesome Englishman who spent his time in rescuing aristocrats—traitors, all of them—from the clutches of Madame la Guillotine must be either the devil himself, or at any rate one of his most powerful agents.

"Nom de Dieu! just think of his name! The Scarlet Pimpernel they call him! No one knows him by any other name! and he is preternaturally tall and strong and superhumanly cunning! And the power which he has of being transmuted into various personalities—rendering himself quite unrecognizable to the eyes of the most sharp-seeing patriot of France, must of a surety be a gift of Satan!"

But the Committee of Public Safety refused to listen to Ferney's explanations. The Scarlet Pimpernel was only an ordinary mortal—an exceedingly cunning and meddlesome personage it is true, and endowed with a superfluity of wealth which enabled him to break the thin crust of patriotism that overlay the natural cupidity of many Captains of the Town Guard—but still an ordinary man for all that! and no true lover of the Republic should allow either superstitious terror or greed to interfere with the discharge of his duties which at the Porte Montmartre consisted in detaining any and every person—aristocrat, foreigner, or otherwise traitor to the Republic—who could not give a satisfactory reason for desiring to leave Paris. Having detained such persons, the patriot's next duty was to hand them over to the Committee of Public Safety, who would then decide whether Madame la Guillotine would have the last word over them or not.

And the guillotine did nearly always have the last word to say, unless the Scarlet Pimpernel interfered.

The trouble was, that that same accursed Englishman interfered at times in a manner which was positively terrifying. His impudence, certes, passed all belief. Stories of his daring and of his impudence were abroad which literally made the lank and greasy hair of every patriot curl with wonder. 'Twas even whispered—not too loudly, forsooth—that certain members of the Committee of Public Safety had measured their skill and valour against that of the Englishman and emerged from the conflict beaten and humiliated, vowing vengeance which, of a truth, was still slow in coming.

Citizen Chauvelin, one of the most implacable and unyielding members of the Committee, was known to have suffered overwhelming shame at the hands of that daring gang, of whom the so-called Scarlet Pimpernel was the accredited chief. Some there were who said that citizen Chauvelin had for ever forfeited his prestige, and even endangered his head by measuring his well-known astuteness against that mysterious League of spies.

But then Bibot was different!

He feared neither the devil, nor any Englishman. Had the latter the strength of giants and the protection of every power of evil, Bibot was ready for him. Nay! he was aching for a tussle, and haunted the purlieus of the Committees to obtain some post which would enable him to come to grips with the Scarlet Pimpernel and his League.

Bibot's zeal and perseverance were duly rewarded, and anon he was appointed to the command of the guard at the Porte Montmartre.

A post of vast importance as aforesaid; so much so, in fact, that no less a person than citizen Jean Paul Marat himself came to speak with Bibot on that third day of Nivose in the year I of the Republic, with a view to impressing upon him the necessity of keeping his eyes open, and of suspecting every man, woman, and child indiscriminately until they had proved themselves to be true patriots.

"Let no one slip through your fingers, citizen Bibot," Marat admonished with grim earnestness. "That accursed Englishman is cunning and resourceful, and his impudence surpasses that of the devil himself."

"He'd better try some of his impudence on me!" commented Bibot with a sneer, "he'll soon find out that he no longer has a Ferney to deal with. Take it from me, citizen Marat, that if a batch of aristocrats escape out of Paris within the next few days, under the guidance of the d—d Englishman, they will have to find some other way than the Porte Montmartre."

"Well said, citizen!" commented Marat. "But be watchful to-night ... to-night especially. The Scarlet Pimpernel is rampant in Paris just now."

"How so?"

"The ci-devant Duc and Duchesse de Montreux and the whole of their brood—sisters, brothers, two or three children, a priest, and several servants—a round dozen in all, have been condemned to death. The guillotine for them to-morrow at daybreak! Would it could have been to-night," added Marat, whilst a demoniacal leer contorted his face which already exuded lust for blood from every pore. "Would it could have been to-night. But the guillotine has been busy; over four hundred executions to-day ... and the tumbrils are full—the seats bespoken in advance—and still they come.... But to-morrow morning at daybreak Madame la Guillotine will have a word to say to the whole of the Montreux crowd!"

"But they are in the Conciergerie prison surely, citizen! out of the reach of that accursed Englishman?"

"They are on their way, and I mistake not, to the prison at this moment. I came straight on here after the condemnation, to which I listened with true joy. Ah, citizen Bibot! the blood of these hated aristocrats is good to behold when it drips from the blade of the guillotine. Have a care, citizen Bibot, do not let the Montreux crowd escape!"

"Have no fear, citizen Marat! But surely there is no danger! They have been tried and condemned! They are, as you say, even now on their way—well guarded, I presume—to the Conciergerie prison!—to-morrow at daybreak, the guillotine! What is there to fear?"

"Well! well!" said Marat, with a slight tone of hesitation, "it is best, citizen Bibot, to be over-careful these times."

Even whilst Marat spoke his face, usually so cunning and so vengeful, had suddenly lost its look of devilish cruelty which was almost superhuman in the excess of its infamy, and a greyish hue—suggestive of terror—had spread over the sunken cheeks. He clutched Bibot's arm, and leaning over the table he whispered in his ear:

"The Public Prosecutor had scarce finished his speech to-day, judgment was being pronounced, the spectators were expectant and still, only the Montreux woman and some of the females and children were blubbering and moaning, when suddenly, it seemed from nowhere, a small piece of paper fluttered from out the assembly and alighted on the desk in front of the Public Prosecutor. He took the paper up and glanced at its contents. I saw that his cheeks had paled, and that his hand trembled as he handed the paper over to me."

"And what did that paper contain, citizen Marat?" asked Bibot, also speaking in a whisper, for an access of superstitious terror was gripping him by the throat.

"Just the well-known accursed device, citizen, the small scarlet flower, drawn in red ink, and the few words: 'To-night the innocent men and women now condemned by this infamous tribunal will be beyond your reach!'"

"And no sign of a messenger?"

"None."

"And when did——"

"Hush!" said Marat peremptorily, "no more of that now. To your post, citizen, and remember—all are suspect! let none escape!"

The two men had been sitting outside a small tavern, opposite the Porte Montmartre, with a bottle of wine between them, their elbows resting on the grimy top of a rough wooden table. They had talked in whispers, for even the walls of the tumble-down cabaret might have had ears.

Opposite them the city wall—broken here by the great gate of Montmartre—loomed threateningly in the fast-gathering dusk of this winter's afternoon. Men in ragged red shirts, their unkempt heads crowned with Phrygian caps adorned with a tricolour cockade, lounged against the wall, or sat in groups on the top of piles of refuse that littered the street, with a rough deal plank between them and a greasy pack of cards in their grimy fingers. Guns and bayonets were propped against the wall. The gate itself had three means of egress; each of these was guarded by two men with fixed bayonets at their shoulders, but otherwise dressed like the others, in rags—with bare legs that looked blue and numb in the cold—the sans-culottes of revolutionary Paris.

Bibot rose from his seat, nodding to Marat, and joined his men.

From afar, but gradually drawing nearer, came the sound of a ribald song, with chorus accompaniment sung by throats obviously surfeited with liquor.

For a moment—as the sound approached—Bibot turned back once more to the Friend of the People.

"Am I to understand, citizen," he said, "that my orders are not to let anyone pass through these gates to-night?"

"No, no, citizen," replied Marat, "we dare not do that. There are a number of good patriots in the city still. We cannot interfere with their liberty or—"

And the look of fear of the demagogue—himself afraid of the human whirlpool which he has let loose—stole into Marat's cruel, piercing eyes.

"No, no," he reiterated more emphatically, "we cannot disregard the passports issued by the Committee of Public Safety. But examine each passport carefully, citizen Bibot! If you have any reasonable ground for suspicion, detain the holder, and if you have not——"

The sound of singing was quite near now. With another wink and a final leer, Marat drew back under the shadow of the cabaret, and Bibot swaggered up to the main entrance of the gate.

"Qui va la?" he thundered in stentorian tones as a group of some half-dozen people lurched towards him out of the gloom, still shouting hoarsely their ribald drinking song.

The foremost man in the group paused opposite citizen Bibot, and with arms akimbo, and legs planted well apart tried to assume a rigidity of attitude which apparently was somewhat foreign to him at this moment.

"Good patriots, citizen," he said in a thick voice which he vainly tried to render steady.

"What do you want?" queried Bibot.

"To be allowed to go on our way unmolested."

"What is your way?"

"Through the Porte Montmartre to the village of Barency."

"What is your business there?"

This query delivered in Bibot's most pompous manner seemed vastly to amuse the rowdy crowd. He who was the spokesman turned to his friends and shouted hilariously:

"Hark at him, citizens! He asks me what is our business. Oh, citizen Bibot, since when have you become blind? A dolt you've always been, else you had not asked the question."

But Bibot, undeterred by the man's drunken insolence, retorted gruffly:

"Your business, I want to know."

"Bibot! my little Bibot!" cooed the bibulous orator now in dulcet tones, "dost not know us, my good Bibot? Yet we all know thee, citizen—Captain Bibot of the Town Guard, eh, citizens! Three cheers for the citizen captain!"

When the noisy shouts and cheers from half a dozen hoarse throats had died down, Bibot, without more ado, turned to his own men at the gate.

"Drive these drunken louts away!" he commanded; "no one is allowed to loiter here."

Loud protest on the part of the hilarious crowd followed, then a slight scuffle with the bayonets of the Town Guard. Finally the spokesman, somewhat sobered, once more appealed to Bibot.

"Citizen Bibot! you must be blind not to know me and my mates! And let me tell you that you are doing yourself a deal of harm by interfering with the citizens of the Republic in the proper discharge of their duties, and by disregarding their rights of egress through this gate, a right confirmed by passports signed by two members of the Committee of Public Safety."

He had spoken now fairly clearly and very pompously. Bibot, somewhat impressed and remembering Marat's admonitions, said very civilly:

"Tell me your business then, citizen, and show me your passports. If everything is in order you may go your way."

"But you know me, citizen Bibot?" queried the other.

"Yes, I know you—unofficially, citizen Durand."

"You know that I and the citizens here are the carriers for citizen Legrand, the market gardener of Barency?"

"Yes, I know that," said Bibot guardedly, "unofficially."

"Then, unofficially, let me tell you, citizen, that unless we get to Barency this evening, Paris will have to do without cabbages and potatoes to-morrow. So now you know that you are acting at your own risk and peril, citizen, by detaining us."

"Your passports, all of you," commanded Bibot.

He had just caught sight of Marat still sitting outside the tavern opposite, and was glad enough, in this instance, to shelve his responsibility on the shoulders of the popular "Friend of the People." There was general searching in ragged pockets for grimy papers with official seals thereon, and whilst Bibot ordered one of his men to take the six passports across the road to citizen Marat for his inspection, he himself, by the last rays of the setting winter sun, made close examination of the six men who desired to pass through the Porte Montmartre.

As the spokesman had averred, he—Bibot—knew every one of these men. They were the carriers to citizen Legrand, the Barency market gardener. Bibot knew every face. They passed with a load of fruit and vegetables in and out of Paris every day. There was really and absolutely no cause for suspicion, and when citizen Marat returned the six passports, pronouncing them to be genuine, and recognizing his own signature at the bottom of each, Bibot was at last satisfied, and the six bibulous carriers were allowed to pass through the gate, which they did, arm in arm, singing a wild curmagnole, and vociferously cheering as they emerged out into the open.

But Bibot passed an unsteady hand over his brow. It was cold, yet he was in a perspiration. That sort of thing tells on a man's nerves. He rejoined Marat, at the table outside the drinking booth, and ordered a fresh bottle of wine.

The sun had set now, and with the gathering dusk a damp mist descended on Montmartre. From the wall opposite, where the men sat playing cards, came occasional volleys of blasphemous oaths. Bibot was feeling much more like himself. He had half forgotten the incident of the six carriers, which had occurred nearly half an hour ago.

Two or three other people had, in the meanwhile, tried to pass through the gates, but Bibot had been suspicious and had detained them all.

Marat having commended him for his zeal took final leave of him. Just as the demagogue's slouchy, grimy figure was disappearing down a side street there was the loud clatter of hoofs from that same direction, and the next moment a detachment of the mounted Town Guard, headed by an officer in uniform, galloped down the ill-paved street.

Even before the troopers had drawn rein the officer had hailed Bibot.

"Citizen," he shouted, and his voice was breathless, for he had evidently ridden hard and fast, "this message to you from the citizen Chief Commissary of the Section. Six men are wanted by the Committee of Public Safety. They are disguised as carriers in the employ of a market gardener, and have passports for Barency!... The passports are stolen: the men are traitors—escaped aristocrats—and their spokesman is that d—d Englishman, the Scarlet Pimpernel."

Bibot tried to speak; he tugged at the collar of his ragged shirt; an awful curse escaped him.

"Ten thousand devils!" he roared.

"On no account allow these people to go through," continued the officer.

"Keep their passports. Detain them!... Understand?"

Bibot was still gasping for breath even whilst the officer, ordering a quick "Turn!" reeled his horse round, ready to gallop away as far as he had come.

"I am for the St. Denis Gate—Grosjean is on guard there!" he shouted.

"Same orders all round the city. No one to leave the gates!... Understand?"

His troopers fell in. The next moment he would be gone, and those cursed aristocrats well in safety's way.

"Citizen Captain!"

The hoarse shout at last contrived to escape Bibot's parched throat. As if involuntarily, the officer drew rein once more.

"What is it? Quick!—I've no time. That confounded Englishman may be at the St. Denis Gate even now!"

"Citizen Captain," gasped Bibot, his breath coming and going like that of a man fighting for his life. "Here!... at this gate!... not half an hour ago ... six men ... carriers ... market gardeners ... I seemed to know their faces...."

"Yes! yes! market gardener's carriers," exclaimed the officer gleefully, "aristocrats all of them ... and that d—d Scarlet Pimpernel. You've got them? You've detained them?... Where are they?... Speak, man, in the name of hell!..."

"Gone!" gasped Bibot. His legs would no longer bear him. He fell backwards on to a heap of street debris and refuse, from which lowly vantage ground he contrived to give away the whole miserable tale.

"Gone! half an hour ago. Their passports were in order!... I seemed to know their faces! Citizen Marat was here.... He, too—"

In a moment the officer had once more swung his horse round, so that the animal reared, with wild forefeet pawing the air, with champing of bit, and white foam scattered around.

"A thousand million curses!" he exclaimed. "Citizen Bibot, your head will pay for this treachery. Which way did they go?"

A dozen hands were ready to point in the direction where the merry party of carriers had disappeared half an hour ago; a dozen tongues gave rapid, confused explanations.

"Into it, my men!" shouted the officer; "they were on foot! They can't have gone far. Remember the Republic has offered ten thousand francs for the capture of the Scarlet Pimpernel."

Already the heavy gates had been swung open, and the officer's voice once more rang out clear through a perfect thunder-clap of fast galloping hoofs:

"Ventre a terre! Remember!—ten thousand francs to him who first sights the Scarlet Pimpernel!"

The thunder-clap died away in the distance, the dust of four score hoofs was merged in the fog and in the darkness; the voice of the captain was raised again through the mist-laden air. One shout ... a shout of triumph ... then silence once again.

Bibot had fainted on the heap of debris.

His comrades brought him wine to drink. He gradually revived. Hope came back to his heart; his nerves soon steadied themselves as the heavy beverage filtrated through into his blood.

"Bah!" he ejaculated as he pulled himself together, "the troopers were well-mounted ... the officer was enthusiastic; those carriers could not have walked very far. And, in any case, I am free from blame. Citoyen Marat himself was here and let them pass!"

A shudder of superstitious terror ran through him as he recollected the whole scene: for surely he knew all the faces of the six men who had gone through the gate. The devil indeed must have given the mysterious Englishman power to transmute himself and his gang wholly into the bodies of other people.

More than an hour went by. Bibot was quite himself again, bullying, commanding, detaining everybody now.

At that time there appeared to be a slight altercation going on, on the farther side of the gate. Bibot thought it his duty to go and see what the noise was about. Someone wanting to get into Paris instead of out of it at this hour of the night was a strange occurrence.

Bibot heard his name spoken by a raucous voice. Accompanied by two of his men he crossed the wide gates in order to see what was happening. One of the men held a lanthorn, which he was swinging high above his head. Bibot saw standing there before him, arguing with the guard by the gate, the bibulous spokesman of the band of carriers.

He was explaining to the sentry that he had a message to deliver to the citizen commanding at the Porte Montmartre.

"It is a note," he said, "which an officer of the mounted guard gave me. He and twenty troopers were galloping down the great North Road not far from Barency. When they overtook the six of us they drew rein, and the officer gave me this note for citizen Bibot and fifty francs if I would deliver it tonight."

"Give me the note!" said Bibot calmly.

But his hand shook as he took the paper; his face was livid with fear and rage.

The paper had no writing on it, only the outline of a small scarlet flower done in red —the device of the cursed Englishman, the Scarlet Pimpernel.

"Which way did the officer and the twenty troopers go," he stammered, "after they gave you this note?"

"On the way to Calais," replied the other, "but they had magnificent horses, and didn't spare them either. They are a league and more away by now!"

All the blood in Bibot's body seemed to rush up to his head, a wild buzzing was in his ears....

And that was how the Duc and Duchesse de Montreux, with their servants and family, escaped from Paris on that third day of Nivose in the year I of the Republic.

CHAPTER III. TWO GOOD PATRIOTS

Being the deposition of citizeness Fanny Roussell, who was brought up, together with her husband, before the Tribunal of the Revolution on a charge of treason—both being subsequently acquitted.

My name is Fanny Roussell, and I am a respectable married woman, and as good a patriot as any of you sitting there.

Aye, and I'll say it with my dying breath, though you may send me to the guillotine ... as you probably will, for you are all thieves and murderers, every one of you, and you have already made up your minds that I and my man are guilty of having sheltered that accursed Englishman whom they call the Scarlet Pimpernel ... and of having helped him to escape.

But I'll tell you how it all happened, because, though you call me a traitor to the people of France, yet am I a true patriot and will prove it to you by telling you exactly how everything occurred, so that you may be on your guard against the cleverness of that man, who, I do believe, is a friend and confederate of the devil ... else how could he have escaped that time?

Well! it was three days ago, and as bitterly cold as anything that my man and I can remember. We had no travellers staying in the house, for we are a good three leagues out of Calais, and too far for the folk who have business in or about the harbour. Only at midday the coffee-room would get full sometimes with people on their way to or from the port.

But in the evenings the place was quite deserted, and so lonely that at times we fancied that we could hear the wolves howling in the forest of St. Pierre.

It was close on eight o'clock, and my man was putting up the shutters, when suddenly we heard the tramp of feet on the road outside, and then the quick word, "Halt!"

The next moment there was a peremptory knock at the door. My man opened it, and there stood four men in the uniform of the 9th Regiment of the Line ... the same that is quartered at Calais. The uniform, of course, I knew well, though I did not know the men by sight.

"In the name of the People and by the order of the Committee of Public Safety!" said one of the men, who stood in the forefront, and who, I noticed, had a corporal's stripe on his left sleeve.

He held out a paper, which was covered with seals and with writing, but as neither my man nor I can read, it was no use our looking at it.

Hercule—that is my husband's name, citizens—asked the corporal what the Committee of Public Safety wanted with us poor hoteliers of a wayside inn.

"Only food and shelter for to-night for me and my men," replied the corporal, quite civilly.

"You can rest here," said Hercule, and he pointed to the benches in the coffee-room, "and if there is any soup left in the stockpot, you are welcome to it."

Hercule, you see, is a good patriot, and he had been a soldier in his day.... No! no ... do not interrupt me, any of you ... you would only be saying that I ought to have known ... but listen to the end.

"The soup we'll gladly eat," said the corporal very pleasantly. "As for shelter ... well! I am afraid that this nice warm coffee-room will not exactly serve our purpose. We want a place where we can lie hidden, and at the same time keep a watch on the road. I noticed an outhouse as we came. By your leave we will sleep in there."

"As you please," said my man curtly.

He frowned as he said this, and it suddenly seemed as if some vague suspicion had crept into Hercule's mind.

The corporal, however, appeared unaware of this, for he went on quite cheerfully:

"Ah! that is excellent! Entre nous, citizen, my men and I have a desperate customer to deal with. I'll not mention his name, for I see you have guessed it already. A small red flower, what?... Well, we know that he must be making straight for the port of Calais, for he has been traced through St. Omer and Ardres. But he cannot possibly enter Calais city to-night, for we are on the watch for him. He must seek shelter somewhere for himself and any other aristocrat he may have with him, and, bar this house, there is no other place between Ardres and Calais where he can get it. The night is bitterly cold, with a snow blizzard raging round. I and my men have been detailed to watch this road, other patrols are guarding those that lead toward Boulogne and to Gravelines; but I have an idea, citizen, that our fox is making for Calais, and that to me will fall the honour of handing that tiresome scarlet flower to the Public Prosecutor en route for Madame la Guillotine."

Now I could not really tell you, citizens, what suspicions had by this time entered Hercule's head or mine; certainly what suspicions we did have were still very vague.

I prepared the soup for the men and they ate it heartily, after which my husband led the way to the outhouse where we sometimes stabled a traveller's horse when the need arose.

It is nice and dry, and always filled with warm, fresh straw. The entrance into it immediately faces the road; the corporal declared that nothing would suit him and his men better.

They retired to rest apparently, but we noticed that two men remained on the watch just inside the entrance, whilst the two others curled up in the straw.

Hercule put out the lights in the coffee-room, and then he and I went upstairs—not to bed, mind you—but to have a quiet talk together over the events of the past half-hour.

The result of our talk was that ten minutes later my man quietly stole downstairs and out of the house. He did not, however, go out by the front door, but through a back way which, leading through a cabbage-patch and then across a field, cuts into the main road some two hundred metres higher up.

Hercule and I had decided that he would walk the three leagues into Calais, despite the cold, which was intense, and the blizzard, which was nearly blinding, and that he would call at the post of gendarmerie at the city gates, and there see the officer in command and tell him the exact state of the case. It would then be for that officer to decide what was to be done; our responsibility as loyal citizens would be completely covered.

Hercule, you must know, had just emerged from our cabbage-patch on to the field when he was suddenly challenged:

"Qui va la?"

He gave his name. His certificate of citizenship was in his pocket; he had nothing to fear. Through the darkness and the veil of snow he had discerned a small group of men wearing the uniform of the 9th Regiment of the Line.

"Four men," said the foremost of these, speaking quickly and commandingly, "wearing the same uniform that I and my men are wearing ... have you seen them?"

"Yes," said Hercule hurriedly.

"Where are they?"

"In the outhouse close by."

The other suppressed a cry of triumph.

"At them, my men!" he said in a whisper, "and you, citizen, thank your stars that we have not come too late."

"These men ..." whispered Hercule. "I had my suspicions."

"Aristocrats, citizen," rejoined the commander of the little party, "and one of them is that cursed Englishman—the Scarlet Pimpernel."

Already the soldiers, closely followed by Hercule, had made their way through our cabbage-patch back to the house.

The next moment they had made a bold dash for the barn. There was a great deal of shouting, a great deal of swearing and some firing, whilst Hercule and I, not a little frightened, remained in the coffee-room, anxiously awaiting events.

Presently the group of soldiers returned, not the ones who had first come, but the others. I noticed their leader, who seemed to be exceptionally tall.

He looked very cheerful, and laughed loudly as he entered the coffee-room. From the moment that I looked at his face I knew, somehow, that Hercule and I had been fooled, and that now, indeed, we stood eye to eye with that mysterious personage who is called the Scarlet Pimpernel.

I screamed, and Hercule made a dash for the door; but what could two humble and peaceful citizens do against this band of desperate men, who held their lives in their own hands? They were four and we were two, and I do believe that their leader has supernatural strength and power.

He treated us quite kindly, even though he ordered his followers to bind us down to our bed upstairs, and to tie a cloth round our mouths so that our cries could not be distinctly heard.

Neither my man nor I closed an eye all night, of course, but we heard the miscreants moving about in the coffee-room below. But they did no mischief, nor did they steal any of the food or wines.

At daybreak we heard them going out by the front door, and their footsteps disappearing toward Calais. We found their discarded uniforms lying in the coffee-room. They must have entered Calais by daylight, when the gates were opened—just like other peaceable citizens. No doubt they had forged passports, just as they had stolen uniforms.

Our maid-of-all-work released us from our terrible position in the course of the morning, and we released the soldiers of the 9th Regiment of the Line, whom we found bound and gagged, some of them wounded, in the outhouse.

That same afternoon we were arrested, and here we are, ready to die if we must, but I swear that I have told you the truth, and I ask you, in the name of justice, if we have done anything wrong, and if we did not act like loyal and true citizens, even though we were pitted against an emissary of the devil?

CHAPTER IV. THE OLD SCARECROW

I.

Nobody in the quartier could quite recollect when it was that the new Public Letter-Writer first set up in business at the angle formed by the Quai des Augustins and the Rue Dauphine, immediately facing the Pont Neuf; but there he certainly was on the 28th day of February, 1793, when Agnes, with eyes swollen with tears, a market basket on her arm, and a look of dreary despair on her young face, turned that selfsame angle on her way to the Pont Neuf, and nearly fell over the rickety construction which sheltered him and his stock-in-trade.

"Oh, mon Dieu! citizen Lepine, I had no idea you were here," she exclaimed as soon as she had recovered her balance.

"Nor I, citizeness, that I should have the pleasure of seeing you this morning," he retorted.

"But you were always at the other corner of the Pont Neuf," she argued.

"So I was," he replied, "so I was. But I thought I would like a change. The Faubourg St. Michel appealed to me; most of my clients came to me from this side of the river—all those on the other side seem to know how to read and write."

"I was just going over to see you," she remarked.

"You, citizeness," he exclaimed in unfeigned surprise, "what should procure a poor public writer the honour of—"

"Hush, in God's name!" broke in the young girl quickly as she cast a rapid, furtive glance up and down the quai and the narrow streets which converged at this angle.

She was dressed in the humblest and poorest of clothes, her skimpy shawl round her shoulders could scarce protect her against the cold of this cruel winter's morning; her hair was entirely hidden beneath a frilled and starched cap, and her feet were encased in coarse worsted stockings and sabots, but her hands were delicate and fine, and her face had that nobility of feature and look of patient resignation in the midst of overwhelming sorrow which proclaimed a lofty refinement both of soul and of mind.

The old Letter-Writer was surveying the pathetic young figure before him through his huge horn-rimmed spectacles, and she smiled on him through her fast-gathering tears. He used to have his pitch at the angle of the Pont Neuf, and whenever Agnes had walked past it, she had nodded to him and bidden him "Good morrow!" He had at times done little commissions for her and gone on errands when she needed a messenger; to-day, in the midst of her despair, she had suddenly thought of him and that rumour credited him with certain knowledge which she would give her all to possess.

She had sallied forth this morning with the express purpose of speaking with him; but now suddenly she felt afraid, and stood looking at him for a moment or two, hesitating, wondering if she dared tell him—one never knew these days into what terrible pitfall an ill-considered word might lead one.

A scarecrow he was, that old Public Letter-Writer, more like a great, gaunt bird than a human being, with those spectacles of his, and his long, very sparse and very lanky fringe of a beard which fell from his cheeks and chin and down his chest for all the world like a crumpled grey bib. He was wrapped from head to foot in a caped coat which had once been green in colour, but was now of many hues not usually seen in rainbows. He wore his coat all buttoned down the front, like a dressing-gown, and below the hem there peeped out a pair of very large feet encased in boots which had never been a pair. He sat upon a rickety, straw-bottomed chair under an improvised awning which was made up of four poles and a bit of sacking. He had a table in front of him—a table partially and very insecurely propped up by a bundle of old papers and books, since no two of its four legs were completely whole—and on the table there was a neckless bottle half-filled with ink, a few sheets of paper and a couple of quill pens.

The young girl's hesitation had indeed not lasted more than a few seconds.

Furtively, like a young creature terrified of lurking enemies, she once more glanced to right and left of her and down the two streets and the river bank, for Paris was full of spies these days—human bloodhounds ready for a few sous to sell their fellow-creatures' lives. It was middle morning now, and a few passers-by were hurrying along wrapped to the nose in mufflers, for the weather was bitterly cold.

Agnes waited until there was no one in sight, then she leaned forward over the table and whispered under her breath:

"They say, citizen, that you alone in Paris know the whereabouts of the

English milor'—of him who is called the Scarlet Pimpernel...."

"Hush-sh-sh!" said the old man quickly, for just at that moment two men had gone by, in ragged coats and torn breeches, who had leered at Agnes and her neat cap and skirt as they passed. Now they had turned the angle of the street and the old man, too, sank his voice to a whisper.

"I know nothing of any Englishman," he muttered.

"Yes, you do," she rejoined insistently. "When poor Antoine Carre was somewhere in hiding and threatened with arrest, and his mother dared not write to him lest her letter be intercepted, she spoke to you about the English milor', and the English milor' found Antoine Carre and took him and his mother safely out of France. Mme. Carre is my godmother.... I saw her the very night when she went to meet the English milor' at his commands. I know all that happened then.... I know that you were the intermediary."

"And if I was," he muttered sullenly as he fiddled with his pen and paper, "maybe I've had cause to regret it. For a week after that Carre episode I dared not show my face in the streets of Paris; for nigh on a fortnight I dared not ply my trade ... I have only just ventured again to set up in business. I am not going to risk my old neck again in a hurry...."

"It is a matter of life and death," urged Agnes, as once more the tears rushed to her pleading eyes and the look of misery settled again upon her face.

"Your life, citizeness?" queried the old man, "or that of citizen-deputy Fabrice?"

"Hush!" she broke in again, as a look of real terror now overspread her face. Then she added under her breath: "You know?"

"I know that Mademoiselle Agnes de Lucines is fiancee to the citizen-deputy Arnould Fabrice," rejoined the old man quietly, "and that it is Mademoiselle Agnes de Lucines who is speaking with me now."

"You have known that all along?"

"Ever since mademoiselle first tripped past me at the angle of the Pont Neuf dressed in winsey kirtle and wearing sabots on her feet...."

"But how?" she murmured, puzzled, not a little frightened, for his knowledge might prove dangerous to her. She was of gentle birth, and as such an object of suspicion to the Government of the Republic and of the Terror; her mother was a hopeless cripple, unable to move: this together with her love for Arnould Fabrice had kept Agnes de Lucines in France these days, even though she was in hourly peril of arrest.

"Tell me what has happened," the old man said, unheeding her last anxious query. "Perhaps I can help ..."

"Oh! you cannot—the English milor' can and will if only we could know where he is. I thought of him the moment I received that awful man's letter—and then I thought of you...."

"Tell me about the letter—quickly," he interrupted her with some impatience. "I'll be writing something—but talk away, I shall hear every word. But for God's sake be as brief as you can."

He drew some paper nearer to him and dipped his pen in the ink. He appeared to be writing under her dictation. Thin, flaky snow had begun to fall and settled in a smooth white carpet upon the frozen ground, and the footsteps of the passers-by sounded muffled as they hurried along. Only the lapping of the water of the sluggish river close by broke the absolute stillness of the air.

Agnes de Lucines' pale face looked ethereal in this framework of white which covered her shoulders and the shawl crossed over her bosom: only her eyes, dark, appealing, filled with a glow of immeasurable despair, appeared tensely human and alive.

"I had a letter this morning," she whispered, speaking very rapidly, "from citizen Heriot—that awful man—you know him?"

"Yes, yes!"

"He used to be valet in the service of deputy Fabrice. Now he, too, is a member of the National Assembly ... he is arrogant and cruel and vile. He hates Arnould Fabrice and he professes himself passionately in love with me."

"Yes, yes!" murmured the old man, "but the letter?"

"It came this morning. In it he says that he has in his possession a number of old letters, documents and manuscripts which are quite enough to send deputy Fabrice to the guillotine. He threatens to place all those papers before the Committee of Public Safety unless ... unless I...."

She paused, and a deep blush, partly of shame, partly of wrath, suffused her pale cheeks.

"Unless you accept his grimy hand in marriage," concluded the man dryly.

Her eyes gave him answer. With pathetic insistence she tried now to glean a ray of hope from the old scarecrow's inscrutable face. But he was bending over his writing: his fingers were blue with cold, his great shoulders were stooping to his task.

"Citizen," she pleaded.

"Hush!" he muttered, "no more now. The very snowflakes are made up of whispers that may reach those bloodhounds yet. The English milor' shall know of this. He will send you a message if he thinks fit."

"Citizen—"

"Not another word, in God's name! Pay me five sous for this letter and pray Heaven that you have not been watched."

She shivered and drew her shawl closer round her shoulders, then she counted out five sous with elaborate care and laid them out upon the table. The old man took up the coins. He blew into his fingers, which looked paralysed with the cold. The snow lay over everything now; the rough awning had not protected him or his wares.

Agnes turned to go. The last she saw of him, as she went up the Rue Dauphine, was one broad shoulder still bending over the table, and clad in the shabby, caped coat all covered with snow like an old Santa Claus.

II.

It was half-an-hour before noon, and citizen-deputy Heriot was preparing to go out to the small tavern round the corner where he habitually took his dejeuner. Citizen Rondeau, who for the consideration of ten sous a day looked after Heriot's paltry creature-comforts, was busy tidying up the squalid apartment which the latter occupied on the top floor of a lodging-house in the Rue Cocatrice. This apartment consisted of three rooms leading out of one another; firstly there was a dark and narrow antechamber wherein slept the aforesaid citizen-servant; then came a sitting-room sparsely furnished with a few chairs, a centre table and an iron stove, and finally there was the bedroom wherein the most conspicuous object was a large oak chest clamped with wide iron hinges and a massive writing-desk; the bed and a very primitive washstand were in an alcove at the farther end of the room and partially hidden by a tapestry curtain.

At exactly half-past seven that morning there came a peremptory knock at the door of the antechamber, and as Rondeau was busy in the bedroom, Heriot went himself to see who his unexpected visitor might be. On the landing outside stood an extraordinary-looking individual—more like a tall and animated scarecrow than a man—who in a tremulous voice asked if he might speak with the citizen Heriot.

"That is my name," said the deputy gruffly, "what do you want?"

He would have liked to slam the door in the old scarecrow's face, but the latter, with the boldness which sometimes besets the timid, had already stepped into the antichambre and was now quietly sauntering through to the next room into the one beyond. Heriot, being a representative of the people and a social democrat of the most advanced type, was supposed to be accessible to every one who desired speech with him. Though muttering sundry curses, he thought it best not to go against his usual practice, and after a moment's hesitation he followed his unwelcome visitor.

The latter was in the sitting-room by this time; he had drawn a chair close to the table and sat down with the air of one who has a perfect right to be where he is; as soon as Heriot entered he said placidly:

"I would desire to speak alone with the citizen-deputy."

And Heriot, after another slight hesitation, ordered Rondeau to close the bedroom door.

"Keep your ears open in case I call," he added significantly.

"You are cautious, citizen," merely remarked the visitor with a smile.

To this Heriot vouchsafed no reply. He, too, drew a chair forward and sat opposite his visitor, then he asked abruptly: "Your name and quality?"

"My name is Lepine at your service," said the old man, "and by profession I write letters at the rate of five sous or so, according to length, for those who are not able to do it for themselves."

"Your business with me?" queried Heriot curtly.

"To offer you two thousand francs for the letters which you stole from deputy Fabrice when you were his valet," replied Lepine with perfect calm.

In a moment Heriot was on his feet, jumping up as if he had been stung; his pale, short-sighted eyes narrowed till they were mere slits, and through them he darted a quick, suspicious glance at the extraordinary out-at-elbows figure before him. Then he threw back his head and laughed till the tears streamed down his cheeks and his sides began to ache.

"This is a farce, I presume, citizen," he said when he had recovered something of his composure.

"No farce, citizen," replied Lepine calmly. "The money is at your disposal whenever you care to bring the letters to my pitch at the angle of the Rue Dauphine and the Quai des Augustins, where I carry on my business."

"Whose money is it? Agnes de Lucines' or did that fool Fabrice send you?"

"No one sent me, citizen. The money is mine—a few savings I possess—I honour citizen Fabrice—I would wish to do him service by purchasing certain letters from you."

Then as Heriot, moody and sullen, remained silent and began pacing up and down the long, bare floor of the room, Lepine added persuasively, "Well! what do you say? Two thousand francs for a packet of letters—not a bad bargain these hard times."

"Get out of this room," was Heriot's fierce and sudden reply.

"You refuse?"

"Get out of this room!"

"As you please," said Lepine as he, too, rose from his chair. "But before I go, citizen Heriot," he added, speaking very quietly, "let me tell you one thing. Mademoiselle Agnes de Lucines would far sooner cut off her right hand than let yours touch it even for one instant. Neither she nor deputy Fabrice would ever purchase their lives at such a price."

"And who are you—you mangy old scarecrow?" retorted Heriot, who was getting beside himself with rage, "that you should assert these things? What are those people to you, or you to them, that you should interfere in their affairs?"

"Your question is beside the point, citizen," said Lepine blandly; "I am here to propose a bargain. Had you not better agree to it?"

"Never!" reiterated Heriot emphatically.

"Two thousand francs," reiterated the old man imperturbably.

"Not if you offered me two hundred thousand," retorted the other fiercely. "Go and tell that, to those who sent you. Tell them that I—Heriot—would look upon a fortune as mere dross against the delight of seeing that man Fabrice, whom I hate beyond everything in earth or hell, mount up the steps to the guillotine. Tell them that I know that Agnes de Lucines loathes me, that I know that she loves him. I know that I cannot win her save by threatening him. But you are wrong, citizen Lepine," he continued, speaking more and more calmly as his passions of hatred and of love seemed more and more to hold him in their grip; "you are wrong if you think that she will not strike a bargain with me in order to save the life of Fabrice, whom she loves. Agnes de Lucines will be my wife within the month, or Arnould Fabrice's head will fall under the guillotine, and you, my interfering friend, may go to the devil, if you please."

"That would be but a tame proceeding, citizen, after my visit to you," said the old man, with unruffled sang-froid. "But let me, in my turn, assure you of this, citizen Heriot," he added, "that Mlle. de Lucines will never be your wife, that Arnould Fabrice will not end his valuable life under the guillotine—and that you will never be allowed to use against him the cowardly and stolen weapon which you possess."

Heriot laughed—a low, cynical laugh and shrugged his thin shoulders:

"And who will prevent me, I pray you?" he asked sarcastically.

The old man made no immediate reply, but he came just a step or two closer to the citizen-deputy and, suddenly drawing himself up to his full height, he looked for one brief moment down upon the mean and sordid figure of the ex-valet. To Heriot it seemed as if the whole man had become transfigured; the shabby old scarecrow looked all of a sudden like a brilliant and powerful personality; from his eyes there flashed down a look of supreme contempt and of supreme pride, and Heriot—unable to understand this metamorphosis which was more apparent to his inner consciousness than to his outward sight, felt his knees shake under him and all the blood rush back to his heart in an agony of superstitious terror.

From somewhere there came to his ear the sound of two words: "I will!" in reply to his own defiant query. Surely those words uttered by a man conscious of power and of strength could never have been spoken by the dilapidated old scarecrow who earned a precarious living by writing letters for ignorant folk.

But before he could recover some semblance of presence of mind citizen Lepine had gone, and only a loud and merry laugh seemed to echo through the squalid room.

Heriot shook off the remnant of his own senseless terror; he tore open the door of the bedroom and shouted to Rondeau, who truly was thinking that the citizen-deputy had gone mad:

"After him!—after him! Quick! curse you!" he cried.

"After whom?" gasped the man.

"The man who was here just now—an aristo."

"I saw no one—but the Public Letter-Writer, old Lepine—I know him well—"

"Curse you for a fool!" shouted Heriot savagely, "the man who was here was that cursed Englishman—the one whom they call the Scarlet Pimpernel. Run after him—stop him, I say!"

"Too late, citizen," said the other placidly; "whoever was here before is certainly half-way down the street by now."

III.

"No use, Ffoulkes," said Sir Percy Blakeney to his friend half-an-hour later, "the man's passions of hatred and desire are greater than his greed."

The two men were sitting together in one of Sir Percy Blakeney's many lodgings—the one in the Rue des Petits Peres—and Sir Percy had just put Sir Andrew Ffoulkes au fait with the whole sad story of Arnould Fabrice's danger and Agnes de Lucines' despair.

"You could do nothing with the brute, then?" queried Sir Andrew.

"Nothing," replied Blakeney. "He refused all bribes, and violence would not have helped me, for what I wanted was not to knock him down, but to get hold of the letters."

"Well, after all, he might have sold you the letters and then denounced Fabrice just the same."

"No, without actual proofs he could not do that. Arnould Fabrice is not a man against whom a mere denunciation would suffice. He has the grudging respect of every faction in the National Assembly. Nothing but irrefutable proof would prevail against him—and bring him to the guillotine."

"Why not get Fabrice and Mlle. de Lucines safely over to England?"

"Fabrice would not come. He is not of the stuff that emigres are made of. He is not an aristocrat; he is a republican by conviction, and a demmed honest one at that. He would scorn to run away, and Agnes de Lucines would not go without him."

"Then what can we do?"

"Filch those letters from that brute Heriot," said Blakeney calmly.

"House-breaking, you mean!" commented Sir Andrew Ffoulkes dryly.

"Petty theft, shall we say?" retorted Sir Percy. "I can bribe the lout who has charge of Heriot's rooms to introduce us into his master's sanctum this evening when the National Assembly is sitting and the citizen-deputy safely out of the way."

And the two men—one of whom was the most intimate friend of the Prince of Wales and the acknowledged darling of London society—thereupon fell to discussing plans for surreptitiously entering a man's room and committing larceny, which in normal times would entail, if discovered, a long term of imprisonment, but which, in these days, in Paris, and perpetrated against a member of the National Assembly, would certainly be punished by death.

IV.

Citizen Rondeau, whose business it was to look after the creature comforts of deputy Heriot, was standing in the antechamber facing the two visitors whom he had just introduced into his master's apartments, and idly turning a couple of gold coins over and over between his grimy fingers.

"And mind, you are to see nothing and hear nothing of what goes on in the next room," said the taller of the two strangers; "and when we go there'll be another couple of louis for you. Is that understood?"

"Yes! it's understood," grunted Rondeau sullenly; "but I am running great risks. The citizen-deputy sometimes returns at ten o'clock, but sometimes at nine.... I never know."

"It is now seven," rejoined the other; "we'll be gone long before nine."

"Well," said Rondeau surlily, "I go out now for my supper. I'll return in half an hour, but at half-past eight you must clear out."

Then he added with a sneer:

"Citizens Legros and Desgas usually come back with deputy Heriot of nights, and citizens Jeanniot and Bompard come in from next door for a game of cards. You wouldn't stand much chance if you were caught here."

"Not with you to back up so formidable a quintette of stalwarts," assented the tall visitor gaily. "But we won't trouble about that just now. We have a couple of hours before us in which to do all that we want. So au revoir, friend Rondeau ... two more louis for your complaisance, remember, when we have accomplished our purpose."

Rondeau muttered something more, but the two strangers paid no further heed to him; they had already walked to the next room, leaving Rondeau in the antechamber.

Sir Percy Blakeney did not pause in the sitting-room where an oil lamp suspended from the ceiling threw a feeble circle of light above the centre table. He went straight through the bedroom. Here, too, a small lamp was burning which only lit up a small portion of the room—the writing-desk and the oak chest—leaving the corners and the alcove, with its partially drawn curtains, in complete shadow.

Blakeney pointed to the oak chest and to the desk.

"You tackle the chest, Ffoulkes, and I will go for the desk," he said quietly, as soon as he had taken a rapid survey of the room. "You have your tools?"

Ffoulkes nodded, and anon in this squalid room, ill-lit, ill-ventilated, barely furnished, was presented one of the most curious spectacles of these strange and troublous times: two English gentlemen, the acknowledged dandies of London drawing-rooms, busy picking locks and filing hinges like any common house-thieves.

Neither of them spoke, and a strange hush fell over the room—a hush only broken by the click of metal against metal, and the deep breathing of the two men bending to their task. Sir Andrew Ffoulkes was working with a file on the padlocks of the oak chest, and Sir Percy Blakeney, with a bunch of skeleton keys, was opening the drawers of the writing-desk. These, when finally opened, revealed nothing of any importance; but when anon Sir Andrew was able to lift the lid of the oak chest, he disclosed an innumerable quantity of papers and documents tied up in neat bundles, docketed and piled up in rows and tiers to the very top of the chest.

"Quick to work, Ffoulkes," said Blakeney, as in response to his friend's call he drew a chair forward and, seating himself beside the chest, started on the task of looking through the hundreds of bundles which lay before him. "It will take us all our time to look through these."

Together now the two men set to work—methodically and quietly—piling up on the floor beside them the bundles of papers which they had already examined, and delving into the oak chest for others. No sound was heard save the crackling of crisp paper and an occasional ejaculation from either of them when they came upon some proof or other of Heriot's propensity for blackmail.

"Agnes de Lucines is not the only one whom this brute is terrorising," murmured Blakeney once between his teeth; "I marvel that the man ever feels safe, alone in these lodgings, with no one but that weak-kneed Rondeau to protect him. He must have scores of enemies in this city who would gladly put a dagger in his heart or a bullet through his back."

They had been at work for close on half an hour when an exclamation of triumph, quickly smothered, escaped Sir Percy's lips.

"By Gad, Ffoulkes!" he said, "I believe I have got what we want!"

With quick, capable hands he turned over a bundle which he had just extracted from the chest. Rapidly he glanced through them. "I have them, Ffoulkes," he reiterated more emphatically as he put the bundle into his pocket; "now everything back in its place and—"

Suddenly he paused, his slender hand up to his lips, his head turned toward the door, an expression of tense expectancy in every line of his face.

"Quick, Ffoulkes," he whispered, "everything back into the chest, and the lid down."

"What ears you have," murmured Ffoulkes as he obeyed rapidly and without question. "I heard nothing."

Blakeney went to the door and bent his head to listen.

"Three men coming up the stairs," he said; "they are on the landing now."

"Have we time to rush them?"

"No chance! They are at the door. Two more men have joined them, and I can distinguish Rondeau's voice, too."

"The quintette," murmured Sir Andrew. "We are caught like two rats in a trap."

Even as he spoke the opening of the outside door could be distinctly heard, then the confused murmur of many voices. Already Blakeney and Ffoulkes had with perfect presence of mind put the finishing touches to the tidying of the room—put the chairs straight, shut down the lid of the oak chest, closed all the drawers of the desk.

"Nothing but good luck can save us now," whispered Blakeney as he lowered the wick of the lamp. "Quick now," he added, "behind that tapestry in the alcove and trust to our stars."

Securely hidden for the moment behind the curtains in the dark recess of the alcove the two men waited. The door leading into the sitting-room was ajar, and they could hear Heriot and his friends making merry irruption into the place. From out the confusion of general conversation they soon gathered that the debates in the Chamber had been so dull and uninteresting that, at a given signal, the little party had decided to adjourn to Heriot's rooms for their habitual game of cards. They could also hear Heriot calling to Rondeau to bring bottles and glasses, and vaguely they marvelled what Rondeau's attitude might be like at this moment. Was he brazening out the situation, or was he sick with terror?

Suddenly Heriot's voice came out more distinctly.

"Make yourselves at home, friends," he was saying; "here are cards, dominoes, and wine. I must leave you to yourselves for ten minutes whilst I write an important letter."

"All right, but don't be long," came in merry response.

"Not longer than I can help," rejoined Heriot. "I want my revenge against Bompard, remember. He did fleece me last night."

"Hurry on, then," said one of the men. "I'll play Desgas that return game of dominoes until then."

"Ten minutes and I'll be back," concluded Heriot.

He pushed open the bedroom door. The light within was very dim. The two men hidden behind the tapestry could hear him moving about the room muttering curses to himself. Presently the light of the lamp was shifted from one end of the room to the other. Through the opening between the two curtains Blakeney could just see Heriot's back as he placed the lamp at a convenient angle upon his desk, divested himself of his overcoat and muffler, then sat down and drew pen and paper closer to him. He was leaning forward, his elbow resting upon the table, his fingers fidgeting with his long, lank hair. He had closed the door when he entered, and from the other room now the voices of his friends sounded confused and muffled. Now and then an exclamation: "Double!" "Je ... tiens!" "Cinq-deux!" an oath, a laugh, the click of glasses and bottles came out more clearly; but the rest of the time these sounds were more like a droning accompaniment to the scraping of Heriot's pen upon the paper when he finally began to write his letter.

Two minutes went by and then two more. The scratching of Heriot's pen became more rapid as he appeared to be more completely immersed in his work. Behind the curtain the two men had been waiting: Blakeney ready to act, Ffoulkes equally ready to interpret the slightest signal from his chief.

The next minute Blakeney had stolen out of the alcove, and his two hands—so slender and elegant looking, and yet with a grip of steel—had fastened themselves upon Heriot's mouth, smothering within the space of a second the cry that had been half-uttered. Ffoulkes was ready to complete the work of rendering the man helpless: one handkerchief made an efficient gag, another tied the ankles securely. Heriot's own coat-sleeves supplied the handcuffs, and the blankets off the bed tied around his legs rendered him powerless to move. Then the two men lifted this inert mass on to the bed and Ffoulkes whispered anxiously: "Now, what next?"

Heriot's overcoat, hat, and muffler lay upon a chair. Sir Percy, placing a warning finger upon his lips, quickly divested himself of his own coat, slipped that of Heriot on, twisted the muffler round his neck, hunched up his shoulders, and murmuring: "Now for a bit of luck!" once more lowered the light of the lamp and then went to the door.

"Rondeau!" he called. "Hey, Rondeau!" And Sir Percy himself was surprised at the marvelous way in which he had caught the very inflection of Heriot's voice.

"Hey, Rondeau!" came from one of the players at the table, "the citizen-deputy is calling you!"

They were all sitting round the table: two men intent upon their game of dominoes, the other two watching with equal intentness. Rondeau came shuffling out of the antechamber. His face, by the dim light of the oil lamp, looked jaundiced with fear.

"Rondeau, you fool, where are you?" called Blakeney once again.

The next moment Rondeau had entered the room. No need for a signal or an order this time. Ffoulkes knew by instinct what his chief's bold scheme would mean to them both if it succeeded. He retired into the darkest corner of the room as Rondeau shuffled across to the writing-desk. It was all done in a moment. In less time than it had taken to bind and gag Heriot, his henchman was laid out on the floor, his coat had been taken off him, and he was tied into a mummy-like bundle with Sir Andrew Ffoulkes' elegant coat fastened securely round his arms and chest. It had all been done in silence. The men in the next room were noisy and intent on their game; the slight scuffle, the quickly smothered cries had remained unheeded.

"Now, what next?" queried Sir Andrew Ffoulkes once more.

"The impudence of the d—— l, my good Ffoulkes," replied Blakeney in a whisper, "and may our stars not play us false. Now let me make you look as like Rondeau as possible—there! Slip on his coat—now your hair over your forehead—your coat-collar up—your knees bent—that's better!" he added as he surveyed the transformation which a few deft strokes had made in Sir Andrew Ffoulkes' appearance. "Now all you have to do is to shuffle across the room—here's your prototype's handkerchief—of dubious cleanliness, it is true, but it will serve—blow your nose as you cross the room, it will hide your face. They'll not heed you—keep in the shadows and God guard you—I'll follow in a moment or two ... but don't wait for me."

He opened the door, and before Sir Andrew could protest his chief had pushed him out into the room where the four men were still intent on their game. Through the open door Sir Percy now watched his friend who, keeping well within the shadows, shuffled quietly across the room. The next moment Sir Andrew was through and in the antechamber. Blakeney's acutely sensitive ears caught the sound of the opening of the outer door. He waited for a while, then he drew out of his pocket the bundle of letters which he had risked so much to obtain. There they were neatly docketed and marked: "The affairs of Arnould Fabrice."

Well! if he got away to-night Agnes de Lucines would be happy and free from the importunities of that brute Heriot; after that he must persuade her and Fabrice to go to England and to freedom.

For the moment his own safety was terribly in jeopardy; one false move—one look from those players round the table.... Bah! even then—!

With an inward laugh he pushed open the door once more and stepped into the room. For the moment no one noticed him; the game was at its most palpitating stage; four shaggy heads met beneath the lamp and four pairs of eyes were gazing with rapt attention upon the intricate maze of the dominoes.

Blakeney walked quietly across the room; he was just midway and on a level with the centre table when a voice was suddenly raised from that tense group beneath the lamp: "Is it thou, friend Heriot?"

Then one of the men looked up and stared, and another did likewise and exclaimed: "It is not Heriot!"

In a moment all was confusion, but confusion was the very essence of those hair-breadth escapes and desperate adventures which were as the breath of his nostrils to the Scarlet Pimpernel. Before those four men had had time to jump to their feet, or to realise that something was wrong with their friend Heriot, he had run across the room, his hand was on the knob of the door—the door that led to the antechamber and to freedom.

Bompard, Desgas, Jeanniot, Legros were at his heels, but he tore open the door, bounded across the threshold, and slammed it to with such a vigorous bang that those on the other side were brought to a momentary halt. That moment meant life and liberty to Blakeney; already he had crossed the antechamber. Quite coolly and quietly now he took out the key from the inner side of the main door and slipped it to the outside. The next second—even as the four men rushed helter-skelter into the antechamber he was out on the landing and had turned the key in the door.

His prisoners were safely locked in—in Heriot's apartments—and Sir Percy Blakeney, calmly and without haste, was descending the stairs of the house in the Rue Cocatrice.

The next morning Agnes de Lucines received, through an anonymous messenger, the packet of letters which would so gravely have compromised Arnould Fabrice. Though the weather was more inclement than ever, she ran out into the streets, determined to seek out the old Public Letter-Writer and thank him for his mediation with the English milor, who surely had done this noble action.

But the old scarecrow had disappeared.

CHAPTER V. A FINE BIT OF WORK

I.

"Sh!... sh!... It's the Englishman. I'd know his footstep anywhere—"

"God bless him!" murmured petite maman fervently.

Pere Lenegre went to the door; he stepped cautiously and with that stealthy foot-tread which speaks in eloquent silence of daily, hourly danger, of anguish and anxiety for lives that are dear.

The door was low and narrow—up on the fifth floor of one of the huge tenement houses in the Rue Jolivet in the Montmartre quarter of Paris. A narrow stone passage led to it—pitch-dark at all times, but dirty, and evil-smelling when the concierge—a free citizen of the new democracy—took a week's holiday from his work in order to spend whole afternoons either at the wineshop round the corner, or on the Place du Carrousel to watch the guillotine getting rid of some twenty aristocrats an hour for the glorification of the will of the people.

But inside the small apartment everything was scrupulously neat and clean. Petite maman was such an excellent manager, and Rosette was busy all the day tidying and cleaning the poor little home, which Pere Lenegre contrived to keep up for wife and daughter by working fourteen hours a day in the government saddlery.

When Pere Lenegre opened the narrow door, the entire framework of it was filled by the broad, magnificent figure of a man in heavy caped coat and high leather boots, with dainty frills of lace at throat and wrist, and elegant chapeau-bras held in the hand.

Pere Lenegre at sight of him, put a quick finger to his own quivering lips.

"Anything wrong, vieux papa?" asked the newcomer lightly.

The other closed the door cautiously before he made reply. But petite maman could not restrain her anxiety.

"My little Pierre, milor?" she asked as she clasped her wrinkled hands together, and turned on the stranger her tear-dimmed restless eyes.

"Pierre is safe and well, little mother," he replied cheerily. "We got him out of Paris early this morning in a coal cart, carefully hidden among the sacks. When he emerged he was black but safe. I drove the cart myself as far as Courbevoie, and there handed over your Pierre and those whom we got out of Paris with him to those of my friends who were going straight to England. There's nothing more to be afraid of, petite maman," he added as he took the old woman's wrinkled hands in both his own; "your son is now under the care of men who would die rather than see him captured. So make your mind at ease, Pierre will be in England, safe and well, within a week."

Petite maman couldn't say anything just then because tears were choking her, but in her turn she clasped those two strong and slender hands—the hands of the brave Englishman who had just risked his life in order to save Pierre from the guillotine—and she kissed them as fervently as she kissed the feet of the Madonna when she knelt before her shrine in prayer.

Pierre had been a footman in the household of unhappy Marie Antoinette. His crime had been that he remained loyal to her in words as well as in thought. A hot-headed but nobly outspoken harangue on behalf of the unfortunate queen, delivered in a public place, had at once marked him out to the spies of the Terrorists as suspect of intrigue against the safety of the Republic. He was denounced to the Committee of Public Safety, and his arrest and condemnation to the guillotine would have inevitably followed had not the gallant band of Englishmen, known as the League of the Scarlet Pimpernel, succeeded in effecting his escape.

What wonder that petite maman could not speak for tears when she clasped the hands of the noble leader of that splendid little band of heroes? What wonder that Pere Lenegre, when he heard that his son was safe murmured a fervent: "God bless you, milor, and your friends!" and that Rosette surreptitiously raised the fine caped coat to her lips, for Pierre was her twin-brother, and she loved him very dearly.

But already Sir Percy Blakeney had, with one of his characteristic cheery words, dissipated the atmosphere of tearful emotion which oppressed these kindly folk.

"Now, Papa Lenegre," he said lightly, "tell me why you wore such a solemn air when you let me in just now."

"Because, milor," replied the old man quietly, "that d———d concierge, Jean Baptiste, is a black-hearted traitor."

Sir Percy laughed, his merry, infectious laugh.

"You mean that while he has been pocketing bribes from me, he has denounced me to the Committee."

Pere Lenegre nodded: "I only heard it this morning," he said, "from one or two threatening words the treacherous brute let fall. He knows that you lodge in the Place des Trois Maries, and that you come here frequently. I would have given my life to warn you then and there," continued the old man with touching earnestness, "but I didn't know where to find you. All I knew was that you were looking after Pierre."

Even while the man spoke there darted from beneath the Englishman's heavy lids a quick look like a flash of sudden and brilliant light out of the lazy depths of his merry blue eyes; it was one of those glances of pure delight and exultation which light up the eyes of the true soldier when there is serious fighting to be done.

"La, man," he said gaily, "there was no cause to worry. Pierre is safe, remember that! As for me," he added with that wonderful insouciance which caused him to risk his life a hundred times a day with a shrug of his broad shoulders and a smile upon his lips; "as for me, I'll look after myself, never fear."

He paused awhile, then added gravely: "So long as you are safe, my good Lenegre, and petite maman, and Rosette."

Whereupon the old man was silent, petite maman murmured a short prayer, and Rosette began to cry. The hero of a thousand gallant rescues had received his answer.

"You, too, are on the black list, Pere Lenegre?" he asked quietly.

The old man nodded.

"How do you know?" queried the Englishman.

"Through Jean Baptiste, milor."

"Still that demmed concierge," muttered Sir Percy.

"He frightened petite maman with it all this morning, saying that he knew my name was down on the Sectional Committee's list as a 'suspect.' That's when he let fall a word or two about you, milor. He said it is known that Pierre has escaped from justice, and that you helped him to it.

"I am sure that we shall get a domiciliary visit presently," continued Pere Lenegre, after a slight pause. "The gendarmes have not yet been, but I fancy that already this morning early I saw one or two of the Committee's spies hanging about the house, and when I went to the workshop I was followed all the time."

The Englishman looked grave: "And tell me," he said, "have you got anything in this place that may prove compromising to any of you?"

"No, milor. But, as Jean Baptiste said, the Sectional Committee know about Pierre. It is because of my son that I am suspect."

The old man spoke quite quietly, very simply, like a philosopher who has long ago learned to put behind him the fear of death. Nor did petite maman cry or lament. Her thoughts were for the brave milor who had saved her boy; but her fears for her old man left her dry-eyed and dumb with grief.

There was silence in the little room for one moment while the angel of sorrow and anguish hovered round these faithful and brave souls, then the Englishman's cheery voice, so full of spirit and merriment, rang out once more—he had risen to his full, towering height, and now placed a kindly hand on the old man's shoulder:

"It seems to me, my good Lenegre," he said, "that you and I haven't many moments to spare if we mean to cheat those devils by saving your neck. Now, petite maman," he added, turning to the old woman, "are you going to be brave?"

"I will do anything, milor," she replied quietly, "to help my old man."

"Well, then," said Sir Percy Blakeney in that optimistic, light-hearted yet supremely authoritative tone of which he held the secret, "you and Rosette remain here and wait for the gendarmes. When they come, say nothing; behave with absolute meekness, and let them search your place from end to end. If they ask you about your husband say that you believe him to be at his workshop. Is that clear?"

"Quite clear, milor," replied petite maman.

"And you, Pere Lenegre," continued the Englishman, speaking now with slow and careful deliberation, "listen very attentively to the instructions I am going to give you, for on your implicit obedience to them depends not only your own life but that of these two dear women. Go at once, now, to the Rue Ste. Anne, round the corner, the second house on your right, which is numbered thirty-seven. The porte cochere stands open, go boldly through, past the concierge's box, and up the stairs to apartment number twelve, second floor. Here is the key of the apartment," he added, producing one from his coat pocket and handing it over to the old man. "The rooms are nominally occupied by a certain Maitre Turandot, maker of violins, and not even the concierge of the place knows that the hunchbacked and snuffy violin-maker and the meddlesome Scarlet Pimpernel, whom the Committee of Public Safety would so love to lay by the heels, are one and the same person. The apartment, then, is mine; one of the many which I occupy in Paris at different times," he went on. "Let yourself in quietly with this key, walk straight across the first room to a wardrobe, which you will see in front of you. Open it. It is hung full of shabby clothes; put these aside, and you will notice that the panels at the back do not fit very closely, as if the wardrobe was old or had been badly put together. Insert your fingers in the tiny aperture between the two middle panels. These slide back easily: there is a recess immediately behind them. Get in there; pull the doors of the wardrobe together first, then slide the back panels into their place. You will be perfectly safe there, as the house is not under suspicion at present, and even if the revolutionary guard, under some meddle-some sergeant or other, chooses to pay it a surprise visit, your hiding-place will be perfectly secure. Now is all that quite understood?"

"Absolutely, milor," replied Lenegre, even as he made ready to obey Sir Percy's orders, "but what about you? You cannot get out of this house, milor," he urged; "it is watched, I tell you."

"La!" broke in Blakeney, in his light-hearted way, "and do you think I didn't know that? I had to come and tell you about Pierre, and now I must give those worthy gendarmes the slip somehow. I have my rooms downstairs on the ground floor, as you know, and I must make certain arrangements so that we can all get out of Paris comfortably this evening. The demmed place is no longer safe either for you, my good Lenegre, or for petite maman and Rosette. But wherever I may be, meanwhile, don't worry about me. As soon as the gendarmes have been and gone, I'll go over to the Rue Ste. Anne and let you know what arrangements I've been able to make. So do as I tell you now, and in Heaven's name let me look after myself."

Whereupon, with scant ceremony, he hustled the old man out of the room.

Pere Lenegre had contrived to kiss petite maman and Rosette before he went. It was touching to see the perfect confidence with which these simple-hearted folk obeyed the commands of milor. Had he not saved Pierre in his wonderful, brave, resourceful way? Of a truth he would know how to save Pere Lenegre also. But, nevertheless, anguish gripped the women's hearts; anguish doubly keen since the saviour of Pierre was also in danger now.

When Pere Lenegre's shuffling footsteps had died away along the flagged corridor, the stranger once more turned to the two women.

"And now, petite maman," he said cheerily, as he kissed the old woman on both her furrowed cheeks, "keep up a good heart, and say your prayers with Rosette. Your old man and I will both have need of them."

He did not wait to say good-bye, and anon it was his firm footstep that echoed down the corridor. He went off singing a song, at the top of his voice, for the whole house to hear, and for that traitor, Jean Baptiste, to come rushing out of his room marvelling at the impudence of the man, and cursing the Committee of Public Safety who were so slow in sending the soldiers of the Republic to lay this impertinent Englishman by the heels.

II.

A quarter of an hour later half dozen men of the Republican Guard, with corporal and sergeant in command, were in the small apartment on the fifth floor of the tenement house in the Rue Jolivet. They had demanded an entry in the name of the Republic, had roughly hustled petite maman and Rosette, questioned them to Lenegre's whereabouts, and not satisfied with the reply which they received, had turned the tidy little home topsy-turvy, ransacked every cupboard, dislocated every bed, table or sofa which might presumably have afforded a hiding place for a man.

Satisfied now that the "suspect" whom they were searching for was not on the premises, the sergeant stationed four of his men with the corporal outside the door, and two within, and himself sitting down in the centre of the room ordered the two women to stand before him and to answer his questions clearly on pain of being dragged away forthwith to the St. Lazare house of detention.

Petite maman smoothed out her apron, crossed her arms before her, and looked the sergeant quite straight in the face. Rosette's eyes were full of tears, but she showed no signs of fear either, although her shoulder—where one of the gendarmes had seized it so roughly—was terribly painful.

"Your husband, citizeness," asked the sergeant peremptorily, "where is he?"

"I am not sure, citizen," replied petite maman. "At this hour he is generally at the government works in the Quai des Messageries."

"He is not there now," asserted the sergeant. "We have knowledge that he did not go back to his work since dinner-time."

Petite maman was silent.

"Answer," ordered the sergeant.

"I cannot tell you more, citizen sergeant," she said firmly. "I do not know."

"You do yourself no good, woman, by this obstinacy," he continued roughly. "My belief is that your husband is inside this house, hidden away somewhere. If necessary I can get orders to have every apartment searched until he is found: but in that case it will go much harder with you and with your daughter, and much harder too with your husband than if he gave us no trouble and followed us quietly."

But with sublime confidence in the man who had saved Pierre and who had given her explicit orders as to what she should do, petite maman, backed by Rosette, reiterated quietly:

"I cannot tell you more, citizen sergeant, I do not know."

"And what about the Englishman?" queried the sergeant more roughly, "the man they call the Scarlet Pimpernel, what do you know of him?"

"Nothing, citizen," replied petite maman, "what should we poor folk know of an English milor?"

"You know at any rate this much, citizeness, that the English milor helped your son Pierre to escape from justice."

"If that is so," said petite maman quietly, "it cannot be wrong for a mother to pray to God to bless her son's preserver."

"It behooves every good citizen," retorted the sergeant firmly, "to denounce all traitors to the Republic."

"But since I know nothing about the Englishman, citizen sergeant—?"

And petite maman shrugged her thin shoulders as if the matter had ceased to interest her.

"Think again, citizeness," admonished the sergeant, "it is your husband's neck as well as your daughter's and your own that you are risking by so much obstinacy."

He waited a moment or two as if willing to give the old woman time to speak: then, when he saw that she kept her thin, quivering lips resolutely glued together he called his corporal to him.

"Go to the citizen Commissary of the Section," he commanded, "and ask for a general order to search every apartment in No. 24 Rue Jolivet. Leave two of our men posted on the first and third landings of this house and leave two outside this door. Be as quick as you can. You can be back here with the order in half an hour, or perhaps the committee will send me an extra squad; tell the citizen Commissary that this is a big house, with many corridors. You can go."

The corporal saluted and went.

Petite maman and Rosette the while were still standing quietly in the middle of the room, their arms folded underneath their aprons, their wide-open, anxious eyes fixed into space. Rosette's tears were falling slowly, one by one down her cheeks, but petite maman was dry-eyed. She was thinking, and thinking as she had never had occasion to think before.

She was thinking of the brave and gallant Englishman who had saved Pierre's life only yesterday. The sergeant, who sat there before her, had asked for orders from the citizen Commissary to search this big house from attic to cellar. That is what made petite maman think and think.

The brave Englishman was in this house at the present moment: the house would be searched from attic to cellar and he would be found, taken, and brought to the guillotine.

The man who yesterday had risked his life to save her boy was in imminent and deadly danger, and she—petite maman—could do nothing to save him.

Every moment now she thought to hear milor's firm tread resounding on stairs or corridor, every moment she thought to hear snatches of an English song, sung by a fresh and powerful voice, never after to-day to be heard in gaiety again.

The old clock upon the shelf ticked away these seconds and minutes while petite maman thought and thought, while men set traps to catch a fellow-being in a deathly snare, and human carnivorous beasts lay lurking for their prey.

III.

Another quarter of an hour went by. Petite maman and Rosette had hardly moved. The shadows of evening were creeping into the narrow room, blurring the outlines of the pieces of furniture and wrapping all the corners in gloom.

The sergeant had ordered Rosette to bring in a lamp. This she had done, placing it upon the table so that the feeble light glinted upon the belt and buckles of the sergeant and upon the tricolour cockade which was pinned to his hat. Petite maman had thought and thought until she could think no more.

Anon there was much commotion on the stairs; heavy footsteps were heard ascending from below, then crossing the corridors on the various landings. The silence which reigned otherwise in the house, and which had fallen as usual on the squalid little street, void of traffic at this hour, caused those footsteps to echo with ominous power.

Petite maman felt her heart beating so vigorously that she could hardly breathe. She pressed her wrinkled hands tightly against her bosom.

There were the quick words of command, alas! so familiar in France just now, the cruel, peremptory words that invariably preceded an arrest, preliminaries to the dragging of some wretched—often wholly harmless—creature before a tribunal that knew neither pardon nor mercy.

The sergeant, who had become drowsy in the close atmosphere of the tiny room, roused himself at the sound and jumped to his feet. The door was thrown open by the men stationed outside even before the authoritative words, "Open! in the name of the Republic!" had echoed along the narrow corridor.

The sergeant stood at attention and quickly lifted his hand to his forehead in salute. A fresh squad of some half-dozen men of the Republican Guard stood in the doorway; they were under the command of an officer of high rank, a rough, uncouth, almost bestial-looking creature, with lank hair worn the fashionable length under his greasy chapeau-bras, and unkempt beard round an ill-washed and bloated face. But he wore the tricolour sash and badge which proclaimed him one of the military members of the Sectional Committee of Public Safety, and the sergeant, who had been so overbearing with the women just now, had assumed a very humble and even obsequious manner.

"You sent for a general order to the sectional Committee," said the new-comer, turning abruptly to the sergeant after he had cast a quick, searching glance round the room, hardly condescending to look on petite maman and Rosette, whose very souls were now gazing out of their anguish-filled eyes.

"I did, citizen commandant," replied the sergeant.

"I am not a commandant," said the other curtly. "My name is Rouget, member of the Convention and of the Committee of Public Safety. The sectional Committee to whom you sent for a general order of search thought that you had blundered somehow, so they sent me to put things right."

"I am not aware that I committed any blunder, citizen," stammered the sergeant dolefully. "I could not take the responsibility of making a domiciliary search all through the house. So I begged for fuller orders."

"And wasted the Committee's time and mine by such nonsense," retorted Rouget harshly. "Every citizen of the Republic worthy of the name should know how to act on his own initiative when the safety of the nation demands it."

"I did not know—I did not dare—" murmured the sergeant, obviously cowed by this reproof, which had been delivered in the rough, overbearing tones peculiar to these men who, one and all, had risen from the gutter to places of importance and responsibility in the newly-modelled State.

"Silence!" commanded the other peremptorily. "Don't waste any more of my time with your lame excuses. You have failed in zeal and initiative. That's enough. What else have you done? Have you got the man Lenegre?"

"No, citizen. He is not in hiding here, and his wife and daughter will not give us any information about him."

"That is their look-out," retorted Rouget with a harsh laugh. "If they give up Lenegre of their own free will the law will deal leniently with them, and even perhaps with him.

But if we have to search the house for him, then it means the guillotine for the lot of them."

He had spoken these callous words without even looking on the two unfortunate women; nor did he ask them any further questions just then, but continued speaking to the sergeant:

"And what about the Englishman? The sectional Committee sent down some spies this morning to be on the look-out for him on or about this house. Have you got him?"

"Not yet, citizen. But—"

"Ah ca, citizen sergeant," broke in the other brusquely, "meseems that your zeal has been even more at fault than I had supposed. Have you done anything at all, then, in the matter of Lenegre or the Englishman?"

"I have told you, citizen," retorted the sergeant sullenly, "that I believe Lenegre to be still in this house. At any rate, he had not gone out of it an hour ago—that's all I know. And I wanted to search the whole of this house, as I am sure we should have found him in one of the other apartments. These people are all friends together, and will always help each other to evade justice. But the Englishman was no concern of mine. The spies of the Committee were ordered to watch for him, and when they reported to me I was to proceed with the arrest. I was not set to do any of the spying work. I am a soldier, and obey my orders when I get them."

"Very well, then, you'd better obey them now, citizen sergeant," was Rouget's dry comment on the other man's surly explanation, "for you seem to have properly blundered from first to last, and will be hard put to it to redeem your character. The Republic, remember, has no use for fools."

The sergeant, after this covert threat, thought it best, apparently, to keep his tongue, whilst Rouget continued, in the same aggressive, peremptory tone:

"Get on with your domiciliary visits at once. Take your own men with you, and leave me the others. Begin on this floor, and leave your sentry at the front door outside. Now let me see your zeal atoning for your past slackness. Right turn! Quick march!"

Then it was that petite maman spoke out. She had thought and thought, and now she knew what she ought to do; she knew that that cruel, inhuman wretch would presently begin his tramp up and down corridors and stairs, demanding admittance at every door, entering every apartment. She knew that the man who had saved her Pierre's life was in hiding somewhere in the house—that he would be found and dragged to the guillotine, for she knew that the whole governing body of this abominable Revolution was determined not to allow that hated Englishman to escape again.

She was old and feeble, small and thin—that's why everyone called her petite maman —but once she knew what she ought to do, then her spirit overpowered the weakness of her wizened body.

Now she knew, and even while that arrogant member of an execrated murdering Committee was giving final instructions to the sergeant, petite maman said, in a calm, piping voice:

"No need, citizen sergeant, to go and disturb all my friends and neighbours. I'll tell you where my husband is."

In a moment Rouget had swung round on his heel, a hideous gleam of satisfaction spread over his grimy face, and he said, with an ugly sneer:

"So! you have thought better of it, have you? Well, out with it! You'd better be quick about it if you want to do yourselves any good."

"I have my daughter to think of," said petite maman in a feeble, querulous way, "and I won't have all my neighbours in this house made unhappy because of me. They have all been kind neighbours. Will you promise not to molest them and to clear the house of soldiers if I tell you where Lenegre is?"

"The Republic makes no promises," replied Rouget gruffly. "Her citizens must do their duty without hope of a reward. If they fail in it, they are punished. But privately I will tell you, woman, that if you save us the troublesome and probably unprofitable task of searching this rabbit-warren through and through, it shall go very leniently with you and with your daughter, and perhaps—I won't promise, remember—perhaps with your husband also."

"Very good, citizen," said petite maman calmly. "I am ready."

"Ready for what?" he demanded.

"To take you to where my husband is in hiding."

"Oho! He is not in the house, then?"

"No."

"Where is he, then?"

"In the Rue Ste. Anne. I will take you there."

Rouget cast a quick, suspicious glance on the old woman, and exchanged one of understanding with the sergeant.

"Very well," he said after a slight pause. "But your daughter must come along too. Sergeant," he added, "I'll take three of your men with me; I have half a dozen, but it's better to be on the safe side. Post your fellows round the outer door, and on my way to the Rue Ste. Anne I will leave word at the gendarmerie that a small reinforcement be sent on to you at once. These can be here in five minutes; until then you are quite safe."

Then he added under his breath, so that the women should not hear: "The Englishman may still be in the house. In which case, hearing us depart, he may think us all gone and try to give us the slip. You'll know what to do?" he queried significantly.

"Of course, citizen," replied the sergeant.

"Now, then, citizeness—hurry up."

Once more there was tramping of heavy feet on stone stairs and corridors. A squad of soldiers of the Republican Guard, with two women in their midst, and followed by a member of the Committee of Public Safety, a sergeant, corporal and two or three more men, excited much anxious curiosity as they descended the steep flights of steps from the fifth floor.

Pale, frightened faces peeped shyly through the doorways at sound of the noisy tramp from above, but quickly disappeared again at sight of the grimy scarlet facings and tricolour cockades.

The sergeant and three soldiers remained stationed at the foot of the stairs inside the house. Then citizen Rouget roughly gave the order to proceed. It seemed strange that it should require close on a dozen men to guard two women and to apprehend one old man, but as the member of the Committee of Public Safety whispered to the sergeant before he finally went out of the house: "The whole thing may be a trap, and one can't be too careful. The Englishman is said to be very powerful; I'll get the gendarmerie to send you another half-dozen men, and mind you guard the house until my return."

IV.

Five minutes later the soldiers, directed by petite maman, had reached No. 37 Rue Ste. Anne. The big outside door stood wide open, and the whole party turned immediately into the house.

The concierge, terrified and obsequious, rushed—trembling—out of his box.

"What was the pleasure of the citizen soldiers?" he asked.

"Tell him, citizeness," commanded Rouget curtly.

"We are going to apartment No. 12 on the second floor," said petite maman to the concierge.

"Have you a key of the apartment?" queried Rouget.

"No, citizen," stammered the concierge, "but—"

"Well, what is it?" queried the other peremptorily.

"Papa Turandot is a poor, harmless maker of volins," said the concierge. "I know him well, though he is not often at home. He lives with a daughter somewhere Passy way, and only uses this place as a workshop. I am sure he is no traitor."

"We'll soon see about that," remarked Rouget dryly.

Petite maman held her shawl tightly crossed over her bosom: her hands felt clammy and cold as ice. She was looking straight out before her, quite dry-eyed and calm, and never once glanced on Rosette, who was not allowed to come anywhere near her mother.

As there was no duplicate key to apartment No. 12, citizen Rouget ordered his men to break in the door. It did not take very long: the house was old and ramshackle and the doors rickety. The next moment the party stood in the room which a while ago the Englishman had so accurately described to pere Lenegre in petite maman's hearing.

There was the wardrobe. Petite maman, closely surrounded by the soldiers, went boldly up to it; she opened it just as milor had directed, and pushed aside the row of shabby clothes that hung there. Then she pointed to the panels that did not fit quite tightly together at the back. Petite maman passed her tongue over her dry lips before she spoke.

"There's a recess behind those panels," she said at last. "They slide back quite easily. My old man is there."

"And God bless you for a brave, loyal soul," came in merry, ringing accent from the other end of the room. "And God save the Scarlet Pimpernel!"

These last words, spoken in English, completed the blank amazement which literally paralysed the only three genuine Republican soldiers there—those, namely, whom Rouget had borrowed from the sergeant. As for the others, they knew what to do. In less than a minute they had overpowered and gagged the three bewildered soldiers.

Rosette had screamed, terror-stricken, from sheer astonishment, but petite maman stood quite still, her pale, tear-dimmed eyes fixed upon the man whose gay "God bless you!" had so suddenly turned her despair into hope.

How was it that in the hideous, unkempt and grimy Rouget she had not at once recognised the handsome and gallant milor who had saved her Pierre's life? Well, of a truth he had been unrecognizable, but now that he tore the ugly wig and beard from his face, stretched out his fine figure to its full height, and presently turned his lazy, merry eyes on her, she could have screamed for very joy.

The next moment he had her by the shoulders and had imprinted two sounding kisses upon her cheeks.

"Now, petite maman," he said gaily, "let us liberate the old man."

Pere Lenegre, from his hiding-place, had heard all that had been going on in the room for the last few moments. True, he had known exactly what to expect, for no sooner had he taken possession of the recess behind the wardrobe than milor also entered the apartment and then and there told him of his plans not only for pere's own safety, but for that of petite maman and Rosette who would be in grave danger if the old man followed in the wake of Pierre.

Milor told him in his usual light-hearted way that he had given the Committee's spies the slip.

"I do that very easily, you know," he explained. "I just slip into my rooms in the Rue Jolivet, change myself into a snuffy and hunchback violin-maker, and walk out of the house under the noses of the spies. In the nearest wine-shop my English friends, in various disguises, are all ready to my hand: half a dozen of them are never far from where I am in case they may be wanted."

These half-dozen brave Englishmen soon arrived one by one: one looked like a coal-heaver, another like a seedy musician, a third like a coach-driver. But they all walked boldly into the house and were soon all congregated in apartment No. 12. Here fresh disguises were assumed, and soon a squad of Republican Guards looked as like the real thing as possible.

Pere Lenegre admitted himself that though he actually saw milor transforming himself into citizen Rouget, he could hardly believe his eyes, so complete was the change.

"I am deeply grieved to have frightened and upset you so, petite maman," now concluded milor kindly, "but I saw no other way of getting you and Rosette out of the house and leaving that stupid sergeant and some of his men behind. I did not want to arouse in him even the faintest breath of suspicion, and of course if he had asked me for the written orders which he was actually waiting for, or if his corporal had returned sooner than I anticipated, there might have been trouble. But even then," he added with his usual careless insouciance, "I should have thought of some way of baffling those brutes."

"And now," he concluded more authoritatively, "it is a case of getting out of Paris before the gates close. Pere Lenegre, take your wife and daughter with you and walk boldly out of this house. The sergeant and his men have not vacated their post in the Rue Jolivet, and no one else can molest you. Go straight to the Porte de Neuilly, and on the other side wait quietly in the little cafe at the corner of the Avenue until I come. Your old passes for the barriers still hold good; you were only placed on the 'suspect' list this morning, and there has not been a hue and cry yet about you. In any case some of us will be close by to help you if needs be."

"But you, milor," stammered pere Lenegre, "and your friends—?"

"La, man," retorted Blakeney lightly, "have I not told you before never to worry about me and my friends? We have more ways than one of giving the slip to this demmed government of yours. All you've got to think of is your wife and your daughter. I am afraid that petite maman cannot take more with her than she has on, but we'll do all we can for her comfort until we have you all in perfect safety—in England—with Pierre."

Neither pere Lenegre, nor petite maman, nor Rosette could speak just then, for tears were choking them, but anon when milor stood nearer, petite maman knelt down, and, imprisoning his slender hand in her brown, wrinkled ones, she kissed it reverently.

He laughed and chided her for this.

"'Tis I should kneel to you in gratitude, petite maman," he said earnestly, "you were ready to sacrifice your old man for me."

"You have saved Pierre, milor," said the mother simply.

A minute later pere Lenegre and the two women were ready to go. Already milor and his gallant English friends were busy once more transforming themselves into grimy workmen or seedy middle-class professionals.

As soon as the door of apartment No. 12 finally closed behind the three good folk, my lord Tony asked of his chief:

"What about these three wretched soldiers, Blakeney?"

"Oh! they'll be all right for twenty-four hours. They can't starve till then, and by that time the concierge will have realised that there's something wrong with the door of No. 12 and will come in to investigate the matter. Are they securely bound, though?"

"And gagged! Rather!" ejaculated one of the others. "Odds life, Blakeney!" he added enthusiastically, "that was a fine bit of work!"

CHAPTER VI. HOW JEAN PIERRE MET THE SCARLET PIMPERNEL

As told by Himself

I.

Ah, monsieur! the pity of it, the pity! Surely there are sins which le bon Dieu Himself will condone. And if not—well, I had to risk His displeasure anyhow. Could I see them both starve, monsieur? I ask you! and M. le Vicomte had become so thin, so thin, his tiny, delicate bones were almost through his skin. And Mme. la Marquise! an angel, monsieur! Why, in the happy olden days, before all these traitors and assassins ruled in France, M. and Mme. la Marquise lived only for the child, and then to see him dying—yes, dying, there was no shutting one's eyes to that awful fact—M. le Vicomte de Mortain was dying of starvation and of disease.

There we were all herded together in a couple of attics—one of which little more than a cupboard—at the top of a dilapidated half-ruined house in the Rue des Pipots—Mme. la Marquise, M. le Vicomte and I—just think of that, monsieur! M. le Marquis had his chateau, as no doubt you know, on the outskirts of Lyons. A loyal high-born gentleman; was it likely, I ask you, that he would submit passively to the rule of those execrable revolutionaries who had murdered their King, outraged their Queen and Royal family, and, God help them! had already perpetrated every crime and every abomination for which of a truth there could be no pardon either on earth or in Heaven? He joined that plucky but, alas! small and ill-equipped army of royalists who, unable to save their King, were at least determined to avenge him.

Well, you know well enough what happened. The counter-revolution failed; the revolutionary army brought Lyons down to her knees after a siege of two months. She was then marked down as a rebel city, and after the abominable decree of October 9th had deprived her of her very name, and Couthon had exacted bloody reprisals from the entire population for its loyalty to the King, the infamous Laporte was sent down in order finally to stamp out the lingering remnants of the rebellion. By that time, monsieur, half the city had been burned down, and one-tenth and more of the inhabitants—men, women, and children—had been massacred in cold blood, whilst most of the others had fled in terror from the appalling scene of ruin and desolation. Laporte completed the execrable work so ably begun by Couthon. He was a very celebrated and skillful doctor at the Faculty of Medicine, now turned into a human hyena in the name of Liberty and Fraternity.

M. le Marquis contrived to escape with the scattered remnant of the Royalist army into Switzerland. But Mme la Marquise throughout all these strenuous times had stuck to her post at the chateau like the valiant creature that she was. When Couthon entered Lyons at the head of the revolutionary army, the whole of her household fled, and I was left alone to look after her and M. le Vicomte.

Then one day when I had gone into Lyons for provisions, I suddenly chanced to hear outside an eating-house that which nearly froze the marrow in my old bones. A captain belonging to the Revolutionary Guard was transmitting to his sergeant certain orders, which he had apparently just received.

The orders were to make a perquisition at ten o'clock this same evening in the chateau of Mortaine as the Marquis was supposed to be in hiding there, and in any event to arrest every man, woman, and child who was found within its walls.

"Citizen Laporte," the captain concluded, "knows for a certainty that the ci-devant Marquise and her brat are still there, even if the Marquis has fled like the traitor that he is. Those cursed English spies who call themselves the League of the Scarlet Pimpernel have been very active in Lyons of late, and citizen Laporte is afraid that they might cheat the guillotine of the carcase of those aristos, as they have already succeeded in doing in the case of a large number of traitors."

I did not, of course, wait to hear any more of that abominable talk. I sped home as fast as my old legs would carry me. That self-same evening, as soon as it was dark, Mme. la Marquise, carrying M. le Vicomte in her arms and I carrying a pack with a few necessaries on my back, left the ancestral home of the Mortaines never to return to it again: for within an hour of our flight a detachment of the revolutionary army made a descent upon the chateau; they ransacked it from attic to cellar, and finding nothing there to satisfy their lust of hate, they burned the stately mansion down to the ground.

We were obliged to take refuge in Lyons, at any rate for a time. Great as was the danger inside the city, it was infinitely greater on the high roads, unless we could arrange for some vehicle to take us a considerable part of the way to the frontier, and above all for some sort of passports—forged or otherwise—to enable us to pass the various toll-gates on the road, where vigilance was very strict. So we wandered through the ruined and deserted streets of the city in search of shelter, but found every charred and derelict house full of miserable tramps and destitutes like ourselves. Half dead with fatigue, Mme. la Marquise was at last obliged to take refuge in one of these houses which was situated in the Rue des Pipots. Every room was full to overflowing with a miserable wreckage of humanity thrown hither by the tide of anarchy and of bloodshed. But at the top of the house we found an attic. It was empty save for a couple of chairs, a table and a broken-down bedstead on which were a ragged mattress and pillow.

Here, monsieur, we spent over three weeks, at the end of which time M. le Vicomte fell ill, and then there followed days, monsieur, through which I would not like my worst enemy to pass.

Mme. la Marquise had only been able to carry away in her flight what ready money she happened to have in the house at the time. Securities, property, money belonging to aristocrats had been ruthlessly confiscated by the revolutionary government in Lyons. Our scanty resources rapidly became exhausted, and what was left had to be kept for milk and delicacies for M. le Vicomte. I tramped through the streets in search of a doctor, but most of them had been arrested on some paltry charge or other of rebellion, whilst others had fled from the city. There was only that infamous Laporte—a vastly clever doctor, I knew—but as soon take a lamb to a hungry lion as the Vicomte de Mortaine to that bloodthirsty cut-throat.

Then one day our last franc went and we had nothing left. Mme. la Marquise had not touched food for two days. I had stood at the corner of the street, begging all the day until I was driven off by the gendarmes. I had only obtained three sous from the passers-by. I bought some milk and took it home for M. le Vicomte. The following morning when I entered the larger attic I found that Mme. la Marquise had fainted from inanition.

I spent the whole of the day begging in the streets and dodging the guard, and even so I only collected four sous. I could have got more perhaps, only that at about midday the smell of food from an eating-house turned me sick and faint, and when I regained consciousness I found myself huddled up under a doorway and evening gathering in fast around me. If Mme. la Marquise could go two days without food I ought to go four. I struggled to my feet; fortunately I had retained possession of my four sous, else of a truth I would not have had the courage to go back to the miserable attic which was the only home I knew.

I was wending my way along as fast as I could—for I knew that Mme. la Marquise would be getting terribly anxious—when, just as I turned into the Rue Blanche, I spied two gentlemen—obviously strangers, for they were dressed with a luxury and care with which we had long ceased to be familiar in Lyons—walking rapidly towards me. A moment or two later they came to a halt, not far from where I was standing, and I heard the taller one of the two say to the other in English—a language with which I am vaguely conversant: "All right again this time, what, Tony?"

Both laughed merrily like a couple of schoolboys playing truant, and then they disappeared under the doorway of a dilapidated house, whilst I was left wondering how two such elegant gentlemen dared be abroad in Lyons these days, seeing that every man, woman and child who was dressed in anything but threadbare clothes was sure to be insulted in the streets for an aristocrat, and as often as not summarily arrested as a traitor.

However, I had other things to think about, and had already dismissed the little incident from my mind, when at the bottom of the Rue Blanche I came upon a knot of gaffers, men and women, who were talking and gesticulating very excitedly outside the door of a cook-shop. At first I did not take much notice of what was said: my eyes were glued to the front of the shop, on which were displayed sundry delicacies of the kind which makes a wretched, starved beggar's mouth water as he goes by; a roast capon especially attracted my attention, together with a bottle of red wine; these looked just the sort of luscious food which Mme. la Marquise would relish.

Well, sir, the law of God says: "Thou shalt not covet!" and no doubt that I committed a grievous sin when my hungry eyes fastened upon that roast capon and that bottle of Burgundy. We also know the stories of Judas Iscariot and of Jacob's children who sold their own brother Joseph into slavery—such a crime, monsieur, I took upon my conscience then; for just as the vision of Mme. la Marquise eating that roast capon and drinking that Burgundy rose before my eyes, my ears caught some fragments of the excited conversation which was going on all around me.

"He went this way!" someone said.

"No; that!" protested another.

"There's no sign of him now, anyway."

The owner of the shop was standing on his own doorstep, his legs wide apart, one arm on his wide hip, the other still brandishing the knife wherewith he had been carving for his customers.

"He can't have gone far," he said, as he smacked his thick lips.

"The impudent rascal, flaunting such fine clothes—like the aristo that he is."

"Bah! these cursed English! They are aristos all of them! And this one with his followers is no better than a spy!"

"Paid by that damned English Government to murder all our patriots and to rob the guillotine of her just dues."

"They say he had a hand in the escape of the ci-devant Duc de Sermeuse and all his brats from the very tumbril which was taking them to execution."

A cry of loathing and execration followed this statement. There was vigorous shaking of clenched fists and then a groan of baffled rage.

"We almost had him this time. If it had not been for these confounded, ill-lighted streets—"

"I would give something," concluded the shopkeeper, "if we could lay him by the heels."

"What would you give, citizen Dompierre?" queried a woman in the crowd, with a ribald laugh, "one of your roast capons?"

"Aye, little mother," he replied jovially, "and a bottle of my best Burgundy to boot, to drink confusion to that meddlesome Englishman and his crowd and a speedy promenade up the steps of the guillotine."

Monsieur, I assure you that at that moment my heart absolutely stood still. The tempter stood at my elbow and whispered, and I deliberately smothered the call of my conscience. I did what Joseph's brethren did, what brought Judas Iscariot to hopeless remorse. There was no doubt that the hue and cry was after the two elegantly dressed gentlemen whom I had seen enter the dilapidated house in the Rue Blanche. For a second or two I closed my eyes and deliberately conjured up the vision of Mme. la Marquise fainting for lack of food, and of M. le Vicomte dying for want of sustenance; then I worked my way to the door of the shop and accosted the burly proprietor with as much boldness as I could muster.

"The two Englishmen passed by me at the top of the Rue Blanche," I said to him. "They went into a house ... I can show you which it is—"

In a moment I was surrounded by a screeching, gesticulating crowd. I told my story as best I could; there was no turning back now from the path of cowardice and of crime. I saw that brute Dompierre pick up the largest roast capon from the front of his shop, together with a bottle of that wine which I had coveted; then he thrust both these treasures into my trembling hands and said:

"En avant!"

And we all started to run up the street, shouting: "Death to the English spies!" I was the hero of the expedition. Dompierre and another man carried me, for I was too weak to go as fast as they wished. I was hugging the capon and the bottle of wine to my heart; I had need to do that, so as to still the insistent call of my conscience, for I felt a coward—a mean, treacherous, abominable coward!

When we reached the house and I pointed it out to Dompierre, the crowd behind us gave a cry of triumph. In the topmost storey a window was thrown open, two heads appeared silhouetted against the light within, and the cry of triumph below was answered by a merry, prolonged laugh from above.

I was too dazed to realise very clearly what happened after that. Dompierre, I know, kicked open the door of the house, and the crowd rushed in, in his wake. I managed to keep my feet and to work my way gradually out of the crowd. I must have gone on mechanically, almost unconsciously, for the next thing that I remember with any distinctness was that I found myself once more speeding down the Rue Blanche, with all the yelling and shouting some little way behind me.

With blind instinct, too, I had clung to the capon and the wine, the price of my infamy. I was terribly weak and felt sick and faint, but I struggled on for a while, until my knees refused me service and I came down on my two hands, whilst the capon rolled away into the gutter, and the bottle of Burgundy fell with a crash against the pavement, scattering its precious contents in every direction.

There I lay, wretched, despairing, hardly able to move, when suddenly I heard rapid and firm footsteps immediately behind me, and the next moment two firm hands had me under the arms, and I heard a voice saying:

"Steady, old friend. Can you get up? There! Is that better?"

The same firm hands raised me to my feet. At first I was too dazed to see anything, but after a moment or two I was able to look around me, and, by the light of a street lanthorn immediately overhead, I recognised the tall, elegantly dressed Englishman and his friend, whom I had just betrayed to the fury of Dompierre and a savage mob.

I thought that I was dreaming, and I suppose that my eyes betrayed the horror which I felt, for the stranger looked at me scrutinisingly for a moment or two, then he gave the quaintest laugh I had ever heard in all my life, and said something to his friend in English, which this time I failed to understand.

Then he turned to me:

"By my faith," he said in perfect French—so that I began to doubt if he was an English spy after all—"I verily believe that you are the clever rogue, eh? who obtained a roast capon and a bottle of wine from that fool Dompierre. He and his boon companions are venting their wrath on you, old compeer; they are calling you liar and traitor and cheat, in the intervals of wrecking what is left of the house, out of which my friend and I have long since escaped by climbing up the neighbouring gutter-pipes and scrambling over the adjoining roofs."

Monsieur, will you believe me when I say that he was actually saying all this in order to comfort me? I could have sworn to that because of the wonderful kindliness which shone out of his eyes, even through the good-humoured mockery wherewith he obviously regarded me. Do you know what I did then, monsieur? I just fell on my knees and loudly thanked God that he was safe; at which both he and his friend once again began to laugh, for all the world like two schoolboys who had escaped a whipping, rather than two men who were still threatened with death.

"Then it WAS you!" said the taller stranger, who was still laughing so heartily that he had to wipe his eyes with his exquisite lace handkerchief.

"May God forgive me," I replied.

The next moment his arm was again round me. I clung to him as to a rock, for of a truth I had never felt a grasp so steady and withal so gentle and kindly, as was his around my shoulders. I tried to murmur words of thanks, but again that wretched feeling of sickness and faintness overcame me, and for a second or two it seemed to me as if I were slipping into another world. The stranger's voice came to my ear, as it were through cotton-wool.

"The man is starving," he said. "Shall we take him over to your lodgings, Tony? They are safer than mine. He may be able to walk in a minute or two, if not I can carry him."

My senses at this partly returned to me, and I was able to protest feebly:

"No, no! I must go back—I must—kind sirs," I murmured. "Mme. la

Marquise will be getting so anxious."

No sooner were these foolish words out of my mouth than I could have bitten my tongue out for having uttered them; and yet, somehow, it seemed as if it was the stranger's magnetic personality, his magic voice and kindly act towards me, who had so basely sold him to his enemies, which had drawn them out of me. He gave a low, prolonged whistle.

"Mme. la Marquise?" he queried, dropping his voice to a whisper.

Now to have uttered Mme. la Marquise de Mortaine's name here in Lyons, where every aristocrat was termed a traitor and sent without trial to the guillotine, was in itself an act of criminal folly, and yet—you may believe me, monsieur, or not—there was something within me just at that moment that literally compelled me to open my heart out to this stranger, whom I had so basely betrayed, and who requited my abominable crime with such gentleness and mercy. Before I fully realised what I was doing, monsieur, I had blurted out the whole history of Mme. la Marquise's flight and of M. le Vicomte's sickness to him. He drew me under the cover of an open doorway, and he and his friend listened to me without speaking a word until I had told them my pitiable tale to the end.

When I had finished he said quietly:

"Take me to see Mme. la Marquise, old friend. Who knows? perhaps I may be able to help."

Then he turned to his friend.

"Will you wait for me at my lodgings, Tony," he said, "and let Ffoulkes and Hastings know that I may wish to speak with them on my return?"

He spoke like one who had been accustomed all his life to give command, and I marvelled how his friend immediately obeyed him. Then when the latter had disappeared down the dark street, the stranger once more turned to me.

"Lean on my arm, good old friend," he said, "and we must try and walk as quickly as we can. The sooner we allay the anxieties of Mme. la Marquise the better."

I was still hugging the roast capon with one arm, with the other I clung to him as together we walked in the direction of the Rue des Pipots. On the way we halted at a respectable eating-house, where my protector gave me some money wherewith to buy a bottle of good wine and sundry provisions and delicacies which we carried home with us.

II.

Never shall I forget the look of horror which came in Mme. la Marquise's eyes when she saw me entering our miserable attic in the company of a stranger. The last of the little bit of tallow candle flickered in its socket. Madame threw her emaciated arms over her child, just like some poor hunted animal defending its young. I could almost hear the cry of terror which died down in her throat ere it reached her lips. But then, monsieur, to see the light of hope gradually illuminating her pale, wan face as the stranger took her hand and spoke to her—oh! so gently and so kindly—was a sight which filled my poor, half-broken heart with joy.

"The little invalid must be seen by a doctor at once," he said, "after that only can we think of your ultimate safety."

Mme. la Marquise, who herself was terribly weak and ill, burst out crying. "Would I not have taken him to a doctor ere now?" she murmured through her tears. "But there is no doctor in Lyons. Those who have not been arrested as traitors have fled from this stricken city. And my little Jose is dying for want of medical care."

"Your pardon, madame," he rejoined gently, "one of the ablest doctors in France is at present in Lyons——"

"That infamous Laporte," she broke in, horrified. "He would snatch my sick child from my arms and throw him to the guillotine."

"He would save your boy from disease," said the stranger earnestly, "his own professional pride or professional honour, whatever he might choose to call it, would compel him to do that. But the moment the doctor's work was done, that of the executioner would commence."

"You see, milor," moaned Madame in pitiable agony, "that there is no hope for us."

"Indeed there is," he replied. "We must get M. le Vicomte well first—after that we shall see."

"But you are not proposing to bring that infamous Laporte to my child's bedside!" she cried in horror.

"Would you have your child die here before your eyes," retorted the stranger, "as he undoubtedly will this night?"

This sounded horribly cruel, and the tone in which it was said was commanding. There was no denying its truth. M. le Vicomte was dying. I could see that. For a moment or two madame remained quite still, with her great eyes, circled with pain and sorrow, fixed upon the stranger. He returned her gaze steadily and kindly, and gradually that frozen look of horror in her pale face gave place to one of deep puzzlement, and through her bloodless lips there came the words, faintly murmured: "Who are you?"

He gave no direct reply, but from his little finger he detached a ring and held it out for her to see. I saw it too, for I was standing close by Mme. la Marquise, and the flickering light of the tallow candle fell full upon the ring. It was of gold, and upon it there was an exquisitely modelled, five-petalled little flower in vivid red enamel.

Madame la Marquise looked at the ring, then once again up into his face. He nodded assent, and my heart seemed even then to stop its beating as I gazed upon his face. Had we not—all of us—heard of the gallant Scarlet Pimpernel? And did I not know—far better than Mme. la Marquise herself—the full extent of his gallantry and his self-sacrifice? The hue and cry was after him. Human bloodhounds were even now on his track, and he spoke calmly of walking out again in the streets of Lyons and of affronting that infamous Laporte, who would find glory in sending him to death. I think he guessed what was passing in my mind, for he put a finger up to his lip and pointed significantly to M. le Vicomte.

But it was beautiful to see how completely Mme. la Marquise now trusted him. At his bidding she even ate a little of the food and drank some wine—and I was forced to do likewise. And even when anon he declared his intention of fetching Laporte immediately, she did not flinch. She kissed M. le Vicomte with passionate fervour, and then gave the stranger her solemn promise that the moment he returned she would take refuge in the next room and never move out of it until after Laporte had departed.

When he went I followed him to the top of the stairs. I was speechless with gratitude and also with fears for him. But he took my hand and said, with that same quaint, somewhat inane laugh which was so characteristic of him:

"Be of good cheer, old fellow! Those confounded murderers will not get me this time."

III.

Less than half an hour later, monsieur, citizen Laporte, one of the most skillful doctors in France and one of the most bloodthirsty tyrants this execrable Revolution has known, was sitting at the bedside of M. le Vicomte de Mortaine, using all the skill, all the knowledge he possessed in order to combat the dread disease of which the child was dying, ere he came to save him—as he cynically remarked in my hearing—for the guillotine.

I heard afterwards how it all came about.

Laporte, it seems, was in the habit of seeing patients in his own house every evening after he had settled all his business for the day. What a strange contradiction in the human heart, eh, monsieur? The tiger turned lamb for the space of one hour in every twenty-four—the butcher turned healer. How well the English milor had gauged the strange personality of that redoubtable man! Professional pride—interest in intricate cases—call it what you will—was the only redeeming feature in Laporte's abominable character. Everything else in him, every thought, every action was ignoble, cruel and vengeful.

Milor that night mingled with the crowd who waited on the human hyena to be cured of their hurts. It was a motley crowd that filled the dreaded pro-consul's ante-chamber—men, women and children—all of them too much preoccupied with their own troubles to bestow more than a cursory glance on the stranger who, wrapped in a dark mantle, quietly awaited his turn. One or two muttered curses were flung at the aristo, one or two spat in his direction to express hatred and contempt, then the door which gave on the inner chamber would be flung open—a number called—one patient would walk out, another walk in—and in the ever-recurring incident the stranger for the nonce was forgotten.

His turn came—his number being called—it was the last on the list, and the antechamber was now quite empty save for him. He walked into the presence of the proconsul. Claude Lemoine, who was on guard in the room at the time, told me that just for the space of two seconds the two men looked at one another. Then the stranger threw back his head and said quietly:

"There's a child dying of pleurisy, or worse, in an attic in the Rue des Pipots. There's not a doctor left in Lyons to attend on him, and the child will die for want of medical skill. Will you come to him, citizen doctor?"

It seems that for a moment or two Laporte hesitated.

"You look to me uncommonly like an aristo, and therefore a traitor," he said, "and I've half a mind—"

"To call your guard and order my immediate arrest," broke in milor with a whimsical smile, "but in that case a citizen of France will die for want of a doctor's care. Let me take you to the child's bedside, citizen doctor, you can always have me arrested afterwards."

But Laporte still hesitated.

"How do I know that you are not one of those English spies?" he began.

"Take it that I am," rejoined milor imperturbably, "and come and see the patient."

Never had a situation been carried off with so bold a hand. Claude Lemoine declared that Laporte's mouth literally opened for the call which would have summoned the sergeant of the guard into the room and ordered the summary arrest of this impudent stranger. During the veriest fraction of a second life and death hung in the balance for the gallant English milor. In the heart of Laporte every evil passion fought the one noble fibre within him. But the instinct of the skillful healer won the battle, and the next moment he had hastily collected what medicaments and appliances he might require, and the two men were soon speeding along the streets in the direction of the Rue des Pipots.

During the whole of that night, milor and Laporte sat together by the bedside of M. le Vicomte. Laporte only went out once in order to fetch what further medicaments he required. Mme. la Marquise took the opportunity of running out of her hiding-place in order to catch a glimpse of her child. I saw her take milor's hand and press it against her heart in silent gratitude. On her knees she begged him to go away and leave her and the boy to their fate. Was it likely that he would go? But she was so insistent that at last he said:

"Madame, let me assure you that even if I were prepared to play the coward's part which you would assign to me, it is not in my power to do so at this moment. Citizen Laporte came to this house under the escort of six picked men of his guard. He has left these men stationed on the landing outside this door."

Madame la Marquise gave a cry of terror, and once more that pathetic look of horror came into her face. Milor took her hand and then pointed to the sick child.

"Madame," he said, "M. le Vicomte is already slightly better. Thanks to medical skill and a child's vigorous hold on life, he will live. The rest is in the hands of God."

Already the heavy footsteps of Laporte were heard upon the creaking stairs. Mme. la Marquise was forced to return to her hiding-place.

Soon after dawn he went. M. le Vicomte was then visibly easier. Laporte had all along paid no heed to me, but I noticed that once or twice during his long vigil by the sick-bed his dark eyes beneath their overhanging brows shot a quick suspicious look at the door behind which cowered Mme. la Marquise. I had absolutely no doubt in my mind then that he knew quite well who his patient was.

He gave certain directions to milor—there were certain fresh medicaments to be got during the day. While he spoke there was a sinister glint in his eyes—half cynical, wholly menacing—as he looked up into the calm, impassive face of milor.

"It is essential for the welfare of the patient that these medicaments be got for him during the day," he said dryly, "and the guard have orders to allow you to pass in and out. But you need have no fear," he added significantly, "I will leave an escort outside the house to accompany you on your way."

He gave a mocking, cruel laugh, the meaning of which was unmistakable. His well-drilled human bloodhounds would be on the track of the English spy, whenever the latter dared to venture out into the streets.

Mme. la Marquise and I were prisoners for the day. We spent it in watching alternately beside M. le Vicomte. But milor came and went as freely as if he had not been carrying his precious life in his hands every time that he ventured outside the house.

In the evening Laporte returned to see his patient, and again the following morning, and the next evening. M. le Vicomte was making rapid progress towards recovery.

The third day in the morning Laporte pronounced his patient to be out of danger, but said that he would nevertheless come again to see him at the usual hour in the evening. Directly he had gone, milor went out in order to bring in certain delicacies of which the invalid was now allowed to partake. I persuaded Madame to lie down and have a couple of hours' good sleep in the inner attic, while I stayed to watch over the child.

To my horror, hardly had I taken up my stand at the foot of the bed when Laporte returned; he muttered something as he entered about having left some important appliance behind, but I was quite convinced that he had been on the watch until milor was out of sight, and then slipped back in order to find me and Madame here alone.

He gave a glance at the child and another at the door of the inner attic, then he said in a loud voice:

"Yes, another twenty-four hours and my duties as doctor will cease and those of patriot will re-commence. But Mme. la Marquise de Mortaine need no longer be in any anxiety about her son's health, nor will Mme. la Guillotine be cheated of a pack of rebels."

He laughed, and was on the point of turning on his heel when the door which gave on the smaller attic was opened and Mme. la Marquise appeared upon the threshold.

Monsieur, I had never seen her look more beautiful than she did now in her overwhelming grief. Her face was as pale as death, her eyes, large and dilated, were fixed upon the human monster who had found it in his heart to speak such cruel words. Clad in a miserable, threadbare gown, her rich brown hair brought to the top of her head like a crown, she looked more regal than any queen.

But proud as she was, monsieur, she yet knelt at the feet of that wretch. Yes, knelt, and embraced his knees and pleaded in such pitiable accents as would have melted the heart of a stone. She pleaded, monsieur—ah, not for herself. She pleaded for her child and for me, her faithful servant, and she pleaded for the gallant gentleman who had risked his life for the sake of the child, who was nothing to him.

"Take me!" she said. "I come of a race that have always known how to die! But what harm has that innocent child done in this world? What harm has poor old Jean-Pierre done, and, oh … is the world so full of brave and noble men that the bravest of them all be so unjustly sent to death?"

Ah, monsieur, any man, save one of those abject products of that hideous Revolution, would have listened to such heartrending accents. But this man only laughed and turned on his heel without a word.

Shall I ever forget the day that went by? Mme. la Marquise was well-nigh prostrate with terror, and it was heartrending to watch the noble efforts which she made to amuse M. le Vicomte. The only gleams of sunshine which came to us out of our darkness were the brief appearances of milor. Outside we could hear the measured tramp of the guard that had been set there to keep us close prisoners. They were relieved every six hours, and, in fact, we were as much under arrest as if we were already incarcerated in one of the prisons of Lyons.

At about four o'clock in the afternoon milor came back to us after a brief absence. He stayed for a little while playing with M. le Vicomte. Just before leaving he took Madame's hand in his and said very earnestly, and sinking his voice to the merest whisper:

"To-night! Fear nothing! Be ready for anything! Remember that the League of the Scarlet Pimpernel have never failed to succour, and that I hereby pledge you mine honour that you and those you care for will be out of Lyons this night."

He was gone, leaving us to marvel at his strange words. Mme. la Marquise after that was just like a person in a dream. She hardly spoke to me, and the only sound that passed her lips was a quaint little lullaby which she sang to M. le Vicomte ere he dropped off to sleep.

The hours went by leaden-footed. At every sound on the stairs Madame started like a frightened bird. That infamous Laporte usually paid his visits at about eight o'clock in the evening, and after it became quite dark, Madame sat at the tiny window, and I felt that she was counting the minutes which still lay between her and the dreaded presence of that awful man.

At a quarter before eight o'clock we heard the usual heavy footfall on the stairs. Madame started up as if she had been struck. She ran to the bed—almost like one demented, and wrapping the one poor blanket round M. le Vicomte, she seized him in her arms. Outside we could hear Laporte's raucous voice speaking to the guard. His usual query: "Is all well?" was answered by the brief: "All well, citizen." Then he asked if the English spy were within, and the sentinel replied: "No, citizen, he went out at about five o'clock and has not come back since."

"Not come back since five o'clock?" said Laporte with a loud curse.

"Pardi! I trust that that fool Caudy has not allowed him to escape."

"I saw Caudy about an hour ago, citizen," said the man.

"Did he say anything about the Englishman then?"

It seemed to us, who were listening to this conversation with bated breath, that the man hesitated a moment ere he replied; then he spoke with obvious nervousness.

"As a matter of fact, citizen," he said, "Caudy thought then that the Englishman was inside the house, whilst I was equally sure that I had seen him go downstairs an hour before."

"A thousand devils!" cried Laporte with a savage oath, "if I find that you, citizen sergeant, or Caudy have blundered there will be trouble for you."

To the accompaniment of a great deal more swearing he suddenly kicked open the door of our attic with his boot, and then came to a standstill on the threshold with his hands in the pockets of his breeches and his legs planted wide apart, face to face with Mme. la Marquise, who confronted him now, herself like a veritable tigress who is defending her young.

He gave a loud, mocking laugh.

"Ah, the aristos!" he cried, "waiting for that cursed Englishman, what? to drag you and your brat out of the claws of the human tiger.... Not so, my fine ci-devant Marquise. The brat is no longer sick—he is well enough, anyhow, to breathe the air of the prisons of Lyons for a few days pending a final rest in the arms of Mme. la Guillotine. Citizen sergeant," he called over his shoulder, "escort these aristos to my carriage downstairs. When the Englishman returns, tell him he will find his friends under the tender care of Doctor Laporte. En avant, little mother," he added, as he gripped Mme. la Marquise tightly by the arm, "and you, old scarecrow," he concluded, speaking to me over his shoulder, "follow the citizen sergeant, or——"

Mme. la Marquise made no resistance. As I told you, she had been, since dusk, like a person in a dream; so what could I do but follow her noble example? Indeed, I was too dazed to do otherwise.

We all went stumbling down the dark, rickety staircase, Laporte leading the way with Mme. la Marquise, who had M. le Vicomte tightly clasped in her arms. I followed with the sergeant, whose hand was on my shoulder; I believe that two soldiers walked behind, but of that I cannot be sure.

At the bottom of the stairs through the open door of the house I caught sight of the vague outline of a large barouche, the lanthorns of which threw a feeble light upon the cruppers of two horses and of a couple of men sitting on the box.

Mme. la Marquise stepped quietly into the carriage. Laporte followed her, and I was bundled in in his wake by the rough hands of the soldiery. Just before the order was given to start, Laporte put his head out of the window and shouted to the sergeant:

"When you see Caudy tell him to report himself to me at once. I will be back here in half an hour; keep strict guard as before until then, citizen sergeant."

The next moment the coachman cracked his whip, Laporte called loudly, "En avant!" and the heavy barouche went rattling along the ill-paved streets.

Inside the carriage all was silence. I could hear Mme. la Marquise softly whispering to M. le Vicomte, and I marvelled how wondrously calm—nay, cheerful, she could be. Then suddenly I heard a sound which of a truth did make my heart stop its beating. It was a quaint and prolonged laugh which I once thought I would never hear again on this earth. It came from the corner of the barouche next to where Mme. la Marquise was so tenderly and gaily crooning to her child. And a kindly voice said merrily:

"In half an hour we shall be outside Lyons. To-morrow we'll be across the Swiss frontier. We've cheated that old tiger after all. What say you, Mme. la Marquise?"

It was milor's voice, and he was as merry as a school-boy.

"I told you, old Jean-Pierre," he added, as he placed that firm hand which I loved so well upon my knee, "I told you that those confounded murderers would not get me this time."

And to think that I did not know him, as he stood less than a quarter of an hour ago upon the threshold of our attic in the hideous guise of that abominable Laporte. He had spent two days in collecting old clothes that resembled those of that infamous wretch, and in taking possession of one of the derelict rooms in the house in the Rue des Pipots. Then while we were expecting every moment that Laporte would order our arrest, milor assumed the personality of the monster, hoodwinked the sergeant on the dark staircase, and by that wonderfully audacious coup saved Mme. la Marquise, M. le Vicomte and my humble self from the guillotine.

Money, of which he had plenty, secured us immunity on the way, and we were in safety over the Swiss frontier, leaving Laporte to eat out his tigerish heart with baffled rage.

CHAPTER VII. OUT OF THE JAWS OF DEATH

Being a fragment from the diary of Valentine Lemercier, in the possession of her great-granddaughter.

We were such a happy family before this terrible Revolution broke out; we lived rather simply, but very comfortably, in our dear old home just on the borders of the forest of Compiegne. Jean and Andre were the twins; just fifteen years old they were when King Louis was deposed from the throne of France which God had given him, and sent to prison like a common criminal, with our beautiful Queen Marie Antoinette and the Royal children, and Madame Elizabeth, who was so beloved by the poor!

Ah! that seems very, very long ago now. No doubt you know better than I do all that happened in our beautiful land of France and in lovely Paris about that time: goods and property confiscated, innocent men, women, and children condemned to death for acts of treason which they had never committed.

It was in August last year that they came to "Mon Repos" and arrested papa, and maman, and us four young ones and dragged us to Paris, where we were imprisoned in a narrow and horribly dank vault in the Abbaye, where all day and night through the humid stone walls we heard cries and sobs and moans from poor people, who no doubt were suffering the same sorrows and the same indignities as we were.

I had just passed my nineteenth birthday, and Marguerite was only thirteen. Maman was a perfect angel during that terrible time; she kept up our courage and our faith in God in a way that no one else could have done. Every night and morning we knelt round her knee and papa sat close beside her, and we prayed to God for deliverance from our own afflictions, and for the poor people who were crying and moaning all the day.

But of what went on outside our prison walls we had not an idea, though sometimes poor papa would brave the warder's brutalities and ask him questions of what was happening in Paris every day.

"They are hanging all the aristos to the street-lamps of the city," the man would reply with a cruel laugh, "and it will be your turn next."

We had been in prison for about a fortnight, when one day—oh! shall I ever forget it?—we heard in the distance a noise like the rumbling of thunder; nearer and nearer it came, and soon the sound became less confused, cries and shrieks could be heard above that rumbling din; but so weird and menacing did those cries seem that instinctively—though none of us knew what they meant—we all felt a nameless terror grip our hearts.

Oh! I am not going to attempt the awful task of describing to you all the horrors of that never-to-be-forgotten day. People, who to-day cannot speak without a shudder of the September massacres, have not the remotest conception of what really happened on that awful second day of that month.

We are all at peace and happy now, but whenever my thoughts fly back to that morning, whenever the ears of memory recall those hideous yells of fury and of hate, coupled with the equally horrible cries for pity, which pierced through the walls behind which the six of us were crouching, trembling, and praying, whenever I think of it all my heart still beats violently with that same nameless dread which held it in its deathly grip then.

Hundreds of men, women, and children were massacred in the prisons of that day—it was a St. Bartholomew even more hideous than the last.

Maman was trying in vain to keep our thoughts fixed upon God—papa sat on the stone bench, his elbows resting on his knees, his head buried in his hands; but maman was kneeling on the floor, with her dear arms encircling us all and her trembling lips moving in continuous prayer.

We felt that we were facing death—and what a death, O my God!

Suddenly the small grated window—high up in the dank wall—became obscured. I was the first to look up, but the cry of terror which rose from my heart was choked ere it reached my throat.

Jean and Andre looked up, too, and they shrieked, and so did Marguerite, and papa jumped up and ran to us and stood suddenly between us and the window like a tiger defending its young.

But we were all of us quite silent now. The children did not even cry; they stared, wide-eyed, paralysed with fear.

Only maman continued to pray, and we could hear papa's rapid and stertorous breathing as he watched what was going on at that window above.

Heavy blows were falling against the masonry round the grating, and we could hear the nerve-racking sound of a file working on the iron bars; and farther away, below the window, those awful yells of human beings transformed by hate and fury into savage beasts.

How long this horrible suspense lasted I cannot now tell you; the next thing I remember clearly is a number of men in horrible ragged clothing pouring into our vault-like prison from the window above; the next moment they rushed at us simultaneously—or so it seemed to me, for I was just then recommending my soul to God, so certain was I that in that same second I would cease to live.

It was all like a dream, for instead of the horrible shriek of satisfied hate which we were all expecting to hear, a whispering voice, commanding and low, struck our ears and dragged us, as it were, from out the abyss of despair into the sudden light of hope.

"If you will trust us," the voice whispered, "and not be afraid, you will be safely out of Paris within an hour."

Papa was the first to realise what was happening; he had never lost his presence of mind even during the darkest moment of this terrible time, and he said quite calmly and steadily now:

"What must we do?"

"Persuade the little ones not to be afraid, not to cry, to be as still and silent as may be," continued the voice, which I felt must be that of one of God's own angels, so exquisitely kind did it sound to my ear.

"They will be quiet and still without persuasion," said papa; "eh, children?"

And Jean, Andre, and Marguerite murmured: "Yes!" whilst maman and I drew them closer to us and said everything we could think of to make them still more brave.

And the whispering, commanding voice went on after awhile:

"Now will you allow yourselves to be muffled and bound, and, after that, will you swear that whatever happens, whatever you may see or hear, you will neither move nor speak? Not only your own lives, but those of many brave men will depend upon your fulfilment of this oath."

Papa made no reply save to raise his hand and eyes up to where God surely was watching over us all. Maman said in her gentle, even voice:

"For myself and my children, I swear to do all that you tell us."

A great feeling of confidence had entered into her heart, just as it had done into mine. We looked at one another and knew that we were both thinking of the same thing: we were thinking of the brave Englishman and his gallant little band of heroes, about whom we had heard many wonderful tales—how they had rescued a number of innocent people who were unjustly threatened with the guillotine; and we all knew that the tall figure, disguised in horrible rags, who spoke to us with such a gentle yet commanding voice, was the man whom rumour credited with supernatural powers, and who was known by the mysterious name of "The Scarlet Pimpernel."

Hardly had we sworn to do his bidding than his friends most unceremoniously threw great pieces of sacking over our heads, and then proceeded to tie ropes round our bodies. At least, I know that that is what one of them was doing to me, and from one or two whispered words of command which reached my ear I concluded that papa and maman and the children were being dealt with in the same summary way.

I felt hot and stifled under that rough bit of sacking, but I would not have moved or even sighed for worlds. Strangely enough, as soon as my eyes and ears were shut off from the sounds and sights immediately round me, I once more became conscious of the horrible and awful din which was going on, not only on the other side of our prison walls, but inside the whole of the Abbaye building and in the street beyond.

Once more I heard those terrible howls of rage and of satisfied hatred, uttered by the assassins who were being paid by the government of our beautiful country to butcher helpless prisoners in their hundreds.

Suddenly I felt myself hoisted up off my feet and slung up on to a pair of shoulders that must have been very powerful indeed, for I am no light weight, and once more I heard the voice, the very sound of which was delight, quite close to my ear this time, giving a brief and comprehensive command:

"All ready!—remember your part—en avant!"

Then it added in English. "Here, Tony, you start kicking against the door whilst we begin to shout!"

I loved those few words of English, and hoped that maman had heard them too, for it would confirm her—as it did me—in the happy knowledge that God and a brave man had taken our rescue in hand.

But from that moment we might have all been in the very ante-chamber of hell. I could hear the violent kicks against the heavy door of our prison, and our brave rescuers seemed suddenly to be transformed into a cageful of wild beasts. Their shouts and yells were as horrible as any that came to us from the outside, and I must say that the gentle, firm voice which I had learnt to love was as execrable as any I could hear.

Apparently the door would not yield, as the blows against it became more and more violent, and presently from somewhere above my head—the window presumably—there came a rough call, and a raucous laugh:

"Why? what in the name of—— is happening here?"

And the voice near me answered back equally roughly: "A quarry of six—but we are caught in this confounded trap—get the door open for us, citizen—we want to get rid of this booty and go in search for more."

A horrible laugh was the reply from above, and the next instant I heard a terrific crash; the door had at last been burst open, either from within or without, I could not tell which, and suddenly all the din, the cries, the groans, the hideous laughter and bibulous songs which had sounded muffled up to now burst upon us with all their hideousness.

That was, I think, the most awful moment of that truly fearful hour. I could not have moved then, even had I wished or been able to do so; but I knew that between us all and a horrible, yelling, murdering mob there was now nothing—except the hand of God and the heroism of a band of English gentlemen.

Together they gave a cry—as loud, as terrifying as any that were uttered by the butchering crowd in the building, and with a wild rush they seemed to plunge with us right into the thick of the awful melee.

At least, that is what it all felt like to me, and afterwards I heard from our gallant rescuer himself that that is exactly what he and his friends did. There were eight of them altogether, and we four young ones had each been hoisted on a pair of devoted shoulders, whilst maman and papa were each carried by two men.

I was lying across the finest pair of shoulders in the world, and close to me was beating the bravest heart on God's earth.

Thus burdened, these eight noble English gentlemen charged right through an army of butchering, howling brutes, they themselves howling with the fiercest of them.

All around me I heard weird and terrific cries: "What ho! citizens—what have you there?"

"Six aristos!" shouted my hero boldly as he rushed on, forging his way through the crowd.

"What are you doing with them?" yelled a raucous voice.

"Food for the starving fish in the river," was the ready response. "Stand aside, citizen," he added, with a round curse; "I have my orders from citizen Danton himself about these six aristos. You hinder me at your peril."

He was challenged over and over again in the same way, and so were his friends who were carrying papa and maman and the children; but they were always ready with a reply, ready with an invective or a curse; with eyes that could not see, one could imagine them as hideous, as vengeful, as cruel as the rest of the crowd.

I think that soon I must have fainted from sheer excitement and terror, for I remember nothing more till I felt myself deposited on a hard floor, propped against the wall, and the stifling piece of sacking taken off my head and face.

I looked around me, dazed and bewildered; gradually the horrors of the past hour came back to me, and I had to close my eyes again, for I felt sick and giddy with the sheer memory of it all.

But presently I felt stronger and looked around me again. Jean and Andre were squatting in a corner close by, gazing wide-eyed at the group of men in filthy, ragged clothing, who sat round a deal table in the centre of a small, ill-furnished room.

Maman was lying on a horsehair sofa at the other end of the room, with Marguerite beside her, and papa sat in a low chair by her side, holding her hand.

The voice I loved was speaking in its quaint, somewhat drawly cadence:

"You are quite safe now, my dear Monsieur Lemercier," it said; "after Madame and the young people have had a rest, some of my friends will find you suitable disguises, and they will escort you out of Paris, as they have some really genuine passports in their possessions, which we obtain from time to time through the agency of a personage highly placed in this murdering government, and with the help of English banknotes. Those passports are not always unchallenged, I must confess," added my hero with a quaint laugh; "but to-night everyone is busy murdering in one part of Paris, so the other parts are comparatively safe."

Then he turned to one of his friends and spoke to him in English:

"You had better see this through, Tony," he said, "with Hastings and Mackenzie. Three of you will be enough; I shall have need of the others."

No one seemed to question his orders. He had spoken, and the others made ready to obey. Just then papa spoke up:

"How are we going to thank you, sir?" he asked, speaking broken English, but with his habitual dignity of manner.

"By leaving your welfare in our hands, Monsieur," replied our gallant rescuer quietly.

Papa tried to speak again, but the Englishman put up his hand to stop any further talk.

"There is no time now, Monsieur," he said with gentle courtesy. "I must leave you, as I have much work yet to do."

"Where are you going, Blakeney?" asked one of the others.

"Back to the Abbaye prison," he said; "there are other women and children to be rescued there!"

THE LEAGUE OF THE SCARLET PIMPERNEL

CHAPTER VIII. THE TRAITOR

I.

Not one of them had really trusted him for some time now. Heaven and his conscience alone knew what had changed my Lord Kulmsted from a loyal friend and keen sportsman into a surly and dissatisfied adherent—adherent only in name.

Some say that lack of money had embittered him. He was a confirmed gambler, and had been losing over-heavily of late; and the League of the Scarlet Pimpernel demanded sacrifices of money at times from its members, as well as of life if the need arose. Others averred that jealousy against the chief had outweighed Kulmsted's honesty. Certain it is that his oath of fealty to the League had long ago been broken in the spirit. Treachery hovered in the air.

But the Scarlet Pimpernel himself, with that indomitable optimism of his, and almost maddening insouciance, either did not believe in Kulmsted's disloyalty or chose not to heed it.

He even asked him to join the present expedition—one of the most dangerous undertaken by the League for some time, and which had for its object the rescue of some women of the late unfortunate Marie Antoinette's household: maids and faithful servants, ruthlessly condemned to die for their tender adherence to a martyred queen. And yet eighteen pairs of faithful lips had murmured words of warning.

It was towards the end of November, 1793. The rain was beating down in a monotonous drip, drip, drip on to the roof of a derelict house in the Rue Berthier. The wan light of a cold winter's morning peeped in through the curtainless window and touched with its weird grey brush the pallid face of a young girl—a mere child—who sat in a dejected attitude on a rickety chair, with elbows leaning on the rough deal table before her, and thin, grimy fingers wandering with pathetic futility to her tearful eyes.

In the farther angle of the room a tall figure in dark clothes was made one, by the still lingering gloom, with the dense shadows beyond.

"We have starved," said the girl, with rebellious tears. "Father and I and the boys are miserable enough, God knows; but we have always been honest."

From out the shadows in that dark corner of the room there came the sound of an oath quickly suppressed.

"Honest!" exclaimed the man, with a harsh, mocking laugh, which made the girl wince as if with physical pain. "Is it honest to harbour the enemies of your country? Is it honest—"

But quickly he checked himself, biting his lips with vexation, feeling that his present tactics were not like to gain the day.

He came out of the gloom and approached the girl with every outward sign of eagerness. He knelt on the dusty floor beside her, his arms stole round her meagre shoulders, and his harsh voice was subdued to tones of gentleness.

"I was only thinking of your happiness, Yvonne," he said tenderly; "of poor blind papa and the two boys to whom you have been such a devoted little mother. My only desire is that you should earn the gratitude of your country by denouncing her most bitter enemy—an act of patriotism which will place you and those for whom you care for ever beyond the reach of sorrow or of want."

The voice, the appeal, the look of love, was more than the poor, simple girl could resist. Milor was so handsome, so kind, so good.

It had all been so strange: these English aristocrats coming here, she knew not whence, and who seemed fugitives even though they had plenty of money to spend. Two days ago they had sought shelter like malefactors escaped from justice—in this same tumbledown, derelict house where she, Yvonne, with her blind father and two little brothers, crept in of nights, or when the weather was too rough for them all to stand and beg in the streets of Paris.

There were five of them altogether, and one seemed to be the chief. He was very tall, and had deep blue eyes, and a merry voice that went echoing along the worm-eaten old rafters. But milor—the one whose arms were encircling her even now—was the handsomest among them all. He had sought Yvonne out on the very first night when she had crawled shivering to that corner of the room where she usually slept.

The English aristocrats had frightened her at first, and she was for flying from the derelict house with her family and seeking shelter elsewhere; but he who appeared to be the chief had quickly reassured her. He seemed so kind and good, and talked so gently to blind papa, and made such merry jests with Francois and Clovis that she herself could scarce refrain from laughing through her tears.

But later on in the night, milor—her milor, as she soon got to call him—came and talked so beautifully that she, poor girl, felt as if no music could ever sound quite so sweetly in her ear.

That was two days ago, and since then milor had often talked to her in the lonely, abandoned house, and Yvonne had felt as if she dwelt in Heaven. She still took blind papa and the boys out to beg in the streets, but in the morning she prepared some hot coffee for the English aristocrats, and in the evening she cooked them some broth. Oh! they gave her money lavishly; but she quite understood that they were in hiding, though what they had to fear, being English, she could not understand.

And now milor—her milor—was telling her that these Englishmen, her friends, were spies and traitors, and that it was her duty to tell citizen Robespierre and the Committee of Public Safety all about them and their mysterious doings. And poor Yvonne was greatly puzzled and deeply distressed, because, of course, whatever milor said, that was the truth; and yet her conscience cried out within her poor little bosom, and the thought of betraying those kind Englishmen was horrible to her.

"Yvonne," whispered milor in that endearing voice of his, which was like the loveliest music in her ear, "my little Yvonne, you do trust me, do you not?"

"With all my heart, milor," she murmured fervently.

"Then, would you believe it of me that I would betray a real friend?"

"I believe, milor, that whatever you do is right and good."

A sigh of infinite relief escaped his lips.

"Come, that's better!" he said, patting her cheek kindly with his hand. "Now, listen to me, little one. He who is the chief among us here is the most unscrupulous and daring rascal whom the world has ever known. He it is who is called the 'Scarlet Pimpernel!'"

"The Scarlet Pimpernel!" murmured Yvonne, her eyes dilated with superstitious awe, for she too had heard of the mysterious Englishman and of his followers, who rescued aristocrats and traitors from the death to which the tribunal of the people had justly condemned them, and on whom the mighty hand of the Committee of Public Safety had never yet been able to fall.

"This Scarlet Pimpernel," said milor earnestly after a while, "is also mine own most relentless enemy. With lies and promises he induced me to join him in his work of spying and of treachery, forcing me to do this work against which my whole soul rebels. You can save me from this hated bondage, little one. You can make me free to live again, make me free to love and place my love at your feet."

His voice had become exquisitely tender, and his lips, as he whispered the heavenly words, were quite close to her ear. He, a great gentleman, loved the miserable little waif whose kindred consisted of a blind father and two half-starved little brothers, and whose only home was this miserable hovel, whence milor's graciousness and bounty would soon take her.

Do you think that Yvonne's sense of right and wrong, of honesty and treachery, should have been keener than that primeval instinct of a simple-hearted woman to throw herself trustingly into the arms of the man who has succeeded in winning her love?

Yvonne, subdued, enchanted, murmured still through her tears:

"What would milor have me do?"

Lord Kulmsted rose from his knees satisfied.

"Listen to me, Yvonne," he said. "You are acquainted with the Englishman's plans, are you not?"

"Of course," she replied simply. "He has had to trust me."

"Then you know that at sundown this afternoon I and the three others are to leave for Courbevoie on foot, where we are to obtain what horses we can whilst awaiting the chief."

"I did not know whither you and the other three gentlemen were going, milor," she replied; "but I did know that some of you were to make a start at four o'clock, whilst I was to wait here for your leader and prepare some supper against his coming."

"At what time did he tell you that he would come?"

"He did not say; but he did tell me that when he returns he will have friends with him—a lady and two little children. They will be hungry and cold. I believe that they are in great danger now, and that the brave English gentleman means to take them away from this awful Paris to a place of safety."

"The brave English gentleman, my dear," retorted milor, with a sneer, "is bent on some horrible work of spying. The lady and the two children are, no doubt, innocent tools in his hands, just as I am, and when he no longer needs them he will deliver them over to the Committee of Public Safety, who will, of a surety, condemn them to death. That will also be my fate, Yvonne, unless you help me now."

"Oh, no, no!" she exclaimed fervently. "Tell me what to do, milor, and I will do it."

"At sundown," he said, sinking his voice so low that even she could scarcely hear, "when I and the three others have started on our way, go straight to the house I spoke to you about in the Rue Dauphine—you know where it is?"

"Oh, yes, milor."

"You will know the house by its tumbledown portico and the tattered red flag that surmounts it. Once there, push the door open and walk in boldly. Then ask to speak with citizen Robespierre."

"Robespierre?" exclaimed the child in terror.

"You must not be afraid, Yvonne," he said earnestly; "you must think of me and of what you are doing for me. My word on it—Robespierre will listen to you most kindly."

"What shall I tell him?" she murmured.

"That a mysterious party of Englishmen are in hiding in this house—that their chief is known among them as the Scarlet Pimpernel. The rest leave to Robespierre's discretion. You see how simple it is?"

It was indeed very simple! Nor did the child recoil any longer from the ugly task which milor, with suave speech and tender voice, was so ardently seeking to impose on her.

A few more words of love, which cost him nothing, a few kisses which cost him still less, since the wench loved him, and since she was young and pretty, and Yvonne was as wax in the hands of the traitor.

II.

Silence reigned in the low-raftered room on the ground floor of the house in the Rue Dauphine.

Citizen Robespierre, chairman of the Cordeliers Club, the most bloodthirsty, most Evolutionary club of France, had just re-entered the room.

He walked up to the centre table, and through the close atmosphere, thick with tobacco smoke, he looked round on his assembled friends.

"We have got him," he said at last curtly.

"Got him! Whom?" came in hoarse cries from every corner of the room.

"That Englishman," replied the demagogue, "the Scarlet Pimpernel!"

A prolonged shout rose in response—a shout not unlike that of a caged herd of hungry wild beasts to whom a succulent morsel of flesh has unexpectedly been thrown.

"Where is he?" "Where did you get him?" "Alive or dead?" And many more questions such as these were hurled at the speaker from every side.

Robespierre, calm, impassive, immaculately neat in his tightly fitting coat, his smart breeches, and his lace cravat, waited awhile until the din had somewhat subsided. Then he said calmly:

"The Scarlet Pimpernel is in hiding in one of the derelict houses in the Rue Berthier."

Snarls of derision as vigorous as the former shouts of triumph drowned the rest of his speech.

"Bah! How often has that cursed Scarlet Pimpernel been said to be alone in a lonely house? Citizen Chauvelin has had him at his mercy several times in lonely houses."

And the speaker, a short, thick-set man with sparse black hair plastered over a greasy forehead, his shirt open at the neck, revealing a powerful chest and rough, hairy skin, spat in ostentatious contempt upon the floor.

"Therefore will we not boast of his capture yet, citizen Roger," resumed Robespierre imperturbably. "I tell you where the Englishman is. Do you look to it that he does not escape."

The heat in the room had become intolerable. From the grimy ceiling an oil-lamp, flickering low, threw lurid, ruddy lights on tricolour cockades, on hands that seemed red with the blood of innocent victims of lust and hate, and on faces glowing with desire and with anticipated savage triumph.

"Who is the informer?" asked Roger at last.

"A girl," replied Robespierre curtly. "Yvonne Lebeau, by name; she and her family live by begging. There are a blind father and two boys; they herd together at night in the derelict house in the Rue Berthier. Five Englishmen have been in hiding there these past few days. One of them is their leader. The girl believes him to be the Scarlet Pimpernel."

"Why has she not spoken of this before?" muttered one of the crowd, with some scepticism.

"Frightened, I suppose. Or the Englishman paid her to hold her tongue."

"Where is the girl now?"

"I am sending her straight home, a little ahead of us. Her presence should reassure the Englishman whilst we make ready to surround the house. In the meanwhile, I have sent special messengers to every gate of Paris with strict orders to the guard not to allow anyone out of the city until further orders from the Committee of Public Safety. And now," he added, throwing back his head with a gesture of proud challenge, "citizens, which of you will go man-hunting to-night?"

This time the strident roar of savage exultation was loud and deep enough to shake the flickering lamp upon its chain.

A brief discussion of plans followed, and Roger—he with the broad, hairy chest and that gleam of hatred for ever lurking in his deep-set, shifty eyes—was chosen the leader of the party.

Thirty determined and well-armed patriots set out against one man, who mayhap had supernatural powers. There would, no doubt, be some aristocrats, too, in hiding in the derelict house—the girl Lebeau, it seems, had spoken of a woman and two children. Bah! These would not count. It would be thirty to one, so let the Scarlet Pimpernel look to himself.

From the towers of Notre Dame the big bell struck the hour of six, as thirty men in ragged shirts and torn breeches, shivering beneath a cold November drizzle, began slowly to wend their way towards the Rue Berthier.

They walked on in silence, not heeding the cold or the rain, but with eyes fixed in the direction of their goal, and nostrils quivering in the evening air with the distant scent of blood.

III.

At the top of the Rue Berthier the party halted. On ahead—some two hundred metres farther—Yvonne Lebeau's little figure, with her ragged skirt pulled over her head and her bare feet pattering in the mud, was seen crossing one of those intermittent patches of light formed by occasional flickering street lamps, and then was swallowed up once more by the inky blackness beyond.

The Rue Berthier is a long, narrow, ill-paved and ill-lighted street, composed of low and irregular houses, which abut on the line of fortifications at the back, and are therefore absolutely inaccessible save from the front.

Midway down the street a derelict house rears ghostly debris of roofs and chimney-stacks upward to the sky. A tiny square of yellow light, blinking like a giant eye through a curtainless window, pierced the wall of the house. Roger pointed to that light.

"That," he said, "is the quarry where our fox has run to earth."

No one said anything; but the dank night air seemed suddenly alive with all the passions of hate let loose by thirty beating hearts.

The Scarlet Pimpernel, who had tricked them, mocked them, fooled them so often, was there, not two hundred metres away; and they were thirty to one, and all determined and desperate.

The darkness was intense.

Silently now the party approached the house, then again they halted, within sixty metres of it.

"Hist!"

The whisper could scarce be heard, so low was it, like the sighing of the wind through a misty veil.

"Who is it?" came in quick challenge from Roger.

"I—Yvonne Lebeau!"

"Is he there?" was the eager whispered query.

"Not yet. But he may come at any moment. If he saw a crowd round the house, mayhap he would not come."

"He cannot see a crowd. The night is as dark as pitch."

"He can see in the darkest night," and the girl's voice sank to an awed whisper, "and he can hear through a stone wall."

Instinctively, Roger shuddered. The superstitious fear which the mysterious personality of the Scarlet Pimpernel evoked in the heart of every Terrorist had suddenly seized this man in its grip.

Try as he would, he did not feel as valiant as he had done when first he emerged at the head of his party from under the portico of the Cordeliers Club, and it was with none too steady a voice that he ordered the girl roughly back to the house. Then he turned once more to his men.

The plan of action had been decided on in the Club, under the presidency of Robespierre; it only remained to carry the plans through with success.

From the side of the fortifications there was, of course, nothing to fear. In accordance with military regulations, the walls of the houses there rose sheer from the ground without doors or windows, whilst the broken-down parapets and dilapidated roofs towered forty feet above the ground.

The derelict itself was one of a row of houses, some inhabited, others quite abandoned. It was the front of that row of houses, therefore, that had to be kept in view. Marshalled by Roger, the men flattened their meagre bodies against the walls of the houses opposite, and after that there was nothing to do but wait.

To wait in the darkness of the night, with a thin, icy rain soaking through ragged shirts and tattered breeches, with bare feet frozen by the mud of the road—to wait in silence while turbulent hearts beat well-nigh to bursting—to wait for food whilst hunger gnaws the bowels—to wait for drink whilst the parched tongue cleaves to the roof of the mouth—to wait for revenge whilst the hours roll slowly by and the cries of the darkened city are stilled one by one!

Once—when a distant bell tolled the hour of ten—a loud prolonged laugh, almost impudent in its suggestion of merry insouciance, echoed through the weird silence of the night.

Roger felt that the man nearest to him shivered at that sound, and he heard a volley or two of muttered oaths.

"The fox seems somewhere near," he whispered. "Come within. We'll wait for him inside his hole."

He led the way across the street, some of the men following him.

The door of the derelict house had been left on the latch. Roger pushed it open.

Silence and gloom here reigned supreme; utter darkness, too, save for a narrow streak of light which edged the framework of a door on the right. Not a sound stirred the quietude of this miserable hovel, only the creaking of boards beneath the men's feet as they entered.

Roger crossed the passage and opened the door on the right. His friends pressed closely round to him and peeped over his shoulder into the room beyond.

A guttering piece of tallow candle, fixed to an old tin pot, stood in the middle of the floor, and its feeble, flickering light only served to accentuate the darkness that lay beyond its range. One or two rickety chairs and a rough deal table showed vaguely in the gloom, and in the far corner of the room there lay a bundle of what looked like heaped-up rags, but from which there now emerged the sound of heavy breathing and also a little cry of fear.

"Yvonne," came in feeble, querulous accents from that same bundle of wretchedness, "are these the English milors come back at last?"

"No, no, father," was the quick whispered reply.

Roger swore a loud oath, and two puny voices began to whimper piteously.

"It strikes me the wench has been fooling us," muttered one of the men savagely.

The girl had struggled to her feet. She crouched in the darkness, and two little boys, half-naked and shivering, were clinging to her skirts. The rest of the human bundle seemed to consist of an oldish man, with long, gaunt legs and arms blue with the cold. He turned vague, wide-open eyes in the direction whence had come the harsh voices.

"Are they friends, Yvonne?" he asked anxiously.

The girl did her best to reassure him.

"Yes, yes, father," she whispered close to his ear, her voice scarce above her breath; "they are good citizens who hoped to find the English milor here. They are disappointed that he has not yet come."

"Ah! but he will come, of a surety," said the old man in that querulous voice of his. "He left his beautiful clothes here this morning, and surely he will come to fetch them." And his long, thin hand pointed towards a distant corner of the room.

Roger and his friends, looking to where he was pointing, saw a parcel of clothes, neatly folded, lying on one of the chairs. Like so many wild cats snarling at sight of prey, they threw themselves upon those clothes, tearing them out from one another's hands, turning them over and over as if to force the cloth and satin to yield up the secret that lay within their folds.

In the skirmish a scrap of paper fluttered to the ground. Roger seized it with avidity, and, crouching on the floor, smoothed the paper out against his knee.

It contained a few hastily scrawled words, and by the feeble light of the fast-dying candle Roger spelt them out laboriously:

"If the finder of these clothes will take them to the cross-roads opposite the foot-bridge which leads straight to Courbevoie, and will do so before the clock of Courbevoie Church has struck the hour of midnight, he will be rewarded with the sum of five hundred francs."

"There is something more, citizen Roger," said a raucous voice close to his ear.

"Look! Look, citizen—in the bottom corner of the paper!"

"The signature."

"A scrawl done in red," said Roger, trying to decipher it.

"It looks like a small flower."

"That accursed Scarlet Pimpernel!"

And even as he spoke the guttering tallow candle, swaying in its socket, suddenly went out with a loud splutter and a sizzle that echoed through the desolate room like the mocking laugh of ghouls.

IV.

Once more the tramp through the dark and deserted streets, with the drizzle—turned now to sleet—beating on thinly clad shoulders. Fifteen men only on this tramp. The others remained behind to watch the house. Fifteen men, led by Roger, and with a blind old man, a young girl carrying a bundle of clothes, and two half-naked children dragged as camp-followers in the rear.

Their destination now was the sign-post which stands at the cross-roads, past the footbridge that leads to Courbevoie.

The guard at the Maillot Gate would have stopped the party, but Roger, member of the Committee of Public Safety, armed with his papers and his tricolour scarf, overruled Robespierre's former orders, and the party mached out of the gate.

They pressed on in silence, instinctively walking shoulder to shoulder, vaguely longing for the touch of another human hand, the sound of a voice that would not ring weirdly in the mysterious night.

There was something terrifying in this absolute silence, in such intense darkness, in this constant wandering towards a goal that seemed for ever distant, and in all this weary, weary fruitless waiting; and these men, who lived their life through, drunken with blood, deafened by the cries of their victims, satiated with the moans of the helpless and the innocent, hardly dared to look around them, lest they should see ghoulish forms flitting through the gloom.

Soon they reached the cross-roads, and in the dense blackness of the night the gaunt arms of the sign-post pointed ghostlike towards the north.

The men hung back, wrapped in the darkness as in a pall, while Roger advanced alone.

"Hola! Is anyone there?" he called softly.

Then, as no reply came, he added more loudly:

"Hola! A friend—with some clothes found in the Rue Berthier. Is anyone here? Hola! A friend!"

But only from the gently murmuring river far away the melancholy call of a waterfowl seemed to echo mockingly:

"A friend!"

Just then the clock of Courbevoie Church struck the midnight hour.

"It is too late," whispered the men.

They did not swear, nor did they curse their leader. Somehow it seemed as if they had expected all along that the Englishman would evade their vengeance yet again, that he would lure them out into the cold and into the darkness, and then that he would mock them, fool them, and finally disappear into the night.

It seemed futile to wait any longer. They were so sure that they had failed again.

"Who goes there?"

The sound of naked feet and of wooden sabots pattering on the distant footbridge had caused Roger to utter the quick challenge.

"Hola! Hola! Are you there?" was the loud, breathless response.

The next moment the darkness became alive with men moving quickly forward, and raucous shouts of "Where are they?" "Have you got them?" "Don't let them go!" filled the air.

"Got whom?" "Who are they?" "What is it?" were the wild counter-cries.

"The man! The girl! The children! Where are they?"

"What? Which? The Lebeau family? They are here with us."

"Where?"

Where, indeed? To a call to them from Roger there came no answer, nor did a hasty search result in finding them—the old man, the two boys, and the girl carrying the bundle of clothes had vanished into the night.

"In the name of——, what does this mean?" cried hoarse voices in the crowd.

The new-comers, breathless, terrified, shaking with superstitious fear, tried to explain.

"The Lebeau family—the old man, the girl, the two boys—we discovered after your departure, locked up in the cellar of the house—prisoners."

"But, then—the others?" they gasped.

"The girl and the children whom you saw must have been some aristocrats in disguise. The old man who spoke to you was that cursed Englishman—the Scarlet Pimpernel!"

And as if in mocking confirmation of these words there suddenly rang, echoing from afar, a long and merry laugh.

"The Scarlet Pimpernel!" cried Roger. "In rags and barefooted! At him, citizens; he cannot have got far!"

"Hush! Listen!" whispered one of the men, suddenly gripping him by the arm.

And from the distance—though Heaven only knew from what direction—came the sound of horses' hoofs pawing the soft ground; the next moment they were heard galloping away at breakneck speed.

The men turned to run in every direction, blindly, aimlessly, in the dark, like bloodhounds that have lost the trail.

One man, as he ran, stumbled against a dark mass prone upon the ground.

With a curse on his lips, he recovered his balance.

"Hold! What is this?" he cried.

Some of his comrades gathered round him. No one could see anything, but the dark mass appeared to have human shape, and it was bound round and round with cords. And now feeble moans escaped from obviously human lips.

"What is it? Who is it?" asked the men.

"An Englishman," came in weak accents from the ground.

"Your name?"

"I am called Kulmsted."

"Bah! An aristocrat!"

"No! An enemy of the Scarlet Pimpernel, like yourselves. I would have delivered him into your hands. But you let him escape you. As for me, he would have been wiser if he had killed me."

They picked him up and undid the cords from round his body, and later on took him with them back into Paris.

But there, in the darkness of the night, in the mud of the road, and beneath the icy rain, knees were shaking that had long ago forgotten how to bend, and hasty prayers were muttered by lips that were far more accustomed to blaspheme.

CHAPTER IX. THE CABARET DE LA LIBERTE

I.

"Eight!"

"Twelve!"

"Four!"

A loud curse accompanied this last throw, and shouts of ribald laughter greeted it.

"No luck, Guidal!"

"Always at the tail end of the cart, eh, citizen?"

"Do not despair yet, good old Guidal! Bad beginnings oft make splendid ends!"

Then once again the dice rattled in the boxes; those who stood around pressed closer round the gamesters; hot, avid faces, covered with sweat and grime, peered eagerly down upon the table.

"Eight and eleven—nineteen!"

"Twelve and zero! By Satan! Curse him! Just my luck!"

"Four and nine—thirteen! Unlucky number!"

"Now then—once more! I'll back Merri! Ten assignats of the most worthless kind! Who'll take me that Merri gets the wench in the end?"

This from one of the lookers-on, a tall, cadaverous-looking creature, with sunken eyes and broad, hunched-up shoulders, which were perpetually shaken by a dry, rasping cough that proclaimed the ravages of some mortal disease, left him trembling as with ague and brought beads of perspiration to the roots of his lank hair. A recrudescence of excitement went the round of the spectators. The gamblers sitting round a narrow deal table, on which past libations had left marks of sticky rings, had scarce room to move their elbows.

"Nineteen and four—twenty-three!"

"You are out of it, Desmonts!"

"Not yet!"

"Twelve and twelve!"

"There! What did I tell you?"

"Wait! wait! Now, Merri! Now! Remember I have backed you for ten assignats, which I propose to steal from the nearest Jew this very night."

"Thirteen and twelve! Twenty-five, by all the demons and the ghouls!" came with a triumphant shout from the last thrower.

"Merri has it! Vive Merri!" was the unanimous and clamorous response.

Merri was evidently the most popular amongst the three gamblers. Now he sprawled upon the bench, leaning his back against the table, and surveyed the assembled company with the air of an Achilles having vanquished his Hector.

"Good luck to you and to your aristo!" began his backer lustily—would, no doubt, have continued his song of praise had not a violent fit of coughing smothered the words in his throat. The hand which he had raised in order to slap his friend genially on the back now went with a convulsive clutch to his own chest.

But his obvious distress did not apparently disturb the equanimity of Merri, or arouse even passing interest in the lookers-on.

"May she have as much money as rumour avers," said one of the men sententiously.

Merri gave a careless wave of his grubby hand.

"More, citizen; more!" he said loftily.

Only the two losers appeared inclined to scepticism.

"Bah!" one of them said—it was Desmonts. "The whole matter of the woman's money may be a tissue of lies!"

"And England is a far cry!" added Guidal.

But Merri was not likely to be depressed by these dismal croakings.

"'Tis simple enough," he said philosophically, "to disparage the goods if you are not able to buy."

Then a lusty voice broke in from the far corner of the room:

"And now, citizen Merri, 'tis time you remembered that the evening is hot and your friends thirsty!"

The man who spoke was a short, broad-shouldered creature, with crimson face surrounded by a shock of white hair, like a ripe tomato wrapped in cotton wool.

"And let me tell you," he added complacently, "that I have a cask of rum down below, which came straight from that accursed country, England, and is said to be the nectar whereon feeds that confounded Scarlet Pimpernel. It gives him the strength, so 'tis said, to intrigue successfully against the representatives of the people."

"Then by all means, citizen," concluded Merri's backer, still hoarse and spent after his fit of coughing, "let us have some of your nectar. My friend, citizen Merri, will need strength and wits too, I'll warrant, for, after he has married the aristo, he will have to journey to England to pluck the rich dowry which is said to lie hidden there."

"Cast no doubt upon that dowry, citizen Rateau, curse you!" broke in Merri, with a spiteful glance directed against his former rivals, "or Guidal and Desmonts will cease to look glum, and half my joy in the aristo will have gone."

After which, the conversation drifted to general subjects, became hilarious and ribald, while the celebrated rum from England filled the close atmosphere of the narrow room with its heady fumes.

II.

Open to the street in front, the locality known under the pretentious title of "Cabaret de la Liberté" was a favoured one among the flotsam and jetsam of the population of this corner of old Paris; men and sometimes women, with nothing particular to do, no special means of livelihood save the battening on the countless miseries and sorrows which this Revolution, which was to have been so glorious, was bringing in its train; idlers and loafers, who would crawl desultorily down the few worn and grimy steps which led into the cabaret from the level of the street. There was always good brandy or eau de vie to be had there, and no questions asked, no scares from the revolutionary guards or the secret agents of the Committee of Public Safety, who knew better than to interfere with the citizen host and his dubious clientele. There was also good Rhine wine or rum to be had, smuggled across from England or Germany, and no interference from the spies of some of those countless Committees, more autocratic than any ci-devant despot. It was, in fact, an ideal place wherein to conduct those shady transactions which are unavoidable corollaries of an unfettered democracy. Projects of burglary, pillage, rapine, even murder, were hatched within this underground burrow, where, as soon as evening drew in, a solitary, smoky oil-lamp alone cast a dim light upon faces that liked to court the darkness, and whence no sound that was not meant for prying ears found its way to the street above. The walls were thick with grime and smoke, the floor mildewed and cracked; dirt vied with squalor to make the place a fitting abode for thieves and cut-throats, for some of those sinister night-birds, more vile even than those who shrieked with satisfied lust at sight of the tumbril, with its daily load of unfortunates for the guillotine.

On this occasion the project that was being hatched was one of the most abject. A young girl, known by some to be possessed of a fortune, was the stake for which these workers of iniquity gambled across one of mine host's greasy tables. The latest decree of the Convention, encouraging, nay, commanding, the union of aristocrats with so-called patriots, had fired the imagination of this nest of jail-birds with thoughts of glorious possibilities. Some of them had collected the necessary information; and the report had been encouraging.

That self-indulgent aristo, the ci-devant banker Amede Vincent, who had expiated his villainies upon the guillotine, was known to have been successful in abstracting the bulk of his ill-gotten wealth and concealing it somewhere—it was not exactly known where, but thought to be in England—out of the reach, at any rate, of deserving patriots.

Some three or four years ago, before the glorious principles of Liberty, Equality, and Fraternity had made short shrift of all such pestilential aristocrats, the ci-devant banker, then a widower with an only daughter, Esther, had journeyed to England. He soon returned to Paris, however, and went on living there with his little girl in comparative retirement, until his many crimes found him out at last and he was made to suffer the punishment which he so justly deserved. Those crimes consisted for the most part in humiliating the aforesaid deserving patriots with his benevolence, shaming them with many kindnesses, and the simplicity of his home-life, and, above all, in flouting the decrees of the Revolutionary Government, which made every connection with ci-devant churches and priests a penal offence against the security of the State.

Amede Vincent was sent to the guillotine, and the representatives of the people confiscated his house and all his property on which they could lay their hands; but they never found the millions which he was supposed to have concealed. Certainly his daughter Esther—a young girl, not yet nineteen—had not found them either, for after her father's death she went to live in one of the poorer quarters of Paris, alone with an old and faithful servant named Lucienne. And while the Committee of Public Safety was deliberating whether it would be worth while to send Esther to the guillotine, to follow in her father's footsteps, a certain number of astute jail-birds plotted to obtain possession of her wealth.

The wealth existed, over in England; of that they were ready to take their oath, and the project which they had formed was as ingenious as it was diabolic: to feign a denunciation, to enact a pretended arrest, to place before the unfortunate girl the alternative of death or marriage with one of the gang, were the chief incidents of this inquitous project, and it was in the Cabaret de la Liberte that lots were thrown as to which among the herd of miscreants should be the favoured one to play the chief role in the sinister drama.

The lot fell to Merri; but the whole gang was to have a share in the putative fortune—even Rateau, the wretched creature with the hacking cough, who looked as if he had one foot in the grave, and shivered as if he were stricken with ague, put in a word now and again to remind his good friend Merri that he, too, was looking forward to his share of the spoils. Merri, however, was inclined to repudiate him altogether.

"Why should I share with you?" he said roughly, when, a few hours later, he and Rateau parted in the street outside the Cabaret de la Liberte. "Who are you, I would like to know, to try and poke your ugly nose into my affairs? How do I know where you come from, and whether you are not some crapulent spy of one of those pestilential committees?"

From which eloquent flow of language we may infer that the friendship between these two worthies was not of very old duration. Rateau would, no doubt, have protested loudly, but the fresh outer air had evidently caught his wheezy lungs, and for a minute or two he could do nothing but cough and splutter and groan, and cling to his unresponsive comrade for support. Then at last, when he had succeeded in recovering his breath, he said dolefully and with a ludicrous attempt at dignified reproach:

"Do not force me to remind you, citizen Merri, that if it had not been for my suggestion that we should all draw lots, and then play hazard as to who shall be the chosen one to woo the ci-devant millionairess, there would soon have been a free fight inside the cabaret, a number of broken heads, and no decision whatever arrived at; whilst you, who were never much of a fighter, would probably be lying now helpless, with a broken nose, and deprived of some of your teeth, and with no chance of entering the lists for the heiress. Instead of which, here you are, the victor by a stroke of good fortune, which you should at least have the good grace to ascribe to me."

Whether the poor wretch's argument had any weight with citizen Merri, or whether that worthy patriot merely thought that procrastination would, for the nonce, prove the best policy, it were impossible to say. Certain it is that in response to his companion's tirade he contented himself with a dubious grunt, and without another word turned on his heel and went slouching down the street.

III.

For the persistent and optimistic romanticist, there were still one or two idylls to be discovered flourishing under the shadow of the grim and relentless Revolution. One such was that which had Esther Vincent and Jack Kennard for hero and heroine. Esther, the orphaned daughter of one of the richest bankers of pre-Revolution days, now a daily governess and household drudge at ten francs a week in the house of a retired butcher in the Rue Richelieu, and Jack Kennard, formerly the representative of a big English firm of woollen manufacturers, who had thrown up his employment and prospects in England in order to watch over the girl whom he loved. He, himself an alien enemy, an Englishman, in deadly danger of his life every hour that he remained in France; and she, unwilling at the time to leave the horrors of revolutionary Paris while her father was lingering at the Conciergerie awaiting condemnation, as such forbidden to leave the city. So Kennard stayed on, unable to tear himself away from her, and obtained an unlucrative post as accountant in a small wine shop over by Montmartre. His life, like hers, was hanging by a thread; any day, any hour now, some malevolent denunciation might, in the sight of the Committee of Public Safety, turn the eighteen years old "suspect" into a living peril to the State, or the alien enemy into a dangerous spy.

Some of the happiest hours these two spent in one another's company were embittered by that ever-present dread of the peremptory knock at the door, the portentous: "Open, in the name of the Law!" the perquisition, the arrest, to which the only issue, these days, was the guillotine.

But the girl was only just eighteen, and he not many years older, and at that age, in spite of misery, sorrow, and dread, life always has its compensations. Youth cries out to happiness so insistently that happiness is forced to hear, and for a few moments, at the least, drives care and even the bitterest anxiety away.

For Esther Vincent and her English lover there were moments when they believed themselves to be almost happy. It was in the evenings mostly, when she came home from her work and he was free to spend an hour or two with her. Then old Lucienne, who had been Esther's nurse in the happy, olden days, and was an unpaid maid-of-all-work and a loved and trusted friend now, would bring in the lamp and pull the well-darned curtains over the windows. She would spread a clean cloth upon the table and bring in a meagre supper of coffee and black bread, perhaps a little butter or a tiny square of cheese. And the two young people would talk of the future, of the time when they would settle down in Kennard's old home, over in England, where his mother and sister even now were eating out their hearts with anxiety for him.

"Tell me all about the South Downs," Esther was very fond of saying; "and your village, and your house, and the rambler roses and the clematis arbour."

She never tired of hearing, or he of telling. The old Manor House, bought with his father's savings; the garden which was his mother's hobby; the cricket pitch on the village green. Oh, the cricket! She thought that so funny—the men in high, sugar-loaf hats, grown-up men, spending hours and hours, day after day, in banging at a ball with a wooden bat!

"Oh, Jack! The English are a funny, nice, dear, kind lot of people. I remember—"

She remembered so well that happy summer which she had spent with her father in England four years ago. It was after the Bastille had been stormed and taken, and the banker had journeyed to England with his daughter in something of a hurry. Then her father had talked of returning to France and leaving her behind with friends in England. But Esther would not be left. Oh, no! Even now she glowed with pride at the thought of her firmness in the matter. If she had remained in England she would never have seen her dear father again. Here remembrances grew bitter and sad, until Jack's hand reached soothingly, consolingly out to her, and she brushed away her tears, so as not to sadden him still more.

Then she would ask more questions about his home and his garden, about his mother and the dogs and the flowers; and once more they would forget that hatred and envy and death were already stalking their door.

IV.

"Open, in the name of the Law!"

It had come at last. A bolt from out the serene blue of their happiness. A rough, dirty, angry, cursing crowd, who burst through the heavy door even before they had time to open it. Lucienne collapsed into a chair, weeping and lamenting, with her apron thrown over her head. But Esther and Kennard stood quite still and calm, holding one another by the hand, just to give one another courage.

Some half dozen men stalked into the little room. Men? They looked like ravenous beasts, and were unspeakably dirty, wore soiled tricolour scarves above their tattered breeches in token of their official status. Two of them fell on the remnants of the meagre supper and devoured everything that remained on the table—bread, cheese, a piece of home-made sausage. The others ransacked the two attic-rooms which had been home for Esther and Lucienne: the little living-room under the sloping roof, with the small hearth on which very scanty meals were wont to be cooked, and the bare, narrow room beyond, with the iron bedstead, and the palliasse on the floor for Lucienne.

The men poked about everywhere, struck great, spiked sticks through the poor bits of bedding, and ripped up the palliasse. They tore open the drawers of the rickety chest and of the broken-down wardrobe, and did not spare the unfortunate young girl a single humiliation or a single indignity.

Kennard, burning with wrath, tried to protest.

"Hold that cub!" commanded the leader of the party, almost as soon as the young Englishman's hot, indignant words had resounded above the din of overturned furniture. "And if he opens his mouth again throw him into the street!" And Kennard, terrified lest he should be parted from Esther, thought it wiser to hold his peace.

They looked at one another, like two young trapped beasts—not despairing, but trying to infuse courage one into the other by a look of confidence and of love. Esther, in fact, kept her eyes fixed on her good-looking English lover, firmly keeping down the shudder of loathing which went right through her when she saw those awful men coming nigh her. There was one especially whom she abominated worse than the others, a bandy-legged ruffian, who regarded her with a leer that caused her an almost physical nausea. He did not take part in the perquisition, but sat down in the centre of the room and sprawled over the table with the air of one who was in authority. The others addressed him as "citizen Merri," and alternately ridiculed and deferred to him. And there was another, equally hateful, a horrible, cadaverous creature, with huge bare feet thrust into sabots, and lank hair, thick with grime. He did most of the talking, even though his loquacity occasionally broke down in a racking cough, which literally seemed to tear at his chest, and left him panting, hoarse, and with beads of moisture upon his low, pallid forehead.

Of course, the men found nothing that could even remotely be termed compromising. Esther had been very prudent in deference to Kennard's advice; she also had very few possessions. Nevertheless, when the wretches had turned every article of furniture inside out, one of them asked curtly:

"What do we do next, citizen Merri?"

"Do?" broke in the cadaverous creature, even before Merri had time to reply. "Do? Why, take the wench to—to—"

He got no further, became helpless with coughing. Esther, quite instinctively, pushed the carafe of water towards him.

"Nothing of the sort!" riposted Merri sententiously. "The wench stays here!"

Both Esther and Jack had much ado to suppress an involuntary cry of relief, which at this unexpected pronouncement had risen to their lips.

The man with the cough tried to protest.

"But—" he began hoarsely.

"I said, the wench stays here!" broke in Merri peremptorily. "Ah ca!" he added, with a savage imprecation. "Do you command here, citizen Rateau, or do I?"

The other at once became humble, even cringing.

"You, of course, citizen," he rejoined in his hollow voice. "I would only remark—"

"Remark nothing," retorted the other curtly. "See to it that the cub is out of the house. And after that put a sentry outside the wench's door. No one to go in and out of here under any pretext whatever. Understand?"

Kennard this time uttered a cry of protest. The helplessness of his position exasperated him almost to madness. Two men were holding him tightly by his sinewy arms. With an Englishman's instinct for a fight, he would not only have tried, but also succeeded in knocking these two down, and taken the other four on after that, with quite a reasonable chance of success. That tuberculous creature, now! And that bandy-legged ruffian! Jack Kennard had been an amateur middle-weight champion in his day, and these brutes had no more science than an enraged bull! But even as he fought against that instinct he realised the futility of a struggle. The danger of it, too—not for himself, but for her. After all, they were not going to take her away to one of those awful places from which the only egress was the way to the guillotine; and if there was that amount of freedom there was bound to be some hope. At twenty there is always hope!

So when, in obedience to Merri's orders, the two ruffians began to drag him towards the door, he said firmly:

"Leave me alone. I'll go without this unnecessary struggling."

Then, before the wretches realised his intention, he had jerked himself free from them and run to Esther.

"Have no fear," he said to her in English, and in a rapid whisper. "I'll watch over you. The house opposite. I know the people. I'll manage it somehow. Be on the look-out."

They would not let him say more, and she only had the chance of responding firmly:

"I am not afraid, and I'll be on the look-out." The next moment Merri's compeers seized him from behind—four of them this time.

Then, of course, prudence went to the winds. He hit out to the right and left. Knocked two of those recreants down, and already was prepared to seize Esther in his arms, make a wild dash for the door, and run with her, whither only God knew, when Rateau, that awful consumptive reprobate, crept slyly up behind him and dealt him a swift and heavy blow on the skull with his weighted stick. Kennard staggered, and the bandits closed upon him. Those on the floor had time to regain their feet. To make assurance doubly sure, one of them emulated Rateau's tactics, and hit the Englishman once more on the head from behind. After that, Kennard became inert; he had partly lost consciousness. His head ached furiously. Esther, numb with horror, saw him bundled out of the room. Rateau, coughing and spluttering, finally closed the door upon the unfortunate and the four brigands who had hold of him.

Only Merri and that awful Rateau had remained in the room. The latter, gasping for breath now, poured himself out a mugful of water and drank it down at one draught. Then he swore, because he wanted rum, or brandy, or even wine. Esther watched him and Merri, fascinated. Poor old Lucienne was quietly weeping behind her apron.

"Now then, my wench," Merri began abruptly, "suppose you sit down here and listen to what I have to say."

He pulled a chair close to him and, with one of those hideous leers which had already caused her to shudder, he beckoned her to sit. Esther obeyed as if in a dream. Her eyes were dilated like those of one in a waking trance. She moved mechanically, like a bird attracted by a serpent, terrified, yet unresisting. She felt utterly helpless between these two villainous brutes, and anxiety for her English lover seemed further to numb her senses. When she was sitting she turned her gaze, with an involuntary appeal for pity, upon the bandy-legged ruffian beside her. He laughed.

"No! I am not going to hurt you," he said with smooth condescension, which was far more loathsome to Esther's ears than his comrades' savage oaths had been. "You are pretty and you have pleased me. 'Tis no small matter, forsooth!" he added, with loud-voiced bombast, "to have earned the good-will of citizen Merri. You, my wench, are in luck's way. You realise what has occurred just now. You are amenable to the law which has decreed you to be suspect. I hold an order for your arrest. I can have you seized at once by my men, dragged to the Conciergerie, and from thence nothing can save you—neither your good looks nor the protection of citizen Merri. It means the guillotine. You understand that, don't you?"

She sat quite still; only her hands were clutched convulsively together.

But she contrived to say quite firmly:

"I do, and I am not afraid."

Merri waved a huge and very dirty hand with a careless gesture.

"I know," he said with a harsh laugh. "They all say that, don't they, citizen Rateau?"

"Until the time comes," assented that worthy dryly.

"Until the time comes," reiterated the other. "Now, my wench," he added, once more turning to Esther, "I don't want that time to come. I don't want your pretty head to go rolling down into the basket, and to receive the slap on the face which the citizen executioner has of late taken to bestowing on those aristocratic cheeks which Mme. la Guillotine has finally blanched for ever. Like this, you see."

And the inhuman wretch took up one of the round cushions from the nearest chair, held it up at arm's length, as if it were a head which he held by the hair, and then slapped it twice with the palm of his left hand. The gesture was so horrible and withal so grotesque, that Esther closed her eyes with a shudder, and her pale cheeks took on a leaden hue. Merri laughed aloud and threw the cushion down again.

"Unpleasant, what? my pretty wench! Well, you know what to expect ... unless," he added significantly, "you are reasonable and will listen to what I am about to tell you."

Esther was no fool, nor was she unsophisticated. These were not times when it was possible for any girl, however carefully nurtured and tenderly brought up, to remain ignorant of the realities and the brutalities of life. Even before Merri had put his abominable proposition before her, she knew what he was driving at. Marriage—marriage to him! that ignoble wretch, more vile than any dumb creature! In exchange for her life!

It was her turn now to laugh. The very thought of it was farcical in its very odiousness. Merri, who had embarked on his proposal with grandiloquent phraseology, suddenly paused, almost awed by that strange, hysterical laughter.

"By Satan and all his ghouls!" he cried, and jumped to his feet, his cheeks paling beneath the grime.

Then rage seized him at his own cowardice. His egregious vanity, wounded by that laughter, egged him on. He tried to seize Esther by the waist. But she, quick as some panther on the defense, had jumped up, too, and pounced upon a knife—the very one she had been using for that happy little supper with her lover a brief half hour ago. Unguarded, unthinking, acting just with a blind instinct, she raised it and cried hoarsely:

"If you dare touch me, I'll kill you!"

It was ludicrous, of course. A mouse threatening a tiger. The very next moment Rateau had seized her hand and quietly taken away the knife. Merri shook himself like a frowsy dog.

"Whew!" he ejaculated. "What a vixen! But," he added lightly, "I like her all the better for that—eh, Rateau? Give me a wench with a temperament, I say!"

But Esther, too, had recovered herself. She realised her helplessness, and gathered courage from the consciousness of it! Now she faced the infamous villain more calmly.

"I will never marry you," she said loudly and firmly. "Never! I am not afraid to die. I am not afraid of the guillotine. There is no shame attached to death. So now you may do as you please—denounce me, and send me to follow in the footsteps of my dear father, if you wish. But whilst I am alive you will never come nigh me. If you ever do but lay a finger upon me, it will be because I am dead and beyond the reach of your polluting touch. And now I have said all that I will ever say to you in this life. If you have a spark of humanity left in you, you will, at least, let me prepare for death in peace."

She went round to where poor old Lucienne still sat, like an insentient log, panic-stricken. She knelt down on the floor and rested her arm on the old woman's knees. The light of the lamp fell full upon her, her pale face, and mass of chestnut-brown hair. There was nothing about her at this moment to inflame a man's desire. She looked pathetic in her helplessness, and nearly lifeless through the intensity of her pallor, whilst the look in her eyes was almost maniacal.

Merri cursed and swore, tried to hearten himself by turning on his friend. But Rateau had collapsed—whether with excitement or the ravages of disease, it were impossible to say. He sat upon a low chair, his long legs, his violet-circled eyes staring out with a look of hebetude and overwhelming fatigue. Merri looked around him and shuddered. The atmosphere of the place had become strangely weird and uncanny; even the tablecloth, dragged half across the table, looked somehow like a shroud.

"What shall we do, Rateau?" he asked tremulously at last.

"Get out of this infernal place," replied the other huskily. "I feel as if I were in my grave-clothes already."

"Hold your tongue, you miserable coward! You'll make the aristo think that we are afraid."

"Well?" queried Rateau blandly. "Aren't you?"

"No!" replied Merri fiercely. "I'll go now because … because … well! because I have had enough to-day. And the wench sickens me. I wish to serve the Republic by marrying her, but just now I feel as if I should never really want her. So I'll go! But, understand!" he added, and turned once more to Esther, even though he could not bring himself to go nigh her again. "Understand that to-morrow I'll come again for my answer. In the meanwhile, you may think matters over, and, maybe, you'll arrive at a more reasonable frame of mind. You will not leave these rooms until I set you free. My men will remain as sentinels at your door."

He beckoned to Rateau, and the two men went out of the room without another word.

V.

The whole of that night Esther remained shut up in her apartment in the Petite Rue Taranne. All night she heard the measured tramp, the movements, the laughter and loud talking of men outside her door. Once or twice she tried to listen to what they said. But the doors and walls in these houses of old Paris were too stout to allow voices to filter through, save in the guise of a confused murmur. She would have felt horribly lonely and frightened but for the fact that in one window on the third floor in the house opposite the light of a lamp appeared like a glimmer of hope. Jack Kennard was there, on the watch. He had the window open and sat beside it until a very late hour; and after that he kept the light in, as a beacon, to bid her be of good cheer.

In the middle of the night he made an attempt to see her, hoping to catch the sentinels asleep or absent. But, having climbed the five stories of the house wherein she dwelt, he arrived on the landing outside her door and found there half a dozen ruffians squatting on the stone floor and engaged in playing hazard with a pack of greasy cards. That wretched consumptive, Rateau, was with them, and made a facetious remark as Kennard, pale and haggard, almost ghostlike, with a white bandage round his head, appeared upon the landing.

"Go back to bed, citizen," the odious creature said, with a raucous laugh. "We are taking care of your sweetheart for you."

Never in all his life had Jack Kennard felt so abjectly wretched as he did then, so miserably helpless. There was nothing that he could do, save to return to the lodging, which a kind friend had lent him for the occasion, and from whence he could, at any rate, see the windows behind which his beloved was watching and suffering.

When he went a few moments ago, he had left the porte cochere ajar. Now he pushed it open and stepped into the dark passage beyond. A tiny streak of light filtrated through a small curtained window in the concierge's lodge; it served to guide Kennard to the foot of the narrow stone staircase which led to the floors above. Just at the foot of the stairs, on the mat, a white paper glimmered in the dim shaft of light. He paused, puzzled, quite certain that the paper was not there five minutes ago when he went out. Oh! it may have fluttered in from the courtyard beyond, or from anywhere, driven by the draught. But, even so, with that mechanical action peculiar to most people under like circumstances, he stooped and picked up the paper, turned it over between his fingers, and saw that a few words were scribbled on it in pencil. The light was too dim to read by, so Kennard, still quite mechanically, kept the paper in his hand and went up to his room. There, by the light of the lamp, he read the few words scribbled in pencil:

"Wait in the street outside."

Nothing more. The message was obviously not intended for him, and yet.... A strange excitement possessed him. If it should be! If…! He had heard—everyone had—of the mysterious agencies that were at work, under cover of darkness, to aid the unfortunate, the innocent, the helpless. He had heard of that legendary English gentleman who had before now defied the closest vigilance of the Committees, and snatched their intended victims out of their murderous clutches, at times under their very eyes.

If this should be…! He scarce dared put his hope into words. He could not bring himself really to believe. But he went. He ran downstairs and out into the street, took his stand under a projecting doorway nearly opposite the house which held the woman he loved, and leaning against the wall, he waited.

After many hours—it was then past three o'clock in the morning, and the sky of an inky blackness—he felt so numb that despite his will a kind of trance-like drowsiness overcame him. He could no longer stand on his feet; his knees were shaking; his head felt so heavy that he could not keep it up. It rolled round from shoulder to shoulder, as if his will no longer controlled it. And it ached furiously. Everything around him was very still. Even "Paris-by-Night," that grim and lurid giant, was for the moment at rest. A warm summer rain was falling; its gentle, pattering murmur into the gutter helped to lull Kennard's senses into somnolence. He was on the point of dropping off to sleep when something suddenly roused him. A noise of men shouting and laughing—familiar sounds enough in these squalid Paris streets.

But Kennard was wide awake now; numbness had given place to intense quivering of all his muscles, and super-keenness of his every sense. He peered into the darkness and strained his ears to hear. The sound certainly appeared to come from the house opposite, and there, too, it seemed as if something or things were moving. Men! More than one or two, surely! Kennard thought that he could distinguish at least three distinct voices; and there was that weird, racking cough which proclaimed the presence of Rateau.

Now the men were quite close to where he—Kennard—still stood cowering. A minute or two later they had passed down the street. Their hoarse voices soon died away in the distance. Kennard crept cautiously out of his hiding-place. Message or mere coincidence, he now blessed that mysterious scrap of paper. Had he remained in his room, he might really have dropped off to sleep and not heard these men going away.

There were three of them at least—Kennard thought four. But, anyway, the number of watch-dogs outside the door of his beloved had considerably diminished. He felt that he had the strength to grapple with them, even if there were still three of them left. He, an athlete, English, and master of the art of self-defence; and they, a mere pack of drink-sodden brutes! Yes! He was quite sure he could do it. Quite sure that he could force his way into Esther's rooms and carry her off in his arms—whither? God alone knew. And God alone would provide.

Just for a moment he wondered if, while he was in that state of somnolence, other bandits had come to take the place of those that were going. But this thought he quickly dismissed. In any case, he felt a giant's strength in himself, and could not rest now till he had tried once more to see her. He crept very cautiously along; was satisfied that the street was deserted.

Already he had reached the house opposite, had pushed open the porte cochere, which was on the latch—when, without the slightest warning, he was suddenly attacked from behind, his arms seized and held behind his back with a vice-like grip, whilst a vigorous kick against the calves of his legs caused him to lose his footing and suddenly brought him down, sprawling and helpless, in the gutter, while in his ear there rang the hideous sound of the consumptive ruffian's racking cough.

"What shall we do with the cub now?" a raucous voice came out of the darkness.

"Let him lie there," was the quick response. "It'll teach him to interfere with the work of honest patriots."

Kennard, lying somewhat bruised and stunned, heard this decree with thankfulness. The bandits obviously thought him more hurt than he was, and if only they would leave him lying here, he would soon pick himself up and renew his attempt to go to Esther. He did not move, feigning unconsciousness, even though he felt rather than saw that hideous Rateau stooping over him, heard his stertorous breathing, the wheezing in his throat.

"Run and fetch a bit of cord, citizen Desmonts," the wretch said presently. "A trussed cub is safer than a loose one."

This dashed Kennard's hopes to a great extent. He felt that he must act quickly, before those brigands returned and rendered him completely helpless. He made a movement to rise—a movement so swift and sudden as only a trained athlete can make. But, quick as he was, that odious, wheezing creature was quicker still, and now, when Kennard had turned on his back, Rateau promptly sat on his chest, a dead weight, with long legs stretched out before him, coughing and spluttering, yet wholly at his ease.

Oh! the humiliating position for an amateur middle-weight champion to find himself in, with that drink-sodden—Kennard was sure that he was drink-sodden—consumptive sprawling on the top of him!

"Don't trouble, citizen Desmonts," the wretch cried out after his retreating companions. "I have what I want by me."

Very leisurely he pulled a coil of rope out of the capacious pocket of his tattered coat. Kennard could not see what he was doing, but felt it with supersensitive instinct all the time. He lay quite still beneath the weight of that miscreant, feigning unconsciousness, yet hardly able to breathe. That tuberculous caitiff was such a towering weight. But he tried to keep his faculties on the alert, ready for that surprise spring which would turn the tables, at the slightest false move on the part of Rateau.

But, as luck would have it, Rateau did not make a single false move. It was amazing with what dexterity he kept Kennard down, even while he contrived to pinion him with cords. An old sailor, probably, he seemed so dexterous with knots.

My God! the humiliation of it all. And Esther a helpless prisoner, inside that house not five paces away! Kennard's heavy, wearied eyes could perceive the light in her window, five stories above where he lay, in the gutter, a helpless log. Even now he gave a last desperate shriek:

"Esther!"

But in a second the abominable brigand's hand came down heavily upon his mouth, whilst a raucous voice spluttered rather than said, right through an awful fit of coughing:

"Another sound, and I'll gag as well as bind you, you young fool!"

After which, Kennard remained quite still.

VI.

Esther, up in her little attic, knew nothing of what her English lover was even then suffering for her sake. She herself had passed, during the night, through every stage of horror and of fear. Soon after midnight that execrable brigand Rateau had poked his ugly, cadaverous face in at the door and peremptorily called for Lucienne. The woman, more dead than alive now with terror, had answered with mechanical obedience.

"I and my friends are thirsty," the man had commanded. "Go and fetch us a litre of eau-de-vie."

Poor Lucienne stammered a pitiable: "Where shall I go?"

"To the house at the sign of 'Le fort Samson,' in the Rue de Seine," replied Rateau curtly. "They'll serve you well if you mention my name."

Of course Lucienne protested. She was a decent woman, who had never been inside a cabaret in her life.

"Then it's time you began," was Rateau's dry comment, which was greeted with much laughter from his abominable companions.

Lucienne was forced to go. It would, of course, have been futile and madness to resist. This had occurred three hours since. The Rue de Seine was not far, but the poor woman had not returned. Esther was left with this additional horror weighing upon her soul. What had happened to her unfortunate servant? Visions of outrage and murder floated before the poor girl's tortured brain. At best, Lucienne was being kept out of the way in order to make her—Esther—feel more lonely and desperate! She remained at the window after that, watching that light in the house opposite and fingering her prayer-book, the only solace which she had. Her attic was so high up and the street so narrow, that she could not see what went on in the street below. At one time she heard a great to-do outside her door. It seemed as if some of the bloodhounds who were set to watch her had gone, or that others came. She really hardly cared which it was. Then she heard a great commotion coming from the street immediately beneath her: men shouting and laughing, and that awful creature's rasping cough.

At one moment she felt sure that Kennard had called to her by name. She heard his voice distinctly, raised as if in a despairing cry.

After that, all was still.

So still that she could hear her heart beating furiously, and then a tear falling from her eyes upon her open book. So still that the gentle patter of the rain sounded like a soothing lullaby. She was very young, and was very tired. Out, above the line of sloping roofs and chimney pots, the darkness of the sky was yielding to the first touch of dawn. The rain ceased. Everything became deathly still. Esther's head fell, wearied, upon her folded arms.

Then, suddenly, she was wide awake. Something had roused her. A noise. At first she could not tell what it was, but now she knew. It was the opening and shutting of the door behind her, and then a quick, stealthy footstep across the room. The horror of it all was unspeakable. Esther remained as she had been, on her knees, mechanically fingering her prayer-book, unable to move, unable to utter a sound, as if paralysed. She knew that one of those abominable creatures had entered her room, was coming near her even now. She did not know who it was, only guessed it was Rateau, for she heard a raucous, stertorous wheeze. Yet she could not have then turned to look if her life had depended upon her doing so.

The whole thing had occurred in less than half a dozen heart-beats. The next moment the wretch was close to her. Mercifully she felt that her senses were leaving her. Even so, she felt that a handkerchief was being bound over her mouth to prevent her screaming. Wholly unnecessary this, for she could not have uttered a sound. Then she was lifted off the ground and carried across the room, then over the threshold. A vague, subconscious effort of will helped her to keep her head averted from that wheezing wretch who was carrying her. Thus she could see the landing, and two of those abominable watchdogs who had been set to guard her.

The ghostly grey light of dawn came peeping in through the narrow dormer window in the sloping roof, and faintly illumined their sprawling forms, stretched out at full length, with their heads buried in their folded arms and their naked legs looking pallid and weird in the dim light. Their stertorous breathing woke the echoes of the bare, stone walls. Esther shuddered and closed her eyes. She was now like an insentient log, without power, or thought, or will—almost without feeling.

Then, all at once, the coolness of the morning air caught her full in the face. She opened her eyes and tried to move, but those powerful arms held her more closely than before. Now she could have shrieked with horror. With returning consciousness the sense of her desperate position came on her with its full and ghastly significance, its awe-inspiring details. The grey dawn, the abandoned wretch who held her, and the stillness of this early morning hour, when not one pitying soul would be astir to lend her a helping hand or give her the solace of mute sympathy. So great, indeed, was this stillness that the click of the man's sabots upon the uneven pavement reverberated, ghoul-like and weird.

And it was through that awesome stillness that a sound suddenly struck her ear, which, in the instant, made her feel that she was not really alive, or, if alive, was sleeping and dreaming strange and impossible dreams. It was the sound of a voice, clear and firm, and with a wonderful ring of merriment in its tones, calling out just above a whisper, and in English, if you please:

"Look out, Ffoulkes! That young cub is as strong as a horse. He will give us all away if you are not careful."

A dream? Of course it was a dream, for the voice had sounded very close to her ear; so close, in fact, that ... well! Esther was quite sure that her face still rested against the hideous, tattered, and grimy coat which that repulsive Rateau had been wearing all along. And there was the click of his sabots upon the pavement all the time. So, then, the voice and the merry, suppressed laughter which accompanied it, must all have been a part of her dream. How long this lasted she could not have told you. An hour and more, she thought, while the grey dawn yielded to the roseate hue of morning. Somehow, she no longer suffered either terror or foreboding. A subtle atmosphere of strength and of security seemed to encompass her. At one time she felt as if she were driven along in a car that jolted horribly, and when she moved her face and hands they came in contact with things that were fresh and green and smelt of the country. She was in darkness then, and more than three parts unconscious, but the handkerchief had been removed from her mouth. It seemed to her as if she could hear the voice of her Jack, but far away and indistinct; also the tramp of horses' hoofs and the creaking of cart-wheels, and at times that awful, rasping cough, which reminded her of the presence of a loathsome wretch, who should not have had a part in her soothing dream.

Thus many hours must have gone by.

Then, all at once, she was inside a house—a room, and she felt that she was being lowered very gently to the ground. She was on her feet, but she could not see where she was. There was furniture; a carpet; a ceiling; the man Rateau with the sabots and the dirty coat, and the merry English voice, and a pair of deep-set blue eyes, thoughtful and lazy and infinitely kind.

But before she could properly focus what she saw, everything began to whirl and to spin around her, to dance a wild and idiotic saraband, which caused her to laugh, and to laugh, until her throat felt choked and her eyes hot; after which she remembered nothing more.

VII.

The first thing of which Esther Vincent was conscious, when she returned to her senses, was of her English lover kneeling beside her. She was lying on some kind of couch, and she could see his face in profile, for he had turned and was speaking to someone at the far end of the room.

"And was it you who knocked me down?" he was saying, "and sat on my chest, and trussed me like a fowl?"

"La! my dear sir," a lazy, pleasant voice riposted, "what else could I do? There was no time for explanations. You were half-crazed, and would not have understood. And you were ready to bring all the nightwatchmen about our ears."

"I am sorry!" Kennard said simply. "But how could I guess?"

"You couldn't," rejoined the other. "That is why I had to deal so summarily with you and with Mademoiselle Esther, not to speak of good old Lucienne, who had never, in her life, been inside a cabaret. You must all forgive me ere you start upon your journey. You are not out of the wood yet, remember. Though Paris is a long way behind, France itself is no longer a healthy place for any of you."

"But how did we ever get out of Paris? I was smothered under a pile of cabbages, with Lucienne on one side of me and Esther, unconscious, on the other. I could see nothing. I know we halted at the barrier. I thought we would be recognised, turned back! My God! how I trembled!"

"Bah!" broke in the other, with a careless laugh. "It is not so difficult as it seems. We have done it before—eh, Ffoulkes? A market-gardener's cart, a villainous wretch like myself to drive it, another hideous object like Sir Andrew Ffoulkes, Bart., to lead the scraggy nag, a couple of forged or stolen passports, plenty of English gold, and the deed is done!"

Esther's eyes were fixed upon the speaker. She marvelled now how she could have been so blind. The cadaverous face was nothing but a splendid use of grease paint! The rags! the dirt! the whole assumption of a hideous character was masterly! But there were the eyes, deep-set, and thoughtful and kind. How did she fail to guess?

"You are known as the Scarlet Pimpernel," she said suddenly. "Suzanne de Tournai was my friend. She told me. You saved her and her family, and now ... oh, my God!" she exclaimed, "how shall we ever repay you?"

"By placing yourselves unreservedly in my friend Ffoulkes' hands," he replied gently. "He will lead you to safety and, if you wish it, to England."

"If we wish it!" Kennard sighed fervently.

"You are not coming with us, Blakeney?" queried Sir Andrew Ffoulkes, and it seemed to Esther's sensitive ears as if a tone of real anxiety and also of entreaty rang in the young man's voice.

"No, not this time," replied Sir Percy lightly. "I like my character of Rateau, and I don't want to give it up just yet. I have done nothing to arouse suspicion in the minds of my savoury compeers up at the Cabaret de la Liberte. I can easily keep this up for some time to come, and frankly I admire myself as citizen Rateau. I don't know when I have enjoyed a character so much!"

"You mean to return to the Cabaret de la Liberte!" exclaimed Sir Andrew.

"Why not?"

"You will be recognised!"

"Not before I have been of service to a good many unfortunates, I hope."

"But that awful cough of yours! Percy, you'll do yourself an injury with it one day."

"Not I! I like that cough. I practised it for a long time before I did it to perfection. Such a splendid wheeze! I must teach Tony to do it some day. Would you like to hear it now?"

He laughed, that perfect, delightful, lazy laugh of his, which carried every hearer with it along the path of light-hearted merriment. Then he broke into the awful cough of the consumptive Rateau. And Esther Vincent instinctively closed her eyes and shuddered.

CHAPTER X. "NEEDS MUST—"

I.

The children were all huddled up together in one corner of the room. Etienne and Valentine, the two eldest, had their arms round the little one. As for Lucile, she would have told you herself that she felt just like a bird between two snakes—terrified and fascinated—oh! especially by that little man with the pale face and the light grey eyes and the slender white hands unstained by toil, one of which rested lightly upon the desk, and was only clenched now and then at a word or a look from the other man or from Lucile herself.

But Commissary Lebel just tried to browbeat her. It was not difficult, for in truth she felt frightened enough already, with all this talk of "traitors" and that awful threat of the guillotine.

Lucile Clamette, however, would have remained splendidly loyal in spite of all these threats, if it had not been for the children. She was little mother to them; for father was a cripple, with speech and mind already impaired by creeping paralysis, and maman had died when little Josephine was born. And now those fiends threatened not only her, but Etienne who was not fourteen, and Valentine who was not much more than ten, with death, unless she—Lucile—broke the solemn word which she had given to M. le Marquis. At first she had tried to deny all knowledge of M. le Marquis' whereabouts.

"I can assure M. le Commissaire that I do not know," she had persisted quietly, even though her heart was beating so rapidly in her bosom that she felt as if she must choke.

"Call me citizen Commissary," Lebel had riposted curtly. "I should take it as a proof that your aristocratic sentiments are not so deep-rooted as they appear to be."

"Yes, citizen!" murmured Lucile, under her breath.

Then the other one, he with the pale eyes and the slender white hands, leaned forward over the desk, and the poor girl felt as if a mighty and unseen force was holding her tight, so tight that she could neither move, nor breathe, nor turn her gaze away from those pale, compelling eyes. In the remote corner little Josephine was whimpering, and Etienne's big, dark eyes were fixed bravely upon his eldest sister.

"There, there! little citizeness," the awful man said, in a voice that sounded low and almost caressing, "there is nothing to be frightened of. No one is going to hurt you or your little family. We only want you to be reasonable. You have promised to your former employer that you would never tell anyone of his whereabouts. Well! we don't ask you to tell us anything.

"All that we want you to do is to write a letter to M. le Marquis—one that I myself will dictate to you. You have written to M. le Marquis before now, on business matters, have you not?"

"Yes, monsieur—yes, citizen," stammered Lucile through her tears.

"Father was bailiff to M. le Marquis until he became a cripple and now I—-"

"Do not write any letter, Lucile," Etienne suddenly broke in with forceful vehemence. "It is a trap set by these miscreants to entrap M. le Marquis."

There was a second's silence in the room after this sudden outburst on the part of the lad. Then the man with the pale face said quietly:

"Citizen Lebel, order the removal of that boy. Let him be kept in custody till he has learned to hold his tongue."

But before Lebel could speak to the two soldiers who were standing on guard at the door, Lucile had uttered a loud cry of agonised protest.

"No! no! monsieur!—that is citizen!" she implored. "Do not take Etienne away. He will be silent.... I promise you that he will be silent … only do not take him away! Etienne, my little one!" she added, turning her tear-filled eyes to her brother, "I entreat thee to hold thy tongue!"

The others, too, clung to Etienne, and the lad, awed and subdued, relapsed into silence.

"Now then," resumed Lebel roughly, after a while, "let us get on with this business. I am sick to death of it. It has lasted far too long already."

He fixed his blood-shot eyes upon Lucile and continued gruffly:

"Now listen to me, my wench, for this is going to be my last word. Citizen Chauvelin here has already been very lenient with you by allowing this letter business. If I had my way I'd make you speak here and now. As it is, you either sit down and write the letter at citizen Chauvelin's dictation at once, or I send you with that impudent brother of yours and your imbecile father to jail, on a charge of treason against the State, for aiding and abetting the enemies of the Republic; and you know what the consequences of such a charge usually are. The other two brats will go to a House of Correction, there to be detained during the pleasure of the Committee of Public Safety. That is my last word," he reiterated fiercely. "Now, which is it to be?"

He paused, the girl's wan cheeks turned the colour of lead. She moistened her lips once or twice with her tongue; beads of perspiration appeared at the roots of her hair. She gazed helplessly at her tormentors, not daring to look on those three huddled-up little figures there in the corner. A few seconds sped away in silence. The man with the pale eyes rose and pushed his chair away. He went to the window, stood there with his back to the room, those slender white hands of his clasped behind him. Neither the commissary nor the girl appeared to interest him further. He was just gazing out of the window.

The other was still sprawling beside the desk, his large, coarse hand—how different his hands were!—was beating a devil's tattoo upon the arm of his chair.

After a few minutes, Lucile made a violent effort to compose herself, wiped the moisture from her pallid forehead and dried the tears which still hung upon her lashes. Then she rose from her chair and walked resolutely up to the desk.

"I will write the letter," she said simply.

Lebel gave a snort of satisfaction; but the other did not move from his position near the window. The boy, Etienne, had uttered a cry of passionate protest.

"Do not give M. le Marquis away, Lucile!" he said hotly. "I am not afraid to die."

But Lucile had made up her mind. How could she do otherwise, with these awful threats hanging over them all? She and Etienne and poor father gone, and the two young ones in one of those awful Houses of Correction, where children were taught to hate the Church, to shun the Sacraments, and to blaspheme God!

"What am I to write?" she asked dully, resolutely closing her ears against her brother's protest.

Lebel pushed pen, ink and paper towards her and she sat down, ready to begin.

"Write!" now came in a curt command from the man at the window. And Lucile wrote at his dictation:

"MONSIEUR LE MARQUIS,—We are in grave trouble. My brother Etienne and I have been arrested on a charge of treason. This means the guillotine for us and for poor father, who can no longer speak; and the two little ones are to be sent to one of those dreadful Houses of Correction, where children are taught to deny God and to blaspheme. You alone can save us, M. le Marquis; and I beg you on my knees to do it. The citizen Commissary here says that you have in your possession certain papers which are of great value to the State, and that if I can persuade you to give these up, Etienne, father and I and the little ones will be left unmolested. M. le Marquis, you once said that you could never adequately repay my poor father for all his devotion in your service. You can do it now, M. le Marquis, by saving us all. I will be at the chateau a week from to-day. I entreat you, M. le Marquis, to come to me then and to bring the papers with you; or if you can devise some other means of sending the papers to me, I will obey your behests.—I am, M. le Marquis' faithful and devoted servant, **LUCILE CLAMETTE.**"

The pen dropped from the unfortunate girl's fingers. She buried her face in her hands and sobbed convulsively. The children were silent, awed and subdued—tired out, too. Only Etienne's dark eyes were fixed upon his sister with a look of mute reproach.

Lebel had made no attempt to interrupt the flow of his colleague's dictation. Only once or twice did a hastily smothered "What the—!" of astonishment escape his lips. Now, when the letter was finished and duly signed, he drew it to him and strewed the sand over it. Chauvelin, more impassive than ever, was once more gazing out of the window.

"How are the ci-devant aristos to get this letter?" the commissary asked.

"It must be put in the hollow tree which stands by the side of the stable gate at Montorgueil," whispered Lucile.

"And the aristos will find it there?"

"Yes. M. le Vicomte goes there once or twice a week to see if there is anything there from one of us."

"They are in hiding somewhere close by, then?"

But to this the girl gave no reply. Indeed, she felt as if any word now might choke her.

"Well, no matter where they are!" the inhuman wretch resumed, with brutal cynicism. "We've got them now—both of them. Marquis! Vicomte!" he added, and spat on the ground to express his contempt of such titles. "Citizens Montorgueil, father and son—that's all they are! And as such they'll walk up in state to make their bow to Mme. la Guillotine!"

"May we go now?" stammered Lucile through her tears.

Lebel nodded in assent, and the girl rose and turned to walk towards the door. She called to the children, and the little ones clustered round her skirts like chicks around the mother-hen. Only Etienne remained aloof, wrathful against his sister for what he deemed her treachery. "Women have no sense of honour!" he muttered to himself, with all the pride of conscious manhood. But Lucile felt more than ever like a bird who is vainly trying to evade the clutches of a fowler. She gathered the two little ones around her. Then, with a cry like a wounded doe she ran quickly out of the room.

II.

As soon as the sound of the children's footsteps had died away down the corridor, Lebel turned with a grunt to his still silent companion.

"And now, citizen Chauvelin," he said roughly, "perhaps you will be good enough to explain what is the meaning of all this tomfoolery."

"Tomfoolery, citizen?" queried the other blandly. "What tomfoolery, pray?"

"Why, about those papers!" growled Lebel savagely. "Curse you for an interfering busybody! It was I who got information that those pestilential aristos, the Montorgueils, far from having fled the country are in hiding somewhere in my district. I could have made the girl give up their hiding-place pretty soon, without any help from you. What right had you to interfere, I should like to know?"

"You know quite well what right I had, citizen Lebel," replied Chauvelin with perfect composure. "The right conferred upon me by the Committee of Public Safety, of whom I am still an unworthy member. They sent me down here to lend you a hand in an investigation which is of grave importance to them."

"I know that!" retorted Lebel sulkily. "But why have invented the story of the papers?"

"It is no invention, citizen," rejoined Chauvelin with slow emphasis. "The papers do exist. They are actually in the possession of the Montorgueils, father and son. To capture the two aristos would be not only a blunder, but criminal folly, unless we can lay hands on the papers at the same time."

"But what in Satan's name are those papers?" ejaculated Lebel with a fierce oath.

"Think, citizen Lebel! Think!" was Chauvelin's cool rejoinder. "Methinks you might arrive at a pretty shrewd guess." Then, as the other's bluster and bounce suddenly collapsed upon his colleague's calm, accusing gaze, the latter continued with impressive deliberation:

"The papers which the two aristos have in their possession, citizen, are receipts for money, for bribes paid to various members of the Committee of Public Safety by Royalist agents for the overthrow of our glorious Republic. You know all about them, do you not?"

While Chauvelin spoke, a look of furtive terror had crept into Lebel's eyes; his cheeks became the colour of lead. But even so, he tried to keep up an air of incredulity and of amazement.

"I?" he exclaimed. "What do you mean, citizen Chauvelin? What should I know about it?"

"Some of those receipts are signed with your name, citizen Lebel," retorted Chauvelin forcefully. "Bah!" he added, and a tone of savage contempt crept into his even, calm voice now. "Heriot, Foucquier, Ducros and the whole gang of you are in it up to the neck: trafficking with our enemies, trading with England, taking bribes from every quarter for working against the safety of the Republic. Ah! if I had my way, I would let the hatred of those aristos take its course. I would let the Montorgueils and the whole pack of Royalist agents publish those infamous proofs of your treachery and of your baseness to the entire world, and send the whole lot of you to the guillotine!"

He had spoken with so much concentrated fury, and the hatred and contempt expressed in his pale eyes were so fierce that an involuntary ice-cold shiver ran down the length of Lebel's spine. But, even so, he would not give in; he tried to sneer and to keep up something of his former surly defiance.

"Bah!" he exclaimed, and with a lowering glance gave hatred for hatred, and contempt for contempt. "What can you do? An I am not mistaken, there is no more discredited man in France to-day than the unsuccessful tracker of the Scarlet Pimpernel."

The taunt went home. It was Chauvelin's turn now to lose countenance, to pale to the lips. The glow of virtuous indignation died out of his eyes, his look became furtive and shamed.

"You are right, citizen Lebel," he said calmly after a while. "Recriminations between us are out of place. I am a discredited man, as you say. Perhaps it would have been better if the Committee had sent me long ago to expiate my failures on the guillotine. I should at least not have suffered, as I am suffering now, daily, hourly humiliation at thought of the triumph of an enemy, whom I hate with a passion which consumes my very soul. But do not let us speak of me," he went on quietly. "There are graver affairs at stake just now than mine own."

Lebel said nothing more for the moment. Perhaps he was satisfied at the success of his taunt, even though the terror within his craven soul still caused the cold shiver to course up and down his spine. Chauvelin had once more turned to the window; his gaze was fixed upon the distance far away. The window gave on the North. That way, in a straight line, lay Calais, Boulogne, England—where he had been made to suffer such bitter humiliation at the hands of his elusive enemy. And immediately before him was Paris, where the very walls seemed to echo that mocking laugh of the daring Englishman which would haunt him even to his grave.

Lebel, unnerved by his colleague's silence, broke in gruffly at last:

"Well then, citizen," he said, with a feeble attempt at another sneer, "if you are not thinking of sending us all to the guillotine just yet, perhaps you will be good enough to explain just how the matter stands?"

"Fairly simply, alas!" replied Chauvelin dryly. "The two Montorgueils, father and son, under assumed names, were the Royalist agents who succeeded in suborning men such as you, citizen—the whole gang of you. We have tracked them down, to this district, have confiscated their lands and ransacked the old chateau for valuables and so on. Two days later, the first of a series of pestilential anonymous letters reached the Committee of Public Safety, threatening the publication of a whole series of compromising documents if the Marquis and the Vicomte de Montorgueil were in any way molested, and if all the Montorgueil property is not immediately restored."

"I suppose it is quite certain that those receipts and documents do exist?" suggested Lebel.

"Perfectly certain. One of the receipts, signed by Heriot, was sent as a specimen."

"My God!" ejaculated Lebel, and wiped the cold sweat from his brow.

"Yes, you'll all want help from somewhere," retorted Chauvelin coolly. "From above or from below, what? if the people get to know what miscreants you are. I do believe," he added, with a vicious snap of his thin lips, "that they would cheat the guillotine of you and, in the end, drag you out of the tumbrils and tear you to pieces limb from limb!"

Once more that look of furtive terror crept into the commissary's bloodshot eyes.

"Thank the Lord," he muttered, "that we were able to get hold of the wench Clamette!"

"At my suggestion," retorted Chauvelin curtly. "I always believe in threatening the weak if you want to coerce the strong. The Montorgueils cannot resist the wench's appeal. Even if they do at first, we can apply the screw by clapping one of the young ones in gaol. Within a week we shall have those papers, citizen Lebel; and if, in the meanwhile, no one commits a further blunder, we can close the trap on the Montorgueils without further trouble."

Lebel said nothing more, and after a while Chauvelin went back to the desk, picked up the letter which poor Lucile had written and watered with her tears, folded it deliberately and slipped it into the inner pocket of his coat.

"What are you going to do?" queried Lebel anxiously.

"Drop this letter into the hollow tree by the side of the stable gate at

Montorgueil," replied Chauvelin simply.

"What?" exclaimed the other. "Yourself?"

"Why, of course! Think you I would entrust such an errand to another living soul?"

III.

A couple of hours later, when the two children had had their dinner and had settled down to play in the garden, and father been cosily tucked up for his afternoon sleep, Lucile called her brother Etienne to her. The boy had not spoken to her since that terrible time spent in the presence of those two awful men. He had eaten no dinner, only sat glowering, staring straight out before him, from time to time throwing a look of burning reproach upon his sister. Now, when she called to him, he tried to run away, was halfway up the stairs before she could seize hold of him.

"Etienne, mon petit!" she implored, as her arms closed around his shrinking figure.

"Let me go, Lucile!" the boy pleaded obstinately.

"Mon petit, listen to me!" she pleaded. "All is not lost, if you will stand by me."

"All is lost, Lucile!" Etienne cried, striving to keep back a flood of passionate tears. "Honour is lost. Your treachery has disgraced us all. If M. le Marquis and M. le Vicomte are brought to the guillotine, their blood will be upon our heads."

"Upon mine alone, my little Etienne," she said sadly. "But God alone can judge me. It was a terrible alternative: M. le Marquis, or you and Valentine and little Josephine and poor father, who is so helpless! But don't let us talk of it. All is not lost, I am sure. The last time that I spoke with M. le Marquis—it was in February, do you remember?—he was full of hope, and oh! so kind. Well, he told me then that if ever I or any of us here were in such grave trouble that we did not know where to turn, one of us was to put on our very oldest clothes, look as like a bare-footed beggar as we could, and then go to Paris to a place called the Cabaret de la Liberte in the Rue Christine. There we were to ask for the citizen Rateau, and we were to tell him all our troubles, whatever they might be. Well! we are in such trouble now, mon petit, that we don't know where to turn. Put on thy very oldest clothes, little one, and run bare-footed into Paris, find the citizen Rateau and tell him just what has happened: the letter which they have forced me to write, the threats which they held over me if I did not write it—everything. Dost hear?"

Already the boy's eyes were glowing. The thought that he individually could do something to retrieve the awful shame of his sister's treachery spurred him to activity. It needed no persuasion on Lucile's part to induce him to go. She made him put on some old clothes and stuffed a piece of bread and cheese into his breeches pocket.

It was close upon a couple of leagues to Paris, but that run was one of the happiest which Etienne had ever made. And he did it bare-footed, too, feeling neither fatigue nor soreness, despite the hardness of the road after a two weeks' drought, which had turned mud into hard cakes and ruts into fissures which tore the lad's feet till they bled.

He did not reach the Cabaret de la Liberte till nightfall, and when he got there he hardly dared to enter. The filth, the squalor, the hoarse voices which rose from that cellar-like place below the level of the street, repelled the country-bred lad. Were it not for the desperate urgency of his errand he never would have dared to enter. As it was, the fumes of alcohol and steaming, dirty clothes nearly choked him, and he could scarce stammer the name of "citizen Rateau" when a gruff voice presently demanded his purpose.

He realised now how tired he was and how hungry. He had not thought to pause in order to consume the small provision of bread and cheese wherewith thoughtful Lucile had provided him. Now he was ready to faint when a loud guffaw, which echoed from one end of the horrible place to the other, greeted his timid request.

"Citizen Rateau!" the same gruff voice called out hilariously. "Why, there he is! Here, citizen! there's a blooming aristo to see you."

Etienne turned his weary eyes to the corner which was being indicated to him. There he saw a huge creature sprawling across a bench, with long, powerful limbs stretched out before him. Citizen Rateau was clothed, rather than dressed, in a soiled shirt, ragged breeches and tattered stockings, with shoes down at heel and faded crimson cap. His face looked congested and sunken about the eyes; he appeared to be asleep, for stertorous breathing came at intervals from between his parted lips, whilst every now and then a racking cough seemed to tear at his broad chest.

Etienne gave him one look, shuddering with horror, despite himself, at the aspect of this bloated wretch from whom salvation was to come. The whole place seemed to him hideous and loathsome in the extreme. What it all meant he could not understand; all that he knew was that this seemed like another hideous trap into which he and Lucile had fallen, and that he must fly from it—fly at all costs, before he betrayed M. le Marquis still further to these drink-sodden brutes. Another moment, and he feared that he might faint. The din of a bibulous song rang in his ears, the reek of alcohol turned him giddy and sick. He had only just enough strength to turn and totter back into the open. There his senses reeled, the lights in the houses opposite began to dance wildly before his eyes, after which he remembered nothing more.

IV.

There is nothing now in the whole countryside quite so desolate and forlorn as the chateau of Montorgueil, with its once magnificent park, now overgrown with weeds, its encircling walls broken down, its terraces devastated, and its stately gates rusty and torn.

Just by the side of what was known in happier times as the stable gate there stands a hollow tree. It is not inside the park, but just outside, and shelters the narrow lane, which skirts the park walls, against the blaze of the afternoon sun.

Its beneficent shade is a favourite spot for an afternoon siesta, for there is a bit of green sward under the tree, and all along the side of the road. But as the shades of evening gather in, the lane is usually deserted, shunned by the neighbouring peasantry on account of its eerie loneliness, so different to the former bustle which used to reign around the park gates when M. le Marquis and his family were still in residence. Nor does the lane lead anywhere, for it is a mere loop which gives on the main road at either end.

Henri de Montorgueil chose a peculiarly dark night in mid-September for one of his periodical visits to the hollow-tree. It was close on nine o'clock when he passed stealthily down the lane, keeping close to the park wall. A soft rain was falling, the first since the prolonged drought, and though it made the road heavy and slippery in places, it helped to deaden the sound of the young man's furtive footsteps. The air, except for the patter of the rain, was absolutely still. Henri de Montorgueil paused from time to time, with neck craned forward, every sense on the alert, listening, like any poor, hunted beast, for the slightest sound which might betray the approach of danger.

As many a time before, he reached the hollow tree in safety, felt for and found in the usual place the letter which the unfortunate girl Lucile had written to him. Then, with it in his hand, he turned to the stable gate. It had long since ceased to be kept locked and barred. Pillaged and ransacked by order of the Committee of Public Safety, there was nothing left inside the park walls worth keeping under lock and key.

Henri slipped stealthily through the gates and made his way along the drive. Every stone, every nook and cranny of his former home was familiar to him, and anon he turned into a shed where in former times wheelbarrows and garden tools were wont to be kept. Now it was full of debris, lumber of every sort. A more safe or secluded spot could not be imagined. Henri crouched in the furthermost corner of the shed. Then from his belt he detached a small dark lanthorn, opened its shutter, and with the aid of the tiny, dim light read the contents of the letter. For a long while after that he remained quite still, as still as a man who has received a stunning blow on the head and has partly lost consciousness. The blow was indeed a staggering one. Lucile Clamette, with the invincible power of her own helplessness, was demanding the surrender of a weapon which had been a safeguard for the Montorgueils all this while. The papers which compromised a number of influential members of the Committee of Public Safety had been the most perfect arms of defense against persecution and spoliation.

And now these were to be given up: Oh! there could be no question of that. Even before consulting with his father, Henri knew that the papers would have to be given up. They were clever, those revolutionaries. The thought of holding innocent children as hostages could only have originated in minds attuned to the villainies of devils. But it was unthinkable that the children should suffer.

After a while the young man roused himself from the torpor into which the suddenness of this awful blow had plunged him. By the light of the lanthorn he began to write upon a sheet of paper which he had torn from his pocket-book.

> "MY DEAR LUCILE," he wrote, "As you say, our debt to your father and to you all never could be adequately repaid. You and the children shall never suffer whilst we have the power to save you. You will find the papers in the receptacle you know of inside the chimney of what used to be my mother's boudoir. You will find the receptacle unlocked. One day before the term you name I myself will place the papers there for you. With them, my father and I do give up our lives to save you and the little ones from the persecution of those fiends. May the good God guard you all."

He signed the letter with his initials, H. de M. Then he crept back to the gate and dropped the message into the hollow of the tree.

A quarter of an hour later Henri de Montorgueil was wending his way back to the hiding place which had sheltered him and his father for so long. Silence and darkness then held undisputed sway once more around the hollow tree. Even the rain had ceased its gentle pattering. Anon from far away came the sound of a church bell striking the hour of ten. Then nothing more.

A few more minutes of absolute silence, then something dark and furtive began to move out of the long grass which bordered the roadside—something that in movement was almost like a snake. It dragged itself along close to the ground, making no sound as it moved. Soon it reached the hollow tree, rose to the height of a man and flattened itself against the tree-trunk. Then it put out a hand, felt for the hollow receptacle and groped for the missive which Henri de Montorgueil had dropped in there a while ago.

The next moment a tiny ray of light gleamed through the darkness like a star. A small, almost fragile, figure of a man, dressed in the mud-stained clothes of a country yokel, had turned up the shutter of a small lanthorn. By its flickering light he deciphered the letter which Henri de Montorgueil had written to Lucile Clamette.

"One day before the term you name I myself will place the papers there for you."

A sigh of satisfaction, quickly suppressed, came through his thin, colourless lips, and the light of the lanthorn caught the flash of triumph in his pale, inscrutable eyes.

Then the light was extinguished. Impenetrable darkness swallowed up that slender, mysterious figure again.

V.

Six days had gone by since Chauvelin had delivered his cruel "either—or" to poor little Lucile Clamette; three since he had found Henri de Montorgueil's reply to the girl's appeal in the hollow of the tree. Since then he had made a careful investigation of the chateau, and soon was able to settle it in his own mind as to which room had been Madame la Marquise's boudoir in the past. It was a small apartment, having direct access on the first landing of the staircase, and the one window gave on the rose garden at the back of the house. Inside the monumental hearth, at an arm's length up the wide chimney, a receptacle had been contrived in the brickwork, with a small iron door which opened and closed with a secret spring. Chauvelin, whom his nefarious calling had rendered proficient in such matters, had soon mastered the workings of that spring. He could now open and close the iron door at will.

Up to a late hour on the sixth night of this weary waiting, the receptacle inside the chimney was still empty. That night Chauvelin had determined to spend at the chateau. He could not have rested elsewhere.

Even his colleague Lebel could not know what the possession of those papers would mean to the discredited agent of the Committee of Public Safety. With them in his hands, he could demand rehabilitation, and could purchase immunity from those sneers which had been so galling to his arrogant soul—sneers which had become more and more marked, more and more unendurable, and more and more menacing, as he piled up failure on failure with every encounter with the Scarlet Pimpernel.

Immunity and rehabilitation! This would mean that he could once more measure his wits and his power with that audacious enemy who had brought about his downfall.

"In the name of Satan, bring us those papers!" Robespierre himself had cried with unwonted passion, ere he sent him out on this important mission. "We none of us could stand the scandal of such disclosures. It would mean absolute ruin for us all."

And Chauvelin that night, as soon as the shades of evening had drawn in, took up his stand in the chateau, in the small inner room which was contiguous to the boudoir.

Here he sat, beside the open window, for hour upon hour, his every sense on the alert, listening for the first footfall upon the gravel path below. Though the hours went by leaden-footed, he was neither excited nor anxious. The Clamette family was such a precious hostage that the Montorgueils were bound to comply with Lucile's demand for the papers by every dictate of honour and of humanity.

"While we have those people in our power," Chauvelin had reiterated to himself more than once during the course of his long vigil, "even that meddlesome Scarlet Pimpernel can do nothing to save those cursed Montorgueils."

The night was dark and still. Not a breath of air stirred the branches of the trees or the shrubberies in the park; any footsteps, however wary, must echo through that perfect and absolute silence. Chauvelin's keen, pale eyes tried to pierce the gloom in the direction whence in all probability the aristo would come. Vaguely he wondered if it would be Henri de Montorgueil or the old Marquis himself who would bring the papers.

"Bah! whichever one it is," he muttered, "we can easily get the other, once those abominable papers are in our hands. And even if both the aristos escape," he added mentally, "'tis no matter, once we have the papers."

Anon, far away a distant church bell struck the midnight hour. The stillness of the air had become oppressive. A kind of torpor born of intense fatigue lulled the Terrorist's senses to somnolence. His head fell forward on his breast....

VI.

Then suddenly a shiver of excitement went right through him. He was fully awake now, with glowing eyes wide open and the icy calm of perfect confidence ruling every nerve. The sound of stealthy footsteps had reached his ear.

He could see nothing, either outside or in; but his fingers felt for the pistol which he carried in his belt. The aristo was evidently alone; only one solitary footstep was approaching the chateau.

Chauvelin had left the door ajar which gave on the boudoir. The staircase was on the other side of that fateful room, and the door leading to that was closed. A few minutes of tense expectancy went by. Then through the silence there came the sound of furtive footsteps on the stairs, the creaking of a loose board and finally the stealthy opening of the door.

In all his adventurous career Chauvelin had never felt so calm. His heart beat quite evenly, his senses were undisturbed by the slightest tingling of his nerves. The stealthy sounds in the next room brought the movements of the aristo perfectly clear before his mental vision. The latter was carrying a small dark lanthorn. As soon as he entered he flashed its light about the room. Then he deposited the lanthorn on the floor, close beside the hearth, and started to feel up the chimney for the hidden receptacle.

Chauvelin watched him now like a cat watches a mouse, savouring these few moments of anticipated triumph. He pushed open the door noiselessly which gave on the boudoir. By the feeble light of the lanthorn on the ground he could only see the vague outline of the aristo's back, bending forward to his task; but a thrill went through him as he saw a bundle of papers lying on the ground close by.

Everything was ready; the trap was set. Here was a complete victory at last. It was obviously the young Vicomte de Montorgueil who had come to do the deed. His head was up the chimney even now. The old Marquis's back would have looked narrower and more fragile. Chauvelin held his breath; then he gave a sharp little cough, and took the pistol from his belt.

The sound caused the aristo to turn, and the next moment a loud and merry laugh roused the dormant echoes of the old chateau, whilst a pleasant, drawly voice said in English:

"I am demmed if this is not my dear old friend M. Chambertin! Zounds, sir! who'd have thought of meeting you here?"

Had a cannon suddenly exploded at Chauvelin's feet he would, I think, have felt less unnerved. For the space of two heart-beats he stood there, rooted to the spot, his eyes glued on his arch-enemy, that execrated Scarlet Pimpernel, whose mocking glance, even through the intervening gloom, seemed to have deprived him of consciousness. But that phase of helplessness only lasted for a moment; the next, all the marvelous possibilities of this encounter flashed through the Terrorist's keen mind.

Everything was ready; the trap was set! The unfortunate Clamettes were still the bait which now would bring a far more noble quarry into the mesh than even he—Chauvelin —had dared to hope.

He raised his pistol, ready to fire. But already Sir Percy Blakeney was on him, and with a swift movement, which the other was too weak to resist, he wrenched the weapon from his enemy's grasp.

"Why, how hasty you are, my dear M. Chambertin," he said lightly.

"Surely you are not in such a hurry to put a demmed bullet into me!"

The position now was one which would have made even a braver man than Chauvelin quake. He stood alone and unarmed in face of an enemy from whom he could expect no mercy. But, even so, his first thought was not of escape. He had not only apprised his own danger, but also the immense power which he held whilst the Clamettes remained as hostages in the hands of his colleague Lebel.

"You have me at a disadvantage, Sir Percy," he said, speaking every whit as coolly as his foe. "But only momentarily. You can kill me, of course; but if I do not return from this expedition not only safe and sound, but with a certain packet of papers in my hands, my colleague Lebel has instructions to proceed at once against the girl Clamette and the whole family."

"I know that well enough," rejoined Sir Percy with a quaint laugh. "I know what venomous reptiles you and those of your kidney are. You certainly do owe your life at the present moment to the unfortunate girl whom you are persecuting with such infamous callousness."

Chauvelin drew a sigh of relief. The situation was shaping itself more to his satisfaction already. Through the gloom he could vaguely discern the Englishman's massive form standing a few paces away, one hand buried in his breeches pockets, the other still holding the pistol. On the ground close by the hearth was the small lanthorn, and in its dim light the packet of papers gleamed white and tempting in the darkness. Chauvelin's keen eyes had fastened on it, saw the form of receipt for money with Heriot's signature, which he recognised, on the top.

He himself had never felt so calm. The only thing he could regret was that he was alone. Half a dozen men now, and this impudent foe could indeed be brought to his knees. And this time there would be no risks taken, no chances for escape. Somehow it seemed to Chauvelin as if something of the Scarlet Pimpernel's audacity and foresight had gone from him. As he stood there, looking broad and physically powerful, there was something wavering and undecided in his attitude, as if the edge had been taken off his former recklessness and enthusiasm. He had brought the compromising papers here, had no doubt helped the Montorgueils to escape; but while Lucile Clamette and her family were under the eye of Lebel no amount of impudence could force a successful bargaining.

It was Chauvelin now who appeared the more keen and the more alert; the Englishman seemed undecided what to do next, remained silent, toying with the pistol. He even smothered a yawn. Chauvelin saw his opportunity. With the quick movement of a cat pouncing upon a mouse he stooped and seized that packet of papers, would then and there have made a dash for the door with them, only that, as he seized the packet, the string which held it together gave way and the papers were scattered all over the floor.

Receipts for money? Compromising letters? No! Blank sheets of paper, all of them—all except the one which had lain tantalisingly on the top: the one receipt signed by citizen Heriot. Sir Percy laughed lightly:

"Did you really think, my good friend," he said, "that I would be such a demmed fool as to place my best weapon so readily to your hand?"

"Your best weapon, Sir Percy!" retorted Chauvelin, with a sneer. "What use is it to you while we hold Lucile Clamette?"

"While I hold Lucile Clamette, you mean, my dear Monsieur Chambertin," riposted Blakeney with elaborate blandness.

"You hold Lucile Clamette? Bah! I defy you to drag a whole family like that out of our clutches. The man a cripple, the children helpless! And you think they can escape our vigilance when all our men are warned! How do you think they are going to get across the river, Sir Percy, when every bridge is closely watched? How will they get across Paris, when at every gate our men are on the look-out for them?"

"They can't do it, my dear Monsieur Chambertin," rejoined Sir Percy blandly, "else I were not here."

Then, as Chauvelin, fuming, irritated despite himself, as he always was when he encountered that impudent Englishman, shrugged his shoulders in token of contempt, Blakeney's powerful grasp suddenly clutched his arm.

"Let us understand one another, my good M. Chambertin," he said coolly. "Those unfortunate Clamettes, as you say, are too helpless and too numerous to smuggle across Paris with any chance of success. Therefore I look to you to take them under your protection. They are all stowed away comfortably at this moment in a conveyance which I have provided for them. That conveyance is waiting at the bridgehead now. We could not cross without your help; we could not get across Paris without your august presence and your tricolour scarf of office. So you are coming with us, my dear M. Chambertin," he continued, and, with force which was quite irresistible, he began to drag his enemy after him towards the door. "You are going to sit in that conveyance with the Clamettes, and I myself will have the honour to drive you. And at every bridgehead you will show your pleasing countenance and your scarf of office to the guard and demand free passage for yourself and your family, as a representative member of the Committee of Public Safety. And then we'll enter Paris by the Porte d'Ivry and leave it by the Batignolles; and everywhere your charming presence will lull the guards' suspicions to rest. I pray you, come! There is no time to consider! At noon to-morrow, without a moment's grace, my friend Sir Andrew Ffoulkes, who has the papers in his possession, will dispose of them as he thinks best unless I myself do claim them from him."

While he spoke he continued to drag his enemy along with him, with an assurance and an impudence which were past belief. Chauvelin was trying to collect his thoughts; a whirl of conflicting plans were running riot in his mind. The Scarlet Pimpernel in his power! At any point on the road he could deliver him up to the nearest guard ... then still hold the Clamettes and demand the papers....

"Too late, my dear Monsieur Chambertin!" Sir Percy's mocking voice broke in, as if divining his thoughts. "You do not know where to find my friend Ffoulkes, and at noon to-morrow, if I do not arrive to claim those papers, there will not be a single ragamuffin in Paris who will not be crying your shame and that of your precious colleagues upon the housetops."

Chauvelin's whole nervous system was writhing with the feeling of impotence. Mechanically, unresisting now, he followed his enemy down the main staircase of the chateau and out through the wide open gates. He could not bring himself to believe that he had been so completely foiled, that this impudent adventurer had him once more in the hollow of his hand.

"In the name of Satan, bring us back those papers!" Robespierre had commanded. And now he—Chauvelin—was left in a maze of doubt; and the vital alternative was hammering in his brain: "The Scarlet Pimpernel—or those papers——" Which, in Satan's name, was the more important? Passion whispered "The Scarlet Pimpernel!" but common sense and the future of his party, the whole future of the Revolution mayhap, demanded those compromising papers. And all the while he followed that relentless enemy through the avenues of the park and down the lonely lane. Overhead the trees of the forest of Sucy, nodding in a gentle breeze, seemed to mock his perplexity.

He had not arrived at a definite decision when the river came in sight, and when anon a carriage lanthorn threw a shaft of dim light through the mist-laden air. Now he felt as if he were in a dream. He was thrust unresisting into a closed chaise, wherein he felt the presence of several other people—children, an old man who was muttering ceaselessly. As in a dream he answered questions at the bridge to a guard whom he knew well.

"You know me—Armand Chauvelin, of the Committee of Public Safety!"

As in a dream, he heard the curt words of command:

"Pass on, in the name of the Republic!"

And all the while the thought hammered in his brain: "Something must be done! This is impossible! This cannot be! It is not I—Chauvelin—who am sitting here, helpless, unresisting. It is not that impudent Scarlet Pimpernel who is sitting there before me on the box, driving me to utter humiliation!"

And yet it was all true. All real. The Clamette children were sitting in front of him, clinging to Lucile, terrified of him even now. The old man was beside him—imbecile and not understanding. The boy Etienne was up on the box next to that audacious adventurer, whose broad back appeared to Chauvelin like a rock on which all his hopes and dreams must for ever be shattered.

The chaise rattled triumphantly through the Batignolles. It was then broad daylight. A brilliant early autumn day after the rains. The sun, the keen air, all mocked Chauvelin's helplessness, his humiliation. Long before noon they passed St. Denis. Here the barouche turned off the main road, halted at a small wayside house—nothing more than a cottage. After which everything seemed more dreamlike than ever. All that Chauvelin remembered of it afterwards was that he was once more alone in a room with his enemy, who had demanded his signature to a number of safe-conducts, ere he finally handed over the packet of papers to him.

"How do I know that they are all here?" he heard himself vaguely muttering, while his trembling fingers handled that precious packet.

"That's just it!" his tormentor retorted airily. "You don't know. I don't know myself," he added, with a light laugh. "And, personally, I don't see how either of us can possibly ascertain. In the meanwhile, I must bid you au revoir, my dear M. Chambertin. I am sorry that I cannot provide you with a conveyance, and you will have to walk a league or more ere you meet one, I fear me. We, in the meanwhile, will be well on our way to Dieppe, where my yacht, the Day Dream, lies at anchor, and I do not think that it will be worth your while to try and overtake us. I thank you for the safe-conducts. They will make our journey exceedingly pleasant. Shall I give your regards to M. le Marquis de Montorgueil or to M. le Vicomte? They are on board the Day Dream, you know. Oh! and I was forgetting! Lady Blakeney desired to be remembered to you."

The next moment he was gone. Chauvelin, standing at the window of the wayside house, saw Sir Percy Blakeney once more mount the box of the chaise. This time he had Sir Andrew Ffoulkes beside him. The Clamette family were huddled together—happy and free—inside the vehicle. After which there was the usual clatter of horses' hoofs, the creaking of wheels, the rattle of chains. Chauvelin saw and heard nothing of that. All that he saw at the last was Sir Percy's slender hand, waving him a last adieu.

After which he was left alone with his thoughts. The packet of papers was in his hand. He fingered it, felt its crispness, clutched it with a fierce gesture, which was followed by a long-drawn-out sigh of intense bitterness.

No one would ever know what it had cost him to obtain these papers. No one would ever know how much he had sacrificed of pride, revenge and hate in order to save a few shreds of his own party's honour.

CHAPTER XI. A BATTLE OF WITS

I.

What had happened was this:

Tournefort, one of the ablest of the many sleuth-hounds employed by the Committee of Public Safety, was out during that awful storm on the night of the twenty-fifth. The rain came down as if it had been poured out of buckets, and Tournefort took shelter under the portico of a tall, dilapidated-looking house somewhere at the back of St.

Lazare. The night was, of course, pitch dark, and the howling of the wind and beating of the rain effectually drowned every other sound.

Tournefort, chilled to the marrow, had at first cowered in the angle of the door, as far away from the draught as he could. But presently he spied the glimmer of a tiny light some little way up on his left, and taking this to come from the concierge's lodge, he went cautiously along the passage intending to ask for better shelter against the fury of the elements than the rickety front door afforded.

Tournefort, you must remember, was always on the best terms with every concierge in Paris. They were, as it were, his subordinates; without their help he never could have carried on his unavowable profession quite so successfully. And they, in their turn, found it to their advantage to earn the good-will of that army of spies, which the Revolutionary Government kept in its service, for the tracking down of all those unfortunates who had not given complete adhesion to their tyrannical and murderous policy.

Therefore, in this instance, Tournefort felt no hesitation in claiming the hospitality of the concierge of the squalid house wherein he found himself. He went boldly up to the lodge. His hand was already on the latch, when certain sounds which proceeded from the interior of the lodge caused him to pause and to bend his ear in order to listen. It was Tournefort's metier to listen. What had arrested his attention was the sound of a man's voice, saying in a tone of deep respect:

"Bien, Madame la Comtesse, we'll do our best."

No wonder that the servant of the Committee of Public Safety remained at attention, no longer thought of the storm or felt the cold blast chilling him to the marrow. Here was a wholly unexpected piece of good luck. "Madame la Comtesse!" Peste! There were not many such left in Paris these days. Unfortunately, the tempest of the wind and the rain made such a din that it was difficult to catch every sound which came from the interior of the lodge. All that Tournefort caught definitely were a few fragments of conversation.

"My good M. Bertin ..." came at one time from a woman's voice. "Truly I do not know why you should do all this for me."

And then again: "All I possess in the world now are my diamonds. They alone stand between my children and utter destitution."

The man's voice seemed all the time to be saying something that sounded cheerful and encouraging. But his voice came only as a vague murmur to the listener's ears. Presently, however, there came a word which set his pulses tingling. Madame said something about "Gentilly," and directly afterwards: "You will have to be very careful, my dear M. Bertin. The chateau, I feel sure, is being watched."

Tournefort could scarce repress a cry of joy. "Gentilly? Madame la Comtesse? The chateau?" Why, of course, he held all the necessary threads already. The ci-devant Comte de Sucy—a pestilential aristo if ever there was one!—had been sent to the guillotine less than a fortnight ago. His chateau, situated just outside Gentilly, stood empty, it having been given out that the widow Sucy and her two children had escaped to England. Well! she had not gone apparently, for here she was, in the lodge of the concierge of a mean house in one of the desolate quarters of Paris, begging some traitor to find her diamonds for her, which she had obviously left concealed inside the chateau. What a haul for Tournefort! What commendation from his superiors! The chances of a speedy promotion were indeed glorious now! He blessed the storm and the rain which had driven him for shelter to this house, where a poisonous plot was being hatched to rob the people of valuable property, and to aid a few more of those abominable aristos in cheating the guillotine of their traitorous heads.

He listened for a while longer, in order to get all the information that he could on the subject of the diamonds, because he knew by experience that those perfidious aristos, once they were under arrest, would sooner bite out their tongues than reveal anything that might be of service to the Government of the people. But he learned little else. Nothing was revealed of where Madame la Comtesse was in hiding, or how the diamonds were to be disposed of once they were found. Tournefort would have given much to have at least one of his colleagues with him. As it was, he would be forced to act single-handed and on his own initiative. In his own mind he had already decided that he would wait until Madame la Comtesse came out of the concierge's lodge, and that he would follow her and apprehend her somewhere out in the open streets, rather than here where her friend Bertin might prove to be a stalwart as well as a desperate man, ready with a pistol, whilst he—Tournefort—was unarmed. Bertin, who had, it seemed, been entrusted with the task of finding the diamonds, could then be shadowed and arrested in the very act of filching property which by decree of the State belonged to the people.

So he waited patiently for a while. No doubt the aristo would remain here under shelter until the storm had abated. Soon the sound of voices died down, and an extraordinary silence descended on this miserable, abandoned corner of old Paris. The silence became all the more marked after a while, because the rain ceased its monotonous pattering and the soughing of the wind was stilled. It was, in fact, this amazing stillness which set citizen Tournefort thinking. Evidently the aristo did not intend to come out of the lodge to-night. Well! Tournefort had not meant to make himself unpleasant inside the house, or to have a quarrel just yet with the traitor Bertin, whoever he was; but his hand was forced and he had no option.

The door of the lodge was locked. He tugged vigorously at the bell again and again, for at first he got no answer. A few minutes later he heard the sound of shuffling footsteps upon creaking boards. The door was opened, and a man in night attire, with bare, thin legs and tattered carpet slippers on his feet, confronted an exceedingly astonished servant of the Committee of Public Safety. Indeed, Tournefort thought that he must have been dreaming, or that he was dreaming now. For the man who opened the door to him was well known to every agent of the Committee. He was an ex-soldier who had been crippled years ago by the loss of one arm, and had held the post of concierge in a house in the Ruelle du Paradis ever since. His name was Grosjean. He was very old, and nearly doubled up with rheumatism, had scarcely any hair on his head or flesh on his bones. At this moment he appeared to be suffering from a cold in the head, for his eyes were streaming and his narrow, hooked nose was adorned by a drop of moisture at its tip. In fact, poor old Grosjean looked more like a dilapidated scarecrow than a dangerous conspirator. Tournefort literally gasped at sight of him, and Grosjean uttered a kind of croak, intended, no doubt, for complete surprise.

"Citizen Tournefort!" he exclaimed. "Name of a dog! What are you doing here at this hour and in this abominable weather? Come in! Come in!" he added, and, turning on his heel, he shuffled back into the inner room, and then returned carrying a lighted lamp, which he set upon the table. "Amelie left a sup of hot coffee on the hob in the kitchen before she went to bed. You must have a drop of that."

He was about to shuffle off again when Tournefort broke in roughly:

"None of that nonsense, Grosjean! Where are the aristos?"

"The aristos, citizen?" queried Grosjean, and nothing could have looked more utterly, more ludicrously bewildered than did the old concierge at this moment. "What aristos?"

"Bertin and Madame la Comtesse," retorted Tournefort gruffly. "I heard them talking."

"You have been dreaming, citizen Tournefort," the old man said, with a husky little laugh. "Sit down, and let me get you some coffee—"

"Don't try and hoodwink me, Grosjean!" Tournefort cried now in a sudden access of rage. "I tell you that I saw the light. I heard the aristos talking. There was a man named Bertin, and a woman he called 'Madame la Comtesse,' and I say that some devilish royalist plot is being hatched here, and that you, Grosjean, will suffer for it if you try and shield those aristos."

"But, citizen Tournefort," replied the concierge meekly, "I assure you that I have seen no aristos. The door of my bedroom was open, and the lamp was by my bedside. Amelie, too, has only been in bed a few minutes. You ask her! There has been no one, I tell you—no one! I should have seen and heard them—the door was open," he reiterated pathetically.

"We'll soon see about that!" was Tournefort's curt comment.

But it was his turn indeed to be utterly bewildered. He searched—none too gently—the squalid little lodge through and through, turned the paltry sticks of furniture over, hauled little Amelie, Grosjean's granddaughter, out of bed, searched under the mattresses, and even poked his head up the chimney.

Grosjean watched him wholly unperturbed. These were strange times, and friend Tournefort had obviously gone a little off his head. The worthy old concierge calmly went on getting the coffee ready. Only when presently Tournefort, worn out with anger and futile exertion, threw himself, with many an oath, into the one armchair, Grosjean remarked coolly:

"I tell you what I think it is, citizen. If you were standing just by the door of the lodge you had the back staircase of the house immediately behind you. The partition wall is very thin, and there is a disused door just there also. No doubt the voices came from there. You see, if there had been any aristos here," he added naively, "they could not have flown up the chimney, could they?"

That argument was certainly unanswerable. But Tournefort was out of temper. He roughly ordered Grosjean to bring the lamp and show him the back staircase and the disused door. The concierge obeyed without a murmur. He was not in the least disturbed or frightened by all this blustering. He was only afraid that getting out of bed had made his cold worse. But he knew Tournefort of old. A good fellow, but inclined to be noisy and arrogant since he was in the employ of the Government. Grosjean took the precaution of putting on his trousers and wrapping an old shawl round his shoulders. Then he had a final sip of hot coffee; after which he picked up the lamp and guided Tournefort out of the lodge.

The wind had quite gone down by now. The lamp scarcely flickered as Grosjean held it above his head.

"Just here, citizen Tournefort," he said, and turned sharply to his left. But the next sound which he uttered was a loud croak of astonishment.

"That door has been out of use ever since I've been here," he muttered.

"And it certainly was closed when I stood up against it," rejoined Tournefort, with a savage oath, "or, of course, I should have noticed it."

Close to the lodge, at right angles to it, a door stood partially open. Tournefort went through it, closely followed by Grosjean. He found himself in a passage which ended in a cul de sac on his right; on the left was the foot of the stairs. The whole place was pitch dark save for the feeble light of the lamp. The cul de sac itself reeked of dirt and fustiness, as if it had not been cleaned or ventilated for years.

"When did you last notice that this door was closed?" queried Tournefort, furious with the sense of discomfiture, which he would have liked to vent on the unfortunate concierge.

"I have not noticed it for some days, citizen," replied Grosjean meekly.

"I have had a severe cold, and have not been outside my lodge since Monday last. But we'll ask Amelie!" he added more hopefully.

Amelie, however, could throw no light upon the subject. She certainly kept the back stairs cleaned and swept, but it was not part of her duties to extend her sweeping operations as far as the cul de sac. She had quite enough to do as it was, with grandfather now practically helpless. This morning, when she went out to do her shopping, she had not noticed whether the disused door did or did not look the same as usual.

Grosjean was very sorry for his friend Tournefort, who appeared vastly upset, but still more sorry for himself, for he knew what endless trouble this would entail upon him.

Nor was the trouble slow in coming, not only on Grosjean, but on every lodger inside the house; for before half an hour had gone by Tournefort had gone and come back, this time with the local commissary of police and a couple of agents, who had every man, woman and child in that house out of bed and examined at great length, their identity books searchingly overhauled, their rooms turned topsy-turvy and their furniture knocked about.

It was past midnight before all these perquisitions were completed. No one dared to complain at these indignities put upon peaceable citizens on the mere denunciation of an obscure police agent. These were times when every regulation, every command, had to be accepted without a murmur. At one o'clock in the morning, Grosjean himself was thankful to get back to bed, having satisfied the commissary that he was not a dangerous conspirator.

But of anyone even remotely approaching the description of the ci-devant Comtesse de Sucy, or of any man called Bertin, there was not the faintest trace.

II.

But no feeling of discomfort ever lasted very long with citizen Tournefort. He was a person of vast resource and great buoyancy of temperament.

True, he had not apprehended two exceedingly noxious aristos, as he had hoped to do; but he held the threads of an abominable conspiracy in his hands, and the question of catching both Bertin and Madame la Comtesse red-handed was only a question of time. But little time had been lost. There was always someone to be found at the offices of the

Committee of Public Safety, which were open all night. It was possible that citizen Chauvelin would be still there, for he often took on the night shift, or else citizen Gourdon.

It was Gourdon who greeted his subordinate, somewhat ill-humouredly, for he was indulging in a little sleep, with his toes turned to the fire, as the night was so damp and cold. But when he heard Tournefort's story, he was all eagerness and zeal.

"It is, of course, too late to do anything now," he said finally, after he had mastered every detail of the man's adventures in the Ruelle du Paradis; "but get together half a dozen men upon whom you can rely, and by six o'clock in the morning, or even five, we'll be on our way to Gentilly. Citizen Chauvelin was only saying to-day that he strongly suspected the ci-devant Comtesse de Sucy of having left the bulk of her valuable jewelry at the chateau, and that she would make some effort to get possession of it. It would be rather fine, citizen Tournefort," he added with a chuckle, "if you and I could steal a march on citizen Chauvelin over this affair, what? He has been extraordinarily arrogant of late and marvelously in favour, not only with the Committee, but with citizen Robespierre himself."

"They say," commented Tournefort, "that he succeeded in getting hold of some papers which were of great value to the members of the Committee."

"He never succeeded in getting hold of that meddlesome Englishman whom they call the Scarlet Pimpernel," was Gourdon's final dry comment.

Thus was the matter decided on. And the following morning at daybreak, Gourdon, who was only a subordinate officer on the Committee of Public Safety, took it upon himself to institute a perquisition in the chateau of Gentilly, which is situated close to the commune of that name. He was accompanied by his friend Tournefort and a gang of half a dozen ruffians recruited from the most disreputable cabarets of Paris.

The intention had been to steal a march on citizen Chauvelin, who had been over arrogant of late; but the result did not come up to expectations. By midday the chateau had been ransacked from attic to cellar; every kind of valuable property had been destroyed, priceless works of art irretrievably damaged. But priceless works of art had no market in Paris these days; and the property of real value—the Sucy diamonds namely—which had excited the cupidity or the patriotic wrath of citizens Gourdon and Tournefort could nowhere be found.

To make the situation more deplorable still, the Committee of Public Safety had in some unexplainable way got wind of the affair, and the two worthies had the mortification of seeing citizen Chauvelin presently appear upon the scene.

It was then two o'clock in the afternoon. Gourdon, after he had snatched a hasty dinner at a neighbouring cabaret, had returned to the task of pulling the chateau of Gentilly about his own ears if need be, with a view to finding the concealed treasure.

For the nonce he was standing in the centre of the finely proportioned hall. The rich ormolu and crystal chandelier lay in a tangled, broken heap of scraps at his feet, and all around there was a confused medley of pictures, statuettes, silver ornaments, tapestry and brocade hangings, all piled up in disorder, smashed, tattered, kicked at now and again by Gourdon, to the accompaniment of a savage oath.

The house itself was full of noises; heavy footsteps tramping up and down the stairs, furniture turned over, curtains torn from their poles, doors and windows battered in.

And through it all the ceaseless hammering of pick and axe, attacking these stately walls which had withstood the wars and sieges of centuries.

Every now and then Tournefort, his face perspiring and crimson with exertion, would present himself at the door of the hall. Gourdon would query gruffly: "Well?"

And the answer was invariably the same: "Nothing!"

Then Gourdon would swear again and send curt orders to continue the search, relentlessly, ceaselessly.

"Leave no stone upon stone," he commanded. "Those diamonds must be found. We know they are here, and, name of a dog! I mean to have them."

When Chauvelin arrived at the chateau he made no attempt at first to interfere with Gourdon's commands. Only on one occasion he remarked curtly:

"I suppose, citizen Gourdon, that you can trust your search party?"

"Absolutely," retorted Gourdon. "A finer patriot than Tournefort does not exist."

"Probably," rejoined the other dryly. "But what about the men?"

"Oh! they are only a set of barefooted, ignorant louts. They do as they are told, and Tournefort has his eye on them. I dare say they'll contrive to steal a few things, but they would never dare lay hands on valuable jewelry. To begin with, they could never dispose of it. Imagine a va-nu-pieds peddling a diamond tiara!"

"There are always receivers prepared to take risks."

"Very few," Gourdon assured him, "since we decreed that trafficking with aristo property was a crime punishable by death."

Chauvelin said nothing for the moment. He appeared wrapped in his own thoughts, listened for a while to the confused hubbub about the house, then he resumed abruptly:

"Who are these men whom you are employing, citizen Gourdon?"

"A well-known gang," replied the other. "I can give you their names."

"If you please."

Gourdon searched his pockets for a paper which he found presently and handed to his colleague. The latter perused it thoughtfully.

"Where did Tournefort find these men?" he asked.

"For the most part at the Cabaret de la Liberte—a place of very evil repute down in the Rue Christine."

"I know it," rejoined the other. He was still studying the list of names which Gourdon had given him. "And," he added, "I know most of these men. As thorough a set of ruffians as we need for some of our work. Merri, Guidal, Rateau, Desmonds. TIENS!" he exclaimed. "Rateau! Is Rateau here now?"

"Why, of course! He was recruited, like the rest of them, for the day. He won't leave till he has been paid, you may be sure of that. Why do you ask?"

"I will tell you presently. But I would wish to speak with citizen Rateau first."

Just at this moment Tournefort paid his periodical visit to the hall. The usual words, "Still nothing," were on his lips, when Gourdon curtly ordered him to go and fetch the citizen Rateau.

A minute or two later Tournefort returned with the news that Rateau could nowhere be found. Chauvelin received the news without any comment; he only ordered Tournefort, somewhat roughly, back to his work. Then, as soon as the latter had gone, Gourdon turned upon his colleague.

"Will you explain—" he began with a show of bluster.

"With pleasure," replied Chauvelin blandly. "On my way hither, less than an hour ago, I met your man Rateau, a league or so from here."

"You met Rateau!" exclaimed Gourdon impatiently. "Impossible! He was here then, I feel sure. You must have been mistaken."

"I think not. I have only seen the man once, when I, too, went to recruit a band of ruffians at the Cabaret de la Liberte, in connection with some work I wanted doing. I did not employ him then, for he appeared to me both drink-sodden and nothing but a miserable, consumptive creature, with a churchyard cough you can hear half a league away. But I would know him anywhere. Besides which, he stopped and wished me good morning. Now I come to think of it," added Chauvelin thoughtfully, "he was carrying what looked like a heavy bundle under his arm."

"A heavy bundle!" cried Gourdon, with a forceful oath. "And you did not stop him!"

"I had no reason for suspecting him. I did not know until I arrived here what the whole affair was about, or whom you were employing. All that the Committee knew for certain was that you and Tournefort and a number of men had arrived at Gentilly before daybreak, and I was then instructed to follow you hither to see what mischief you were up to. You acted in complete secrecy, remember, citizen Gourdon, and without first ascertaining the wishes of the Committee of Public Safety, whose servant you are. If the Sucy diamonds are not found, you alone will be held responsible for their loss to the Government of the People."

Chauvelin's voice had now assumed a threatening tone, and Gourdon felt all his audacity and self-assurance fall away from him, leaving him a prey to nameless terror.

"We must round up Rateau," he murmured hastily. "He cannot have gone far."

"No, he cannot," rejoined Chauvelin dryly. "Though I was not specially thinking of Rateau or of diamonds when I started to come hither. I did send a general order forbidding any person on foot or horseback to enter or leave Paris by any of the southern gates. That order will serve us well now. Are you riding?"

"Yes. I left my horse at the tavern just outside Gentilly. I can get to horse within ten minutes."

"To horse, then, as quickly as you can. Pay off your men and dismiss them—all but Tournefort, who had best accompany us. Do not lose a single moment. I'll be ahead of you and may come up with Rateau before you overtake me. And if I were you, citizen Gourdon," he concluded, with ominous emphasis, "I would burn one or two candles to your compeer the devil. You'll have need of his help if Rateau gives us the slip."

III.

The first part of the road from Gentilly to Paris runs through the valley of the Biere, and is densely wooded on either side. It winds in and out for the most part, ribbon-like, through thick coppice of chestnut and birch. Thus it was impossible for Chauvelin to spy his quarry from afar; nor did he expect to do so this side of the Hopital de la Sante. Once past that point, he would find the road quite open and running almost straight, in the midst of arid and only partially cultivated land.

He rode at a sharp trot, with his caped coat wrapped tightly round his shoulders, for it was raining fast. At intervals, when he met an occasional wayfarer, he would ask questions about a tall man who had a consumptive cough, and who was carrying a cumbersome burden under his arm.

Almost everyone whom he thus asked remembered seeing a personage who vaguely answered to the description: tall and with a decided stoop—yes, and carrying a cumbersome-looking bundle under his arm. Chauvelin was undoubtedly on the track of the thief.

Just beyond Meuves he was overtaken by Gourdon and Tournefort. Here, too, the man Rateau's track became more and more certain. At one place he had stopped and had a glass of wine and a rest, at another he had asked how close he was to the gates of Paris.

The road was now quite open and level; the irregular buildings of the hospital appeared vague in the rain-sodden distance. Twenty minutes later Tournefort, who was riding ahead of his companions, spied a tall, stooping figure at the spot where the Chemin de Gentilly forks, and where stands a group of isolated houses and bits of garden, which belong to la Sante. Here, before the days when the glorious Revolution swept aside all such outward signs of superstition, there had stood a Calvary. It was now used as a signpost. The man stood before it, scanning the half-obliterated indications.

At the moment that Tournefort first caught sight of him he appeared uncertain of his way. Then for a while he watched Tournefort, who was coming at a sharp trot towards him. Finally, he seemed to make up his mind very suddenly and, giving a last, quick look round, he walked rapidly along the upper road. Tournefort drew rein, waited for his colleagues to come up with him. Then he told them what he had seen.

"It is Rateau, sure enough," he said. "I saw his face quite distinctly and heard his abominable cough. He is trying to get into Paris. That road leads nowhere but to the barrier. There, of course, he will be stopped, and—"

The other two had also brought their horses to a halt. The situation had become tense, and a plan for future action had at once to be decided on. Already Chauvelin, masterful and sure of himself, had assumed command of the little party. Now he broke in abruptly on Tournefort's vapid reflections.

"We don't want him stopped at the barrier," he said in his usual curt, authoritative manner. "You, citizen Tournefort," he continued, "will ride as fast as you can to the gate, making a detour by the lower road. You will immediately demand to speak with the sergeant who is in command, and you will give him a detailed description of the man Rateau. Then you will tell him in my name that, should such a man present himself at the gate, he must be allowed to enter the city unmolested."

Gourdon gave a quick cry of protest.

"Let the man go unmolested? Citizen Chauvelin, think what you are doing!"

"I always think of what I am doing," retorted Chauvelin curtly, "and have no need of outside guidance in the process." Then he turned once more to Tournefort. "You yourself, citizen," he continued, in sharp, decisive tones which admitted of no argument, "will dismount as soon as you are inside the city. You will keep the gate under observation. The moment you see the man Rateau, you will shadow him, and on no account lose sight of him. Understand?"

"You may trust me, citizen Chauvelin," Tournefort replied, elated at the prospect of work which was so entirely congenial to him. "But will you tell me—"

"I will tell you this much, citizen Tournefort," broke in Chauvelin with some acerbity, "that though we have traced the diamonds and the thief so far, we have, through your folly last night, lost complete track of the ci-devant Comtesse de Sucy and of the man Bertin. We want Rateau to show us where they are."

"I understand," murmured the other meekly.

"That's a mercy!" riposted Chauvelin dryly. "Then quickly man. Lose no time! Try to get a few minutes' advance on Rateau; then slip in to the guard-room to change into less conspicuous clothes. Citizen Gourdon and I will continue on the upper road and keep the man in sight in case he should think of altering his course. In any event, we'll meet you just inside the barrier. But if, in the meanwhile, you have to get on Rateau's track before we have arrived on the scene, leave the usual indications as to the direction which you have taken."

Having given his orders and satisfied himself that they were fully understood, he gave a curt command, "En avant," and once more the three of them rode at a sharp trot down the road towards the city.

IV.

Citizen Rateau, if he thought about the matter at all, must indeed have been vastly surprised at the unwonted amiability or indifference of sergeant Ribot, who was in command at the gate of Gentilly. Ribot only threw a very perfunctory glance at the greasy permit which Rateau presented to him, and when he put the usual query, "What's in that parcel?" and Rateau gave the reply: "Two heads of cabbage and a bunch of carrots," Ribot merely poked one of his fingers into the bundle, felt that a cabbage leaf did effectually lie on the top, and thereupon gave the formal order: "Pass on, citizen, in the name of the Republic!" without any hesitation.

Tournefort, who had watched the brief little incident from behind the window of a neighbouring cabaret, could not help but chuckle to himself. Never had he seen game walk more readily into a trap. Rateau, after he had passed the barrier, appeared undecided which way he would go. He looked with obvious longing towards the cabaret, behind which the keenest agent on the staff of the Committee of Public Safety was even now ensconced. But seemingly a halt within those hospitable doors did not form part of his programme, and a moment or two later he turned sharply on his heel and strode rapidly down the Rue de l'Oursine.

Tournefort allowed him a fair start, and then made ready to follow.

Just as he was stepping out of the cabaret he spied Chauvelin and Gourdon coming through the gates. They, too, had apparently made a brief halt inside the guard-room, where—as at most of the gates—a store of various disguises was always kept ready for the use of the numerous sleuth-hounds employed by the Committee of Public Safety. Here the two men had exchanged their official garments for suits of sombre cloth, which gave them the appearance of a couple of humble bourgeois going quietly about their business. Tournefort had donned an old blouse, tattered stockings, and shoes down at heel. With his hands buried in his breeches' pockets, he, too, turned into the long narrow Rue de l'Oursine, which, after a sharp curve, abuts on the Rue Mouffetard.

Rateau was walking rapidly, taking big strides with his long legs. Tournefort, now sauntering in the gutter in the middle of the road, now darting in and out of open doorways, kept his quarry well in sight. Chauvelin and Gourdon lagged some little way behind. It was still raining, but not heavily—a thin drizzle, which penetrated almost to the marrow. Not many passers-by haunted this forlorn quarter of old Paris. To right and left tall houses almost obscured the last, quickly-fading light of the grey September day.

At the bottom of the Rue Mouffetard, Rateau came once more to a halt. A network of narrow streets radiated from this centre. He looked all round him and also behind. It was difficult to know whether he had a sudden suspicion that he was being followed; certain it is that, after a very brief moment of hesitation, he plunged suddenly into the narrow Rue Contrescarpe and disappeared from view.

Tournefort was after him in a trice. When he reached the corner of the street he saw Rateau, at the further end of it, take a sudden sharp turn to the right. But not before he had very obviously spied his pursuer, for at that moment his entire demeanour changed. An air of furtive anxiety was expressed in his whole attitude. Even at that distance Tournefort could see him clutching his bulky parcel close to his chest.

After that the pursuit became closer and hotter. Rateau was in and out of that tight network of streets which cluster around the Place de Fourci, intent, apparently, on throwing his pursuers off the scent, for after a while he was running round and round in a circle. Now up the Rue des Poules, then to the right and to the right again; back in the Place de Fourci. Then straight across it once more to the Rue Contrescarpe, where he presently disappeared so completely from view that Tournefort thought that the earth must have swallowed him up.

Tournefort was a man capable of great physical exertion. His calling often made heavy demands upon his powers of endurance; but never before had he grappled with so strenuous a task. Puffing and panting, now running at top speed, anon brought to a halt by the doubling-up tactics of his quarry, his great difficulty was the fact that citizen Chauvelin did not wish the man Rateau to be apprehended; did not wish him to know that he was being pursued. And Tournefort had need of all his wits to keep well under the shadow of any projecting wall or under cover of open doorways which were conveniently in the way, and all the while not to lose sight of that consumptive giant, who seemed to be playing some intricate game which well-nigh exhausted the strength of citizen Tournefort.

What he could not make out was what had happened to Chauvelin and to Gourdon. They had been less than three hundred metres behind him when first this wild chase in and out of the Rue Contrescarpe had begun. Now, when their presence was most needed, they seemed to have lost track both of him—Tournefort—and of the very elusive quarry. To make matters more complicated, the shades of evening were drawing in very fast, and these narrow streets of the Faubourg were very sparsely lighted.

Just at this moment Tournefort had once more caught sight of Rateau, striding leisurely this time up the street. The worthy agent quickly took refuge under a doorway and was mopping his streaming forehead, glad of this brief respite in the mad chase, when that awful churchyard cough suddenly sounded so close to him that he gave a great jump and well-nigh betrayed his presence then and there. He had only just time to withdraw further still into the angle of the doorway, when Rateau passed by.

Tournefort peeped out of his hiding-place, and for the space of a dozen heart beats or so, remained there quite still, watching that broad back and those long limbs slowly moving through the gathering gloom. The next instant he perceived Chauvelin standing at the end of the street.

Rateau saw him too—came face to face with him, in fact, and must have known who he was for, without an instant's hesitation and just like a hunted creature at bay, he turned sharply on his heel and then ran back down the street as hard as he could tear. He passed close to within half a metre of Tournefort, and as he flew past he hit out with his left fist so vigorously that the worthy agent of the Committee of Public Safety, caught on the nose by the blow, staggered and measured his length upon the flagged floor below.

The next moment Chauvelin had come by. Tournefort, struggling to his feet, called to him, panting:

"Did you see him? Which way did he go?"

"Up the Rue Bordet. After him, citizen!" replied Chauvelin grimly, between his teeth.

Together the two men continued the chase, guided through the intricate mazes of the streets by their fleeing quarry. They had Rateau well in sight, and the latter could no longer continue his former tactics with success now that two experienced sleuth-hounds were on his track.

At a given moment he was caught between the two of them. Tournefort was advancing cautiously up the Rue Bordet; Chauvelin, equally stealthily, was coming down the same street, and Rateau, once more walking quite leisurely, was at equal distance between the two.

V.

There are no side turnings out of the Rue Bordet, the total length of which is less than fifty metres; so Tournefort, feeling more at his ease, ensconced himself at one end of the street, behind a doorway, whilst Chauvelin did the same at the other. Rateau, standing in the gutter, appeared once more in a state of hesitation. Immediately in front of him the door of a small cabaret stood invitingly open; its signboard, "Le Bon Copain," promised rest and refreshment. He peered up and down the road, satisfied himself presumably that, for the moment, his pursuers were out of sight, hugged his parcel to his chest, and then suddenly made a dart for the cabaret and disappeared within its doors.

Nothing could have been better. The quarry, for the moment, was safe, and if the sleuth-hounds could not get refreshment, they could at least get a rest. Tournefort and Chauvelin crept out of their hiding-places. They met in the middle of the road, at the spot where Rateau had stood a while ago. It was then growing dark and the street was innocent of lanterns, but the lights inside the cabaret gave a full view of the interior. The lower half of the wide shop-window was curtained off, but above the curtain the heads of the customers of "Le Bon Copain," and the general comings and goings, could very clearly be seen.

Tournefort, never at a loss, had already climbed upon a low projection in the wall of one of the houses opposite. From this point of vantage he could more easily observe what went on inside the cabaret, and in short, jerky sentences he gave a description of what he saw to his chief.

"Rateau is sitting down ... he has his back to the window ... he has put his bundle down close beside him on the bench ... he can't speak for a minute, for he is coughing and spluttering like an old walrus.... A wench is bringing him a bottle of wine and a hunk of bread and cheese.... He has started talking ... is talking volubly ... the people are laughing ... some are applauding.... And here comes Jean Victor, the landlord ... you know him, citizen ... a big, hulking fellow, and as good a patriot as I ever wish to see.... He, too, is laughing and talking to Rateau, who is doubled up with another fit of coughing—"

Chauvelin uttered an exclamation of impatience:

"Enough of this, citizen Tournefort. Keep your eye on the man and hold your tongue. I am spent with fatigue."

"No wonder," murmured Tournefort. Then he added insinuatingly: "Why not let me go in there and apprehend Rateau now? We should have the diamonds and—"

"And lose the ci-devant Comtesse de Sucy and the man Bertin," retorted Chauvelin with sudden fierceness. "Bertin, who can be none other than that cursed Englishman, the—"

He checked himself, seeing Tournefort was gazing down on him, with awe and bewilderment expressed in his lean, hatchet face.

"You are losing sight of Rateau, citizen," Chauvelin continued calmly.

"What is he doing now?"

But Tournefort felt that this calmness was only on the surface; something strange had stirred the depths of his chief's keen, masterful mind. He would have liked to ask a question or two, but knew from experience that it was neither wise nor profitable to try and probe citizen Chauvelin's thoughts. So after a moment or two he turned back obediently to his task.

"I can't see Rateau for the moment," he said, "but there is much talking and merriment in there. Ah! there he is, I think. Yes, I see him!... He is behind the counter, talking to Jean Victor ... and he has just thrown some money down upon the counter.... gold too! name of a dog...."

Then suddenly, without any warning, Tournefort jumped down from his post of observation. Chauvelin uttered a brief:

"What the——- are you doing, citizen?"

"Rateau is going," replied Tournefort excitedly. "He drank a mug of wine at a draught and has picked up his bundle, ready to go."

Once more cowering in the dark angle of a doorway, the two men waited, their nerves on edge, for the reappearance of their quarry.

"I wish citizen Gourdon were here," whispered Tournefort. "In the darkness it is better to be three than two."

"I sent him back to the Station in the Rue Mouffetard," was Chauvelin's curt retort; "there to give notice that I might require a few armed men presently. But he should be somewhere about here by now, looking for us. Anyway, I have my whistle, and if—"

He said no more, for at that moment the door of the cabaret was opened from within and Rateau stepped out into the street, to the accompaniment of loud laughter and clapping of hands which came from the customers of the "Bon Copain."

This time he appeared neither in a hurry nor yet anxious. He did not pause in order to glance to right or left, but started to walk quite leisurely up the street. The two sleuth-hounds quietly followed him. Through the darkness they could only vaguely see his silhouette, with the great bundle under his arm. Whatever may have been Rateau's fears of being shadowed awhile ago, he certainly seemed free of them now. He sauntered along, whistling a tune, down the Montagne Ste. Genevieve to the Place Maubert, and thence straight towards the river.

Having reached the bank, he turned off to his left, sauntered past the Ecole de Medecine and went across the Petit Pont, then through the New Market, along the Quai des Orfevres. Here he made a halt, and for awhile looked over the embankment at the river and then round about him, as if in search of something. But presently he appeared to make up his mind, and continued his leisurely walk as far as the Pont Neuf, where he turned sharply off to his right, still whistling, Tournefort and Chauvelin hard upon his heels.

"That whistling is getting on my nerves," muttered Tournefort irritably; "and I haven't heard the ruffian's churchyard cough since he walked out of the 'Bon Copain.'"

Strangely enough, it was this remark of Tournefort's which gave Chauvelin the first inkling of something strange and, to him, positively awesome. Tournefort, who walked close beside him, heard him suddenly mutter a fierce exclamation.

"Name of a dog!"

"What is it, citizen?" queried Tournefort, awed by this sudden outburst on the part of a man whose icy calmness had become proverbial throughout the Committee.

"Sound the alarm, citizen!" cried Chauvelin in response. "Or, by Satan, he'll escape us again!"

"But—" stammered Tournefort in utter bewilderment, while, with fingers that trembled somewhat, he fumbled for his whistle.

"We shall want all the help we can," retorted Chauvelin roughly. "For, unless I am much mistaken, there's more noble quarry here than even I could dare to hope!"

Rateau in the meanwhile had quietly lolled up to the parapet on the right-hand side of the bridge, and Tournefort, who was watching him with intense keenness, still marvelled why citizen Chauvelin had suddenly become so strangely excited. Rateau was merely lolling against the parapet, like a man who has not a care in the world. He had placed his bundle on the stone ledge beside him. Here he waited a moment or two, until one of the small craft upon the river loomed out of the darkness immediately below the bridge. Then he picked up the bundle and threw it straight into the boat. At that same moment Tournefort had the whistle to his lips. A shrill, sharp sound rang out through the gloom.

"The boat, citizen Tournefort, the boat!" cried Chauvelin. "There are plenty of us here to deal with the man."

Immediately, from the quays, the streets, the bridges, dark figures emerged out of the darkness and hurried to the spot. Some reached the bridgehead even as Rateau made a dart forward, and two men were upon him before he succeeded in running very far. Others had scrambled down the embankment and were shouting to some unseen boatman to "halt, in the name of the people!"

But Rateau gave in without a struggle. He appeared more dazed than frightened, and quietly allowed the agents of the Committee to lead him back to the bridge, where Chauvelin had paused, waiting for him.

VI.

A minute or two later Tournefort was once more beside his chief. He was carrying the precious bundle, which, he explained, the boatman had given up without question.

"The man knew nothing about it," the agent said. "No one, he says, could have been more surprised than he was when this bundle was suddenly flung at him over the parapet of the bridge."

Just then the small group, composed of two or three agents of the Committee, holding their prisoner by the arms, came into view. One man was walking ahead and was the first to approach Chauvelin. He had a small screw of paper in his hand, which he gave to his chief.

"Found inside the lining of the prisoner's hat, citizen," he reported curtly, and opened the shutter of a small, dark lantern which he wore at his belt.

Chauvelin took the paper from his subordinate. A weird, unexplainable foreknowledge of what was to come caused his hand to shake and beads of perspiration to moisten his forehead. He looked up and saw the prisoner standing before him. Crushing the paper in his hand he snatched the lantern from the agent's belt and flashed it in the face of the quarry who, at the last, had been so easily captured.

Immediately a hoarse cry of disappointment and of rage escaped his throat.

"Who is this man?" he cried.

One of the agents gave reply:

"It is old Victor, the landlord of the 'Bon Copain.' He is just a fool, who has been playing a practical joke."

Tournefort, too, at sight of the prisoner had uttered a cry of dismay and of astonishment.

"Victor!" he exclaimed. "Name of a dog, citizen, what are you doing here?"

But Chauvelin had gripped the man by the arm so fiercely that the latter swore with the pain.

"What is the meaning of this?" he queried roughly.

"Only a bet, citizen," retorted Victor reproachfully. "No reason to fall on an honest patriot for a bet, just as if he were a mad dog."

"A joke? A bet?" murmured Chauvelin hoarsely, for his throat now felt hot and parched. "What do you mean? Who are you, man? Speak, or I'll—"

"My name is Jean Victor," replied the other. "I am the landlord of the 'Bon Copain.' An hour ago a man came into my cabaret. He was a queer, consumptive creature, with a churchyard cough that made you shiver. Some of my customers knew him by sight, told me that the man's name was Rateau, and that he was an habitue of the 'Liberte,' in the Rue Christine. Well; he soon fell into conversation, first with me, then with some of my customers—talked all sorts of silly nonsense, made absurd bets with everybody. Some of these he won, and others he lost; but I must say that when he lost he always paid up most liberally. Then we all got excited, and soon bets flew all over the place. I don't rightly know how it happened at the last, but all at once he bet me that I would not dare to walk out then and there in the dark, as far as the Pont Neuf, wearing his blouse and hat and carrying a bundle the same as his under my arm. I not dare?... I, Jean Victor, who was a fine fighter in my day! I bet him a gold piece that I would and he said that he would make it five if I came back without my bundle, having thrown it over the parapet into any passing boat. Well, citizen!" continued Jean Victor with a laugh, "I ask you, what would you have done? Five gold pieces means a fortune these hard times, and I tell you the man was quite honest and always paid liberally when he lost. He slipped behind the counter and took off his blouse and hat, which I put on. Then we made up a bundle with some cabbage heads and a few carrots, and out I came. I didn't think there could be anything wrong in the whole affair—just the tomfoolery of a man who has got the betting mania and in whose pocket money is just burning a hole. And I have won my bet," concluded Jean Victor, still unabashed, "and I want to go back and get my money. If you don't believe me, come with me to my CABARET. You will find the citizen Rateau there, for sure; and I know that I shall find my five gold pieces."

Chauvelin had listened to the man as he would to some weird dream-story, wherein ghouls and devils had played a part. Tournefort, who was watching him, was awed by the look of fierce rage and grim hopelessness which shone from his chief's pale eyes. The other agents laughed. They were highly amused at the tale, but they would not let the prisoner go.

"If Jean Victor's story is true, citizen," their sergeant said, speaking to Chauvelin, "there will be witnesses to it over at 'Le Bon Copain.' Shall we take the prisoner straightway there and await further orders?"

Chauvelin gave a curt acquiescence, nodding his head like some insentient wooden automaton. The screw of paper was still in his hand; it seemed to sear his palm. Tournefort even now broke into a grim laugh. He had just undone the bundle which Jean Victor had thrown over the parapet of the bridge. It contained two heads of cabbage and a bunch of carrots. Then he ordered the agents to march on with their prisoner, and they, laughing and joking with Jean Victor, gave a quick turn, and soon their heavy footsteps were echoing down the flagstones of the bridge.

Chauvelin waited, motionless and silent, the dark lantern still held in his shaking hand, until he was quite sure that he was alone. Then only did he unfold the screw of paper.

It contained a few lines scribbled in pencil—just that foolish rhyme which to his fevered nerves was like a strong irritant, a poison which gave him an unendurable sensation of humiliation and impotence:

> "We seek him here, we seek him there!
> Chauvelin seeks him everywhere!
> Is he in heaven? Is he in hell?
> That demmed, elusive Pimpernel!"

He crushed the paper in his hand and, with a loud groan, of misery, fled over the bridge like one possessed.

VII.

Madame la Comtesse de Sucy never went to England. She was one of those French women who would sooner endure misery in their own beloved country than comfort anywhere else. She outlived the horrors of the Revolution and speaks in her memoirs of the man Bertin. She never knew who he was nor whence he came. All that she knew was that he came to her like some mysterious agent of God, bringing help, counsel, a semblance of happiness, at the moment when she was at the end of all her resources and saw grim starvation staring her and her children in the face. He appointed all sorts of strange places in out-of-the-way Paris where she was wont to meet him, and one night she confided to him the history of her diamonds, and hardly dared to trust his promise that he would get them for her.

Less than twenty-four hours later he brought them to her, at the poor lodgings in the Rue Blanche which she occupied with her children under an assumed name. That same night she begged him to dispose of them. This also he did, bringing her the money the next day.

She never saw him again after that.

But citizen Tournefort never quite got over his disappointment of that night. Had he dared, he would have blamed citizen Chauvelin for the discomfiture. It would have been better to have apprehended the man Rateau while there was a chance of doing so with success.

As it was, the impudent ruffian slipped clean away, and was never heard of again either at the "Bon Copain" or at the "Liberte." The customers at the cabaret certainly corroborated the story of Jean Victor. The man Rateau, they said, had been honest to the last. When time went on and Jean Victor did not return, he said that he could no longer wait, had work to do for the Government over the other side of the water and was afraid he would get punished if he dallied. But, before leaving, he laid the five gold pieces on the table. Every one wondered that so humble a workman had so much money in his pocket, and was withal so lavish with it. But these were not the times when one inquired too closely into the presence of money in the pocket of a good patriot.

And citizen Rateau was a good patriot, for sure.

And a good fellow to boot!

They all drank his health in Jean Victor's sour wine; then each went his way.

Made in the USA
Columbia, SC
30 September 2023

23656441R00331